WAR

Grand System Vending

Book Two

By

Ryan maxwell

WAR

Contents

<u>Dedication</u>

For Eddie Creamier
You were always there—quiet strength, steady hands, and an answer for every broken thing I brought your way, whether it was a question, a problem, or just a moment of doubt. You never needed to say much. Somehow, I always knew I had your approval, and that meant more than I ever told you.

Thank you for every lesson, every laugh, and every time you made me feel like I belonged. Sixteen years of family, and it still doesn't feel like enough.

I love you. And I miss you.

Prologue

A woman fell to her knees in the dirt, struggling under the weight of a large stone she was forced to carry from the dig site to a waste pile on the far side of the construction area. Her joints screamed at her to stop and rest. She had been lifting these heavy rocks for over a week now with barely any respite. Reaching a trembling hand to her neck, she ran a finger along the inside of the cold metal collar that encircled it—a collar that The Master had placed on her when she had come to him seeking help after the world had changed.

As her fingers brushed the collar, small pulses of power shot through her, forcing her hand away. Her muscles spasmed involuntarily, compelling her to stand despite the agony. She groaned, struggling against the force that compelled her to obey. As she resisted, a dark presence seeped into her mind, overpowering her meager willpower. She was forced to stand and lift the heavy stone once more. Screaming against the pain in her joints and the anguish in her mind, she hefted the burden and began to slowly step toward the pile.

"You have no power here. You are mine now, and you will do as I command. Do you wish to return to the outside, where monsters can kill you? Where you will have to fight for everything you need?" The voice in her head was dripping with malevolence, relishing in her suffering as it forced her to comply.

At this point, she would have preferred the peril of surviving the outside world. This was no way to live—working sixteen hours a day to help build a fortification for the Guild building they had claimed. It felt like she had been trapped here for years, though in reality, she had been under this horrifying control for only two weeks. She'd stumbled into the camp, desperate to find people who would protect her and help her find provisions. The man who called himself The Master had promised safety from monsters, food, and shelter in exchange for her assistance in building a place worth living in.

She had accepted the offer almost immediately, overwhelmed with relief at finding someone willing to help her in her desperate situation. She had watched friends die at the hands of monsters and had been forced to break into stores to find food as she darted from building to building, searching for safety. When she finally found The Master, the simple act of wearing a collar to show she was part of the Guild seemed like the deal of a lifetime. She had never been so wrong.

The Master had taken her to a vending machine inside the Guild building once she had accepted his invitation. He purchased a can containing a metal collar, and she had seen others in the Guild wearing them, assuming it was some sort of uniform marking them as members. The Master had even said as much. Trusting his words, she willingly let him place the collar around her neck, unaware that the others who wore it were unable to warn her of the horrors she was about to endure.

The moment the collar clamped shut around her neck, she felt his mind press against hers, battering down her will with an overwhelming force. It was like being caught in a tidal wave of power. She was left a drooling, mindless heap on the ground. Over the next couple of days, she gradually regained some of her senses, only to find that The Master's will had completely dominated her mind. She could do nothing but obey his commands.

Once she had recovered, she was sent directly to the construction site. Lacking any useful building skills, she was relegated to the most menial manual labor. Resistance was futile; anyone who fought against the collar's control was severely punished. Helping others resulted in punishment. Even *thinking* of escape led to punishment. The pain wasn't just mental—it ravaged her body, causing convulsions that sometimes escalated into forced self-harm.

This was a nightmare, a living hellscape that broke those trapped within it. The collars stripped the wearers of their identity, reducing them to mere extensions of The Master's will. He was a cruel, sadistic man who thrived on their suffering. All she could do was obey and pray for an end to her torment.

"That's right. You cannot escape. You are mine forever. I provide for you. I protect you. I keep you safe. You will repay my kindness in whatever capacity you can," the voice cooed in her head, filled with twisted delight at her suffering.

The so-called protection had come not from The Master but from the other slaves. She had witnessed a goblin raid on the building site, and in response, several of the strongest men were compelled to rise from their tasks and hurl themselves at the attackers with reckless abandon. They had no weapons, only their bare hands. Stabbed and sliced, they fought on until every goblin lay dead. When the compulsion lifted, the men collapsed. Two of the four died from their wounds, bleeding out as they writhed on the ground in agony. The survivors bore long, ragged scars that had barely begun to heal.

Night offered no solace. The slaves were herded into a cramped room with meager rations and water to sustain them. The Master had a penchant for selecting the most attractive slaves to serve him during meals, treating himself as a king. They were forced to attend to him in his makeshift throne room, dressed in revealing servant garb designed solely to satisfy his leering gaze. More than once, one had stumbled or dropped something while serving him, and his response was brutal. He beat them with whips, clubs, or his fists, reveling in their pain.

She remembered the time he had chosen her to serve him. She was commanded to hold his wine chalice and pour it into his mouth whenever he beckoned. Standing behind his chair, she obeyed, her movements mechanical and devoid of any will. Another young woman brought him grapes, but as she approached his seat, she tripped on a step and fell. The Master leapt from his throne, raining blows upon her as he berated her for her clumsiness. She was left bruised and swollen, one eye nearly shut from the assault. Two young men were ordered to drag her away.

She could hardly believe that this was now her reality. She often thought of ending her life just to escape the suffering, but even that was beyond her reach. Once, she had found a knife and intended to cut her throat, but the collar intervened. She couldn't even bring the blade close to her skin without being seized by violent convulsions. Each attempt was met with The Master's mocking laughter, his voice dripping with derision as he shamed her for daring to defy him.

Dropping the heavy stone at the edge of the pile, she finally heard The Master's voice in her head, commanding everyone to stop for the day and return to their cramped quarters. She complied, marching back to the Guild building. As she stepped inside, she suddenly froze. No matter how she struggled, she was unable to move as the other slaves filed past her.

They turned to her with looks of pity and dread, understanding all too well what this meant. Once the room was clear, she was left standing with a red-haired woman and a young man. The three of them exchanged helpless glances, their eyes wide with fear. The Master's voice slithered into their minds.

"Time for you all to show your gratitude for the help I've so graciously given you. Lose the dirty work clothes and join me in the throne room once you have changed."

The three of them began to strip off their filthy garments, letting them fall to the floor. They donned the scant servant attire from a nearby rack, then marched down the hallway to The Master's throne room. When they reached the door, their bodies pressed against one another as it swung open. The Master surveyed them with satisfaction before stepping aside and gesturing for them to enter.

With no will of their own, they obeyed, stepping into the room as The Master closed the door behind them. He turned to face them, his eyes gleaming with anticipation.

"I am so glad you are all here," he said, his voice oozing with cruel delight. "It is time for dinner service to begin. Do not disappoint me."

Chapter 1

A Welcome Addition

Tom hung up the radio, his mind reeling from the conversation. Everything was falling apart. Seth was dead, the guild was on the brink of war, and he was still stuck in Arizona with a multi-day journey ahead just to get back to Dallas. To make matters worse, he had no clear plan for how to handle any of it. He felt woefully unprepared for the responsibilities of leading a Guild, and his grasp on strategy, especially when it came to warfare, was practically nonexistent.

Taking a deep breath, Tom stood up, pushing away the wave of uncertainty that threatened to overwhelm him. He had to break the news to his team, and as much as he wished he had all the answers, he knew he couldn't face this alone. He braced himself for the difficult conversations to come, hoping that together, they might find a way through the chaos.

"Hey, guys, everyone gather round. I have some news about our situation back in Dallas," Tom said as the other members of his Guild all moved in to hear what he had to say.

Looking at each of them in turn, Tom noticed that Bob had come over to join them as well, and looked at him curiously.

"Bob? Is this your way of saying you're joining us?" Tom asked.

"After what we just went through, you bet. I saw some real promise in there and the sacrifices you were willing to make for your team. I figure there's no one better to join up with," Bob replied, smiling widely as he looked directly at Tom. A shadow passed across the repairman's eyes, his smile faltering. "I'm sorry about your friend. Someone willing to literally jump in front of that monster for a team member, though, is somewhere I want to be. You must engender true respect from these people if they're willing to die for each other."

A somber mood settled over the group as they remembered Seth's sacrifice. He had been an invaluable member of the team with limitless potential, and his loss weighed heavily on everyone's hearts. Some couldn't shake the guilt, feeling responsible for his death because they were the ones who had pulled him away from his home in Decatur. But Tom knew that Seth wouldn't want them to dwell on blame or regret.

Instead, he urged his friends to honor Seth by remembering him as the hero he truly was. Seth had given everything for the team, and though his absence left a painful void, they chose to celebrate his bravery and the legacy of his selfless actions, keeping his memory alive in the way he would have wanted.

"Any of us would be happy to lay our lives down for the others. We're in this together to the very end," Tom said to Bob, with a smile that didn't quite touch his eyes. "So, you're welcome to join us, Bob. We would be honored to have you as a member of the Guild."

Thinking about the Guild menu, a screen appeared in his vision, and he thought about sending an invite to Bob, who accepted almost immediately.

"Welcome to Vanguard, Bob." Tom smiled at him again.

Suddenly James was there, wearing a creepy grin and extending a hand expectantly.

"What… What's this?" Bob asked uncertainly, looking toward Tom for answers.

It was Jay, however, who spoke up. "It's part of the Guild Agreement. We require regular sacrifices to our lord and savior, Lucifer."

"Um…" Bob's eyes were wide. "And this is…?" He gestured toward James.

"Lucifer Morningstar," James greeted the man with a bow. "At your service." His smile was wide as he held out his hand once more. "Now, about that sacrifice…"

"What—ah." Bob cleared his throat nervously. "What do you require?" He smiled, trying to ease the tension. "I'm afraid I'm all out of virgins…"

"Cookies!" James barked, causing Bob to startle. He pointed at his open hand with the finger of his other hand. "Now."

Bob began patting his pockets awkwardly. "I—ah. I'm afraid I'm all out of those as well."

"Wrong!" James shouted once more. "I know what you're capable of, *mister* Vending." He gestured back toward the dungeon they had exited. "You can pull anything you please out of that thing." He glared at the man, his extended finger punctuating his next words by poking his open hand. "Cookies. *Now*. Otherwise, I'm afraid it's to the seventh hell with—"

He let out a whoof of air as Kiera elbowed him in the stomach.

"What the hell was that for?" James asked indignantly.

"Don't be an ass," was all Kiera said in reply.

"Actually, you just reminded me of something, James." Tom stroked his chin thoughtfully.

James brightened hopefully. "Cookies?"

"No."

James deflated.

"Bob's knowledge will help us accomplish even more than we already have. We can really make use of the added benefits of the System. We could help a lot of people," Tom said excitedly.

"And that was super corny. Thanks, Tom," Kedron added.

"Fine, just trying to look on the bright side. Welcome to the Guild nonetheless, Bob," Tom reiterated, trying not to feel ashamed.

"Glad to join. Now, what's the plan here?" Bob asked, trying not to snicker.

"We have to make it back to Dallas to help the Guild. But we'll have to stop at least in Decatur to let people say goodbye to Seth. We owe that to them," Tom said solemnly.

Everyone nodded in agreement at the sentiment. They should be allowed to grieve for him as well.

"I really meant, what's the plan for when we get back?" Bob added.

"I'm not exactly sure. That'll depend on the situation. If we come back to an all-out war, we just hop in and start bashing some skulls. If it's just tension, I'm hoping we can work on some more diplomatic approaches," Tom thought aloud. "In either case, there isn't much we can do about any of it until we're back in Dallas. So, we might as well get on the road."

"That's the best plan I've heard so far. Let's hit the road and see what we can do," Kedron said, clapping his hands together and stepping back from the circle of people.

"How do we get back? We're out of seats with Bob joining us now," Bobby mentioned.

"No, actually… we aren't," Kedron said, his words careful, deliberate—like he was forcing them past the weight in his throat.

Silence crashed down over the group. It wasn't just quiet—it was the kind of stillness that pressed in, suffocating, leaving nothing but the raw ache in their chests. The realization settled like a lead weight in their stomachs.

There should have been no room. Every vehicle had been packed. Every seat taken. But now… one was empty.

The cold finality of it hit them all at once. Seth should have been here. His voice, his laugh, his presence—gone. And in its place, a hollow space that no one dared to speak about.

"I think we can help with that," Zach interrupted them as he walked over with his team. "We have some extra room and couldn't help but overhear your little dilemma. And we figured you might want to leave that seat open for a bit."

"You guys are coming to Dallas? Don't you all have a family to get back to?" Tom asked, looking at Zach with concern.

"We do, but we have others who came with us that are going to go back and get everyone together and bring them to Dallas. You all have a stronger presence there than we do in Utah. It's not that far from here, truth be told. And we'd rather be somewhere we know with people we can trust," Zach said.

"I can't promise anyone safety if they come to Dallas," Tom said, making sure he looked into Zach's eyes.

"No one can, brother." Zach shrugged. "No one can promise safety anywhere. Might as well work on being with people we know can have each other's backs, right?" Zach said nonchalantly as he shrugged and tried to act as if he didn't care.

"We're going, too," Isaac said as he came to join the group. "Vegas is a shit hole anyway. We'd rather join you all as well. And it sounds like you could use the backup."

"This is getting ridiculous. Would anyone wanting to go to Dallas just come over now and stop interrupting for dramatic effect?!" James called out to the group of people still tearing down the camp.

Light laughter rippled through the group as Chris and his team announced they would also be joining Tom on the journey back to Dallas. Each of them had a small following in their own towns who would be coming along as well, but they needed to send someone back to guide their people to the meeting point.

Mike, from Chris' team, managed to radio back to his group, maintaining contact throughout their travels. However, Isaac and Zach still needed to send someone back to relay the location and instructions, ensuring their teams would know where to go.

Tom attempted to send Zach a Guild invite but received an error instead.

Cannot send Zach a Guild invite:

The person you are attempting to invite to Vanguard is already a member of another Guild. Guild members can only belong to one Guild at a time. Please ask the individual to leave their current Guild if they wish to join Vanguard, and then resend the invitation.

"Well, that's new," Tom said, puzzled by the System message.

"What is?" Derek asked.

"It says I can't invite Zach to the Guild because he's already in another one," Tom replied, rereading the message.

"Are you the Guild leader, Zach?" Bob asked.

"I am," Zach replied.

"Then just merge your Guilds together. That way, everyone is included at once," Bob stated, crossing his arms as if this should have been common knowledge.

"We can do that?" Tom asked, looking up from the System message.

"Of course. You just have to choose which one will be the main Guild, and which one is the merging Guild. It's a sub-menu on the Guild page," Bob explained. "You can even merge multiple Guilds at a time, assuming Isaac and Chris are also already in Guilds."

"We do already have a Guild," Chris confirmed, moving back to the group.

"We don't," Isaac informed them. "We didn't have enough people we trusted and then got sucked into this quest before we had a chance to form one."

Tom navigated to the Guild management page and found the section for Guild merging. At the top of the page, there was a drop-down menu listing the available Guilds, allowing him to select the primary Guild. Below that, branching sections displayed options for merging additional Guilds, each with its own drop-down field for easy selection and configuration.

"What are the names of your Guilds?" Tom asked Isaac and Chris.

"Desert Wolves," Zach said.

Chris mumbled something under his breath.

"What was that, Chris?" Tom asked, straining to hear him.

"The Prancing Unicorns, okay?!" he almost yelled in anger.

James' too-bright eyes locked with Chris' own. His head was nodding slowly in appreciation. "It's not quite Your Mother's a Horde, but… nice."

"My daughter named it. It wasn't my choice, but she hasn't been dealing well with the apocalypse, and this helped distract her," Chris pouted, pointedly not meeting anyone's eyes.

Silence reigned for a moment before everyone nearby burst out laughing.

"The Prancing Unicorns, eh? That suits you all so well!" Kedron teased through fits of laughter.

"Yeah, yeah," Chris grumbled. "I know. But when you meet Sasha, you'll see why it's hard to say no to her."

"Alright, let's do the merge," Tom said, getting his laughter under control.

Tom carefully scrolled through the extensive list of Guild names, hundreds of them organized alphabetically. He selected the appropriate Guilds— Desert Wolves and Prancing Unicorns—from the drop-down menus. Once both Guilds were chosen, the large red "MERGE" button at the bottom of the page lit up. With a deep breath, Tom pressed it.

A confirmation message flashed briefly, and just like that, Desert Wolves and Prancing Unicorns were officially merged into Vanguard. All members from the merged Guilds now appeared under the Vanguard members list, consolidating their forces and bringing everyone under one banner.

This influx brought Tom's Guild list up to almost seven hundred people.

"I had no idea we had so many members already," Tom stared in awe at the list of names.

"Brian sure has been busy," Derek said, equally shocked as he looked at the names in his view.

"More people means more bodies to do the tasks needed to keep a Guild running. It's why many of the Guilds won't last without coming together," Bob mentioned offhandedly.

"You think they'll die off?" Tom asked, concern lacing his voice.

"Either that or the list will get shorter because they'll figure out they can merge as well. Either way, there will come a time when the number of Guilds will begin to shrink," Bob continued. "It has to happen. Small groups won't be able to stay afloat forever."

"Some will," Tom denied, shaking his head and thinking of the small Guilds of the different games he'd played.

"Yes, some will," Bob agreed. "But only tight-knit groups of experts will manage it."

"Like military or paramilitary personnel," Tom said thoughtfully. "Is that why you said small groups wouldn't be able to stay afloat?"

"Exactly. Those with the capabilities to manage such a thing will already be used to being part of a much larger organization with infrastructure and chains of command. Not to mention that you can't have a Guild without a Guild *building*. So, you have to have a place to call home. It means putting down roots. If everyone leaves to make the Guild a roaming Guild, then someone could take over the Guild building. If that happens, your group is disbanded. You lose all the bonuses with it as well. To keep a building, you'll have to defend it from, at the very least—monsters. That means getting stronger. If everyone always fights, then who gathers supplies? Who makes the building defensible? Who makes the changes to the Guild that make it stronger? I read a statistic somewhere that it takes between ten and fifty people to support one soldier in war time. And make no mistake—we are at war. It's just not sustainable long term," Bob explained.

"Is it possible to change Guild buildings?" Derek asked.

"Yes, but it means you need people at both locations who both have the authority to make that kind of change," Bob explained.

"Could someone make something like a cruise ship or a yacht into a Guild building?" Austin asked.

"They aren't buildings, so no. They could be part of the Guild fleet. But not a building to form a Guild around," Bob answered.

"Fleet? That sounds like a pretty cool idea," Kedron said.

"Boats can get pretty big," Kiera countered. "You could easily build a building *on* a boat. Would that work?"

"...Actually. I don't know," Bob said. "It just might. But I'm not sure you're taking into account what all goes into maintaining a yacht or cruise ship. It's not practical," Bob added.

"Let's just cross that ocean when we get to it. So, how many vehicles will be in the caravan going home now?" Tom asked, looking around at everyone who had gathered.

"We have two vehicles," Zach piped up.

"We have three," Chris added.

"I only have one going with us," Isaac mentioned.

"So, six, plus our two, plus the motorcycle. Nine in total in the caravan. Just to let you all know, we will be stopping several times to check in on some places. One of which we have to lay a friend to rest in," Tom told the teams. "So, it isn't a straight shot. But it has to be done. Anyone have any issues with that?"

No one said anything. Each looked to the others to see if anyone would speak up.

"Alright, time to load everything up. We got some road to burn!" Tom called out so everyone could hear him.

Turning to leave the campsite, Tom stared off into the distance, realization donning on him.

"We parked up there," Tom said, pointing at the top of the canyon, which was a few miles off.

"And we parked in the other direction," Zach said, pointing to another rise.

Chris and Isaac didn't even say anything as they pointed in other directions.

"Well, shit. Okay, everyone, go to your vehicles, and we'll meet up at the park entrance. Everyone knows where that is, right?" Tom asked, feeling his impatience rising.

The others all nodded.

"Awesome," Tom sighed as he turned to move out. "Let's get this over with."

The teams split up, each heading in one of four different directions as they began their hikes back to their respective vehicles. Tom and his team walked together, going over the information Joe had relayed over the radio once more. Despite their best efforts to brainstorm solutions, they kept arriving at the same conclusion: there was nothing they could do about the situation until they returned to Dallas.

Frustrated but resigned, they focused on the task at hand; knowing that dealing with the challenges back home would have to wait until they were reunited with their Guild.

"Look, all I'm saying is, if we just kick Shandra's ass really good one time, she'll probably back off," Kiera said.

"*Or* she'll become one of those vengeful anime super-bitches that goes out, becomes even stronger, and destroys all of us in her own heroic tale," James said.

"What? How would her tale be heroic?" Kiera asked indignantly.

"Everyone is the hero in their own story. In the same way we see her as a villain, she might see us as villains as well. Even the bad guys think what they're doing is right a lot of the time," James explained, continuing to huff and puff while they hiked through the canyon.

"Doubt she sees us as villains," Jay butted in. "More like NPCs inside of her own personal universe. But you're right. She might not see us as villains *yet.* Putting her in her place could change that."

"You really think villains see themselves as the heroes?" Kiera asked.

"Sure do. Think about it. You're out there killing off goblins because they killed humans. But goblins are likely out there killing humans because they got flopped down in a world where they are the minority and are scared. They see these creatures twice their size and look nothing like them everywhere. What do they do? They defend themselves. Strike first and ask questions later," James continued, pausing momentarily to catch his breath.

"Bullshit," Jay scoffed.

"Hmm?" James raised an eyebrow.

"The goblins enjoy terrorizing people too much for all that nonsense you just spouted to fit with what we're seeing. They're not scared little boy scouts looking to earn a new badge for the sash." Jay scowled but raised his hands in concession. "I'm not saying that they're all evil little bastards, but what I *am* saying is that all the ones we've met sure as hell are. So far, not a single one has tried diplomacy."

"Jay's got a point," Kiera nodded. "Why wouldn't their first thought be to talk to these strange creatures and understand them?"

"Was your first thought to speak with the ogres? We couldn't even understand them, and we couldn't understand the goblins. Hard to make peace with someone you can't talk to. And a lot of them appeared on freeways with vehicles driving past. Look, the point isn't that goblins are misunderstood *Care Bears*, it's that a lot of villains also think they are doing the right thing."

"People are stupid," Derek said suddenly. The quiet ex-military man's words were soft, but carried in that strange way that drill sergeants the world over possessed.

Everyone looked at the man.

"It's true." he shrugged.

"I'm… not disagreeing," Kiera said. "I'm just wondering what you mean by that."

"It's a quote from a book I read once," Derek replied. "It really struck me, so I remember the whole thing." He cleared his throat. "Wizard's First Rule: people are stupid. Given proper motivation, almost anyone will believe almost anything. Because people are stupid, they will believe a lie because they want to believe it's true, or because they are afraid it *might* be true. People's heads are full of knowledge, facts, and beliefs, and most of it is false, yet they think it's all true. People are stupid; they rarely can tell the difference between a lie and the truth, and yet they are confident they can, and so are all the easier to fool." Derek paused a moment before continuing, "People need an enemy to feel a sense of purpose. It's easy to lead people when they have a sense of purpose. Sense of purpose is more important by far than the truth. In fact, truth has no bearing on belief. People are stupid; they want to believe, so they do."

Derek tilted his head toward James. "What he said about 'bad guys' is true. Everyone is the hero of their own story." Derek's words became thoughtful. "What really struck me about the quote is just how true and powerful it is. I'll give you an illustration that was given in the book about how dangerous this kind of thing can be." He looked toward Tom. "Tom, who would you be more afraid of—a two-hundred-and-twenty-pound man who wants to steal your wallet, or a ninety-pound woman who believes—wrongly, but believes with all her heart that you stole her baby?"

Tom swallowed, thinking about the woman and what she'd be capable of. "The woman, one-hundred percent."

Derek nodded, his eyes scanning the group. "And *that* is what we're up against. Stupid, scared, *believing* people. People who *know* they are right and are willing to kill for that belief."

Everyone grew quiet as they thought about exactly what they were up against. Unsurprisingly, James broke the tension.

"I liked the way I said it better," he pouted, folding his arms.

"I don't," Kiera snorted.

"Me either," Jay agreed, holding his hand out flat behind his back. Kiera lightly slapped his hand, not trying very hard to hide what they were doing.

"Whatever. Let's not get too into the weeds on it. Do what you think is right; that's what matters. People will either agree with you or they won't. And it won't do anything but make your life shorter to try to make everyone agree with you all the time," James added.

"Wow. That was probably the deepest thing you've ever said, James," Derek interjected.

"I read a lot of comic books. It's something I've thought about before when thinking about why villains did what they did," James replied, starting to walk again with the group. "But don't get me wrong, some people are just bastards and want to watch people suffer."

After walking for a couple of miles, Derek pointed to a spot in the canyon wall where they could begin their ascent. The teams lined up and proceeded single file up the narrow, winding path that led out of the canyon. It was a steep and careful climb, but they moved steadily, watching their footing on the rocky terrain.

Once they reached the top, everyone paused to catch their breath and took a moment to survey their surroundings. The vast expanse stretched out before them, and they exchanged glances, taking in the view and mentally preparing for the journey ahead.

"Where the fuck are the vehicles?!" Tom yelled.

Chapter 2

Under Pressure

"They're over there, Tom," Derek said, facepalming as he pointed farther down the canyon to where the vehicles had been left.

"Oh, right. Sorry," Tom said, feeling extremely embarrassed.

"We just came up at a closer point than we went down. Nothing to worry about. Who's going to steal them anyway? There isn't anyone here," Derek asked.

"I don't know. But we did fight off all those raiders. If anyone is going to loot us, now's the time to do it. I mean, we *technically* stole those vehicles to begin with," Tom replied defensively.

"True, but it's unlikely to happen without more people around. And people coming here are likely looking for the quest, which likely was removed from their interface when we completed it," Derek explained, beginning to walk toward where the GS2, motorcycle, and Hummer were parked.

Moving behind him, the team followed along.

"Sorry, it's just hard not to think that in this world now," Tom said.

"Understandable, but there were no signs. Glass on the ground from broken windows, no tire tracks to show they left or were even here to begin with, nothing to indicate they were stolen. Look harder before you panic and, by extension, panic others," Derek scolded Tom.

"You're right, of course," Tom sighed heavily.

"You only said what some of us were thinking," James added. "I just wasn't quick enough on the swear."

"I'm just glad they're there still. My nerves are frayed enough as it is. With everything that's been happening, I'm just ready to get some rest," Tom said, hunching slightly as he walked. "Jay, you wanna drive the first leg of the journey?"

"I thought you'd never ask!" Jay blurted excitedly.

Tom pulled the keys from his Inventory and tossed them to Jay, who caught them deftly midair. A grin spread across Jay's face as he thought about the possibility of running over more goblins on their way back. He let out a maniacal cackle, and Kedron joined in, rubbing his hands together like a classic villain as they excitedly planned their goblin encounters on the trip home.

Derek rolled his eyes at the pair, shaking his head in mild amusement. The teams made their way to the vehicles, climbing in and getting ready to head toward the canyon entrance. James opened the trunk for DeeDee and Squirrel to climb in, making sure they were comfortable before shutting it. As Tom settled into the passenger seat, Jerky appeared on his shoulder, ready for the journey ahead.

"Just gonna take my spot?" Derek asked Tom after he had closed the door.

"Yup. Guild leader perks. You'll be alright," Tom said, not even looking at him as he slumped down in the seat, about ready to take a nap.

Derek rolled his eyes again and climbed into one of the captain's chairs in the middle row.

"And you're gonna take my seat?" James said indignantly.

"Yup. I can hit things through the window that get close. Plus, Guild General perks. You can crawl up to the sunroof if needed," Derek replied, also without looking at James.

"This is some bullshit," James grumbled as he crawled into the back row.

"Actually…" Kiera frowned. "There were a lot of groups who died fighting that bastard down there, wasn't there? There's probably a lot of vehicles, or at least supplies, that are going to be up for grabs."

James' head suddenly popped up from the back seat, his eyes gleaming.

"Down, boy," Jay said, looking at James through the rearview mirror.

James' smile melted, his head lowering sadly from sight.

"Jay's got a point," Derek nodded. "We don't know these people enough to know which group didn't make it nor where they parked their transportation, and we don't have enough time to wait for everyone to clear out and then take what's left."

"Okay… fine." Kiera huffed, climbing into the vehicle.

A long, sad sigh came from the back seat.

Once everyone was settled, they set off toward the canyon entrance. Since their vehicle was parked closest, Tom's team was the first to arrive. They waited patiently, keeping an eye on the horizon as the rest of the teams made their way back.

About an hour later, the others began to arrive, each vehicle pulling in one by one. Bob rode in with Zach, seated in the passenger seat of an Escalade, looking relieved to have finally made it. The teams regrouped, ready to continue their journey together.

"That is a sweet ride," James said, whistling as he popped up through the sunroof, admiring the Cadillac.

"I'll trade you for the modified ride you all have. That thing looks mean!" Zach called back from the driver's side window.

"Just run over some gobos, get the *Vehicular Manslaughter* Skill, then use the upgrade points. You can make yours look mean, too," Tom called over.

"What?! That's it?" Zach cried in disbelief. "You've been running those fuckers over?"

"Yeah, little bastards got in the way, so we just kept going. Easier than going around them," Tom called back.

"Aren't you worried about damaging your ride?" Zach asked.

"Nope. Plenty of vehicles out there if need be. Besides, we have a mechanic, and the upgrade points can be used to fix the vehicle if you're really in a bind," Tom said nonchalantly.

"We seriously need to talk about what you all know," Zach said, looking wide eyed at Tom in amazement.

"We'll have time. Now, follow us, and we'll start heading for Dallas. Driver, eastbound, please," Tom said, taking on the accent of a rich person.

"Right away, sir!" Jay replied in his best terrible British accent, then giggled evilly as he put the GS2 into drive.

"Wait!" James suddenly shouted from the back.

DeeDee squealed as a mountain of supplies fell onto her. Everyone turned their head toward James as he ferociously dug through the supplies that were suddenly piled back there with him. After long moments of complaints and things flying through the air of the car, he shouted victoriously.

"Found it!" James shouted. He crawled over the seats and the people in them, despite their shoving and complaining. Reaching the front, he held out something toward Tom.

Grabbing the item, Tom frowned.

"Did… you just empty your entire Inventory just so you could dramatically dig through it inside the car?" Tom asked.

Jay was holding one thick-fingered hand over the lower half of his face, but his shaking shoulders gave away his uncontrolled laughter.

"What the fuck, dude?" Tom scowled at the rapidly retreating James.

James didn't answer. He was apparently too busy stuffing everything back into his Inventory. But Tom was wrong. The man did answer, after a fashion.

"Couldn't find a monocle!" James retorted by way of explanation, now crawling under the bench seats for the rest of his things. "Times are tough. It's the best I could do!"

"Are these…" Kiera's voice called out in confusion, holding up a set of thin, wrapped objects. "...tampons?"

"*Excuse* you." James' head popped up as he snatched the toiletries from the woman's hand. "Did you think it was Valentine's Day or something? I'm saving those for a special someone," James huffed before disappearing back toward the floorboards.

Kiera looked at Derek, who simply shrugged.

Still laughing, Jay put the vehicle in gear and began to carefully drive toward the entrance of the park; weaving between groups who were packing for their own journeys. He pulled to a stop near a group of three people, looking at Tom meaningfully.

"We're not leaving until I do this, are we?" Tom asked, resigned to his fate.

"Not a chance in hell." Jay smirked.

Tom tilted his head back toward Derek, looking for support. The soldier smiled, shaking his head. "You wanted the front seat, big guy. This one's on you."

Tom held up the jar of Grey Poupon while everyone broke out into laughter. The Warlock rubbed his face before shrugging and rolling down his window.

The group looked up, surprised. One of them opened their mouth to speak. "Uh. Hi. Can we help you?"

Tom sighed, but straightened his face before holding up the jar of honey mustard, his voice taking on a cultured tone.

"Pardon me…"

Gales of laughter followed in their wake as Jay peeled out, leaving the small group scratching their head in confusion.

As they drove out of the Grand Canyon National Park, the teams began their long journey back to Dallas. Traveling along the highway was smoother now, with one side of the road cleared, allowing them to maintain a steady pace without constant obstacles.

"It feels weird to be driving on this side of the road," Jay said offhandedly to Tom. I'm not complaining at all, though. It sure as hell beats having to get out and move vehicles."

"Mhm," was all Tom said in reply as he continued to stare out the passenger window.

"Something bothering you, brother?" Jay asked him, turning his head back and forth between the road and Tom.

"I have no idea what I'm doing," Tom said sullenly. "I'm expected to have the answers for what we should be doing to fix… *everything*, and I'm feeling completely overwhelmed as to how to handle all these new situations. First, Seth dies, and I can't do anything about it. Then, I get told there might be a full-on war happening when we return, and it's with some power-hungry Guild leader looking to steal our people away from us. We have so many people in the Guild now who are all looking to me for answers, and I can't promise a single one of them that they'll be safe from anything without flat-out lying to their faces."

"You do realize you're putting all that pressure on yourself. No one is doing it to you," Jay replied.

"But everyone looks to me as the leader," Tom said, finally turning to look at Jay.

"Dude, you have the title, but we're all here offering to help you. You aren't bearing this alone, and you're absolutely not held responsible for what happens to anyone. It's no secret that the best leaders are also the best delegators. You're just one guy who people picked to be the leader so that they didn't have to have the stupid title themselves. You just happened to be the first chump to say yes," Jay added, shrugging as he said the last bit.

"Thanks. That really makes me feel special. Then how about you be the leader?" Tom blurted out.

"No thanks. I'm not looking to add to my list of stupid decisions. I make plenty of those without the added pressure," Jay chuckled, shifting to drive with only his right arm on the top of the steering wheel. "You're stuck being the scapegoat. Plus, I don't think it would go over well with everyone to have a sudden change of management either."

"But I don't fucking want it! It's too much pressure!" Tom exclaimed.

The car went silent at this outburst, everyone turning to look at the pair in the front seats.

"Ha! No one does. But someone has to. You've been doing an amazing job at being the Guild leader."

"Bullshit," Tom scoffed.

"You don't think so?" Jay replied. As he spoke, he began ticking off each of his fingers, which only made Tom more nervous as the man was driving. "You aren't a tyrant who tells people what to do all the time. You have a group of people you consider your inner circle that you always turn to for advice, and most importantly, you tend to listen to them when they give it to you," Jay explained. "You're just beating yourself up for no reason. Not a single person would want to trade places with you, but not a single person would criticize you, either. Well, not a single person that matters."

"I see what's happening here," DeeDee said from the trunk. "You're trying to do it all instead of delegating. Think of yourself as the manager of a team. Yes, you should make important decisions as a finality so that people don't question them, but you need to let others know what you're thinking in the process."

"What do you mean?" Tom asked, turning to look over his shoulder.

"You worked in software development, right?" DeeDee asked.

"I did," Tom replied, confused about where she was going with this.

"Think of yourself as the IT director for the entire team working on the next big coding project. The entire thing is being developed by your team, and you're in charge of what happens when," DeeDee explained. "But that doesn't mean you sit at a computer and code the whole thing yourself. You step back and look at how the project is going as a whole, give your inner circle things to do to manage those nitty-gritty details, and then meet with them for progress updates and discussions on what needs to happen. If you look at every line of code, you'll go completely crazy and never get anything done. Plus, if you try to do everything yourself, no one else will know how everything fits together. If you get killed, the whole team will fall apart."

"Are we… still talking about coding?" Tom said, confused.

"It's an illustration, dummy," DeeDee huffed but continued on where she'd left off. "If you bring people in to manage things, then you can know what's going on since you're looking at the forest and not just the trees, and not just you. That way, if something happens, the team can keep going without you. That, in turn, takes a lot of the weight off your shoulders."

"What was it you did again before this all happened?" Derek asked DeeDee.

"I was a Scrum Master for a development team. So, I'm used to seeing IT professionals meltdown as they try to micromanage things," DeeDee replied, stroking Squirrel's fur.

"She's right, you know. And I'm not just saying that because she's my wife," Graham added. "You gotta let this go and work with everyone. If you try to bear all the weight, you'll snap. And that leaves everyone in a bad place."

"I thought I *was* working with everyone?" Tom asked, exasperated.

"You are, but also not. You're working with us in that you listen to advice, but you *aren't* in that you keep bottling up your emotions and thoughts. You gotta open up more," Jay said, stealing Tom's attention back to the road. "Don't you already feel a little better knowing we aren't mad and are ready to help you with how you're feeling right now?"

"Actually, I do. It's a relief to know that everyone isn't mad at me for what happened," Tom said, sagging a little in his seat.

"Blaming you for what happens is like blaming a higher power for when someone's loved ones get hit by drunk drivers. If some deity were responsible for every action that a human being with free will took, then that means they are some crazy, heartless bastard who just likes to watch the world burn. You didn't make anyone do anything. They always had a choice to walk away or not listen. Bad things happen. You don't make them happen unless you go on a killing spree," Jay explained.

Up ahead, a group of goblins had set up a makeshift barricade across the road. Caught off guard by the approaching vehicles from behind, they scrambled to the other side of their flimsy stick wall, brandishing their weapons and glaring menacingly at the incoming convoy. The goblins stood their ground, attempting to look intimidating despite the obvious surprise and disarray.

"Oh, hold that thought," Jay said as he sat up straighter and put both hands on the wheel, speeding up slightly. "Papa's got a Skill to unlock…"

The GS2 barreled through the barricade, shattering the makeshift structure and sending goblins flying. The wooden wall splintered on impact, sending jagged pieces of debris shooting into the goblins that weren't directly in the vehicle's path. Screams filled the air as some goblins were crushed beneath the wheels, while others were pierced by the sharp fragments of wood, their cries echoing briefly before fading into silence.

"Sorry about that. Where were we?" Jay asked, unable to stop smiling.

A second crash resounded behind them as Kedron and the others swerved to the sides, targeting any goblins that had escaped the initial onslaught. They skillfully maneuvered their vehicles, finishing off the stragglers missed by the first charge.

"Those green idiots. You'd think they'd learn about the way vehicles can just destroy them and won't slow down. Or maybe there are still some people with sensibilities about them," Jay added.

A shadow began to cover the vehicle slowly as they drove forward. Everyone was so busy watching the devastation behind them that they almost didn't see what was in front of them.

"JAY, WATCH OUT!" Tom shouted as he braced his arms on the dashboard.

Chapter 3

Goblins, Goblins, Everywhere

Jay slammed on the brakes, bringing the GS2 to a screeching halt as quickly as he could. In front of them, a towering structure at least four stories high was being pushed into the road, blocking their path. The massive contraption was a chaotic blend of wood and steel, haphazardly held together with rope, nails, and globs of tree sap. It loomed over them like a makeshift siege tower straight out of a medieval battle, complete with an array of wooden and metal spikes jutting from the front, designed specifically to prevent anything from simply ramming through it.

"You just had to talk about how stupid they were, didn't you?" James scolded Jay from the back seat.

Goblins standing on the structure leaned out, jeering at the vehicles below and tossing rocks that bounced harmlessly off the metal exteriors. Some of the goblins danced atop the tower, celebrating what they perceived as a victory simply because the vehicles had come to a stop. Tom leaned out of the window and gestured for everyone to join him outside before turning and flipping the goblins the bird.

As soon as the team exited their vehicles, rocks and a few spears began pelting them from above. Quickly raising their shields or ducking their heads to avoid the incoming projectiles, Tom signaled for everyone to get back inside the vehicles. They pulled back, retreating to a safe distance just beyond the range of the tower's makeshift weapons. Once they were clear, they noticed the structure slowly inching forward, as if determined to continue its advance despite the setback.

"Holy shit, it moves," Jay gasped at the large structure moving at a snail's pace.

"They moved the damned thing into the road, idiot," James called out from the back.

"Right, but then it wasn't *chasing us* like some kind of *Friday the 13th* villain!" Jay shouted back. "And that it moves at all is a miracle of modern goblin invention. Have you seen the other shit they make?"

"Well"—James shrugged—"don't trip and you should be fine."

Jay looked back at the slowly crawling fortification before pressing his lips together, his eyebrows raising in agreement. "Okay, yeah. That's fair."

Tom leaned out of the window and made a wide circling motion with his hand, signaling for everyone to gather together. The teams quickly exited their vehicles and converged in front of the GS2. Once everyone was assembled, Tom stepped forward and addressed the group, ready to discuss their next move.

"Look, these are just goblins," Tom called out to everyone. "It won't likely be much of a challenge, but we can't let this many of them go on their merry way. So, let's make this quick and fuck up their day. Everyone, get your weapons ready, and I'll give the signal for when we start."

"What's the signal going to be?" Zach asked.

"An *Eldritch Blast* to the structure. I figured it would be obvious, but whatever..." Tom snapped, slightly annoyed.

"Sorry, mate. You doing okay?" Zach asked, concern evident on his face.

"Yeah, I'll be alright. Sorry I snapped. Been having a rough time recently," Tom apologized and hung his head slightly.

"No worries, mate. It's been a rough couple of... well, weeks, I suppose. If you need anything, we're here for you," Zach offered, putting a hand on Tom's shoulder.

"Thanks. I'll probably need to take some of you up on that offer soon. For now, though, let's handle these goblins." Tom refocused the group and hardened his resolve.

"So, just a smash-and-grab?" Bobby asked.

"Smash-and-grab?" Isaac asked, staring confusedly at Bobby.

"Yup, a standard beat the shit out of anyone inside and take all their stuff," Bobby replied.

"Did someone say smash-and-grab?" James chirped, his head popping up. His eyes were nearly glowing with enthusiasm.

"What kind of friends do you have, Tom?" Isaac said, looking over at him with concern.

"The kind that likes smashing and grabbing," Tom said, smiling evilly.

"Fuckin'-A," Jay confirmed, holding his fist out toward Tom. Tom bumped it.

"What did I get myself into?" Isaac said, putting his face into his hand. "I chose Paladin because I wanted to be a good guy and help people."

"I'm a Paladin, too," Kedron said, raising a hand. "Being a paladin doesn't mean not killing goblins. In fact, if anything, you should want to kill goblins more. They're murderous little shit stains."

"I'm more concerned about the fact that someone on your team may have previously committed smash-and-grabs," Isaac said, making air quotes with his hands around the last words.

"Dude, I was in Iraq. Every day was a smash-and-grab. Smash into a terrorist hideout and grab all their weapons so they stop killing civilians," Bobby said as if he wasn't getting mad that someone was questioning his motives. "Seems like basically the same thing here. It's just smaller, greener terrorists."

"Well, crap. I'm sorry, man. I misjudged you," Isaac said sheepishly.

"Don't worry about it. It's kinda fun watching people squirm when I tell them that," Bobby smiled broadly at him.

"So, you do this for kicks?" Isaac asked.

"You're going to be so much fun to have in the Guild," Bobby said, now rubbing his hands together.

"Focus! We need to take down these goblins," Derek ordered them after letting the banter go on longer than he felt he should have. "Time to kick some ass and not worry about taking names."

"We probably couldn't pronounce them anyway. Or they'd just be like Crackle and Goatmeat," James added.

"Anyway… We can attack it and take this thing down with little trouble. Just don't let the goblins do anything drastic. Kill them quickly and thoroughly," Derek said, turning to face the contraption.

As Tom watched, the center of the towering structure suddenly dropped forward, revealing a massive trap door that opened like a gaping maw. From within, five goblin archers and three goblin mages emerged, immediately firing arrows and charging up magical attacks aimed at the group.

"SCATTER! DON'T GROUP UP! DON'T LET THEM HIT YOU ALL AT ONCE! BRING THEM DOWN NOW!" Derek shouted, his eyes widening in shock at the sudden assault.

The teams instantly split in every direction, making themselves harder targets for the goblins. Tom dashed to the side, quickly gathering energy for his own *Eldritch Blast*, which he launched at the structure. The blast struck the side of the tower, but instead of the expected explosion or flames, it merely left a small scorch mark on the surface.

"What the hell?!" Tom exclaimed in frustration. He had expected the mostly wooden and rope-bound structure to catch fire and burn, but it seemed more resilient than anticipated.

"That won't work. You can't use a little blast like that to set it on fire," called a man from his right, who Tom couldn't recall the name of. "Here, watch this!"

He raised his hands, the first one glowing with a sickly green hue as a spout of grease shot from his palm, coating the goblin structure in a slick, oily mess. Without missing a beat, he raised his other hand, where crackling orange fire erupted from his fingertips, shooting toward the now grease-covered contraption.

The moment the flames touched the grease, the entire structure burst into a roaring blaze. Goblins shrieked in panic, scrambling in a futile attempt to douse the fire with blankets. Realizing the flames were spreading too quickly, they began abandoning the burning tower, leaping from the sides in a desperate bid to escape the raging inferno.

"Now *that's* how you start a campfire," Clay said in awe of the flames. "We used to keep a burn pile out in the fields for burning brush, and at night, we'd have a bonfire party. Makes me want a jar of moonshine right about now."

"Don't just stand there with your thumb up your ass, pining for the days of old," Kedron yelled at Clay in a strong Southern accent. "Get your ass in gear, or you're not gonna get any goblin XP."

"Oh, shit! Save some for me!" Clay called out to the others, raising his weapon and charging into the fray.

The teams swiftly descended upon the scattered goblins, turning the fight into a merciless slaughter. The goblin archers and mages attempted to mount a defense, but Derek, Isaac, and several other shield-bearers quickly surrounded them, forming an impenetrable wall of shields. Meanwhile, Briana cast a barrier behind the fighters, blocking any stray projectiles from hitting the team.

Arrows ricocheted harmlessly off the shields as the goblin mages desperately hurled spells at the fighters. One man in plate armor took a direct hit from a small firebolt, but he barely flinched, charging forward and slamming his shield into the face of the offending mage. The goblin exploded in a shower of gore and ash, the force of the impact obliterating it instantly.

"What the hell?! I didn't know I had that kind of power with a shield?" the man, Emmery, exclaimed at the sudden blast, and he took a step back as he tried to process what was happening.

"You don't," Derek explained through a grunt as he bashed a goblin over the head with his mace. "It was a magical backlash. Apparently, he was getting a spell ready to cast when you hit him. By the looks of it, it was a big one. So good job stopping that."

Emmery swung his sword in a horizontal slash through a bow, string, then body of an archer goblin as he grunted back, "Sweeeet! It was fun to watch the thing blow up like a firecracker."

Graham stepped up beside Emmery and swung his axe in a powerful overhand strike that whistled past Emmery's head, missing him by mere inches. Emmery's eyes widened in shock as he instinctively dove to the side, narrowly avoiding the deadly swing.

"DUDE!?" Emmery cried in disbelief, anger starting to bubble up at nearly being hit.

He turned to look in the direction where the axe had landed and noticed a goblin, wearing all black with two daggers, split completely in half, lying on the ground just behind where he had been standing moments before.

"Oooohhhhh…" Emmery gasped, realization dawning on him.

Graham smiled down at Emmery, winked, and extended a hand to help him up before jogging off to join the next fight.

Meanwhile, Tom activated his *Cleave* ability with his greatsword, slicing through three goblins in a single horizontal swing as they charged at him with rusted short swords. The goblins tried to block the attack, but their weapons, weakened from neglect, shattered upon impact. Continuing the momentum of his strike, Tom pivoted and raised his hand, releasing an *Eldritch Blast* at a goblin that was attempting to sneak up behind Kiera.

The goblin screeched in pain, abandoning its ambush as it fled, frantically waving its hands in the air. Kiera, alerted by the goblin's yelp, glanced back and gave Tom a thumbs up before returning her focus to her rifle scope. She fired a precise shot at a goblin near the base of the burning tower. It exploded in a fountain of gore and fiery shrapnel.

"I see they have goblin bombers too," Tom shouted, both as a realization for himself and to let the others know.

Jay, moving swiftly and silently, used his daggers to strike at vulnerable points on goblins that were already engaged with other team members. Each motion was precise, resulting in critical hits with every strike. With one clean cut, he sliced open a goblin's neck, and in a fluid backswing, stabbed another goblin in the kidney. His relentless assault provided his allies with openings to finish off their own battles quickly.

Nearby, Kevin and Kirsten had become a synchronized whirlwind of destruction, their greataxes twirling in a deadly dance around each other. Their coordinated attacks left no opportunity for the goblins to mount a counterattack. Every swing of their massive blades cut down another goblin as they carved a path of devastation through the enemy lines, their war cries echoing over the battlefield.

With their defensive structure in flames and the relentless onslaught of the Vanguard Guild, the goblins fell into disarray, desperately attempting to flee. But none made it far. Spells, arrows, bolts, and bullets rained down upon them, ensuring that not a single goblin escaped.

As the last goblin fell, the team discovered the charred remains of a larger goblinoid creature among the wreckage of the siege tower.

"That's the second time we've seen one of these larger goblins leading a force," Derek observed, crouching down to examine the burnt corpse with his mace. "I think we might be seeing a pattern here."

"You've seen this before?" Zach asked, looking down at Derek.

"On the way to the Grand Canyon. We encountered a group similar to this, though without the construction. They'd formed a party and had apparently even learned to use the vending machines. They had actual gear on them as well," Derek continued while surveying the battlefield.

"That's a little unnerving," Isaac said as he walked over to where Derek, Tom, Zach, and a few others were standing. "Goblins that are learning?"

"I mean, they *are* humanoid creatures with at least a semblance of intellect. They can build structures; why not study and figure out how to use the machines?" Tom added, picking up a sword that seemed shinier than the others. "This looks like something they bought from a machine. I would guess they'd figured it out as well."

"This doesn't bode well for the future," Chris interjected.

"We can only take it one day at a time. But yes, it means that there's likely someplace where there will be a goblin society. Hell, this guy might not even be the leader. He could just be the one in charge of a raiding party," Tom said, thinking deeply about the implications.

"So, you're saying there's a goblin society out there?" Kiera asked, walking over to the group as she stored her rifle in her Inventory.

"We're saying it's a possibility. Hell, maybe they'll have their own Guilds. We can't know without scouring every inch of land to find out, and that just isn't happening. So, all we can do is build up our defenses, keeping a potential goblin raid in the back of our minds," Derek replied, standing up and dusting off his pants. "We should be doing that anyway. Building walls and defensive structures and other methods of dealing with enemies that might attack us directly."

"For now, everyone gather any equipment you can find. Weapons, items, even armor," Tom called out to everyone in the area.

"But their armor won't fit us," someone called back.

"You mean you guys didn't figure out that armor magically resizes for the wearer?" James asked back loudly, unsure who had spoken.

"Are you fucking kidding me?!" a man dressed in black leather cried. "I left stuff behind because I didn't think it would fit anyone but a child and there is no point in selling it, and I could have just tried it on?"

"Yup," was all James replied with, in a cheery voice.

"Son of a bitch!" the man screamed as he put his hands over his head in pure frustration.

A chuckle ran through the group of people.

"Don't worry. Anyone who needs equipment will get it. As long as you continue to do your part in the Guild, the Guild will take care of you," Tom announced loudly so everyone could hear.

This reassurance put many people at ease, further solidifying their belief that joining Tom and his team had been the right choice. As the group continued looting the goblins, several people approached Tom to shake his hand, expressing their gratitude for being welcomed into Vanguard.

About half an hour into the looting and search, Chris called out, "Hey, Tom. You're gonna wanna come see this!"

Tom, along with Derek, Jay, Zach, and Isaac, made his way over to the remains of the goblin siege structure. Most of it had burned down, but the base was still intact. They gathered around Chris, who was crouched down, examining a goblin lying on the platform.

"Is that what I think it is?" Derek asked, first looking at the floor beneath the charred corpse and then over at Tom.

"Well, that can't be good," Tom replied.

Chapter 4

On The Road Again

Staring down at the tower's base, Tom moved the charred husk that had been a goblin and tossed it off the platform. Underneath, the scorched wood revealed symbols etched into its surface—intricate, dark lines that formed a large circle with a smaller concentric circle inside. Runes filled the spaces between the circles, each one meticulously carved with an eerie precision that suggested purpose and intent. The symbols glowed faintly, as though they still held a residual energy, their shapes twisting and interlocking in a pattern that was unsettling to look at, hinting at a deeper, darker purpose behind the goblin's construction.

"Is it just me, or does that look like Azroc's summoning circle?" Derek asked, reaching out to trace the engravings.

"It's similar, but it's not the same. They weren't summoning Azroc, but it definitely was some kind of Warlock Patron ritual," Tom replied, pondering the implications of this discovery.

"So, now goblins get Classes?" Jay asked, confused as to what this meant for their future.

"I thought they already had Classes. More rudimentary Classes than ours, but Classes nonetheless. I guess this means something has changed, and they can get the same Classes as us. Probably has something to do with their use of the vending machines. I don't like this," Derek thought aloud as he worked through theories of what might be happening.

"So why would it change all of a sudden?" Zach asked, looking between Tom and Derek for answers.

"I have two theories," Tom explained, getting a nod from Derek in confirmation of his thoughts. "One, they are changing because they used the vending machines, and the System needs to recognize their Classes, so the System compensates for that. Or two, since the world is built on video game logic, the monsters we fight have to become stronger as we become stronger. In the video game world, it's called scaling. As you get stronger, the monsters level with you to ensure you don't just steamroll the game. It could be either one of those or possibly a combination of the two."

"Great. So, when we thought we could get stronger to survive better, are the monsters going to get worse, too?" Isaac blurted out, losing his cool a little at the thought of stronger monsters showing up.

"Looks that way. In games, it's a good thing, because if you kept killing tiny monsters, you wouldn't be able to level effectively once the XP started being zero for tiny creatures. Of course, in reality, what it means is we'll basically always be fighting for our lives," Derek added.

"Let me check," Tom said, eyes glossing over to read his combat logs.

After a few minutes of scrolling, he found what he was looking for, "Looks like its right. The levels of the creatures are higher than they used to be."

"Awesome," Chris chimed in, putting his hands on his hips and turning away to stare off into the distance. "One more thing to add to the 'I wish they fucking wouldn't' pile for this new existence."

"Not a lot we can do about it right now. But it means we have to be on our guard. Clearly, this world is still evolving, and we have to stay ahead of it. No taking monsters for granted," Derek said, grunting as he stood from kneeling.

"Does this mean we can evolve too?" Tom asked, almost as much to himself as to the others.

"I was talking more about evolving difficulties. I haven't seen much indication of actual evolution so far. Normally, in that kind of setting, there would maybe be a species rank that would show us that we have the ability to evolve. But I guess time will tell," Derek replied, stretching his back and getting satisfying popping sounds.

Tom paused and opened his System interface, his gaze settling on the backlog of notifications from his recent fights. Since the battle with the Devourer, he had been minimizing his alerts, allowing them to accumulate without review. Now, as he pulled them up, the screen was flooded with a sea of messages—hundreds of them, each marking an event, an earned XP, or a status update.

The sheer volume of information was staggering, with lines of text blurring together in a chaotic mess. Tom could see the glowing red of combat logs, the blue of completed quests, and the occasional gold of significant achievements, all layered in a dizzying cascade. It was too much to process at once.

Taking a breath, he focused his thoughts. With a mental command, he filtered the notifications, shrinking the overwhelming list down to a more manageable stack. The screen reorganized itself, neatly categorizing the messages by priority and type. Critical alerts hovered at the top, while less urgent updates were tucked away, waiting for review at his convenience.

Satisfied with the newfound order, Tom began to sift through the condensed list, ready to address the essential details and glean whatever insights he could from the battles he had fought. He started at the bottom, saving the important messages for last to process them.

XP Gained:
Your raid party has defeated 497 Devourer minions. XP gained: 385,276. Your share of this XP is 16,567.

XP Gained:

Your raid party has defeated the Dungeon boss: Devourer. XP Gained: 1,435,786. Your share of the XP is 47,859.

Level Up:

You have earned enough XP to advance to the next level. You are now level 24! Continue to work hard and push yourself to gain more XP to continue to level up. You receive 10 Attribute Points to distribute as you see fit.

Admin Blessing

For your outstanding leadership and strategic rallying of teams to confront a threat that would have led to Earth's destruction, you have been granted a blessing.

- **Reward: +5 Charisma**

Your ability to inspire and unite others in the face of overwhelming danger has not gone unnoticed. This boost to your Charisma will enhance your influence, further empowering you to lead and inspire those who follow your path. Continue to use your strengths wisely, as the fate of many rests in your hands.

Dungeon Rewards:

Your raid party left the Dungeon without claiming a prize for its completion. Each party member will be awarded 1 Rare Core as a reward instead of choosing an item.

Dungeon Cleared

Congratulations! Your raid party has become the first to clear this exclusive world event Dungeon. As a reward for this extraordinary feat, and in recognition of this once-in-a-lifetime achievement, each member of your party gains an additional **50,000 XP**.

This Dungeon will not be available to run again, marking this victory as a permanent milestone in the annals of your journey. Your success here will be remembered as a defining moment in the history of the Grand System. Continue to strive for greatness, and let this be the first of many legendary accomplishments!

"Well, fuck me sideways with a broom," Tom swore suddenly, causing a couple of people to jump.

"What?! What is it? Are we being attacked?" Clay yelled and equipped his weapon as he spun about, looking for something to attack.

"No, nothing like that. We were so focused on the people who died that we forgot to claim our Dungeon prize," Tom explained as he read over the prompt again.

"Oh, yeah. But you saw the System gave us a rare core, right?" Isaac said.

"You noticed and didn't say anything?" Tom asked indignantly.

"I just assumed you all had read your prompts like normal people. How was I supposed to know you put things off like that?" Isaac replied with a shrug, showing he didn't care how Tom felt about it.

"Yeah, yeah. You're right. I always put off prompts. I need to start being better about looking at those," Tom muttered to himself, although loud enough that others could hear him. "But fifty thousand XP doesn't feel right for what we went through. We could have just done some grinding for that."

"I'd say you should be happy for it," Derek interjected.

"Why?" Tom asked.

"When you kill monsters you get, what, a few hundred XP, maybe a thousand? To get more than that, you have to find bigger, more dangerous monsters. So, you saved yourself fifty potential death matches with creatures out here by doing that one quest, maybe more."

"Okay, yeah, I can see that logic," Tom conceded.

"As for the Dungeon item… At least they gave us something," Derek tried to add helpfully. "They could have just said, 'Too bad, so sad, you didn't select an item and just left.'"

"True. Glad they have some kind of fail-safe in there for that," Tom admitted.

"Actually, they don't normally," Bob interjected. "I think it only happened this time because it was a one-time completion Dungeon."

Everyone turned to look at Bob when he said this.

"You mean we could have lost a reward if we hadn't just been lucky enough to be in a one-time Dungeon?" Tom asked in a serious tone.

"Yes, unfortunately. Always be sure you pick a reward. Normally it's a lot harder to miss because the vending machine appears in front of you. This last time, it was less noticeable because the vending machine was already there," Bob continued. "In a normal Dungeon, it should be a lot easier to remember."

"That all makes sense. I sure wish I could have picked something from that machine, though. It would have been epic," Tom thought wistfully as he imagined looking over all the options.

"The others all have the same options. Just have to look through the menu to find them. I can show you how to use it if you would like," Bob offered to Tom.

"That sounds great! Next time we're near one, I'll hold you to that," Tom agreed and stuck out his hand to shake with Bob.

WAR

They shook hands to seal the agreement, and Tom returned his focus to his character sheet. With ten Attribute Points still at his disposal, he contemplated his next move.

After a moment of deliberation, he decided to allocate his points to bolster his Strength and Constitution, feeling these Attributes needed attention. He evenly distributed the points, placing five into Strength and five into Constitution.

Satisfied with his choices, he took a moment to review his updated stats, noting the increase in his physical capabilities and endurance.

Tom Harris	
Race: Human	**Class:** Warlock
Level: 24	**Total XP:** 545,926
XP To Next Level: 84,074	**HP:** 350/350
MP: 470/470	**SP:** 280/280
Attributes:	**Unused Attributes Points:** 0
Strength: 40	**Constitution:** 35
Dexterity: 30	**Endurance:** 28
Intelligence: 47	**Wisdom:** 40
Charisma: 80	**Luck:** 20
Non-Combat Skills:	
Inspect	**Level: 6 Rank:** Beginner
Combat Skills:	
Vehicular Homicide	**Level: 15 Rank:** Novice
Swords	**Level: 10 Rank:** Novice
Summon Demonic Creature	**Level: 9 Rank:** Beginner
Fear	**Level: 5 Rank:** Beginner
Corruption	**Level: 5 Rank:** Beginner
Spells:	
Eldritch Blast	**Level: 6 Rank:** Beginner
Dark Ball	**Level: 3 Rank:** Beginner
Dark Healing	**Level: 5 Rank:** Beginner
Lightning Strike	**Level: 5 Rank:** Beginner
Doppelganger	**Level: 2 Rank:** Beginner
Dark Flame Weapon	**Level: 3 Rank:** Beginner
Tattoos:	Tattoo of Brute Strength
Tattoo of Life Absorption	

Satisfied with the way his build was still progressing, Tom turned to the others in the group.

"Make sure you're assigning your Attribute Points if you haven't already. Don't need anyone falling behind in their growth. Time to get back into the vehicles and head on! Was there anything worth scavenging from the goblins here?" Tom called out to everyone in the group.

"Some armor and a few weapons. Nothing extra special, though. It looks like we interrupted a ritual of some kind, but without the details of what they were doing, the items are just random crap we don't have any use for," Bobby explained, stepping forward to show Tom the ingredients that were being used in the ritual.

"Well, that's… gross. They killed the chicken in the ritual space, I suppose?" Tom asked, looking at the odd assortment of items in Bobby's hands.

"Looks that way. The dagger they used is ornate looking but has trash stats," he continued. "I'd say it was a summoning ritual, but I have absolutely nothing to base that on except old *Indiana Jones* movies."

"Well, if there isn't anything of real value, just leave what we don't think others can use, and let's get going. Time to roll out!" Tom finished the last of this sentence in a loud voice as he spun his hand around in a circle over his head, signaling the others to load up.

Piling back into their vehicles, the convoy set off again, heading toward Dallas. Their first planned stop was Flagstaff, where they had previously assisted the townspeople with the raider problem. Tom hoped that they had found a way to come together and focus on survival. It was a cautious hope, but he believed that with most of the aggressors gone, the remaining raiders might be driven to seek help from the city to survive.

The devastation they had caused still weighed heavily on Tom. The raiders had given them little choice, with their relentless violence against the townsfolk who had only wanted peace. And peace, Tom knew, never came without a cost to someone. It was a harsh truth, one his grandfather had often shared with him after recounting his own war stories. Tom had always loved listening to those tales, filled with both bravery and loss, and they always ended with his grandfather's somber reminder: "Freedom is never free." Now, Tom truly understood what that meant.

Back in the vehicles, Jay started up the GS2, and they continued down the highway. Soon, the goblin tower disappeared behind the horizon in their rearview mirrors, the sun slowly dipping below it as well.

They pressed on for a while longer, but eventually decided to pull over and make camp for the night. They agreed to take shifts keeping watch in groups, and after setting up camp, they put some food in a pot to cook over the fire they had built.

As Tom sat around the campfire, watching the members of his Guild chat, share stories, and joke with one another, a warmth spread through his heart. It had felt so heavy over the past few days that he hadn't been sure how he would continue on. But moments like this, seeing the camaraderie and resilience of his friends, made the weight and sacrifices worth it. He found himself smiling, despite everything, and turned to talk with James, who had just come to sit next to him. Telling stories of their days before the apocalypse, James, Derek, Tom, and a few others sitting together laughed at their antics.

"So, you all were video game developers before the apocalypse?" Isaac asked, looking at Tom with genuine interest.

"Yup! We worked on several games over the last few years. Did you play Dragons of Argonia?" Tom asked.

"Did I?! That was where I really cut my teeth on MMOs. I played RPGs, but they were always single-player games. But DOA changed my life. I only play MMORPGs now. Man, I can't believe you all worked on that game," Isacc remarked, shaking his head in disbelief.

"We did. We were all also on the Assassin's Assault game. That was fun to talk about because we would all joke about going to AA meetings," Tom laughed as he recalled the inside jokes around the office.

"Remember how Donovan would always lean back and say he couldn't go because AA was for quitters! That son of a bitch was a true alcoholic through and through," Derek added, chuckling at the thoughts of the past dancing through his mind.

"What about you, Isaac? What did you do before this world went to hell in a handbasket?" Tom asked, leaning forward with his elbows on his knees.

"I was a commercial airline pilot," Isaac said, looking down at his food as though he was embarrassed by the job.

"Really?! That's so cool! What airline did you fly for?" James asked.

"You think that job is cool?" Isaac asked, turning to look at James in confusion.

"Controlling a giant aircraft to bring people from one place to another in a matter of hours that normally would take days to drive to or weeks to walk to? Hell yeah, it's cool," James replied with excitement.

"Most modern planes fly themselves for the most part. But I guess it is kinda cool to think about. I worked for Air US Mainway. Not the biggest company, but they paid well and treated their employees like family," Isaac added. "I got to fly all over the country. It was nice to see so many places, but it was hard to have a family with that kind of commitment."

"I could see that. We didn't even travel like that, and we are still single," Tom said.

"Yeah, James and Tom here even lived together. Made it nice when we all wanted to hang out, though. Meant half of the people lived there so we just hung out at their apartment to play games," Derek said.

"Half? Wait, who else worked with you?" Isaac asked, looking around the makeshift camp.

"Kevin," Tom said, looking over at him and smiling.

"Meathead Kevin?" Isaac asked in complete disbelief. "Kevin the *Barbarian*?"

"He didn't always look like that. That's a Barbarian perk. It makes him look all beefy. He was a skinny little nerd with anger issues before all this," Tom said, smiling even wider at Isaac's shock.

"Can confirm. I saw him just before the change, too," Jay said, pulling up a seat near the fire to join the group. "Now he's a normal muscle-head with anger issues. He roided out in a matter of minutes with that perk. It was cool to watch."

"Interesting. I will file that under things I probably didn't need to know," Isaac said, a look of confusion bordering on disgust coming to him as he looked at Kevin one more time.

"What about you, Chris? What did you do before all of this?" Derek asked as someone called that the food was ready.

"I was a mechanic. I owned my own shop. Worked on cars since I was a little boy. My dad was also a mechanic, so I followed in his footsteps. I love taking things apart and fixing them, and it was some of my happiest childhood memories doing it with my dad," Chris said, a look of sadness coming over him.

Tom placed a hand on the man's shoulder in solidarity.

"It's fine. My dad passed away about four years before this all happened. So at least he didn't have to see this shit hole," Chris said, looking down at the bowl of soup he was handed from the communal pot.

"I'm sorry to hear that, Chris. Losing a loved one is never easy," DeeDee said as she scooped out more bowls of the soup for others.

"Thanks. But it was for the best. He was getting older, and I don't know if he'd have lasted in this world," Chris replied, spooning some of the food into his mouth. "This is delicious, by the way. Where did you learn to cook like this?"

"I learned a little from watching videos online before the apocalypse and now from a Skill. Anyone can learn cooking, and the new Skill gives you some hints as to what will make things taste better as you experiment with recipes," DeeDee replied, smiling wide at Chris.

"You mean that cooking can now be reduced to a Skill that you can learn from so anyone can be a chef?" Tom asked, sitting up with interest.

"I suppose. But it kinda feels like there's more to it than that. Like, everyone can learn it, but some have an affinity for it that makes it easier. I don't know if that makes sense," DeeDee tried to explain.

Instantly curious, Tom pulled up his info sheets and looked at his Skills. He did a close inspection on *Swords*, and sure enough, it pulled up another menu.

"Well, I'll be damned. You're right, DeeDee," Tom said in shock as he stared with unfocused eyes at the Skill screen.

Skill: Swords

This Skill allows the user to gain experience with swords. Pointy end toward the bad guy.
Level: 10
Rank: Novice
Affinity: 78%

"If you inspect a Skill, you can see the affinity you have for the Skill. Like I have a seventy-eight-percent affinity with swords," Tom explained. "I wonder if that will affect how far I can go with it?"

"It will. But for many Skills, it's mostly unimportant," Bob interjected. "Most Skills are never raised to a level where that type of difference will matter. It'll be more obvious with physical Skills like *Swords*, but it still will be of little consequence until you reach much higher levels."

The snapping of a branch off in the distance suddenly caused the team to jump and look toward the trees behind them.

"What the hell was that?" Tom called out. "Everyone, weapons ready! Form up!"

Chapter 5

Flagstaff

With everyone armed and ready, the group moved into a defensive position. The magic users and ranged fighters took cover against the vehicles, forming a solid line of defense. Out in front, the Tanks and melee fighters stood ready, weapons drawn, prepared to intercept any threats that might emerge. Weapons seemed to appear almost instantly in their hands, equipped directly from their Inventories just as they had been instructed. The tension in the air was palpable. Every eye scanned the surrounding treeline, watching for movement.

Suddenly, a woman emerged from between the trees, her hands raised high in a gesture of surrender. Her eyes were wide with fear, darting nervously across the group in front of her—each member with weapons raised or spells ready to cast.

"Don't attack, please. I mean you no harm, " the woman said, still with her hands outstretched, showing she was not trying to be a threat.

"Sarah? Is that you?" Tom called out.

"Tom?" Sarah replied.

"What the hell are you doing out here?" Tom asked her. "Oh, stand down, everyone; I know her. She's good people."

Relaxing, the team returned their weapons to their Inventories and began to go back to sitting around the camp.

"I came out here to try to catch you on your way back to Dallas. I figured that with the completion of the quest, either you had something to do with it or you'd be headed back this way. Are you planning to go through Flagstaff?" Sarah asked.

"We are, but you didn't need to come out here. We would have found you when we went through town," Tom said, concern on his face for her. "You could have been hurt out here. You aren't exactly a fighter."

"I can handle myself. And what if you hadn't gone through town? How did I know you would stop there for sure?" Sarah asked, putting her hands on her hips in annoyance.

"It was much more likely for us to stop there than in some random campground off the road," Tom argued. He sighed, waving off the argument. "Regardless, we *are* going there. So, no need to worry," Tom assured her.

"Good. Because there are a bunch of people waiting," Sarah said, still miffed but letting him off the hook for his attitude.

"Wait, why?" Tom asked, suddenly confused.

"They're going with you back to Dallas. They saw what you could do and figured that they had a better chance of survival with you than staying in Flagstaff," Sarah explained. "The raiders came back, and a lot of them want to go as well."

"And you're okay with that? After they terrorized you all?" Tom questioned her, unsure he would be so forgiving.

"They were doing what they thought they had to in order to survive. Plus, most of the people left are women and children. The men were the ones who were doing the violence," Sarah explained.

"I'm not sure we can just take on a bunch of women and children to protect," Tom thought aloud and turned to see what Derek thought.

"You don't think you can just reject them, do you?" Sarah asked in complete shock. "You would turn them away simply because they aren't fighters?"

"No, we would never do that. But it's complicated. They're going to travel with us, which makes us more vulnerable. We have to carefully plan so they don't become a liability on the road," Derek interjected. "We have to set up a protective force that can be at the front and back with a few in between so if we are attacked, they can protect the non-combatants."

"Do they have any Skills they might contribute? We always tell people before they join that they have to contribute or they'll have to be let go. We need all kinds of people, but we can't just support a bunch of moochers," Tom said, trying to be both blunt and caring at the same time and finding it very difficult.

"They'll work for their way. No one there seems to be lazy. Though, I suppose I haven't personally interviewed each of them. How do you normally do that?" Sarah asked.

"*I* don't. Normally we have people that do that, and I've been away for a while so I'm not sure what the protocol is. But we can have them all screened. I won't just extend invites willy-nilly. But they can come nonetheless, I suppose," Tom said, looking again at Derek.

"I can't in good faith let them just stay, but this is going to make things very complicated," Derek sighed loudly as he thought about the logistics. "How many are there that want to come?"

"About three hundred," Sarah said as she winced at having to tell them the actual number.

Tom and Derek stared in wide-eyed shock at Sarah for a long moment.

"Holy shit," was all Tom could think to say.

"I know, it's a lot of people, but we can't just leave them there," Sarah said, almost desperate to get them to agree.

"Yeah, that's definitely a lot," Tom said, running his hand through his hair as he began to think frantically about how they might transport that many people to Dallas.

"We have vans. And with Inventories, people don't really have luggage to take. We also found a large school bus to take a lot of them. We're trying to reduce the number of vehicles it'll take to transport them," Sarah added, trying to offer a solution.

"That'll definitely help. See how few vehicles we can fit them all into," Derek mused as he considered the best strategy. "See if there are any city buses as well and if anyone can drive them."

"Right! I'll go back and get them ready. You'll be here for the night, it looks like?" Sarah asked, looking over Tom's shoulder at the camp.

"Yeah, we're going to stay here. We'll be headed into town in the morning. We really need some rest," Tom replied, looking back at the team.

"Your little party keeps growing. You're a good man, Tom," Sarah said, rubbing his arm before she turned and made her way back into the forest.

Tom smiled after her as she followed a trail deeper into the woods.

"Somebody's got a girlfriend," James teased in a sing-song voice.

"I do not!" Tom said indignantly. "Sarah is just a friend."

"A friend who's a girl," James continued teasing.

"You're just jealous that you are still alone and no one likes you," Tom said to James.

"Wow… that was harsh," James said in mock insult. "If I wasn't such good friends with you, I just might slap you, good sir."

"You could try," Tom taunted James with an evil smile.

James swung his hand out to slap Tom and missed as Tom leaned back with an agile grace that seemed born of years of practice.

"How the hell did you do that?" James asked in awe.

"Honestly, I have no idea. It just felt instinctual," Tom said, looking at his hands, equally confused.

They both paused, staring at each other in shock. Suddenly their eyes both narrowed and Tom leaped up from his seat, backing away quickly as James began to attempt to slap him in earnest, chasing him around the camp.

"Are we sure they aren't already together?" Isaac murmured, leaning toward Derek.

"Positive. Though you wouldn't know it sometimes," Derek replied softly as they watched Tom and James laughing and slapping at each other.

"Should we say something?" Isaac asked.

"Nah. Let them have their fun. Tom needs the distraction," Derek said, returning to his soup and blowing on a spoonful before bringing it to his mouth.

Tom and James playfully chased each other around the camp, weaving between tents and darting around makeshift obstacles, their laughter echoing in the cool night air. They kept up their spirited game for a good five minutes, dodging and taunting each other, before their luck ran out. Both tripped over a log, tumbling to the ground in a tangled heap of limbs and laughter.

As they lay there for a moment, catching their breath and trying to untangle themselves, the rest of the camp erupted in laughter at their antics. Grinning sheepishly, Tom and James finally managed to stand up, brushing off dirt and leaves. Still chuckling, they made their way back to the circle around the fire, welcomed back with friendly jabs and pats on the back.

"Tomorrow, we head into Flagstaff. Sounds like a lot of people are going to be joining us," Tom said seriously.

"Indeed. But that's okay. We knew there were going to be people wanting to join. Maybe not this many, but still. It'll help in the long run," Derek replied, not looking up from his soup as he finished the last of the bowl.

"Yeah, but at this rate, we'll gather people up like a snowball rolling downhill on our way back and might have an issue with how many we'll be bringing," Tom looked at Derek as he spoke worriedly.

"All true. But we can only take things one day at a time for right now. We can figure that all out when we are back and have an accurate account of what we'll be looking at. For now, sleep and rest. Tomorrow will take care of tomorrow," Derek said sagely.

"Wow, thanks, Mr. Fortune Cookie," James piped in. "But I guess he's right. Nothing we can do about it right now. May as well rest."

"Fine. I just need to eat a little, and I'm off to bed," Tom said, moving to the pot over the fire to get some soup.

After eating his fill, Tom and the others retired to their tents for the night. Teams of six took turns keeping watch, rotating shifts to ensure the camp was always on guard.

The next morning, everyone awoke early. The camp buzzed with activity as tents were taken down, gear was packed into Inventories, and everyone loaded back into the vehicles. As they set off down the road, Tom's mind wandered to the people in Flagstaff and the growing number of new recruits joining the Guild. It was remarkable how many were willing to come together under one banner. Still, he couldn't help but wish a few more seasoned fighters were among them.

When they finally arrived in Flagstaff, the change was astounding. The once eerily silent ghost town, where everyone hid in fear of an impending attack, was now bustling with life. People moved through the streets with purpose, no longer shadowed by the dread of violence. The air of fear had been replaced by an undercurrent of hope and determination—a group preparing for a mass exodus.

Vans and buses were being packed with people and supplies, while others organized makeshift caravans. Amid the controlled chaos, Sarah stood at the center of it all, orchestrating the preparations with a commanding presence, ensuring everything was done efficiently and with care.

"Oh, hi, Tom!" Sarah exclaimed in excited recognition once the team had parked and were walking toward the group of people.

"Hey, Sarah. There sure are a lot of people. Is everyone coming?" Tom asked.

"Almost. There are a few still planning to stay, but they are those that like their privacy and have always been a bit on the outside of the community anyway," Sarah explained. "But everyone else will be, and they have all agreed to put any skills they have to use for the Guild."

Tom looked at her beaming face and smiled back. "That is excellent news! I'm glad they're willing to try to pull their weight."

"We did have a few who were reluctant at first, but when we told them it was help or stay, they came around. I did make note of who they were, though, just in case it becomes an issue later," Sarah continued, looking at her clipboard with names in a list on a writing pad.

"That'll be extremely helpful. If we know who to keep an eye on from the start, we won't have any surprises," Tom said, looking over her shoulder at the names on the list.

"We should be ready to go within the hour. I'm not sure how long you were planning to stay, but with everyone going, I figured getting on the road early would be better than dawdling around here," Sarah said, again looking up at him and smiling. "I'm all about efficiency and want to make sure we do this right."

"That's great! I don't suppose you'd want a position as an Assistant Chancellor in the Guild to help our main guy with all the new people, would you?" Tom asked, thinking about how much she could help Brian.

"Depends. What's the pay like?" Sarah teased Tom.

"Abysmal," Tom teased back. "Almost as bad as the hours you have to work."

"Torture in the workplace? Sounds like my kind of job. Sign me up!" Sarah replied excitedly. "But seriously, I'd love to help get them all sorted so it's not as big of a burden on you all."

"Awesome! I'll get you in touch with Brian when we get back. He's our Guild Chancellor and takes care of the day-to-day workings of the people management stuff," Tom explained. "I'm sure he'll be happy for the help."

About half an hour later, Sarah stood at the front of the line of buses and vans, meticulously checking off the last of the names on her list. One by one, people climbed aboard a large yellow school bus, their faces a mix of determination and anxiety. She moved with a practiced efficiency, her eyes darting between the list and the people, ensuring everyone was accounted for and ready to go.

"That's everyone accounted for. And we're slightly ahead of schedule! Tom, are you all ready?" Sarah called out to Tom and his team.

"Sure are!" Tom called back.

"Then let's get this show on the road! Dallas, here we come!"

Chapter 6

Albuquerque & Amarillo by Morning

With six buses and a minivan now added to the convoy leaving Flagstaff, the group set out on the next leg of their journey to Dallas. The GS2 and the Hummer, along with Carl on his motorcycle, took up the front position, leading the way. Isaac, Zach, and Chris, each in their own vehicles, brought up the rear to cover the back. The plan for signaling trouble from the rear was simple: the last vehicle would honk at the last bus, and that bus would continue honking up the chain until it reached the first bus, which would then honk at Tom and his team.

"In theory, we should hear the honking long before the front bus honks at us, but this way we can be sure they're all listening and repeating it to us," Derek explained when someone asked how they planned to communicate between the vehicles.

"We don't have radios, and cell towers are still down, so there aren't many other options," Tom added, elaborating on the plan he and Derek had put together. "We can only work within the limits that we have."

"Don't buses *have* radios already," Jay asked.

"In case you haven't noticed," Derek snorted. "Most of these things are *school* buses."

"And?" Jay asked, clearly confused.

"What would a school bus need a radio for, genius?" Derek asked, exasperated.

"To call in the SWAT team?" Jay asked.

Derek sputtered.

"Hey, schools are dangerous these days," Jay argued.

"Just have them use the horns," Derek scowled

Everyone agreed to the idea, and with that, they set off. The majority of the trip back to Albuquerque was uneventful. They encountered a few goblin barricades along the way, but nothing as formidable as the tower they'd faced earlier. The vehicles and buses plowed through the makeshift barriers, leaving behind only bloody, splintered messes where their enemies had stood. Everyone had been warned not to stop for the goblins, as stopping could result in an attack, and it seemed that everyone took this warning to heart.

A few of the bus and van drivers had cringed and stiffened up when they first ran through the goblins, but after seeing Jay, Kedron, and Carl resolutely crashing through the flimsy defenses, they had powered through. One driver had screamed to his passengers to hold on and almost swerved out of the way, but as the GS2 and Hummer had taken out most of the obstacles, it had been a fairly smooth passage for them.

As they reached the outskirts of Albuquerque, Carl took the lead, guiding the convoy through the city along the easiest route. The oppressive heat bore down on them as they navigated the streets. Suddenly, a group of people stepped out onto the road, blocking their path. Not wanting to harm any humans without cause, the motorcade came to a halt to see what these people wanted.

"Get out of the fekking road!" Carl yelled at the people gathered before them.

"Are you Tom?" one man, appearing to be in his mid-thirties with short brown hair and piercing blue eyes, yelled back at Carl.

"No, now get out of the damn road, we need to get moving," Carl shouted grumpily.

"I'm Tom," Tom yelled from behind Carl.

"We need to talk to you! It's very important!" the man yelled to Tom.

Carl rolled his eyes and let out a heavy sigh before turning off his motorcycle, allowing the rumble of the engine to die so they could hear each other clearly. Tom stepped out of the GS2, the door creaking slightly as he pushed it open, and walked over to the man who had been calling out to them.

"What is it you want?" Tom asked a little more forcefully than he meant, but he was trying to stick to a schedule.

"We heard about what you did to the cult and to Jimmy," the man said when Carl cut him off.

"Jimmy..." Carl growled at the mention of the name.

"...Anyway, we heard what you did, and we want to join you. This world isn't safe, and we heard you have a Guild that's helping people," the man almost begged.

"We only help people who are willing to pull their weight," Tom said, looking the man up and down. "Are you someone that pulls their weight?"

"Andrew, sir," Andrew replied.

"Andrew? We can't just take care of people looking for a free ride. That's reserved for small children and the elderly," Tom continued.

"Of course! We're all willing to do whatever we need to so we can help. Some of us can even fight!" Andrew exclaimed, looking back to the others gathered, who were now nodding enthusiastically.

"You also need transport. We can't fit anyone else in with us," Tom said, looking back at the long caravan that held the passengers from Flagstaff.

"We can figure that out. If you can just give us a small bit of time, we'll be ready to go," Andrew replied quickly, hoping that Tom wouldn't turn them away if they took some time.

Tom turned to look at Derek, who rolled his eyes and gave a hand gesture of "fine, whatever, you're just going to do it anyway."

"Alright. But you have one hour, and we leave again," Tom said with finality.

"You got it!" Andrew said, turning and running back to the group. "He said yes! We just have to get vehicles to carry us all!"

Cheers erupted from the crowd that had gathered, and people scattered in every direction, like ants swarming at a picnic. Tom made his way back along the line of vehicles to talk to the rest of the convoy. He instructed each driver to allow their passengers out for a break but to be ready to depart again in an hour.

As people disembarked, they stretched their legs after the long ride, grateful for the chance to move around. Some took the opportunity for bathroom breaks, while others grabbed light snacks and water, chatting amongst themselves to pass the time. After the short respite, they began to regroup, climbing back onto their respective buses and vans, ready to continue the journey.

Forty-five minutes later, the people from Albuquerque had an assortment of vehicles, ranging from buses to a Mini Cooper, all ready to drive to Dallas.

"There's really almost too many vehicles in this group now. We can't promise to protect them all," Derek expressed his concerns to Tom.

"I know that. I've already sent each of our teams to the vehicles to relay the danger protocol but also to tell them they might have to defend themselves until we can get there," Tom replied, trying to calm Derek down.

"I don't like this," Derek said, crossing his arms over his chest.

"Fine, then you go tell them they have to stay here and fend for themselves," Tom said, also crossing his arms over his chest.

"Ugh! Fine. But when we get there, I don't know how we'll support this many people," Derek huffed as he walked back over to the GS2 and got in.

"Love you too!" Tom called after him. "Wait… am I James now?!"

He turned around to find James standing there, arms crossed and scowling. "Can't be me," he snorted. "Many men have tried…"

Tom's eyebrows drew down. "Like *who*, exactly?"

"*Many* men, Tom," James reiterated. "You think the burden you bear now is bad. Imagine trying to fill these shoes," he said, pointing down at his feet.

Tom blinked. "Are… Are those bath slippers from the hotel we stayed at a few weeks back?"

"Why are you looking at me like that?" James replied. "They said I could."

"*When?*" Tom exclaimed.

"When they told me to make myself at home," James explained patiently.

"And you thought that meant it was okay to steal from them?"

"Steal?" James patted Tom on the head, speaking slowly as if to someone mentally deficient. "Tom, I own everything in my home."

Tom rubbed his temples. "I give up."

James was still patting him on the head. "That's probably for the best. Being me is a tough responsibility. You should stay in your lane, where it's safe."

Tom swatted the man's hand away, grumbling as he moved to their vehicle.

Once everyone was loaded up, the line of vehicles began moving again, continuing their procession down the road. Leaving Albuquerque behind, they set out onto the open highway once more. After driving for most of the day, the convoy pulled off to the side of the road to refuel with the supplies they had brought along and take a break for a meal.

Each group had planned ahead, organizing amongst themselves to ensure they wouldn't need to dip into another group's supplies during this leg of the journey. They had been warned to bring enough provisions for a multi-day trip. As they sat and ate, people talked amongst themselves, their spirits remarkably high. Conversations buzzed with excitement about moving somewhere new and safer, filling the air with hope and anticipation as the hundreds of travelers made their way toward Dallas.

"We can't just stop here for the night. We need to switch drivers and keep making for Amarillo. When it was just us, we were fine to camp out. But with this many people to protect? We're fucked if you think we are capable of handling that," Carl said, looking at the large groups of people sitting and eating a meal.

"I hate to admit it, but he's right, Tom," Derek agreed reluctantly. "We need to keep going."

"Amarillo by mornin'," James sang with a Southern twang, a huge shit-eating grin on his face. "Up from San Antone. Everything that I got, is just what I've got on."

"Really? You're so desperate for attention that you're resorting to that level of humor?" Derek asked.

"Gives me all the attentions!" James said in a Gollum impression. "We wantses it, precious!"

"I didn't think it was possible, but he must have had it because he just officially lost it. James needs a nap," Derek said, looking at Tom.

"Hey! I am doing just fine, thank you. You're the one with something stuck up his ass about all of this," James retorted.

"Ladies, you're both pretty, smart, and brave," Tom laid it on. James preened at each word. Derek scowled. "We just need to focus on getting done what needs to be done. Derek, I agree, we can't camp out. Get some people to tell the teams they need to have someone fresh to drive now because we are driving through the night. I can't believe I'm saying this," Tom said with a sigh as he slumped slightly. "But we need to hit… Amarillo by morning."

"HA! They took my saddle in Houston," James sang bawdily. "Broke my leg in Santa Fe. Lost my wife and a girlfriend somewhere along the way. But I'll be lookin' for eight, when they pull that gate. And I hope that judge ain't blind…"

Jay sidled up to James, wrapping an arm around his shoulders. James, in turn, wrapped an arm around Tom. "Amarillo by mornin'," the two sang.

Tom sighed heavily but swayed in time with the song.

James paraded around for a moment like he owned the world, and then he went back to the Tahoe to check on Squirrel.

Derek whistled loudly, putting two fingers in his mouth.

"Alright, people!" Derek yelled out over the crowd. "Start getting ready to hop back in your vehicles! We can't stop here. There's too many people to protect! Time to get loaded up and head for the next major town!"

Everyone eagerly got up, stored their items in their Inventories, and climbed into the vehicles without a single fuss or complaint.

"That… went way easier than I thought it would," Derek said, extremely confused.

"That's the difference between people happy to go somewhere for the promise of safety and the old world where people felt like they had no control over their lives and kept being forced down certain paths. These people all chose this freely," Bob said, walking up to stand next to Derek.

"Hadn't thought about it that way," Derek admitted, musing to himself about the situation.

"I know this is tough, and it's not something you normally want to do, but I must say, your team's willingness to help these people makes me proud I chose to be a part of Vanguard. Others would have turned away an impossible task like fitting all these people into their Guild. But Tom and, by extension, *you* took on the burden anyway," Bob continued.

"What choice did we have, really?" Derek asked.

"Oh, you all had a perfectly good choice to tell these people to stick it where the sun doesn't shine and just go back without them. But you didn't, and humanity is defined by the moments where you have the option to show kindness. Those who do see a greater return in the long run than those who don't," Bob replied, putting his hands behind his back in a wise old man's stance.

"Alright then, sensei. What say you about how far we can take this? There are still several more towns we stopped in on the way back. Think we can take everyone?" Derek asked, looking sideways at Bob.

"I don't know," Bob replied, smiling at Derek in return. "But I feel we're going to find out."

The two chuckled lightly before heading back to their vehicles. This time, the teams decided to mix things up a bit—they redistributed the vehicles from the front and back of the line to intersperse them more evenly throughout the convoy. With so many vehicles now in the line, moving efficiently would be a challenge, but it would be worth it to avoid having to run from one end of the group to the other in case of trouble.

A loud honk from the front signaled the caravan to start moving, the sound echoing backward as each vehicle passed it along. Tom began driving the line forward, the convoy moving like a wild, stretched-out funeral procession. The sheer number of vehicles made it difficult to keep track of everyone's position, and at one point, honking began coming from the rear, working its way up to the front. The entire convoy came to a stop as Tom turned the GS2 around and raced to the back to see what the issue was.

When he arrived, he found it was simply a case of someone needing a bathroom break after driving for too long. Tom realized he hadn't accounted for such situations and made a mental note that they'd need to schedule more frequent stops.

"Are we going to need to train all of these people?" Jay asked, glancing over the growing group of survivors. "Like we did back on day one at the Guild?"

Tom exhaled, rubbing the back of his neck as he surveyed the exhausted but expectant faces around them. "We need to keep moving," he said. "We've got people at the Guild who can handle most of the training. But… it wouldn't hurt to give them a bit of a pep talk first, I suppose."

Before everyone climbed back into their vehicles, Tom quickly sent runners to each of the groups, instructing them to gather on the side of the road. Murmurs of confusion and restless shuffling filled the air as they assembled, dust swirling around their tired forms. The sun hung low on the horizon, casting long shadows as Tom stepped forward to address them.

He took a deep breath. "How many of you feel like you have a solid grasp of what's happening with the System so far?" His voice rang out, firm and clear.

A few hands rose, hesitant. Too few.

Tom nodded grimly. "Alright. If you were to gain a level right now, do you know how to allocate your Attribute Points? How to build your strengths?"

Even fewer hands remained up.

A quiet tension spread through the crowd. The weight of uncertainty hung heavy on their faces—some of them had been surviving by instinct alone, clinging to whatever scraps of information they could pick up along the way.

"That's okay," Tom reassured them, his tone steady. "We're going to help each of you figure this out. When we get to Dallas, we have a team dedicated to getting you up to speed—breaking down the screens, the Skills, the Attributes, all of it. You'll get the tools you need to make the most of the System's interface." He let that sink in for a moment, scanning their faces. "But for now, let's go over the basics. Just enough to get you started."

"But… we aren't fighters," came a voice from near the back of the crowd.

"You are. We all are. That's the reality of the world we live in. The truth is that we can't protect you all. We simply don't have the strength to do so, but we can show you how to protect yourselves," Derek spoke up. "Like it or not, we all have a role to play in this, and sometimes that will mean fighting for what you have. Now, listen to what Tom has to tell you so you don't get left behind in this new world."

And with that, Tom launched into a fifteen-minute breakdown of what they had learned so far—how Attributes shaped their strengths, how Skills and Spells could mean the difference between life and death, how weapons interacted with the System, and the importance of understanding the items they came across.

The air was thick with tension, but as he spoke, some of the fear in their eyes flickered into something else—determination. A spark of understanding. It wasn't much, but it was a start.

After he finished his tutorial, Tom urged them all to load up as quickly as they could. Stopping in the dark made him uneasy, so he hurried everyone back into their vehicles and set off again.

As the eastern horizon began to turn a beautiful shade of pink, signaling the morning sun preparing to crest over the Earth's curve, the sign marking the city limits of Amarillo came into view. Tom let out a sigh of relief—they had made it to the town. Everyone was tired and in need of a place to rest.

Tom pulled off the highway and they began to drive down the streets until they found an old hotel that looked to be abandoned. Pulling into several surrounding parking lots, all vehicles found a place to stop and let passengers off.

"Let's go in and see what we're working with here. Hopefully, there will be enough rooms for everyone," Tom said as the team leads all gathered together.

"I'm sure we can manage. The only tough part is going to be opening all the rooms. Well, maybe not tough, but time-consuming," Derek stated, thinking over how they would handle the situation. "Besides, people can double up in the rooms if necessary."

"Leave that to my team. We'll do a sweep, breaking open each door and leaving them open so everyone can come in as they please," Isaac offered, taking a good bit of the burden off everyone else.

"That's great! Go ahead and get started. We'll begin to get people headed in that direction once you've given us the all-clear," Tom said, grateful to have people so willing to take on the grunt work when he needed help.

Isaac and his team moved quickly toward the building, breaking the glass to get through the normally locked sliding doors. Once inside, they started moving down the halls, kicking in doors and propping them open to make sure the rooms were accessible. Meanwhile, Tom, Chris, Zach, and Derek were outside, trying to organize people into groups who could stay in the same rooms together. They prioritized families and close friends to ensure they could stick together and save space. If there were rooms left over, they would allow people to spread out a bit more.

As the groups were sorted, a member of Isaac's team guided them inside once they had completed the task of opening the rooms. Fortunately, there were just enough rooms to accommodate everyone—except for the members of the teams that had been at the Grand Canyon. They were fine with this, as they had brought camping gear and chose to set themselves up in the lobby to guard the entrance.

Everyone was settling down to sleep for the day, a concept that felt strange given the circumstances, when an unsettling scratching noise began to emanate from the walls of the hotel.

Chapter 7

The Itsy Bitsy Spider Queen

"Can we not have *one* night of peace?!" Kiera yelled, disturbed by the skittering noises coming from all around them.

The sound grew louder, like a thousand tiny feet tap dancing just on the other side of the walls. The noise of something crawling within the walls became more distinct, escalating in volume as whatever was inside moved closer. Suddenly, a ceiling tile crashed down above them, and a spider the size of a terrier dropped to the floor with a sickening thud. It landed awkwardly, breaking two legs on one side, and struggled to get its remaining legs underneath itself to stand.

A shriek pierced the air from the middle of the group. Everyone turned to see DeeDee, standing on the toes of one foot, desperately trying to climb on top of Graham to escape the sight of the massive spider. Taken by surprise at the sudden weight, Graham stumbled forward and fell flat on his chest. Unfazed by his fall, DeeDee scrambled onto his back, clutching her hands to her chest. She squeezed her eyes shut, her whole body trembling, and shook her head back and forth violently, clearly overwhelmed by panic.

"EEEEEWWWWWW! Get it away, get it away, GET IT AWAY!" Deedee screamed while dancing around on Graham's back.

"Could you please stop river dancing on my back," Graham grunted between the stomping on his back.

"I hate spiders! You know this!" DeeDee protested, now appearing to be on the verge of tears.

"I can't kill it with you using me like a trampoline," Graham barely got out through gasps for air.

Realizing his situation, DeeDee stopped and hopped off Graham's back.

"Oh! I'm so sorry, baby. I didn't mean to keep you from killing it. Look, it's right over there, over there, yeah, that one, ok, yeah, kill it. Kill it, baby. KILL it. Okay? Thanks, love you, bye!" DeeDee spat out the words at a hundred miles an hour.

Everyone except Graham stared wide eyed at DeeDee, in complete shock at her display. Graham walked forward, shaking his head.

"Happens all the time. She does this with the little ones, too. These will just need a bigger boot," Graham said, chuckling slightly at the thought of a huge boot smushing this spider.

WAR

Graham reached the spider just as it reared up on its back legs, raising its front two feet in the air and waving its three-inch-long fangs menacingly. Without a moment's hesitation, he took a long stride forward and brought his battle axe down in a powerful overhand chop, splitting the spider cleanly in two. As soon as the creature died, all the skittering sounds within the walls abruptly stopped. Silence reigned for a long, tense moment, broken only by the sound of the party's racing heartbeats.

Suddenly, a high-pitched screeching noise erupted from the walls, replacing the earlier skittering. The noise seemed to be coming from everywhere at once, vibrating through the walls and ceiling tiles.

"I think we fucked up," James said, fear evident in his voice.

The screeching turned into a frenzied clawing at the walls and ceiling. The ceiling tiles gave way first, and a dozen spiders dropped down into the lobby, right among the adventurers. The room exploded into chaos. Yells, screams, and screeches blended together in a cacophony of confusion as men and women began attacking the spiders with extreme prejudice.

As soon as the spiders from the ceiling were dispatched, the walls began to crumble, releasing a flood of hundreds of spiders racing toward the group. Not waiting for the spiders to get close, Tom started firing *Eldritch Blasts* at them, his hands glowing with green energy. Other magic users quickly followed his lead, casting spells to cut down the advancing swarm before they could close in.

Spiders were incinerated by flames, frozen solid, smashed with conjured rocks, exploded into chunks, and poisoned by noxious fumes. Those that managed to survive the barrage of spells leapt around to dodge the attacks and clambered onto the adventurers, seeking to bite at the vulnerable gaps in their armor. Some of the fighters smashed together like frat boys at a party, crushing the spiders caught between them. Others pulled the creatures off their comrades and crushed or stabbed them with swift, brutal efficiency.

One overzealous mage launched an ice spell at a spider crawling on his Warrior friend's back, freezing the creature to his armor. The added weight caused the Warrior to tip over backward, becoming stuck like a turtle on a rounded block of ice, his arms and legs flailing uselessly.

Several fighters were bitten, and some began to faint or double over, vomiting violently as the poison coursed through their veins. Clerics moved swiftly among the group, working to heal and cleanse those afflicted by the venom, but the threat wasn't over. If they didn't kill the spiders soon, more would continue to get poisoned.

Tom activated his newest *Tattoo of Life Absorption* and began moving through the melee, crushing spiders left and right. The power drained from the spiders flowed into him, filling his health, stamina, and mana bars to the brim, with the excess energy lost to the ether. As he pushed through the fray, the spiders around him weakened, many dying outright from the life drain. A cheer erupted from the group as they rallied together and finished eliminating the spiders around them.

Just as they began to gain the upper hand, a monstrous shriek echoed from the back of the hotel, sounding like a pterodactyl's cry. Everyone, including the remaining spiders, froze for a moment. A massive crashing sound followed, and the back wall of the hotel burst open, revealing a seven-foot-tall spider forcing its way into the room.

DeeDee took one look at the enormous creature and fainted on the spot.

"Ho-ly shit," Tom spoke softly, in complete disbelief at what he was seeing.

Rearing up, its front two legs held in the air, the massive spider shrieked again. This time, the sound was so deafening that everyone had to cover their ears to block out the piercing noise. Poison droplets dangled from the ends of its fangs like huge, purple grapes, glistening ominously in the dim light. It swung its legs down in a series of feints, daring anyone to come closer and face its wrath.

"Defenders! To the front, shields ready! Magic users, light this motherfucker up!" Derek shouted to the parties.

Everyone sprang into action. Those with defensive skills raced to form a line between the giant spider and the rest of the group. Once in position, they moved together, shields raised, to form a solid wall of protection. The spellcasters began to unleash every imaginable spell at the monstrosity. The air filled with bursts of fire, bolts of lightning, and shards of ice as the spider shrieked in pain and fury, enraged that the creatures before it dared to fight back.

With a sudden leap, the spider lunged at the shield wall. Its legs scraped against the metal shields, leaving deep grooves and smearing them with sticky purple poison. But the wall held firm. Fighters without shields quickly moved to brace their comrades, reinforcing the line against the spider's weight. Seeing it couldn't break through directly, the spider changed tactics, swinging its legs to the edges of the shield formation. With terrifying strength, it broke through the shield wall, tossing them left and right as it tried to break through to the spellcasters.

Just as the spider created a gap wide enough for it to crawl through, Tom leapt forward, placing himself directly in its path. His greatsword gleamed in his hands, ready for the strike. The spider paused, momentarily confused by the audacity of this lone figure standing against it. Just as it crouched, ready to pounce on Tom, a shot rang out from the far end of the hotel lobby.

The bullet tore through the air, whistling just above everyone's heads, and slammed into the spider's face, blowing half of its head apart. The creature collapsed to the floor with a heavy thud, its forward momentum from the attempted leap carrying it slightly forward. After a few spasms of its legs, the spider went completely still.

The room fell silent. Everyone stood motionless, holding their breath, waiting to see if there was any further danger. When everything remained quiet and nothing moved, a collective sigh of relief rippled through the group.

At that exact moment, one of the smaller, terrier-sized spiders decided to make a break for it. It scurried out from beneath the carcass of a larger spider and sprinted toward the exit. Several distinctly feminine screams erupted from the direction where only one woman stood, and in an instant, six gunshots rang out, accompanied by three fireballs, an ice spike, and a lightning bolt—all aimed at the fleeing creature. The result was nothing but a blackened smear on the rug, vaguely spider shaped.

Everyone went still again, holding their breath for what felt like an eternity. When, once more, nothing moved among the dead spiders, another collective sigh filled the room. This time, it seemed like the danger had truly passed.

"So, who's ready for bed?" James said brightly, his smoking handguns held up on display.

"What the *fuck* was that?!" Chris exclaimed loudly, ignoring James' antics.

People began cautiously emerging from their rooms, glancing around to ensure the coast was clear. They gathered around, asking what had happened. The group explained the ordeal repeatedly, bringing everyone up to speed as more people trickled downstairs. After the seventh retelling, the party reassured everyone that they were prepared for any other threats that might come. Taking this reassurance in good faith, the people nodded and slowly made their way back to their rooms, hoping for some peace after the chaos.

"Well, we can't fucking sleep in this battle zone. Where do we go now?" Kiera asked.

"I'm sure they have a conference room and some other areas where we can lay in," Zach replied. "I'll go ahead and look for them now."

He took off down the hall to see what other rooms were available. Meanwhile, the rest of the group gathered up whatever they could salvage from the lobby. When Zach returned and reported what he had found, they moved into smaller, safer rooms. Fortunately, no one was left without a place to sleep, and they finally managed to get some much-needed rest. No more creatures attacked while they slept, and the tension began to ease.

Later that evening, everyone woke up and gathered together outside for a meal. Large stew pots were set over campfires, simmering with hearty soup to be shared among the group. Ingredients were brought to those with cooking skills, who prepared the meals with care, ensuring there was enough for everyone. As the food cooked, Bards and others sang songs, filling the air with music, while many passed around beers they had raided from a nearby warehouse shopping center. The camaraderie was palpable; people were getting along well and actively working to help one another.

Tom watched the scene unfold, immensely pleased to see everyone cooperating and contributing to the group's well-being. One of his biggest concerns had been whether people would truly integrate into the Guild or if he would have to turn some away. But witnessing this sight—the singing, the laughter, the shared labor—gave him hope that these people could indeed become a cohesive part of the Guild.

"So, are we driving through the night from now on?" Kedron asked Tom, handing him a beer.

"Only until we reach Decatur. Once we're there, we'll stay an extra day to get back on the right sleep cycle. At this pace, we should be there by morning or early afternoon," Tom replied, accepting the drink and taking a swig.

"If they'll let us stay that long," Kedron said, speaking aloud the fear that they were all feeling.

"Yeah, if they let us," Tom repeated, looking down at the floor in shame.

Chapter 8

Sorrow's Return

Loading up into the vehicles took about half an hour as everyone made sure to use the bathroom and find their correct place on the designated transport. After ensuring everyone was accounted for and settled, the team was finally ready to set off. With everything in order, they began to slowly move their procession forward, vehicles rumbling back to life as the convoy started down the road once more.

"I just don't see why we can't stop at the steak house again," James complained as they pulled onto the highway. "It was fine last time. We just need seating for five hundred."

"We told you they won't have enough seating and likely won't have enough meat for all of us plus the others who go regularly," Derek replied. "We can always come back some other time."

"Ugh! Fine, but I want a steak when we get back to Dallas," James warned Derek with a single finger extended.

"We'll see what they have. You'll eat what they make, and you'll like it, or you'll be on bathroom cleaning duty for a month," Derek retorted.

"You wouldn't dare!" James gasped.

"Try me," Derek said coldly.

Both stared at each other for a long moment, James finally looking away.

"Wise choice." Derek grinned wickedly at his triumph.

"Shrimp is the fruit of the sea," James grumbled as he leaned against the window, putting his chin on a hand as he sulked. "You can barbecue it, boil it, broil it, bake it, sauté it," James continued on while Derek rolled his eyes. "...Shrimp-kabobs, shrimp creole, shrimp gumbo. Pan-fried, deep-fried, stir-fried. There's pineapple shrimp, lemon shrimp, coconut shrimp, pepper shrimp, shrimp soup, shrimp stew, shrimp salad, shrimp and potatoes, shrimp burger, shrimp sandwich..."

The parade of vehicles continued down the highway late into the night. Goblins, it seemed, didn't bother setting up their barricades after dark; several makeshift barriers were seen pulled off to the sides of the road, abandoned. This was valuable information for future travel—those who wanted to avoid goblin ambushes could move under the cover of night.

Tom agreed with Jay, though, that it was a missed opportunity. "We're really missing out on some great XP," Jay muttered, more to himself than anyone else. "And, y'know, a healthy outlet for stress."

Jay couldn't help but whine a little every time they passed another set of barricades, visibly agitated at the missed chance to mow down some goblins. Tom just chuckled, shaking his head at his friend's unusual idea of "healthy coping mechanisms."

"We could have been smashing those fuckers to pieces, but instead, we're driving at night because we had to accept every human being that has ever been to join us," Jay continued to grumble after passing yet another barricade.

"Oh, come on, Jay. You know you don't feel that way and wouldn't have turned them away either," Tom said, leaning back in the passenger seat again.

Jay continued to grumble for a long time, his words incoherent in his attempt to keep Tom from hearing what he was really thinking. He finally let out a long sigh.

"You're right. But I don't like it," Jay said, trying to express his feelings on the matter.

"Right. It makes terrible actual short-term, self-preservation sense. We could move as fast or slow as we needed alone. But that isn't what we are about," Tom explained. "Everyone's thinking about what's happened and assuming it's all temporary." Tom shook his head. "We can't afford to think like that. What we have here—this is the new normal. Our vision has to be greater than the concerns of today. The individuals we save today could be the ones saving us tomorrow."

"I know, it's just not something I ever thought I'd be doing. I always looked out for myself with most people. Because most people are bastards," Jay began. "But now that terrible things are happening to people who probably didn't deserve it, I can't help but feel like I have to help them."

"It's a terrible burden, my friend. But it's the right thing to do. Even if it never pays off," Tom replied, a sad smile on his face.

"That… is really depressing, man!" Jay groaned. "Why would you go and explain it that way? That would make me far less likely to want to do it."

"Because I'm not sugarcoating anything anymore. Our old reality was carefully curated and politically correct. You had to say the right thing to everyone. Now that it's fight or flight, kill or be killed, I'm not going to tell people what they want to hear, only what they need to hear," Tom explained, laying his cards out on the table for his friend.

"Well, I do appreciate that. I hate playing a game of bullshit the bullshitter when it comes to people telling me what I need to know," Jay gave in and finally admitted.

"Yeah, and deciding to be this way has been very stress relieving. You were right about sharing this load and not keeping it all to myself. I appreciate you all saying something about it," Tom graciously bowed his head to his teammates.

"We're just glad you listened and realized it. It's always messy when someone doesn't listen," DeeDee added from the back of the vehicle.

"What's that mean?" Tom asked, now concerned about what could have happened.

"Oh, when people are flailing like that and don't reach out for help, they usually implode and get fired. I guess the translation here would be removed as Guild leader?" DeeDee continued nonchalantly. "Or you get people killed?"

"Wow, I see now why you were a little flustered with the completely honest truth," Tom said, turning to Jay.

"You can be honest without being a jerk," DeeDee interjected.

"I get your point. I'll still try to be tactful… sometimes," Tom reluctantly agreed.

Continuing in much the same way until late morning, the team finally reached the border of Decatur. A collective sigh of relief swept through the group as they approached the arm gates still set up at the edge of town.

The guard on duty leaned out of his booth, trying to gauge just how far the line of vehicles stretched. He removed his sunglasses and squinted into the distance, clearly taken aback by the length of the convoy. Jay rolled down the driver's side window and casually leaned an arm on the window ledge, ready to talk.

"Good morning," Jay said cheerfully.

"Uh… good morning," the guard replied in confusion. "Are all of these vehicles together? And are you all planning to stay in town?"

"Yes, they are all together, and yes, we want to stay in town, but not, like, permanently or anything. Just a short time. Like a day or two. Tops. Probably, I mean, if that's okay and all…" Jay rambled on as he looked nervously at the guard.

"Uh, huh. Alright, I just need to make a quick call." The officer stepped into the booth that held up the arm gate.

Returning just a minute later, he looked in the window and asked, "Who are you again?"

"Tell whoever it is that it's Tom. The team that Seth went with," Tom leaned forward and called to the guard.

"Oh! Tom! It's you guys!" the guard said, suddenly realizing who he was talking to. "I'll let them know!"

Walking back into the booth, the guard picked up the phone and began a conversation that lasted several minutes. He kept glancing between the phone and Tom's group, his brow furrowing as he spoke. At one point, he made a few vague hand gestures and attempted to count the number of vehicles in the convoy, but he quickly gave up with a frustrated shake of his head. After hanging up the phone, he walked back over to the vehicle, still looking somewhat bewildered.

"Okay, this is a lot of people," the guard began.

"I know, and I'm sorry to be bringing so many. But we are on our way back to Dallas and are just passing through, so we just need a place to park the vehicles, and we can handle the rest," Tom butted in to try to explain.

"What? Oh, no, it's nothing like that. I was just going to tell you that you'll need to stay at the hotel on the other side of the courthouse because the one you stayed in last time doesn't have as many rooms. Now go on in and meet up with the mayor at the courthouse," the guard replied with a big smile as he raised the arm of the gate.

"Oh… well, thank you, sir. We'll meet up with them," Tom stammered as Jay let off the brake, making long, weird eye contact with the guard.

"Smooth move, ex-lax," James teased Tom.

"I didn't see you jumping in to tell them what was going on," Tom replied with a bite in his voice.

"Easy there, killer. I'm just having a bit of fun," James said in a British accent.

"Sorry, just feeling stupid," Tom apologized to James.

"Yeah, we all saw. Anyway, let's get there so we can get out of this vehicle. I think my ass is asleep," James complained.

"Don't make me turn this car around. We will go right back to where we were," Jay mocked being a parent.

Driving to the courthouse took about fifteen minutes. When they arrived, the mayor was already standing out front, and several guards were ready to guide everyone to their designated parking areas. A whole lot had been cleared specifically for the buses, eliminating the need to squeeze into smaller spots next to regular-sized vehicles.

Once parked, everyone got out of their vehicles to stretch and take in their surroundings. John approached the group with a welcoming smile and shook Tom's hand.

"Tom," John said, shaking firmly.

"Mr. Mayor," Tom teased, shaking firmly as well.

"None of that Mr. Mayor crap. Just call me John," the mayor replied, shaking his head at Tom's antics.

"So, how's it been going here, John?" Tom asked.

"We've been very busy, but things have gone well. With your guidance, everyone has found a Class and is working to get stronger. We've been fortunate not to have any more large creature attacks, but we're out preparing for that eventuality. Fighters are training hard to raise their levels to be better," John explained. "Where's Seth? I was looking forward to seeing him again."

Tom's eyes dropped, and his mood darkened. Sadness hit him like a truck.

"Oh, um… about Seth…" Tom began but started to get a little choked up.

"Oh, I see…" John tried to reply but also cut off.

"We tried to save him, but he was gone too fast. He died defending one of us from the monster that was causing all the System's problems," Tom tried to explain, but he just felt like they were hollow excuses.

"I'm glad to hear he went heroically," John said, and he reached out and put a hand on Tom's shoulder.

"Don't worry that we'll blame you. You came here and saved all of us. Sure, we loved Seth and would have liked for him to stay, but you all were right. It took losing our protector to make everyone see the light of the situation we were in. For that, we are grateful," John said, trying to relieve Tom's worry. "Seth was an adult capable of making his own decisions. I know that he would be proud to say that he was defending a friend."

"I'm so sorry, John…" Tom tried to apologize again, but John silenced him with a raised hand.

"Don't go down that road. It leads to madness and grief. You have to stay strong and resolute for those who follow you. You came back here, even though you could likely have avoided us forever to give us news of what happened. You're a good person, Tom. Don't change that," John spoke looking into Tom's eyes as if he was trying to make him believe the words mentally as much as verbally.

"Thanks, John. I appreciate the wisdom. I'll try not to sink into that logic," Tom replied, feeling an immense relief that the people were not going to blame him for the loss of Seth.

"Let's go to where you will be staying so you can get these people settled. Then we can talk in the courthouse about what happened," John offered, turning to extend an arm in the direction of the hotel.

They followed him to the hotel, where several townspeople had gathered to help ensure everyone had rooms. The guests queued up for room assignments, and the hotel staff efficiently provided them with everything they needed, including clean sheets, pillows, and blankets for the beds.

"We raided the town Bed Bath & Beyond, so we have a ton of bedding," John explained to Tom when he was looking curiously at the amount of bedding they had available.

"That's a really great idea. I'll have to use that in Dallas if they haven't thought of it already back at the Guild building," Tom replied, making a mental note to ask Brian about it.

Once everyone had been settled into their rooms, the team that had been at the Grand Canyon went to set up in the lobby.

"What are you all doing?" the woman at the check-in counter asked the group.

"We are setting up. This place must be full now," Tom explained, confused by the question.

"Oh, no, it's not. We reserved rooms for your entire team. We would have put people up in a different hotel before giving yours away. Here, take these keys, and you'll find your rooms on the top floor," the woman explained, smiling at them.

"Which rooms on the top floor?" Tom asked, curious about the numbering.

"All of them. You can each have your own room, or you can share, whichever you want," the woman continued, pressing the keys into Tom's hands.

Tom was speechless for a moment, then he remembered himself and thanked her for the kind gesture.

"We also have the water working here again. It's not hot, but it's a shower," she explained as she ushered them to the stairs. "Soap and shampoo are on the sinks. Hint hint: use both."

"Yeah, yeah, we get it, we stink. You'd stink, too, if you had to camp out all the time and fight monsters to save the world," James complained under his breath, as he started walking up the stairs.

Once they reached the top floor, Tom handed out keys to nearly everyone. The only people who chose to share a room were DeeDee and Graham, the only married couple present, and Clay and James—because crazy loves company.

Inside, the rooms were spacious, each furnished with either a king-sized bed or two queens. The bathrooms had a soft, pre-lit glow from some sort of magical light affixed to the walls. While it seemed to be a good alternative to electricity, it wasn't a complete solution; the rooms were still fairly dim. However, leaving the bathroom doors open allowed enough light to filter through, making it possible to see.

Tom took his first shower in over a week, scrubbing himself nearly raw to remove the layers of caked-on filth, including dried blood, that he had been living in. After this thorough exfoliation, he found himself lying on the bed in nothing but a towel, staring up at the ceiling, feeling the greatest contentment he had felt in a long time. In that moment, there were no worries, no looming threats—just the comfort of a darkened room with soft bedding.

Pulling a set of clean clothes out of his Inventory, Tom dressed and climbed into bed. Lying under the sheets, wrapped in the quiet of that moment, he drifted off to sleep, finally feeling a sense of peace.

Chapter 9

One More Goodbye

The next morning, Tom was awakened by someone knocking on his door.

"Tom? Tom! John wants to see us. Are you even up yet?" Derek asked from the other side of the door.

Tom rolled carefully out of bed, wiping away the drool on his chin with one hand while running the other through his hair and rubbing his tired eyes. He walked slowly to the door, feeling the stiffness in his muscles. Upon reaching it, he stretched, arching his back until he felt a satisfying pop and groaned with relief. Then, he grabbed the handle and pulled the door open.

"Well, good morning, sunshine. The Earth says hello," Derek teased with a movie quote after seeing Tom's disheveled appearance. "Sleep well, I presume?"

"Best sleep I've had post-apocalypse, hands down," Tom said through a massive yawn. "So, what're we doing again?"

"Geeze, you *did* sleep well. We have to have the farewell for Seth," Derek said solemnly.

Tom suddenly felt completely awake. "Oh, right. Give me a few minutes to get ready, and I'll be out."

He closed the door to his room as Derek turned to leave. Sitting on the bed a moment later, Tom buried his head in his hands. He wasn't ready to deal with all this, but everyone else needed him to be strong. And so, he would be.

He pulled on his clothes and armor—he never went anywhere without armor in this world. Standing up, he walked to the door to leave but paused. Out of habit, he walked around the room one last time to see if he had forgotten anything. Deciding to take the bedding with him—since he had mostly been sleeping on a bare mattress—he gathered it up and made his way out.

Exiting his room, he headed down the corridor to the stairs. It was quiet this morning; the hallways were empty, and his footsteps echoed softly all the way down the stairwell. When he reached the lobby, people would smile at him as he walked by, but most of their smiles didn't quite reach their eyes. A somberness resonated through the room. Even those who hadn't known Seth felt the weight of their own losses. Some wept openly, wounds they had covered with the need to survive now bubbling to the surface as they found themselves in a safer space.

Walking outside, Tom stretched and looked up at the sky. It was a vibrant blue, with just the right amount of big, fluffy white clouds drifting by, occasionally providing some welcome shade as they passed over the sun.

"Tom, there you are," a familiar voice said, and Tom looked over to see John walking over to him from a set of tables that had been set up as a makeshift buffet.

"John, how's your morning been?" Tom asked, making polite small talk.

"Oh, as good as it can be, given the circumstances. But we are feeling the sadness of the mood as well. Seth will be greatly missed," John said reverently.

"Yeah, he was an amazing person. We miss him so much," Tom admitted, though he wasn't sure why.

"It warms my heart to hear that. I would have hated to hear that Seth had left with people who cared nothing about him. Your strength of character shows through your friends," John patted Tom on the back as he spoke. "Are you hungry? Today, we set up a breakfast buffet for everyone in town to celebrate Seth's life. We decided to set aside this entire day to honor him."

"That's an amazing gesture to offer. I am feeling a bit peckish," Tom said as he eyed the buffet longingly.

"Then, by all means, dig in. Don't hold back on my account. I'll walk with you," John offered, extending an arm in the direction of the food for Tom to begin.

Making his way through the buffet options was something Tom had come to miss dearly in this new world. Most of the time, it was about eating whatever you could find, so seeing a full spread with so many choices was an unexpected luxury—a wonderful treat.

There were juicy sausages in both patty and link form, piles of crispy bacon, large dishes of scrambled eggs, assorted muffins, biscuits smothered in gravy, creamy grits, golden and crispy hashbrowns, and yogurt parfaits topped with fresh fruits, which Tom had no idea how they had gotten, given the lack of refrigeration. The sheer variety of options was overwhelming to look at. By the time Tom had reached the halfway point of the serving line, his plate was already piled high with food. He hadn't even gotten to the waffles or pancakes yet!

Tom glanced around, trying to decide what to do. People were waiting behind him, eager to move forward in the line, but he didn't want to miss out on the delicious, light, and fluffy waffles and pancakes just waiting to be topped with butter and syrup. He stood there, torn between his choices.

Suddenly, a plate entered his view from the side. Surprised, Tom looked up to see John standing beside him, smiling.

"I thought you'd need a second plate, so I grabbed one while we were waiting. I already ate, so I don't need it," John said, extending the plate for Tom to take.

Tom's eyes began to well up. "Thank you. You don't know how much this means to me..." And he broke down crying in the buffet line.

People stared awkwardly at the grown man crying over being handed a plate.

"Okay, Tom. Let's get you to a table to sit at, and I'll get you some pancakes and waffles. Is syrup and butter okay?" John offered, trying his best to get Tom away from the line.

"Y-yes," Tom said through sobs.

They moved to a nearby table, and Tom sat down, wiping his eyes as he set his plate of food down. John quickly returned to the buffet. After witnessing Tom's emotional moment in line, the others were more than happy to let John cut ahead to grab the remaining items he needed. When John returned to the table, Tom had managed to compose himself a bit more.

"Sorry about that," Tom said, looking embarrassed.

"Don't worry about it. You are actually the fourth person to break down in the line today. So, it's no big deal," John said, trying to make him feel better. "Plus, I'm guessing you weren't actually crying about the flapjacks?"

"No," Tom admitted sheepishly. "It's just… being here… The memories it's bringing up, and the past we've been through."

"I understand," John said softly. "I actually had my own breakdown this morning at home. I didn't expect it to hit me this hard, but it seems like this moment, this time of remembering one person, is also the time we're all using to remember everything that's happened." He paused, his voice carrying the weight of unspoken emotions as he made deep eye contact with Tom. "We've been holding so much back—trying to move from one crisis to the next, putting out fires left and right—that we haven't had a chance to process our grief, our fear, and all the anxiety that's been building up."

Tom realized that he had been so caught up in solving everyone else's problems and fighting for his life at every turn that he hadn't taken any time to process his own emotions. He had been running on autopilot, completely engulfed in the chaos around him, without a moment to reflect on everything he had lost or what it had cost him.

"Now, everything is building up," John continued softly, still holding Tom's gaze. "By letting yourself feel for this one person, all those buried emotions are surfacing together. You can't stop it, and you shouldn't. This is the time to let it all out, to make room for new feelings and move forward."

"It's just hard to let them out, knowing everyone else is depending on you," Tom admitted.

"It is, but I've talked with your friends, and they're here for you just as much as you are for them. Let them be a part of it," John advised, sitting back in the chair he was in and crossing one leg over the other as he sipped a cup of coffee.

"You're right. I'll do that more often. Now, what's the plan for today?" Tom asked, curious about the day's events and trying to move the subject to something else.

"Nice deflection," John chuckled, "but I agree—we should move on to what's next." He paused, his tone shifting to something more serious yet hopeful. "We'll have lunch and dinner prepared today. This morning, there will be a ceremony for Seth and all those we've lost. After that, we'll take some time to celebrate how far we've come, from lunch into dinner. The evening will finish with a big party to help everyone let loose and relax for a while."

"So, it's just a day of parties?" Tom asked, a little confused as to why they were planning it this way.

"Sort of," John began. "The first ceremony will be like a funeral, and after that, we'll have lunch. Then comes the celebration, where we'll have a time for remembrances—so I'm sure there will be some sadness then as well. After dinner, though, the final party is where no sadness is allowed. We'll look ahead to the future and focus on what's to come."

"Perfect. Then let's get this started," Tom said, pushing away his now empty plates.

"Not sure I've seen anyone put food away that fast before," John said as he stared at Tom with a curious look.

"Gotta eat fast these days, and these new bodies seem to require a bit more energy than they did before," Tom explained, wiping his mouth with a napkin.

"I hadn't noticed that yet, but then again, I'm not out battling monsters and leveling up every day," John said, groaning a little as he stood up from the chair. "But all of that aside, I would like for you to speak at the ceremony for Seth today. Nothing fancy, just a nice remembrance of him and what he stood for."

"Me? You want me to give a speech?" Tom asked, feeling put on the spot.

"Yup. Figured if I asked before now, you would crash and burn trying to write something. I want this to be just true feelings for him," John said, smiling at putting Tom on the spot.

"Alright, I would be honored. Terrified, but honored," Tom accepted.

"That's the spirit! Now, let's head over to the area we've set up for the memorial," John said, guiding Tom toward a makeshift stage that had been prepared in front of the courthouse. Blankets were scattered across the street for people to sit on and gather together.

Some folks were already settling down on the blankets, trying to get a good spot for the memorial. Others slowly trickled in as volunteers went around, informing everyone that it was time to begin and where they needed to go.

Once most of the people had arrived, John stepped onto the stage and began speaking. He delivered a heartfelt speech about his interactions with Seth and the impact Seth had on him. He also talked about others he had lost—friends, family, and even a pet—encouraging everyone to mourn their losses openly. His words resonated with the crowd, offering them permission to grieve. He spoke for about thirty minutes, and as he continued, Tom started to feel the pressure building to give a longer, more meaningful speech than he felt capable of delivering.

When John finished, he stepped off the stage, and to Tom's surprise, a woman got up and moved to the stage to speak next. Confused, Tom looked over at John for clarification.

"You're going last since he spent his final days with you. Also, don't feel pressured to talk for any specific length of time. I spoke for that long because, well, people expect the mayor to do that sort of thing," John explained, noticing the confusion on Tom's face.

"Alright, thanks for letting me know. I was getting a bit worried about my speech." Tom sighed, feeling a wave of relief wash over him.

"Just be honest and real. Speak from the heart," John said, giving him another reassuring pat on the back.

The woman on stage finished her speech a bit later, and four more people came up to share their thoughts and stories. One of the speakers was a clinical psychologist who gave a presentation on coping strategies for dealing with the profound changes they were all experiencing. She seemed particularly passionate about this subject, likely because it was a unique opportunity to study the effects of an apocalyptic event on people's mental states.

Though her talk felt a bit too clinical for Tom's taste, it was clear that she had many good points and ideas for coping with this kind of tragedy and world-altering situation. He mentally filed away a few of her suggestions to try later.

After about an hour and a half, the final speaker finished, and it was Tom's turn. He was gently nudged onto the makeshift stage. There was no podium, no microphone—just him standing there with the crowd sitting on blankets, staring up at him with expectant eyes. As his mouth began to dry up like a sponge left out on a Texas summer sidewalk, he swallowed hard and made eye contact with a few familiar faces in the crowd. Then, summoning his courage, he began his speech.

Chapter 10

Parting is Such Sweet Sorrow

"Hello," Tom began, trying to figure out where exactly to start this speech. "My name is Tom. Many of you may remember me from when we came through on our way to the Grand Canyon to take on the monster that was affecting the vending machines. Well, I am happy to say that we were able to defeat that monster and set the System right again!"

There was a wave of applause, and a few voices called out, "Thank you!" and "Great job!"

Tom nodded in acknowledgment then continued, his voice steady but filled with emotion. "None of this would have been possible without a team of people pulling together, making each other stronger. Every person has a role to play in what we do to become better. No one can do this on their own. You've heard people come up here and say those exact things, but for me, it truly sank in today."

The crowd was now completely focused on him, their eyes attentive. Tom took a deep breath and went on, "Seth came with us because he wanted to be a part of something bigger than himself. Little did he know that joining us meant saving the world—not just from being unable to order something at a vending machine but from stopping the complete destruction of everything we know."

Audible gasps rippled through the crowd. Many who weren't there had no idea how close they had come to being wiped off the map.

"This wasn't something that was in the warning messages or the quest invites," Tom explained. "It was something we found out by being there. But we were able to stop the threat. Seth gave his life so that countless others would live. He was a true hero—not just in defending you all here but out there as well. Thank you, from the bottom of my heart, for sharing him with us. He was one of a kind, truly genuine, and always there for his friends. We'll always remember him fondly, and we'll strive to live each day following the example he set for us."

Tom paused, his eyes scanning the crowd for a moment before he nodded and turned to leave the stage. As he did, applause erupted, and people rose to their feet, some with tears in their eyes, moved by his words.

John met him at the side of the stage. "That was perfect, Tom. Thank you for sharing with us. We'll have some people coming up to share things like songs and poems next, so feel free to take a seat out there on the blankets, at the tables, or wherever you'd like to be. We'll find you for lunch if you're not still out here," John said, moving past Tom to announce the next person.

Tom decided to join his party at the tables where he had eaten breakfast earlier. He moved over to a spot where his original team was seated. Kirsten was also with them, sitting close to Kevin. It seemed their relationship was blossoming into something more as they fed each other food off a single plate, sharing small smiles and laughter.

Tom settled in, feeling a strange mix of sadness and solace, surrounded by his friends and the comforting sense of unity they shared.

"I see love is in the air even in these times," Tom commented, nodding at Kevin and Kirsten.

"Oh, yeah, it seems that way. It's a little disgusting, though," Kiera said.

"Don't mind her; she's just jealous," Jay added.

"I am not!" Kiera tried to deny it.

"Oh, come on, it's okay to be jealous. I wish I had someone to make goo-goo eyes at like that, too," Jay admitted.

"Well, it won't be me," Kiera quickly said.

"Damn right, it won't be. I've got no time for someone like that, even if I wish it could happen. Too much fighting to do," Jay said, twirling two knives in his hands that he had equipped from his Inventory.

"Stop it, you two. We get it. You're afraid people will see you as a couple, and you aren't. No one thinks of you that way. It's like siblings. We would think it's gross if you two did anything," Tom said, a little annoyed at the spats continually happening but still finding it amusing to tease them about it from time to time.

"Besides, I think I have a better shot with Jay than Kiera does," James quipped, waggling his eyebrows suggestively.

"I will cut you," Jay replied, leaning menacingly over the table.

"Don't threaten me with a good time!" James laughed, clearly enjoying how red Jay's face was getting.

"Both of you, knock it off. This isn't what this time is for," Derek interjected, trying to defuse the situation.

"Let them go, Derek. It helps them relax and get back to the usual jabbing and joking," Tom said, placing a calming hand on Derek's shoulder. "Today is supposed to be about healing. What heals better than a bit of normalcy?"

Derek nodded. "Fair point. My bad. Jay, you may continue. Stab him if you want—I can heal him," he added, leaning back in his chair with a grin.

"Wait, no, I didn't actually want—OW!" James yelped as Jay suddenly stabbed a knife through his hand, pinning it to the table.

Derek blinked in surprise, quickly moving to heal James' hand after Jay pulled the knife out. "Okay, new rule: no *actual* stabbing. Just keep it to verbal jabs."

"That really hurt, dude!" James complained, cradling his now-healed hand.

"Sorry, man. Just making a point," Jay said with a wicked grin. "I *will* cut you. I'm crazy!"

Tom sighed and scolded them, his voice firm, "We can't hurt each other on purpose. That'll lead to mistrust or thoughts of revenge in a bad situation. Jay, apologize, and I don't want to see it happen again."

Jay's grin faded as he looked down. "Yeah, yeah. I'm sorry. Just… feeling a lot today."

James, still grumpy, muttered, "I guess I forgive you. Just don't do it again."

"You got it," Jay nodded. "I know we give you crap because you're weird and all, but we do like having you on the team."

"Still no excuse for stabbing me," James insisted.

"You're right. No excuse," Jay admitted. "It won't happen again. Here, to show there are no hard feelings," he added, pulling out a few Monster Cores, "go grab something from the vending—"

Jay blinked. All of the cores had disappeared from his hands.

"Alright, I'll take them *this* time," James called out over his shoulder as he stomped his feet dramatically toward the nearest vending machine. "But I'm still *super* mad, you hear? Like, *really* angry, so don't think this makes us even! It's going to take twenty—" He stuttered in his stomping for a moment. "No— *thirty* more of these before we're friends again!" The last words were shouted as the man hurried around a corner and disappeared from sight.

"So, what's bothering you?" Derek asked once James had left the table, leaning in a bit closer to Jay.

"What do you mean? I'm fine," Jay shot back, immediately dismissing the question with a wave of his hand.

Derek raised an eyebrow. "Oh, come on. You're not fooling anyone. You might be a bit of a crusty sailor, but you've never just stabbed someone like that." He leaned on the table, trying to appear more engaged and less confrontational.

Jay shifted in his seat, avoiding eye contact. "Truth be told, I don't know why I did that. You gave me a bit of a green light with the healing comment, so I just figured I'd get it out of my system. Nothing more to it," he said, still trying to brush off the issue.

Derek shrugged and leaned back in his chair, acting casual. "Fine, don't tell me. But it's going to fester until you let it out."

A long silence stretched between them. Jay kept his face carefully neutral, but the more Derek stared at him with that unblinking gaze, the more uncomfortable he became. The tension grew until Jay finally threw up his hands.

"Alright, fine! I'll talk… Damn, that stare is creepy," Jay muttered, rolling his eyes.

Derek smirked. "So, what's going on?"

Jay sighed, his defenses dropping. "It's just… life, man. Everything's different now. People are depending on us. Seth is gone. We've got these space pirates looming over us, and it's all taking a toll after being on the road and fighting for so long."

Derek nodded slowly, his expression softening. "I get it. That does explain a lot. We need to find some time to rest, let others handle things for a bit. Tom and I will talk and see what we can figure out. Sounds like burnout, and the best cure for that is a break."

Jay chuckled dryly. "You want us to take a vacation in the apocalypse? Sounds like the premise for some cheesy new anime: 'That Time I Vacationed in the Apocalypse.'"

Derek grinned. "Laugh all you want, but it's probably the best way to solve the issue."

Jay's smile faded slightly. "Okay, wise guy, how do you propose we do that?"

"We have to get back to Dallas first," Derek said thoughtfully. "Once we're there and can assess the situation, we'll figure out some kind of rotational hiatus or something. We'll make it work—assuming, of course, the world doesn't end."

Jay groaned, covering his face with one hand. "You just had to jinx it."

Derek chuckled, patting Jay on the back. "Hey, what's life without a little risk?"

"So, you really think we have a chance at some time off?" Kiera said, returning to the table with a small plate of food.

"I think anything is possible if the circumstances are right," Derek replied.

"What a cop-out of an answer," Kiera said flatly, shaking her head. "At least try to give us something believable and slightly less vague."

"The US military were actively deployed for over twenty years, Kiera." Derek didn't back down. "Did you think we never learned anything about stress and how to manage it?"

"He's right, Kiera. We can make it happen. Provided we aren't right in the middle of a turf war when we get back. We deserve a break after what we've done," Tom added, staring at a screen the others couldn't see.

"Whatcha working on there, Tom?" Jay asked, deciding the better idea was to change the subject.

"Hmm? Oh, just looking at some of the admin screens for the Guild. Brian has been busy while we have been gone. It's nice to see him taking care of so much while we're out," Tom commented, still not fully engaged in the conversation.

Tom had been poring over the Guild tabs, scrutinizing what he could control remotely. Unfortunately, most of the screens required him to be much closer to the Guild building to make any significant changes or have much influence. Still, as he sifted through the various pages, he noticed something encouraging: the Guild was continuing to grow in size even in their absence.

The numbers were steadily climbing, and they were now approaching nine hundred members in the Vanguard. With the additional people they were bringing back on this trip, they would soon surpass the one-thousand-member mark. It was a sobering thought—what had started as a small group was rapidly evolving into a formidable force.

"I'm not sure how we're supposed to feed this many people," Tom suddenly blurted out, cutting through the lighthearted conversation at the table.

"What?" Derek asked, looking over at Tom with a raised eyebrow.

Tom took a deep breath, his concern evident. "When we get back, there will be over a thousand people in the Guild. Are we sure we can feed that many?"

Derek paused to consider this. "I would think if there was a major issue, we would have heard about it in the brief radio call. Could be they didn't want to worry us, but I'm guessing they'll have something figured out."

Jay chimed in, his tone reassuring, "Yeah, Brian is a pretty smart cookie. He'll have things under control or at least have a temporary fix. We can figure it out when we get there."

Tom nodded, though his worry was still etched into his face. "You're probably right. I'm just feeling pulled in two directions. We need to help people, but helping people is a bit of a weakness for us—it spreads us thin."

Kevin, who had been quietly listening, finally spoke up, "At the end of the day, I'd rather die defending someone who couldn't fight for themselves than hoarding supplies just for myself."

A moment of silence settled over the group as they absorbed Kevin's words. It was a simple yet profound statement that seemed to resonate deeply with everyone.

James returned to the table from his trip to the vending machine, catching the tail end of the conversation. "That was really deep, Kevin," he said, nodding in approval.

Kevin grinned, pleased with the reaction. "Thanks, man. I have those moments sometimes. Then again, most of the other times, I just want to smash!" With that, he stood up and began striking exaggerated poses as if he were competing in a Mr. Universe contest, flexing his muscles and grinning from ear to ear.

Jay rolled his eyes. "Really? Your brain is a muscle too, try flexing it sometimes."

Kevin just laughed, unfazed. "But these are way more fun! I never had muscles like this before!" he exclaimed, clearly reveling in his newfound strength.

Kirsten, standing beside him, played along, pretending to swoon over his display, squeezing his arms. "Those sure are impressive. Here, I'll squeeze them," she said, fawning over him.

"Hey, no fair." Kevin grinned.

"I guess you're right," Kirsten purred. "It's only fair if you get to squeeze mine, too." She flexed invitingly.

Derek shook his head, clearly amused but ready to move on. "Alright, I've had enough of this new puppy love display. Let's go see what the rest of the plans for today are," he said, standing up and motioning for the others to follow him away from the table.

Following his lead, the rest of the team left Kevin and Kirsten to continue their posing and muscle worship. Tom moved to talk with John at the back of the stage.

"Hey, John. What all is planned for the rest of the day again? I know we have more meals to eat, but what activities?" Tom asked.

"Up next on the agenda is a break, then lunch, and that's followed by the life celebration where everyone tells stories about Seth and other loved ones. I think everyone would really like to hear the tales of your adventures with him." John looked at Tom expectantly.

"Hell of a story, but the ending needs some work," Tom replied.

"Gallows humor. Not the best coping mechanism, but I like it," John said sarcastically with a huge smile plastered on his face. "Now, if you'd like to come with me, there is a green room for people who will be making speeches that has some privacy."

Tom nodded, and the team followed him down the hallway of the hotel back to a room they hadn't visited before. He opened the door and was surprised to find a spacious conference room that had been transformed into a makeshift bar. The long, polished wooden table that once hosted meetings was now covered with a variety of liquor bottles, mixers, and glasses of all shapes and sizes.

The bar area had been set up at one end of the room, where a few of the hotel's large serving tables had been pushed together to form a counter. Several stools, likely borrowed from the dining area, lined the makeshift bar. Behind the counter, shelves stocked with a surprisingly varied assortment of alcohol—from whiskey and rum to gin and vodka—were propped against the wall. There were even some craft beers chilling in a couple of large ice buckets set on the floor.

A soft glow from lanterns and candles scattered around the room provided a warm, cozy ambiance. The lights reflected off the glass bottles, casting shimmering patterns on the walls. The smell of freshly sliced limes and lemons mixed with the faint scent of aged wood, giving the room an inviting atmosphere. A chalkboard sign propped up near the entrance read "Today's Specials" in neat, hand-drawn letters, listing some cocktail options and snacks that were being offered.

A few people were already there, chatting and laughing quietly at small round tables scattered around the room. A couple of bartenders, people from the town who had clearly picked up a new skill set, were busy mixing drinks and serving them with a practiced ease.

Tom looked around, impressed. "Well, this is unexpected," he said, turning to the team. "Looks like they really know how to make the best of things."

The group chuckled, settling in and making their way toward the bar, where they could finally unwind after everything they had been through.

"Where did you get all this?" Tom asked.

"What? Your first thought in an apocalypse wasn't to raid the liquor store? We need to teach you about what becomes most valuable in a panic, Tom," John joked with him. "Booze is better than gold in an apocalypse."

"Honestly, in all the chaos, I didn't even think about it. But I really want a drink now!" Tom said excitedly, moving toward the bar.

"Cindy, these are Tom and his friends," John said, introducing them to the bartender. "They're the ones who helped save us and were Seth's traveling companions. Make sure they're well taken care of."

Cindy, a middle-aged woman with a warm smile and a quick, professional demeanor, nodded. "You got it, John."

John turned back to Tom and his team. "I need to get back to the stage area to make sure everything is set for the next phase. I'll send someone to get you when it's time for lunch."

With that, John left, weaving his way back through the gathering crowd, while Tom and his team settled in at the bar. They took turns ordering drinks, starting with light cocktails and gradually working their way up to stronger concoctions. Laughter filled the air as they reminisced about past adventures and shared stories, the tension of the past days easing away with each drink.

About an hour later, John returned to the bar. His eyes widened as he took in the scene. Almost all of Tom's team were visibly intoxicated, some of them leaning on each other for support while others were engaged in overly enthusiastic conversations. Jay was attempting to teach Tom some overly complicated dance moves that were clearly beyond both of their current abilities, while James and Kiera were loudly debating which type of goblin had been the toughest to fight.

"How many drinks could you all have had in that short a period of time?!" John exclaimed, looking over at the bartender, who was leaning back against the bar, sweat dripping down her face, and panting slightly from exertion.

"Oh, we only had a couple two three seven maybe twelve drinks each? Sh-sh-sh... don't tell anyone. Hehehehehe. We might be a tany but fershnickered," Tom slurred out as he put one finger to John's lips in a shushing motion.

"Hey! Hey. Have I ever told you I love you, man?" James slurred even worse as he put an arm around Tom's shoulders.

"Awww, I love you too, man!" Tom replied, holding a drink over his head in a terrible attempt not to spill it.

"You all know the apocalypse is a government ploy to get us into fighting shape for the draft that's coming?!" Clay exclaimed from the other end of the bar.

"You're only half right!" Jay belligerently hiccuped. "It's definitely a cannon fodder farm, but the government's too shit to manage it. Naw. It's definitely aliens. They need us for the Galactic Wars."

"Fuuuuck," Clay said, slack jawed. "You're right. Daaamn. How'd you figure   it   out?"

Jay glanced around surreptitiously before gesturing for Clay to get closer and loudly whispering in his ear. "Well, you see... about ten years ago, I was abducted..."

"Sorry about them," Derek said, walking over to John. "I'll get them cleaned up in a minute. Just letting them all let off a little steam first."

"You mean, you can fix this?" John asked.

"Sure. It's easy. Just use a Cleric cleansing spell. Alcohol is considered a poison, so it'll purify it from your system," Derek replied, turning to look at his teammates with a chuckle. "I was nearly that drunk just a moment ago, and casting it on myself sobered me right up."

"Okay, good." John sighed with relief. "I was worried that this would mean we would have to keep them away from the next part of the day. And god only knows what would've happened if there had been a monster attack and we couldn't sober them up."

"MONSTER?! WHERE?! POINT ME AT THEM!" Bobby suddenly screamed from the middle of the bar, and in a flash, his weapon was equipped, and he was spinning around, looking for danger.

This sudden action set off a chain reaction among the rest of the intoxicated party members. In a frenzied panic, everyone began hastily equipping items from their Inventories as if preparing for an impending battle.

Tom retrieved his greatsword, the heavy blade gleaming under the dim lights of the bar. Kedron and Graham both pulled out their axes, brandishing them with drunken determination, while Kevin hefted his massive greataxe over his shoulder, nearly knocking over a nearby stool. Kiera quickly readied her rifle, peering through the scope as if targeting some invisible enemy across the room.

Amidst the chaos, James, with a more serious expression than anyone had ever seen on the man, pulled out a bright pink umbrella from his Inventory. He opened it with a dramatic *whoosh* and held it out in front of him like a shield, its colorful fabric somehow looking almost menacing in his hands. The sheer absurdity of it all caused a momentary pause, and then the whole group erupted into uncontrollable laughter.

"No, no! There is no monster! We're safe in Decatur at a bar!" Derek yelled, trying to calm the scene.

Everyone slowly lowered their weapons as they looked at Derek. He cast his cleansing spell on Tom first. Nothing happened.

"What the hell?" Derek said in confusion. "Oh, shit. He's dark aligned."

"What does that mean?" John asked, looking at Tom as though this was what he expected to happen from a spell.

"He can't be affected by light-aligned healing spells because, as a Warlock, he's considered dark aligned. I can help most of the others, though," Derek explained, letting out a sigh.

He moved around the room, healing most of the other party members. However, when he got to Jay, he found that he couldn't be cleansed because Jay's Rogue Class was also dark aligned.

"This will have to do. We can keep Tom and Jay here for now," John said. "It's time to move out to the next part of the ceremony."

Chapter 11

Live and Let Loose

"Tom, I need you to remember that we're in Decatur and I need you to stay in this room. Don't leave. Take a nap if you can. Jay, just stay there. And if you're stable enough, try to heal yourself," Derek instructed the two after convincing both to sit on the couch by offering to bring them another drink.

"Oh yeah, Seth died," Tom said as though he had just remembered. He suddenly made a sad face, appearing on the edge of tears. "Why did it have to be him? It could have been me instead."

"Oh, shit. Emotional Tom. I knew we should have stuck to liquor instead of wine." Derek tried to soothe Tom. "Ummm, look, man, it's not your fault. It just happened that way. And we are here to celebrate all the good he did."

"Yeah, I know you're right. But I still feel re…respins…spironsible…sinsorible… I feel guilty," Tom finally spat out.

"I know ya do, buddy. But you're gonna have to let that go. Here, have another drink and remember the monsters," Derek said, hoping it would distract him from Seth.

"Monsters?! Where?!" Tom yelled, jumping up from the couch and brandishing his drink like a sword, spilling its contents everywhere.

"Heyyy… that's alcohol abuse right there. You… you've been naughty," Jay slurred from the couch next to him after watching perfectly good bourbon go to waste.

Derek spun around and dashed out of the room, leaving the wide-eyed bartender calling after him in confusion. Once outside, he slowed his pace and made his way over to the stage area where John stood, intently reading a memo on a clipboard. John's brows were furrowed, his expression tense and concerned, clearly troubled by whatever news he had just received.

"Everything going okay, John?" Derek asked.

"Hmm? Oh, no, not really. I just got a notice that Jeffery was seen trying to sneak back into town," John said, seeming to ponder this deeply, a look of concern on his face.

"Jeffery? You mean Seth's dad? The guy that almost ruined the town?" Derek asked, suddenly concerned as well.

"Yeah, that Jeffery. I think it's cruel not to let him in for his son's funeral. But he was saying some disturbing things when we threw him out of town," John said, finally looking up from his clipboard, weariness evident on his face.

"Disturbing how?" Derek asked, immediately fearing the worst.

"Mostly threats against the town, me, and you all more than anyone. He was really mad. Not sure what he can actually do about it, but I always try to take those threats seriously," John informed him, crossing his arms over his chest as he spoke.

"That's definitely concerning. I don't know what he's capable of now; he didn't seem like much of a threat before. But in this new world, people can get stronger a lot faster than they used to," Derek said, agreeing with John's caution.

"I want to give him a chance to come in, but we need to be extremely careful," John replied, his expression thoughtful.

"I think we can manage it. We have a lot of adventurers from the quest with us, and we can all keep an eye on him," Derek suggested. "How about I go with you, and we can talk to him together?"

"That sounds like a good idea," John agreed, nodding. "Let's go speak with him. I think allowing him to join for the second part of the celebration, then having him leave afterward, would give him a chance to be part of things without the risk of him getting too lost in the party atmosphere."

"Perfect," Derek said with a determined smile. "Let's go let him know." He walked over to a golf cart that had been used by the event staff throughout the day, ready to head out with John.

John hopped onto the cart beside Derek and pointed toward the south entrance. Derek pressed the gas pedal, and the brake disengaged with a sharp click before the cart lurched forward. They zipped across the event grounds, the hum of the electric motor mingling with the distant sounds of the celebration.

Once they reached the gate, both John and Derek hopped out of the cart, the crunch of gravel underfoot contrasting with the quiet tension of the moment. They walked over to the guard on duty, a burly man with a stern expression, standing alert by the entrance. The guard snapped to attention as they approached, sensing the urgency in their demeanor.

"Hey, Tim. How's it going out here?" John asked the guard on duty.

"All's quiet out here, Mr. Mayor. Well, everything except him. He's been insisting he be let in to see his son," Tim replied, gesturing at a very disheveled-looking Jeffery, who was sitting on the ground in the middle of the road.

His once-pristine white suit was now in shambles. The right sleeve of the jacket had been torn, hanging loosely from his arm like a tattered flag, and his tie was undone, dangling limply around his neck. Streaks of blood and dirt smeared across the fabric, marring its former elegance. His hair, which had once been neatly styled, was now a tangled mess, and his glasses sat askew on his face, one lens cracked. He looked like he had just lost a fight—or barely escaped one.

"Where is Seth? I want to see him," Jeffery demanded as he looked up at John and Derek.

"Jeffery, we have some bad news for you. Seth didn't make it back. He was unfortunately killed in combat against the Devourer," Derek stated flatly.

"What?" was all Jeffery could manage.

"We're so sorry for your loss, but we're having a celebration of life for him in town today. If you think you can be on your best behavior, we can bring you into town for the next part of the celebration, but you have to leave after that," John added with more compassion.

"My boy… is dead? How can this be?" Jeffery said, tears beginning to well up in his eyes.

He suddenly balled his hands into fists and his visage changed to one of rage.

"This is *your* fault. If he had stayed here, he wouldn't have died!" Jeffery began with a low volume, ending in a yell as he stood up and pointed an accusing finger at Derek.

"If he had stayed here doing what he was doing, he would have died as well. At least this way, he died for something bigger than just this little town. He saved the whole fucking world," Derek responded with a building sense of anger.

"We were *fine* here. He could defeat any monsters that came to this town. He didn't need to go searching for bigger monsters. You did this. This is all your fault. I'll kill you for this!" Jeffery was practically screaming at the end of his rant, spittle flying from his mouth.

"Well, I guess you can't come in after all. We can't have someone causing this kind of a scene and threatening our guests. Derek, can you stay here while I go get some additional guards to watch him?" John asked, exasperated at this point with everything he was having to deal with.

"Sure. I'll be here. Just hurry back. I don't want to miss the celebration," Derek replied without taking his eyes off Jeffery, who was now fully crying in a fit of rage as he slung profanities and threats at Derek and his friends.

John hopped back into the golf cart and sped off to find additional guards. About twenty minutes later, he returned with a small group in tow. By that time, Jeffery had mostly burned himself out. He was now on his knees, a pitiful, wailing cry escaping him as he mourned the loss of his son. His face was red and streaked with tears, his body trembling with a mixture of exhaustion and anguish.

"I don't like how he's acting," Derek said quietly to John when he came back. "I think he's losing himself to his rage. You might want to lock him up for today, just to be safe."

"Do you really think he's that much of a danger?" John asked, concern furrowing his brow.

"I don't take anything for granted now that we can't just call the police for backup," Derek replied, his voice steady. "We should do everything we can to keep people safe."

John nodded slowly, weighing Derek's words. "Alright. Tim, gather the others and take Jeffery to the jail for now. We'll let him out again in the morning," he instructed one of the guards. Tim nodded, signaling to the rest of the guards to move in.

They approached Jeffery carefully. His energy seemed completely drained, his earlier fury replaced by a hollow despair. He offered no resistance as they cuffed his hands behind his back and led him to another vehicle. The guards helped him into the back seat and drove off into town, Jeffery's head hanging low.

"Now, we'll just wait here until they return, then we can join the festivities again," John said, turning to Derek with a grateful smile as he extended his hand. "Thanks for helping with this, by the way."

"No worries. I'm happy to help," Derek replied, shaking John's hand firmly. "Though I am now concerned about Jeffery, and while I can't let that distract me for the moment, we need to make sure that we set some time aside to deal with that after the celebration."

They waited for about thirty minutes until Tim and another guard returned to take over their post. Once relieved, Derek and John hopped into the golf cart and drove back to the town center. As they approached, they could hear the sounds of laughter and voices on the stage, where people were sharing stories about Seth and remembering him fondly. Some of his friends took turns speaking, describing him as a "badass dude" who was always ready to lend a hand, no matter the risk.

"I remember this one time," a man began, his eyes twinkling with the memory. "There was this scrawny kid who'd rather read a book than play sports, and he was getting bullied by that jerk, Jackson. Jackson had grabbed the kid's backpack and was just about to shove him into a locker when Seth came barreling down the hall. Without a second thought, he drop-kicked Jackson." The man chuckled, shaking his head. "Jackson went flying down the hall, leaving the scrawny kid and his backpack on the floor, staring in shock."

Laughter rippled through the crowd as they pictured the scene. "Jackson ran off crying like a little girl," the man continued, grinning. "Kept screaming he was gonna tell the principal on Seth. If I remember correctly, Seth got a two-day suspension for that, but the funny thing is, it led to Jackson eventually getting expelled. A whole bunch of other kids came forward after that, talking about how Jackson had bullied them, too. Seth's actions were the catalyst that made that happen."

Others shared similar stories, recounting moments where Seth had stepped in to help them when they were being bullied or when they needed something. "He'd always let people borrow things if they needed them," one woman said fondly. "He never cared if he got it back."

A mother stood up with her two children, her eyes welling with tears. "One time," she began, her voice shaky but filled with gratitude, "Seth paid for our groceries when our card got declined. What he didn't know was that we had just moved to town to get away from an abusive ex-husband. I had no job, no money, and no food. That kindness carried us through to my first paycheck. He literally saved us from starving."

As more stories were shared, it became clear that Seth had touched countless lives with his small, selfless acts. What seemed like little gestures to him had made a world of difference to others. Derek listened, reflecting on the impact that simple actions could have on someone's life. He realized he'd never truly understood how much of a difference a small kindness could make.

After another hour and a half of stories, the crowd began to disperse, people trickling out of the area to rest before the dinner and final celebration. Derek made his way back to check on Tom and Jay. Upon entering the bar area, he found Jay sitting on a couch, engrossed in a book, while Tom was sprawled out on the floor. He was fast asleep, mouth wide open, snoring loudly, with a small puddle of drool forming on the floor beside him.

"For heaven's sake. He's still out?" Derek asked incredulously.

"He should be coming around any minute. But he did have more to drink than everyone else," Jay said, not looking up from his book.

"Yeah, he needed it. But he needs to get back up so we can get ready for dinner," Derek said.

"Actually, let him rest. We have a couple of hours before that happens. He can keep sleeping it off, and we'll be sure he's ready closer to the time," John said, walking in as well.

"Fine," Derek sighed. "I could use some rest as well."

He flopped down onto the couch across from Jay in the sitting area.

"I feel like we've been going nonstop for years. We need a better rest time when we get back to Dallas," Derek said, rubbing the heels of his hands over his eyes.

"I hear that. This has been better than the road and fighting constantly, but being home in my space will be so much better," Jay said, looking at Derek and putting one finger in the book so as not to lose his place.

"It sounds like we won't even get that, though. We're going to hit the ground running when we are back, too," Derek replied in an exhausted tone.

"We'll take it one day at a time for now. That's all we can do," Jay stated, opening the book again and picking up where he left off.

About two hours later, John returned to the bar area and informed them now was the best time to begin getting Tom up.

"Alright, sunshine. Time to rise and greet the world," Derek said, moving over to Tom and slapping him less than softly on the face.

"Huh?! What? I'm up!" Tom spoke quickly, his eyelids barely half open as he lifted his head, trying to appear alert.

"Gotta get ready for dinner. That should sound good to you. Oh, can you also cast your healing spell on yourself and see if that cures the drunk?" Derek asked Tom, trying to make his tone sound sweet.

Tom stared at him in confusion for a moment, then his eyes widened as realization hit. He quickly sat up and started looking through a menu that only he could see. His expression shifted from puzzled to understanding as he found what he was looking for. With a focused look, he closed the menu. A soft purple light enveloped him for a brief moment, and he let out a sigh of relief.

"That's better," Tom said, rubbing his neck. "It doesn't really take away the drunk, but it definitely cures the hangover I was starting to get."

"Glad to hear it," Kedron said as he entered the room with the rest of the group trailing behind John. "Because we have to head out for dinner soon. After that, it's time to cut loose again and party."

"Just let me go freshen up a bit. It's nice to be using a bathroom again," Tom commented, standing up and walking to the bathroom in the back area of the bar.

About ten minutes later, Tom emerged from the bathroom, looking refreshed. The team gathered and made their way through the town to the dinner area, set up outside near the courthouse. The final meal of the day was a tribute to Seth—his favorite: hamburgers. At one end of the street, several men had propane-powered grills fired up, the sizzling of meat filling the air as they grilled burgers to perfection for everyone to enjoy.

A line formed for the dinner buffet, and the team joined the queue, chatting and joking as they waited. The aroma of freshly grilled beef, toasted buns, and an array of toppings wafted through the air, creating a comforting atmosphere. After loading their plates and building their perfect burgers, they found a spot to sit and eat together.

As they settled in, a low rumble from a generator could be heard in front of the courthouse. The street lights flickered to life around the generator, casting a warm glow over the crowd. Moments later, the speakers crackled, and the first notes of music filled the air—the familiar tune of "Don't Stop Believin'" by Journey. It was Seth's favorite band, and the choice of song seemed to resonate with everyone.

Conversations shifted as people began to sing along, their voices blending together. Some sang in harmony, others off-key, but it didn't matter. The singing grew louder, more unified, until the entire crowd was belting out the final chorus together. For that brief moment, the trials and hardships of the past few weeks seemed to melt away, replaced by a shared sense of camaraderie and hope.

Tom wiped away a tear as the song came to an end, overwhelmed by the emotion of the moment. More music followed, the playlist carrying on with other classic hits, setting a joyful tone for the evening. As many finished their meals, John approached the group and announced that the rest of the night was dedicated to celebration. The dance floor was open, and the bar would be serving drinks until supplies ran out.

For the remainder of the evening, the group let go of their burdens and simply enjoyed being in the moment. They danced, laughed, and sang, feeling a sense of peace they hadn't felt in weeks. The night became a tribute to their journey, their losses, and the strength they'd found in each other.

Chapter 12

Homeward Bound

Everyone slept in the next morning. Even Derek, who was notorious for waking up at the crack of dawn, wasn't up until the sun was already high in the sky. The festivities the night before had stretched late into the night, offering a much-needed release for everyone after the relentless chaos and tension since the world had turned upside down.

For once, the burdens of survival were set aside. There had been dancing and singing, with spontaneous laughter breaking out among the crowd as they celebrated the simple joy of being alive. The music and voices had filled the air, carrying with them a sense of unity and hope that felt foreign yet familiar. Food was shared freely among the gathered friends and strangers alike, and for one fleeting moment, the worries and hardships of this new world seemed to dissolve into the night.

It was a moment suspended in time—a brief, shining escape from the relentless weight they all carried, allowing them to remember what it was like to simply live, even if just for a night.

"Magic sure does make parties more fun," James commented.

"How so?" Derek asked, stretching after rubbing the sleep from his eyes.

"No more hangovers," James replied, smiling widely.

"Is that the only reason?" Derek questioned, annoyed at James' one-dimensional approach to magic.

"Of course not. Those fireballs someone was tossing into the sky to explode like fireworks were awesome as well," James continued. "Even the building fire that happened when one of them went rogue after someone bumped into the wizard was awesome. He was able to use a stream of water spell to put it out."

"People could have been seriously hurt!" Derek replied angrily.

"I know, but we could heal them. It wasn't like he was pointing it at anyone," James shuffled backward at Derek's sudden outburst.

"Or maybe someone could just *not* do dangerous drunken stunts with magic simply because we have it," Derek suggested, crossing his arms over his chest.

"Now, where's the fun in that?" James grinned as he pulled a handgun from his Inventory. Attempting to twirl it around his finger like a gunslinger from an old western, he immediately lost control of the weapon. It slipped from his grasp and clattered to the floor, where it discharged with a deafening bang, sending a bullet into the wall at the far end of the room.

Derek, who had instinctively ducked and covered his head with his hands, slowly straightened up. He stared at James with a mix of shock and fury, his eyes blazing with the kind of anger that only comes from narrowly avoiding disaster.

"Still working on that one. It's not as easy as it looks," James explained sheepishly as he picked up the gun and stored it back in his Inventory.

Derek threw his hands up in exasperation, his face flushed with anger. Without a word, he turned on his heel and stormed off, his footsteps echoing with frustration as he put distance between himself and James.

"Hey, tell Clay I wanna talk to him if you see him!" James called after Derek. "Hopefully he's in a better mood than Derek."

Tom entered the lobby a few minutes later, looking much worse off than the others.

"Well, look what the cat threw up," James said, looking Tom over. "You look like you were ridden hard and put away dead."

"Yeah, being dark aligned makes it harder to get rid of all the symptoms. It's still way better than pre-magic times, but I definitely don't feel as chipper as you all sound," Tom said, his hair askew and bags forming under his eyes.

"Maybe you should have chosen differently," James offered.

"And never have met Azroc? …No thank you," Tom replied, smiling at James' antics.

"I didn't think about that. Yeah, I like him. You made the right call," James replied, retracting his statement.

Moving to the exit, the team stepped out into the bright sunlight. The sudden glare made Tom squint, and he instinctively raised a hand to shield his eyes from the blinding light. The warmth of the sun hit them, a stark contrast to the dim interior they had just left.

"Son of a bitch, it's bright today," he commented. "Where are my… oh, duh."

Tom produced a pair of sunglasses from his Inventory and put them on.

"You keep sunglasses in there?" James asked, suddenly intrigued at what was in Tom's Inventory.

"You don't?"

"Well, of course *I* do," James scoffed. "I was just surprised you did, too.

"I keep pretty much everything that I find and think I might need in there." Tom shrugged.

"I've just been keeping fighting stuff and foodstuff in there," James said, slightly upset at not thinking of that.

"Dude, if you find something, put it in there in case you need it. You never know what'll come in handy later on," Tom replied, taking a cup of coffee out of his Inventory.

"Seriously?!" James sputtered.

"Seriously. It's still hot, too," Tom grinned as he put the steaming cup to his mouth to take a loud slurp.

Tom rummaged through his Inventory and began pulling out a random assortment of items to show what he'd managed to scavenge. First, he produced a bagel, still in its packaging, followed by a bright, inflatable pool floaty shaped like a flamingo. Next came a gas torch, which he held up with a bemused expression.

With a grin, he reached in again and pulled out a small metal safe, setting it down with a thud. He wasn't done yet. Out came a tank of helium, which he set beside a goldfish in a bowl, its water sloshing slightly as it landed. Finally, he pulled out the container they had put Seth's ashes in. His heart clenched at the sight and he set it aside to give to John.

"Tom, we need to address the elephant in the room," James said, placing a hand on Tom's shoulder with a mock-serious expression. "You're a loot hoarder."

"I am not!" Tom retorted, his face scrunching up defensively. "I might need this stuff later—" But his rebuttal was cut off as James pressed a finger to his lips.

"Shhhhh… It's okay," James said soothingly, his tone dripping with playful condescension. "I understand what you're going through. But look at this," he continued, gesturing to the bizarre assortment of items scattered around them. "This is junk, Tom. Junk."

"I think you've watched one too many episodes of Hoarders," Tom said, pushing James' hand away from his face with an exasperated sigh.

"I think you've got too much crap in your Inventory," James shot back, eyebrows raised.

"I do not! I might need this stuff. You never know," Tom argued, sounding more defensive than convincing.

"Seriously, Tom? When are we ever going to use a goldfish in a bowl?" James asked, holding up the bowl and staring at the tiny fish floating lifelessly at the bottom. "And it's dead, man. I'm pretty sure we can't store living things in our Inventories."

"How was I supposed to know that?" Tom said, ripping the bowl out of James' hands, his cheeks flushed slightly with embarrassment.

"Hey, at least you tested with a goldfish first. That thing was alive when you put it in there, right?" James asked, suddenly looking concerned that Tom might have thought a dead goldfish was valuable.

"Yes, of course it was alive!" Tom snapped, though his voice softened slightly. "I thought a kid back at the Guild building might like it or something."

James blinked, then laughed incredulously. "Really? A kid who's living through the apocalypse is gonna think, 'Man, if I had a goldfish, my life would be so much better?' That's what you were going with?"

Tom rubbed his temples, realizing how ridiculous it sounded. "Have I stepped through some kind of dimensional door where James actually makes good points?" he muttered to himself, half joking, half annoyed.

"Hey! I may not have a lot of bright ideas, but I was due," James replied, grinning as he crossed his arms.

"Fine," Tom relented, "I'll work on decluttering. But for now, it's almost time to load up and head out. We need to find John and thank him for the hospitality." He glanced around, scanning the area for any sign of their host.

John stood in front of the courthouse entrance, sipping a steaming cup of coffee. When he spotted them emerging from the hotel, he raised a hand and waved, motioning for them to head his way. Tom, with Derek and James close behind, made his way toward John.

As they walked, Tom couldn't help but reflect on how far they'd come. It was hard to believe that it had all started with just the three of them. Technically, it had been James and him at the very beginning, but Derek had quickly become an integral part of their little team—his steady hand and knack for making smart decisions had often been the difference between survival and disaster during those chaotic early days of the System integration.

A wave of gratitude washed over Tom as he glanced at his friends. What would have happened if he'd stayed home sick from work that day? Or if some tiny detail had been different in those first moments of chaos? He didn't want to get lost in the "what ifs," but he allowed himself a brief moment to appreciate the friends walking beside him.

He stopped for a second, smiling warmly at Derek and James. "I'm glad we're in this together," he said quietly, more to himself than anyone else, but the sentiment carried.

"Dude, you okay? You're creeping me out with the stare," Derek commented, noticing that Tom had stopped walking.

"I think it's nice. This is my good side, by the way," James said, stopping and bending over slightly as he turned back to look at Tom, his eyebrows bouncing up and down.

"Just have to make everything weird, don't you?" Tom asked, chuckling slightly at James' antics.

"It's what I do best," James replied, smiling and standing up fully.

"Thanks for doing this with me, guys," Tom said to them.

"You mean going to the courthouse?" James asked, confused about what Tom was saying this for.

"No, I mean the whole apocalypse thing," Tom corrected. "You all have stuck beside me and we make an awesome team."

"It's true. We're pretty awesome," James said, preening and putting his thumbs under invisible suspenders.

"Of course, Tom. We're in this together. The only way people survive apocalypses is by banding together. We're here for the long haul," Derek replied, smiling as well. "Now, let's go see what John has for us and thank him so we can get moving."

When the trio finally reached John, he greeted them with a warm smile and extended his hand. One by one, they each took it in a firm handshake, feeling the sincerity in his grip. Tom felt a sense of camaraderie in the gesture, a silent acknowledgment of the trials they had faced and the battles they had fought to get here. John's eyes met each of theirs in turn, his expression a mix of gratitude and determination.

"Thank you all so much for coming back through here. We know you didn't have to, but it shows your level of character that you didn't shy away from an awkward situation and told us of Seth's fate. For that, we are grateful," John said, taking another sip of coffee.

"It was the right thing to do. We hope someone else would have done the same for us," Tom replied.

"I know you've already done so much for us, but I needed to ask if you could do one more thing," John said hesitantly as he looked at the three men.

"Let me guess, people want to come with us?" Tom asked.

"How did you know?" John looked shocked that they had guessed that.

"Every stop we've made back through, at least some of the people want to come with us. It was bound to happen here," Tom replied as if he was tired of hearing it.

"Is that okay? I get a little feeling you don't want to take them," John asked, worried they were going to say no.

"No, it's not that. It's merely that we're already trying to figure out what to do with so many people. But at this point, with how many we have, more can't be any worse. I mean, it can, but we won't likely notice a huge difference," Derek explained. "How many want to come?"

"Only about twenty. Most people are content to stay here," John explained.

"Sure, we'll take them with us, but they need their own transport. That's been our rule for everyone else," Tom told him. "Also, here."

Tom handed John the coffee can they had repurposed to hold Seth's ashes. "Sorry, it's not an urn. They're a little hard to come by now."

"Thank you. As for the transport, we can arrange that. Thank you so much again! I don't want to force anyone to be where they're unhappy. And I know some of the people here have been looking for someone like you to follow," John praised them.

"Don't forget to send extra gasoline with them. We store it in our Inventories to bring out when we need to refuel," Tom advised John to ensure they didn't hit any issues on the way back.

"Good note. I will make sure we send plenty with them," John replied, turning to leave and get those going with Tom ready.

After checking in with the others, Tom and his team stepped outside to assess how the preparations were coming along. The courtyard was buzzing with activity—people were moving swiftly double-checking their gear for the journey ahead. The air was filled with the hum of conversation and the occasional shout of instructions.

Tom took a deep breath, feeling the energy of the group, and called his team together. "Alright, everyone, gather up," he said, his voice steady but commanding. One by one, his team members stopped what they were doing and made their way over, forming a tight circle around him, ready to hear their next steps.

"Are we ready to hit the road? I don't want to dawdle anywhere we don't have to," Tom asked.

"We're ready. We're just waiting for the rest. We filled up the vehicles with gas, and these Inventories make packing and travel a breeze now," Kedron replied.

"Great. I want everyone ready to load up and head out as soon as we get word that the people here are ready. We might be able to make it most of the way home today," Tom smiled as the thought of being back to check on everyone raced through his mind.

As the team broke from their circle and started toward the vehicles, a sudden shower of sparks erupted from a traffic signal light at an intersection about six streets away. The loud, crackling zap of electricity tore through the air, startling everyone nearby. Tom felt his skin prickle as the hairs on his neck and arms stood on end.

The burst of sparks shot out from the signal light and traveled along the power lines suspended above the street, racing toward the courthouse where the people were gathered. Each signal light it passed on its way exploded in a dazzling display of sparks and shattered glass. Panic spread like wildfire. Screams filled the air as people began to run in all directions, desperate to escape the oncoming wave of electrical chaos.

"What the fuck is that?!" James shouted, his eyes wide as he followed the path of the sparks racing toward them.

"Doesn't matter—it's headed straight for us! MOVE!" Derek yelled, his voice booming as he barked the last word, snapping everyone into action.

As the sparks neared the final signal light at the intersection adjacent to the courthouse, a piercing wail emerged from within the crackling electricity. The noise grew louder and more distorted as the sparks reached the yellow metal housing of the traffic light. Suddenly, the largest burst of sparks yet exploded outward, raining down in a blinding flash. From the heart of the eruption, a being made almost entirely of blue light screeched and shot toward the party members.

The creature's form twisted and flickered with the intensity of a lightning storm, its writhing, electric fingers reaching for James as he instinctively dove to the side. The fingers missed him by mere inches, but their proximity left blackened burn marks on his clothes from the residual electricity crackling off its body.

As it surged through the panicked crowd, grabbing at people with a frantic desperation, its form began to coalesce into something more tangible. The being transformed into a shriveled humanoid figure with wild, scraggly white hair and blazing, furious azure eyes, its once-fluid body solidifying with each step it took.

Specter
A Specter is a malevolent spirit born from the lingering hatred of the dead. As an incorporeal entity, it drifts silently through the air, its form flickering like a shadow in a storm. Its presence is marked by a chilling aura that seems to drain the warmth from its surroundings. It is driven by a single purpose: to steal the life force of the living.

HP:	1025/1025
MP:	550/550
SP:	N/A
Attacks:	Spectral Touch, Ethereal Kiss, Banshee's Scream

Turning its body sharply toward Tom, the creature extended a single, withered finger in his direction. Its eyes blazed with a malevolent blue light as it fixed its gaze on him. In a voice that sounded like a chorus of harsh, raspy whispers woven together, it shrieked, "YOOOOOUUUUUUUU!"

Chapter 13

Raise the Specter

"Me?" James shouted, pointing at himself in abject terror.

The Specter paused, its gaze locking onto James with a look of confusion, like a *Scooby-Doo* villain interrupted mid-monolog by Shaggy and Scooby's antics. It shook its head slowly then pointed again, more emphatically, directly at Tom.

James, wide eyed, mouthed, "Oh, sorry, my bad," and sheepishly raised both hands in apology. He took a step back, clearing the way so Tom was once again the center of the creature's ominous attention.

"Really?" Tom said as he rolled his eyes and then took a fighting stance.

Equipping his greatsword from his Inventory, Tom dashed forward, slashing horizontally at the Specter. The creature remained still, its eerie eyes locked on Tom as he charged. The blade sliced through the air, but passed harmlessly through the Specter's incorporeal form.

The Specter grinned wickedly, unfazed by the attack. It turned slowly, extending a bony hand toward Tom. The moment it made contact, icy tendrils snaked across Tom's shoulder and down his arm, sending a wave of excruciating cold through his body. Tom yanked himself away with a yell, the searing pain vanishing the instant he broke free. A quick glance at his health bar showed he was down to ninety percent.

"Holy shit, that sucks! Don't let it touch you—it drains your health!" Tom shouted to the others. "And weapons can't hurt it. Light it up with spells!"

Tom formed his hand into the gesture for *Eldritch Blast*, green flames igniting in his palm. He hurled the spell at the Specter. A ghastly, ear-splitting scream erupted from the creature as the green fire struck it, sending it into a frenzy. A high-pitched keening filled the air, causing everyone nearby to cover their ears in agony, many dropping to their knees.

When the keening finally ceased, the Specter darted toward a woman on the sidewalk. It seized her shoulders with its skeletal hands, and she screamed as tendrils of gray crept from where the Specter touched her, spreading down her arms. Its mouth opened impossibly wide, and a strange sucking sound began as light formed in the woman's chest, pulling toward her mouth.

Suddenly, four bolts of purple energy slammed into the Specter, one after another, interrupting its ghastly ritual. It released the woman, dropping her to the ground, and stumbled backward. Another wave of that high-pitched keening began, forcing everyone to cover their ears again.

Tom, having had enough, stored his greatsword back in his Inventory. "That's it! I've been wanting to try this for a while. Time to fuck some shit up!" he yelled, getting to his feet as blood trickled from his ears.

He held both hands at chest level, focusing as a ball of purple energy appeared in each palm. Turning his hands to face each other, he began forcing the two orbs together. His muscles strained and bulged as the two spells resisted, repelling each other like magnetic poles. The purple glow began to spread from his hands down his arms, enveloping his entire body in an intense purple aura.

"Haaaaaaaaaaaaa," Tom growled, his voice growing louder with each second as he poured his strength into the effort. "HAAAAAAAAAAAAAAA!"

With a final, guttural shout, the two energy balls merged into one, creating a massive orb with a brilliant, glowing core. Tom shifted his right foot forward, positioning the orb at his hip, his hands bracketing the energy sphere.

"I've always wanted to do this…" Tom muttered with a wicked grin, his eyes locking onto the Specter. "FINAL… FLAAAAAAASH!"

He thrust his hands forward, and the orb blasted out, a searing purple beam trailing back to his hands. The ball of energy smashed into the Specter's chest, bending it backward as it tried to resist. The light intensified as Tom continued to pour his mana into the spell, growing so bright it seared the air.

With a deafening roar, the beam punched through the Specter's back, slicing into the building behind it. The Specter let out a final, agonized scream, forcing everyone but Tom to their knees. When the beam finally faded, the Specter hung there, a gaping hole in its torso. For a moment, it lingered, then it exploded into a cloud of tiny, glowing blue particles.

"Ho-ly shit," James muttered, staring at the spot where the Specter had been. "Careful where you go flashing those balls, Vegeta. You'll put someone's eye out."

Skill Acquired - Spell Weaving

Congratulations! You have unlocked the Skill: Spell-Weaving.
You now have the ability to create unique spells by combining your knowledge of magic and manipulating its properties. The success and potency of your custom spells will depend on your mastery of magical elements, your level, and your overall proficiency with magic.
Tip: Experiment with different magical components and effects to discover powerful combinations. The more you learn and practice, the more complex and potent your spells can become!
Keep exploring the world of magic to expand your capabilities!

New Spell - Final Flash	
New Spell Created! Your mastery of magic and spell-weaving has led to the creation of a powerful new spell. This spell is now part of your repertoire and can be cast at will. Experiment with different amounts of mana to maximize its destructive potential!	
Spell:	Final Flash
Mana Cost:	200+ MP
Attack:	500-525 Damage
Range:	300 Feet
Casting Time:	20 Seconds
Cool Down:	30 Seconds
Special Ability: Imbue	This ability allows the caster to feed additional mana into the spell, significantly increasing its damage output. The more mana imbued, the more devastating the Final Flash becomes.

"That wasn't exactly what I was going for, but I'll take it!" Tom said excitedly.

"What wasn't?" Derek asked.

"I was just trying to dual cast a more powerful version of the spell, but instead, I created a whole new spell. Wish I could have named it something else, though," Tom replied, slightly disappointed in the name.

"You literally shouted the name as you cast it," Derek pointed out.

"You can create your own spells?" James asked, immediately interested.

"Appears so. Although you have to know about magical theory, so I must have just gotten lucky," Tom admitted.

"Well, damn. I don't know anything about magic," James pouted sourly.

"Wait, wait, wait. You mean to tell me you just *created* a new spell? By shoving two pieces of extremely volatile magic together and flinging it at a monster?!" Bob moved through the crowd of people calling for Tom. When he reached him, Bob looked up at him expectantly.

"Um… yes?" Tom replied, confused as to why Bob appeared to be angry.

"You're messing with forces that you have no idea what they are capable of," Bob huffed, putting his hands on his hips. "Magic is unstable at the best of times, then you go and take two opposing forces—not meant to be interacting—

and literally cram them inside of each other. You are extremely lucky that it didn't just explode when they came into contact with each other!"

"Well, how was I supposed to know that?" Tom asked, indignant at being called out and chastised like a child.

"You've never seen depictions of magic attacks hitting each other and causing explosions? In movies or TV shows? That should have given you pause, at least," Bob continued. "You could have killed yourself and half the people here with that if it had gone wrong."

"Yeah, bro," James said, suddenly standing behind Bob. "Never cross the streams, Venkman."

"Well… I didn't know that. How could I have known that? How do *you* know that?" Tom sputtered.

"The info download from the machine, remember? I know a lot more than I should about the System," Bob replied, pointing at his head as he spoke.

"Right, right. Okay, what should I do about it, then?" Tom asked, not exactly sure what Bob was wanting from him.

"Just promise me that you won't mess with spells again until we get a chance to talk about this new Skill. Please?" Bob begged him.

"Of course. Yeah, yeah, I'll just use regular spells until we can talk," Tom assured him.

"Thank you. Now… carry on with what you were doing," Bob said awkwardly as he began to back away.

"Right! John! Where are you?" Tom called out as he searched the sea of faces around them.

"Here, Tom," John called from the steps of the courthouse.

"How is everyone?" Tom asked, the concern evident on his face.

"It seems like everyone is okay. That thing had a weird fixation with you," John puzzled over the odd behavior.

"I saw it point at me. I just assumed it was because I was someone who looked fightable," Tom replied, trying to come up with a reason he would be targeted.

"With everyone else wearing adventuring gear as well? Unlikely," John scoffed. "I'd watch myself for a while going forward."

"He's right," Bob said, stepping forward again.

"What do you know about this?" Tom asked, looking worried now.

"I know that was a Specter. Those creatures are only created when someone has a tremendous amount of hate in their soul for someone," Bob began, looking incredibly serious. "They are the result of magic escaping someone in the most vile way imaginable, and the person with the hate unconsciously controls it. If they realize they're the cause, they can unleash unimaginably vile creatures to go after the one they loathe."

"So, you mean to tell me that someone hates me so much that they created a monster and sent it after me, but they likely have no idea that they did it?" Tom asked, looking incredulously at Bob.

"That's the gist of it," Bob replied. "You have to be careful, and we'll need to figure out who the culprit is at some point."

"Someone who hates me... I wonder who that could be" Tom began to pretend to ponder sarcastically but was interrupted by someone running up to the team.

"Sir!" the security guard yelled while clearly struggling to breathe from running.

"What is it?" John asked as he turned and looked concerned at the guard.

"Monsters are coming. We need to get ready to repel them." The guard straightened and saluted after being addressed.

"Sorry, Tom, I'll have to catch up with you later. We need to handle this issue," John said, turning to follow the guard.

"Do you need help?" Tom asked him as he was leaving.

"Nope. If we can't handle this, then we should just leave. You all get ready to head out, and we'll handle this issue," John said over his shoulder without turning, waving one hand.

"Alright, then. You know where we'll be if you need us," Tom replied and turned to his team to check on the preparations to leave. "I guess we can just head out, then. How are we getting on?"

"Almost ready. I'm sure we'll be off within the hour," Derek replied.

"Awesome. Let's see where we can help," Tom offered as he started walking toward the lots where the vehicles were parked.

"Wait... so, you're okay with just having someone sneak up on you, who hates you, possibly kissing you sweetly on your cheek, before killing you in your sleep?" James asked.

Tom stared blankly at him for a moment. "What the actual—"

"Let's find them and kill them first," James interrupted.

"We don't have time for this. We need to get back. The Guild needs us," Tom replied with finality.

"Fine. But I'll have a lot of fun saying I told you so to your corpse," James huffed.

Work continued as people got ready to leave, ensuring vehicles were all prepared for the journey ahead. The air was filled with the sounds of gunfire and the thunderous explosions of spells, mingling with the ringing clash of steel and the agonized screams of creatures dying off in the distance. These sounds, though intense, were fading, signaling the end of the skirmish.

When John returned about twenty minutes later, blood was splattered on his face and hands. He wore a smile; a stark contrast to his disheveled appearance. Tom noticed this and smiled back, understanding that John's joy wasn't from the killing itself but from the victory in defense. It was the satisfaction of knowing that they had been able to defend themselves without needing Tom and his team to step in. The smile spoke of confidence, a reassurance that they were going to be okay on their own.

"It looks like they're going to be alright after all," Tom commented to Derek, watching John wipe the blood from his face with a cloth.

"Yeah," Derek replied, his eyes still scanning the organized chaos as people were loaded onto buses and vans. "I think we can rest easier knowing they've taken the right steps to protect themselves."

The bustle continued as John and his assistant moved through the crowd, making sure everyone was accounted for and safely boarded. The sun was now high in the sky, casting long shadows as the last of the vehicles were loaded. Tom and his team moved to their own vehicle, feeling a sense of relief and accomplishment.

Just as they settled in and the engine roared to life, James suddenly shouted from the back seat, his voice urgent and panicked.

"Oh, god! Wait!"

Chapter 14

Are We There Yet?

"What?! What is it, James?! Is everything alright?" Tom called at James' sudden yelling.

"I have to go to the little boy's room," he replied, much to everyone's annoyance.

"Seriously?" Tom looked pointedly at James. "We thought something was actually wrong!"

"It snuck up on me," James whined as he squirmed in his seat.

"Hurry up and go. We need to get on the road," Tom replied, rolling his eyes as he turned to face forward in the driver's seat.

James practically leaped from the vehicle, sprinting toward a nearby building. He approached the door of the courthouse, and it swung open as a woman was exiting. Unable to stop in time, James collided face-first with the door. He loudly swore, stumbling back and clutching his forehead while grabbing his crotch in a bizarre mix of pain and desperation. Caught in a frantic potty dance, he shoved the startled woman aside. She tumbled into the bushes as he bolted into the building.

A few minutes later, James emerged from the courthouse, his shoulders slumping in visible relief. He exhaled a long, satisfied sigh, then noticed the woman still lying in the bushes. His face turned red with embarrassment as he hurried over to help her to her feet, apologizing profusely the whole time. His awkward display drew laughter from the entire caravan. With his head hung low, James trudged back to the vehicle and climbed inside, and they finally took off down the road.

As they drove out of town, it seemed as though the entire community had come out to see them off. Crowds of people lined the streets, waving and calling out their thanks, wishing them good luck on their journey back.

"I feel like they're going to be okay now," Tom said with a smile, watching the townspeople fade into the distance.

"I think so too. We did good here, helping them see what they needed to do," Derek replied, sitting in his usual co-pilot seat.

The caravan made its way to the highway. Movement was slightly slowed by the buses lagging behind the smaller vehicles, but they made up time by not having to stop at signal lights or navigate around road signs. Tom couldn't help but comment on how nice it was to have so few drivers on the road compared to their typical commute.

The journey on this leg was smoother. Almost no creatures bothered them, except for a few groups of goblins who had set up makeshift roadblocks.

Occasionally, they spotted creatures in the distance that would dart back into the treeline or see wolves feasting on a carcass by the roadside. As the signs marking the miles to Dallas became more frequent, excitement grew among the passengers—they were getting closer to their new home.

For many of the travelers, this was a huge change; they had lived in the same state or even the same metropolitan area their entire lives. Now, they had uprooted themselves to join Tom and his team. The weight of that decision pressed on Tom's mind. Had he made the right choice in bringing them along? He knew he couldn't have left them behind, as it would have meant certain death for many. But could he truly uphold his promise to provide them with a better life in Dallas?

As they finally entered downtown Dallas, they began to notice subtle but significant changes. The streets were cleaner, eerily clear of vehicles, and there was a strange absence of sound. Having lived near the city for so long, Tom was used to the noise of active life. The quiet, empty streets carried a sense of foreboding.

Turning down a side street, they found themselves face-to-face with a Toyota Highlander. A man stood in the sunroof, and as they got closer, Tom realized it was TJ. He honked the horn and waved out the window. TJ recognized them and waved back enthusiastically. As the cars approached each other, both caravans came to a halt, eager to reconnect.

"What the fuck did you do, print fliers and go door to door telling people about our Lord and Savior Vanguard?" TJ asked, staring back at the long line of vehicles following Tom.

"Lucifer, actually," James corrected.

TJ looked at him askew, but James simply rolled his window back up, maintaining eye contact with the man the entire time.

"What can I say? It's just my magnetic personality," Tom replied through the window of his vehicle, getting the man's attention.

"Oh, sure. Could you reverse the polarity a little?" TJ joked.

"No, I don't believe it works that way. I think if I turn that knob, it attracts every living being within a thousand miles," Tom replied, smiling at the exchange in its simplicity.

"Well, shit! Leave it! Don't change it!" TJ broke out in laughter. "You guys need an escort back?"

"Sure! Probably best a familiar face leads a convoy like this," Tom replied, thinking it was good that TJ thought of that. What if they hadn't recognized him?

TJ's vehicle made a U-turn and moved to the front of the caravan, taking the lead to guide them back to the center of what was now beginning to look like a fortified compound. As they arrived at the gate, TJ stopped his vehicle and stepped out to speak with a large man wearing black tactical gear and holding a clipboard. The man's size was imposing—he stood so tall that his head nearly grazed the top of the doorway of the security checkpoint stand.

The man looked down the line of vehicles stretching out behind TJ and shook his head, clearly skeptical about allowing them all in. Without missing a beat, TJ marched right up to him, his face set in determination. Despite being a good twelve inches shorter, TJ squared his shoulders and got in the man's face.

What followed was almost comical—TJ pointed, gesturing wildly, and barked orders with a fierceness that belied his stature. The towering guard, who at first seemed immovable, began to shrink back, his confidence wilting under TJ's tirade. After a few moments of this one-sided dressing down, with a lot of emphatic pointing and stern reprimands, the man finally relented. He nodded meekly, then saluted TJ several times before turning to open the gate.

With a broad smile and a triumphant thumbs-up, TJ turned back to Tom and his team, clearly proud of his success. As Tom's vehicle approached the gate, TJ raised a hand to signal him to stop, wanting to speak with him before they proceeded further.

"You all park in the usual spot. Have the buses and vans head up to the second floor. The parking garage is big enough for buses, I promise. This place used to double as a convention center, so it can handle them. All other cars should park on the first level for now," TJ instructed, rattling off the directions quickly.

Tom nodded in understanding, and they drove off as TJ stayed at the checkpoint, waving in the vehicles following behind. Circling around to the building's front entrance, they entered the parking garage and pulled into their customary spot. The team hopped out of the GS2 and began intercepting incoming vehicles to direct them to their designated areas.

Amidst the bustle of parking and organizing, Brian emerged from the building, his expression curious as he looked around to see what was going on.

"Brian! Good to see you again!" Tom said, once the last of the vehicles had been directed to where they should be.

"Glad to see you're alive and well. Joe told me he spoke with you. Makes me feel a little bad about calling his radio 'ancient garbage that we could probably make a better version of with magic.' But not too bad because I still feel that way," Brian joked as he put out a hand to shake.

Tom grasped Brian's hand firmly, shaking it with a genuine smile. "We're glad he had it, and it's a good thing we had someone in our camp who's a radio nerd too. We had no idea what to expect coming back."

Brian nodded. "It's not great, but it could be a whole lot worse. We'll catch you up once you've had some time to settle in."

Tom glanced around at the incoming vehicles and the crowd of new arrivals. "We should probably make sure these folks find where they need to go," he said, looking back at Brian.

Brian shook his head. "Oh, don't worry about that. I've got the welcoming committee already handling it," he replied, gesturing to a few people assisting the newcomers. "You and your team should go inside, wash up, and get yourselves presentable. We'll have a meeting in the gym this evening. After that, I'd recommend getting some rest. Tomorrow we can go over everything in detail. You've done more than enough already."

Tom gave a relieved nod, appreciating the chance to unwind for a bit.

The smile on Brian's face was enough to wash away all the worry that had been building up. Tom suddenly felt the exhaustion of what seemed like weeks of sleepless nights settling over him. Knowing there were now others ready to shoulder the responsibility of guiding and helping the new arrivals, he allowed himself—and his team—to let go of the burden, if only for a while. The relief was palpable, and the sense of freedom that came with it was almost overwhelming.

As they stepped into the Trammel Crow Center, Tom was immediately struck by the buzz of activity within the building and the fact that the electricity was on. The team stood in awe, taking in the sight of the bustling entrance filled with people moving around, engaged in various tasks and conversations. After so long spent in towns without power or camping out in the wild, the sight of lights and the hum of life was almost surreal. It was a comforting reminder of the world they had known before—an unexpected slice of normalcy amidst the chaos that had become their lives.

"This is remarkable," Tom managed to say, barely above a whisper.

"Yes, everyone has been hard at work to make this happen. The people you've found have been very motivated." Brian smiled as he commented on what they were staring at.

The room was bright and clean, with a feather duster gliding across a table near the entrance, moving entirely on its own.

"What the hell is that?" Tom asked, pointing at the floating feather duster.

"That is the work of Penelope," Brian replied, his smile widening at their reaction. "She has psychic magic that allows her to control inanimate objects with her mind. She uses cleaning as a way to practice controlling her powers."

"Wait, psychic magic?" Tom asked, his voice filled with disbelief. "That's possible now?"

"Yes," Brian confirmed. "It seems almost any style of magic is possible now. Many here have been training hard to be as prepared as they can be. We've set up specialized training sessions for everyone so we can assess their abilities and help them grow. It's incredible how fast people can develop when they focus on their specialties."

As Brian spoke, Tom and his team watched the scene unfold around them. People moved through the entryway with purpose, each engaged in a task. Some carried boxes or building supplies, while others were cleaning or huddled in small groups, discussing their plans for the day. There was a flurry of activity and cooperation, a stark contrast to the chaos and uncertainty they had faced on the road.

Nearly everyone was dressed in some form of armor for protection, with weapons—ranging from guns to hand weapons—within easy reach. The sight of so many people working together, focused and determined, filled Tom with a sense of hope. The atmosphere in the Center was one of productivity and camaraderie, a welcome change from the struggles of the past weeks.

"And you're building walls around the Center?" Tom asked, recalling the compound-like appearance of the exterior.

"We are!" Brian confirmed. "We had some trouble with goblins and a few other monsters, given the amount of space we needed to cover outside. Putting up the walls has greatly reduced the number of attacks, keeping everyone safer." He then grinned and added, "Now, no more dawdling. Off with you to the showers. You smell like you've died."

Reluctantly, the teams headed to the gym locker room, eager to wash off the grime from the road and countless battles. Tom stepped into one of the individual shower stalls, hanging the towel he'd been given on the hook outside the curtain. Stripping down, he turned on the water and was amazed to feel almost instantly hot water cascading over him. It was a small luxury, but after so long without it, it felt heavenly. He let the warmth and comfort envelop him, savoring the sensation of scrubbing his body clean. He stayed under the steaming water for nearly half an hour, relishing the moment.

As he washed, Tom couldn't help but notice the changes in his body since the System integration. The soft belly he once had from sitting at a desk all day was gone, replaced by a lean set of abs. His muscles were more defined and toned, giving him a stronger, fitter look. He wasn't as bulky as someone like Kevin, who looked like a bodybuilder now, but he was lean, with a clearly athletic build.

Finally, he turned off the water and dried himself in the shower stall before stepping out onto the cool tile floor, a towel wrapped securely around his waist. He pulled some clean clothes from his Inventory and laid them out on a bench in the locker area. As he dressed, Tom took a moment to reflect on everything that had happened—how far they'd come and what bringing all these new people back would mean for them. It was clear that everyone in the Center had their own role and took pride in their work. He even noticed that there were people who had taken their clothes and equipment to be cleaned for them, adding another layer of comfort to this new life.

Once dressed, Tom left the locker room, feeling cleaner than he had in a long time. He was one of the last to be ready, having taken his time to enjoy the hot shower. When he reached the gym, he found that a large group of people had already gathered in the stands, waiting eagerly for what was to come next.

"I see you enjoyed the showers," Brian called to him with a wide grin.

"It was wonderful. How did you get them working again?" Tom asked.

"Oh, there's a long, complicated explanation for that, but it boils down to magic and being able to gather the mana and convert it to power for the utilities of the building," Brian explained. "But for now, we need to focus on the people you brought with you. There sure were a fuck ton of them."

"Yeah, sorry about that. But we couldn't just leave them," Tom replied sheepishly.

"I know, I know. But still. Holy shit, man," Brian muttered, shaking his head in disbelief. "Never mind. We'll manage. We've actually started storing food from the gardens. The farming skills some of our people have gained seem to drastically reduce the growth time of the plants. They're reaching full maturity in just a couple of weeks, which means we'll have several harvests each year."

He paused, catching himself rambling, and smiled. "But listen to me prattle on. That's a discussion for tomorrow. Everyone should be here in the next fifteen minutes or so. Let's focus on getting ready to talk to them, shall we?"

Chapter 15

Catching Up

After another ten minutes, the rest of the travelers gathered in the gym, waiting patiently to hear what would come next. Tom and his team stood at the half-court mark, with a microphone and speakers set up just as before. Stepping up to the mic, Tom began to address the assembled crowd.

"Hello, everyone. Thank you for coming," Tom began, his voice carrying a touch of nervousness. "I know this has been a long journey to get here, and many of you have uprooted your entire lives to join us. I want to start by saying thank you for putting your trust in us." His tone was sincere, but he could feel the weight of his words as they settled over the crowd.

"Some of you have already heard a condensed version of this talk when we first set out, but this is just the first of many difficult steps to surviving in this new world," he continued, his eyes scanning the faces before him. "As you know, and I'm sure, experienced, we are facing dangers around every corner, and we can't guarantee everyone's safety. I know that's not what you want to hear, but I feel it's important to be honest about the reality of our situation."

A heavy silence fell over the crowd, and Tom noticed people glancing at one another, their expressions a mix of concern and uncertainty.

"I do, however, promise you this," Tom said, his voice growing steadier. "If you strive to do your best to help make the Guild work, we'll do our best for you as well. Some of you will be fighters, helping with our protection, but others will be putting your skills to use in keeping our day-to-day life running smoothly." He tried to make eye contact with as many people as he could, wanting them to see his sincerity.

"We also need everyone to work on getting stronger and building Skills that will help us all out," Tom added. "We'll work with you to hone yourselves into the best version of whatever you excel at."

"So, we have to go out and fight monsters?" a man asked, standing up so everyone could see him.

"Yes," Tom replied frankly. "But not alone. You'll be placed in a team with people who have experience doing this. We would never send anyone out into danger without taking every precaution to ensure your safety. But fighting is the fastest way to get stronger and ensure you have what it takes to survive in this new world."

The man nodded, seeming satisfied with the answer, and sat back down.

Tom continued, "I know many of you have questions, and we'll make sure to answer all of them. However, this isn't the right forum for a Q&A session. This meeting is to give you a basic understanding of what we'll be doing, what's expected of everyone, and to welcome you all to the Guild." He spoke with authority, ignoring the several raised hands around the room.

Tom then moved on, covering a few more essential rules and objectives of the Guild, emphasizing cooperation, training, and the importance of each person's role. He finished by introducing some key members of his team and their roles within the Guild, making sure everyone knew who they could approach for guidance and support.

"And now, I'd like to introduce you to your Guild liaison," Tom announced, his eyes scanning the crowd. "And she has no idea I'm doing this, so come on up here, Sarah!"

A look of shock spread across Sarah's face as she realized she was being called up. Confused but smiling nervously, she slowly stood up. She hesitated for a moment, then walked to the half-court circle, giving a small, sheepish wave to the crowd.

Tom continued, "We all know Sarah did an incredible job getting you organized and safely here, so I thought it only made sense to have her in charge of helping you all integrate into the team."

As Tom spoke, Sarah's initial confusion began to melt away. She straightened her posture, and her confidence seemed to grow with every moment.

"Thank you all for trusting us and being willing to help make survival better here," Tom said, finishing his introduction. "If you need anything, ask, and we will do what we can to help you."

Tom stepped away from the microphone, and a moderate amount of applause rippled through the crowd. He understood that people were feeling a range of emotions—uncertainty, fear, hope—but they needed to hear the truth about what was expected if they chose to stay. Guild membership wasn't mandatory, but everyone needed to be clear about what it would take to be part of this community.

"Why didn't you tell me you were going to do that? What if I didn't want to be a liaison?" Sarah hissed at him after the meeting had broken up.

"I did tell you that. And sorry, but I need your skills and knowledge in that area. Would you have actually said no if I had asked just to make sure you were given a formal offer?" Tom asked, staring at her for a moment in expectation.

"Well… no. I would have said yes," Sarah admitted begrudgingly.

"See, I knew you would. You were going to join no matter what or you wouldn't have come. So, putting you there made the most sense," Tom smiled as he replied. "Sorry it was a surprise. Not sorry for doing it."

Sarah rolled her eyes but couldn't help smiling as she accepted the position. With that settled, Tom and his team excused themselves to their rooms for the night to get some much-needed rest. Tom barely had time to kick off his boots before collapsing into bed, his body sinking into the mattress. As his head hit the pillow, he felt the weight of the last few days finally begin to lift. Within seconds, he was fast asleep, his defenses down in the comfort of a familiar place.

The next morning, after indulging in another long, hot shower—because it felt so damn good—and enjoying a hearty breakfast, Tom made his way up to the conference room. This was the same room where he and his team had become accustomed to meeting with Brian. By the time he arrived, most of the key Guild members were already there, seated and ready, waiting to catch him up on the latest events.

"Thanks for coming, Tom," Brian began as Tom took a seat, pulling his chair up to the table. "This isn't going to be a fun meeting—it's going to take a while—but we're ecstatic to have you back and ready to get you up to speed."

"I'm super happy to be back," Tom replied, his voice carrying a mix of relief and weariness. "We really missed this place while we were out there."

"We truly appreciate what you did," Brian continued. "Bob here filled us in on what was happening at the Grand Canyon, but we'd like to hear about the rest of your journey in your own words."

Tom nodded and took a deep breath before launching into the full story of their journey. He recounted each harrowing event in detail, the hardships they faced, and the unexpected allies they found along the way. When he reached the part about the cult, concerned murmurs filled the room, but there was visible relief when he explained how they had managed to deal with that threat.

As Tom began to describe the loss of Seth, his voice faltered. He had to pause and take a moment to compose himself, the weight of that loss still fresh and heavy in his chest. The room fell silent, the gravity of the moment sinking in for everyone present. After a few breaths, Tom continued, his voice steadier now, sharing the final stretch of their journey and the recent events leading up to their return.

When he finished, Tom looked around the room, meeting the eyes of each person there. He could see the mix of emotions—grief, determination, and a renewed sense of purpose—mirroring his own.

"Wow. That's a lot. I don't think any of us would have been able to do all of that," Brian said, looking around at the others in the room, who were all nodding in agreement. "I mean, holy shit, dude. But again, we're glad you made it back safely. We haven't been idle by any means, though our story isn't nearly as exciting as yours. Let's start with the obvious—electricity. Harold, would you like to explain?"

"Sure," Harold said, leaning forward, his face lighting up with enthusiasm. "We managed to scrounge together materials from around the city to build mana collectors and a mana battery. Then, using some of our skills, we figured out a way to convert mana into a system that could power the extremely large generators in the basement that power the building."

"We heard a bit about that," Tom interjected. "How does it actually work? Does the system directly convert the mana into power for the generators?"

"No, it's not quite that simple," Harold replied, shaking his head. "If that were the case, we could just hook the power directly to the batteries. Instead, we created a prototype machine that runs solely on mana. From there, we adapted the concept to a larger scale, creating a machine that effectively runs the generator. So, the mana-powered machine turns the electromagnetic armature in the existing generators, creating energy without the need for traditional fuel. The rotating armature inside a stationary magnetic field generates an electrical current through copper wiring, which powers the building."

"So, you're saying the hardest part was figuring out how to build a machine that runs on mana?" Tom asked, leaning forward with interest.

"Exactly," Harold confirmed. "Once we cracked that, it was just a matter of fabricating parts to connect the new machine to the generator. And voila, it works!" He smiled, clearly proud of their achievement.

"Excellent work, Harold! I'm thrilled you managed to figure that out," Tom praised.

"Unfortunately, this breakthrough seems to have seriously pissed Shandra off," Brian interjected with a concerned look. "Now we have a bit of a target on our back. We offered to teach her how we did it, but she only wants the people who made the changes for herself. She's incredibly unreasonable."

"Great, just what we need," Tom muttered, rubbing his temples. "Alright, what else have we been working on?"

"We've discovered that if the people working in farming cast a specific spell on the crops every day, it significantly speeds up their growth," Andrea chimed in, her voice filled with excitement. "We've managed to cut down the traditional three-month growing time of most crops to just under ten percent of that. Now we can have a harvest once a week by rotating which crops are harvested when."

"That's incredible!" Tom said, impressed. "What about meat? Do we have enough of that?"

Andrea's expression turned a bit more serious. "We're still short on meat. People have been bringing back what they hunt, but it's not nearly enough. We need to look for a more sustainable resource," she admitted, sounding a bit frustrated. "We'd like to start keeping livestock, but we haven't been able to find the space."

Tom leaned back in his chair, tapping his fingers on the table as he thought. "So, what are our options?" he asked, looking around at the group, his mind already working on possible solutions.

"We could expand our barrier to allow for creatures to be kept there," Brian suggested, "but that would be extremely difficult given the amount of space we'd need. Another option is to find a different location altogether, or we could try to expand and house them within our current building."

"Inside? Like, roaming around with us?" Tom asked, feeling uneasy about that idea.

"No, not exactly. More like using Guild points to expand the basement, and building a dedicated space for them there," Brian clarified.

"We can do that?" Tom asked, sitting up straighter, intrigued by the idea of making significant changes to their headquarters.

"Technically, yes," Brian continued, his eyes glazing over slightly as he navigated his System menus. "We can use Guild points to expand any part of the Guild building. It's costly, but it would be far easier than trying to manage a construction project of that size and complexity ourselves."

"Great! Let's go with that plan. But where do we get farm animals?" Tom asked, warming to the idea of an underground farm.

"We can find some," Andrea chimed in. "We'd just need to head out and retrieve them from a farm somewhere. This is Texas; it shouldn't be too hard to find livestock."

"Perfect. What else?" Tom urged, eager to cover more ground in their planning.

"With the number of people you've brought back, we've definitely crossed the one thousand-person mark," Brian pointed out. "We need to set up places where everyone can be productive, which means figuring out what Skills they have and what roles they can fill."

The meeting continued throughout most of the day and into the evening, with each specialist reporting on their respective area of expertise. They discussed their progress, challenges, and future plans in great detail. By the time they were done, Tom's head was spinning from the sheer volume of information.

As he stood up to leave, feeling a bit overwhelmed, Brian reached out and stopped him.

"Oh, and Tom, one more thing," Brian called out as Tom was about to leave. "We've gotten reports of two new Dungeons. I didn't want to bring it up earlier and distract you from the meeting."

"That… was actually really smart," Tom replied with a chuckle. "I definitely would have lost focus."

"Yes, well, they're in different parts of the city, but you can get directions to each from TJ. He's been scouting the area and has made sure the routes to them are safe," Brian explained as Tom walked back over to sit next to him.

"Thanks, Brian. I really appreciate you handling all of this. I don't know where we'd be without you," Tom said sincerely.

"Thank you, Tom," Brian replied, his chest puffing up slightly with pride. "I'm happy to be of use. Besides, I'd much rather be doing this than putting my life on the line like you and your team."

"Now," Tom said, shifting gears, "I've been stuck in this meeting for so long that I need to grab some food. Did you give my team the day off? I think they've earned it."

"Yes, we didn't ask anything of them today," Brian assured him. "They were free to do whatever they wanted. Go grab something to eat, check on them, and try to relax a bit yourself. I know what you've been through was taxing. I'm sorry for pulling you into this so soon, but we needed you up to date to help us make decisions."

"Thanks, I understand," Tom replied. "There's just a lot on my plate. But I want to make sure the others are involved in these decisions too. This isn't just me running everything; it's a team effort. I'd fall flat on my face if I tried to do it all alone."

"I'm glad to hear that," Brian said with a nod, shuffling some papers on the conference table. "It's good to work with someone who understands the value of collaboration."

Leaving Brian to his work, Tom made his way down to the cafeteria to see what was being prepared for dinner. The smell of hearty stew wafted through the air, and as he joined the line, several people came up to him, thanking him for helping them get back to Dallas safely. His face grew hot with embarrassment as children ran up and hugged his leg, repeatedly thanking him.

After their mothers pulled them away, he finally got his bowl of stew and spotted Kiera sitting at the far end of the room with a book. He decided to join her, grateful for a familiar face amidst the crowd.

"Sure feels weird to be seen by so many as some kind of hero," Tom said, setting his bowl of stew down and gazing across the bustling cafeteria. People were chatting, laughing, and looking far more relaxed than he'd seen them in weeks.

"Yup," Kiera replied absently, her eyes glued to the pages of a book she was reading. She licked her finger to turn the page, barely acknowledging Tom's comment.

Tom looked back down at his food, pausing as he realized Kiera wasn't really engaging in the conversation. "I don't rightly feel like I did anything to deserve this," he continued, hoping to pull her into a deeper discussion.

"You did what you thought was right," Kiera replied, still not lifting her eyes from the book. "And that helped a lot of people."

Tom waited for a moment, watching as she licked her finger again and turned another page. When it was clear she wasn't going to add more, he decided to switch gears. "Is it any good?" he asked, gesturing toward the book with his spoon.

"This?" Kiera glanced up briefly, turning the book over to reveal the cover. "It's a story about a situation kind of like ours. Some author wrote it as fiction, but it's set in a post-apocalyptic Earth where people get Skills and powers like we have now. Figured I'd see if there were any ideas I could pull from it."

"So, like a zombie apocalypse kind of thing?" Tom asked, intrigued.

"No, not zombies," Kiera said, finally meeting his eyes for a moment. "It's more like the world ending and people suddenly developing Skills and magic. The premise is surprisingly close to our situation. Different magic system and all, but it's kind of eerie how similar it is." She held the book up for him to see the cover.

"*Ether Collapse* by Ryan DeBruyn," Tom read aloud, examining the cover art of a winged lion with a scorpion tail facing a man wielding a sword. "Huh… I wonder if he survived the apocalypse. Maybe we could find him and ask him what he thinks of all this?"

Kiera chuckled lightly, her eyes drifting back to the pages. "If he did survive, he might have more ideas than what's in his books. But who knows? Stranger things have happened."

Tom nodded, taking a bite of his stew as he contemplated how much their reality had begun to feel like something out of a story—one that didn't feel like it had a clear ending just yet.

"Not sure. This takes place in Canada, so he might be Canadian," Kiera mused, glancing at the book. "Chances of finding him without some kind of global communication network are pretty small."

"That's pretty cool, though! I hope it helps. Let me know how it turns out," Tom replied, genuinely interested.

Kiera gave him a small smile, then spooned more stew into her mouth before returning her attention to the book. Realizing she was engrossed in her reading, Tom took the hint. He finished up his food, disposed of his trash, and turned in his tray.

"I wonder where the trash goes now," Tom thought aloud as he left the cafeteria.

Feeling the fatigue from the day's events, Tom decided to head back to his room. "Jerky, are you there?" he called out.

A moment later, his tiny demon familiar appeared on his shoulder.

"Of course. Jerky always with Tom. Is Tom's familiar," Jerky replied in his broken English.

"Good to hear," Tom said with a chuckle, giving the little demon a scratch behind his horns. Jerky leaned into the touch, clearly enjoying the attention. Tom continued toward his room, eager for another good night's sleep.

Just as he was about to enter his room, a chime echoed through the building: *Ding-ding-ding-dong.*

A voice came over the speakers that had been repurposed for Guild announcements: "*Tom Harris, please report to the security center immediately. Tom Harris, please report to TJ at the security center immediately.*" It was TJ's voice, sounding urgent.

Tom sighed, rubbing the bridge of his nose. "What on earth do they want now?" he muttered.

Reluctantly, he turned away from his room and made his way toward the security center, hoping this wouldn't be another crisis.

Chapter 16

I Need a Hero

Tom made his way from the upstairs hallway back down to the main floor and toward the front of the building, where the security center was located next to the parking garage. When he reached the door, he knocked and waited to be let in. A moment later, the door clicked open, and TJ stood in the doorway, motioning for Tom to enter.

Inside, the room had dramatically transformed with the return of power. Several televisions were mounted on the wall, each displaying feeds from cameras placed around the building's exterior and interior, showing people going about their daily activities.

Against the far wall, an open safe was visible, stocked with enough guns to arm a small militia. Next to the safe, a series of badges hung on the wall, each one belonging to a security officer to identify them as part of the team. A desk on the right side of the room was lined with walkie-talkies, some sitting in chargers, while others lay scattered across the surface, ready for use.

"Tom, thanks for coming," TJ said, closing the door behind him. "Sorry to call you down here after your long meeting with Brian earlier, but I thought you needed to hear this."

Tom glanced around the usually bustling security room, which was now unusually quiet. Most of the team, who normally would be busy at their respective stations, were gathered around the screens showing the camera feeds. In the chair that typically held the person responsible for monitoring the cameras, sat a frail-looking woman. Brian was already there, kneeling beside her and offering her a glass of water.

Tom felt a twinge of concern as he took in the scene. "What's going on?" he asked, his eyes shifting from TJ to Brian and the woman in the chair. "Is everyone okay?"

"Yes, everyone is fine, and it's quiet outside," TJ reassured him. "But this woman just showed up about half a mile from the building. Rogers found her during a routine sweep for monsters." He gestured toward the frail woman. "I think you'll want to hear what she has to say. Maybe you can help her."

Tom nodded and moved closer to the woman. He paused at the edge of the circle that had formed around her. She looked up, fear evident in her wide, darting eyes. As she glanced around at the men surrounding her, she began to draw her legs up, curling into a defensive ball in the chair.

"How about we give her some breathing room?" Tom suggested, his voice firm but calm. "Everyone but Brian and TJ, back to your stations. Don't you all have jobs to do?"

Several of them looked startled, then they sheepishly took hurried sips of their coffees, as they scrambled back to their positions around the room. One man hesitated, eyeing the chair where the woman sat, but a sharp glance from Tom was enough to send him awkwardly back to staring at the monitors, pretending to see something of interest.

Tom knelt down to be at the woman's eye level, trying to appear as unthreatening as possible, though he realized he wasn't sure how to pull that off. "Hey there," he began softly. "My name is Tom. What happened? What brought you here to us, and are you okay?"

The woman recoiled slightly, her body tensing as if preparing to bolt. She was dressed in filthy rags that barely clung to her thin frame, and a black metal collar was fastened around her neck, fitting almost like a choker. Tom could see how tightly it clung, its metal edges pressing into her skin.

"It's okay," he added gently, sensing her fear. "You're safe here. No one is going to hurt you."

The woman's eyes flitted to him and then down to the floor. She seemed unsure whether to believe him. Tom stayed quiet for a moment, giving her space to gather her thoughts.

"What's this thing?" Tom said, reaching up to touch the dark metal.

Just as Tom was about to touch the collar, the woman realized what he was doing, and her eyes went wide as she scrambled back so hard that the chair fell over.

"Okay, okay! Sorry. No touching. Can you at least tell me your name?" Tom put his hands up in surrender and moved back slightly.

With eyes still wide, the woman looked from him to TJ then to Brian, and back to him, breathing heavily from her fear. Seeing that no one was making any moves to touch her or get closer to her, she began to relax slightly. She set the chair upright and sat in it again. Her cup of water had spilled on the floor, and TJ picked it up to get her more. Staring up at Tom, she seemed to be deciding if telling him her name would be a good idea.

"Lily. My name is Lily," the woman finally said, her voice barely above a whisper.

"Lily," Tom repeated softly. "That's a pretty name. Can you tell me what happened to you?"

She stared at him for a long moment, her eyes wide with a mix of fear and exhaustion, before she finally spoke. "I managed to escape."

"Escape? From where?" Tom asked gently, trying not to push too hard.

"The Master," Lily whispered, as though merely speaking the name might bring some terrible punishment upon her.

Tom frowned. "Who is The Master, Lily? Did he do this to you?" he asked, gesturing to her bruised and battered body.

Lily nodded, her eyes distant and unblinking.

"He's a terrible man," she began, her voice trembling. "He promises to help people, to protect them. But when he takes you in, he puts one of these mind-control collars on you and makes you do whatever he wants… with his mind."

Tom's face twisted with a mix of horror and disgust. "He does what?! How is that even possible?"

"I don't know," Lily replied, her voice breaking as she spoke. "But if we don't obey, he punishes us." She held out her arms, revealing bruises and scars that criss-crossed her skin like a dark, painful map.

"That's… that's terrible!" Tom said, his voice full of empathy and anger. "How could someone do this to another person?" He looked up at Brian, who was standing nearby with his hand on his chin, deep in thought.

Brian shook his head slowly, his expression serious and troubled. He didn't say a word, clearly trying to process the gravity of what Lily had just revealed.

"How many people are there?" Tom asked, turning back to Lily.

"Hundreds of us," she said, her voice quavering. "He brings in people all the time. Many come because he promises to keep us safe and feed us. I was desperate because I was alone, and monsters were chasing me. He took me in, and I thought I was safe. Then… then the collar came." Her gaze dropped to the floor as she spoke of the collar, her shoulders hunching in shame and fear.

Tom looked at the metal device around her neck. "So, all we need to do is take the collar off. That shouldn't be too hard," he said, reaching cautiously toward it.

"NO, DON'T! IT WILL—AAAAAAAHHHHHH!" Lily screamed as purple electricity erupted from the collar, sending shocks throughout her entire body. She convulsed violently, her screams cutting through the room like a knife.

Tom jumped back, his hand snapping away as arcs of purple electricity crackled over Lily's body. She writhed on the floor, her face contorted in agony. After several long, tense seconds, the electricity ceased, leaving Lily sprawled on the floor, panting heavily.

Everyone remained frozen, afraid to move or speak, worried it might trigger the collar again. After a long moment, Tom cautiously moved forward, carefully helping Lily sit up, his face etched with concern.

"I'm so sorry, Lily. I had no idea it would do that," Tom apologized, helping her back into the chair, his expression filled with regret.

Lily's eyes remained on the floor as she spoke, her voice heavy with fear. "We can't take them off. Only his key can do that. He's going to know I'm gone when he wakes up. I'll be forced to go back… or he'll kill me."

Tom's jaw tightened. "We won't let that happen," he said with a tone of finality.

Brian, standing nearby, looked at Tom skeptically. "And what exactly do you plan to do to stop it?" he asked. "She's wearing a damn collar that shocks her if we try to take it off. It could hurt us, too."

Tom didn't take his eyes off Lily. "I don't know yet, but I'll think of something," he replied. "Get Jay here. Let's see what he thinks about this."

"Alright, I'll get him," TJ said, moving toward the communication system to make the announcement.

"And get the best magic user we have while you're at it," Tom added. "Maybe they'll know something. And bring Harold in, too. An engineer might be able to help."

TJ nodded and made the call over the system. The room fell silent, the tension thick as they waited.

"Don't worry, we'll figure this out," Tom said softly to Lily, trying to reassure her.

Lily nodded, pulling her knees up to her chest and wrapping her arms around her legs. She still trembled from the shock, her eyes darting nervously around the room.

About half an hour later, Jay arrived with Harold, a wiry man with a sharp mind for engineering, and Bohdan, the best magic user in the Guild. They gathered around Lily, inspecting the collar from a safe distance.

Jay leaned in first, squinting as he examined the device. "Well, there's no keyhole, so I doubt we can pick the lock. It must be controlled electronically or by magic," he said, his eyes tracing the thin seams of the metal as Lily tilted her head back to give him a better view.

Harold crossed his arms, his brow furrowed. "I don't know how we can do anything to it if it shocks her every time we touch it. We'd just end up hurting her more."

Tom turned to Bohdan, who was rubbing his chin thoughtfully. "Bohdan, is there anything you can think of?" he asked.

Bohdan, a stocky man with a thick Ukrainian accent, nodded slowly. "Maybe," he began. "I could try using an anti-magic field to see if it has any effect on it. There is a possibility it would disrupt its connection, and we could make an attempt to remove it then."

"And what exactly does an anti-magic field do?" Tom asked, intrigued.

"It creates a space—a cube—where magic does not work. No spells, no magical effects. It could stop the collar's function, at least temporarily," Bohdan explained.

Tom looked around at the others. "I can't see a downside to at least trying that," he said, gauging their reactions. Both Brian and TJ nodded in agreement.

"Alright, Bohdan. Let's start there," Tom decided, hoping this plan could finally provide a solution.

Bohdan gave a single nod then turned his focus to Lily. With a deep breath, he began moving his hands in intricate patterns, chanting softly under his breath. As the incantation built in intensity, he thrust his hands out to the sides, and a glowing yellow barrier expanded from his body, stretching outward until it filled the entire room. The barrier seemed to stop just short of the walls, shimmering faintly as it settled in place.

As the field reached the electronics scattered around the room, everything instantly powered down. The televisions mounted on the walls went dark, and the static hum of the walkie-talkies ceased, leaving an eerie silence.

"What the hell just happened?" one of the security guards blurted out, looking around in confusion.

Bohdan remained calm and turned to Tom. "It is done," he announced.

Tom nodded and took a step closer to Lily. "Lily, I need you to trust me," he said gently. "I'm going to try to touch the collar to see if the anti-magic field has stopped it from working. Can you trust me to let me try?"

Lily hesitated, her eyes wide with fear as she shrank back slightly. She stared at Tom for what felt like an eternity, searching his face for any sign of deceit or uncertainty. Finally, she gave a small nod, her lips pressed into a thin line as she tried to muster the courage to let him proceed. Her entire body tensed as Tom slowly reached out toward the collar.

Tom moved cautiously, his finger hovering just above the metal band around her neck. He glanced at Lily one more time, giving her a reassuring nod before carefully lowering his hand. He barely touched the collar with the tip of one finger.

Lily's eyes squeezed shut, her body bracing for the familiar surge of agony. But… nothing happened. Slowly, she opened her eyes, a mix of confusion and hope written across her face. She looked up at Tom, who was smiling back at her, relief evident in his eyes.

"It worked," he said softly, his voice full of warmth. "You're safe now."

"Just as a side note, did you notice what that field did to the electronics in the room?" Harold asked, glancing around. "After figuring out how to make a machine that runs on mana, I thought there might be ways to use it in more places, but this… this is baffling. It seems like technology and magic might be able to interact with or even control each other. Like they are somehow connected."

"What do you mean, Harold?" Tom asked, turning to face him.

"I'm not entirely sure yet," Harold replied, rubbing his chin thoughtfully. "Maybe this whole System is more literal than any of us thought. But I need to head back to the engineering lab. Bohdan, could you come by at some point? The sooner, the better. We need to look into this further."

"Sure. I will come to the lab and help with experiments," Bohdan agreed, clearly intrigued by the prospect.

Tom cleared his throat, interrupting their train of thought. "Let's focus on helping Lily first. We need to get this thing off her neck."

"Right, of course," Harold said, snapping back to the task at hand. "Sorry, I got carried away. It's just… fascinating."

"How long will this anti-magic field last?" Tom asked Bohdan.

"About thirty minutes," Bohdan replied.

"Alright, let's get to work," Tom said, turning back to Lily.

"I'll go fetch some tools," Harold said, looking around. "Though I guess they have to be hand tools."

About ten minutes later, Herbert returned with a large pair of bolt cutters and a hacksaw.

"Without electricity, we can't use a grinder or any other power tools," Harold explained. "So, we're going to have to do this the hard way. We need to be really careful."

Everyone nodded in agreement. Lily tilted her head as far to the left as possible while Harold carefully positioned the bolt cutters on the edge of the collar, aiming to cut through it.

"I'd rather avoid using the hacksaw since that's riskier," Harold said, focusing on his task. "Just keep leaning away, and I'll see if these cutters will do the job."

He pulled the handles together with all his might, and the metal groaned under the pressure. Harold grunted, struggling to cut through.

"Why don't I give it a try? My Strength stat is probably a lot higher than yours, Harold," Tom suggested.

"Yeah, that might be for the best," Harold admitted, stepping back and wiping sweat from his brow.

Tom took the handles from Harold, positioning himself as Lily tried to stay as still as possible. She closed her eyes, bracing herself.

"Alright, on three," Tom said, steadying his grip. "One… two… three!"

With a surge of power, Tom pressed the handles together. At first, there was resistance, but then the metal gave way. There was a loud crack, and the collar snapped into two pieces, falling to the floor with a clatter. Lily gasped, her hand flying to her neck.

"I'm… I'm free!" she whispered, her voice trembling as tears filled her eyes.

Tom smiled warmly. "I told you we'd help. Now, we need to get more information from you—anything you can remember about this place or The Master so we can help the others."

Turning to Harold, Tom continued, "And, Harold, take that collar and run some tests on it. Maybe you can figure out a better solution. I don't think bolt cutters and repeated anti-magic fields are the ideal approach for this."

Harold nodded, accepting the broken collar pieces. "Absolutely. I'll let you know what I find." He then looked at Bohdan. "Bohdan, would you come with me to the lab now?"

"Of course. Let's go," Bohdan agreed, and the two of them headed out together.

Tom turned his attention back to Lily. "Alright, Lily. Tell me everything you can about this Master."

Chapter 17

Hatred

Lily spent the next hour recalling everything she could about The Master, his compound, and what she knew of his operations. As she shared more details, Tom felt his anger boiling over at the atrocities this man was committing.

"What kind of sick bastard enslaves people to further his cause? He's making them work against their will so he can get stronger!" Tom growled, unable to contain his rage any longer.

"It's natural for people to want power," Brian said, his face twisted in thought. "What's unnatural is the way he's going about it. Controlling someone's mind is abhorrent."

"The feeling is like being violated every day. You want to do one thing, but some force makes your body do something different," Lily said softly, hugging herself tightly in the chair, her body still trembling.

"We should just go over there and fuck up his day. Free the others while we're at it," Tom said, his voice low but filled with determination as he started moving toward the door.

Brian stepped in front of him, holding out an arm to stop him. "That's a bad idea. If you just go in there guns blazing, he'll use the people as shields if he has to. You've got to think before you act. This is a delicate situation."

"We can't just sit here and do nothing while he tortures these people!" Tom's frustration was building, his voice rising.

"I know, and we won't," Brian said calmly. "But sit down for a second. Let's come up with a plan where fewer people get killed—especially the innocents."

Tom let out a deep, frustrated sigh, his body tense with anger. "Ugh! You're right. But it feels like shit just sitting here."

"What if we used Bohdan to sneak in and start by rescuing some of the people who aren't as closely guarded?" Brian suggested.

Lily shook her head. "He'll notice. He has some kind of mental connection to everyone. When he wakes up, he'll know I don't have the collar on anymore. He always knows when someone dies, so this wouldn't be any different."

"We have to do something!" Tom blurted out after a moment of silence. "I can't just sit here. Jay, let's go."

"Sweet!" Jay grinned, jumping up to join Tom as they headed for the door.

"Please don't do anything rash," Brian pleaded.

"We're just going to have a look. That way, we can plan better," Tom assured him over his shoulder.

Brian sighed as they left. "I really hope they know what they're doing," he muttered to himself.

Outside the security office, Tom and Jay made their way out of the building and into the night. As they left the newly erected compound walls, Tom turned to Jay, his voice low.

"We need to sneak over and get a look at what we're up against. Maybe then we can come up with a plan."

"Sure, sure. And maybe a few of the guards won't make it back inside tonight," Jay said, rubbing his hands together with anticipation.

"No. The guards are probably slaves. No killing people with collars," Tom ordered firmly.

"Fine, fine. But anyone without collars?" Jay asked, hopeful.

"Fair game," Tom replied, his tone serious.

"That's what I'm talkin' about…" Jay chuckled, pulling out a dagger and letting it dance across his fingers.

"Alright, let's get moving. Lily said their compound was on the east side. They built a wall around it, so it shouldn't be hard to find."

"Can't we take the GS2?" Jay complained.

"No, stealth is the key, and that would make too much noise. I want us in and out without being noticed. If we need a quick getaway, we'll lose them easier on foot," Tom replied, leaving no room for argument.

"Aye, aye, captain," Jay said sarcastically, annoyed at the thought of having to walk the whole way.

They set off at a jog, Tom's enhanced Attributes making him feel more capable than ever. His once-desk-job-softened body was now lean and muscular, moving with agility he hadn't felt since high school. Jay kept pace behind him, his head swiveling back and forth, staying vigilant for any signs of danger.

After about half an hour of jogging, Tom raised a hand, signaling Jay to stop.

"What is it?" Jay asked, his voice hushed.

"Listen," Tom whispered.

In the distance, faint grunting noises could be heard. With the power still out across the city, it was too dark to see clearly, but they could make out vague shapes moving ahead.

"Kinda sounds like… pigs?" Jay said, confused.

"I was thinking the same thing, but it doesn't make much sense. We're too deep in the city for wild hogs, aren't we?" Tom replied.

"We should be. But with how things have shifted, they could've moved closer in," Jay speculated.

Tom grinned. "Maybe we should go say hello. I can't say no to bacon. The most delicious of the breakfast meats."

Jay matched his grin and nodded. They crept forward, moving carefully to stay silent. As they got closer, the shadows took more definite shapes. What they saw sent a shiver down Tom's spine—these weren't wild hogs.

In front of them were humanoid creatures with pig-like features, crouched on their knees and feasting on a fresh carcass. Several of the hideous beings were gathered there, gnawing and tearing at the remains of what looked like a recent victim. Tom used his *Inspect* Skill on one of the creatures, his heart pounding with a mix of fear and curiosity.

Porcine Hunters
Porcine Hunters are a dangerous blend of boar and humanoid features, typically docile unless provoked or hungry. Standing upright on two legs, they are covered in coarse, bristled hair and have powerful tusks protruding from their lower jaws. They hunt in packs and are known for their aggression when in pursuit of food or when their territory is threatened. These creatures wield crude, makeshift weapons such as clubs, bone daggers, and stone axes, but they can be equally deadly with their natural tusks and strong jaws.

Level:	19
HP:	550/550
MP:	100/100
SP:	600/750
Attacks:	Can wield weapons, Gore, Claw, Glutton

"Well, shit. There goes breakfast," Tom muttered under his breath, feeling his hopes for a decent meal vanish.

"I'm not eating one of those fuckers," Jay whispered almost inaudibly, his face contorted in disgust.

Tom turned to him and emphatically waved his hand up and down, signaling for him to stay quiet. Jay raised both hands in apology and took a step back. Tom then made a strange gesture, like throwing a baseball, ending with his palm pointed at the creatures. Jay stared at him, confused, and shook his head.

Tom repeated the motion with more emphasis, trying to communicate his plan without words.

"Dude, it looks like you're saying you're gonna... tap that ass," Jay finally whispered, still baffled by the gestures.

Sighing heavily, Tom whispered back, "I'm going to lob an *Eldritch Blast* at them. Then you move in and take one out from behind."

"Got it. Next time, just say that," Jay replied, slipping into the shadows to position himself behind the creatures.

Once in place, Jay flashed his dagger in the moonlight, signaling he was ready. Tom readied himself, hands glowing with dark green energy as he double-cast *Eldritch Blast*. With a swift motion, he launched two green fireballs that streaked through the night air, hitting two of the Porcine Hunters squarely in the head. Their scraggly fur ignited instantly, flames crawling across their bodies.

The creatures let out bloodcurdling screams that echoed through the silent streets—shrieks like a woman being attacked in a dark alley. They leaped around frantically, slapping at the flames with their crude weapons. Unfortunately, the sparse hair burned too quickly, leaving only minor burns except where the fireballs had struck.

"Well… fuck me," Tom muttered as the creatures turned to face him, their eyes glowing a furious red in the darkness.

Jay sprang from the shadows and leaped onto one of the Porcine Hunters, plunging his dagger repeatedly into the creature's neck. The screeching transformed into a sickening gurgle as blood poured from its mouth and throat. The other hunters turned in confusion, momentarily unsure where the threat was.

Tom seized the opportunity, summoning his greatsword from his Inventory. Charging forward, he triggered his *Tattoo of Brute Strength* and activated *Cleave*, delivering a powerful horizontal slash, slicing through the remaining two hunters in one clean motion. System messages of their kills flashed before his eyes, but he dismissed them quickly.

"Great job with the sneak attack. Really gave me the opening I needed," Tom complimented Jay.

"Thanks for not letting them pile on me," Jay replied. They shook hands and then turned to loot the bodies.

The Porcine Hunters wore only tattered loincloths, offering little in the way of loot. Their crude weapons—stone blades tied to sticks or makeshift handles—weren't worth taking. And with the System now handling loot through Monster Cores, there wasn't any money to collect like in traditional RPGs.

"I feel better now," Jay said as they finished up. "Nothing like killing something after hearing there's a giant twat waffle in the city enslaving people."

"That cockholster has something coming if he thinks we're just going to sit back and let this happen," Tom agreed. "But yeah, I do feel a little better too."

Jay nudged Tom. "Time to keep going, bud. We might run into more trouble, and we need to get in and out before sunrise."

"Right. Time to move. I pity the fool that gets in my way now!" Tom said, grinning.

"Slow your roll there, nerdiest Mr. T ever," Jay replied with a smirk. "We still gotta take this easy."

"Oh, you're one to talk, Mr. 'Let's kill the guards,'" Tom shot back, rolling his eyes but smiling at their familiar banter.

They continued moving stealthily through the shadows, jogging through the darkened streets. After about half an hour, a large structure began to rise above the skyline—a sprawling church that looked like a junkyard had exploded on it.

Sheets of rusted metal, twisted car parts, and random debris were piled atop the roof and along the walls, likely meant to fortify it but giving it the appearance of a fortress built from garbage. A crude stone wall about ten feet high encircled the perimeter.

"This is pretty impressive for someone just ordering slaves to do manual labor. I doubt he's even formed a Guild since it requires willing participants," Tom commented as they approached the wall.

"It's disgusting, is what it is," Jay replied, glaring up at the makeshift barrier. "Think about how much work went into building this, and he's not leveling any of them. Imagine doing this at level one. Or even three."

Tom could feel anger bubbling up inside him again. "Let's just get in, look around, and get out. We can't save anyone yet because of those damn collars, but maybe we can sabotage something while we're inside."

"I like that idea. Jay smash!" Jay grinned, trying to contain his excitement.

They tried climbing the wall but quickly realized it was too unstable. Large stones shifted and tumbled with every attempt, threatening to collapse on top of them, forcing them to stop and wait to hear if anyone had heard the noise.

"There must be an entrance. Let's walk around and find it," Tom suggested as a particularly large stone broke loose and almost clipped his head.

"Yeah, let's go. We'll find another way in," Jay agreed.

After circling about a quarter of the way around, they found what they were looking for—a crude set of gates leaned against the inside of the wall, barred shut with a thick wooden plank.

"Ironically, I think this makes getting in harder than if the gates were actually attached," Tom commented, pushing lightly on the gate to test its stability.

"Only for our specific situation," Jay whispered as he helped keep the gate steady.

"I think this calls for a bit of backup," Tom decided. Stepping back from the gate, he began casting *Summon Demonic Creature*.

A dark circle formed on the ground, and out of it rose... an Abyssal Chicken.

"For fuck's sake! That's not what I want!" Tom whispered loudly in frustration.

"Bok?" the demonic chicken clucked, tilting its head at Tom.

"Go on, get!" Tom tried to dismiss the creature, but it simply cocked its head at him and ran off into the compound. "Attempt number two."

"Should we be worried about that one?" Jay asked.

"The worst that happens is it gets killed as a distraction," Tom replied then focused on his casting.

He cast the summoning spell again, and another chicken emerged. This time, in frustration, Tom punted it into the air, where it vanished in a puff of smoke as its health hit zero.

Casting one more time, Tom finally Summoned the creature he wanted— a Demonic Mastadonian. The beast, clad in black leather armor over its nearly black, elephantine skin, towered over them. It turned its massive head toward Tom, tilting it slightly as if awaiting instructions.

Demonic Mastadonian
Mastadonians are formidable creatures, half-man and half-elephant, hailing from a distant plane where strength of arms is revered above all else. Towering at nearly eight feet tall, their powerful frames are covered in thick, leathery skin, with the head and tusks of a mighty elephant. Their eyes gleam with an intense focus, driven by an unquenchable thirst for battle and the desire to prove their strength in combat. Mastadonians live by a strict code of honor, valuing fair fights, loyalty, and the prowess displayed on the battlefield. The Mastadonians come from a war-torn plane where constant battle is a way of life. From a young age, they are trained in the art of war, their society revolving around martial prowess and the pursuit of glory on the battlefield. Despite their fearsome appearance, Mastadonians adhere to a strict code of honor, refusing to strike down an unarmed opponent and always seeking to test their strength against the strongest foes.

HP:	1025/1025
MP:	750/750
SP:	840/840
Attacks:	Can wield weapons, Trunk Slam, Battle Roar, Tusks of Vengeance, Honor's Shield

"I need you to watch our backs. Keep an eye out for anyone that might attack us. If things get hairy, we bail," Tom instructed. The creature nodded in understanding.

"Alright, time to head inside," Tom said, gesturing for Jay to help him push the gates open.

Chapter 18

Spy Hard

Tom, Jay, and the Mastadonian carefully pushed the gate forward, just enough to squeeze through without making too much noise and so they wouldn't fall from their leaning position. The Mastadonian, with its enormous strength, was crucial in keeping the heavy wooden doors from collapsing inward while Tom and Jay slipped inside. Once they were in, the massive creature followed, gently maneuvering the gate back into place.

Inside the compound, a series of partially constructed buildings made the place feel like a set from a war movie. Sandbags were piled up sporadically, creating makeshift walls that looked like they'd been hastily set up for cover. Barbed wire was strewn haphazardly across the ground, coiled in tangled heaps that seemed intended to hinder or trap anyone trying to pass. The area was a maze of makeshift traps and spikes attached to the sides of buildings, all contributing to a chaotic, almost post-apocalyptic atmosphere.

Jay motioned silently to Tom, pointing out a narrow path through the barbed wire and buildings. The path weaved through the maze of obstacles, requiring precise movements to avoid setting off any hidden traps or disturbing the spikes jutting out at odd angles.

"We should try to go through without disturbing anything," Jay whispered to Tom, his voice barely audible.

Tom nodded in agreement. They proceeded cautiously, with Jay leading the way. He carefully stepped over the barbed wire, taking great care not to snag his clothing or make any noise. The Mastadonian followed closely behind, surprisingly nimble for its size. Despite its bulk, the elephantine creature moved with an uncanny silence, its massive feet somehow knowing exactly where to step to avoid making any noise.

They continued toward the main building in the compound, moving slowly to ensure they didn't alert anyone to their presence. The tension in the air was palpable as they crept forward, eyes darting around to take in every detail of their surroundings.

Suddenly, from around the corner of a nearby building, a hideously grotesque sight emerged that nearly made Jay and Tom gasp audibly in shock.

A desiccated goblin and a decaying wolf stumbled into view, shuffling slowly as if their movements were driven by some unnatural force. The goblin's pale green skin clung to its bones, covering only about seventy-five percent of its body, with sections missing entirely. Its entrails dragged along the ground behind it, leaving a sickening trail of dark fluids. The wolf beside it was in slightly better condition, but its mangy fur was matted with blood, and chunks of its flesh appeared to have been gnawed away, exposing patches of raw muscle and bone.

Tom quickly focused his mind and cast *Inspect*, hoping to get more information on the abominations in front of them.

Zombie Goblin	
Once a chaotic and reckless enemy, the goblin in its undead form is even more dangerous. Reanimated as a Zombie Goblin, this creature feels no pain and exhibits a relentless drive to attack anything within its master's command. Stripped of its former cunning but not its malice, the Zombie Goblin will stop at nothing to overwhelm its prey with sheer numbers and vicious attacks. Be especially cautious of its poisonous bite, which can infect and weaken even the most stalwart adventurer. These undead minions often roam in groups, making them a significant threat in large numbers.	
Level:	7
HP:	50/50
MP:	0/0
SP	150/150
Attacks:	Can wield weapons, Bite, Claw

Zombie Wolf	
Transformed into an undead beast, the Zombie Wolf is a terrifying shadow of its former self. Though its intelligence has greatly diminished, its ferocity has only grown. Relentless and driven by a single-minded obedience to its master, the Zombie Wolf attacks without fear or hesitation, making it a formidable foe. With a body that no longer feels pain or fatigue, it can fight until its body is completely destroyed. Its bite has become deadly, carrying a potent poison that can weaken and incapacitate its victims, making it an even more dangerous adversary in close combat.	
Level:	6
HP:	100/100
MP:	0/0

SP	300/300
Attacks:	Bite, Claw

As they moved deeper into the compound, a sudden *whoosh, whoosh* sounded from behind them. Two shadowy daggers sliced through the air and embedded themselves to the hilts in the wolf's temple and the goblin's forehead. Both creatures dropped to the ground with a heavy thud. Startled, Tom and Jay instinctively hugged each other, turning as one to look back at the Mastadonian. Their faces were a mixture of shock and amazement.

The massive creature spoke in a deep, rumbling bass, "Looks like you have a zombie problem here. Aim for their heads. There must be a necromancer at work."

"You can talk!?" Tom whispered loudly, his eyes widening even more with surprise.

The Mastadonian nodded slowly. "When I feel the need."

As Tom absorbed this revelation, the weight of the creature's words sank in. "You mean... The Master might be a necromancer? That's how he's controlling people—and why there are zombies here?"

Another nod from the Mastadonian, this time silent.

"What's your name? And are you the same Mastadonian I summoned last time?" Tom asked, curiosity overtaking his initial shock.

"I'm not sure you have the ability to pronounce my birth name, but I will tell you, for you seem honorable. My name is," and the creature let out a series of rumbling noises, interspersed with clicks and squeaks, reminiscent of sounds you'd hear in a nature documentary about elephants. "But you may call me Bron. And yes, I am the same warrior you summoned last time. We formed a pact then, and now that you know my name, you may summon me at will instead of randomly."

"That explains why I haven't been able to summon the monsters I want. I need to know their names?" Tom asked, beginning to piece things together.

"Yes. Each time you summon a creature, you form a pact with it. If it survives, you can summon it again using its name. If it dies, you must forge a new pact," Bron explained.

"Can all Summons talk?" Tom continued, his mind racing with new information.

"No. The simpler creatures have basic minds and cannot share their names with you," Bron replied. "Also, you can choose which creature you summon. You know that, right?"

"What?" Tom asked, his voice dropping an octave in disbelief.

"You can switch between random Summons and specific Summons. When you select the 'Specific Summons' option, a list of available creatures appears for you to focus on during the summoning."

Immediately, Tom opened his menu and navigated to the Skills page. Sure enough, under his *Summon Demonic Creature* Skill, a drop-down menu offered two options: "Summon Random" and "Select Summon." He facepalmed at the discovery, feeling a mix of embarrassment and relief.

"This is all well and good, but we need to keep moving. More zombies could show up any moment, and we need to get the hell out of here before anyone notices us," Jay interrupted in a loud whisper, snapping Tom out of his thoughts.

"Yeah, yeah, you're right. Let's move," Tom agreed, albeit reluctantly. He couldn't help but wonder how many other details he had overlooked in the System.

Before closing the menu, Tom quickly skimmed over the list of creatures he could summon: Abyssal Chicken, Dretch, Demonic Mastadonian, and something called an Usiku. His curiosity got the better of him, and he decided to summon an Usiku on the spot.

A dark purple summoning circle appeared on the ground, and Jay groaned at the unnecessary delay. Black mist billowed out of the portal, accompanied by distant jungle sounds. A large cat with fur as dark as midnight stepped through. It growled low and menacingly, taking in its surroundings. Two large tentacles sprouted from its shoulder blades, moving in a defensive pattern as its bright yellow eyes observed the scene with a clear, intelligent gaze.

The Usiku looked at Tom, tilting its head in curiosity, then noticed Bron standing beside him. It padded over and rubbed affectionately against the Mastadonian's side, purring deeply. The sheer weight of the giant creature almost toppled Bron over. With a swishing tail and muscular build, the Usiku was large enough for Tom to ride.

"Alright, I'll admit it. That was worth it," Jay said, his eyes wide as he watched the majestic beast appear.

Usiku
The Usiku is a nocturnal predator, perfectly adapted for hunting in darkness. Resembling a large, sleek cat with fur as black as the void, it moves with a silent grace that belies its lethal nature. Sprouting from its powerful shoulders are two long tentacles, each lined with hidden, hooked barbs designed to latch onto prey, immobilizing them while the Usiku's razor-sharp claws and teeth deliver fatal blows.

Level:	15
HP:	500/500
MP:	250/250
SP:	750/750
Attacks:	Psionic Confusion, Claw, Bite

"Damn, that's cool. He's really an adorable murder furball," Tom commented while stroking the Usiku's sleek, ebony fur. "Can I call you Shadow?"

The cat purred loudly as it rubbed its head against Tom's face.

Suddenly, the big cat's ears perked up, swiveling toward another building. It began to growl, a low rumble resonating from deep within its chest. Tom followed its gaze, and from the distance, he could hear a faint shuffling sound growing closer.

"Get ready. Don't let them sound the alarm," Bron instructed, his deep voice steady but commanding.

Tom quickly equipped his greatsword, and Jay pressed himself against the wall of the building they were hiding behind, sliding into a low, ready stance. The Usiku crouched low behind them, its tentacles swaying slightly, ready to lash out. Bron, bringing up the rear, carefully extracted his daggers from the zombies, preparing them for the next encounter.

Before they could round the corner, the demonic chicken came rushing past them with a rotting arm in its mouth. Jay and Tom looked at each other in confusion before turning back to the shuffling sounds.

As they rounded the corner, a pack of four zombie goblins came into view, one missing an arm. Their pale green skin hung loosely over their skeletal frames, and their eyes were glazed with a milky film. Jay sprang forward, striking with precision; his daggers sank into the eyes of the first goblin, killing it instantly. The Usiku pounced on another, tearing its head clean off with a swift, powerful bite. Tom swung his greatsword in a wide arc, cleaving the remaining two goblins at the waist. The top halves, still animated, began dragging themselves forward with their clawed hands, gurgling menacingly.

Bron stepped forward and swiftly stomped on their heads, crushing them into the dirt. The demonic chicken suddenly rushed in from behind them and started ripping the bodies to shreds with its mouth and claws, as if it had been waiting for the opportunity to show its ferocity.

"I said attack the heads," Bron reminded, his voice rumbling like distant thunder.

"Sorry. I forgot. I just reacted," Tom replied sheepishly, glancing down at his sword.

"You are still a young warrior. You will learn with time how to react," Bron said, his tone that of a patient teacher. "Focus on your opponent and their weaknesses every time you fight. Use this knowledge to defeat them as quickly as possible, and you will grow stronger."

Tom nodded, taking the lesson to heart. He and Jay quickly dragged the bodies into a nearby building to hide them, ensuring they left no obvious trail of death leading to their location. They moved on, creeping further into the compound, careful not to disturb any traps or hidden dangers as they made their way toward the main building. They kept low, moving from shadow to shadow, avoiding piles of barbed wire and makeshift barricades that looked like they belonged in a war zone.

When they reached the building, they circled it, trying to peer inside through the windows. Every window was covered, blocking any view of what was inside. They knew they needed to get a closer look. Carefully, they eased open the front doors, peeking inside. The interior was crawling with zombies—dozens of them shuffling about in the entryway, with glimpses of more beyond in other rooms. Jay quietly shut the door and turned back to the others, his expression grim.

"No way we are going in there unless we're ready for a battle," Jay whispered. "There are too many zombies. We might be able to kill them and The Master, but there's no telling what would happen to the people he controls. It's too much of a risk right now."

Tom clenched his teeth in frustration but nodded in agreement. The risk was too great without a solid plan. Reluctantly, they decided to head back to the Guild building. They retraced their steps through the compound, avoiding any traps they had spotted earlier, until they reached the gate. Slipping back through with Bron's help, they made it outside the wall.

"This isn't good," Tom said, his voice tense. "He's amassing an army. Anything dead becomes his plaything, and if he's got control of those collars, he can use people as living shields. We can only hope he doesn't want to damage his puppets."

"It's not an ideal situation," Jay replied, deep in thought, "but if we can figure out how to handle the collars, we should be able to kill this fucker."

"We need to get back to the center to see if there's been any progress with the research. I'm sure it'll take a few days, but hopefully, they can find something we can use," Tom said, already moving toward the Guild.

A loud caw echoed above them, drawing their attention. A raven circled overhead, joined by more birds. Bron narrowed his eyes at the strange sight.

"I think we have company," Bron commented, his eyes following the flight paths of the birds.

"What, the birds? They're probably just looking for more corpses," Tom said dismissively.

"Take a closer look," Bron insisted, pointing upward.

Tom squinted, realizing what Bron meant. The birds weren't normal; their bodies were mottled with rotting flesh, and some had patches where feathers were missing. A sickly green foam dripped from their beaks.

"Shit, they're zombies," Tom whispered, his stomach tightening.

"Well, well, well… what do we have here?" a voice taunted from above.

Tom and the others looked up to see a man standing atop the wall, a manic grin stretched across his face.

"Have you come to play with me?" he asked, his eyes gleaming with a twisted excitement.

Chapter 19

Retreat

Staring down at them was a well-dressed man in his mid-thirties. His dark brown hair, flecked with the first hints of gray, was neatly combed back. He wore large, round glasses that magnified his eyes, making them appear unnaturally wide on his thin, wiry face. His lips stretched into a manic grin, showing teeth that gleamed unnaturally white in the dim light.

"Don't be shy, come inside. We would love to have you play with us," the man called out, his voice dripping with mockery as his eyes began to glow a sinister red.

Suddenly, there was a loud pounding on the gate, accompanied by the scraping of nails and the unsettling sound of bodies pressing against it. The wood groaned under the pressure, and the boards began to bend outward.

"I don't think we should stay here with our thumbs up our asses, guys," Jay muttered, eyeing the gate as it shuddered and the stone wall nearby trembled.

"Aww, what's the matter? Doom is underrated, I assure you. There is great freedom in death," the man taunted, his grin widening even further, stretching his lips to the point Tom thought they might tear.

"Actually, you can't call it 'doom' unless it comes from the Mount Doom region of Mordor. Here, we just call it 'Sparkling Abject Terror,'" Tom replied quickly, his mind scrambling for anything that might distract the man.

Suddenly, Jay had a maroon bottle in his hand. He waved his hand toward it like Vanna White, before twisting the cork out and offering it to Tom.

Tom froze, the joke having progressed too far for him to keep up. His uncertainty only lasted a moment. Jay elbowed him with a look that said 'get your shit together, man.' Tom shook free of his hesitancy.

Smiling, he took a long pull from the bottle, swishing it around in his mouth with a discerning expression, trying to channel his best James impersonation. "Ah, yes. A fine vintage." He looked toward Jay haughtily. "The Terror Hills?"

"Terror Plains, actually," Jay corrected.

"Truth?" Tom raised an eyebrow. "I'd thought that vintage lost in the last World War Z."

Jay looked sheepish.

"I won it at the local Lich Auction," he said modestly.

The man's grin faltered, his expression shifting to one of bewilderment. "Um... what?"

"Oh, nothing really, just... what the hell is that?!" Tom shouted suddenly, pointing wildly down the length of the wall.

The man's head snapped to where Tom was pointing. In that split second, Tom raised his hand and fired an *Eldritch Blast* directly at his face. The green energy shot forward, and Tom wasted no time, turning to sprint with Jay, Bron, and Shadow following close behind.

The man reacted just in time, raising his hand to conjure a small, blue-glowing shield that deflected the blast at the last moment.

"Clever," he muttered, watching them turn down a side street. "I will enjoy playing with you."

Behind them, the wooden gates exploded into splinters as a horde of zombies, both monster and human, poured through, tumbling over one another in a chaotic heap. The creatures snarled and groaned, struggling to disentangle themselves. Tom, Jay, Bron, and Shadow continued running, their footsteps echoing in the empty streets.

"That was an excellent diversion. You are learning tactics quickly," Bron praised as he ran. "If we had stayed, he would have overwhelmed us."

"My thoughts exactly. If we can get to the Guild, we can fight them off with the others," Tom replied, breathing heavily but feeling a rush of adrenaline and strength coursing through him. Running no longer felt like a burden; his enhanced body could carry him for miles without tiring.

Arrows began to whistle through the air, missing them by mere inches. Bron turned and, without breaking stride, pulled out a massive bow from his Inventory. He nocked a shimmering arrow made of pure energy and held it steady. As they reached an intersection, Bron released the arrow. A flash of light followed by an explosion shook the street behind them. Tom could have sworn he heard a disappointed "aww" from one of the zombies just before the arrow struck, which nearly made him chuckle.

The explosion bought them some time, but the growls and groans continued. "Where is fucking James when you need him?" Tom growled. "Motherfucker is everywhere when you don't want him around!"

Tom pulled out a gun from his Inventory and fired over his shoulder, managing to shoot a few zombies in the head. One dropped instantly, but he missed more than he hit. "I'm not as good with this as he is," Tom muttered, emptying his third clip before stowing the gun away.

"It's just up here! We're almost there. Jay, get inside and sound the alarm! Bron, Shadow, and I will hold them off at the gate until reinforcements arrive!" Tom barked, urgency in his voice.

Jay nodded, sprinting ahead. Bron simply grunted, shifting his eyes between the approaching horde and watching where they were running, while Shadow growled low and menacingly. As they neared the Trammel Crow Center, Tom pushed himself to sprint faster, his feet pounding against the pavement.

Reaching the gates, Jay darted inside to the security center. Tom, Bron, and Shadow turned to face the oncoming wave of zombies. Bron drew two massive greataxes, his muscles rippling with anticipation as he settled into a battle stance.

"When they arrive, use big sweeping attacks for the first wave," Bron instructed, his voice calm and focused. "Then defend and strike when there is an opening. Keep your weapon up at all times."

Tom nodded, gripping his greatsword tightly, then stowed it momentarily in his Inventory. "I've got a few tricks up my sleeve, too," he said, activating his *Tattoo of Brute Strength*. His muscles bulged with newfound power, and he began to charge a spell. Energy crackled around his hands as he formed the familiar movements, ending with his hands beside his right hip.

"FINAL FLASH!" Tom roared, unleashing the energy in a massive beam that tore through the center of the zombie horde, disintegrating anything in its path.

Bron nodded in approval. "That was impressive indeed. Now, let's see how you handle that sword."

Equipping his greatsword, Tom braced himself for the oncoming swarm. When the zombies were twenty yards away, he let out a battle cry and charged. Bron and Shadow followed, the former letting out a deep, trumpeting roar that reverberated through the battlefield, sending chills down Tom's spine.

The clash was immediate and violent. Tom swung his greatsword in wide arcs, cleaving zombies in half with powerful blows, while Shadow pounced from zombie to zombie, using its claws, fangs, and tentacles to tear them apart. Bron was a force of nature, his axes swinging in a relentless rhythm, decapitating zombie after zombie with each swing.

Despite their efforts, the bodies began to pile up, and the ground grew slick with blood and gore. Just as it seemed they might be overwhelmed, a gunshot rang out, and a zombie's head exploded right next to Tom, covering him in a spray of gore.

A chorus of shouts erupted from the gates as a wave of Vanguard members charged out, led by Derek. "TO TOM! PROTECT THE GUILD LEADER! FOR VANGUARD!" Derek's voice boomed, and the cry was taken up by the entire crowd.

"FOR VANGUARD!" echoed through the streets, bouncing off the walls in a deafening roar.

Vanguard members poured into the fray, their weapons flashing in the dim light. The battle turned into a frenzy of gunfire, swords clashing, spells flying, and even the occasional explosion. The zombies, overwhelmed by the sheer force of the Guild's numbers and determination, were quickly pushed back.

"THE HEADS! THE WEAKNESS IS THE HEADS!" Tom shouted, urging his people to finish the job as efficiently as possible.

"No shit!" James shouted, shooting two zombie heads simultaneously. "We've all seen the movies, asshole."

A tension Tom hadn't realized he'd been holding finally relaxed. He took a deep inhale and exhale before diving back into the melee, his enormous blade reaping the unlife from the zombie horde.

After ten intense minutes, the battlefield quieted. The few remaining zombies were swiftly dispatched, and the members of Vanguard began to regroup. Tom stood amidst the carnage, breathing heavily but filled with pride at what he had just witnessed. His people had fought like true warriors.

Bron was nowhere to be seen, but Tom noticed the timer for his Summon had elapsed. He quickly reactivated his *Summon Demonic Creature* Skill, and Bron reappeared beside him. He also resummoned Shadow to give him the praise he deserved. The Mastadonian glanced around the battlefield and grunted approvingly.

"Your people acquitted themselves well," Bron remarked.

"They did. I'm proud of them," Tom replied, still scanning for anyone who needed healing. Several members were already tending to the wounded.

"Indeed. And you fought valiantly. Though your technique could use some refinement," Bron added with a hint of a smile.

"Would you help me with that?" Tom asked eagerly. "You gave me some tips earlier. If I summon you more often, could you teach me how to fight better?"

Bron considered the request. "Yes. Summon me outside of battle, and I will train you."

"Deal!" Tom grinned, feeling hopeful about the prospect of improving his combat skills.

Shadow, the Usiku, padded over, rubbing against Tom's leg with a rumbling purr of satisfaction. It licked its lips and gazed up at him, clearly pleased with its work. Tom scratched its head, laughing.

"Thank you, Shadow. You did amazing," Tom praised the large cat, scratching under its chin.

Shadow purred even louder, leaning into the affection.

Derek walked over, his face still flushed with adrenaline. "What the fuck happened?!"

"We went to investigate The Master and ran into a zombie problem," Tom said matter-of-factly.

"And you brought them here?!" Derek was furious, his face red with anger.

"We could have fought them there and died," Tom pointed out.

"None of this is okay, Tom! You don't know what could have happened. Now their leader likely knows where our base is!" Derek snapped.

"What should I have done differently?" Tom asked, genuinely wanting to understand.

"How about not going off in the night to gather information without a plan?" Derek shot back, his tone slightly calmer but still stern.

Tom shook his head. "Not really an option. We needed to know what we were up against. This man is enslaving people, stripping them of their free will. That's not okay, and nothing you say will convince me I made the wrong decision."

"Ugh… I know, I know. But this was dangerous," Derek grumbled, letting out a deep sigh of frustration.

"I get it," Tom acknowledged, his tone more composed. "But think about it—tonight was a real test of our defenses and response times. Our people responded like seasoned pros, rushing out to defend what was theirs. They proved they could stand up for themselves, and that's exactly what we've been working toward. We won't always be here to shield them from every threat. I'm proud of what they accomplished tonight."

Derek ran a hand through his hair, clearly grappling with his emotions. "You're right." His glare returned. "But what if you'd been wrong. You. Cannot." Derek punctuated each word with a finger in Tom's chest. "Go out fucking half-cocked. You're not Jason fucking Borne. What you did was stupid, arrogant, and will likely cost the lives of hundreds of people under that maniac's control. Because make no fucking mistake—he now knows we're coming, and he's going to be ready with the bodies of the innocent between him and us."

Tom took a deep breath, trying to fight down the flash of defensive anger toward the soldier. He took a deep breath before sighing. "Maybe you're right. I was just doing what I thought was right."

"And *I'm* just trying to keep everyone as safe as I can," Derek replied, giving the Guild leader a concession. "But you're right; the people were incredible tonight. They're more prepared than I gave them credit for. If you're looking for an apology for the ass-chewing, though—you know where to find it," he grumbled, pointing at the seat of Tom's pants, the weight of his responsibility evident in his voice.

Tom gave him a reassuring smile. "Yeah, yeah. I didn't expect anything less. But tonight, we showed everyone not just what they're capable of, but also that we aren't a Guild to be messed with. We can't afford to play it safe all the time."

Derek nodded slowly, taking in Tom's words. "Maybe not, but the military has a term for things like this—*calculated* risk. You, though, didn't calculate shit. But, sure, we can't just hide behind these walls and hope for the best."

Tom clapped a hand on Derek's shoulder, his smile broadening. "Exactly. Now, let's check on everyone, make sure they're alright, and get inside. We need to debrief the others on what we found out about The Master."

With that, the two of them turned and began moving through the battlefield, helping the others and preparing to regroup inside for what was bound to be an important discussion.

Chapter 20

Smithy

Walking back into the Guild building, Tom was led to the security center, where the other department leaders were gathering. He detailed what he had seen at the enemy base, including the glimpse of the man he believed to be The Master.

"So, he's a necromancer too," Brian mused, rubbing his chin thoughtfully. "That complicates things."

"Lily didn't mention anything about zombies. Were they hidden before?" Harold wondered aloud. Bohdan, now acting as his assistant, stood beside him, nodding along.

"We can just kill zombies, no?" Bohdan suggested.

"The problem is, if he can raise the dead, he has a limitless army at his disposal. There are plenty of corpses in the city to choose from," Tom replied, growing more anxious about the potential threat lurking out there.

"Still, that kind of thing takes both time and energy," Kiera pointed out. "I doubt that making zombies is free. If I had to guess, a necromancer needs a lot of setup to be truly terrifying."

"She's right." Derek took charge. "It's a good argument for attacking sooner rather than later. I want double watches at every access point and some towers built to oversee the walls. Two people in each tower, around the clock. We need to be ready if there's another attack while we figure out our next move."

Tom sighed heavily. "Sorry for getting us into this mess."

"It's alright, Tom," Derek reassured him. "It's actually a good thing we found out. If we hadn't, his army would've grown unchecked. Now we know what we're up against and can prepare accordingly. It would've been much worse if we were caught off guard."

"Exactly," Brian added. "Now, we have a chance to strategize and be proactive rather than reactive."

"We can't let him continue unchecked. Not only is he enslaving people, but we now know that he has an undead army. So, what do we do about it?" Tom asked, leaning against a table near the door.

"I think we only have one real option, though I hate to suggest it," Brian said, his voice heavy.

Tom raised an eyebrow. "And that is?"

"War," Brian answered gravely. "But before we make any decisions, I think it's important to discuss this with everyone and have a vote. It's crucial to gauge how those who'd be fighting feel about it."

Tom frowned, hesitating. "I don't know if I'm ready to drag everyone into a full-scale conflict."

"I know." Brian turned to him, his eyes blazing with determination. "Tom, I consider you a friend and someone I deeply respect. So, I say this with all sincerity—don't be a fucking idiot. Well, more than you already have, I mean. I get it. I really do. You thought you could go out there and shoulder everyone's burdens and things would just… work out." Brian put a hand on Tom's shoulder. "That's not how the world works, friend. What's more—you're insulting and degrading the commitment and contribution of the people you lead. You're not the only one trying to build a better world here."

Tom was taken aback by Brian's sudden intensity. He had always known Brian as the level-headed type, someone who thought things through before acting. Seeing him this worked up about something, ready to go to war, was new and startling.

"You really believe war is the only way forward?" Tom asked, still processing Brian's words.

"Yes," Brian said, his voice steady but fierce. "Me and Abraham Lincoln are on the same page on this one," Brian chuckled. Tom did as well, a measure of tension releasing from his body. "The idea of this man enslaving people makes my blood boil. And knowing he has an undead army just solidifies it. We need to act now, before things spiral completely out of control. I've been in situations where I've been bound by someone's will—no one should have to live like that."

Tom nodded slowly, seeing the fire in Brian's eyes. "Alright. Gather everyone in the gym. We'll lay it out and let them decide." He glanced around. "By the way, has anyone seen James?"

TJ chimed in, "Last I saw, he was taking Squirrel down to the infirmary. He was carrying him."

Tom's expression shifted to concern. "I hope everything's alright. I'm going to check on him before the meeting." With that, he left the room.

Walking through the bustling halls, Tom made his way to the infirmary. Inside, the room was busy with Clerics attending to the injured, moving swiftly from bed to bed, healing wounds and comforting the weary. Since the Grand System's introduction of healing magic, recovery times had drastically shortened, but it still required cooldowns and mana management.

Despite the activity, most of the injured were chatting and smiling, but one corner of the room stood out.

James was sitting on the floor next to a cot, looking distraught. His familiar, Squirrel, was lying on the bed with Rebecca standing over him. She seemed to be examining him without using magic.

Tom approached them. "What's going on? Is Squirrel okay?"

Rebecca glanced up, a slight frown on her face. "We're not sure. Physically, he seems fine, but he's burning up and hasn't moved much. We're keeping him hydrated and monitoring him. That's all we can do for now."

Tom leaned down and stroked Squirrel's fur. The wolf's tail wagged faintly, and he panted lightly. "Hey there, buddy. Just rest up and get better. We've got things handled, and you'll be back on your feet soon."

James was beside himself with worry, staring blankly at his familiar. Tom placed a hand on his shoulder. "James, we need to talk. There's something big happening, and I need you to hear it."

James looked up, reluctant to leave Squirrel's side. "Can it wait? I'd rather stay here."

Tom shook his head. "I'm afraid not. Walk with me for a bit. We won't go far."

Rebecca offered a reassuring smile. "Don't worry, James. We'll keep a close eye on him and let you know if anything changes. He's in good hands."

With a heavy sigh, James stood, giving Squirrel a final pat. "I'll be back, I promise. You just hang in there, okay?"

As they walked out of the infirmary and down the hall, Tom asked quietly. "What happened to Squirrel?"

James' expression darkened. "We were in the middle of the zombie fight, and Squirrel was doing his usual thing, taking down enemies left and right. But when it was over, he looked like he was about to go feral. Then he just collapsed and started burning up. I brought him here as fast as I could." James rubbed his hands across his face in agitation. "I can't help but think either this is really bad or really good."

"What do you mean?" Tom's eyebrows were drawn down while asking the question.

"Well..." James took a deep breath. "Either Squirrel caught the equivalent of Zombiepox, or..."

"*Or...*" Tom repeated, encouraging James to speak.

James clenched a fist. "Or he's going to evolve."

Tom stared at James, processing what he'd said. Images kept coming to his mind, but nothing translated to words he could use.

James looked up at Tom's silence. "You know—" he pantomimed a small spherical object exploding "—like a Pokémon."

"...Yeah, no. I got it the first time you said it." Tom was now the one rubbing his face.

"I hope he's a fire-type," James continued, oblivious to the state of Tom's blood pressure. James rubbed his chin in thought. "Maybe I can check the vending machine for evolution fire-stones..." He trailed off. "I think zombies might be weak to that kind of thing."

"Yeah," Tom sighed. "Me too, man. Let's hope Rebecca and the others can help get to the bottom of what's going on with the furball," Tom said, trying to sound reassuring.

As they neared the main lobby, Tom lowered his voice further. "We're likely going to war with The Master. We're gathering the Guild in the gym to discuss our options and take a vote."

James' eyes widened slightly. "I'm all for kicking that guy's ass. But are we ready for something like that?"

"After what I saw tonight, I think we are," Tom said firmly. "Everyone came to our aid, and they fought hard for the Guild. It's our turn to fight for those who can't fight for themselves."

"Yeah, I guess that makes sense… wait. Do you hear that noise?" James asked suddenly as they walked into the lobby.

The area was nearly empty; most people had likely headed to the gym after the announcement. There was a soft but steady rhythmic *ping, ping, ping* of a hammer striking metal coming from the stairs leading to the basement. Tom and James exchanged a look, and without needing to say a word, they both headed for the stairs to check it out.

As they descended, the air grew noticeably warmer, and a dim, flickering light danced on the walls, casting long shadows. The sound of hammering grew louder. Across the now much-expanded basement, they spotted a forge.

A large man wearing a tank top, jeans, and boots stood over an anvil, hammering a glowing piece of metal. He paused, inspected his work through a pair of goggles, then shoved the metal back into the fire.

"Hello? Sorry to interrupt, but did you miss the announcement? All Guild members are supposed to be in the gym," Tom called out from across the basement.

The man turned, lifting his goggles onto his forehead. "Sorry, I missed it. It's a bit loud down here in ze basement when I am doing ze hammering on ze metal," he replied in a thick German accent, his deep voice resonating off the walls.

As Tom and James approached, they realized just how imposing the man was. Standing at least six-and-a-half-feet tall, he was a mass of muscle and hair. His arms were covered in thick hair that ran all the way to his shoulders, with even more sprouting from the top of his shirt, like he was trying to smuggle a small forest.

"I don't think we've been properly introduced. I'm Tom, and this is James," Tom said, extending a hand.

"I'm Roland. I've been a smith for mein entire adult career, and now it seems it is finally paying off. Sorry about not coming when ze call came out, but I was down here making rüstung for ze Guild," Roland said, gripping Tom's hand.

Tom felt the strength in Roland's grip. If not for his own boosted Strength stat, his hand might have been crushed. When Roland shook James' hand, James winced, his knees buckling slightly. "Ow, ow, ow, ow…"

"Oh, sorry about zat. Sometimes I forget mein strength," Roland said, quickly letting go.

"That's alright, but what is rüstung?" Tom asked, curious.

"Oh, it is… how do you say… *armor*, I think?" Roland replied, searching for the right word in English.

"Ah, that's excellent! Do you make other things too?" Tom asked, intrigued.

"Rüstung? More like rüstunk," James mumbled under his breath, rubbing his nose.

"Vat? I am not sure I understand vat you are meaning," Roland said, turning to James.

"What? Oh, nothing. Just a joke," James stammered, realizing the size difference between them.

"Ahh, I see. Sorry, I do not get jokes normally. Just somezing I am working on for now," Roland replied, turning back to Tom.

"It's okay. Sounds like English is your second language, so that's understandable," Tom said, trying to lighten the mood.

"I work on whatever ze Guild needs. I have made armor, weapons, parts for little machines zat Harold builds. I can make many sings," Roland explained.

"Making people sing? I thought only my old elementary school teacher did that," James quipped.

Roland stared blankly at James, clearly confused. "Your music teacher made people sings? Like toys?"

James sighed. "No sense of humor... this is going to be fun," he muttered.

"Sorry, Roland, but we need everyone up in the gym for a meeting. Can you get back to your work afterward?" Tom asked.

"Sure. I just need to take ze metal out of ze fire so it does not veaken," Roland said, pulling his gloves back on. He carefully removed the glowing metal from the forge with a pair of tongs and set it on the anvil to cool.

"Vell, I am off to ze meeting. See you both zere," Roland said, waving as he headed for the stairs.

"Fun guy," James said sarcastically once Roland was out of earshot.

"Come on, we should get there too. We need to see how everyone feels about the new plan. It might get messy before this is over," Tom said, nudging James back toward the stairs.

Chapter 21

To War

After heading back upstairs, Tom and James made their way to the gym. Nearly everyone in the Guild had gathered, and the gym was almost filled to capacity. It was clear this wasn't going to be a viable meeting spot for much longer. Brian stood near the entrance, trying to organize everyone and make room for Tom to speak. Tom tapped him on the shoulder.

"I don't think this is going to work," Tom said, leaning in so Brian could hear him over the crowd.

"It definitely won't," Kiera interjected, noticing Tom. "Basic sound physics. Bodies absorb sound. When you talk, it won't carry to the back of the room."

"How do you know about sound physics?" Tom asked.

"I was in a band, moron. We had to know these things for room setups," Kiera replied, annoyed.

"Oh, right. That makes sense. Sorry. Brian, can we move this outside?" Tom suggested, turning back to him.

"Yeah, good idea. This definitely isn't working. Over a thousand people packed into one room is making me nervous," Brian said. "TJ, go ahead and make an announcement to have everyone meet out front. We'd never be able to do it from here."

TJ nodded and dashed off to the security center to make the announcement. After another half-hour of people-herding, everyone finally assembled outside. Tom drove the GS2 around to the front, using the roof as a makeshift stage to see above the crowd.

"Uh, hello! How is everyone?" Tom began. A few people shouted back.

Cries of "We're good!" and "Hey, look, it's Tom!" mixed with some "Meh," "Can't complain, I suppose," and one odd "GNOMES RULE!" from someone at the back. Tom couldn't quite tell who had yelled that.

"Alright, alright," Tom continued, trying to keep the energy up. "The reason we've gathered here today is because of the attack that just happened. I know the word about the zombies probably isn't news to most of you. But in case it is, tonight I went to see what was happening in another base in the city."

Tom's eyes found Lily in the crowd, her face streaked with tears—happy tears this time.

"There's a man not far from here who believes his desires are more important than anyone else's. A man who thinks of his fellow humans as puppets, tools for his own plans! He's enslaved a large group of people with collars and forces them to do his bidding. And now, we've learned he can raise zombies to fight for him too!" Tom continued, his voice growing louder with passion as the crowd began to murmur uneasily.

"I cannot stand by while people are forced into slavery! We are better than this! Do you think letting this happen and allowing it to go unchecked is okay?" Tom challenged.

Shouts erupted in response:

"Hell no!"

"What the damn hell!"

"We really living in a time where people are slaves again? I thought we got past that!"

"I'm 'bout to go Malcom X on this bitch," shouted a thick-shouldered black man holding up a wicked-looking club.

A stunned silence fell over the crowd. Everyone turned their heads toward the man. A long moment went by before suddenly, everyone roared in approval, waving weapons of their own.

"I'm going to fight to stop this. We brought you all here to tell you we're planning to go to war against this man who calls himself The Master. We can't let him continue, or he'll reach a point where we won't be able to stop him. Who here is with me in putting a stop to this atrocity?" Tom called out, trying to speak over the growing noise.

"YES!"

"Let's rip his fucking slaver throat out!"

"It's not right!"

"Death to zombies!"

"Isn't that an oxymoron?" James leaned over to ask Derek, hearing the last shout.

"Your mom's an oxymoron," Derek shot back out of the corner of his mouth.

"Dude… weak," James scoffed.

"The time is near! We're not just going to rush over there without a plan and kill everything. We'll strategize and make sure the we minimize our casualties. But we didn't want to commit to war without your support. I thank you from the bottom of my heart for showing you still care about how people are treated, even when you could be selfish right now. This is why VANGUARD WILL STAND FOREVER!" Tom roared the last line.

The crowd erupted into a frenzy of cheers and applause. Pride swelled in Tom's chest as he saw how much everyone had come together in such a short time since the System had been put in place.

Tom climbed down from the vehicle, and Brian quickly approached to shake his hand.

"That went way better than I thought it would. I guess the zombie attack lit a fire under people," Brian said, clearly energized, with a glimmer of revenge still burning in his eyes.

"They all came here looking for a better life. I think they just see this as a chance to do for others what we did for them, and it's inspiring," Tom replied, smiling broadly.

As people began to file back inside, Tom turned to follow them, but Brian caught his arm.

"You're the only one who can declare who we're at war with. You need to do that before we forget," Brian reminded him.

"Right, okay, I'll do it," Tom said, pulling up the System interface and navigating to the Guild tab.

He scrolled through the options and found the tab for war. However, he quickly realized a problem. "Oh, for fuck's sake. We have no idea what The Master's Guild is called. And there's a list of over a thousand Guilds in here now," Tom groaned, rubbing his face.

"Can we try? Maybe there's something obvious that gives it away," Brian suggested.

"I'll look through it, but unless it's called 'I'm The Master. Tom, please declare war on me,' I'm not confident we'll find the right one," Tom replied, growing more frustrated as he scrolled through the names.

"Not to mention, he might not even have a Guild," Derek added. "Remember the 'ten willing participants' part? Let's just hope it's obvious."

He passed by some interesting names: Electric Salamanders, Red Dragon Brigade, and some clearly joke names like Assy McAssFace and It Burns When IP, which brought a chuckle out of him. "Heh… it's not a Wi-Fi you're naming. But that's clever."

After what felt like an eternity of scrolling, Tom finally found a name that seemed to fit.

"Well, this is likely it. But if we declare war on them and it's not the right Guild, what do we do?" Tom asked.

"What's the name of the Guild?" Brian asked.

"It's called 'The Master's Flock,'" Tom replied.

"Odds are pretty good that's our guy. If we're wrong, I guess we'll either have to fight another Guild or explain the situation to them when they find us," Brian said, shrugging.

"Well, here goes nothing," Tom muttered, selecting "The Master's Flock" and pressing the big red "DECLARE WAR" button below.

A message with a bold red border flashed into his vision, as well as into the vision of every other member of the Vanguard Guild. Unbeknownst to them, the same message appeared before every member of The Master's Flock as well.

War has been declared:

The leader of the Guild VANGUARD has officially declared war against the Guild THE MASTER'S FLOCK. All members of both Guilds are hereby notified of the impending conflict.
Prepare for battle!
Sides can be taken: Other Guilds may choose to join this war.

> Alliances can be formed: Unite with allies or recruit new ones to strengthen your ranks.
> Fight with honor: Victory will not only be determined by strength but also by strategy, courage, and resolve.
> The war begins now. May the best Guild prevail!

"Well… I didn't know it was going to do that," Tom said sheepishly after closing the prompt.

"It can't be helped. Declarations of war have always been a public affair, so it's not unusual for them to be broadcast like this," Bob said, sneaking up behind Tom.

"Holy shit! Where did you come from?" Tom asked, jumping slightly from the sudden presence.

"Oh, I've been here the whole time. Just waiting to see what you would do," Bob replied, his hands clasped behind his back in a patient stance.

"I guess you're right. Proclamations in times of war did involve a lot of fanfare back in the day—like heralds and all that," Tom pondered.

"Indeed. So, this kind of announcement is quite normal," Bob replied.

"Right. Now, we need a plan. When we were there, it wasn't too hard to get in. Getting out was the problem," Tom began.

"But we won't need to worry about getting out. The goal is for them to be dead when we leave. The real challenge is keeping the innocents alive and getting those collars off," Brian added.

"True. We'll need to give Harold more time to come up with a solution for the collars. In the meantime, I want everyone training—parties out there killing monsters, learning new skills and spells, and stocking our armory," Tom commanded.

"Look at you, all fired up and taking charge. Much better than before," Jay remarked, sneaking up behind Tom as well.

"Jesus Christ on a cracker, why is everyone sneaking up on me today?!" Tom shouted in frustration.

"Hehehe! I'm a Rogue; what do you expect? Plus, it's good practice," Jay replied, rubbing his hands together menacingly.

"Dude, that's creepy. Stop with the hand rubbing," Tom said, giving him a blank stare.

"Guess it didn't have the effect I was going for. Sorry," Jay said with a shrug.

"It's fine. I need to find Kiera. We need her working on some sniper stuff. Anyone seen her?" Tom asked.

"I think she went to the infirmary. James headed there a moment ago, too," Jay informed him.

"Oh, right! The infirmary! I need to check on Squirrel," Tom said and rushed off toward the building.

Moving swiftly down the back hallway that led to the infirmary, Tom continued until he reached the door. Opening it and looking inside, he wasn't prepared for what he saw. In the back corner of the room, where Squirrel had been laid on a cot after the battle with the zombie horde, was a six-foot-tall wolf with glowing red eyes. Tom quickly identified it while equipping his sword.

Dire Wolf - Squirrel

The Dire Wolf, an evolved form of the common wolf from planet 35956390246, also known as "Earth." Standing at six feet tall at the shoulder, Dire Wolves are far larger, faster, and stronger than their lesser brethren. Their powerful muscles ripple beneath their thick, mottled fur, and their sharp red eyes burn with fierce intelligence. Unlike regular wolves, Squirrel has developed an innate ability to rally nearby wolves, enhancing their aggression and coordination during a hunt or battle.

"What the actual fuck?" was all Tom managed to say as he lowered his greatsword, the tip resting on the floor. He stood there, wide eyed, staring at the massive creature in front of him. The beast—Squirrel—now occupied nearly a third of the infirmary's main area.

"Oh, hey, Tom! Look! Squirrel's fine! I was right. He just needed to evolve!" James shouted excitedly, scratching Squirrel's fur like it was the most natural thing in the world. James looked sad for a moment. "I couldn't find any evolution stones in the vending machine."

"Yes… I see that," Tom said, still trying to process what he was looking at. "But again… what the actual fuck? Will he even fit through the door?"

"Oh, yeah. He does tricks now! Show him, buddy," James said, turning to Squirrel.

Squirrel let out a deep howl and began to shrink, his massive frame reducing until he was about twice the size of a normal wolf.

"That's… that's amazing! How big can he get?" Tom asked, still in awe.

James' eyes widened. He slapped himself on the forehead. "I'm such an idiot, and you're a genius, Tom. Why didn't I think of it before?" He held his hands up in the air as if trying to look up at a massive building. "*Squirrel-kaiju!*" he intoned, his eyes manic. Seconds later, however, he deflated with a sigh. "I think what you saw earlier was about his max size, but we'd probably want to test it out properly outside."

"Alright, we can add that to our to-do list. But for now, we need to meet in the security office. Hopefully, we can come up with some plans to start harassing The Master and disrupting his operations," Tom told him.

"Okay, but what if Squirrel and I just go over there and wreck everyone?" James suggested with an almost gleeful grin.

"No, absolutely not," Tom snapped. "He has slaves he could use as cannon fodder. You'd be stuck trying *not* to hurt them, or worse—you'd kill indiscriminately and end up slaughtering innocent people who are being held captive against their will. Do you want that on your conscience?"

James' grin faded, and he looked down at his shoes. "No," he mumbled, clearly disappointed.

"Didn't think so," Tom said, his tone softening a bit. "Now, let's get to planning. I have a feeling we have some raids in the near future."

Chapter 22

Patron Past

Tom noticed a new notification blinking in his vision, glowing in a different color than the others. He opened it and read through the information.

"Oh, ho! I've finally killed the thousand creatures Azroc needed. We can summon him again and get some rewards!" Tom said to James as they walked to the security center.

"I can't wait to see him again. Love that guy. Remember the way he absolutely dunked on Joe? Legend. Think he might have any advice for the war?" James asked, his eyes bright with excitement.

"Only one way to find out. Let's gather the others and summon him," Tom said, his pace quickening with anticipation.

Picking up speed, Tom and James soon arrived at the security center and entered through the large steel door. Inside, they found Brian, TJ, Kiera, Derek, and a few security guards on duty.

"Hey, can we call Jay over too? I think he'll want to be a part of this," Tom asked.

"What exactly are you planning?" Brian asked, a hint of skepticism creeping into his voice.

"I'm going to summon my Patron," Tom said with a mischievous grin.

"That smile of yours is creeping me out. Should I be worried?" Brian asked cautiously.

"Nah, it's fine. He's a good guy. He's just... a lot, I guess, is the best way to describe it?" Tom replied, unsure how to properly set expectations. "You'll just have to meet him and form your own opinion."

"Alright, I'll call Jay in," TJ said, walking over to the mic to make the announcement.

About half an hour later, everyone was assembled, and Tom had gathered the materials needed to draw the summoning circle on the floor. Brian had managed to find some washable markers, insisting on them even after Tom reassured him that anything used for the summoning would be consumed in the process. Brian wasn't taking any chances with a permanent summoning circle in the middle of the security center.

With Brian momentarily appeased, Tom set about drawing the intricate symbols and lines of the summoning circle. James was practically bouncing with excitement, and the others seemed intrigued, if not a little cautious. Once the circle was complete, Tom began the incantation.

"*Admoneo te, magne spiritus, ad nutum meum accede et da mihi potestatem quam cupio. Habeo crustulum.*"

As before, the circle flared to life, glowing with an ethereal light. A gust of wind whipped through the room, and a portal opened at its center. Azroc emerged, striking a dramatic bodybuilder pose.

"How's it going, wankers?" Azroc bellowed, his gaze sweeping around the room.

"Hey, Azroc. Good to see you again," Tom greeted him, stepping forward.

"Ah! Tom! My favorite new Warlock! Great job kicking ass and killing all those fucking monsters! You really got out there and showed them who's boss, didn't you?" Azroc said, moving over and giving Tom a hearty slap on the back that nearly sent him stumbling forward.

"Whoa! Uh, yeah, we've been busy. No shortage of monsters to kill," Tom said, trying to recover his balance.

"Excellent! I see there are more people here this time. You think this is a peep show or something? And where's that cockholster Joe? Has he gotten any better since we last talked?" Azroc asked, glancing around.

"He's not here. He's come around and has been helping with the farming project," Tom explained.

"That's great to hear. I'd have hated to have to actually turn him inside out and use his entrails for jump rope. It's an amazing threat, but a bit messy in practice," Azroc said, leaning over to Tom and winking.

"Ha, yeah," Tom laughed nervously.

"This is your Patron?" Brian asked, his tone a mix of concern and curiosity.

"I am. You got a problem with it, Lucky Charms?" Azroc shot back, turning his gaze to Brian.

"Oh, absolutely fucking not. I'm just in awe. I've never seen a being of your, uh, power level before," Brian said quickly, backpedaling hard and hoping flattery would smooth things over.

"Ha! Few have," Azroc said, puffing up with pride.

"So, Azroc, what's new? Slay any assholes recently?" James asked, moving forward and holding out a fist for Azroc to bump.

"You know it," Azroc replied, fist-bumping James. "Those motherfuckers got what was coming to them. Pansy-ass sons of bitches."

"Right on!" James replied, wincing and shaking his hand after the fist bump.

"Now, about those rewards, Tom..." Azroc began, turning back to Tom.

"Actually, before that, I was wondering if you could tell us a bit about yourself. Where you come from, how you got to be where you are? Can we become as powerful as you?" Tom asked, hoping to learn something useful for the war.

"You want to know about me?" Azroc seemed genuinely surprised by the question.

"Sure. You're my Patron. I'm as interested in you as you are in me," Tom said with a smile.

"No one's ever asked about me before, except to see what kind of goodies they could get. I'm blown away, Tom. You really are different from those other asshats," Azroc replied.

"That must be tough. And lonely," Tom said sympathetically.

"Not really. It's more like a job. You just do it because it's what you have to fucking do. There are others I talk to, but I don't exactly get a lot of free time," Azroc explained. "Well, I guess it started when I hatched on my homeworld, Garatha. Never knew my mother—bitch laid her eggs and ran off."

"That must have been horrible," Tom said, interjecting.

"Not really. My species doesn't care for their young. We're pretty much born self-sufficient," Azroc continued. "Then my planet got integrated into the Grand System about thirty-five hundred years ago. I chose the Warlock path and got this total asshole for a Patron. Wanted me to do the worst things imaginable for rewards. My blood boils just thinking of that cunt-licker."

"He really fits in with their team dynamic, doesn't he?" Brian whispered to TJ as Azroc talked.

"Hey, I am a fucking delight," Azroc said, turning to face Brian.

"No disagreement here. I was just saying you fit in well with Tom and his team," Brian said quickly, raising his hands in mock surrender.

"Oh, yeah, I do, don't I?" Azroc said, clearly pleased. "Anyway, I did what I had to do to get stronger. Fought for a century before I reached the pinnacle of power for integration. Had to kill a lot of wankers to get there. Finally, I got a quest to pass over to the next evolution, and—"

Azroc abruptly stopped, his mouth clamping shut as his eyes squeezed closed. He seemed to be wracked with sudden, intense pain.

Growling and grunting, Azroc hunched over, the pain eventually subsiding.

"Holy fucking shit, that hurt," Azroc swore loudly. "Sorry, I wasn't supposed to say that part. See, we're all slaves to the fucking System in the end."

"Are you okay?" Tom asked, concerned about his Patron and what it might mean for his progress.

"I'll be fine. I just can't explain certain things. You have to learn them for yourself. Fucking rules," Azroc muttered, still panting from the lingering pain. "Now, where was I? Oh, yes. You can become like me, but I can't explain how. For now, suffice it to say, you do what I fucking tell you to, and you'll get there. I'm here to help you, after all."

"That's great to hear! But I don't know if I'll live for a century. Human life expectancy isn't that long," Tom said, feeling like his hopes had been dashed.

"Oh, that's not an issue. The System will keep you alive a lot longer now, thanks to your stats. You should expect to live about three times longer than before. Fucking elves got the long straw on that one," Azroc explained, muttering the last bit.

"Elves?" Tom asked, intrigued.

"*Elves?*" James leaned in, wiping drool from his face.

"Sure, there are nearly infinite races. Different on most planets. You didn't think everyone was human, did you?" Azroc replied.

"Well, no. Clearly not. I mean, *you're* not human, and the monsters here aren't. But on my planet, elves and dwarves and such are just fantasy creatures in stories and games," Tom explained. "Actually, now that I think about it, it is kind of weird that we have legends about goblins and elves and dwarves and everything else, and now—here they all are…"

"Good, you're thinking rationally. That's what I love about you—more than two brain cells to rub together. And you aren't just begging me for your powers like those needy bastards," Azroc said, a hint of admiration in his tone.

"I know you'll help me if I help you, so I just want to get to know you," Tom said earnestly.

"I wish the others could be more like you, Tom. But I'm here for a gift. So here you go. I hope it helps," Azroc said with a knowing wink.

A new prompt appeared in Tom's vision.

<table>
<tr><td align="center">Pact Update:</td></tr>
<tr><td>

You have successfully completed the requirements to upgrade your pact with Azroc.

- Quest Completion:
    - Kill monsters and send their souls to Azroc: 1000/1000
    - Claim a site of power in Azroc's name: Completed

</td></tr>
</table>

"Hey, wait. What was the site of power I claimed in your name?" Tom asked, confused about when he had completed that quest.

Azroc chuckled. "The Grand Canyon Dungeon with the world vending machine," he said, a hint of amusement in his voice. "It was never meant to be a Dungeon at all. It was actually a site of power holding the supply of all the world's goods. Marking it as you did, completed that aspect of the quest."

Tom blinked in surprise, his mouth forming a small "o" as he processed the information.

"Ohhhh. Cool!" he exclaimed, a wide grin spreading across his face. He quickly returned his attention to his prompts, eager to see what new powers were available to him.

Pact of the Tattoo Upgrade:

You have completed a quest for Azroc. In recognition of your unwavering service and devotion, Azroc grants you the opportunity to select a new tattoo to enhance your abilities. Choose wisely:

- **Tattoo of Stealth:** Become nearly undetectable for 30 minutes. Cost: 250 mana.
- **Tattoo of Magic Nullification:** Create an anti-magic field around yourself for 1 hour. Cost: 250 mana. (Note: Your magic will also be nullified in this field; however, the effects of other tattoos will remain active.)
- **Tattoo of Healing:** Regenerate 5 HP per second for 300 seconds. Cost: 250 mana.

Choose your new power and strengthen your bond with Azroc!

It seemed as though Azroc always knew exactly what Tom needed. Every time, he managed to provide something that gave him an edge. But this time, the decision was much tougher.

"Damn. All of these would be amazing to have," Tom muttered, his eyes moving back and forth over the options.

"Sorry, you can only choose one," Azroc began, then paused thoughtfully. "Although…"

"What?!" Tom blurted, eyes wide with anticipation at the hint of a possible opportunity for an extra reward.

"There is a way to grant you more than one," Azroc continued, a grin forming on his face. "But you'd need to take on an extra quest next time."

"Well, this doesn't seem fair," TJ whispered to Brian, his eyes narrowing.

"Fuck off, dickweed. You know nothing of the Law of Reciprocation. Nothing in the multiverse is free. If you wanted the help, you should've chosen Warlock," Azroc snapped, glaring at TJ until he shrank back under his gaze.

"So, what's the quest?" Tom asked, focusing back on his Patron.

"You have to be the one to kill The Master," Azroc replied, his grin widening.

"Deal," Tom responded without hesitation.

"Whoa, wait, really?" Azroc looked genuinely surprised. "I didn't peg you as quite that bloodthirsty."

"Worthy leaders don't put off on others the responsibilities that belong to themselves," Tom replied, his grin growing darker.

"Bullshit," Azroc declared. "You're just a murderhobo masquerading as the heroic protagonist."

"Not *just* a murderhobo…" Tom kicked at the ground, embarrassed.

Azroc snorted, folding his arms.

Tom grinned. "Now I just need to make sure I get to see the light go out of his eyes."

Tom accepted the quest gladly.

"I think you just became my favorite Warlock ever," Azroc said, looking at Tom with something akin to admiration. "Brings a tear to my eye to see you so willing to murder that fucktard. Gods, I fucking hate necromancers. So full of themselves all the time. We get it, you can raise the dead. Big whoop! It's not like you're bringing them back to fucking life."

"Haha! Yeah, and they die so easily!" James chimed in.

"This guy gets it," Azroc chuckled, nodding in approval at James.

"They really are perfect for each other, aren't they?" Brian said nervously as Azroc, Tom, and James stood in a circle, rubbing their hands together and talking about how they would kill The Master.

"And maybe if we tied him down first, we could take our time ripping pieces of him off," Tom said.

"Or we could dunk him in a vat of lemon juice after letting him slide down a ramp covered in barbed wire," James cackled as he plotted.

"I've always been partial to the old 'rat in a bucket with a candle behind it' technique," Azroc added.

James was rubbing his hands together at the Patron's words.

"Oh, Azroc, by the way." James leaned in, his voice lowering to a whisper that still carried to everyone present. "Is it possible to capture a necromancer and force it to reanimate goblins and shit and turn the bastard into an XP farm?" James' eyes were bright with manic glee.

"I mean, you could. But then you'd be the fucking asshat slaver. Plus, there's the whole revenge arc when the necromancer gets free, and blah, blah, blah… I'd just kill that cum dumpster and be done with it," Azroc replied.

"It's like those fucking anime scenes where the pervs are talking about how they'll do terrible things in a corner by themselves," TJ whispered to Brian, making a seriously concerned face.

"Anyway, as long as you hold up your end of the deal and kill him yourself, I can give you an extra reward now. You can choose two of the tattoos. But if you don't, and someone else kills him, you'll lose one of the tattoos randomly," Azroc said, noticing the chatting and hoping to get everyone back on track.

"I'm willing to take that risk," Tom said firmly. "If someone else kills him, that still works for me. But I really want to see that bastard die by my hands."

"Alright, then, let it be so!" Azroc boomed, his voice echoing as the room's lights dimmed. A surge of power radiated from him, coursing into Tom like a wave.

The prompt in Tom's vision updated, now allowing for the selection of two items. Checkboxes appeared beside each option. He studied the choices carefully. He really wanted all three tattoos, but that wasn't possible. The *Tattoo of Stealth* would be incredibly useful in a variety of situations. Yet the *Tattoo of Healing* could be invaluable in prolonged fights.

"This is tough," Tom admitted. "I'm not sure which one to pick for my second."

"Oh, my bad. I forgot to include your fourth choice," Azroc said slyly, his aura flaring again. Suddenly, a new option appeared on Tom's screen.

"I don't think another choice will make this any easier… Oh…" Tom trailed off, reading the new prompt with fresh curiosity.

Pact of the Tattoo Upgrade:

Congratulations! You have completed a quest for Azroc. As a reward for your continued service and dedication, Azroc grants you an additional power. Select two of the following tattoos to enhance your abilities:

- **Tattoo of Stealth:** Become nearly undetectable for 30 minutes. Cost: 250 mana.
- **Tattoo of Magic Nullification:** Create an anti-magic field around yourself for 1 hour. Cost: 250 mana. (Note: Your magic will also be nullified in this field; however, the effects of other tattoos will remain active.)
- **Tattoo of Healing:** Regenerate 5 HP per second for 300 seconds. Cost: 250 mana.
- **Tattoo of the Summoner:** Empower your summoned creatures, enhancing their abilities for 1 hour at the cost of 200 mana. Perfect for Warlocks who rely on summoned allies to turn the tide of battle.

Choose wisely, Warlock. Your path to power deepens with every decision.

"Actually, that does help. I know what I want now for sure," Tom said, confidently checking the boxes for *Tattoo of Magic Nullification* and *Tattoo of the Summoner*.

As soon as he made his selections, another window appeared in his vision, prompting him to confirm his choices.

Confirmation Required:

You have selected:

- **Tattoo of Magic Nullification:** Create an anti-magic field around you for one hour at the cost of 250 mana.
- **Tattoo of the Summoner:** Increase the abilities of your summoned creatures for one hour at the cost of 200 mana.

Are you sure you wish to proceed with these choices? Once confirmed, this decision cannot be undone.

Confirm?	
Yes	*No*

Tom selected "Yes," and the familiar sensation of a tattoo gun running over his skin surged through him. He winced at the pain, but fortunately, the process was swift, and the discomfort faded in seconds. However, the lingering sting in a specific area made his eyes widen in realization. Lifting the back of his shirt, he glanced over his shoulder, trying to get a look.

"Really?! A tramp stamp?!" Tom exclaimed, first craning his neck to see it, then turning back to Azroc with an annoyed expression.

"Hey, you were the one that chose the Magic Nullification tattoo. One of them was bound to be a tramp stamp, motherfucker," Azroc laughed, clearly amused. "I think it suits you."

"Oh, screw you," Tom grumbled.

"That's the spirit! I like it when you're spunky," Azroc chuckled again.

Trying to brush it off, Tom rolled up his sleeves and noticed his other tattoo had appeared on both forearms. It looked like a set of tapestries with intricate designs—on one arm, a Warlock summoning creatures, and on the other, commanding them in battle.

"The artwork is beautiful, though," Tom admitted, admiring the intricate details of the tattoos.

"Thank you very much. I've been working on these for millennia," Azroc replied with a mock bow. "Now, if there's nothing else, I'll leave you with your new quests and bid you farewell. So many other things to take care of. As much as I'd love to stay, I have to move on."

Just then, another notification appeared in Tom's vision.

New Requests from Your Patron, Azroc:

Your Dark Patron, Azroc, has sent his demands. Complete the following tasks to receive further powers and gifts:

- **Claim Dungeons:** Complete three total dungeons and claim them in the name of Azroc.
- **Eliminate The Master:** The Master must die by your hand.
- **Research Your Class:** Discover texts related to your Warlock Class, uncover its history, and learn the secrets to unlocking greater power.

Fulfill these quests to deepen your pact and ascend to new heights of power.

"Oh, and here, take this," Azroc said, holding out a hand as a book materialized out of thin air and landed in his grasp.

He tossed it to Tom, who caught it and read the title: "Warlocking for Dumb Dumbs." Azroc burst into laughter at Tom's incredulous expression.

"Don't knock it, sourpuss. It's the gold-standard for Warlock training," Azroc said with a grin. "Now, I bid you farewell. Remember, Tom, the path to power is fraught with peril and death, but you can achieve greatness if you push yourself." He glanced around the room one more time. "Later, shitbags."

And with that, he vanished into another portal.

Chapter 23

Mistakes Were Made

"Well, that was… terrifying, really," Brian said, breaking the silence after Azroc vanished from their world.

"He is a lot. But he's a good guy. I like him," Tom replied, chuckling slightly at Brian's reaction to his Patron.

"Feel free to do that without me next time," Brian muttered, still a bit shaken. He turned to leave the security center. "Now, if you'll excuse me, I have some other business to attend to."

Before Brian could reach the door, it was pushed open, and a security guard in full tactical gear burst in, panting as if he'd just sprinted across the compound.

"There's someone at the gate," the guard said, looking around and noticing the gathered group. "Oh, good, you're all here. Tom, I think you'll want to talk to this guy."

Tom's eyes widened, his body tensing with a mix of concern and anticipation. "What is it? Is everything okay? Are we under attack already?"

"No, I think we're safe. But it's… hard to explain. Could you just come to the gate?" the guard asked, clearly flustered.

"Okay. Lead the way," Tom replied, curiosity piqued. He motioned for the others to follow.

Tom, Derek, James, Brian, TJ, Jay, and Kiera all left the security center, trailing behind the guard. As they approached the gate, they saw a man standing near the guardhouse. He was wearing a suit with a clergy collar, clutching what looked like a Bible tightly to his chest.

"What the hell? What's a man of the cloth doing here at this hour? Does he need our help?" Tom wondered as he walked closer.

"Hello, erm… Father?" Tom greeted, trying to gauge the situation.

The man jumped slightly, his grip tightening on the Bible as he turned to face them. "Oh! Sorry, you startled me, my boy," the man replied in a high-pitched, gentle voice. "I'm Father Blakely. I am the, uh, Guild leader of, um, The Master's Flock Guild. I just came here to see what might have happened to cause you to declare war on our little congregation. Was it Billy? He has a bit of a thieving problem, but he's a good boy, I promise. We don't want any trouble. We are just trying to survive this whole ordeal. I'm so sorry if he did anything to offend you… or if any of us did, haha! Oh, dear."

Tom listened to Father Blakely's rambling, trying to make sense of what he was saying. The priest seemed nervous, eager to smooth things over.

"Wait, wait, wait. You mean to tell me that *you* are the Guild leader for The Master's Flock? Not that psychopath who calls himself The Master?" Tom asked, his confusion growing with each passing second.

"What? Oh no, there is no one who would dare to presume to be above our Lord and Savior and call themselves that," Father Blakely clarified, his tone earnest. "I am, or rather *was*, I suppose, the pastor of The Master's House Presbyterian Church here in Dallas. We are a small congregation, but we happened to be open for prayer when the, um, incident happened. We think this was the start of the apocalypse as foretold in Revelation."

Tom blinked, his mind struggling to reconcile this new information. "Jesus fucking Christ in a banana hammock… oh, I mean… sorry, Father."

"It's quite alright, my son," Father Blakely said with a soft smile, his nerves easing. "These are trying times, and I'm sure the Lord would have laughed at that mental image as well."

"So, apparently, we declared war on a small church congregation instead of the person we were trying to target. I'm so sorry, Father Blakely. There's been a mix-up. We were trying to declare war on a man who has committed despicable crimes against humanity," Tom explained, realizing the gravity of the error.

"Oh, my! What exactly has he done?" Father Blakely asked, concern etching his features.

"He found a collar that lets him use some kind of mental ability to control the actions of anyone wearing them, turning them into his slaves. And now we've discovered he's a necromancer too, raising the dead to fight for him," Tom explained, his anger rising as he thought about The Master's actions.

"Oh dear, indeed! That is despicable," Father Blakely responded, his expression filled with horror. "It pains me to think that someone would commit such terrible acts when all life is so precious, especially now. We might be able to help, though. We're a small congregation, but most of our members are simple country folk who moved to Dallas due to the rising costs of farming and shrinking profit margins. Many had to find new jobs in the city, but they're a tough group. Maybe we could join forces? We've been looking for a safer place than our church, and it seems like your group is in a good position."

"Are you asking to join the Guild?" Brian inquired, his voice heavy with resignation and followed by a long sigh.

"Well, only if you'd have us," Father Blakely replied. "I don't want to be a burden, but I swear on the Good Book that we will pull our weight."

"We've already had a massive influx of new members, and our food stores are a bit stretched…" Brian began, hoping to steer the conversation away from the topic.

"Don't listen to him," Tom interrupted, staring pointedly at Brian. "We're happy to welcome anyone who's willing to contribute."

"Fine, fine. Whatever," Brian grumbled, throwing his hands up in surrender, clearly frustrated at the thought of accommodating more people.

"So, now we have to sift through that endless list of Guild names again to find The Master's Guild?" James muttered from behind Tom.

"Actually, I think Derek was right; I doubt The Master has a Guild," Brian interjected.

"What makes you think that?" Tom asked, puzzled.

"Think about it. To form a Guild, you need a building, which isn't hard to come by, and ten willing members. If his slaves are under mind control, they wouldn't be considered willing. Without that, he probably can't form a Guild. So, a formal declaration of war isn't possible. We'll just have to handle him directly," Brian explained. "It makes the most sense, and we should have thought about it more, but given the chaos of the recent battle, I guess we were too flustered."

"That makes a lot of sense," Tom nodded. "Alright, we'll proceed with our war plans without the formal declaration. Now, let's get organized and kick that bastard's ass. Oh… sorry, Father," Tom added, catching himself.

"Not to worry, Tom. These are trying times for all of us," Father Blakely said with a chuckle. "I'm just relieved we could clear up this misunderstanding. I was genuinely worried you might kill me on the spot, but I had to come and speak with you for the sake of the people I watch over."

"Sorry again for the mix-up, Father," Tom said, genuinely apologetic. "We only meant to stop that maniac from gaining more power."

"It's perfectly fine. This meeting went far better than I expected. Honestly, my congregation doesn't even know I'm here. They wanted to launch a surprise attack on you, but I convinced them to wait until we had more information," Father Blakely admitted.

"I don't think that would have ended well for them, considering the size of your Guild," Tom said skeptically.

"I agree. And without knowing more about you, I thought it was a terrible idea. I'm a bit of a pacifist myself, but many in my flock are not. So, I wanted to see if we could resolve this peacefully before it came to that," Father Blakely continued.

"Out of curiosity, Father, have you reached level five yet?" Derek asked. "I'm sorry if that's too personal, but I'm genuinely interested."

"Yes, unfortunately, I have," Father Blakely replied. "I've had to help defend the younger members from goblins on several occasions. Why do you ask?"

"I was curious what Class a man of the cloth like you would choose from the System," Derek explained.

"I chose Paladin," Father Blakely answered.

"My money was on Cleric," Derek said with a chuckle. "Why Paladin?"

"Well, I did consider the Cleric first," Father Blakely confessed, "but after having to defend the children, I thought it best to pick something with more offensive capabilities."

"I think that's truly admirable, Father," Tom said, nodding in approval.

"Don't Paladins have to choose a god to follow?" James asked, his brow furrowing in thought.

"Yes, but I was able to choose my God—the one true God—as my deity because it was a recognized religion here on Earth. Originally, it wasn't an option, but when I got offended and began ranting about all the 'false gods,' the System added Yahweh himself as a choice," Father Blakely explained.

"I'd guess the System didn't initially recognize 'God' as a specific deity name and thought it was just a generic term," Derek suggested. "When you insisted on it and opposed all the other options, the System must have realized that 'God' was actually meant as a proper name and allowed it as a choice."

"Oooorrrrrr… the System just confirmed the existence of God," James proposed, smirking.

"I don't think it proves anything other than that the System can learn and adapt," Derek replied.

"Or maybe it means we could uncover the secrets of the universe by asking the System questions?" James continued, leaning closer to Derek, clearly enjoying the game of annoying him.

"Your logic is flawed. Go ahead, ask the System a universal question and see if it answers," Derek challenged, crossing his arms and giving James a smug look.

"Alright, System? How much wood could a woodchuck chuck if a woodchuck could chuck wood?" James asked aloud, addressing the air around him.

Silence followed his question.

"System?" James tried again, starting to feel the fool.

"See? Just an algorithm learning," Derek said, his voice filled with triumph.

"Shut up. It just didn't have anything to do with the System's parameters right now. I'm sure there'll be a chance to get the answer eventually," James insisted, trying to salvage his dignity.

"Sure, sure. And when you do get an answer, be sure to ask what the profit margins are for a seashell stand down by the seashore," Derek teased.

"And maybe find out how much a peck of pickled peppers weighs. Always been curious," Tom added with a grin.

"Haha, very funny. Some of you are just afraid of asking the tough questions!" James tried to deflect the teasing back onto them.

"Oh, and don't forget to ask what made Fuzzy Wuzzy lose his fuzziness," TJ chimed in, eager to join the fun. "It could be cancer, you know."

"Dude… too far. Cancer jokes aren't cool," Derek said, shooting TJ a disgusted look.

TJ's face fell. "Oh… uh, sorry, I didn't mean—"

Derek cracked a wide grin. "Gotcha! That was actually pretty funny."

TJ exhaled a sigh of relief. "Man, you had me for a second!"

"Hey, if you're gonna dish it out, you gotta take it," Derek chuckled, winking at TJ.

Tom decided it was time to refocus. "Alright, Father Blakely, why don't you head back and gather your congregation, along with anything you think could help the Guild. We'll instruct the guards to let you and anyone you approve inside when you return. We can evaluate everything and see about adding you to our team. Sound good?"

"That sounds wonderful. Thank you, Tom, for understanding. And really, no hard feelings about the mix-up. It's an honest mistake given the circumstances and this monster calling himself The Master," Father Blakely said warmly.

"I'm glad we cleared this up," Tom replied. "Looking forward to seeing you and your people again."

As Father Blakely left, another figure appeared from behind a building, moving toward the gate.

"Halt! Who goes there?" called one of the guards, and everyone turned to see a man approaching in full ninja attire, his face covered except for his eyes. He had two swords strapped across his back and several knives at his waist.

"Greetings, my name is Kyle," the man said, bowing slightly. "I come on behalf of Shandra. She wants to inform you that she will be declaring war on your Guild unless you agree to come under her leadership and follow our Guild's rules and authority."

"What?!" Tom exclaimed. "Why the hell would we ever do that?"

"My mistress sees this as an opportunity for both parties to grow stronger. With your fighters alongside ours, we could rule all of Dallas," Kyle explained.

"We don't want to rule Dallas. We just want it to be a safe and peaceful place for everyone," Tom retorted, his anger rising.

"What better way to ensure peace than to control everything that happens? If Shandra takes over, she'll clean up the city and create a safe environment for people to live their lives," Kyle continued, trying to sound persuasive.

"And pay for it with our people's blood? No thanks," Tom snapped.

"No omelet ever gets made without breaking a few eggs, my dear fellow," Kyle countered, maintaining his calm demeanor.

"Sure, but I'd rather break my own eggs than someone else's," Tom shot back.

James started snickering.

"Shut up. You know what I meant," Tom said without looking back at James.

"Mistress Shandra will be displeased," Kyle replied, his eyes narrowing.

Tom's expression hardened. "I don't give a flying fuck what that power-hungry narcissist thinks or feels. The answer is no."

Kyle nodded, his face expressionless. "Very well. I wish you the best of luck in what is to come." With that, he stepped back into the shadows, his form vanishing from sight as if he were never there.

Almost immediately, a new notification flashed in everyone's vision simultaneously.

War has been declared:

WAR

The leader of the Guild STORMCRUSHER has officially declared war against the Guild VANGUARD. All members of both Guilds are hereby notified of the impending conflict.

Prepare for battle!

Sides can be taken: Other Guilds may choose to join this war.

Alliances can be formed: Unite with allies or recruit new ones to strengthen your ranks.

Fight with honor: Victory will not only be determined by strength but also by strategy, courage, and resolve.

The war begins now. May the best Guild prevail!

"Well… shit," Tom said, reading the prompt.

Chapter 24

The Tower

A fist slammed into a concrete column in the dimly lit dining room that had been converted into a makeshift throne room within Reunion Tower. The impact sent a small cloud of dust cascading down from the ceiling, the entire room seeming to tremble in response.

"He should not be allowed to talk about you that way," growled a towering, muscular man clad only in a loincloth. His face twisted with rage, his voice a low, guttural rumble. "Miserable worm. I should go over there right now and make him regret every word." His fists clenched, veins bulging against his skin as if barely containing the fury boiling beneath.

"Calm yourself, Keith," came a measured, commanding voice from the far end of the room. Seated upon an ornate throne fashioned from the remains of the dining room's tables and chairs, Shandra gazed out over the city through the floor-to-ceiling windows. She radiated a chilling authority, her presence dominating the room like a queen overseeing her kingdom. "His time will come."

"But, my lady," Keith pressed, his tone seething with barely restrained hatred, "he has no right to criticize us while he wastes his time on weaklings!"

"It means nothing," Shandra replied coolly, her gaze still fixed on the sprawling cityscape below. "We will crush him and his pathetic little Guild. Any survivors will be made to serve us as laborers. But we need the secret behind his ability to power that damn building of his. The professionals stay alive; we must extract that knowledge from them."

Keith's breath was ragged with frustration, his chest heaving as he knelt before her. Shandra's eyes narrowed slightly, her mind already weaving intricate webs of strategy. Tom. That insufferable fool. He had been a thorn in her side since the moment they crossed paths. She had seen potential in many of the fighters who had flocked to him—potential that should have been hers to cultivate. If only she had gone to the Grand Canyon with them. But her choice to stay behind had been a calculated one.

While Tom and his merry band of do-gooders had been off solving the world's problems, Shandra had stayed, continuing to train and solidify her power base. And she had grown stronger. Much stronger. The people under her command were ruthless, efficient—exactly as she had molded them to be. They would tear through any obstacle she placed before them, but Tom's numbers kept growing, and that was a problem.

War was always good for thinning the ranks. Her father had drilled that lesson into her from an early age. He had been a high-ranking military officer, a man whose entire existence revolved around discipline and strategy. He taught her to be cunning, to be ruthless. Weakness was not tolerated in their household. From the moment she could walk, he had put her through grueling training regimens that demanded nothing short of perfection. She had obliged, excelling in every area—straight A's, sports prodigy, a perfect transcript that got her into Harvard Law School, where she passed the bar and became a prosecutor. In the courtroom, she had earned the nickname "The Shark," a testament to her relentless pursuit of victory and her reputation for tearing her opponents to shreds.

And now, here was Tom—a fool guided by weakness disguised as kindness—building a larger following than she had. Why? She had assembled some of the strongest fighters in Dallas, creating a team that had overcome every obstacle with brutal efficiency. And yet, this fool and his bleeding-heart approach were gaining traction faster than she could have imagined.

I guess you really do attract more flies with honey than power, Shandra thought as she seethed at the prospect.

That son of a bitch had returned from the Grand Canyon with what looked like an army. The number of buses and vans entering his Guild building was staggering.

"Yes, Mistress," Keith intoned, still kneeling. His eyes blazed with hatred. "But I want my chance to make him pay for what he said."

"You will get your chance," Shandra assured him, her voice cold and calculating. "But we must be smart. An all-out war would be too costly right now. We will have our moment, but we will play it safe for the time being. We wait. Tom is soft. He won't want all out war, so we have time to plan from the shadows. But he will be on his back foot now." She brought a hand to her chin, her fingers tapping thoughtfully as she leaned on the arm of her throne.

"Thank you, my lady," Keith said, his head bowed in submission.

"For now, keep a close eye on them. We can't let them get further ahead," she continued. "We'll let Sean and his team start with their part of the plan. Stealth is key for the initial strike." A wicked grin crept across her lips, a spark of malice flickering in her eyes.

She rose from her throne and moved to the glass walls of the former dining area, staring out over the skyline of Dallas. This city would soon be hers, and then she could expand her dominion to other territories. People would flock to her for protection and power, aligning themselves under her banner. She would build an empire, one where her word was law, and her power was absolute. She would become the strongest force this new world had ever seen.

And all that stood in her way was one man.

Shandra clenched her fists, her eyes narrowing as she imagined Tom's face. She would break him. She would savor every moment as she watched him crumble. His resistance, his ideals, his very essence would be shattered before her. And then, when there was nothing left but the empty shell of his defiance, she would watch as the light left his eyes for the final time.

"Prepare the teams," she ordered Keith, her voice resolute. "We'll begin with small skirmishes, wear them down. Hit-and-run tactics. Keep them guessing. I want them exhausted and paranoid. When the time is right, we'll strike. And when we do, it will be decisive."

"Yes, Mistress," Keith replied, rising from his kneeling position, his expression one of grim determination. "We will make them suffer."

Shandra's grin widened, a cold and calculating smile that spoke of her ruthless ambition. "Good. Now go. And remember, this isn't just about defeating them—it's about sending a message. No one crosses Shandra and lives to tell the tale."

Keith nodded, turning to leave the throne room to relay her orders. As he departed, Shandra's thoughts drifted back to Tom. She had underestimated him once; she would not make the same mistake again. She would break him, body and soul. And then, Dallas would be hers. All of it. She could already see the flames of his downfall flickering in the distance, a beacon that would guide her to absolute power.

With a final look over the city, Shandra whispered to herself, "Enjoy your little victories while you can, Tom. Because soon, there will be nothing left of you but ashes."

Chapter 25

War... Again

"Two wars in one day," James muttered, still reading the notification with unfocused eyes. "That's a lot of dicks to shoot."

"Is that really all you think about?" Derek asked, his expression a mix of exasperation and mild disgust.

"Of course not," James replied with a smirk, patting the massive wolf beside him. "I also think about letting Squirrel loose on them."

Derek glanced at the wolf, his eyebrows raising. "Is he… bigger than before?"

"He is. Thanks for noticing," James said, beaming with pride. "He evolved after the last battle. Watch this." With a wordless command, Squirrel's form expanded, growing to the size of an SUV. His massive paws sank into the earth as he let out a deep, bone-chilling howl.

"Holy shit," Derek breathed, eyes wide as he took in the sheer size of the beast. "That'll come in handy."

"Hell yeah!" James grinned, reaching up to pat Squirrel's side. "Now he can jump in and start the destruction with true gusto! Though I think, at that size, finding nuts might be a challenge."

Tom, who had been staring out into the city, seemed to snap back to reality. His face twisted with frustration. "This is fucking bullshit!" he suddenly shouted, oblivious to the conversation around him.

"What?" Derek asked, turning toward Tom.

"We're now facing a war on two fronts because that bitch wants to rule?!" Tom continued, his fists clenched so tightly his knuckles turned white. "No one wins wars on two fronts! She's trying to pin us against the wall. I bet she's had spies watching us this whole time, waiting for the perfect moment to strike while we're distracted with The Master!"

"Hey, calm down," Brian urged, stepping forward in an attempt to soothe Tom's rising temper. "Getting all worked up won't help. We need to take a step back and think."

Tom shook his head, barely hearing him. "I swear, this is all part of her plan—take advantage while we're tied up with something else. She's trying to push us into a corner!" His words were a mix of anger and frustration, his mind racing with the implications of Shandra's move.

"We'll increase security," Jay suggested, trying to steer the conversation back toward a productive course. "We need to handle The Master first and free those enslaved people. Then we can deal with Shandra and her power trip."

"I told you she was a bitch," Kiera chimed in from behind them. "Everyone shows their true colors eventually. She's just a greedy sack of shit."

"I want to crush her completely," Tom growled, his fury simmering just below the surface. "She's no better than he is!" His shoulders heaved with deep breaths as he fought to keep his emotions in check.

"You're right," Brian said, stepping closer and placing a calming hand on Tom's shoulder. "But acting in anger won't get us anywhere. If we're reckless, we'll all suffer for it. We need a clear plan."

Tom let out a long sigh, his tension slowly ebbing away. "Yeah… You're right, Brian. It's just so infuriating that she's exploiting this situation. Making it harder for us to help those people." He glanced around at his friends, his voice steadying. "She doesn't care that people are suffering."

"We will help them," Derek reassured him. "But we need to do it smart. An all-out attack would cost too many lives."

"Right," Tom agreed, nodding as he began to collect himself. "Okay, let's get back to planning. We'll figure something out."

James shrugged nonchalantly, his usual carefree grin plastered on his face. "Yeah, besides, it's not like things could get any worse."

Derek shot him a glare. "You complete idiot. You just had to—" His words were cut short by a deafening explosion from within the compound. Smoke and dust filled the air, and screams began to echo around them.

Derek turned to James, fury etched across his face. "You and your big fucking mouth."

Before anyone could respond, they all took off at a full sprint toward the source of the blast. When they reached the section of the wall that had been blown apart, they saw figures dressed in full black ninja gear flooding through the breach, weapons drawn and ready for combat.

"Shit! To me!" Tom shouted. "TJ, Brian, get inside and sound the alarm—again!" He immediately began casting *Summon Demonic Creature*.

A dark, swirling circle appeared on the ground, and Bron rose from the summoning portal, looking around with his usual calm but intimidating demeanor. He quickly cast the spell again, summoning Shadow to help with the fight.

"That was quick," Bron observed, his voice a deep rumble. His eyes took in the scene before him.

"Ninjas. Sneaky bastards," Tom said tersely, drawing his greatsword from his Inventory.

"Stay in the lights! Don't let them get into the shadows!" Bron said, and Tom relayed Bron's instructions to his comrades.

"You have a cat now too?!" James squealed with delight. "Omg, omg, omg, OMG! It needs to be named Jerry!"

"Its name is Shadow!" Tom shouted back, trying to focus on what was going on.

"What a fucking waste of an opportunity. Tom and Jerry really had a nice ring to it." James tsked.

"Jerry was the fucking mouse, you twat waffle," Tom replied through gritted teeth.

"Don't care. Worth it for the pun," James teased.

"Will you focus and fight?" Tom growled.

"Hehehe, time for a snack, Squirrel," James chuckled, aiming his gun at a ninja charging toward him. He fired, and the man tried to dodge but wasn't quick enough. A scream erupted as the ninja clutched his crotch, writhing on the ground. Squirrel lunged, his jaws snapping shut around the man with a sickening crunch. The scream rose to a new, desperate pitch before cutting off abruptly.

Kiera pulled out her lute, her fingers dancing over the strings as she began to play a fierce battle anthem. The sound seemed to fill the air with energy, a wave of strength coursing through their ranks.

"You have a Bard," Bron grinned, his teeth flashing as he charged into the fray with two smaller swords at the ready. "That will be very handy."

Tom felt a surge of power flow through him as he activated his newest tattoo. Mana drained from him, and his MP bar dropped, but Bron's movements became faster, more fluid and lethal. Suddenly, a barrier flashed around Tom, glowing with a sky-blue shimmer. He turned to see an assassin poised behind him, a knife aimed at his back. Jerky appeared on his shoulder, his tiny hands glowing blue as he snarled at the would-be attacker.

"No hurt master. Jerky kill!" The familiar let the barrier go and dove at the man, biting and clawing at his neck.

"Nice save, Jerky," Tom muttered, spinning to face the next threat. The ninja hesitated for a moment, and that hesitation was all Tom needed. He slashed his greatsword down, cleaving through the man's defenses.

Bron was a whirlwind of blades, cutting down every ninja that dared step into the light. He was a blur, his strikes precise and devastating, his movements enhanced by the *Tattoo of the Summoner*. Meanwhile, Jay darted in and out of the shadows, using the chaos to his advantage as he launched sneak attacks, his dagger finding vital spots with practiced ease.

"Watch your backs!" Kiera shouted from behind, her lute still strumming as she infused her allies with courage and speed. The music flowed through the battlefield, lifting spirits and driving them forward with renewed vigor.

Bron and Tom fought side by side, a synchronized dance of destruction and fury. Every swing of Tom's greatsword cleared space, and every stab and slice from Bron severed limbs or took lives. The ninjas were quick and well-trained, but they weren't prepared for the unrelenting onslaught from the Vanguard Guild.

More ninjas poured through the shattered wall, but they were met with a barrage of bullets from the Vanguard security team and spells from their mages. The compound erupted into a full-scale battle, with fighters clashing everywhere.

The chaos was all-consuming, and yet there was an odd clarity in it. Tom knew, despite everything, they were in their element. They had been pushed into a corner, but the corner was where they fought best.

James fired off another shot, this time catching a ninja in the shoulder. "Fucking hell," he muttered as he reloaded. "This is just getting started."

Bron let out a battle cry that reverberated through the battlefield, a primal sound that sent shivers down the spines of enemies and allies alike. "Vanguard! Push them back! Leave none standing!"

Tom grinned, feeling the fire of battle burn within him. "We're not going down today," he shouted to his comrades. "Today, we send a message. Vanguard isn't backing down from anyone!"

Jay was locked in a furious battle with one of the ninjas, their weapons clashing in a rapid exchange of blows. The two danced around each other, narrowly avoiding each other's strikes aimed at vital points. Small cuts appeared on both of them, blood dripping from their wounds as they fought to gain the upper hand. Suddenly, a dark glow surrounded Jay, and his wounds began to close. Feeling a rush of renewed strength, he pressed his attack harder, his strikes growing faster and more precise. He managed to nick the back of the ninja's arm with a sharp slash.

The ninja staggered, his face twisting in pain and shock. For a few more seconds, he tried to fight, his movements becoming more sluggish. Then, he collapsed to the ground, his body going limp from blood loss.

"Ha! Brachial artery, bitch. Can't keep fighting if that gets clipped!" Jay taunted the fallen body. "Thanks for the assist, Tom!" he added, knowing it was Tom's magic that had helped him. He didn't wait for a response and vanished into the shadows, ready to find his next target.

Meanwhile, Derek had stayed close to Kiera, acting as her shield while she played her lute to buff the team. He was locked in combat with another black-clad assassin, using his shield to deflect the nimble ninja's attacks. The assassin darted around him, looking for an opening, but Derek kept his defense tight, his eyes never leaving his opponent.

Kiera saw her chance. With a quick move, she extended her foot just as the ninja lunged forward. The assassin tripped, stumbling and losing her balance and fell to the ground with a surprised cry. Derek didn't hesitate. He swung his mace down with a powerful arc, smashing it into the ninja's head with a sickening crunch, caving it in with a single strike.

Across the battlefield, Tom engaged a ninja wielding a katana. He briefly considered the irony of the weapon choice before focusing on the fight. The ninja brought his sword down in a powerful overhand strike, gripping the hilt with both hands. Tom raised his greatsword with one hand to block, his muscles straining against the force. With his free hand, he conjured a dark ball of energy, charging it with a quick incantation. He slammed the ball into the ninja's stomach, releasing the spell's power upon impact.

The force of the blast sent the ninja flying backward, crashing into a wall with enough momentum to crack the stone. The assassin slumped to the ground, his body crumpled and lifeless.

"Fantastic strategy, Tom!" Bron called out from where he was fending off two more ninjas. Another lay dead at his feet, blood pooling around the body.

Bron's movements were a blur of efficiency and deadly precision. With one fluid motion, he twisted his body to the side, both of his blades sweeping across his attackers. The sudden shift in movement caught both ninjas off guard, throwing them off balance. Bron continued his spin, dragging his blades through their midsections in a swift, lethal cut. Blood sprayed from their wounds as they fell, screaming in agony. Bron wasted no time, stepping forward and stabbing them both in the neck to finish them off before moving on to his next targets.

"Damn. He sure is efficient," Tom muttered, watching Bron with awe. Beside him, Jerky nodded, his eyes wide with admiration for Bron's prowess.

A bolt suddenly whizzed out of the darkness, aimed directly at Tom's head. Before he could react, another shimmering blue shield appeared around him, deflecting the bolt. Jerky, perched on Tom's shoulder, had his tiny hands raised, glowing with the protective magic he'd just cast.

"Whoa! Thanks, buddy. That was close!" Tom said, reaching up to give Jerky a scratch behind his small horns.

Turning to locate where the bolt had come from, Tom heard the distinct crack of a gunshot from behind him. He spun around just in time to see an assassin fall out of the shadows, first dropping to his knees, then collapsing face-first onto the ground, a dark pool of blood spreading beneath him.

Tom looked back and saw a group of twelve security guards, all armed with assault rifles, lined up and aiming at the battlefield.

"Fire at the enemy!" TJ shouted from beside the guards, his own weapon aimed at a group of ninjas near Bron.

The air erupted with the deafening sound of rapid gunfire as the guards advanced, bullets ripping through the remaining assassins. Bron leapt out of the line of fire, moving with the grace of a seasoned warrior. Within seconds, the assassins were cut down, their bodies riddled with bullets.

A return volley of crossbow bolts raced out of the shadows in various places, several finding their marks in the security team. More cries rang out as assassins died from the shots. Three security guards were down from the bolts, but the others continued firing at the shadows.

TJ held up a hand, and the firing ceased.

"Really getting that training down, I see. Nice job, TJ!" Tom called out, impressed by the coordinated effort.

The guards still standing fanned out on TJ's signal, methodically sweeping the area for any remaining enemies. Once they confirmed the perimeter was clear, they regrouped near Tom and the others.

Derek was already attending to the wounded security guards. One had been unfortunate enough to take a bolt to the throat. Derek swore at the loss.

"Perimeter secured," TJ reported. "I'll go get someone to begin repairs on the wall immediately." He turned and sprinted toward the Guild building to organize the cleanup.

"Great work, everyone. We showed them not to mess with us!" Tom said, his voice filled with pride.

"We showed them that we weren't really ready," Derek countered, his tone more cautious.

"What do you mean? We took them out pretty fast," Tom asked, frowning in confusion.

"They still managed to get close enough to blow up part of the wall and we lost a member of the security team. That shouldn't have happened. We need more people on duty for watch," Derek replied, his eyes lingering on the gaping hole and the smoking piles of rubble before dropping to the body of the guard. "And we can't lose more people."

"We can't be everywhere," Jay added, wiping sweat from his brow. "But we should have people inside the compound, too, in case someone slips through. They could sound the alarm quicker."

"Good thought." Derek nodded. "I'll make that happen."

"That bitch!" Kiera suddenly cried out, her face flushed with anger.

"We know," Tom said, trying to calm her down. "But we have to deal with The Master first. Those poor slaves are our priority."

"I know, but I really want to rip her head off," Kiera muttered through gritted teeth. "You don't have any quests that require you to kill her, do you?"

"No," Tom replied with a small smile that didn't quite reach his eyes. "I'll leave that for you if you really need it."

"Good. Gonna be a good old-fashioned ass whooping!" Kiera grinned, punching one fist into her other open palm. Her grin faded when she looked at the body of their fallen Guildmate.

Tom walked over to the man who had tried to shoot him and picked up his crossbow. "Why would he use a crossbow when a gun was available?" Tom asked, inspecting the weapon.

"Because they are assassins," Bron answered simply, walking up behind him. "Those items you call guns create a flash when fired. The light would expose them in the dark."

"Well, this gives me an idea," Tom said, his mind already racing with possibilities. "But we'll have to plan carefully. Once we're ready, it'll be time to pay The Master a little visit."

A new determination could be seen in the Warlock's eyes.

Chapter 26

Shopping

Tom explained his plan to the team, and over the next couple of weeks, the Guild set it into motion. The first step involved forming a specialized team of Rogues, handpicked for their stealth and agility. Jay took the lead, personally overseeing their training. Every day, they ventured out to battle monsters as a tactical unit, honing their Skills in the hidden arts and perfecting their stealth-based combat techniques. Jay drilled them relentlessly, teaching them how to move silently, strike with precision, and blend into the shadows, making them a formidable force for the upcoming conflict.

While the Rogues were undergoing their intense training, Tom and the other strike teams focused on refining their own strategies. They also went out regularly to practice their party formations and battle tactics, ensuring every member knew their role in a fight and could adapt to changing situations. Derek, Kiera, and Kevin each led different teams, coordinating with Tom to simulate real battle scenarios. They practiced ambushes, defensive maneuvers, and counterattacks, all designed to prepare them for the chaos of war.

Bron also spent time with Tom, helping him refine his sword Skills through focused, hands-on drills. He corrected Tom's stance, emphasizing the importance of balance and weight distribution during both offense and defense. They ran through countless footwork exercises—tight pivots, advancing steps, and retreating guards—until Tom's movements became instinctive rather than reactive. Bron stressed the importance of timing over brute strength, teaching him how to bait opponents into overcommitting and then punishing their mistakes with precise counters.

The efforts paid off. By the end of this rigorous period of preparation, everyone saw significant progress. Derek reached level twenty-three, his shield skills becoming even more formidable as he mastered new defensive techniques. James, who was always eager for a fight, pushed himself and his bond with Squirrel further, reaching level twenty-two. Tom, who had been leading both by example and through his dedication to training, achieved level twenty-six, a milestone that filled him with confidence.

The entire group selected for the upcoming mission had leveled up to at least level twenty. As Tom reviewed his stat sheet, he felt a surge of satisfaction. He had put in the work, and it showed. The Guild was shaping up to be a well-oiled machine, ready to tackle whatever challenges lay ahead.

He knew they were going to need every bit of that strength and skill in the days to come.

Tom Harris	
Race: Human	**Class:** Warlock
Level: 26	**Total XP:** 826,450
XP To Next Level: 66,550	**HP:** 450/450
MP: 470/470	**SP:** 330/330
Attributes:	**Unused Attributes Points:** 0
Strength: 40	**Constitution:** 45
Dexterity: 30	**Endurance:** 33
Intelligence: 47	**Wisdom:** 40
Charisma: 85	**Luck:** 20
Non-Combat Skills:	
Inspect	**Level:** 10 **Rank:** Novice
Combat Skills:	
Vehicular Homicide	**Level:** 22 **Rank:** Initiate
Swords	**Level:** 15 **Rank:** Novice
Summon Demonic Creature	**Level:** 16 **Rank:** Novice
Fear	**Level:** 10 **Rank:** Novice
Corruption	**Level:** 10 **Rank:** Novice
Spells:	
Eldritch Blast	**Level:** 12 **Rank:** Novice
Dark Ball	**Level:** 8 **Rank:** Beginner
Dark Healing	**Level:** 11 **Rank:** Novice
Lightning Strike	**Level:** 6 **Rank:** Beginner
Doppelganger	**Level:** 4 **Rank:** Beginner
Dark Flame Weapon	**Level:** 7 **Rank:** Beginner
Final Flash	**Level:** 4 **Rank:** Beginner
Tattoos:	
Tattoo of Brute Strength	Tattoo of Life Absorption
Tattoo of Magic Nullification	Tattoo of the Summoner

His Skills and spells were improving as well, with most of them advancing beyond the beginner rankings. Feeling confident with the progress they'd made, Tom gathered everyone from the strike teams, as well as Jay's special team, in the gym for a crucial meeting. He wanted to share some important information he'd learned from Bob about the vending machines.

"I know we've mentioned this before," Tom began, addressing the assembled group, "but it's time we really put it into practice. The vending machines can do so much more than we've been using them for. When you place your hand on the machine, it reads your Class. But here's what many people don't realize: you can take your hand off the machine and still use the menus to search for other items to purchase. We're going to take full advantage of that today."

As he spoke, Tom could see realization dawning on the faces of those gathered. Many of them exchanged looks, now understanding what they had been missing out on.

"Yeah, you can feel like an idiot later," Tom said with a slight smile. "Right now, we have work to do. I want everyone to spend some time today getting the best gear you can. We need to be as prepared as possible if we want this plan to work. I won't lie to you—it's not going to be easy, and I can't guarantee anyone's safety. But we chose you because you are the most prepared, the ones who can handle the toughest challenges. We've invested this time and effort because we believe you have what it takes. We're going to end this one way or the other."

The determination on everyone's faces grew as Tom's words sank in, a fire of resolve sparking in their eyes.

Earlier that day, Tom had gone to the vending machine with Bob, Derek, and James to test this process out. When he placed his hand on the machine, it had performed its usual scan, showing items tailored for his Class. However, these were still the basic items he'd seen every time he interacted with the machine. Curious about Bob's information, Tom removed his hand from the screen. As Bob had suggested, the display changed to a list of menus, each containing a variety of item categories.

The menus displayed categories like Armor, Weapons, Food, Parts, Potions, Poisons, and Miscellaneous. Intrigued, Tom selected "Weapons," which opened up a sub-menu with more options: Projectiles, Slashing, Piercing, Blunt, and Unconventional. With growing interest, he decided to explore the "Unconventional" category. Instantly, the machine's display changed, showing a range of unique weapons: war fans, whips, chakrams, and other exotic gear appeared on the cans.

"Whoa, that's cool!" Tom exclaimed as he scanned through the options. The war fan and chakram caught his eye, but he knew better than to go for something he wasn't trained to use.

Deciding to focus on his current specialty, Tom backed out of the "Unconventional" menu and selected "Slashing" instead. This time, another set of sub-menu options appeared: Sword, Greatsword, Dagger, Sickle, Axe, Greataxe, Spear, Polearm, Swallow, and more. As his eyes landed on "Swallow," he paused and selected it, curious about what would appear.

The machine changed once again, revealing a weapon that looked like two sword blades connected at their pommels to form a single, double-bladed sword.

"Oh, cool! It's like Darth Maul's saber!" Tom said, clearly impressed by the find.

"You'll kill yourself with that before you kill anyone else," Derek interjected with a smirk. "If you haven't trained with it, don't pick an exotic weapon just because it looks cool."

"Yeah, you're right," Tom conceded with a sigh. "It does look badass, though." He sulked for a moment, still staring longingly at the weapon, before returning to the menu and selecting "Greatsword."

The machine changed once more. This time, it displayed five different options. Tom carefully examined each choice, reading through their descriptions. He decided on option F4, a well-balanced greatsword that seemed perfectly suited for his needs.

After confirming his selection, he deposited what amounted to one hundred and fifty-six common cores into the machine. A can was dispensed from the slot at the bottom, and Tom quickly grabbed it. He popped the can open, eager to see what his new weapon would be like. After the initial *chhhttssssss* sound of the can opening and the smoke cleared, Tom was holding a beautiful greatsword that looked like it had just come out of an anime.

Item: Greatsword of Hell's Inferno
The **Greatsword of Hell's Inferno** is an imposing weapon. It emanates an eerie heat even when dormant. The blade's edge is razor-sharp, designed to cleave through armor and bone with terrifying efficiency. At the pommel is a spiked sun, a cruel emblem that doubles as a brutal bludgeoning tool, adding extra punishment to strikes and pommel slams. The crossguards not only provide balance and protection but also serve as a visual representation of the sword's fiery power. When *Dark Inferno* is activated, the crossguards also appear to flicker with a dark, mesmerizing glow, enhancing the weapon's menacing appearance. This sword is not just a weapon but a statement—of raw power, chaos, and the relentless fury of hellfire. Wielded by a true master, it has the potential to turn the tide of battle and leave enemies scorched and terrified in its wake.

Item Type:	Weapon, Slashing, Two-handed
Durability:	2500/2500
Attack:	35-50
Item Quality:	Excellent
Item Rarity:	Epic

<table>
<tr><td colspan="2">Weapon Ability: Dark Inferno - Activating Dark Inferno causes the blade to be engulfed in dark, writhing flames, inflicting additional Dark and Fire damage to any target it strikes. The dark flames spread like a wildfire upon impact, potentially setting enemies ablaze for ongoing damage over time. This ability consumes mana to activate and maintain.</td></tr>
<tr><td>Open Slots:</td><td>2</td></tr>
</table>

"Hey, Bob, what does 'Open Slots' mean on a weapon?" Tom asked the old man, grateful to have him around to answer his questions.

"It means you can equip the weapon with a weapon crystal," Bob explained, moving closer to inspect the greatsword Tom was holding. "And before you ask—weapon crystals are magical stones that grant additional properties or Skills to a weapon. They should be listed in the miscellaneous category on the vending machine."

The sword Tom held was a masterpiece. Its blade, a deep crimson bordering on the color of dried blood, was both intimidating and captivating. Standing at five-and-a-half-feet tall, the weapon exuded an aura of dread and power. The pommel was shaped like a blazing sun, complete with protruding spikes that could turn even the back end of the weapon into a dangerous bludgeoning tool. The crossguards, forged in the likeness of roaring flames, curved outward in a menacing pattern, offering both aesthetic and functional flair to the hilt.

Tom marveled at the craftsmanship. He was pretty sure this was the first epic-grade item he had come across, combined with an "Excellent" crafting rank. The quality was beyond superb—it was practically flawless. He wondered what even higher-ranked items would look like if this one was already such a marvel. And with a durability of twenty-five hundred, this greatsword could take an incredible amount of punishment and still remain battle-ready.

Excited about the possibilities, Tom quickly navigated to the miscellaneous category on the vending machine and found the section for weapon crystals. As expected, there were countless options, and the machine had to categorize them into multiple lists. Two stones immediately caught Tom's eye, and he selected them. The machine adjusted once more to display his choices and their prices.

His excitement wavered for a moment as he glanced at the cost—two hundred and twenty-five Monster Cores. It was a hefty price, but Tom knew it would be worth it. With a determined nod, he confirmed the purchase and retrieved the cans from the machine. Opening them up, he found himself holding two crystals: one small, sickly green stone that seemed to swirl with a dark mist within, and another clear stone, resembling a diamond, with a faint inner glow.

He looked back at the greatsword in his hand, focusing on the "Open Slots" in its description. His mind raced with the potential these crystals could unlock.

<table>
<tr><td colspan="2" align="center">Weapon Item Slots:</td></tr>
<tr><td colspan="2">

Available Weapon Slots: 2

Would you like to equip a weapon crystal to the Greatsword of Hell's Inferno?

Please select a crystal to equip:

Slot 1: [Select Crystal]
Slot 2: [Select Crystal]

Note: Once equipped, crystals cannot be removed without breaking.

</td></tr>
<tr><td align="center">Yes</td><td align="center">No</td></tr>
</table>

Selecting "Yes," a new window popped up, displaying the two stones Tom had recently acquired: the Self Repair Weapon Stone and the Life Leech Weapon Stone. Each stone glowed faintly in the virtual menu, their descriptions hovering just beneath them.

The Self Repair Stone had a steady, soft blue shimmer, hinting at its protective, restorative properties. Meanwhile, the Life Leech Stone emitted an unsettling, dark green aura that seemed to pulse rhythmically, almost as if it had a life of its own.

Tom studied both options carefully, weighing their potential benefits in his mind before making his decision.

<table>
<tr><td colspan="2" align="center">Weapon Stone: Self Repair</td></tr>
<tr><td colspan="2">A crystal with a faint glow that seems to pulse with energy, the Self Repair Weapon Stone is a coveted gem among warriors who wish to keep their weapons in prime condition without the need for constant maintenance. When slotted into a weapon, it forms a symbiotic relationship with the blade, allowing the wielder to channel their own mana into the weapon to mend chips, cracks, and wear. The stone radiates warmth when held, and it carries the faint scent of fresh rain on stone—a reminder of its restorative properties.</td></tr>
<tr><td align="center">Item Type:</td><td align="center">Weapon Crystal</td></tr>
<tr><td align="center">Rarity:</td><td align="center">Rare</td></tr>
</table>

> **Effect:** When equipped, grants the ability to infuse the weapon with mana to repair its durability. The mana cost is proportional to the amount of durability as well as the quality of the material being restored. Note: This ability cannot be used if the weapon's durability reaches 0 and the weapon is completely broken.

Weapon Stone: Life Leech

The Life Leech Weapon Stone is a dark, sickly green crystal that seems to pulse rhythmically, almost like a beating heart. When held, it emits a faint, eerie glow, and the air around it feels cold and heavy. Slotting this stone into a weapon imbues it with a vampiric power, allowing the wielder to siphon life from their foes with every blow. The stolen life force creates a faint green mist that flows from the wound to the wielder, providing a surge of vitality. This stone is favored by those who relish sustaining themselves through their enemies' downfall, turning every clash into a chance for renewed strength.

Item Type:	Weapon Crystal
Rarity:	Rare

> **Effect:** When equipped, this stone imbues the weapon with the ability to drain a small amount of HP from an opponent with each successful strike, transferring it to the wielder. The amount of HP stolen is based on the damage dealt and has a cooldown between activations.

Tom first selected the Self Repair crystal. It appeared in one of the slots already attached to the weapon, fitting snugly into a small socket just below the blade's crossguard. Next, he chose the Life Leech crystal, and it too was inserted seamlessly into the second slot on the sword. Inspecting the greatsword again, Tom noticed two new icons beside its name: a green skull and a hammer. Focusing on them brought up descriptions of the effects of each crystal—one allowing the weapon to siphon life from his enemies, and the other enabling the sword to self-repair with mana infusion.

"Neat!" Tom exclaimed, pleased with the new additions to his weapon.

He returned to the vending machine and navigated to the armor options. He decided to upgrade to some new medium armor. Initially, he bought chainmail, thinking it would be both cool and functional. However, it turned out to be much heavier than anticipated and cumbersome to wear. The weight and restrictive nature of the armor clashed with his preferred fighting style. Fortunately, thanks to the automagic resizing provided by the System, another Guild member was happy to purchase it off him for a discount. The chainmail had a special deflection enchantment that added extra defense against projectiles, but Tom felt too restricted in it to wield his greatsword effectively.

"Why do you keep saying 'automagic' when you talk about the System's auto-resizing function for armor?" Bob asked, an eyebrow raised.

Tom chuckled. "It started when James said 'automagically' instead of 'automatically' for the resizing armor function, and it just kind of stuck. I guess it's become a bit of an inside joke."

After some trial and error, Tom settled on a more flexible and practical combination: a studded leather chest piece, metal greaves, bracers, and Kevlar pants. The other options didn't seem comfortable or appealing to him, and he didn't want to end up looking ridiculous in mismatched gear.

"In video games, we always wore whatever gave the best stats," James commented, noticing Tom's choices. "Why not pick those?"

"Because I don't want to look like I'm wearing a skirt with some of the best pants options," Tom retorted, raising an eyebrow.

James grinned. "Okay, but what if it's a kilt? You know, freeballing?" he teased.

Tom rolled his eyes. "No, these pants are fine. They may not stop a real bullet, but they should at least offer some protection against a blade. Now, quit bugging me about it. This is what I want."

"Fine, fine. Touchy much?" James laughed, backing off.

Tom continued browsing and decided to purchase a pair of steel-toed tactical boots for added protection and durability. With some cores left over, he picked up a few mana, stamina, and health potions. For added security, he also bought a Colt 1911, costing him another hundred and fifty cores, along with four magazines and two thousand rounds of ammunition.

"Can't be too safe. Everyone needs at least one gun in their Inventory," Derek said, nodding in approval.

"Is there anything else I might need?" Tom asked, feeling like he might be missing something.

"There's always more you could use, but let's focus on combat for now. How about some knuckle dusters?" Derek suggested.

"I don't even know where to find those in the menu," Tom said, staring at the vending machine's screen.

"Just ask it for what you want, assuming you know the name of the specific item," Bob chimed in from the corner of the room, his attention still on the book he was reading.

"Really? Hey, vending machine, can you show me knuckle dusters?" Tom spoke hesitantly to the machine.

"Just say, 'Show me knuckle dusters,'" Bob corrected without looking up, turning another page.

Even with Tom's awkward phrasing, the machine understood and updated its display to show a can with an image of a dagger attached to brass knuckles.

"Holy fuck! Those look brutal!" Tom exclaimed, eyes wide at the image on the can.

"That's the point. They were used in trench warfare during World War One. Here, they'll be handy if you end up in close combat and need something vicious. I'd suggest getting two," Derek explained.

Tom made the purchase, adding the weapons to his Inventory. Satisfied for now and significantly lighter on Monster Cores, he stepped aside to let the others make their selections.

Derek chose a mace that had a single weapon stone slot but allowed him to execute an area-of-effect attack once every hour, throwing enemies away from him in all directions. It also added earth elemental damage to his strikes. Deciding to slot the mace with a stone that added additional holy damage to go with his Cleric build, he moved on. For armor, he stuck with heavier gear—metal-plated pants, gauntlets that nearly reached his elbows, a helmet, and steel-toed boots. He also picked up a 9mm Sig Sauer, several magazines, and two thousand rounds as well. He found a heater-shaped shield with a reflective Skill that could deflect attacks at the cost of stamina. Lastly, Derek also bought two of the knuckle dusters and stocked up on potions.

James, on the other hand, made some eclectic choices: an assault rifle, brass knuckles, steel-toed boots, tactical gear for maneuverability, potions, magic gloves with a Skill for steadying his hands when aiming, night vision goggles, more magazines for all his weapons, twenty thousand rounds of varying calibers, wolf treats, a tennis ball, and a spell called Hunter's Mark, which let him choose a target and gain a fifty percent accuracy boost for all his shots.

Once Tom, Derek, and James finished answering questions from the assembled group, they allowed the others to use the vending machine to make their purchases. About three hours later, everyone had a full set of upgraded gear. While not everyone's equipment matched the quality of Tom's or his core team's, it was a significant improvement from their previous setups. Tom even shared some of his cores with those who needed a bit extra to afford better items.

When everyone finished reading over their new gear's effects, Tom addressed the group once more.

"Alright, everyone. It's time to begin setting the plan in motion!" he announced, his voice filled with determination.

Chapter 27

Familiar Days

Being such a small creature in a world filled with giants was something no creature could get used to overnight. But being chosen as the familiar of a being who ruled over so many others—and whose Charisma was high enough to make those around him flock to him—had its perks.

Jerky stretched in the plush circular bed his master had gifted him for their chambers. His master had called it a dog bed, but having no idea what a dog even was, Jerky saw it simply as his master taking expert care of him.

Before arriving in this world, Jerky had lived in the plains of Alothrim. His home was a small cave buried under rocks at the base of a cliff. Life there had been a daily struggle; as one of the lowest forms of life, he had constantly fought for survival. However, Jerky had mastered the necessary strategies to stay alive, find food, and avoid antagonizing the greater creatures that roamed the land.

This new world was a paradise compared to his previous one. The skies here were clear, unlike the dark, ash-choked skies of Alothrim, where smoke rose from the tops of tall mountains in explosive displays every hour of every day. Rivers of hot, molten rock flowed through the valleys, and Jerky had seen many creatures fall into them—or be thrown in—and heard the terrible sounds of their pain. He had learned to stay hidden to avoid such a fate.

Since his arrival on this plane, Jerky had been treated like a king, as he felt he deserved. He answered only to his master, and he loved his master for the kindness shown to him. Food was given freely just because of his connection to his master, and he especially enjoyed the scratches from the music-playing female. Why didn't everyone treat him like this? He certainly deserved it.

Jerky climbed out of his bed and padded into the large, slippery room to relieve himself in the wash box. He still didn't understand why his master got so upset about this. He had seen his master excrete in the wash box, so why couldn't he?

Feeling hungry afterward, Jerky realized his master was still asleep. His master needed much more sleep than Jerky did—probably because of all the killing. Master was good at killing. He had taken down creatures far larger than himself, and Jerky truly admired his prowess in battle. His master so confident in his fighting abilities that he allowed the monsters to hurt him just to prove he wasn't invincible. Yes, his master was truly humble.

WAR

Jerky left the room he shared with his master and made his way down to the great food room. There were many places for the others to sit and eat, but the tables and chairs were too big for him. So, he headed into the food-making area to see if he could get something to eat. Once inside, he removed his invisibility and hopped up to where the food lady was working.

"Well, good morning, you tiny menace. Have you come for some breakfast?" the food female asked, her voice amused.

Jerky nodded enthusiastically, reaching out his small hands in a gesture that clearly said, "Give me food."

"Can you say 'Charlene?'" the food female asked, smiling down at him.

Jerky never understood why she wanted him to say this word. It didn't make any sense. Was it some kind of etiquette on this plane to use specific words to acquire food?

"Charlene," Jerky repeated dutifully, sitting on his haunches to show he was being patient, even though he wanted to vanish and take what he wanted.

He had tried that before, once. Unfortunately, he had slipped on some yellowish cube that had been left on a plate with an unsharpened knife beside it.

An odd weapon, he thought.

He had fallen, causing metal cooking containers to clatter to the floor, giving him away. So now he always asked. The food female seemed willing to give him what he wanted when he played along with her little games.

"Excellent! That's right, I'm Charlene, and I control the food," the food female said proudly.

She called herself Charlene? What a stupid name. Jerky was so much better. Why did this woman insist he say what she called herself before feeding him?

"Here, since you've been a good boy this morning." The food female turned and came back with a piece of raw meat.

Jerky's mouth began to water at the sight of the food. His tail began wagging of its own accord. Stupid tail. Why did it betray him so?!

He reached out eagerly, and the food female placed the meat in his hands. Diving in as though he hadn't eaten in days, Jerky tore the meat to shreds and devoured it in under a minute. His best time yet. He liked eating fast; it usually meant he would be given more food.

"Wow, you sure were hungry this morning. Here, I have a little extra for you. Try this," the food female said, bringing him a plate of reddish strips.

Jerky sniffed the new offering. It smelled good, but he had never seen it before and was wary. Why couldn't she just give him another piece of delicious meat? Getting closer, he sniffed the strips from every possible angle, finally deciding to trust the food female. He licked the end of one of the strips cautiously.

An explosion of flavor burst on the tip of his tongue in a way he had never experienced before. Without hesitation, he grabbed all the strips on the plate and shoved them into his mouth as fast as he possibly could, savoring absolutely none of it in his attempt to get as much of it as he could.

He would definitely be coming back for more of these reddish strips. Maybe there was more to this "Charlene" than he had thought.

"That's what I thought. Everyone loves bacon," the food female said, turning back to prepare food for the others who lived there now.

Bacon. That was a funny word. But he would remember it forever.

"Bacon," Jerky tried to repeat the word, but his mouth was full, so it came out as "bekking."

"Don't talk with your mouth full, Jerky. It's impolite," the food female chastised him.

Talk, don't talk—this female clearly didn't know what she wanted. Deciding he was done with her confusing rules, Jerky hopped off the counter and became invisible again as he left the great food room. Racing down the halls, he soon found his master in the metal room with the magic boxes.

The magic boxes always showed others doing things, but it was never exciting things like killing or sneaking. Another one of those who lived here now sat in a seat facing the magic boxes, just staring at them. These creatures did such odd things sometimes.

Seeing that his master was busy speaking with some of the others, Jerky turned to go. At the last moment, he noticed the sneaky male staring at him.

Strange... I'm invisible, aren't I? Jerky looked down at himself and realized he wasn't. Quickly, he vanished again and scampered out of the room.

Jerky decided he wanted to do some hunting today. He left through the main entrance when someone opened the door. There were always creatures coming and going from the home, so he just needed to leave at the same time. Once outside, he headed for the wall. Being invisible was a great way to sneak in and out of the home without being noticed. He worried that if his master needed him, he wouldn't be there, but his master could always use the mind talk to call him. His master had never used it before, but Jerky was sure he would when needed.

Traveling in this plane was so much different than his previous home. The creatures here traveled in some kind of metal box. Jerky was sure it was just to keep them safe and help them move faster, but it was incredible that his master could control such a large object with just his hands. And they insisted on having the ground covered in stone. Such strange creatures.

Moving along the stone ground, Jerky made his way to another home, where he knew small furry creatures that squeaked lived. The System called them "rats" when he *Inspected* them, but they were just fur snacks. They seemed so helpless and undeveloped, with no Skills to use. What sad, pathetic fur snacks. Moving inside through where the clear barricade had once been, now shattered on the ground, Jerky entered and began to sniff around for his next victims.

Killing the fur snacks also gave him experience. He wanted to get stronger to help his master fight, and killing the fur snacks was a good way of doing that. Today, however, there was one of the stinky, green creatures in the other home, and it was digging through some kind of box.

Master hated these green, stinky creatures. He even ran them down with his big metal box for traveling. Jerky loved it when that happened. It always left such a pretty splatter spot on the ground, and the green creatures made a funny noise that made Jerky happy when they died. His master had killed so many of the smelly, green creatures that they had begun to fear him. As they should! All should fear his master!

Jerky decided that he would help his master get rid of these creatures and would kill this one for him. Sneaking around behind the creature, he got ready to strike. Charging up an attack, he let loose his eye beams, which burned the backside of the creature, making it scream and jump into the air. It grabbed the spot Jerky had hit and turned around, glaring at him.

That's right, come and get me! Jerky thought, readying himself.

The creature, now furious, dove at him in rage, clumsily trying to grab him. Jerky simply jumped up and landed on the creature's head as it fell, using his claws to scratch at it. The creature wailed in pain, and Jerky cried out in triumph over his foe. Blood began to flow from the scratches on its head as it flailed about. Jerky was determined to destroy this creature for his master!

Suddenly, he was struck on the side by one of the creature's hands as it continued to flail in an attempt to get him off. It DARED to strike him? That would be the last mistake this creature made. Growling now in fury, Jerky got back to his feet and saw the creature charging him. Right before it reached him, Jerky activated his shield, and the creature ran face-first into the barrier.

Laughing at the creature's antics, Jerky released the shield and leapt at it, sinking his teeth into its neck.

"BLEGH!" This creature tasted horrible, and Jerky tried to spit out what was in his mouth, but the creature's blood was different. It wouldn't come out. *Oh, this awful taste is going to linger for a while.*

Meanwhile, the pathetic creature grabbed at its neck and flung itself around, spraying more of the nasty blood everywhere. Jerky knew it was going to die. It was only a matter of time; no creature lost this much blood and lived. So, he waited. As the creature began to grow tired and fell to its knees, Jerky ran at it full force and impaled the creature with his horns, finishing it off.

Another one for Master.

Climbing on top of his fallen victim, Jerky raised his hands in triumph, mimicking the stupid male's victory pose. Jerky didn't quite understand why his master kept the stupid one around, but his master seemed to like him. Jerky did, however, like the stupid one's animal companion. Sometimes, Jerky even rode the furry creature around instead of walking. Its fur was wonderfully warm, and it was quite skilled at killing. Though it seemed to have an odd preference for biting at its enemies' reproductive parts—a habit Jerky had no interest in trying himself—he was fine with it if it made the stupid male's pet happy.

With his foe defeated, Jerky was pleased to see he had gained another level. *Soon, I will be strong like Master.* Leaving the stinky body behind, he resumed his hunt for the fur snacks. After satisfying his hunger with the tasty creatures, Jerky returned to the home. He found his master preparing to go hunting as well.

Climbing up onto his master's shoulder, Jerky felt a warm, familiar scratch behind his horns. His master praised him. He must have known of Jerky's kills—his master always knew everything. Jerky's tiny heart swelled with pride. He loved his master so much.

They set out onto the stone grounds and hunted creatures for most of the day. Jerky managed to level up several more times, helping his master by activating his shields when needed and keeping him safe. He was a good familiar, a loyal companion.

When it was time to return home, they entered through the front, and his master headed straight to their room and the wash box. Jerky watched as his master got all the blood and dirt off of him. *Odd,* Jerky thought. *Blood and dirt were like badges of honor in my old plane.* Still, he jumped in with his master and washed himself as well. He wanted to show his master that he was going to be just like him someday.

Once they were clean, they went back to the great food room. Most of the others who traveled with his master were there as well. The big male. The weird male who always talked about farming. The female with the music, who was staring at some papers bound together. The sneaky one, who sat at the end, observing everyone. The one in armor, sitting across from his master with his mate. The other nice female who always had snacks for him. And the one with the red beard, next to her.

They talked for a long time while they ate, which seemed very inefficient to Jerky. If they ate faster, the food female would surely give them more. But they seemed happy with the talking, so Jerky didn't interrupt them. Instead, he moved over to the music female's lap and curled up, waiting for his master to finish his meal. She scratched his head absentmindedly while staring at the strange papers, occasionally eating a bit of her food too.

When they finished eating, they all walked out and went in different directions. His master went to the machine that held the things. Jerky watched as his master discussed his choices with the serious male and the stupid male. The old male, who knew too much, was there too. Jerky was happy to see his master getting new things—they would help him kill even more creatures!

Finally finished with the things machine, Jerky jumped onto his master's shoulders as he headed back to their room. Lying down on the bed, his master let out a deep sigh, exhausted from the day's work. Jerky wanted to show his master that he was proud of him. He nuzzled his hand and face. His master looked over, smiled, scratched him again, and gave him more praise.

Then, his master told Jerky it was time for sleep. Jerky obliged, moving to his soft, fluffy bed and settling in as his master removed his clothes and climbed into his own bed. Soon, the sound of his master's snoring filled the room, and Jerky allowed himself to drift off as well. This new life was truly amazing, and he was glad his master had found him and brought him here.

Chapter 28

Plans in Action

After much discussion and not a few arguments about the best way to handle several red flags that arose, the higher-ranking Guild members had come up with what they believed to be a decent strategy. Tom's team would stay back to monitor the plan from a strategic location. The operation had three main pillars, each playing a crucial role in creating chaos and pitting their enemies against each other.

The first pillar was what Tom had dubbed "Team Ninja." Jay would lead his group of Rogues to attack The Master's defenses. The strategy involved wearing the same black garb that Shandra's Guild's Rogues had worn during their attack on Vanguard. The goal was to make The Master believe they were from Shandra's group, causing him to think they had allied against him. This confusion would put him off balance and force him to split his attention.

The second pillar was Kiera's team of snipers. They would be positioned strategically to pick off larger zombies and other significant threats as they emerged. This team acted as insurance, providing cover for any Vanguard members needing to retreat and ensuring that no major threats went unchecked.

The third pillar was Tom's own team, waiting in reserve as backup. Their role was to sweep in and provide support as needed, ready to engage in a decisive moment to turn the tide. With these three prongs in place, along with the rest of the Guild on standby, the plan was to force a conflict between The Master and Shandra, creating what James had affectionately called a "Mexican Standoff." This would result in each enemy facing a two-front battle, rather than just focusing on Vanguard.

Brian was particularly pleased with the plan. It gave them some breathing room and leveraged their numerical advantage. However, there was still some concern about The Master and the number of zombies he might command. That wildcard element would have to be dealt with as it arose.

Preparations had been underway for two weeks, and they finally felt ready to enact the plan. Tom, Kiera, and Jay would lead their teams into position at dawn, hoping to have the sun at their backs. The Master, being the farthest east, would be forced to face the rising sun. Though Derek pointed out that zombies might not be affected by sunlight the same way as living creatures, it was still an advantage they could try to use.

"Alright, we have everyone ready to go, right?" Tom asked after they had assembled in front of the Guild building.

"They're ready, Tom. I think this is a brilliant plan. What gave you the idea?" Brian asked, stepping forward to wish everyone good luck.

"You wouldn't believe me if I told you," Tom replied, chuckling at the memory.

"Oh, come on, it can't be that bad, can it?" Brian prodded.

"Remember that show *The Office*?" Tom asked.

"The British or the American one?" Brian replied.

"The American one. *I'm* American, Brian," Tom said with mock sarcasm.

"Sure, sure. It was pretty funny, but I watched the British one first," Brian replied, wondering where this was going.

"Well, I was thinking about how we had to defend against two enemies, and then I remembered that scene where Dwight, Michael Scott, and Andy were all in the conference room pointing finger guns at each other. I started thinking about what it would take to make them focus on each other at the same time," Tom explained.

"And the idea for attacking them?" Brian continued, encouraging Tom to elaborate.

"The Master sent a wave of zombies at us just for stepping into his domain, while Shandra is like dried kindling waiting for a spark to light her ablaze. If we attack looking like Shandra's Rogues—especially in their all-black garb— The Master will think they're targeting him. He'd be foolish not to have spies watching us, and they'd see the ninjas that attacked us. If he retaliates, Shandra will be itching to show her strength and strike back. It gives us the breathing room we need," Tom explained his thought process.

"It's fucking genius. I wish I'd thought of it," Brian said, shaking his head in disbelief. "So simple. So effective. Playing off their emotions and mindsets. Bloody brilliant."

"Thank you. I appreciate that," Tom replied, beaming at the praise.

"I just wanted to wish you all good luck. You need to head out soon if you want to catch the sun at the right time," Brian said, glancing eastward.

"Right. Is everyone ready? You all know what you're doing?" Tom asked, turning to the assembled teams. "Team Ninja, your job is the most perilous. I want you all to stay on your toes and be prepared to pull out if things go sideways. Am I clear?"

"We got it, Tom. We're not looking to be heroes, just to fuck up some zombies and get the hell outta dodge," Jay replied, urging Tom to move on.

"Good. Kiera, keep an eye on their backs. The goal is zero casualties on our side," Tom ordered.

"For fuck's sake, we know what we're doing. We've only gone over this a thousand times. Let's get a fucking move on and be in position early," Kiera replied, clearly annoyed by the repeated instructions.

"Alright, alright. Sorry, I'm just worried. This all rests on me, you know," Tom said, feeling a bit irritated at being rushed.

"It's not all on you, you fucking cod. We all have to play our parts, or it won't work," Kedron interjected from behind Tom.

"Yeah, don't go hogging all the blame, shitbag. We're in this together," Jay added.

The team exchanged a few more words of encouragement before heading out, each knowing their roles and responsibilities. Tom could feel the tension but also the camaraderie among them. They were ready to make their move and, hopefully, turn the tables in their favor.

"Thanks, everyone. I truly appreciate you being in this with me. Now, MOVE OUT! GET TO YOUR POSITIONS!" Tom shouted the last part, his voice carrying over the gathered crowd to get everyone moving.

"Yeah, yeah. We're tired, not deaf, ya fucking tool," someone from Jay's team called back, and the group burst into laughter.

Jay's team moved out first, after the area had been carefully scanned for enemies. They needed to put some distance between themselves and the others to ensure they weren't seen leaving from the same location. It was clear that Jay had been training his Rogues hard; as soon as they slipped into the shadows, they seemed to disappear completely, blending into the darkness.

"Kiera, The Master's base of operations is east of here. Find a building that suits your needs and get your team ready to lay down cover fire if needed," Tom directed, turning to check that his own team was prepared.

Kiera gave a sharp nod and moved out east with four other snipers, taking care to follow a different route than Jay's team.

"Are the rest of you ready to charge in should we need it?" Tom asked, looking at the assembled fighters.

"You just say the word, and we'll fuck some shit up," Kedron replied, a grin on his face.

Tom had reassembled his team from the Grand Canyon trip but had added Zach and Isaac as sub-commanders, each leading their own teams. In Jay's place, Tom had recruited a new member from Albuquerque named Michael. A tall, well-muscled man with a massive beard, he'd shaved the sides of his head, leaving a strip of hair that ended in a bun on top. Michael wielded two battleaxes and cut an imposing figure. He looked like a Viking warrior from legend, and his mere presence was intimidating.

Michael had approached Tom after hearing about the plan to take on The Master and volunteered to help.

"So, today, we get to pay that fucker back for what he did to those he enslaved?" Michael asked, walking up to Tom with his axes resting over his shoulders.

"If everything goes according to plan. But in my experience, no plan holds up completely in the end. So be ready to give them hell," Tom said, appreciating Michael's fierce attitude.

"That suits me just fine. The man is a coward. He deserves to be put down," Michael replied, his voice steady and determined.

"Well, yeah, I agree, but I need to be the one to kill him. So, if he shows his face, try to save the killing blow for me," Tom explained, making sure everyone knew the priority.

Tom couldn't help but feel slightly intimidated by Michael. The man was a mountain of muscle and always dead serious.

I'm glad he's on our side. I'd hate to run into him in a dark alley, Tom thought to himself.

"Shouldn't be a problem. If the bastard shows his face, we'll clear a path for you," Michael replied, still staring toward the east, already envisioning the fight ahead.

To round out his team, Tom had also brought in a Cleric named Donovan. Donovan was known for his focus on healing, and he came highly recommended by Chris from the beta team. Donovan had proven invaluable in keeping his team alive during skirmishes with the city's roaming monsters. Tom would have liked to have more cover fire, but Derek pointed out that Kiera's team already covered that angle.

Meanwhile, every other Guild member able to fight was on standby in the courtyard of the compound, ready to reinforce if things went south. For now, they stayed inside to avoid arousing suspicion by appearing like a prepared army.

Tom paused for a moment, closing his eyes. He took a deep breath of the cool morning air, steadying himself for what lay ahead. Opening his eyes, his resolve was set.

"Alright, let's move out. It's time we paid The Master back for his actions," Tom said with determination.

"Yeah, float like a butterfly, stings when I pee," James added, moving up to stand on Tom's other side.

Everyone turned to stare at James in horror and confusion.

"Oh, come on! Just trying to lighten the mood. You all are way too serious," James scoffed, unbothered by their reactions.

"Just when I think you can't surprise us, you say something stupid like that," Tom chuckled, shaking his head with a smile. "Thanks for being the light for the team."

"Hey, someone has to keep you all from being a bunch of sourpusses. Happy to do my job so well," James replied, a huge grin spreading across his face.

"Alright, let's get moving. We need to get into position too. We'll hide out Where we can view the gates to see if we're needed. Today, we set in motion a series of events that will change this city. It's the start of our war," Tom said solemnly, leading his team eastward.

The teams picked up the pace as soon as they exited the compound, moving at a jog toward The Master's base. They stayed close to the buildings, keeping out of sight to avoid drawing attention. When they reached the final corner before the compound, they stopped and waited.

The plan was simple: if something went wrong, any member of Jay's team had a scroll of Fireball to launch into the air as a signal. Kiera's team was also on the lookout; if they saw a need to intervene, they'd use gunfire from the rooftops as a secondary signal.

Tom peeked around the corner, his eyes narrowing on the gates in the distance. The Master had repaired them, making entry more challenging, but TJ had provided another set of C4 to blast through if necessary.

"So, this is where that bloody fuckwit lives," Zach said, moving up beside Tom to get a look.

"Yeah, it's a maze once you're inside. Shoddy buildings everywhere with barbed wire forcing you down certain paths. Be ready for that; it's not a straight shot," Tom explained.

"No worries, mate. We'll move that shit out of the way when we get in. Phillip can use *Mage Hand* to clear the wire, and the buildings will give us good cover," Zach replied, still studying the walls and gate.

Phillip was a magic user in Zach's party with a vast repertoire of spells. He had been invaluable around the Guild, using his *Mage Hand* to assist with various tasks. Though the spell had weight limits, barbed wire was light enough to be managed.

As they continued to watch, Tom saw Jay and his team emerge from the shadows, swinging grappling hooks over the eastern section of the wall. The Rogues climbed the wall in unison, dropping silently on the other side. A tense silence followed as everyone waited for what came next.

The air was thick with anticipation. Then, the quiet was shattered by the sounds of fighting from within the compound. It had begun.

Chapter 29

Sneaky Sneak

Jay moved swiftly, activating his *Stealth* Skill the moment he slipped into the shadows outside of the Vanguard Guild building. Ever since Tom had shared the plan, Jay had been relentlessly training his stealth abilities. The plan was brilliant—create confusion among their enemies and buy Vanguard some breathing room. For this to work, stealth kills were vital, and Jay had drilled this relentlessly into the heads of the Rogues in his squad. Understanding that their part of the plan was the most critical, he had pushed his team extra hard to be ready.

During their initial meetings, Jay had shared everything he knew about Rogue Skills and how to maximize their stealth potential. He taught them to combine Skills like *Stealth* and *Camouflage* to stack bonuses for hiding from the enemy. Then, he covered techniques like *Backstab* and the damage multipliers granted by attacking from *Stealth*. He had even found a training dummy in the vending machine and bought it to help train recruits on striking critical areas for maximum damage.

Jay had also trained them in the use of various weapons and tools from the art of ninjutsu, ensuring they could climb walls, lay traps, disarm traps, and wield the most effective weapons for stealth. They practiced with throwing stars for projectiles, smoke bombs for quick escapes, daggers, short swords, kama, and punch blades. One member had even suggested silencers for handguns—a suggestion Jay was so impressed by that he insisted everyone buy one with their Monster Cores as a backup ranged weapon for assassinations.

The team committed themselves fully to the training. They stayed out late for night attacks on monsters, got up early to train in the shifting shadows of dawn, and used every spare moment to sharpen their Skills. Jay was proud of the dedication they showed to their craft and the experience each one gained from it.

Now, they were about to put all of that training to the ultimate test.

As they approached the wall of The Master's base, each Rogue pulled out their grappling hooks. With ropes securely fastened, they silently climbed up and over the wall. The sun had just started to peek over the horizon, casting amber and pink hues across the landscape. As it rose higher, the sunlight would shine directly into the compound, giving them an advantage with the mix of blinding light and lengthening shadows.

Dropping softly into a crouch on the other side of the wall, the team checked for any signs of movement. Seeing none, they activated their *Stealth Skills* and moved away from the wall to the nearest cluster of buildings at the base's edge.

Jay used hand signals to give his orders—stay close, watch for enemies, keep your eyes and ears open. Follow my lead, but don't group up. The Rogues nodded in understanding, spreading out to several buildings within sight of Jay, awaiting further commands.

Peering around the corner of a dilapidated building, Jay scanned the area. Satisfied, he motioned for them to move forward. The team advanced toward the main building, hopping over barbed wire and darting from cover to cover. As the sun climbed, Jay spotted the shambling figures of zombies on guard duty near the main base. He signaled two of his team members to flank them.

The two Rogues silently moved into position, and in a well-coordinated attack, one Rogue stabbed a zombie in the back of the head while the other slashed another's throat, preventing it from screaming. With a quick follow-up strike, the zombie's head rolled to the ground.

Jay flashed a congratulatory hand signal from the shadows. Just then, two more zombies rounded the corner of the main building, spotting their fallen comrades. Jay leaned around his cover and fired his silenced handgun, dispatching both with clean headshots, the shots making nothing more than a muffled "pew."

Wasting no time, the team approached the main building. The large wooden doors were shut, with windows on either side. They crouched below the window sills, waiting for Jay's signal.

With a nod, Jay motioned to breach the doors. In one fluid motion, they burst inside as Jay launched several smoke bombs from a small device strapped to his left forearm.

"Stormcrushers say hello, motherfuckers!" Jay shouted as he followed up with several shurikens, embedding them in the heads of zombies milling about inside.

The rest of the team took their shots and then began backing out of the main door. As the smoke filled the room, zombies began pouring out, followed by a man with glasses—someone Jay recognized from his earlier surveillance attempts.

"Mistress Shandra will rule this whole town in the name of Stormcrusher!" Jay continued, laying it on thick to make sure the deception took hold.

"KILL THEM! KILL THE INVADERS THAT DARE ATTACK US!" the man with glasses shrieked, directing the zombie horde.

Jay and his team continued their tactical retreat, taking shots at the zombies while falling back. Switching to short swords, they prepared to engage in melee as the first wave reached them. Smoke screens were deployed to further obscure the enemy's vision, making it harder for the zombies to land a hit.

A shot zipped past Jay's head, and the zombie next to him dropped with half its skull blown away.

"There she is," Jay muttered with a smile, knowing Kiera and her team were in position and providing cover.

"Time for the strategic retreat!" Jay called out, decapitating another zombie as he spoke.

As they began to fall back, one Rogue got overwhelmed, his screams piercing the air as the zombies piled on top of him, clawing and biting.

"STEVE!" another Rogue shouted in anguish.

"We can't help him! There are too many! We have to get back, or we'll all end up like Steve!" Jay barked, his voice sharp and commanding. "Fuck!" Jay screamed, locking eyes with Steve, who'd barely managed to push himself partially free of the piling undead. "I fucking *hate* zombies!" Jay raised his crossbow, the knot in his throat hot and tight.

"Do it, you bastard!" shouted Steve. "Don't let me become one of these fucking things!"

Jay's chest hitched, his eyes somehow both soft and filled with a steely resolve.

"The head is the fucking weak spot," Jay growled.

He pulled the trigger.

The team members' shoulders slumped when the crossbow bolt buried itself into Steve's forehead, his own emotions forming a tight knot in his stomach. They broke away and sprinted back to the outer wall, ready to make for Shandra's Guild building. The zombies, slowed by their decayed bodies, gave chase, but the Rogues were faster. Reaching the wall, they used a second set of grappling hooks to climb up, pulling the ropes up after them to prevent pursuit.

"To the gate, you fucking buffoons! After them!" the man with glasses screamed, ordering the zombies to move toward the gate.

Thankfully, Tom had warned Jay to ensure his team carried nothing that could be traced back to Vanguard. While he regretted losing Steve, Jay knew this was necessary for the greater good. Reaching the ground on the other side, they bolted for the gates and ran straight toward where Tom's forces lay in wait.

Suddenly, arrows started raining down from the walls, forcing the Rogues to weave in a zig-zag pattern to avoid getting hit.

"Where did a fucking zombie learn to shoot a damn bow?!" Jay growled as they darted back and forth.

Looking back, Jay saw zombie goblins on top of the walls, fumbling with bows and arrows. One particularly clumsy goblin accidentally released its bowstring without an arrow, sending its own arm flying across the road.

The disembodied arm smacked one of Jay's teammates in the back of the head. The Rogue cried out in alarm, only to realize it wasn't an arrow piercing his skull. He tore the arm off his clothing, tossing it away in disgust.

Another pathetic zombie moan echoed behind them, but Jay pushed forward, spotting Tom waiting around a corner ahead. Tom nodded once before pulling back behind cover. Jay picked up his pace, knowing everything hinged on the next few moments.

Chapter 30

Shooty Shoot

Kiera had taken her four recruits to the top of a building in the middle of the city, turning it into their training ground. She drilled them relentlessly on everything they needed to know to unlock the *Marksman* Skill—a vital ability that improved accuracy with any ranged weapon, whether it be a gun, a bow and arrow, or even a simple rock.

The city was still and quiet, with only the occasional distant noise of some unseen creature echoing off the buildings. This eerie calm provided the perfect backdrop for their training. The team could focus entirely on the task at hand—honing their Skills to perfection. Once each of them had unlocked the Skill, training became a matter of practice and repetition. They would sit atop the building, patiently waiting for monsters or wandering enemies to come within range. When they did, the recruits would pick them off one by one, steadily gaining experience and confidence.

However, Kiera knew that relying solely on ranged attacks would be a significant liability. There was always the possibility of getting caught in close quarters, where a sniper rifle or even a handgun would be less effective. She didn't want her team to be sitting ducks if that happened. To prepare them for such situations, she took them to Graham, the Guild's combat instructor, for training in hand-to-hand combat and techniques for quickly dispatching enemies with various weapons.

Graham, a seasoned fighter with years of experience, was an exceptional teacher. He broke each technique down to the basics—footwork, positioning, and awareness—before moving on to more advanced techniques. He didn't just cover the fundamentals and worked individually with each recruit to determine their natural affinities and preferences, tailoring their training regimens accordingly.

Tina, for instance, gravitated toward daggers. Her lithe, nimble form naturally fit a dexterity build. She was quick on her feet, able to dodge and weave around opponents, making her an ideal candidate for close-quarter combat. Graham honed in on this, teaching her the importance of positioning and timing to maximize the effectiveness of her strikes. After borrowing Jay's training dummy—because why buy her own?—Tina became adept at targeting vital areas with her blades, turning her into a deadly force in melee combat. She practiced every day, her movements becoming more fluid, her strikes more precise.

Dale, on the other hand, took to the sword like a fish to water. He was a solid, well-built young man with a natural aptitude for defensive and offensive maneuvers. He trained directly with Graham, who put him through the paces with rigorous sparring sessions. Graham consistently bested Dale in their matches, but he always provided feedback on what Dale could improve. Dale took the lessons to heart, diligently practicing his forms, repeating each motion until it was second nature. His determination paid off. He even joined a few scouting missions to test his skills against actual monsters, learning how to adapt to different situations and enemy types. He quickly became one of the most dependable fighters in Kiera's team.

Scott went with the axe. Graham noticed that Scott's natural movement style—his gait, his posture, even the way he approached an opponent—was more suited to the powerful, sweeping motions of an axe. Scott took to it immediately, wielding the weapon with brutal efficiency. His powerful build allowed him to deliver crushing blows, and he quickly learned how to use his momentum to his advantage. He worked tirelessly on refining his strikes, making each swing more devastating than the last. Scott's dedication and raw power made him a valuable asset, capable of holding the line or dealing significant damage to tougher enemies.

Janice, however, was the most challenging to equip. She lacked Tina's agility and finesse and wasn't as strong as Scott or Dale. But she had an uncanny knack for precision and targeting. She could hit her mark with remarkable accuracy and lock onto a target faster than anyone else on the team. Sensing an opportunity, Graham asked her a series of seemingly unrelated questions—about her hobbies, interests, and background. The next day, he brought her an unusual weapon—a whip tipped with tiny steel blades.

Janice was skeptical at first. Her face clearly stated that she felt like the idea of using a whip was impractical.

Graham took no notice of her skepticism and started her off with the basics, teaching her how to crack a non-bladed whip safely. She picked up the basics quickly. Then he advanced to more specialized techniques: targeting specific areas, controlling the whip's path, and even using the whip to disarm an opponent. He taught her how to twist the whip to strike from different angles, how to use her body to shift the whip's momentum fluidly from one strike into the next, and how to maximize the damage dealt by those tiny blades at the tip.

Graham set up a series of fruits on tables and chairs, then gave Janice an order in which to hit them. She focused, locking onto each target with laser-like precision. One by one, the fruits exploded in quick succession, each hit punctuated by the sharp crack of the whip. The other team members watched in awe. The whip was perfect for her. Not only could she keep her distance, but she could also deal damage with incredible precision, much like her sniper shots.

With her team now proficient in both close and ranged combat, Kiera wanted to ensure they could also handle mid-range threats. She took them out for practice, equipping them with shotguns, handguns, and assault rifles. The task was simple: engage monsters using only these weapons while maintaining a safe distance, all without the backup of melee fighters. This training scenario was more challenging. They had to manage distance carefully, conserving ammunition while ensuring they weren't overwhelmed. Fortunately, only one instance required them to switch to melee weapons, and, in retrospect, Kiera was glad it happened. It provided invaluable experience transitioning from ranged to close-quarters combat.

While the team continued their training, Kiera went scouting. She moved stealthily from rooftop to rooftop, avoiding detection as she searched for the perfect vantage point around The Master's base. She knew they needed a building that offered both elevation and cover—a place where they could see without being seen. After several hours, she found the perfect spot: a tall building with a concrete wall and railing at the roof's edge. It had the perfect line of sight over the compound without exposing them too much. She noted the location, memorized the layout, and returned to brief her team.

On the day of the operation, Kiera led her team swiftly but carefully to their designated building, making sure to stay out of sight. When they arrived, she cursed under her breath—a group of goblins had taken up residence inside.

"Shit. Alright, looks like we have to do some pest control before we can get to the roof," Kiera said, assessing the situation. "Dale, you and Scott take the lead with your weapons to keep the goblins at bay. Tina, Janice, and I will follow with mid-range weapons to cover your backs. Head for the stairs to the roof and stay alert."

The team nodded, understanding the stakes. Dale and Scott took point, equipping their sword and axe. They moved quietly, approaching the first group of goblins near the front doors. Kiera, Janice, and Tina followed closely behind, handguns drawn. As they reached the entrance, Dale and Scott attacked. Their blades cleaved through the first goblins, their screams echoing through the building. The noise drew more goblins, who burst through the doors, spewing angry curses.

"Light 'em up!" Kiera shouted, and the three women opened fire with their handguns. The goblins, caught off guard, fell in a hail of bullets, their bodies piling up at the entrance.

With the first floor clear, the team quickly moved through the building, racing for the stairwell in the back. They reached it without further incident and began climbing, moving quickly but carefully. Reaching the third floor, a goblin entered the stairwell from a side door. Kiera fired, instantly taking it down, but the noise alerted the other goblins.

More goblins flooded into the stairwell from the second floor, charging upward to meet the intruders. With enemies approaching from both directions, Kiera, Tina, and Janice swiftly switched to melee weapons. In the narrow confines of the stairwell, only two goblins could attack at a time, a bottleneck that worked in their favor. With a combination of swift strikes and well-placed attacks, they cleared the stairwell, pushing their way up floor by floor.

Seven flights later, they burst onto the roof. Kiera immediately ordered them to barricade the door with a steel pipe they found lying on the roof. The door opened inward, and the handle was a lever, so they could effectively lock the goblins out for a short time, at least.

They quickly moved to the edge of the roof, crouching behind a waist-high concrete wall topped with a railing. Setting up their rifles, they sighted in on The Master's base and began scanning for Jay and his team.

"There they are," Janice said, spotting Jay's team dropping over the wall.

"Good. We're not too late," Kiera replied, her voice calm but intense. She watched as Jay's team moved with precision from building to building, taking out zombies in their path with brutal efficiency.

"Do we kill them so they have a clear path?" Tina asked, her rifle trained on a pair of zombies ahead of Jay's team.

"No," Kiera answered, keeping her scope steady. "The gunfire would give us away. We only interfere if they start getting overwhelmed or if any big baddies show up."

Jay's team worked like a well-oiled machine, efficiently dispatching zombies. As they reached the main building's doors, Jay fired smoke bombs inside. The Rogue's voice rang out over the courtyard, echoing off the dilapidated buildings.

"Stormcrushers say hello, motherfuckers!" The declaration was followed by shuriken whizzing through the air, embedding themselves in the heads of several zombies.

Zombies began to pour out of the building like a flood, surging toward Jay's team. Kiera waited, finger on the trigger, ready for the right moment. Jay's team met the first wave with a coordinated attack—silent blades and quick movements taking down zombies with minimal noise. Then, more zombies emerged, this time from around the corner of the main building.

They were beginning to get overwhelmed.

Kiera exhaled slowly and squeezed the trigger. A shot rang out, and a zombie's head exploded right next to Jay. He didn't flinch, already knowing what it meant—Kiera and her team had his back. Immediately, the other snipers took their cue and began firing, their shots precise, each one dropping a zombie before they even realized they were under attack.

"They're getting closer," Tina muttered, lining up her next shot.

Jay's team began to pull back, but one of their own, Steve, got surrounded. Zombies piled on top of him as he let out a scream, buried under the weight and claws of the undead.

"STEVE!" one of the other Rogues shouted, panic in his voice.

"We can't help him; there are too many. If we try, we'll all end up like Steve!" Jay shouted back, the frustration clear in his voice. His barely carried to Kiera's location. The Rogue's shoulders slumped, but it was clear he knew Jay was right.

Tears pricked at Kiera's eyes as she watched the horrifying drama unfold in front of her. For a moment, she thought Steve would break free from the crowding zombies. She sighted down her scope, her mind whirling to work out the best target.

But then she saw the man's leg in twelve-times magnification.

It had been torn free at the knee. At the sight, she knew that Steve wouldn't be escaping from the zombies today.

"Do it, you bastard!" shouted Steve. "Don't let me become one of these fucking things!"

Her jaw clenched as she watched Jay fire off one last quarrel of mercy, before turning and sprinting away.

She only wished that she'd had the courage to take the shot herself and spare Jay the pain she knew he'd be feeling.

Kiera watched them run, her eyes darting between them and the mass of zombies giving chase. She fired off another shot, dropping a particularly fast one. "Stay focused," she reminded herself. "Pick them off, one by one."

As the team reached the wall and climbed over, she noticed goblin archers appearing along the walls of the compound. "Shit, they're using goblin zombies as archers now?" she muttered, incredulous. She took a quick shot, downing one that was aiming at Jay's back. The goblin's body slumped over, an arrow slipping from its loose grip.

The retreat was almost successful when an arm came flying through the air and hit one of Jay's men. The Rogue looked at the flailing limb with wide eyes before yanking it off and tossing it away. It was almost comical, and Kiera had to suppress a snort.

"Focus," she reminded herself again, readjusting her aim.

"Where did a fucking zombie learn to shoot a damn bow?!" She heard Jay's voice growl from below as they ran back and forth.

From their vantage point, Kiera and her team continued to provide cover fire, ensuring that Jay and the remaining Rogues could retreat to safety. Finally, Jay's team cleared the kill zone and made it back to where Tom's forces were waiting.

"Good. They made it back," Scott announced, still scanning the area with his scope.

"Perfect," Kiera said, her tone filled with satisfaction. "Now, we move to building number two and prepare for phase two. Move out!"

Without missing a beat, they packed up their gear, knowing they only had a few moments to reposition before their next part in this deadly dance began. Moving quickly and quietly, they descended the stairs, clearing out any remaining goblins that tried to slow them down.

This was it. Everything they had trained for was unfolding before their eyes. And Kiera was determined to make sure every shot counted.

The real battle was about to begin.

Chapter 31

Stabby Stab

Jay sprinted past Tom without stopping, his breath ragged but his steps purposeful. According to the plan, his team was supposed to continue west toward Stormcrusher's headquarters, leaving no trace for the zombies to follow. Their objective was clear: disappear into the shadows, creating confusion about their identity and affiliations. That's where Tom and his team came in. They needed to draw the remaining zombies' attention and buy time for Jay's group to vanish.

Tom began pulling his team back, motioning for them to shift into a more defensible position. The goal was to be in an ideal spot to intercept the approaching zombies, giving Kiera's sniper team time to set up in their second location. If everything worked out as intended, it would look like Tom's group was patrolling the area when they "encountered" the zombie horde. This way, they could keep the undead away from their base while planting the blame firmly on Shandra's shoulders.

Jay had been moving at such a breakneck speed that it took nearly a full minute before the first of the zombies appeared around the corner. The undead creatures lurched into view, their heads swiveling as they scanned the area. When they spotted Tom's team, their groans intensified, their focus locking onto their new targets. They shuffled forward with unsettling eagerness, drawn by the scent of the living.

"Hold your positions! Get ready for a good fight!" Tom shouted to his team, his voice steady despite the tension. "Kiera will have our backs shortly!"

Michael, standing beside Tom, hefted his dual axes with a gleam in his eye and a dark grin spreading across his face. "Finally! Time for some action!" he bellowed, the bloodlust evident in his voice.

Tom wasted no time, summoning Bron and Shadow, along with a Dretch whose AOE attacks could poison anything nearby. He hoped the zombies were susceptible to such an attack. As the first wave of undead closed in, a brilliant bolt of lightning cracked from the sky, striking the ground with a deafening roar. The front line of zombies disintegrated in an explosion of charred flesh and blackened bones, leaving a smoking crater behind.

"Holy fucking shit! What the damn hell was that?!" Tom exclaimed, his heart racing from the sudden blast.

"Sorry, that was me," came a weak but enthusiastic voice from the back.

Tom turned to see Briana waving at him, her face lit up with a smile so wide her eyes almost vanished into crescents. She was holding her staff with both hands, still crackling with residual energy.

"I learned some new spells, and this felt like the perfect time to use them," Briana explained, her voice trembling with excitement.

"Damn! Keep it up! That was amazing," Tom shouted back, his initial shock turning into appreciation. He turned back to face the zombies.

The front ranks, already unstable from the lightning strike, had either fallen over or stood there, stunned by the sudden assault. Those who were hit directly had been completely obliterated. The others, slowly recovering from their stupor, resumed their advance.

"First blood is ours! Now take the fight to them!" Tom commanded, his voice echoing off the nearby buildings.

His team charged forward, meeting the zombies with a ferocity that caught the undead off guard. War cries filled the air as they crashed into the horde like a tidal wave of steel and fury. The impact was so forceful that several zombies were bowled over and trampled underfoot, their clawed hands scrabbling uselessly against the armored legs of the fighters above them.

Bron, with his massive elephantine legs, simply continued to march forward, his enormous axe swinging in wide, deadly arcs. Each step was like a sledgehammer slamming into the earth, crushing zombies beneath his feet as if they were nothing more than grapes in a vineyard. Tom had spent countless hours training with Bron in the weeks leading up to the assault, learning how to wield his own weapon more efficiently. The training paid off. With each swing of his Greatsword of Hell's Inferno, zombies were mowed down like wheat before a scythe. Dark flames engulfed the blade, igniting any zombie it touched, turning them into burning, staggering torches.

Meanwhile, James was having a fit. His usual strategy—shooting his targets in the groin to disable them, then delivering a clean headshot—was proving useless against these undead monstrosities.

"Fuck this shit! I wanna go back to fighting live opponents!" James complained loudly, frustration dripping from his words as he continued to fire *only* at the zombies' heads from behind Derek's shield.

"Oh, come on, you big baby. Just pretend they have dicks on their faces, and headshots are just zombie dickshots," Derek suggested with a grin, trying to lighten James' mood.

James paused, considering the idea for a moment.

"You're a goddamned genius, Derek! Hey, dickface! How about some lunch?" With renewed vigor, he aimed at the zombies' heads and began firing, imagining each shot as a satisfying zombie dickshot. His mood noticeably improved.

Nearby, Squirrel had grown to the size of an SUV and launched himself into the fray. His massive jaws snapped shut around zombies, and his powerful claws tore through their rotting flesh. As zombies tried to clamber up his fur, he shook violently, sending them flying off like leaves in a hurricane. Limbs were torn off from the force, and Squirrel howled triumphantly.

Bobby and Clay fought back-to-back, their blades a blur as they cut down any zombie that dared approach. Zach and Isaac, working in tandem, defended against a group of zombies closing in on them. Isaac raised his shield to protect them while Zach leaped over him, delivering lethal blows to the zombies in a deadly game of leapfrog.

Kedron, who had already suffered a wound on his left arm, made his way closer to Bron for a moment of reprieve. Briana quickly healed him, and with a nod of thanks, Kedron jumped back into the fight.

Even Jerky, Tom's tiny familiar, was contributing to the chaos. He threw up shields to protect Tom's back and pounced on a zombie's face, biting and clawing with a ferocity Tom had never seen before.

Suddenly, about half of the remaining zombies broke away from the fight and began running west. Tom's heart leapt with cautious optimism—the plan was working! These zombies would be no match for Shandra's well-trained warriors, but if they initiated an attack, it might provoke her into retaliation against The Master. Tom's ultimate hope was that he could rescue the enslaved before Shandra's forces obliterated everything. Still, a nagging thought kept prodding at him—The Master couldn't possibly have played all his cards yet. There had to be more up his sleeve, some hidden strategy that would come into play once the real fighting began.

With the zombie horde split, the cleanup became much easier. Tom had to pull back some of his more bloodthirsty fighters, including Squirrel, from giving chase.

"We have to let them attack Shandra, or she won't be drawn into the fight! If we just kill them all here, nothing changes! Hold your positions!" Tom shouted, holding his ground. His team, though some looked ready to tear through the remaining zombies, obeyed. "We need to move back to the Guild building so we don't seem like aggressors. Too bad Kiera missed out on the fun here," he added, a wry smile tugging at his lips.

With that order, Tom's team began their tactical retreat back toward the Trammell Crow Center. As they moved, they kept their eyes and ears open, listening for any signs of pursuit or further traps. The weight of what was coming hung in the air.

This battle had been just the beginning.

Kiera. Was. Pissed.

She and her team had barely made it down the stairs of the first building when they ran into another group of goblins. The encounter delayed them even further, eating away precious minutes they couldn't afford to lose. By the time they managed to fight their way through and reach street level, things went from bad to worse. A swarm of gelatinous creatures—the System called them Pseudo-

Morphs—oozed into their path. The sight of the translucent blobs, glistening in the morning light, might have been almost comical if not for the deadly situation they were in.

Kiera quickly realized that their bullets were mostly ineffective against these creatures. Every shot fired sank into their gelatinous bodies with a muted splat, passing right through them with little effect.

"Shit! These things are like jello!" Dale shouted in frustration, pulling his rifle back after another round went straight through without causing any real damage.

"Physical weapons!" Kiera yelled over the chaos. "Use your blades! Aim for their cores!"

Dale found out the hard way that the Pseudo-Morphs could only be destroyed by physical strikes aimed at their shifting cores, which they could move around inside their amorphous bodies at will. What followed was a frantic game of cat and mouse, with Dale and Scott hacking at the creatures to force the cores into a vulnerable position. Meanwhile, Janice lashed out with her whip, her strikes cutting through the air with a satisfying crack whenever she hit a core dead-on.

One Pseudo-Morph managed to leap onto Tina's arm, and she immediately shrieked in agony as her skin began to sizzle and blister under the acidic touch. The creature's slimy form hissed where it connected with her flesh, emitting a foul stench like rotten eggs mixed with chemicals.

"Get it off! GET IT OFF!" Tina screamed, frantically trying to shake the creature off. Scott swung his axe with precision, cleanly severing the blob from Tina's arm, but the damage was done. Angry, red welts marred her skin where the acidic slime had burned through.

"Are you alright, Tina?" Kiera asked, concern edging into her voice despite her fury. Tina nodded, gritting her teeth through the pain, her face pale but determined.

After what felt like an eternity, they finally cleared the street and made it to the second building. Racing up the stairs, Kiera's heart sank as she reached the top and saw the chaos below. They were too late. Half of the zombies had already split off from the main group, heading west toward Shandra's territory. Meanwhile, Tom and his team had finished mopping up the remaining undead and were beginning to pull back toward their base.

"Fucking monsters slowing us down! We missed out on the action," Kiera growled, slamming her fist down on the edge of the building so hard her knuckles bled. "But at least it looks like Tom's team managed without us."

"Should we take out the ones heading west?" Scott asked, peering down his rifle's scope as he tracked the zombies moving toward Shandra's territory.

Kiera considered for a moment, her mind racing. It would be satisfying to take out a few more zombies and thin their numbers, but it would also risk exposing their entire strategy.

"No," she decided, shaking her head. "We do nothing from here except regroup back at HQ. Those zombies are marching straight to Shandra's doorstep, and I hope they fuck up her day. If we attack now, it'll look like we were setting up a trap instead of just stumbling upon Tom's team. We need to maintain the illusion. So, let's move out!"

With a sense of frustration still burning in her chest, Kiera led her team back down to ground level. They moved quickly and quietly, sticking to the shadows and avoiding any more unnecessary encounters. It was time to get back to the Trammell Crow Center and prepare for the next phase.

Kiera swore silently to herself. If they had to face more distractions like this, she'd make sure to take them out with extreme prejudice next time.

Jay sprinted west, pushing his body to its limits. The remaining members of his team followed closely behind, their footsteps pounding the pavement in a frantic rhythm. The loss of Steve was like a gut punch, but there was no time to mourn now. The mission still hinged on their ability to lure at least some of the zombies west, away from Tom's team and toward Shandra's base. Once they got close enough to Stormcrusher's headquarters, they would vanish into the shadows and make their way back to the Guild building.

"Are they still behind us?" Jay called out, his voice strained from the run.

Charlie, the team member bringing up the rear, glanced over his shoulder. He saw the zombies engaged with Tom and his team in a fierce battle, their rotting forms lurching and clawing at their opponents.

"Looks like they stopped and are fighting with Tom!" Charlie shouted back.

Jay skidded to a halt, turning to see the chaos behind them. Sure enough, the undead had shifted their attention to Tom's group, snarling and lunging at the Vanguard fighters.

"Dammit!" Jay cursed, his frustration bubbling over. "We can't let them just focus on Tom. We have to lure some of them away."

He jogged back a bit, closing the distance until he was within range. With a flick of his wrist, he hurled several shurikens, embedding them into the backs of the zombies. The sharp impact caused a few of them to turn, their hollow eyes locking onto him and his team. Half of their number broke away from the fight, stumbling forward to give chase.

"That's right, you undead fucks. Daddy's back, and he got his cigarettes," Jay called out, a wicked grin spreading across his face.

From his Inventory, Jay pulled out a half-stick of dynamite. Lighting the fuse, he threw it in front of the first zombie that had turned their way.

The explosion shook the ground. Shouts of alarm and fear echoed from Tom's team, but he'd succeeded in his objective.

Dozens of zombie heads turned toward their small group.

"That's more like it," Jay grinned. "Let's go toss the pigskin around a bit, kids." He glanced down at his watch. "Gotta get milk later, so we need to make this fast!"

The zombies, now focused on Jay and his team, picked up speed. Jay led them further west, zigzagging through the maze of abandoned streets. The undead seemed to become more frenzied with each step, their movements growing more erratic and desperate. Their decaying bodies, however, struggled to keep up. Twice, a zombie lost a leg or footing, tumbling to the ground and causing a pile-up of the ones behind it. Jay sighed and facepalmed at the pathetic sight but kept moving.

As they ran, Jay and his team occasionally tossed more shurikens to taunt the zombies, making it seem like they were toying with them. The strikes were non-lethal, calculated to keep as many zombies intact as possible for when they reached Stormcrusher's base. Everything seemed to be going according to plan, which made Jay both relieved and anxious. When did things ever go smoothly?

Just as that thought crossed his mind, the leading zombie abruptly stopped in its tracks and let out a piercing shriek. The others halted as well, responding with shrieks of their own. Then, to Jay's horror, they began to meld together, their bodies liquefying into a grotesque amalgamation. Limbs, torsos, and heads fused, merging into a giant, writhing mass.

"Oh, shit," Jay breathed, coming to a halt as he stared wide-eyed at the monstrosity forming before them. Jay swallowed thickly. "My baby boy's gonna be a linebacker."

The creature that took shape was about three stories tall, with enormous, disproportionately long arms and short, stubby legs. It looked like someone had turned King Kong inside out and sewn him back together. Stitches criss-crossed its patchwork skin, and its hands ended in jagged-bone claws that glinted in the morning light. The creature opened its mouth far wider than any normal being should be able to, letting out a thunderous roar that shook the surrounding buildings.

"Move, you fucktards! We don't want to be caught by that thing! Head for the base, then vanish!" Jay shouted, turning on his heel and sprinting again.

The behemoth zombie lumbered after them, its huge strides covering ground with alarming speed. It swung its massive arms like clubs, forcing the team to dive and roll out of the way of the bone-shattering blows. The ground trembled with each step the creature took, and the air filled with the rancid stench of rotting flesh and blood.

The Stormcrusher base finally came into view, and Jay's heart pounded with both relief and urgency. They had to make this work. He needed to draw the guards' attention.

"Scatter!" Jay yelled as loudly as he could once the guards on duty noticed the oncoming threat. His team instantly broke off in different directions, slipping into the shadows and vanishing like ghosts.

The giant zombie, momentarily confused by its disappearing prey, paused and let out a guttural roar of frustration. The guards, now fully aware of the incoming threat, began blowing whistles to alert the rest of the compound. The zombie's beady eyes landed on the guards, and it seemed to forget all about Jay's team. With a roar that shook the ground, it lumbered forward, barreling toward Reunion Tower, its claws ready to tear apart anything in its path.

Jay watched from the safety of a shadowed alley as the monstrosity impaled one of the guards on a bone claw, lifting him off the ground like a ragdoll. The man's scream was cut short as the life drained from his eyes, and he fell limp, dangling in the air. Another guard fell backward, scrambling away in terror, his whistle dropping uselessly from his lips. Within moments, more of Stormcrusher's members poured out of the building, weapons drawn, ready to fight.

"And that's our cue," Jay muttered, his voice low and steady. "Good job, boys. We can head back home now. Make sure you stay hidden. We don't want anyone seeing us."

The team nodded in agreement, still breathing hard from the adrenaline-fueled chase.

A hand slapped his ass as a soldier walked by. "Fuckin' *daddy's home?*" Charlie's voice was filled with morbid mirth. "Really?"

"Bite your tongue, asshole," Jay grinned. "You try coming up with new material under that kind of pressure."

Grinning, the team slipped from sight.

They moved away from the carnage with practiced stealth, slipping through alleyways and ducking behind debris to keep out of sight. The sounds of battle—shouts, gunfire, and the bloodcurdling roars of the giant zombie—faded behind them as they made their way back toward the Vanguard Guild building.

Jay couldn't help but feel a small swell of pride. Despite the terrifying turn of events, they'd managed to pull it off. Now, it was up to Tom and the rest to see if the chaos they'd sown would be enough to set Shandra's Guild against The Master.

Chapter 32

It... Worked?

Tom was the first to return to the Guild building with his team. They took the opportunity to rest and regroup, anxiously waiting for the others. About an hour later, Kiera and her squad arrived, looking exhausted and frustrated.

"Everything go alright?" Tom asked, moving over to check in with her.

"No, it did *not* go alright!" Kiera snapped. She was clearly fed up, her breath still ragged from the journey. "We managed to help Jay's team, but then kept running into fucking monsters when we tried to get back to your team. By the time we got there, you were already done and headed back here."

"Well, I'm glad to see you all made it back mostly okay," Tom replied, glancing at Tina's arm, which was bandaged and looked like it had been burned.

"We found a new monster. Pseudo-Morphs. They look like slimes from old video games, but they burn like acid when you touch them. The only way to kill them is to destroy their cores. Nasty fuckers," Kiera explained, noticing Tom's concern.

"Shit, at least they have a weakness," Tom said, frowning. "Do you think you were seen?"

"No way. We were too far out. Unless they had a telescope trained on us, and even then, we had good cover," Kiera reassured him.

"That's good news. It seems like things are going well so far. We won't know for sure, though, until Jay gets back," Tom said, his eyes shifting to the gate, watching for any sign of Jay and his team.

"That asshole had better come back," Kiera muttered, staring at the gate as well, trying to mask the worry in her voice with a tough exterior.

Tom chuckled, sensing the genuine concern behind her words. "I'm sure he's hoping you're okay too."

"I mean, he's the best spy we have. We need to keep him around," Kiera retorted, trying to sound more pragmatic than worried.

Tom gave her a knowing smile. "There's no reason to hide your feelings. He's our friend, and that means we worry. But he's got this."

"If he doesn't come back," Kiera said, crossing her arms over her chest, "I'll find his body, drag it to The Master, force him to bring him back, and then kill him myself."

Tom laughed. He knew there was no changing her mind, so he let her express herself in her own way.

Two hours later, Jay finally arrived at the Guild gate. Tom rushed over, his heart pounding with anticipation. The first thing he noticed was that Jay's team was down a man. Several others had minor injuries but seemed relatively intact.

"What the hell happened? You should have been back hours ago!" Tom blurted out, his worry coming out more aggressively than intended.

"We were on our way back but realized we wouldn't know if Shandra took the bait unless we watched. So, we stopped at a building where we could see The Master's base to see if they would go after him," Jay explained quickly. "There were a shit ton of dead goblins there, though. Was that your doing, Kiera?"

"It was," Kiera replied curtly. "Fuckers tried to mess up Plan Mexican Standoff."

"Yeah, well, I hear PMS *is* quite a bitch," Jay said, nodding appreciatively.

Kiera snorted, shoving Jay in the shoulder "You don't know the half of it."

"They definitely took the bait." Jay turned toward Tom. "They didn't make a full assault, but Shandra is pissed! She ran over there and started yelling at The Master, who just sat on top of his walls like he was enjoying the show."

"Could you make out what they were saying?" Tom asked, eager to hear more.

"No, we were too far away for that. I still can't believe you made those shots from that building, Kiera," Jay said, giving her a well-earned compliment. Kiera beamed with pride.

"But Shandra kept getting more and more pissed while that asshat seemed to be enjoying her frustration. I think she's a little worried about what he can do," Jay added, his tone thoughtful.

"That doesn't sound like Shandra. Why would she be concerned?" Tom mused, narrowing his eyes.

"Probably because he has some ability to meld his zombies together to make super zombies," Jay replied, knowing the question was partly rhetorical.

"He can do *what?!*" Tom's eyes widened in shock.

"When we were running from the zombies, they stopped and let out some kind of wail, and then they began to merge into each other. They became this giant zombie abomination—thing was wicked-looking. It even killed a couple of Shandra's men before we ran off," Jay explained, recalling the chilling sight of the grotesque creature.

"That's not good," Tom muttered, his mind racing. "I figured he still had some tricks up his sleeve, but that's a big one. I hope they didn't talk things out and figure out our plan."

"When have you ever known Shandra to talk things out?" Jay snorted. "She's probably over there calling him every name in the book and threatening to wipe him off the map."

"I hope so. That's what we were counting on," Tom said, still mulling over the implications. "We have as many people as possible on watch, so we'll know for sure soon enough. We should post some people on spy duty near both of the other bases. Jay, can you have some people do that?"

"I can," Jay replied. "Though I do need a replacement for Steve." His face fell as he mentioned Steve, a deep sadness clouding his features.

"I noticed you were down a member. What happened?" Tom asked gently.

"Steve," Jay sighed, rubbing his eyes tiredly. "He got surrounded and overrun inside The Master's base. There wasn't anything we could do," Jay said, his voice heavy with guilt and regret.

"We saw it too," Kiera interjected, her tone somber. "We tried to keep the zombies off him, but there were too many, and we could only fire so many shots from that distance." Kiera swallowed. "I—I saw what you had to do…" She placed a hand on the Rogue's arm. "I'm sorry as hell, Jay. I should have done it. I hesitated."

"No." Jay's eyes were fixed on the ground. "He was my responsibility." He placed a hand over Kiera's and gave it a squeeze.

A heavy silence fell over the group as they processed the loss. They all knew the risks of this war, but it never got easier losing someone.

"Go take who you need and get them up to speed," Tom finally said, breaking the silence. "We need those spies to keep us updated on what's happening out there. We can't just sit here and hope they destroy each other. We still have people to help."

"Right," Jay said, nodding before turning to leave. He moved quickly, trying to focus on the mission and not dwell on his grief.

"Everyone else, I want you training every moment you get," Tom said, addressing the crowd that had gathered. "This war is going to get a lot worse before it gets better. If you need resources, come to us and ask. We'll get you anything we can to make sure you get stronger."

Tom watched as determination spread across the faces of his Guild members. They were ready to do whatever it took, and many immediately began preparing to train or arm themselves. Summoning Bron again, Tom looked the massive, elephantine warrior in the eyes.

"I think it's time we start training my body as well as my weapon skills. I need to get stronger," Tom said with resolve.

Bron nodded and motioned for him to follow. To Tom's surprise, several others from his team, including Michael, the new recruit, joined in. The atmosphere was heavy with purpose, and Tom felt a flicker of hope. The war was far from over, but they were ready to face whatever came next.

"You all don't have to come with me," Tom said to his team as they followed him to the training grounds. "This training is going to be grueling."

"We've seen you training with the big guy, and we want in," Michael said, his eyes alight with determination. "You aren't the only one looking to get stronger."

Tom nodded, impressed by their resolve. "Alright, but don't say I didn't warn you," he replied with a smile.

Bron stood nearby, towering over them, his expression stern but slightly amused. "The first step in training your body is to make it as hard as possible and raise your muscular endurance," he announced. "I will need a few things to begin your training." His grin widened, promising nothing but torment.

About an hour later, Tom had to resummon Bron as the time had elapsed on his summoning skill. He presented Bron with all the items he had requested, his concern growing with each one.

"Some of these make me think you're going to torture us," Tom said, eyeing the equipment with a wary expression.

"Technically, it's *not* torture," Bron replied with a slow smile. "But it will… incentivize you not to slack in the training." He paused just long enough at the word "incentivize" to make everyone uneasy.

A few minutes later, Tom found himself squatting precariously over a wooden board with a spike pointed straight up at his backside. Bands with small punch daggers were strapped around his biceps, and he was holding a large stone in each hand, arms stretched out to either side of his body. The strain was immediate, and he regretted his decision to let Bron train them.

"How long do I have to hold this position?" Tom grunted, his legs trembling.

"Until you can't," Bron said nonchalantly, not even looking up as he fanned a flame underneath a makeshift pull-up bar. Michael was hanging from the bar by his knees, swinging his body back and forth to strengthen his core while trying to avoid the flames licking at his back and stomach.

"You"—Tom panted—"sure this isn't torture?" He spat, his arms beginning to lower involuntarily as fatigue set in.

"*Technically,*" Bron stated. "One of the essential aspects in the definition of torture is that it must be a punishment," the Mastadonian clarified. "The body's natural responses are limited when you aren't in a life-or-death situation," Bron replied, his voice carrying a well-worn patience. "To train your body for the trials of battle, you must put yourself in those situations within a controlled environment. Would you rather face beasts that can kill you and hope someone is there to save you, or train here where healers are ready and nothing is actively trying to eat you?"

Tom's arms dropped a little more, and the point of a punch dagger grazed his side. The pain jolted through him, forcing his arms back up with a strained shout. "OW! That hurt!"

"Come on, you weakling! I expected more from you!" Bron bellowed at him, his voice like a war drum.

"HEY, SHUT UP! THIS SUCKS AND IS WAY HARDER THAN IT LOOKS!" Tom shouted back, his frustration boiling over.

"THIS IS THE KIND OF TRAINING WE GIVE *CHILDREN* IN MASTADONIAN SOCIETY! ARE YOU SAYING YOU ARE WEAKER THAN A CHILD?!" Bron roared back, not missing a beat.

"ARE YOU CALLING ME A CHILD?!" Tom yelled, feeling both his anger and his competitive spirit flare up.

"IF YOU CAN'T COMPLETE THE SIMPLEST OF TASKS, THEN YES, I AM CALLING YOU A CHILD!" Bron shouted and cracked a whip across

Tom's back. The leather snapped against his bare skin, sending a stinging pain radiating through his body.

Michael's eyes widened as he watched Bron fan the flames under his bar with renewed vigor, the heat intensifying to the point of singeing his skin.

"HEY! WATCH THE FLAMES! THEY'RE GETTING TOO BIG!" he yelled, panic edging into his voice.

"SILENCE! WHO IS THE ONE WHO'S DONE THIS BEFORE?! GO FASTER, AND YOU WON'T GET HURT!" Bron shouted back at him, showing no sign of relenting.

Kedron, who had been assigned to repeatedly punch a wooden post wrapped in rope, looked up, visibly annoyed.

"Why am I just punching a post? This doesn't feel like it's doing anything," he muttered, frustration evident in his voice.

Bron stopped fanning the flames, which gave Michael a brief moment of relief, and turned his attention to Kedron. His massive figure loomed over the man as he scrutinized the post. Kedron stopped punching and looked up at Bron.

"This will strengthen your fists by building calluses and train you to strike at opponents with high defensive abilities. Eventually, you will be able to do this." Bron drew back his massive fist and slammed it into the post with such force that the top half snapped clean off.

Kedron's eyes went wide with a mix of awe and fear.

"Now, get another post and continue your training!" Bron commanded with a booming voice.

Around them, several other recruits were engaged in equally painful-looking exercises. One pair was doing assisted splits, with poles driven into the ground holding their ankles in place as another person pushed them forward, supposedly to improve their flexibility for combat. The screams of discomfort echoed through the training area, a testament to their determination. No one was willing to give up, even though they all regretted their decision to join Bron's "boot camp."

Tom's arms were shaking violently now, his muscles burning with exhaustion. He was about to give up and drop the stones, risking impaling himself on the spike, when a notification appeared in his view.

Congratulations - Stat Boost
Through the intense struggle of pushing your body beyond its limits and enduring relentless training, your dedication has paid off. Your Strength has increased by 1 point. Keep striving for greatness!

Tom stared in wonder at the notification window before him. He had no idea that actual physical training could raise his Attributes. In all this time, he had never gained a stat boost from just pushing himself physically. A fire ignited within him—a desire to push further, to grow stronger. He refocused, tightening his grip on the stones and holding them as steady as he could manage, despite the burning in his muscles.

"I see you've discovered a secret the System doesn't advertise," Bron said, a knowing glint in his eye as he observed Tom's reaction.

Tom shot him a glare, frustration evident in his voice. "You could have told us this would happen," he snapped, the strain in his arms making his words come out sharper than he intended.

Bron merely shrugged, his face impassive. "If I told you, it would have ruined the achievement. This moment of realization—this feeling of accomplishment—it is that which drives you to push even harder," he explained calmly. "Besides, the true reward isn't the stat boost, but the understanding of your own limits and the satisfaction of breaking them."

Tom couldn't argue with that, but it didn't make the training any easier. He grimaced, feeling his muscles scream in protest. But there was something undeniably motivating in knowing that all this pain was translating directly into power—into real, tangible growth. His anger melted away into a focused determination.

Meanwhile, Bron returned to his task, fanning the flames beneath Michael with renewed enthusiasm. The fire roared higher, and Michael's eyes widened in horror. He swung back and forth faster, his muscles straining as he tried to keep his body from getting too close to the scorching heat.

Tom couldn't help but smile a little. Bron was relentless, but Tom knew he was right. Real growth came from overcoming real challenges—both physical and mental. Today was just the beginning.

"Alright," Tom muttered through clenched teeth, "let's see how far I can push myself."

Chapter 33

Engineering

Another week passed with Tom and the others continuing their grueling training under Bron's rigorous regimen. The fires of war had simmered to embers for the time being; the success of Plan Mexican Standoff had caused attacks on the Vanguard Guild to cease temporarily. However, there were still sporadic skirmishes among The Master, Stormcrusher, and Vanguard. Sometimes, there were clashes between Stormcrusher and The Master, other times between Stormcrusher and Vanguard, and once even directly between The Master and Vanguard. But without a reliable method to quickly remove the collars from the enslaved people, Tom found himself forced to bide his time.

Tom had given Harold several weeks to work on a solution for the collars, so he decided to check in on him. On his way to the engineering lab, Tom ran into Bobby, who was clearly searching for him.

"Hey, Tom. Listen, we gotta talk about something," Bobby said, catching Tom before he could continue on his way. "I think we need to take another approach to the training."

"What do you have in mind?" Tom asked, curious about what kind of training Bobby felt was lacking from Bron's regime.

"Well, Bron's training has been great, and he's given us some excellent techniques," Bobby began, "but I just don't think we're including enough people. There are a *lot* of folks who are just doing the usual workouts or grinding on monsters. Do you mind if I start a routine that rotates everyone in the Guild to teach them some of the new training methods?"

"I think that's a great idea," Tom said thoughtfully. "But do you think you can handle that many people? It could turn into a full-time job."

"I figure I'll only need to do it for a while," Bobby replied. "Then we can train others to lead the classes who have a knack for it. I'll work on that part with Chris. Soon, we could have daily classes at different times so people can get their work done and still train."

Tom grinned at the idea. "I love it. Make it so, Number One!"

Bobby gave Tom a puzzled look, clearly not catching the Star Trek reference. "At least I'm not number two," he joked. "Thanks, Tom. I'll get right on it."

Bobby headed off toward the cafeteria, knowing that would be the best place to rally people around his new training idea. Tom continued on his way alone, heading down to the basement of the building. When he reached the engineering lab, he waved at Roland, who was busy hammering away at his forge.

"Got anything new to show off, Roland?" Tom asked, approaching the large, sweaty, soot-covered Smith.

"I do, actually. I've been vorking on a new armor prototype vis one of ze enchanters from ze Guild," Roland explained, his thick German accent coloring his words. "Here, take a look."

Roland held up what looked like a hybrid piece of half-plate-metal and half-leather armor, blackened and sleek. With surprising ease, he tossed it to Tom, who caught it instinctively.

"Holy shit! It's so light!" Tom exclaimed, having expected the metal components to make it significantly heavier.

"Ja! It has ze lightening properties imbued into ze runes along viz ze strength properties to make it far stronger zan it should be at its size. But it should be as tough as ze dragon scales," Roland boasted, clearly proud of his work.

"This is amazing, Roland!" Tom praised, turning the armor over in his hands, inspecting the intricate rune work and craftsmanship.

"Danke so much. It has been a lot of issues, und I am still not fully happy vis it, but it has come a long way since I committed verschlimmbesserung vis the first sets," Roland explained.

"Since you committed what again?" Tom asked, blinking in confusion.

"Verschlimmbesserung," Roland repeated patiently. "It means, how you say—try to make better, but made worse."

Tom chuckled. "I'm not sure I understand."

"Sink of a painting," Roland continued. "When someone vants to restore it to its former glory, zey usually have to clean off ze years of grime. And sometimes zey commit verschlimmbesserung by destroying some of the work in ze process."

Tom laughed. "Germans have a word for everything, don't they?"

"It is a very efficient language," Roland replied, beaming with pride.

"Well, definitely don't give up! This is great!" Tom encouraged.

Roland smiled and nodded. "Den Teufel nicht an die Wand malen."

Tom stared blankly at Roland, not understanding a word. Roland let out a hearty laugh at Tom's expression. "Literally translated, it means 'Do not paint ze devil on ze wall.' It is a German proverb. It means do not assume zat somesing vill go wrong before you know ze outcome," Roland explained. "You cannot just say zat somesing vill be bad. I vill never give up in zis endeavor."

Tom moved to hand the armor back to Roland, but the Smith held up a hand. "Zat is for you. I saw your armor last time and decided to get you somesing you could use right avay. Keep it. I hope it protects you in your battles."

Tom stared down at the armor, his admiration growing. He activated his *Inspect* ability to see what he was dealing with.

Item: Half Plate of Protection - Light	
Item Type:	Armor - Light
Durability:	1500/1500
Defense:	+300
Item Quality:	Excellent
Item Rarity:	Rare

This expertly crafted half-plate armor, forged by the Vanguard Smith, Roland, combines the defensive strength of traditional plate armor with the agility and lightness of leather. Enchanted with advanced weight-reducing runes, it significantly reduces encumbrance, allowing for swift and fluid movement. The armor is further enhanced with strengthening runes, granting it the durability to withstand heavy blows while maintaining its lightweight nature. A favorite among agile fighters and those who require both protection and mobility, this armor represents a masterful balance between defense and freedom of movement.

"I… I don't know what to say, Roland. This armor is incredible!" Tom exclaimed; his eyes wide with amazement as he examined the craftsmanship.

"Danke, mein Freund. You honor me vis your vords," Roland said, bowing his head slightly, a hand over his heart. "Come back to see me, and I vill see if I can make you some more sings to help you."

With that, Roland returned to pounding on a glowing piece of red-hot metal. Tom took this as his cue to leave and equipped the new armor piece. Immediately, he felt a noticeable difference—he was lighter and more agile compared to his usual medium armor. He twisted his body, testing the mobility of the piece, and found it allowed for a full range of motion with no pinching, thanks to the armor's automagic resizing properties.

Satisfied, Tom headed to the engineering lab on the other side of the basement. As he entered, he waved to Harold, who was working alongside Bohdan.

"Hey, guys! I wanted to check on the progress of the collar removal project. Have we made much headway?" Tom asked as he approached one of the tables covered with schematics and gadgets.

"We're still in the brainstorming phase," Harold admitted. "We've got a few ideas for prototypes, but we won't know for sure until we can actually test them on something."

"We know it will do what we design it to do," Bohdan added in his thick Ukrainian accent, "but we cannot be certain until we have another collar to test on."

"That's a shame. Do we have any collars available for testing? We cut up the last one," Tom recalled, remembering how they'd resorted to using bolt cutters.

Harold nodded, holding up an intact collar he'd apparently acquired from the vending machine. "We've got some, but these damn things need a specific Skill to activate. We're still trying to figure out a way to test them."

Tom crossed his arms, thinking. "So, what's your first approach?"

"We're working on a device that can be thrown at someone wearing the collar," Harold explained, picking up a metallic cube with a button on it. "It'll cast a version of the anti-magic zone spell Bohdan used last time, but in a limited range. Basically, it'll work like a single-use spell scroll. Press the button, throw the cube, and three seconds later, the spell goes off. The idea is to have it disable the collar's magic at three seconds, and then do whatever it takes to unlock the collar at four or five seconds."

"But we still don't know what that second step is," Tom said flatly, eyeing the cube with a thoughtful expression.

"Exactly," Harold replied. "But we'll figure it out. It's only a matter of time. Give us another couple of weeks, and we should have a working prototype."

"Alright, but remember, this is top priority," Tom reminded them.

"We know. Everything else is on hold until we sort this out," Harold assured him.

"Good. Thanks for pushing this forward. Keep me updated," Tom said, leaving them to their work and heading back upstairs.

In the main lobby, Tom considered his next move. With no immediate tasks at hand, he decided it was time to regroup his team and take them on a different type of training run. He'd been holding off on this due to the war efforts, but now there was time.

Tom made his way to the security center and pushed open the steel door, finding TJ monitoring the screens.

"You pulling shifts here now?" Tom asked, stepping up beside him.

"Can't lead from the back all the time. Gotta get in the trenches with the men—especially during a war," TJ replied, glancing up at Tom.

"Can you call Brian and the rest of my team in here for me?" Tom asked with a grin.

"Sure thing. Give me a minute," TJ said, jotting down a few notes on a pad before using the announcement system to call for the others.

About twenty minutes later, the group was assembled, and Tom addressed them.

"Brian, you mentioned some Dungeons were found while we were away. Have they been explored yet?" Tom asked.

"No, we kept them off-limits until your team could take a stab at them first," Brian explained. "I know you have that deal with your Patron about dedicating Dungeons and wanted to make sure the best team went in first."

"Perfect," Tom said, his grin widening mischievously. "Because you're coming with us."

"The hell I am!" Brian protested immediately.

"Everyone needs training. You have to get stronger too. We're going to power-level you," Tom insisted.

"Do you think that's a good idea, Tom?" Derek interjected cautiously.

"It's the fastest way to level him up. He won't have to do much—just deal a little damage here and there, and he'll get the same XP as us," Tom countered.

"This seems very dangerous, and I'm not okay with it," Brian argued, glancing nervously between Derek and Tom.

"Oh, it's happening. Don't try to wriggle out of this," Tom shot back, still focused on Derek. "He needs this, and it'll toughen him up. You have all your gear, right?"

"Umm, yes?" Brian replied, sounding more uncertain than convinced.

"Good. You'll join us in the first Dungeon. I won't make you do both, but you might change your mind after the first one," Tom said, finally turning his attention back to Brian.

"I don't like this at all. Why can't we just go kill some damn goblins to level up?" Brian tried one last time to change Tom's mind.

"Because in war, time is often more valuable than safety, and this is way more XP for the same amount of time. Also, we get loot at the end," Tom explained, enjoying watching Brian squirm.

"I'm gonna enjoy watching you die slowly, maggot!" James chimed in, piling on the teasing.

"For fuck's sake, James. The goal is to keep him alive," Tom snapped, turning on James.

"Sure, sure. That's the goal. But the goal and what actually happens are often two very different things," James replied, rubbing his hands together gleefully.

Seeing Brian's discomfort, Kiera decided to join in. "We can't watch his back all the time. Dungeons are inherently dangerous. Monsters come from all over. Could sneak right up behind him," she said, causing Brian to turn a couple of shades paler.

"That's true; it *is* dangerous," Tom added, looking straight at Brian. "I guess Kiera and James will have to be your personal bodyguards in the Dungeon."

"Yeah… wait, we what?!" Kiera blurted, too caught up in the moment to realize what Tom had said at first. "I'm not a fucking babysitter. Let Kevin do it."

"Kevin will just rush into battle with his *Rage* ability. Can't count on him to defend Brian. But two fighters who usually hang back would be perfect," Tom reasoned, now rubbing his hands together with a mock evil grin.

"We walked right into that one," James muttered, his shoulders slumping.

"Dammit!" Kiera groaned, facepalming. "Why did I have to go and stick my nose in it?"

"Because you love causing trouble," James replied.

"Damn my need to watch others in pain!" Kiera cursed, shaking her fist at the sky.

Tom looked down at Brian, who had practically sunk into a chair and was looking quite pale.

"Now, where's that first Dungeon you were telling us about?" he asked, still grinning.

Chapter 34

Dungeon of Chance

The new Dungeon was apparently located right in the middle of Downtown Dallas. The Dallas World Aquarium was not a place people would normally consider exploring during an apocalypse, but one of their teams had stumbled upon it by accident. They had been chasing down a group of goblins hiding inside the building when they found the Dungeon entrance.

"So, you're really forcing me to go?" Brian asked, almost sulking about the prospect of being put in danger.

"Oh, come on, Brian." Tom tried to ease his worry, his tone a mix of encouragement and impatience. "This is an opportunity that most people would jump at—getting to go into a Dungeon on a first run with the only team the Guild trusts to survive? You're gonna get so many levels."

"Fine. Let one of those people go with you," Brian countered, hoping to slip away and head back to the safety of the Guild building.

"Oh no, you're not getting out that easy," Derek interjected, shutting him down. "You've been cooped up in that building too long. You're falling behind."

"But I could die," Brian continued to protest, his voice filled with genuine concern.

"You could die in that building if the other Guilds attack. You need to be stronger to protect yourself," Tom countered again. "Now shut up and quit whining about it."

The team continued across to the entrance of the aquarium in the GS2. DeeDee and Graham were too busy with training schedules to go, so Brian filled one of the slots, and Kirsten filled the other. She had insisted on coming with Kevin. Seeing no issues with having another Barbarian join the ranks—and picturing what might happen if they told her no and she went full she-hulk on them—they had agreed.

The two were practically inseparable. It was the flame of young love, the kind that always made Tom feel slightly queasy. But despite his usual disdain for such things, he wanted his friend to be happy in a world where finding happiness was a rare occurrence.

Upon arriving at the aquarium, the team exited the vehicle and looked up at the entrance. The building still had its distinctive boxy look, but the plants at the entrance had grown wild and out of control, with no one around to maintain them. Tom had to use his sword to cut through some of the thick vegetation just to reach the doors. Many of the windows had been shattered, possibly by goblins or other creatures scavenging for food.

Everything around the building was eerily quiet, except for the occasional sound of the animals still alive inside. A parrot squawked, its call echoing through the hollow building, followed by other birds responding. Then, suddenly, the birds fell silent. A deep, feral roar split the air, the sound of something large attacking another animal.

"What the fuck was that?" Brian asked, his voice shaky as he instinctively hid behind Tom.

"Probably one of the big cats they kept here. We need to be ready for loose animals," Tom replied, his voice steady but his eyes sharp as he scanned the surroundings. He turned to the team and continued, "Be on guard, and if there are any predatory animals, be ready to kill them."

"Can't we just let them go?" Kiera asked, glancing down at Squirrel, remembering he was just a wild beast before James made him his companion.

"If we do, they might kill someone else. So, unless someone has a 'tame animal' Skill they want to use on any we encounter, it's best we just end the threat," Derek replied, his tone pragmatic.

"Actually, I do have that Skill," Brian said meekly, still half-hiding behind Tom.

"Really? You chose Ranger as your Class?" Tom asked, looking at Brian with surprise.

"Yes. I chose it because it came with the ability to not be on the front line fighting and because it had some stealth Skills so I could slip away. I'm not a fighter, Tom. I'm an administrator," Brian explained, stepping out from behind Tom to try to seem braver.

"Well, then, we need to get you a companion while we're here. Where else will we get that kind of opportunity?" Tom said, now excited at the prospects.

"Couldn't I just get a cat or a dog or something less… murdery?" Brian pleaded.

"Oh, come on. This is an amazing opportunity. And Squirrel loves James, so this will be the same," Tom said, dismissing Brian's protests in favor of the cool factor of possibly having a big cat as a companion.

"I'd rather not. I could get a bird or something. I think I could be a bird guy," Brian continued to protest, but the others weren't having it.

"Nope. You need something that can defend you. This is better. You'll see," Tom insisted, his excitement growing.

As they entered the building, the team was hit by a wall of humid, oppressive air. Moving through the entrance exhibits, they noticed most of the tanks were shattered, likely by goblins or other creatures searching for food. The ones that were still intact seemed to contain mostly dead fish. Without power, the filtration systems had stopped, and it was clear that most aquatic life wouldn't survive for much longer.

They passed through various exhibits, all dark and uninviting, the dim light making everything feel less vibrant and more foreboding. As they reached the outdoor exhibits, they saw a giant net covering the entire area. Birds had once filled this space, but now the perches and fake trees were empty.

The hairs on the back of Tom's neck suddenly stood on end, a cold shiver running down his spine. He looked around, searching for the source of the feeling.

In the bushes to their right, a pair of eyes gleamed, watching the team. The creature remained still, sizing them up, gauging their threat level.

"Brian, this is going to be your chance," Tom whispered, lowering into a defensive stance. "Try to tame the creature before it makes a move."

Brian stepped forward gingerly, trying not to spook the creature, and glanced back at Tom to make sure he was ready to help him.

"Here, kitty, kitty. Good kitty. I'm just going to try to tame you now. We can be friends, right?" Brian said softly, his voice quivering slightly as he attempted to sound calm and non-threatening.

The creature in the bushes responded with a low, menacing growl.

"Try offering it a piece of meat," Tom suggested, remembering he had some steaks in his Inventory. He quickly pulled one out and handed it to Brian.

Brian took the meat and tossed it on the ground a short distance from the bush, hoping to coax the beast out.

A sniffing sound came from the bush, followed by the rustling of leaves as the creature moved closer. But what emerged from the foliage was not what anyone expected. The eyes had been lower because the creature had been crouched down. As it stood up, it revealed its true size—six feet tall at the shoulder, with a sleek, predatory gait.

It wasn't a jaguar like Tom had initially thought. What emerged was a nightmarish hybrid. The creature had a pair of horns jutting from the sides of its head, curving outward before pointing forward in a wicked display. Its body was heavily muscled, with jaguar-like spots covering its sleek frame, but the coloration was a deep black and vivid red instead of the usual tan and black.

Its front legs were those of a big cat, powerful and agile, but its hind legs were thick and muscled like a bull's. A long, reptilian tail extended from its back, swaying behind it, while large, spiked ridges ran down its spine, connected by webbing. Most unsettling of all were the elongated, saber-like fangs protruding from its mouth, giving it a sinister, prehistoric appearance.

The creature's eyes glowed, reflecting an unnatural intelligence as it growled once more, a deep rumble of warning that sent a chill through the group.

Tom's instincts kicked in immediately. He cast *Inspect* on the beast, desperate to understand what they were dealing with.

Catoblepas

The Catoblepas is a fearsome beast, a twisted amalgamation of a big cat and a bull, fused with demonic energies from an alternate dimension. Its muscular form is covered in jaguar-like spots with deep black and vivid red coloration, while a pair of curved horns and elongated saber-like fangs give it a terrifying presence. The creature's hind legs are like those of a bull, built for powerful charges, and its front legs are like a big cat's, designed for slashing and pouncing. A long, reptilian tail and a series of spiked ridges along its back complete its menacing appearance. The Catoblepas is known for its highly aggressive and unpredictable temperament and should never be approached unless absolutely necessary.

HP:	2,870/2,870
MP:	800/800
SP:	3,150/3,150
Level:	24
Attack:	Bite, Claw, Stomp, Gore, Fiery Rush

"Oh, shit!" Tom gasped, staring wide-eyed at the creature as it tossed the piece of meat back into its mouth with a single bite. "That's not a jaguar!"

"No shit, Sherlock! I knew this was a bad idea!" Brian squeaked, his voice breaking as he shrank away from the beast, eyes darting for an escape route.

"Just try to tame it really fast!" Tom urged, his tone rising with urgency.

"Why? So it can fail and make it even madder?!" Brian half-whispered, half-yelled, his eyes never leaving the monstrous Catoblepas.

"It's worth a shot. What do we have to lose at this point?" Tom replied, still cautiously watching the beast to see what it would do next. His hands were already poised to form a grip around his weapons when he summoned them from his Inventory.

Brian reluctantly raised his hand, his palm facing the creature, and cast his *Tame* spell. A green light enveloped the Catoblepas, briefly shimmering over its body. Everyone held their breath, waiting for some sign of submission. Moments later, the green light flickered and winked out.

"Nope. It failed. It failed miserably," Brian muttered, his voice almost trembling. "Good luck with that now."

The beast's eyes flared with a sudden, terrifying red glow as it let out a roar that echoed through the aquarium's empty halls. Without warning, it charged.

"SCATTER!" Derek shouted, and everyone dove out of the way of the charging creature.

The Catoblepas crashed through the thick foliage behind where Tom and Brian had been standing, skidding to a stop as it collided with a tree.

Kirsten and Kevin, not missing a beat, jumped in front of the beast, activating their *Rage* abilities. As the beast lunged at them again, they each grabbed one of its horns, straining to wrestle it to the ground. The creature's massive muscles rippled beneath its skin, and it thrashed wildly, trying to claw at the two Barbarians. But with their positions on either side, pressing against its powerful shoulders, it couldn't quite reach them. It swiped repeatedly with its front claws, grazing them with shallow scratches, but the two held firm, seemingly unfazed in their enraged states.

Jay, always one for dramatic entrances, leaped onto the creature's back. He drove his knives deep into the thick, muscular neck of the Catoblepas. "Bad kitty," he yelled as he twisted the blades, causing the beast to scream in agony and fury.

The Catoblepas wrenched itself free from Kirsten and Kevin's grip and began to buck like a wild rodeo bull. Jay held on for dear life, gripping his knives like handles, but after about four seconds, the beast managed to throw him off. He flew into a dense set of bushes with a loud crash.

"Oooo, so sorry, no ribbon for you. That wasn't quite the full eight seconds," James chimed in with a perfect impression of a rodeo announcer, already firing off rounds from his gun. One of his bullets hit the Catoblepas squarely in its giant testicles. The creature let out another deafening scream, its eyes blazing even brighter as it turned its murderous glare toward James.

James fired again, this time aiming for its head. The bullet bounced harmlessly off the beast's thick skull. Before the Catoblepas could reach him, Kevin came barreling in from the side, shoulder-checking the monster to knock it off course. The creature went sprawling but quickly rolled to its feet, growling low and menacingly at Kevin. It leaped, and they collided, tumbling around in a blur of flesh and fur, each trying to overpower the other.

Kevin's fists hammered down like pistons, and he kicked at the creature with all his might. The Catoblepas clawed viciously at his exposed chest, but Kevin's *Rage* ability, combined with his high Constitution, meant his skin was as tough as leather armor. With a powerful thrust, Kevin managed to grab both of the beast's front legs, planting his feet firmly into its belly, and flipped it over his head in a move that looked straight out of a Lion King reenactment.

Kirsten, quick to seize the opportunity, brought her greataxe down on the beast's exposed stomach. The blade cut deep, but not as deep as expected—its skin was as tough as armor. The creature kicked out with one of its hooved rear legs, sending Kirsten rolling backward. As it flailed its tail to regain its footing, it accidentally swept Tom's legs out from under him. He tumbled to the ground, his head smacking against the hard floor, sending stars exploding through his vision.

Kiera was there in an instant, pulling Tom to his feet and checking if he could move. "You good?" she asked quickly, her eyes never leaving the beast.

"I'm fine," Tom grunted, shaking off the daze. He pulled his arm free from Kiera's grip, rushing back to the fray just in time to see Jay mount the creature for round two. This time, Jay dug his blades into its back, using them like climbing tools to hold on as the beast bucked and thrashed.

Tom saw his chance. "Cover me," he shouted, beginning to charge up his *Final Flash* spell.

Jay managed to stay on the beast for about five more seconds before it bucked him off again. Derek, seeing Tom's spell charging, rushed in and smashed his shield into the creature's head, distracting it. Enraged, the Catoblepas swiped its claws across Derek's shield, producing a harsh, grating sound like nails on a chalkboard. Right after, Derek suddenly turned and ran away.

The beast, momentarily confused by Derek's sudden movement, followed his retreat with its eyes. At that moment, Tom finished charging his spell.

"FINAL FLASH!" he shouted, releasing the pent-up energy in a brilliant beam that crackled with power. The blast hit the Catoblepas squarely in the side, lifting it off its feet and slamming it into the wall. The beam continued to pour into the creature until Tom finally cut off the spell, feeling his mana reserves dangerously low.

The beast fell to the floor, a pitiful, pained whine escaping its throat.

"It's still alive!" Kiera shouted in disbelief.

"Brian! Try now!" Tom yelled, his vision blurring slightly from the mana drain.

Brian's head popped out from a bush, and seeing the monster lying on its side with multiple wounds, he rushed over and extended his hand, casting his taming Skill again. A green glow surrounded his hand as he concentrated, pouring everything he had into the spell. The light flickered and persisted longer this time, but after a few tense moments, it blinked out again.

"It's no use. The creature's level is too high for my Skill to work on it," Brian said, defeated.

"Then put it out of its misery," Tom commanded, his voice firm.

Brian hesitated, staring at the creature's pitiful form. "I'm not sure I can do that," he admitted, looking back at the others for support.

The team closed in, forming a protective circle around the weakened beast, just in case it tried to lash out one last time. "Just shoot it," Tom insisted. "If it gets back up and escapes, it could hurt someone else. We can't leave it."

Hands trembling, Brian pulled out one of his guns and aimed at the creature's head. His first shot pinged off its thick skull, causing it to jerk slightly.

"No, you idiot. In the eye," James snapped.

Taking a deep breath, Brian aimed carefully this time and fired a shot straight into the beast's eye. The creature went still.

"I told you this was a stupid idea! We could have been killed by that thing!" Brian yelled, his voice shaky with lingering fear and adrenaline.

"Oh, please. We had that in the bag. We were just trying to see if you could still tame it," Tom dismissed, waving off Brian's worries. "It wasn't even a big monster."

"Oh, sure. It was nothing, Brian. We can kill gods, Brian. No need to fear, we're here, Brian," Brian rambled, still a bit panicked.

"Now you're getting it," James said, grinning as he patted Brian on the back.

While the others *Inspected* the body for anything useful, Tom's mind drifted to crafting possibilities. "With Roland beginning to forge items and other crafters setting up, I bet some of these parts can be used for crafting," Tom mused aloud.

After removing the Catoblepas' horns, skin, and some larger bones, the team pressed on through the outdoor area. They soon came upon a door to the right that looked like it led to some kind of closet. But something felt off to Tom—this door hadn't been here before. A small plaque on the door read "Dungeon of Chance."

"Alright, time to go exploring," Tom announced, his excitement bubbling back up. "Maybe you can get a better pet after you level up a little, Brian." He turned the knob and pushed the door open, leading the way into the unknown.

Chapter 35

A New Kind of Dungeon

Tom stepped through the door of the Dungeon first, finding himself in a dark, seemingly endless void. There was something unsettlingly magical about the room. Unlike a pitch-black room where darkness swallowed everything, in this space, Tom could see himself and everyone else perfectly, despite the fact that there were no visible walls, floor, or ceiling. The sensation was disorienting, like being suspended in an infinite abyss.

He moved in just far enough to allow the others to follow. As the last of the group stepped inside, the door behind them swung shut with a soft *click*, sealing them in this strange, paradoxical darkness that somehow wasn't darkness at all.

"What the hell is going on here? It's like we're in some kind of goofy room where everything is black but the lights are still on," Jay muttered, glancing around, his eyes narrowing as if trying to pierce through the void.

"I don't know," Tom replied, his eyes scanning the darkness. "But I'm guessing we're about to find out." As he spoke, a message began to materialize in the air ahead of them, written in glowing, orange script. The letters formed one by one, as if an invisible hand was scrawling them in midair.

Once the text was fully written, Tom read it aloud:

"Step within, ye brave and bold,
Acknowledge this truth: the fates are cold.
In the game's heart, the die is cast,
Triumph's gift, should you outlast.
Gather around, ye souls yearning for glory's sound,
Dare the depths, where fortunes are found.
Fortune's favor, for the few who fail to fall,
First among legends, or consigned among the Seconds."

The words hung in the air, glowing softly. The tension in the room thickened as the final word faded out. A large, twenty-sided die then floated down from the unseen ceiling, spinning slowly as it descended. It was bigger than a man's head, hovering ominously before the group.

Tom stepped forward, examining it. He reached out, half-expecting it to be impossibly heavy, but when he poked it, the die floated through the air like a balloon.

"Roll me?" he read aloud, squinting at the new glowing text that had appeared above the die in the same fiery orange. "How am I supposed to—" He paused after picking up the large icosahedron, realizing it was much lighter than expected. "Oh. Well, okay then."

With a flick of his wrist, he tossed the die forward. It clattered against the unseen ground, rolling and bouncing with a heavy, echoing *thud* until it came to a stop on the number fourteen. The number flashed in the same vibrant orange color, and a distant *ding* echoed through the darkness.

"That's not a bad Initiative," Jay said idly.

"Squirrel?!" James called out suddenly from behind Tom. Spinning around, Tom saw that his wolf companion was nowhere to be found.

Turning back to where the die had been, Tom noticed it had vanished, replaced by a pedestal holding several small breathing apparatuses—one for each of them. Above the pedestal, more orange text appeared: *"Familiars are not allowed in the Ocean Room. They have been removed until the completion of the Dungeon."*

"No familiars in this Dungeon. Something about an ocean room?" Tom read aloud, feeling a knot tighten in his stomach.

As if triggered by his words, the floor began to tremble, and water started gushing in from all directions.

"What the fuck?! We came in here just to drown?!" Brian shouted, panic flooding his voice as he sloshed through the rapidly rising water, making a beeline toward Tom. "You! You did this to me! You can go rot in hell, you son of a—"

Brian's rant was cut short as Tom shoved one of the breathing apparatuses into his mouth. "Alright, everybody take one," Tom instructed, his tone steady despite the situation. "These should help you breathe underwater."

Tom found it oddly surreal that, after all he'd been through since the apocalypse started, this near-drowning scenario wasn't affecting him like it might have before. The rest of the group grabbed the devices, securing them in their mouths just as the water reached waist height.

Suddenly, Tom felt a pressure in his mind, like a bubble pressing against his thoughts. It popped, and he could hear the voices of his friends inside his head, clear and sharp. Brian, however, continued to freak out, his panicked thoughts flooding through the connection.

Tom waded over and slapped Brian on the back of his head. Instantly, his voice went silent in the mental link.

"Alright, this is some kind of new Dungeon," Derek's voice came through with a calm authority. "Be ready for anything. Watch each other's backs. We can apparently communicate through thought with these breathers, so keep communication tight."

The water was up to their chests now, and all eyes turned to Derek as he laid out their objectives.

"Looks like it's gonna be an underwater level. Not sure if when we get there we'll be riding something for movement or if it's like a *Super Mario* level where we swim through without touching anything dangerous. Be prepared for either. Anyone here can't swim?"

Silence. No hands raised.

"Excellent news, you sorry bunch of wet wimps!" Derek barked, his inner drill sergeant coming to the surface. "Now, I wanna see some hustle out there! Whoever kills the most monsters gets time off back at the Guild!"

The water crept up over their heads, and suddenly the rushing sound of it filling the space stopped. For a moment, there was an eerie stillness. Then, like dawn breaking, the world around them began to lighten. It felt as though they were opening their eyes to a new day, the dark void giving way to a vibrant underwater landscape.

Beams of sunlight pierced the water from above, creating rippling patterns of light that danced across the sandy ocean floor. They floated just above the seabed, outside what looked like a city made of stone buildings.

"It's beautiful," Kirsten whispered, her hair flowing around her face like a halo as she turned to take it all in.

Colorful fish darted around them, swimming toward the city and out into the open ocean. Suddenly, a shadow passed overhead—a massive whale, gliding serenely near the surface. The team hovered in place, taking in the sights, mesmerized by the underwater wonderland. In what looked like front yards of stone houses, green seaweed swayed gently, while bright corals formed gardens of vibrant blues, pinks, and yellows.

An arrow, glowing bright orange, appeared in the water ahead, pointing toward the distant city. Above it, the text read *"Head to town."*

"I guess we're heading to town," Tom communicated through their mental link. Without further hesitation, he set off toward the city, swimming steadily with the others following closely behind.

Moving through the water was slow and awkward; their human bodies weren't built for aquatic travel. By the time they reached the outskirts of the city, they realized they were at least three hundred feet beneath the ocean surface. Towering buildings, some reaching ten stories tall, stretched upward like coral-covered skyscrapers.

Stalls and shops lined the streets, though their signs were written in a strange, undecipherable language. As Tom focused on one of the signs, the script morphed into something resembling English. Spotting a shop labeled *Travel,* he swam over to it, his curiosity piqued.

As soon as he intended to speak, a familiar pressure built in his mind and popped.

"Hello! Welcome to my shop! I have everything you need to travel through the city in style. Is there anything in particular I can help you find?" a voice chirped in his head.

The shopkeeper was a strange, half-crab, half-human creature that scuttled to the counter with a clattering of clawed legs.

"We're… new to… well, being underwater," Tom explained, trying not to sound too disoriented. "We need to find a way to get around more easily."

"Ahhh, surface dwellers! Welcome to—" The crabman made a bubbling noise, like someone blowing bubbles in water, before continuing, "We are glad you decided to visit us!"

"Wait, is that the name of the town or your shop?" Tom asked, his ADHD fully activated by all the new sights.

"Oh"—the bubbling sound came from the crabman again—"is the name of the city."

"So, if I have that right—" Tom removed his breather and blew some bubbles as well. "Is that a regional dialect?"

The crabman gasped and reached out, slapping Tom hard across the face with one of his claws.

"*Excuse me*, sir! I'll have you know my mother was a fine woman!" the crabman said in utter indignation.

"I'm sorry. I have a very strong, um, surface accent?" Tom ended in a questioning tone as he suddenly realized he had no idea what he was talking about.

"Oh, right. That's true. I'm sorry for being so brash," the crabman suddenly apologized, its mood shifting much like a video game character's.

The creature's voice had a peculiar cadence, rising sharply at the end of every sentence, reminding Tom of King Candy from that *Wreck-It-Ralph* movie. They needed to move more fluidly, though, or they'd be sitting ducks in a fight.

"We need to figure out how to move more efficiently underwater," Tom clarified. "More naturally."

"Ye-e-e-s! I have just the thing! Density-shifting belts! They'll let you move through the water as if you were on land. And you can turn them on and off to swim up or down," the crabman replied, pulling out a tray with several belts.

Tom picked one up, examining the switch on the belt buckle. "How much for these?" he asked.

"Five common cores each," the crabman said, eyes gleaming with anticipation.

"Sold. We'll take one for each of us," Tom agreed, pulling out forty common cores from his Inventory and handing them over.

"Excellent! Thank you for your purchase," the crabman said, bowing low with a clicking of his claws.

"So, this is some kind of adventure Dungeon?" Tom mused as he turned back to the others, fastening his new belt.

"Feels like we're in a real-life one-shot campaign for a tabletop game," Derek replied. "This could be a lot of fun, but it's definitely going to be a challenge."

"Wait, so we're stuck in a real-life Dungeons and Dragons game?" Brian asked, panic creeping back into his voice.

"Hopefully more Dungeons than dragons, but yeah, pretty much," Tom confirmed.

"Oh, God. This is it. This is how I die," Brian muttered, his face pale.

"Cool your jets, shitstorm. We can make it through this. It's just another adventure," Derek tried to reassure him.

Suddenly, a deep bell tolled from somewhere in the center of town. The sea-people—if they could be called that—around them began to panic. They hastily packed up their stalls and scuttled for cover inside the stone buildings. A torrent of shouting erupted around the group, and Tom felt his mind swell with pressure as bubbles of thoughts from the panicking crowd began popping all at once, filling his brain with a cacophony of screaming voices.

Clutching his head, Tom struggled against the wave of sounds. His vision blurred, and his ears felt like they were about to burst. Then, just as quickly as it had started, the noise ceased. A System message flashed in their shared vision.

System Update Notice:
Communication Protocol Adjusted

Due to a miscalculation regarding the mental processing capacity of certain species on this planet, the Admins have implemented an urgent adjustment to the communication system for this Dungeon. The previous method has been deemed incompatible and has caused unintended sensory overload.

Please stand by as the communication protocol is updated to ensure a smoother, more manageable experience for all participants. Thank you for your patience.

Update in progress...

The world around them seemed to come to a sudden standstill. Tom found himself paralyzed, unable to move any part of his body except his eyes. He darted his gaze around, noticing that the creatures in the midst of their panicked retreat were also frozen in place, their faces locked in expressions of fear and urgency.

A moment later, reality seemed to lurch back into motion. A System message flashed in front of them, announcing that the "communication issue" had been resolved. Tom dismissed the notification and immediately felt a strange, almost electric presence in the space around him, emanating from where sounds were generated. His team stood silently beside him, their faces displaying a mix of confusion and readiness, but he could sense that the presence wasn't coming from them. It must have been an adjustment made by the Admins—whatever that meant. At least his head no longer felt like it was about to burst; the relief was palpable.

The town fell into an eerie silence. Every window and door in the stone buildings around them had been shut and locked in a rush, leaving the streets desolate. In the distance, a cloud of sand began to rise, churning up from the ocean floor like dust behind a speeding vehicle. The grains swirled up like a mini sandstorm, but unlike on land, the particles floated back down gently, settling like slow-falling snowflakes on the seabed.

As the cloud grew nearer, the team could make out the shapes within. A group of strange, half-human, half-sea creatures riding giant seahorses galloped toward them at full speed. The creatures had the upper bodies of muscular men and women, but their lower halves were sleek and covered in scales, their tails flowing behind them like mermaids. Their skin shimmered in iridescent hues of blue, green, and silver, catching the faint sunlight that filtered down from above.

The riders pulled their seahorses up short, encircling Tom and his team in a wide, threatening loop. Their eyes were filled with malice, and they began shouting jeers and taunts, trying to unsettle the newcomers. The seahorses snorted and… pawed? Tailed? Whatever it was, they did it to the sand, sending small clouds of particles swirling around them.

After a minute of this unnerving display, a deep, commanding voice cut through the chaos from outside the circle.

"Well, well, well. What do we have here?" the voice echoed, thick with a gravelly undertone that suggested both authority and danger. "A bunch of interlopers on old Pecos Mark's territory, eh? What say we teach them a lesson, boys?"

The voice belonged to a towering figure who emerged from the shadowy ranks of the circling riders. The fishman, who might be this Pecos Mark, had the upper body of a rugged, heavily scarred man, his muscles rippling beneath barnacle-encrusted armor. His lower half, however, was that of a monstrous eel, his dark, serpentine tail coiled beneath him, ready to spring. He wielded a wicked trident, its barbed tips glinting menacingly in the dim underwater light.

Tom felt his pulse quicken. The man's presence radiated danger; it was clear this encounter wasn't going to be a simple chat. His hand twitched instinctively for his weapon, but he held back. This was the kind of challenge they had entered the Dungeon for—a test of both strategy and strength.

The riders around them began to laugh, a hollow, haunting sound that resonated in the watery depths. Their seahorses stamped the ground restlessly, their eyes fixed on Tom and his team, awaiting the signal to charge.

"Everyone, stay calm," Tom communicated mentally to his group. "Be ready, but don't provoke them. Let's see what they want first."

Brian, standing closest to Tom, swallowed hard, his eyes darting between the circling riders. "Are you sure about that? They don't look like they want to negotiate."

"Trust me," Tom replied, his voice firm in their minds. "We'll be ready, but we need to get a read on these guys first. There's always a chance we can turn this to our advantage."

Derek, beside them, had his shield at the ready, his eyes locked on the stranger. "I've got your back, but I don't like the look of this. Something about him… feels off."

Kiera shifted into a defensive stance, her eyes narrowing as she sized up the circling riders.

"I say we teach them not to mess with us," she thought, her voice crackling with barely restrained energy.

"Patience," Tom thought back, a small smile tugging at the corners of his mouth. "Let's see how this plays out."

The fishman's gaze swept over them, his expression unreadable. The sea around them seemed to grow colder, the water pressing in like an invisible hand. This was the calm before the storm—a storm that could break at any moment.

Chapter 36

Pecos Mark's Posse

"Is the bet for most kills still on?" Kevin asked, his eyes locked on the circling sea horses and their half-human, half-fish riders.

"Hold on. Don't do anything rash just yet," Derek cautioned. "But be ready to equip your weapons."

"Taking shit from goons isn't really my style," Kevin chuckled, and in one fluid motion, equipped his greataxe.

Without a second thought, he swung it like a baseball bat, decapitating both a seahorse and its fishman rider in one devastating blow. For a moment, it felt like time slowed down. The now lifeless bodies, without the magic of their density-shifting belts, began to sink slowly toward the ocean floor, moving with a surreal slowness as if they were submerged in syrup.

Blood floated up from the bodies like droplets of food coloring in a kid's science project. It filled the area like a liquid cloud billowing with the shifting of the water.

The sudden display of violence spooked the remaining sea horses. They bucked wildly, trying to shake off their riders. Panic spread among the fishmen, some of whom began to abandon their mounts. From the rear of the group, the man who had spoken earlier—wearing a ridiculous cowboy hat that seemed entirely out of place underwater—began shouting, swinging his hat to control the chaos.

"What in tarnation is going on here?! You mongrels get back in there and show these interlopers what Pecos Mark's Posse can do!" he bellowed.

But as his eyes landed on the decapitated seahorse and its rider, the bluster left his voice. His mouth hung open for a second too long, his bravado slipping away.

"What the hell?!" He gasped, his voice a mix of confusion and fear. His gaze shifted from the floating bodies to Tom and his team, who stood calmly in formation—everyone except Brian, who was quivering behind Tom. "What are you, monsters?"

"Monsters? Now that's just hurtful," James said with an evil grin visible behind his breathing apparatus.

"Slim, we gotta get outta here and warn the boss about this!" another fishman pleaded, his voice high and panicked.

Slim, presumably the man in the hat, narrowed his eyes at Tom and his group. His scowl deepened as he weighed his options. Finally, he spat out a decision. "Move out! We'll let Pecos Mark know what's happening. We'll be back, you filthy scum! Just you wait. This town belongs to Pecos Mark!"

"You know, I never did like those scenes in the movies where the bad guys spout about how they were going to leave and come back to kill everyone," Tom said, his voice deceptively casual as he equipped his sword. "I mean. You'd have to be crazy to just let people *leave* like that, right?"

And with that, chaos erupted.

The team sprang into action. Bullets tore through the water, surprisingly fast despite the resistance, while swords, axes, and maces cut through the fishmen and their mounts with ruthless efficiency. The fishmen barely had time to react; they were utterly outclassed. The sea became a whirl of blood and motion, the team moving like a well-oiled machine.

Except for Brian. He ducked and weaved between his allies, jabbing out with his sword more by luck than any kind of strategy. Somehow, he managed to land a few desperate strikes on the flailing fishmen, his fear turning his movements into something almost effective.

The battle ended as quickly as it had started. The water around them was clouded with blood and debris, and the fishmen lay dead or dying, floating slowly toward the sandy floor below. Slim, clutching a slash across his chest that Tom had delivered, groaned as he tried to push himself up.

"You… you really are monsters," Slim wheezed, blood bubbling up from his mouth as he spoke. His eyes were wide with a mix of pain and disbelief.

"Well, you didn't give us much choice, partner," Tom replied, imitating the Western drawl. "You show up outta nowhere, scare all the townsfolk into hiding, and then try to intimidate us? Yeah, that was a mistake."

Slim coughed up another mouthful of blood, his face paling. "You'll… regret this…" His head lolled back, and his body went limp, sinking slowly to the ground.

Tom checked his Inventory, pleasantly surprised to find the fishmen they had killed were worth quite a few Monster Cores. He'd gained about seventy-five common cores from this brief encounter. Not bad for a Dungeon crawl. Maybe the System hadn't meant for them to kill the group, but it had been an option, and they'd chosen it. Now, they needed to understand more about what was happening in this underwater Western setting.

Before he could speak, a cheer rose from the town. The sea-people began emerging from their homes, cheering and clapping for the team's victory over Pecos Mark's gang.

"What is going on here?" James asked, bewildered.

"I think it's pretty obvious. This Pecos Mark is terrorizing these people, and we're here to save them," Tom said confidently.

"That's not what I meant. Why did Kevin not get in trouble for acting without orders, but I do?" James asked, indignant.

"Oh, that's because he takes the fights seriously," Derek replied with a smirk.

"I take them seriously!" James protested, crossing his arms, his irritation evident.

"You just tried to shoot the fishmen in the dick. Which, by the way, they don't seem to have, judging by how they kept coming at you," Derek countered, raising an eyebrow.

"Touché," James admitted, a little deflated.

"I do think something's off here," Derek said, his eyes narrowing as he looked around at the townsfolk gathering around them.

"Something like what?" Tom asked, turning to him.

"It feels a bit… cliché, doesn't it?" Derek replied, watching the people as they continued to celebrate.

"It's a Dungeon modeled after a Western. I'd expect it to be pretty straightforward," Tom said, shaking a few hands the sea-people extended toward him.

"Okay, everyone, give us some space! BACK UP!" Kiera suddenly shouted, her voice cutting through the noise.

The crowd began to quiet down, taking a few steps back from the adventurers.

"Sorry, I don't like being crowded like that. Makes me uncomfortable," Kiera said, frowning slightly.

"Weren't you a singer in a band? Wouldn't that put you in this position a lot?" Tom asked, glancing at her.

"We mostly played at bars and small clubs. We could go in the back. Not a lot of mobbing to do up on the stage," Kiera replied.

"What about in public?" James persisted.

"Did you miss the part where I said we played bars and small clubs? We weren't the Rolling Stones," Kiera shot back, her tone tinged with annoyance.

"Alright, alright. Look. Where's the mayor of the town? Can we talk to them?" Tom asked, his voice raised to be heard over the murmur of the crowd.

A fishman wearing a large cowboy hat and a shiny badge reading "Sheriff" made his way forward, pushing through the townspeople to speak to them.

"I'm both the mayor and the sheriff. Not many folks 'round these parts are willing to be in charge, so I kinda got picked by default," the man said. "Name's Montgomery. I want to thank you for what you did to Slim and his posse back there."

"It's not really a posse, though, is it?" James interjected.

"What?" Montgomery asked, looking at him as if he'd sprouted a second head.

"A posse. It's supposed to be a group of people the sheriff rounds up to go capture the bad guys, not a group of bad guys that raid the town," James explained, pausing as everyone stared at him strangely. "What? My dad loved Spaghetti Westerns, and I picked up on the terminology. We live in Texas, for crying out loud!"

"No, it's not that. Just… of all the knowledge for you to come through with for us, it couldn't have been more useless," Derek replied, shaking his head.

"Why would we care what they call themselves? They're clearly the bad guys here. So, they died," Tom stated, dismissing the tangent.

Unfortunately, the tangent was determined to have its day in the sun, apparently.

"Now hold on 'ere a moment, sonny." The Sheriff straightened, shoving his chest out. "Not that I want to go against the words of the good sir here, but I'm afraid I *must* contest these here outrageous claims. That there might be the historical definition of a posse, right enough. But the more informal definition is merely that of a group of people who have a common characteristic, occupation, or purpose." The Sheriff thumbed a finger across his nose. "That fits ol' Slim and his misfits right and true like a well-worn glove, I tell ya."

During the man's speech, everyone was turning their heads between the Sheriff and an increasingly thoughtful James.

Silence reigned as James tilted his head back and forth, considering.

"Yeah, no, he's got me on this one," James admitted.

The Sheriff flashed a bright smile that glinted with a number of gold teeth.

Tom's eye was beginning to twitch. He glared at James. "Are we done?"

"Well—" James seemed hesitant. "Since we've got an expert here, I *was* kind of hoping to get his thoughts on the difference between a throng and a mob…"

Tom's steely gaze turned toward Jay. "Jay?"

"Sir!" Jay came to attention, his hand snapping up in salute.

"You remember Operation Trunk Monkey?" Tom narrowed his gaze.

James swallowed.

"Fondly, sir!" Jay said. He grinned wickedly, pulling out a thin, innocuously designed blackjack and disappeared from sight.

"Actually"—James' voice cracked—"I rest my case, Your Honor."

Tom held the jokester's gaze for a moment longer before flicking his hand in dismissal.

Jay reappeared behind James, the blackjack held overhead, ready to bring down on the back of the man's head. Jay froze in place, his grin gradually transforming into a disappointed frown. He grudgingly lowered the implement of instruction. Muttering, he slunk away, throwing antagonistic glances back toward James as he did.

"…Anyway, you all came along right in the nick of time," Montgomery continued, eager to move past the interruption.

"What is it you need from us? We know it's coming, so just spit it out," Tom said, wanting to cut to the chase.

"Well, right to the point. I like a straight-shooter. We need someone who can help us get rid of Pecos Clem," Montgomery said.

"I knew it. You want—wait, what?" Tom asked, realizing Montgomery had said a different name.

"We need your help getting rid of Pecos Clem," Montgomery repeated, looking confused by Tom's reaction.

"But these guys said they were with Pecos Mark. Who the hell is Pecos Clem?!" Tom asked, his patience wearing thin.

"Why do we care what they're called? They want us to go throw ourselves at their enemy, and I, for one, think we should just... not," Brian suggested, his voice tired and frustrated.

Everyone turned to stare at him for a long moment.

"Uuuuggghhh... fine. Continue," Brian relented, sighing as he realized he was outnumbered once again.

"Pecos Mark? That can't be right," Montgomery muttered, scratching his chin as he thought. "He's out to the southeast, holding down his own territories. They shouldn't be here. Pecos Mark and Pecos Clem have a sort of truce going on for now. If they're sending people into Clem's area, that must mean..." Montgomery's eyes widened in realization. "Oh, gods! They must be gearing up for a territory war. This is worse than I thought."

"Really? We can't even escape this crap here?" Tom said, feeling utterly defeated as he facepalmed.

"Well, art does mimic life, or something like that," James quipped with a shrug.

"Not helping," Tom muttered, not even bothering to look at James.

"So, you can't help us?" Montgomery asked nervously, wringing his hands as he spoke.

"We didn't say that." Tom sighed, rubbing his temples. "Ugh... fucking wars are everywhere, aren't they?" He looked up at the sky as if seeking divine intervention.

"Look at it this way," Derek offered, trying to lighten the mood. "We get to storm some bases without worrying about killing anyone we shouldn't."

"Oh! That reminds me!" Montgomery interrupted. "Pecos Clem stole the town's... er, ladies of the night. So, we need them rescued."

"For fuck's sake!" Tom yelled, his voice echoing through the underwater town. "Are you kidding me?! Why does this fucking universe have to dump on us with this load of cunt-licking, dick-slapping, sack-stamping..." Tom's tirade continued for nearly five minutes, a symphony of creative profanities that left his team in stunned silence.

Tom had entered this Dungeon expecting a bit of fun—a break from the constant pressures of leadership, strategy, and the brutal reality of war. He had hoped for a chance to enjoy something that had always excited him in games: exploration and adventure. But instead, he found himself tangled in another conflict, another war scenario. The pressure of being the leader of a Guild caught in a war on two fronts had been building for weeks, and now it was spilling over.

"I *swear* in the name of every god in the heavens and demon below," Tom's rant reached a climactic pitch. "If this fucking place throws in even *one* goddamned escort quest, I will burn this place to the fucking ground!"

Gently, as though afraid to frighten a wild animal, a hand slipped into the air. It was Jay.

"*What?*" Tom snarled.

"But"—Jay gestured to the ocean all around them—"the water..."

"To the *ground!*" Tom shrieked. His swearing tirade returned at an even greater fever pitch.

"This is impressive. Even by my standards," James whispered to Jay in awe. He nodded in agreement.

Montgomery, now visibly nervous, took a cautious step back. "Can... can I give you a minute to talk this over?" he asked, clearly afraid of triggering another outburst.

"Yeah, that'd be good," Derek said, leading Tom away from the group.

Once they were out of earshot, Derek turned to Tom, his face serious. "Dude, you okay? You seem a little stressed for being in a Dungeon. Usually, you're all excited about this stuff."

Tom took a deep breath, trying to steady himself. "I don't know, man. It's just... this is too much. I came here to get my mind off things, to not have to constantly strategize about defending ourselves and attacking enemies, and now I'm right back in the same situation."

"Yeah, it's pretty shitty," Derek agreed. "But think of it like this: this could be practice for how we handle Shandra and The Master back home. If we make mistakes here, it won't cost us any real lives. We can learn from it and be better prepared for the real fight."

Tom stared at the ground, still frustrated. "It just keeps reminding me of everything waiting for us back at Vanguard. I can't help it."

"Just remember, you're not in this alone," Derek said, putting a reassuring hand on Tom's shoulder. "We're all busy getting things ready for our part in the war, but we're never too busy for you. We're friends. We're in this together, and the outcome affects all of us. So, if you need to vent or get some advice, we're here."

"I know that," Tom admitted, his voice softer now. "But it still feels like everything rests on my shoulders. Every decision, every possible outcome... It's like the weight of the world is crushing me. And I'm afraid one day I'll just be nothing but a smear on the ground."

Derek nodded. "Look, everyone wishes they weren't carrying such heavy burdens. We'd all love to be skipping through fields and sipping margaritas. But we don't get to make that call. All we can do is make the best decisions with the information we have, and if there are consequences, we learn from them and move forward. That's how we get stronger."

"But what if I fail?" Tom asked, his voice almost a whisper. "What if people die?"

"People have already died," Derek replied, his tone firm but compassionate. "But think about how many you've saved. Over a thousand people are with Vanguard because you gave them hope. You inspired them. When people die, no one blames you. They trust you because you've shown them you're worth believing in."

Tom had to admit that Derek was right. He'd been so focused on the negatives lately, and that mindset could drag everyone down. He couldn't afford to let his worries get the better of him, not when so many people were counting on him. A small smile crept onto his face as he started to feel a bit lighter.

"There we go," Derek said, smiling back. "You see what we all see now. You're not alone in this. People believe in you, and they'll keep following you as long as you keep doing what's right."

Tom nodded, feeling a renewed sense of purpose. "You're right. Thanks for that."

Derek grinned and threw an arm over Tom's shoulder. "Now, let's get back to business. We've got a Dungeon to clear."

As they walked back to the group, Jay noticed their approach. "You good now, boss?"

"Yeah. Sorry, I needed to get that out of my system," Tom said, exhaling a deep breath. "Alright, so we go after Mark first, take him down, and then we deal with Clem and the whores."

"They… the ladies that is… really prefer other terms," Montgomery began, but quickly shut his mouth when Tom shot him a glare.

"That sounds like the best plan," Derek agreed. "We can gauge their strength without worrying about hostages at first and then plan a rescue."

"Where exactly is Pecos Mark located?" Tom asked.

"He's southeast of here, like I mentioned earlier," Montgomery explained. "Just follow the road and turn south at the fork instead of continuing east."

"What road? I didn't see any—" Tom started, but then he looked back and saw a road had suddenly appeared, carved into the sandy ocean floor where there hadn't been one before.

"Anyone else get the feeling this is a beta Dungeon?" James asked, staring at the newly formed road.

Jay slapped a hand down on James' shoulder. "Takes one to know one, I suppose," he said with a sigh of satisfaction. He raised an eyebrow. "I'll be sure to let you know if I spot an alpha Dungeon though. Until then, we could really use your expertise on everything *beta.*"

Whistling idly, Jay strolled off toward the road.

"Hey!" James complained, trotting after the Rogue. "That doesn't even make sense, asshole!"

Kiera snorted, holding her hand over her mouth.

James just glared as he ran past her, which turned her chuckle into a full-throated laugh.

"There is something weird about this place," Tom agreed, doing his best to ignore the trio.

"Almost like things weren't fully planned out, or maybe someone's messing with us?" Kevin added.

"Why would a System Admin bother with our little party when there are probably billions of other planets out there?" Derek pondered.

"I think the bottom line is 'don't look a gift horse in the mouth,'" Tom said, trying to refocus.

"Don't look a gift 'sea' horse in the mouth, I think you mean," Jay added, chuckling at his own joke.

Tom just glared at him.

"Right, wrong time, got it," Jay said, raising his hands in surrender.

"When we get there, we hit them hard and fast. No time for them to regroup or set up a defense," Tom instructed. "Hopefully, that way we can make a clean sweep."

"Also, be ready for a gunfight," Derek added. "I bet that's what's being set up here. Kiera, you hold back and find a sniper point. Cover us."

"Got it. I'll keep 'em off ya," Kiera confirmed, a fierce glint in her eye.

"We can also provide you with some transport since you volunteered to help us," Montgomery offered.

"What kind of transport?" Tom asked, a bit wary.

About half an hour later, the team stood inside a gigantic clamshell, rigged up like a cart, with four dolphins hitched to the front.

"We look ridiculous," Tom muttered.

"It could be worse," Derek replied, trying to keep things light.

"How?" Tom challenged.

"We could all be wearing seashell bikinis, singing about forks, and talking to seagulls," James joked.

"Yeah, that's one way. And remember, this could also be a fabricated Dungeon with real-world consequences," Derek added, his smile fading slightly at Tom's intensity.

"You're right. Sorry. I'm going to stay positive. We're going to have a good time, and we're going to get some XP," Tom said, his shoulders straightening as he took the reins.

With a flick, the dolphins surged forward, pulling the clamshell along the sandy path. The team prepared themselves mentally for what lay ahead.

"We're coming for you, Pecos Mark," Tom said, his eyes narrowing with determination. "You can't hide from what you've done."

Chapter 37

Hideout

"What exactly *did* Pecos Mark do again?" James asked, breaking the silence after Tom's dramatic proclamation.

"I don't know," Tom grumbled, annoyed at having his moment undermined. "Terrorized towns? Stole from them? Hurt people, probably? It just sounded like a cool thing to say."

"You know, this Dungeon is following a familiar pattern," Derek chimed in as they rode toward the fork in the road.

"How so?" Tom asked, turning to Derek.

"Well, in most games, there are always mini-bosses before you reach the main boss. It's like this Dungeon expects you to take on one challenge first, then move on to the harder task. So, it's just a coincidence we're facing another war on two fronts," Derek explained. "Also, notice how the townspeople here aren't defending themselves; they're hiding, scared for their lives. It's not exactly the same as what we're dealing with back home."

Tom shot Derek a glare, his jaw tightening.

"Sorry, just trying to help. I know you don't need more stress," Derek said, raising his hands in mock surrender.

They reached the fork in the road, and Tom guided the dolphins south, away from the eastern path. His shoulders slumped, and he let out a long sigh.

"I know you're right. I'm sorry for snapping. It's just… I've been hoping for something more relaxing in this Dungeon. A break from all the stress," Tom admitted, trying to let go of his frustration.

"Hey, you don't have to explain yourself to us. We're right there with you," Derek replied. "But it's good to hear you acknowledge it. Besides, I think there's going to be plenty of violence ahead for you to blow off some steam." Derek gave him a friendly nudge with his elbow and winked.

Tom managed a small smile. "You're probably right. It'll be nice to let loose and lop off a few heads."

"It definitely helped me," Kevin chimed in, still grinning while he held an arm around Kirsten's waist.

"You almost screwed that up back there, you know," Derek pointed out to Kevin.

"Nah, I could see it in Tom's eyes. He was ready," Kevin replied, his grin widening.

"Crock of bullshit," James grumbled, arms crossed.

"Oh, come on. You can't expect us to treat everyone the same. You're too much of a child for that," Tom teased, feeling his spirits lift a little more.

As they continued along the sandy path, Tom began to appreciate the surreal beauty of their underwater Western setting. At first, he'd been baffled by the juxtaposition of a Western scene beneath the sea. But now, if he ignored the water surrounding them, it really did resemble a desert landscape. The sand stretched as far as the eye could see, resembling the endless dunes of an actual desert.

The terrain lacked the traditional shifting dunes, but scattered sandbars rose above the otherwise flat ocean floor like small hills. Some of the vegetation and rock formations even resembled cacti, sticking up sporadically as they traveled. Schools of fish darted around these outcroppings, their vibrant colors creating bursts of life against the sandy backdrop. Occasionally, dark shapes loomed in the distance—perhaps sharks—and farther above, the silhouettes of whales surfaced for air.

As they traveled, smaller schools of fish swam alongside them, curious about the clamshell vehicle. A remora had even latched onto the side, hitching a free ride. The colors surrounding them were more vivid than anything Tom had seen above water. The feeling of weightlessness from the water, especially when they turned off the density-shifter belts, was strangely euphoric.

As the team got further away from the town, a range of underwater mountains began to rise in the distance, their jagged peaks casting long shadows across the ocean floor. Drawing closer, the entire scene abruptly froze around them. The world went still, as if someone had hit pause on reality. A message in the familiar glowing orange text appeared before them, saying: "Roll me," and a twenty-sided die floated down to Tom.

"What are we rolling for now?" Tom asked, taking the die into his hand.

The text above the die shifted to read: "Perception check."

Sighing, Tom rolled the die out onto the sandy floor. It bounced and spun for a moment before finally settling on a seventeen. The number flashed once in bright orange, and the die slowly faded out of existence. The world resumed its normal motion, and ahead, a small cave began to glow with a soft orange light, drawing their attention.

"I guess we should check that out?" Tom suggested, looking around at the others.

Most of the team shrugged, but Derek looked ahead, eyes narrowed. "Not much else out here. We should investigate, but let's approach from off the path. Keep some distance."

Tom nodded, steering the dolphins away from the path and toward a large kelp forest that could provide cover. Once hidden in the greenery, they stopped and left the dolphins and clamshell half-concealed among the tall strands of kelp.

"Won't those dolphins die? Don't they need air?" Kiera asked, glancing back at the dolphins with concern.

"Montgomery said they were magical dolphins that can breathe underwater, so they should be fine," Derek assured her.

"You all be good now," Kiera cooed to the dolphins as she walked over, stroking their smooth heads affectionately. "Don't go running off. I'll bring you back some fish if you behave."

The dolphins nuzzled into her hand, seemingly understanding her words. With a satisfied nod, Kiera rejoined the team, and they began their cautious approach toward the glowing cave, weapons at the ready.

The team crept closer to the cave entrance, moving through the thick kelp that stretched nearly a hundred feet toward the surface. Peering through the dense, swaying fronds, they spotted two fishmen lounging on either side of the cave mouth. They were dressed in traditional Western outfits, complete with cowboy hats, and each had a revolver holstered at their hip.

"Well, looks like they all have guns," Tom muttered under his breath.

"No kidding, this is a Western. We kinda figured," James whispered back with a smirk.

"I just meant we can't rush in with swords and axes. We won't get close enough before they gun us down. Everyone got the guns we talked about, right?" Tom asked, his voice low as he scanned the group.

In response, the team pulled out an array of firearms—handguns, shotguns, and a few assault rifles—creating the impression of a makeshift armory.

"Alright, good. Remember, if you can get close, physical weapons can deal more damage to multiple enemies at once. But do whatever it takes to stay alive," Tom instructed, keeping his voice calm and steady as they huddled together.

"I'll start us off," Kiera volunteered, moving to the edge of the kelp forest with her assault rifle at the ready.

Kiera had invested in a good scope, giving her a clear advantage in taking them by surprise. She settled her breathing, peered through the scope, and sighted in on the guard furthest away on the right. She aligned the crosshairs with the fishman's forehead, took a deep breath, and smoothly squeezed the trigger.

The rifle fired with a muffled thud, and the bullet flew true, striking the fishman squarely in the forehead. His head snapped back, and the back of his skull exploded against the stone wall, splattering the cave entrance with a mix of fish blood and brain matter. She quickly swung her aim to the second guard, who had just enough time to turn and see his partner's headless corpse slump to the ground. Her second shot hit him in the back of the head, blowing his face out onto the stone floor. He collapsed without ever fully realizing he was dead.

"MOVE IN!" Derek barked through the mental link.

As one, the team sprinted from the cover of the kelp forest, moving like a SWAT team toward the cave entrance. They barely made it to the first set of crates outside the cave when a horde of fishmen of varying sizes and shapes poured out, guns drawn and ready. The team hunkered down behind whatever cover they could find—crates, barrels, and rocks—just as the first fishmen spotted them. Gunfire erupted from both sides, bullets ricocheting off stone and wood, creating a chaotic symphony of destruction.

James grinned as he took aim. Every time he hit a fishman in the crotch, he'd yell, "DICK SHOT!" The others mostly tried to make their shots count, aiming for center mass or headshots. As more and more fishmen emerged from the cave, ducking behind barrels and crates for cover, James decided it was time to change tactics.

Switching to his Uzis, he activated his *Hunter's Mark* Skill, enhancing his accuracy. With a gleeful cackle, he unleashed a torrent of bullets, spraying the cave entrance. The fishmen, now pinned down, couldn't even risk a glance over their cover without getting a bullet to the face. Every time one of them tried to peek out, James was ready, putting a bullet right between their eyes.

"Keep moving while James lays down fire!" Derek ordered through the mental link. "Kiera, be ready to unload when James runs dry! Cover us while we close in!"

Everyone else—including Brian who still looked reluctant but determined—rushed forward, darting between cover and taking down any fishmen they encountered. Tom slid behind a crate just as James' Uzis ran out of bullets. Ducking behind the cover, he reloaded while Kiera switched to her double assault rifle setup. She waited a heartbeat, then sprang up and unleashed a blistering hail of gunfire.

"THIS IS MY KIND OF PARTY! COME AND DIE BY MY HANDS!" Kiera shouted, adrenaline coursing through her veins as she laid waste to the enemy.

Panicked, the remaining fishmen cowered behind their cover, too terrified to risk exposing themselves. Meanwhile, Tom and the others pressed their advantage, moving from cover to cover and picking off the stragglers. By the time Kiera's magazines ran dry, the cave entrance was littered with the bodies of dead fishmen.

"Merry Christmas, ya filthy animals," James quipped, standing up from behind a crate. A wounded fishman groaned nearby. Without missing a beat, James unloaded another burst from his Uzi into its head. "And a happy new year."

The air grew still, the scent of blood and gunpowder mixing in the water. The team scanned the area, ensuring there were no more threats. Satisfied, Tom gave a nod, and they all moved to regroup.

Derek leaned in to peer into the cave, his eyes squinting against the darkness. A sudden flash and a deafening crack followed as a bullet ricocheted off the cave wall, inches above his head. He jerked back, pressing himself against the rugged stone.

"We're not done yet—there's more inside," he muttered, catching his breath. His heart was pounding from the close call.

"Oh, I know what happens next!" James said, grinning as he darted over to the opposite side of the cave entrance. A second bullet whizzed by, narrowly missing him. He barely flinched, more excited than scared.

With a dramatic flair, James cupped his hands around his mouth and shouted, "Pecos Mark! We know you're in there! This only ends one of two ways, see? Either you come out to us, or we come in to you!"

Jay glanced over at James, raising an eyebrow. "Well, now that just sounded wrong."

James blinked, replaying his words in his head. "Huh? Oh! I got it now. HA!" He doubled over in laughter.

From deep within the cave, a gravelly voice shouted back, "You'll never take me alive!"

James, still chuckling, snapped back into character. "That was never really an option, Mark!" he yelled, doing his best to mimic a Southern drawl. "Ya see, I worked up a mighty fine thirst for blood, killin' all your men out here. Now you's next, ya blue-bellied bottomfeeder!" James was cupping the side of his mouth as best he could as he called out into the cave. "The bill you done rung up with the ol' Dust Devil hisself's come due, Pecos!"

The voice of Pecos Mark echoed back, laced with a mix of mockery and defiance. "Way I sees it, I got the upper hand right now! Go ahead, come on inside and see if I don't feed ya twelve barrels of lead. I dare ya, unless yer' yella bellied on top of bein' ugly enough to back a buzzard off a gut wagon!"

Tom leaned against the rock, thinking quickly. "Anyone have any ideas?" he asked, his gaze darting between the cave entrance and his team.

"I've got one, but you might not like it," Kiera said, her expression serious.

"Well, let's hear it," Tom prompted, eager for any plan that could break the standoff.

Kiera reached into her Inventory and pulled out a heavy, eight-round grenade launcher. "I've got this bad boy, but it only has a few rounds. Cost me a fortune, so I'd rather not waste them."

James' eyes lit up like a kid on Christmas morning. "You bought a grenade launcher?! That's so badass! Why didn't you tell me?"

Kiera held the launcher away from him protectively. "Because you, of all people, absolutely should not have one. In fact, I'm pretty sure it should be illegal for you to even touch it."

"Aww, come on! That's not fair." James pouted, clearly disappointed.

"Oh no, it's totally fair," Tom chimed in, his tone dead serious.

The others nodded in unison, some more emphatically than others.

"Aw, man," James sulked, kicking at the swirling sand.

"Alright," Derek cut in, bringing the conversation back on track. "We go with Kiera's plan. We probably won't be able to go in after, if the cave collapses, but let's hope we get him in the first barrage."

Kiera positioned herself at the cave entrance, bracing the grenade launcher against her shoulder. Her eyes narrowed, focused and intense.

"On my mark," Derek ordered, his voice low and tense. "Three… Two…"

The group tensed, gripping their weapons tighter, ready to move at a moment's notice. The silence hung heavy around them, filled only by the rhythmic pounding of their hearts and the distant sound of bubbles rising through the water.

Chapter 38

Dungeon Campaign

"One… NOW!" Derek shouted, moving further from the cave entrance to avoid the blast radius.

Kiera immediately fired off four grenades in quick succession. The canisters flew into the cave, their metal shells clinking and bouncing off the stone walls, echoing deep inside.

"SON OF A—" a voice shouted from within, but it was cut off as the grenades detonated almost simultaneously.

A deafening explosion rocked the cave, sending chunks of rock and debris flying outward. The concussive blast rippled through the water, blowing the sand on the ocean floor back in a perfect half-circle around the cave entrance. For a moment, everything was obscured by a thick cloud of sediment swirling in the water.

As the sand settled and visibility returned, the team stepped cautiously out from behind their cover, scanning the aftermath.

"I guess the cave wasn't as deep as we thought," James said with a nervous chuckle, still feeling the lingering vibrations of the explosion.

Jay grinned., "Well, whatever those guys were thinking, I'm pretty sure the last thing that went through their minds was… shrapnel."

The group exchanged wary glances, half-expecting some sort of counterattack. Then, a System window appeared in their vision, hovering in mid-water like an ethereal display.

Quest Update: Defeat the Outlaws

Objective Progress:
- Defeat the outlaw Pecos Mark: **1/1 Completed**
- Defeat the outlaw Pecos Clem: **0/1 Completed**
- Return to town to collect rewards: **0/1 Completed**

Next Steps:
Proceed to Pecos Clem's camp to complete the second objective. Be mindful of potential hostages and approach with caution to minimize collateral

---

damage. Return to the town sheriff after both outlaws are defeated to claim your rewards.

Seeing the quest progress update was a relief. Knowing that Pecos Mark was dead made things clearer, especially in a System-generated Dungeon where information was often sparse. The System rarely provided such direct feedback, so having a visible quest tracker for the campaign was a welcome change. It reminded Tom of the RPG games he used to play, where quests were a core mechanic. He wished the System in the real world worked more like that, but he knew better than to hope for changes on such a massive scale.

Shaking off those thoughts, Tom turned to his team to ensure everyone was ready for whatever came next.

"Everyone alright? Any injuries?" Tom asked, scanning the group to make sure the blast hadn't caused any collateral damage.

"I dodged most of the debris, but I've got a nasty cut on my arm," Jay said, stepping closer and showing Tom the deep gash running along his forearm.

Tom winced. "That looks pretty rough. Hold still for a second."

Jay braced himself as Tom extended his hands, dark purple light beginning to swirl around them. He muttered an incantation under his breath, and the healing energy flowed from his hands to Jay's arm. The wound stopped bleeding almost immediately, the torn flesh slowly knitting back together. It took a second casting of *Dark Healing* to fully close the gash and restore Jay's HP, but by the end, only the torn sleeve and dried blood remained as evidence.

Jay flexed his hand, testing his newly healed arm. "Much better. Thanks for that," he said, rubbing the now-healed skin to shake off the phantom pain.

Kiera stepped up, her eyes focused. "So, what's the next move?"

"Pecos Clem is next," Tom said, his tone shifting to a more serious one. "But he's got captives. We can't just blow things up like we did here. We need to be smart about it. Jay, you're taking point on this one. We need stealth and precision. Silent kills. I want them to look shocked when we make our move."

Jay nodded, a sly grin forming. "Stealth is my specialty, but it'd be a lot easier if we wait until nightfall."

Tom considered this for a moment and then nodded. "Good idea. We wait until dark. We go in stealthy and get as close as we can before we're detected. Make it quick, make it clean."

Brian shifted nervously. "And if we get discovered?"

Tom grinned. "Then we do what we do best: fuck shit up."

Brian sighed. "Oh, fantastic. I was worried we might actually have a plan," he said, sarcasm dripping from his voice.

Tom raised an eyebrow. "Got a better idea?"

Brian threw up his hands. "*I*—didn't even want to *be here*. I'm just a desk guy, remember? What do I know about raiding bandit camps to rescue captives? Not a damn thing."

James slapped Brian on the back, grinning. "Relax, man. It's just a Dungeon campaign. Worst case, some of the hostages don't make it. But that's not part of the objective. Just think of it as practice for the real deal."

Brian shot James a glare but didn't argue. His shoulders slumped, his expression one of reluctant acceptance. Just as the tension began to ease, another System window popped up in their vision, grabbing everyone's attention.

Quest Update: Defeat the Outlaws

Objective Progress:
- Defeat the outlaw Pecos Mark: **1/1 Completed**
- Defeat the outlaw Pecos Clem: **0/1 Completed**
- Save the hostages: **0/15 Completed**
- Return to town to collect rewards: **0/1 Completed**

New Objective Added:
- **Save the hostages:** Ensure the safety of the 15 captives held by Pecos Clem's gang. Hostages must be secured alive for successful completion.

Next Steps:
Formulate a strategy to infiltrate Pecos Clem's camp with minimal detection. Prioritize hostage rescue to avoid unnecessary casualties. Once the hostages are secure, eliminate Pecos Clem to complete the quest. Return to town for your rewards after all objectives are achieved.

"You just can't help yourself, can you?" Brian snapped at James, his face flushed with frustration. "Always gotta open that big mouth of yours. Guess what? You screwed us again!"

James rolled his eyes. "Seriously, man. Do you need a Snickers? 'Cause you're being a real diva right now."

"You fucking Americans," Brian began, but he was cut off by the sudden sharp sound of an explosion coming from the north.

"What the hell was that?" Kirsten asked, her eyes wide.

"Sounded like an explosion," Tom replied.

"No shit, Sherlock. I meant, why did it happen?" Kirsten clarified, her annoyance growing.

Jay squinted in the direction of the blast. "My guess is it came from Pecos Clem's camp. We need to check it out before nightfall."

"To the clammobile!" James shouted, pointing toward the kelp forest.

"Wait!" Derek shouted.

"What is it?" Tom asked, worried he'd missed something that Derek picked up on.

"Grab their weapons first," Derek said, his arms extended to both sides like he was trying to goal-keep the other members of the team from leaving. "More guns equals more weapons for the Guild."

"Alright," Tom agreed. "Grab the weapons, then head out."

A short time later, the team scrambled back into their underwater chariot—essentially a half-clamshell pulled by four dolphins. Tom cracked the reins, and they sped off toward the north, heading straight for Pecos Clem's camp. As they raced forward, Tom's mind spun with the complexities of their situation. When there were no innocent victims in the crossfire, his team excelled at cutting down anyone in their path. But add hostages into the mix, and things became far more complicated.

This was precisely why he hadn't yet stormed The Master's stronghold to end things quickly. Hostage situations were messy, unpredictable, and required finesse his team had yet to master. But now, with this Dungeon as their training ground, the stakes felt more manageable. If things went south and the captives didn't make it, it wouldn't result in any real-world consequences—just potentially fewer rewards. Tom found himself oddly comforted by the parallel between this scenario and the one their Guild faced.

Cutting straight north through the kelp forest instead of following the winding road, they made better time toward Pecos Clem's camp. However, this shortcut had an unintended consequence—they overshot their mark. The dense kelp suddenly gave way to an open clearing, and the team, barreling forward at full speed, burst out into the camp without any warning.

Pandemonium erupted.

Pecos Clem's gang, lounging around their camp, sprang up in shock as a giant half-clam shell, dragged by dolphins, exploded out of the kelp. Tom's team, momentarily stunned by their abrupt emergence, stared wide-eyed as they realized they had completely lost the element of surprise.

One significant issue with traversing an underwater kelp forest at breakneck speed was that kelp didn't provide the kind of stability you'd expect from a terrestrial forest. The long strands merely reached up for the surface, giving way with every movement. As Tom had driven the chariot into the kelp, it flopped over the dolphins' faces and lashed the team in the face like a comedic scene from a movie where someone drives through a thick forest without slowing down.

Sputtering and spitting out bits of kelp, Tom and his team found themselves blinded by the slapping strands. So, forgetting to stop, they had plowed straight into the open camp, trailing kelp behind them like streamers as it tore free from the stalks.

Ripping pieces of kelp off their heads to clear their vision, Tom and his crew had only one reaction to the escalating chaos—they began screaming and panicking. Tom pulled hard on the reins to steer the dolphins away from a large stack of crates, but Pecos Clem's men, caught equally off guard, began screaming and scattering as well. Some tried to dive for cover, while others stood frozen in shock.

Several men were caught under the runaway chariot's path, crushed beneath its weight. Their bodies splattered the ocean floor with blood, which began to disperse in crimson clouds as their density-shifting belts malfunctioned. The dolphins, now in a frenzy, whipped their tails furiously, driven by both fear and Tom's desperate tugs on the reins.

Tom managed to steer the dolphins in a hard turn, narrowly avoiding the stack of crates, but not without grazing the side of them. The crates toppled, and as they fell, more of Clem's men were caught beneath the tumbling wood, their screams drowned out by the chaos. Sand swirled around them, creating a murky haze that added to the confusion.

Realizing his screaming wasn't helping, Tom tried to calm himself and regain control. The dolphins, however, were beyond listening. Feeling the chaos take hold again, he decided to embrace it. He pulled out a gun, and with a primal scream of rage, started firing wildly at any target he could find. The others, picking up on his energy, did the same.

The clamshell, now caught in a continuous circle as the dolphins swam in a desperate, counter-clockwise arc, became a dizzying whirl of bullets and bodies. Tom felt like he was in some twisted underwater version of a car chase, narrowly missing enemies while unloading his gun. His team followed suit, turning the chaotic scene into a madman's game of death.

The gang members who hadn't been run over were now either ducking for cover or returning fire in a disorganized frenzy. More and more reinforcements poured out of nearby caves, only to be run down by the chariot's rampage or caught in the crossfire.

The world seemed to tilt as Tom yanked the reins too hard, causing the chariot to smash into another crate. The impact sent the entire team flying out, tumbling across the sandy floor and sending up puffs of sand where they landed. The dolphins, screeching and clicking in panic, finally broke free from their reins and bolted into the distance.

The hammers of dozens of revolvers echoed across the now-calm waters.

Suddenly surrounded, the team had no choice but to raise their hands in surrender.

"Look, we just want to talk to Clem. Can we do that?" Tom said, trying to catch his breath and calm his frayed nerves.

One of the fishmen stepped forward, his eyes narrowing. "The boss has been waiting for you," he said, swinging a heavy club down on Tom's head. The last thing Tom saw before everything went dark was a mocking grin on the fishman's face.

Chapter 39

Pecos Clem

Slowly, the world came back into focus for Tom. He tried to rub his eyes but realized his hands were tied behind his back. He pulled against the ropes, but they only tightened further. They must have been using some kind of constrictor knot. As his senses returned, so did the memory of their disastrous first strike on Pecos Clem's camp.

Tom glanced around. He and the others had been moved inside a cave. If he leaned forward a bit, he could see the cave entrance from where they sat him—night had fallen, which meant he'd been unconscious for a while. Scanning the dimly lit room, he noticed some of his teammates were also stirring awake, though others were still out cold. Toward the back of the room, several scantily dressed fishwomen sat at a table, sipping from teacups.

"Hello," Tom began cautiously, trying to engage them in conversation.

"Well, I'll be! You're finally awake, are ya? Poor thing must be in some kinda pain from that bump on the noggin you got," one of the fishwomen said in a thick Southern Belle accent as she stood up and approached him.

"Are you… the, uh, people from the town that Pecos Clem took?" Tom asked, fumbling for a polite way to describe them.

"Uh-oh, I know that look. Honey, we are the women of questionable affection you're referring to. But I appreciate your attempt at tact," the fishwoman replied with a bemused smile.

"Right, so, we came here to rescue you," Tom said, wincing as he shifted and felt a sharp pain in his head.

"Don't move too much just yet, darlin'. You need to get your wits about ya first," the woman said, grabbing a towel and dabbing his forehead with cool water. "We appreciate the thought, but you're all in here with us now. Not much rescuin' you can do from inside these ropes."

"That's not true. We can fight our way out. Our only concern was your safety. If you're all here, then we'll just take you with us when we get the hell out of here," Tom insisted, feeling more alert as the cold water soothed his headache.

"You sure do think highly of yourself," the woman chuckled. "Pecos Clem ain't someone to mess with. Better to just give him what he wants and play along."

"I'm Tom, by the way," he said, extending a hand as best as he could manage in his bindings.

"Petunia," the fishwoman responded, reaching out to shake his hand. Then she froze. "WAIT!" She gasped suddenly, her eyes widening.

"Shhhhh. Don't go gettin' too excited. We don't want any special attention," Tom whispered, suddenly finding himself speaking with a bit of a Southern accent and putting a finger to his lips.

"How did you get your hands out?" Petunia whispered back, and the other women leaned in closer, curious.

"Just stored the rope in my Inventory. As long as I'm touching something and it isn't too big, I can put it in my Inventory. Learned that little trick from a previous capture," Tom explained with a grin.

"Saying things like 'previous capture' doesn't exactly fill us with confidence," Petunia said, raising an eyebrow.

"Yet here we are, alive and kicking. And we made them pay for it, too," Tom replied, his expression turning serious.

"I see. Then we'll help however we can. What do you need us to do?" Petunia asked, nodding in understanding.

Tom quickly laid out a basic plan for them. They needed to wait until more of his team woke up. Petunia grabbed a jug from the corner and splashed some water on Jay, waking him up with a start. She moved over to Derek and did the same, dumping the contents on his head. Watching her, Tom suddenly became intrigued by the item.

"What is that?" Tom asked, pointing at the jug.

"What? This jug of water?" Petunia looked at it, curious about his sudden interest.

"But you dumped it out twice, and it refilled itself. Is it a trick jug?" Tom asked, now thoroughly fascinated.

"Oh, it's got enchantments on it. One to refill, one for water selection—you gotta fill it with something specific—and a top-off enchantment so it doesn't overflow," Petunia explained, pointing to three different runes on the bottom, side, and near the lip of the jug.

Tom stared at the object in genuine wonder. "Can anyone make them?"

"No, only Enchanters can. You need to know about runes to make these things," Petunia replied. "But that's about all I know."

"Enchanter is a… Profession?" Tom inquired, his mind spinning with possibilities.

"Well, honey, if I didn't know any better, I'd say you were new to all this. Of course it's a Profession," Petunia chuckled, her laughter like soft wind chimes.

"You really want to focus on a magic jug after all we've seen and where we are?" Derek said, rubbing the back of his head where he'd been struck.

"Sorry, you're right. Not the time. We need to get out of here and take down Clem," Tom agreed, shaking off his distraction.

"I wanna know how I just got more wet underwater," Jay chimed in.

"Best not to ask too many questions here, sugar," Petunia said.

"Anyway, this plan isn't great," Derek replied.

"The situation isn't great. If you have any better ideas, I'm all ears," Tom challenged, crossing his arms.

"No, it'll have to do. Just remember how our last plan went," Derek said, gesturing to the room around them.

"That was the dolphins' fault. We can do this," Tom said firmly, though deep down he acknowledged their error of not sticking to the road.

"Fine. But we should bring in Bron," Derek suggested.

"Familiars can't be summoned in this Dungeon," Tom reminded him, thinking about how Jerky and Squirrel had been removed.

"Isn't Bron a Summon, though? That might be different. Just try," Derek urged, still squinting from his lingering headache.

Tom hesitated but decided to give it a shot. He cast his *Summon Demonic Creature* Skill, and to his relief, the summoning circle lit up, and Bron materialized in the room.

"Excellent! It worked!" Tom cheered quietly.

"What worked?" Bron rumbled, looking around.

"Summoning you. I wasn't sure if it would work since familiars aren't allowed in this Dungeon," Tom explained to the towering elephant man.

"Ah, that's different. Familiars are bound to you, while Summons like me are just under contract. That's why I can be here," Bron explained. "But wait, you said we're in a Dungeon. This place looks like it's underwater. Where the hell are we?"

"We're in an underwater Dungeon. By the way, how are you breathing? I just realized I summoned you without one of these breathing apparatuses," Tom asked, distracted yet again by something other than the objective.

"Magic," was all Bron said.

"Well, that's a little deus ex machina, isn't it?" Tom asked, frustrated by the response.

"When you summon a creature, the environment is taken into account. That's how beings from other dimensions and planets that may not breathe your planet's atmosphere can survive. It's a System compensation to ensure the survivability of interplanetary travels," Bron explained after rolling his eyes. "Now, can we get back to the issue at hand?"

Tom spent a few minutes catching Bron up on the situation and the plan they had put together.

"That does sound like a solid plan. But may I suggest one additional tactic?" Bron said, fixing his gaze directly on Tom.

"Absolutely! We're open to ideas," Tom replied, eager for a fresh perspective.

"Chickens," Bron stated flatly.

"Chickens?" Tom repeated, confused for a moment. Then it dawned on him. "Ohhhh, *chickens*."

With the plan finalized, the team went over it once more to ensure everyone was on the same page. When they were confident, Tom moved to a corner of the cave and summoned nine Abyssal Chickens. The effort left him drained, and his mind felt like it was wrapped in a fog. He quickly downed a mana potion from his Inventory, and as his mana quickly began refilling, his mental fatigue began to lift.

Once his mana was restored, Tom summoned another batch of nine Abyssal Chickens. The total of eighteen should be enough to do the job. Feeling more focused, he glanced around at the tunnels leading deeper into the cave. Guards were posted at the entrance, and Clem's gang members were scattered about, either chatting, patrolling, or handling various tasks.

Tom looked back at his team and nodded. They all moved into position. Then, with a single thought, he sent the chickens out into the hallway with a mental command: *If it isn't anyone in this room, kill it.*

He wasn't sure how well Abyssal Chickens would handle facial recognition, but each one took a moment to look at the faces in the room before moving out.

The cave filled with the cacophony of chicken squawks, followed by shouts of confusion and screams of pain. Peering around the corner, Tom watched as chaos erupted. Fishmen were flailing their limbs, screaming and running as Abyssal Chickens latched onto them with their razor-sharp beaks. Others stood frozen in place, desperately trying to pry the vicious creatures off their legs.

"NOW!" Tom yelled, charging around the corner with a handgun in each hand.

Gunshots echoed in the hallways as the team poured out, taking down fishmen as they advanced. Screams were abruptly cut off by headshots, while others turned to anguished cries as bullets hit non-lethal areas. An alarm blared from deeper within the cave, and more gang members rushed out from connecting hallways.

Bron, unarmed and evidently uninterested in using a gun, raised his massive arms to shield his face as he barreled toward a group of fishmen. Once he was close enough, he swung his arms down, smashing them into the ground with his overwhelming strength. Bullets bounced harmlessly off his thick hide, further demonstrating his resilience. Nearby, Petunia and her friends joined the fray, wielding pans from a nearby crate and beating a fishman senseless while an Abyssal Chicken gnawed on his leg like a dog with a toy.

Despite their arrival, more fishmen kept coming, and while some Abyssal Chickens were slain in the onslaught, the chickens' tenacity paid off. After every fishman that fell, the remaining chickens swarmed the next nearest target, ripping them apart with relentless ferocity. It was a macabre dance of death; bodies fell, and the chickens pounced, feeding their insatiable hunger.

One particularly unlucky fishman found himself face-to-face with an Abyssal Chicken that launched off a crate, clamping onto his head with its beak. Tom nearly missed a shot from laughing at the absurdity of the scene—a flailing fishman trying desperately to shake the chicken off his face like something out of a slapstick comedy.

With the last of Clem's men lying dead, Tom and his team pushed further into the cave, where they knew Pecos Clem would be waiting. Reaching the end of a long hallway, they found a large set of double doors blocking their path. Tom gave them a push, but they didn't budge; they were barred from the other side.

Bron stepped up, nodded at Tom, and with a massive heave, threw himself against the doors. There was a loud crack from the other side.

Tom and Derek readied themselves. On Bron's second charge, they all rammed the doors together, and the bar splintered. The doors flew open with a crash.

Inside, seated on a grand marble throne atop a slightly raised platform, was a large man wearing an oversized cowboy hat.

"Pecos Clem, I presume?" Tom said, breathing heavily from the effort.

"That'd be me," Clem replied coolly. "And you're more resourceful than I expected."

"First impressions can be deceiving," Tom shot back.

"Indeed. That stunt outside was entertaining… but foolish," Clem sneered.

"Not every plan goes smoothly. Sometimes you have to roll with the punches," Tom replied, a bit embarrassed at how their initial approach had gone. "But the jig is up, Clem."

"Oh, I absolutely agree, whippersnapper," Clem said, his smile widening.

Tom suddenly heard the unmistakable sound of guns being cocked. He glanced around the room and saw fishmen emerging from every possible hiding spot, their guns aimed directly at him and his team. The group quickly formed a defensive circle, pointing their weapons at the new threats, while the Abyssal Chickens growled menacingly from their feet.

"I think I've shown you all enough mercy," Pecos Clem said, his face twisting into a grin of malevolent satisfaction. "It's time to die."

Chapter 40

Shootout

Clem tipped his comically oversized hat to Tom and stood, the spurs on his boots clinking ominously against the stone floor. With a slow, deliberate motion, he made a hand gesture toward his men. Tom's eyes widened as he realized what was about to happen.

"SCATTER!" he shouted to his team, diving behind a large wooden crate just as bullets erupted from all sides.

The team scrambled for cover, dodging bullets that ricocheted off the stone walls and sent splinters flying from the wooden crates scattered around the room. The Abyssal Chickens, however, didn't seem to understand the concept of self-preservation. Squawking madly, they darted out, targeting the nearest fishmen. Several were shot down almost immediately, but a few managed to latch onto victims, their demonic beaks tearing through flesh.

James and Jay each took hits in their arms as they dove for cover. Blood oozed from their wounds, but Derek and Tom quickly cast healing spells, enveloping them in a soft light that knitted their flesh back together.

Pinned down by the relentless barrage of bullets, Tom pressed his back against the crate that sheltered him, listening to the wood groan under the continuous hail of gunfire. He glanced over the edge and saw that pieces of the crate were being blown away at an alarming rate. Then he heard a distinctive "tunk" followed by a series of explosions and anguished screams. Kiera had fired off another grenade, the shockwave of which provided a brief reprieve. Tom heard the familiar trumpeting roar of Bron entering the fray, which caused a grin to spread across his face.

Taking advantage of the chaos, Tom leaned out from behind the crate and unloaded both of his handguns, taking down two more fishmen. He rolled back into cover just as more bullets tore into the spot where he'd been. His eyes darted around the room, searching for Pecos Clem, who had initiated this chaos. After a few tense moments, he spotted him—still standing arrogantly beside his throne, arms folded, a smug smile plastered across his face.

Anger flared in Tom's chest. He'd had enough of this guy. With a roar, he stood up, stepping out from behind his cover with guns blazing. He fired in both directions, taking out more enemies as bullets whizzed past his head. One hit him square in the chest, knocking the wind out of him, but his new armor absorbed the impact. Gritting his teeth through the pain, Tom kept moving forward.

Seeing Tom become the center of attention, Kiera switched to her fully automatic rifle and unleashed a torrent of bullets, covering him as he advanced. James joined in, popping up from his hiding spot to take shots at the enemy. Kevin and Kirsten, sensing an opportunity, charged the left flank with their axes, cutting through the fishmen with brutal efficiency. Jay, ever the ninja, had vanished from sight, waiting for his moment to strike.

"Can't be a good ninja if we can see you," Tom thought, grinning as he continued firing.

On the right side of the room, Derek advanced with his shield raised, moving to support Bron, who was in the midst of a bloody rampage. Bron was bleeding from multiple wounds, proof that even his thick skin couldn't deflect every bullet. Derek let out a battle cry to announce his presence, and Bron, sensing his approach, sidestepped just as a fishman lunged at him. The fishman's punch slammed into Derek's shield with a sickening crunch, and he howled in pain as his fin-like hand shattered. Derek wasted no time and bashed the fishman across the face with his shield, sending him sprawling to the floor. He followed up with a quick shot to the head, silencing the creature for good.

Bron, meanwhile, had his own, small troubles. An octopus-man hybrid had latched onto his weapon with its suckered limbs, trying to pull it away. With a fluid, almost casual motion, Bron grabbed the creature by the neck, swung it around, and used it like a flail to bludgeon another gang member. Satisfied with the effectiveness of this new weapon, Bron switched his grip to the creature's ankles and continued swinging it like a grotesque, fleshy club.

The morale of Clem's men plummeted as they witnessed Bron's terrifying strength. After about five or six swings, the octopus-man's head finally exploded, sending a shower of blood and brain matter in all directions. Undeterred, Bron tossed the body aside, grabbed two more fishmen by their necks, and began using them as makeshift weapons as well.

"What... What is it?!" one of the fishmen shrieked, his eyes wide with terror as Bron and Derek cut through their ranks like a whirlwind of death.

"It's a monster! We gotta get outta here!" another shouted, and the remaining fishmen broke ranks, fleeing in every direction.

Pecos Clem's face contorted with fury. He had assumed he held the upper hand, but now his men were panicking and his control was slipping away. His fists clenched so tightly that his knuckles turned white, and he let out a primal, rage-filled roar.

"EEEAAAAARRRRRRRRGGGGGGGGHHHHHHH!" Clem bellowed as he drew his twin revolvers. "I will not be made to look a fool in my own territory!"

He aimed directly at Tom and squeezed off several shots. The first couple went wide, but one found its mark, striking Tom in the back and sending him sprawling to the ground.

"TOM!" Kiera shouted, her voice thick with panic as she aimed at Clem and fired.

Pecos Clem ducked behind his throne, returning fire with one hand. Tom groaned, struggling to get back on his feet. His armor had absorbed most of the damage, but blood seeped from the wound, painting his back red. He turned just in time to see Clem aiming at Kiera. His vision blurred with rage. Tom raised his guns and fired several rounds toward Clem, forcing him to duck even lower.

"Keep the others off me! Clem is mine!" Tom shouted as he took cover behind another crate. The wood splintered and cracked under the renewed onslaught from Clem's pistols.

From somewhere nearby, he heard James cursing loudly. "Son of a fucking cunt-bred shit-stain!" he screamed. "Eat a bag of dicks, you giant bukkake smear!"

"Sit still, you fucking princess. It's not that bad," Kiera muttered as she patched him up. Tom smirked, then refocused on the fight.

Clem was peeking out from behind his throne, his pistol aimed directly at Bron. Tom took the opportunity and fired a well-placed shot at Clem's gun, blasting it from his hand. Clem cursed loudly, glaring at Tom with unbridled hatred.

"CLEM!" Tom bellowed. "Let's settle this like men! You and me! No guns!"

Clem's lip curled in a sneer. "You think you can take me in a fair fight? Fine! Let's go, boy!"

Both men charged at each other, fists flying. The first punches were blocked, but both landed solid hits to each other's faces with their second strikes, each staggering back a step.

They circled each other warily, each sizing up the other's movements. Clem launched a flurry of wild punches, but Tom focused on defense, blocking and redirecting each blow with calculated precision. Clem pulled back for a powerful haymaker, but Tom saw it coming. He deflected the punch with a quick parry and countered, activating his *Tattoo of Brute Strength* at the same moment he thrust one fist into Clem's face and another into his stomach.

"Yamazuki, bitch!" Tom shouted as Clem stumbled back, momentarily disoriented.

Growling with fury, Clem charged again, his punches becoming more erratic and desperate. Tom sidestepped, grabbing Clem's forearm and using his momentum to flip him over his shoulder in a judo-style throw. Clem crashed into a stack of crates, sending splinters flying.

Tom wasted no time. He climbed on top of Clem and slipped on the knuckle dusters Derek had advised him to carry. With a grim determination, he began pummeling Clem's face, unleashing all the frustration and anger that had been building up for weeks. His fists came down like sledgehammers, each blow crushing bone and tearing flesh. Clem's lip split open, then his cheekbone shattered, and soon his face was a mess of blood and broken teeth.

The room fell silent. The remaining fishmen, who had been fighting moments before, were now backed against the walls, staring in stunned horror at the brutal scene unfolding before them. Even Tom's team, usually unfazed by his ruthlessness, exchanged uneasy glances. All except Bron, who looked on with a satisfied grin.

"You good?" James asked, limping over, his face still pale from blood loss.

"Yeah," Tom panted, wiping the blood from his weapons. "I'm good."

James offered a hand, and Tom accepted, pulling himself up and stepping over Clem's battered body. Suddenly, Clem let out a low groan, shifting slightly.

"FUCK! ZOMBIE!" James screamed, whipping out his handgun and unloading six rounds into Clem's head and another three into his crotch.

"It's dead, Jim," Tom said, placing a reassuring hand on James' shoulder.

"Don't know what we'd do without you, McCoy," he sighed. His shoulders slumped in relief as he patted Tom's hand. "Also, you know I don't like being called Jim," James muttered.

"I know. But it wouldn't have been the same," Tom replied with a chuckle, patting James on the shoulder.

James rolled his eyes but couldn't help the small smile that crept onto his lips. "You look like shit, dude," he remarked, eyeing Tom's battered appearance.

"Then I'm finally down to only twice as good-looking as you," Tom shot back with a grin.

They stood there for a moment, letting the tension ease from their bodies. The adrenaline was still coursing through them, but the immediate danger seemed to have passed.

"Is this a moment? Are we having a moment?" James asked, his voice mockingly sweet.

"No," Tom replied, still smiling. He patted James on the cheek, giving it a playful tap before walking away to rejoin the others.

Tom looked around at his team, who were still catching their breath and checking their injuries. The last of Pecos Clem's men were still standing against the walls, but now with hands raised in surrender, their faces a mix of fear and resignation.

"Alright, everyone. We can't take prisoners, so you know what to do," Tom said flatly, his voice hardening as he looked at the remaining fishmen.

The sound of pleading voices filled the room, followed by gunfire as Tom's team executed the surviving enemies. There was no joy in it, just grim necessity. Petunia, standing nearby, watched with a mixture of horror and resignation.

"That was a bit harsh, wasn't it?" she asked, her voice wavering as Tom approached her.

Tom turned to her, his expression cold and unyielding. "Would you rather I let them go to stew in anger and then come back to seek their revenge? I have to leave here after this. You all are the ones who have to stay in that town."

Petunia opened her mouth to reply but then closed it, realizing he had a point. "Well… no, I suppose not," she admitted quietly.

"Okay. Then let's get you ladies back home," Tom said, his tone softening as he gestured for the women to follow him.

Chapter 41

Prizes

Tom and his team trudged back to town on foot, the memory of their chaotic encounter at Clem's base still fresh in their minds. The incident with the dolphins during the attack had left them without their peculiar underwater transport, forcing them to make the journey by walking. While it was far from ideal, they made good use of the time, hauling back a significant amount of loot from the base.

The haul included over three hundred handguns and nearly a million rounds of ammunition of various calibers—a massive score for the Guild. The plan was to hand these out back at the Guild building, arming their members for the tough times ahead. For now, though, the team focused on getting back to the relative safety of town.

"Here. We all thought you should have these," Kiera said, approaching Tom with a bundle of cloth.

Tom took the bundle, carefully unwrapping it to reveal Pecos Clem's revolvers. The guns were enormous, practically hand cannons.

"What caliber are these?" Tom asked, his eyes widening at the size.

"Looks like they are .600 Nitro Express rounds. It's not very common—they're basically rifle rounds. Lots of kick to that gun, so be careful if you shoot them," Kiera warned with a smile.

"I'm not even sure how Clem carried these. They look so unwieldy," Tom commented, turning the guns over in his hands.

"Probably a high Strength stat. That would also explain why his shots did so much more damage," Kiera replied, not sure if Tom was looking for an answer but providing one anyway.

"Thank you all for this. And for your help back there," Tom said, a genuine smile breaking across his face as he glanced at Kiera and the rest of the team.

"We're in this together now. We'll always be here," Kiera said, returning the smile, her tension easing as she saw Tom looking calmer and more grounded.

Before leaving Clem's base, Derek had insisted that everyone stop to heal and recover. It had been a good call—there wasn't a single one of them without some kind of injury. They were all battered, bruised, and covered in dirt and dried blood. Petunia and her friends, however, had mostly stayed out of the main fight and remained unscathed. Tom didn't blame them for wanting to avoid the chaos; that fight had been tougher than expected.

Once they had gathered everything they thought could be useful, they had left the hideout and headed back toward town, following the road leading away from the cave's entrance. The trek back took hours, and by the time they finally approached the town, the sun had not only risen but was now high in the sky.

As they entered the town, townspeople who had been going about their daily business stopped to gawk at the ragtag group. Dirty, blood-covered, and armed to the teeth, they must have been quite the sight. Mothers pulled their children behind them, people crossed the street to avoid them, and some even ran into nearby buildings, slamming doors behind them. Petunia guided them to the Sheriff's office, and they walked inside, the bell on the door jangling loudly in the sudden silence.

"Both Pecoses are dead. It is Pecoses, right?" Tom said, suddenly unsure of the plural form of "Pecos" and glancing at his team for confirmation.

The others just shrugged, equally unsure. Tom turned back to the Sheriff, deciding to just go with it.

"Pecosi," James interrupted his thoughts with a level of authority.

"Pecoses," Tom decided. James gave him the finger, but Tom continued on. "Both of those assholes are dead now," Tom affirmed, figuring confidence was the best policy. "Fake it till you make it," his grandpa had once told him.

The Sheriff, a grizzled old fishman with tired eyes, wrinkled his nose and took a step back, covering it with his hand. "What the hell are you covered in?"

"The answer to that question is *also* 'Pecoses,' sir," Tom replied, placing his hands on his hips as if that would somehow add more credibility to his statement.

"You could have just turned off the density-shifter to clean up a bit," the Sheriff suggested, his eyes narrowing with a mix of disgust and frustration.

"I could have also fallen in a seahorse trough or just not bothered to help out. What's your point?" Tom shot back, his annoyance growing at the direction the conversation was taking.

The Sheriff sighed, clearly not wanting to get into it. "Do you have any proof?" he asked, trying to stay as far away from Tom as he could without appearing rude.

"We can vouch for him," Petunia spoke up, her voice firm but polite.

"You think the word of a whore is good enough for us?" the Sheriff retorted, his tone dripping with disdain. "Could have paid you to say that."

Tom's patience was wearing thin. "Beyond the fact that you liked them enough to send me after them, shouldn't you believe them? Fine, here." He pulled out one of Pecos Clem's oversized revolvers and slammed it down on the Sheriff's desk.

The Sheriff's eyes widened at the sight of the massive gun.

"Know anyone else strong enough to shoot that gun?" Tom asked, crossing his arms over his chest, his annoyance evident.

"Well, no, I suppose I don't," the Sheriff admitted reluctantly, still staring at the giant weapon. "This town thanks you for your… uh, help. Do you mind if we keep it as a memento?"

"I certainly *do* mind. I earned this. It's mine now," Tom said with enough finality that the Sheriff just nodded along, deciding not to press the matter further.

With that settled, everyone on Tom's team received the same System message simultaneously:

Quest Complete: Defeat the Outlaws

Congratulations! You have successfully completed the quest "Defeat the Outlaws". Not only did you defeat both Pecos Mark and Pecos Clem, but you also saved all fifteen hostages from their clutches! Your heroic efforts have earned you increased rewards.

Rewards for Each Team Member:
- 25,000 XP
- 50 Common Cores
- 1 Roulette Reward Spin

Your bravery and teamwork have been recognized by the System. Keep up the good work, adventurers!

"A Roulette Reward Spin? What the hell is that?" Tom asked out loud, squinting at the prompt that had appeared before him.

Suddenly, the pop-ups winked out of existence, and the world around them began to fade. Petunia, her friends, and the Sheriff stood completely still, their forms frozen as if time itself had stopped. The surroundings dissolved into darkness, leaving the group in a vast, empty void. It wasn't the kind of darkness where one couldn't see a thing; rather, they could see each other clearly as if lit by an unseen light, but there was nothing else—no ground, no ceiling, just an endless black abyss.

In the void, the familiar orange writing flickered into existence, hanging in the air in front of them, glowing with an ethereal light. The stylized characters spelled out, *"Congratulations, Dungeon Complete."* The words hovered for a moment before beginning to fade, leaving the party in silence.

Dungeon Complete!

Congratulations!

You are the first to complete the Dungeon Showdown!

Reward:

As a reward for this remarkable feat, a special prize awaits you. At the end of every Dungeon, a vending machine will appear, allowing each party member to select one item for free. However, because this is the Dungeon of Chance, the machine will be a roulette-style slot vending machine, and your chances of receiving a better prize will be increased because of your first completion reward. After this, reward probabilities will be reset for future Dungeon dives.

Item Selection:

Item selections will be pre-selected to match your Classes. Unlike standard vending machine purchases, customization of the selection is not available.

Continue to fight hard, strive for excellence, and greater rewards will follow.

As the words dissipated, a new object began to emerge from the unseen floor. Rising slowly, it materialized into what looked like a slot machine, a strange sight in this otherworldly darkness. The machine was ornate, its sides decorated with intricate carvings, and its reels displayed various images that flickered rapidly—a sword, a pile of gold, a mysterious potion, and other items of varying shapes and sizes.

Tom took a step closer to the machine, his curiosity piqued. "So, how do we use this?" he asked, glancing back at his friends.

Almost as if in answer, a small stack of coins materialized on a narrow table attached to the front of the machine. Each coin was slightly larger than a standard currency piece, stamped with a symbol that seemed to shift and change as the light hit it. There was exactly one coin for each of them.

As they stared at the coins, more orange writing appeared, floating in midair.

"You may insert the coin into the machine to take a chance at an amazing prize. But be warned, prizes range from the fantastic to the familiar. Step up and try your luck!"

"Well, that seems really shitty for the Dungeon," James muttered, crossing his arms, his eyes narrowing at the machine.

"It *is* called the Dungeon of Chance," Tom replied with a shrug, taking a step toward the machine. "This seems pretty on-brand."

Reaching forward, he took one of the coins, feeling the cool metal in his palm. He glanced back at his friends, his lips curling into a half-smile. "Wish me luck," he said, giving them a nod.

Tom approached the slot machine and inserted the coin into the slot. The machine whirred to life with a mechanical hum, and he grabbed the lever on the side. With a firm yank, he pulled it down. The reels spun violently, a blur of colors and shapes whirling faster than his eyes could track. The clattering sound of the spinning reels filled the void, building suspense.

The left reel stopped first, landing on an icon of a glowing blue gem. The middle reel followed suit, halting on a golden key. Tension hung in the air as the right reel continued spinning for a few more seconds before clicking to a stop on the image of a dragon's eye.

A bell rang out, its clear tone echoing in the empty space. The top of the machine lit up with flashing lights, casting vibrant patterns across the group. From the bottom of the machine, a small compartment opened, dispensing a metal can that clattered into the tray below.

Tom picked up the can, feeling its unexpected weight. It was a smooth cylinder with a pop-top lid, just like the ones from the vending machines. He gave his friends a quick glance before pulling the top open. A cloud of smoke escaped, dissipating quickly in the void.

Inside, nestled in a bed of soft padding, was a vial filled with a strange amber liquid. The vial itself was crafted from what appeared to be crystal, its facets catching the ambient light and refracting it into a soft rainbow of colors. It was small enough to fit in the palm of his hand, with a delicate stopper sealing the liquid inside. The amber liquid within seemed to glow faintly, casting a warm, inviting light.

Tom raised an eyebrow, turning the vial over in his hands. "What the hell is this?" he murmured. He decided to cast *Inspect* on the vial to see what he had won.

Nectar of Atum

Item Type: Consumable
Rarity: Epic
Description: Crafted by Atum, the Egyptian god of creation, the Nectar of Atum is a potent elixir that was believed to empower his chosen Champions, enabling them to accomplish the impossible. The amber liquid inside the beautifully carved crystal vial glows with a soft, golden light, resonating with divine power.

Effect: Upon consumption, grants the user 30 additional Attribute Points to allocate freely, allowing unparalleled customization and enhancement of their abilities.

"Holy shit! Thirty Attribute Points to put wherever I want? Hell yes!" Tom exclaimed, holding the vial up triumphantly for the others to see. The amber liquid inside shimmered with a tempting glow, and he could practically feel the power radiating from it.

"Oh, man! Move over! Let me have a go at it!" James said, pushing his way eagerly to the machine, a gleam of excitement in his eyes.

He grabbed the next coin from the stack and slotted it into the machine with an audible clink. Grabbing the lever with both hands, he gave it a hearty pull. The reels began to spin wildly, the images blurring together as they raced around. One by one, the reels clattered to a stop, but unlike Tom's turn, there was no bell ringing, no flashing lights. The machine simply clicked, and a can was dispensed with a dull thunk.

James frowned, his excitement fading. "Huh. It didn't give me all the fanfare," he muttered, picking up the can and inspecting it closely. He hesitated a moment, then popped the top. Another cloud of smoke puffed out, quickly fading into the darkness around them.

James was left holding a small silver ring.

"Look," James placed a hand on the wheel, looking as if he was trying to let the thing down gently. "I'm flattered, really. But I've only got room in my life for two ladies." He materialized both his guns in his hands as he spoke. "I'm sorry, but I hope you understand…"

The ring was plain, with no distinctive markings or decorations—just a simple band of silver. It hardly seemed like the kind of grand reward you'd expect from a mystical slot machine.

Kiera, leaning against the side of the machine with her arms crossed, rolled her eyes. "*Inspect* it, dumbass," she suggested with a smirk.

<table>
<tr><td align="center">Ring of Reflect</td></tr>
<tr><td>

Item Type: Accessory - Ring
Rarity: Rare
Description: The Ring of Reflect is a sleek, silver band imbued with a powerful enchantment that allows the wearer to conjure a magical shield at will. When activated, the ring generates a shimmering, semi-transparent shield around the wielder. The shield remains active as long as the user maintains concentration, providing substantial protection against incoming attacks.

Effect: Create a magical shield with 5000 HP. The shield is instantly deployable with a thought and lasts as long as the user focuses on it. When the shield is depleted, it requires a 24-hour cooldown period before it can be used again.

Note: Concentration must be maintained to keep the shield active. Any loss of focus will cause the shield to dissipate.

</td></tr>
</table>

"Oh, I take it back! This is badass!" James exclaimed, eyes wide with excitement. Without a second thought, he slipped the ring onto the middle finger of his left hand. He leaned toward the wheel, whispering, "We'll talk later, okay?"

He activated the ring's ability, and a brilliant blue disc of energy expanded from his arm, forming a translucent shield that covered the upper half of his body. The light from the shield reflected in his eyes, making him look like a kid who had just unwrapped the best gift on Christmas morning.

"That's great! Looks like you're all set for defense now," Tom said, nodding approvingly. "Okay, who's next?"

Kiera stepped forward confidently, grabbing a coin from the stack. She slid it into the machine and pulled the lever with a swift yank. The reels spun around, the pictures blurring until, one by one, they clicked to a stop. A can dropped down with a metallic clatter, but there were no bells or flashing lights this time either.

Kiera popped open the can, and a single Monster Core rolled out into her hand. It looked like any other Monster Core at first glance, but its deep, vibrant color caught her attention. She *Inspected* it and grinned. "It's an epic core," she announced, holding it up for everyone to see. "Worth fifty rare cores. Not bad at all."

Kevin was up next. He grabbed his coin and tossed it into the slot with a casual flick of his wrist, then yanked the lever. This time, the bells rang out joyously, and the machine's lights flashed in a dazzling display. The can that appeared had a bit more heft to it.

As Kevin opened it, his face lit up with delight. In his hands was a gleaming greataxe, crafted entirely from a slightly blue metal that shimmered under the ethereal lights. He marveled at its balance and the almost weightless feel of the metal.

"Now, this is more like it!" Kevin exclaimed, giving the axe a few experimental swings. It cut through the air with an almost musical whoosh, and he looked over at the others with a grin. "I'm definitely looking forward to using this bad boy."

Mithril Greataxe of Sundering

Item Type: Weapon - Greataxe
Material: Mithril
Rarity: Epic
Description: Forged from a single, unbroken piece of mithril ore by master Dwarven Smiths in the fiery depths of the mountain forges on the planet Darthvein, the Mithril Greataxe of Sundering is a masterpiece of Dwarven craftsmanship. Its razor-sharp blade and perfectly balanced weight make it a formidable weapon in any warrior's hands. The lustrous silver hue of mithril

---

---

shines through its polished surface, and intricate Dwarven runes are engraved along its shaft, enhancing its durability and strength.

Effect - Sunder: This mighty greataxe possesses a unique ability known as Sunder, which can be activated by the wielder. When triggered, the axe unleashes a devastating strike that travels in a straight line from the user, extending up to 25 yards. This strike deals additional slicing and force damage to all enemies in its path and forcefully knocks them back.

Cooldown: 60 seconds between uses of Sunder.

"So, the System is introducing items not native to our planet," Tom mused, considering the implications. "That could actually work to our advantage in the long run. But I guess it depends on how widespread it is. It might just be a feature of this particular dungeon, considering how unique it is."

Kirsten eagerly stepped up to the machine next, her eyes gleaming with anticipation. She took her coin and inserted it into the slot. With a firm pull, she yanked down the lever, setting the reels spinning wildly. When they stopped, a can clattered into the tray below. She quickly grabbed it, opened it up, and waited for the smoke to clear, revealing the item inside. Her face fell a little as she pulled out a regular greatsword.

"Well, at least it seems to be taking your Class into account," Tom said, trying to sound encouraging. He noticed her slight disappointment and added, "A Greatsword is still a solid find. Maybe it's got some hidden perks?"

Kirsten nodded, but it was clear she was hoping for something more unique. She hefted the sword a few times to get a feel for it, then stepped aside.

Jay was up next. With a grin, he stepped forward, theatrically kissing his coin before dropping it into the slot. "Wish me luck, ladies and gents," he said with a wink. He pulled the lever, and the reels began their rapid spin. When they slowed to a stop, another can dropped into the tray.

Jay picked up the can with a flourish, popping it open as the familiar puff of smoke billowed out. When the smoke dissipated, he was left holding a small vial filled with a vibrant purple liquid. He turned it over in his hand, inspecting it closely.

"What is it?" Kiera asked, leaning in a bit.

Jay squinted at the vial, then smiled slyly. "No idea yet, but I've got a feeling it's going to be interesting," he said, using his *Inspect* skill.

Botulinum Toxin

Item Type: Consumable - Poison
Rarity: Rare
Description: A vial containing a minute amount of Botulinum Toxin, one of the most lethal neurotoxins known to exist. Even a single drop can be fatal to a grown man. When applied to a weapon, this toxin can deliver devastating effects to enemies, causing paralysis, respiratory failure, and potentially death. Handle with extreme caution.

Effect: Applying this toxin to a weapon will coat the weapon's next attack with a deadly neurotoxin, sure to kill your opponent in a matter of minutes

Duration of Application: 5 hours or until the coated attack is used.

Warning: This item is extremely potent. Use sparingly and avoid accidental exposure, as it could prove fatal to the user as well.

"Holy fuck!" Jay exclaimed, suddenly holding the vial at arm's length as if it were a live grenade. "This shit is dangerous… I love it." Without another word, he quickly stashed it in his Inventory and backed away, clearly not interested in discussing it further.

Brian stepped up to the machine next, a mixture of frustration and reluctance evident in his body language.

"So, you survived. How do you feel?" Tom asked, trying to lighten the mood.

"Like I'm Arnold and you're Miss Frizzle, and we just went on the worst field trip of my life," Brian replied, his tone edging on anger.

Tom chuckled and brushed aside his grumpiness. "Oh, come on. You should get something great! And hey, that must've been worth a ton of XP for you."

"It was," Brian admitted grudgingly. "I gained quite a few levels. So, hopefully, I never have to do this shit again." He fixed Tom with a stare that could cut glass.

"Alright, alright. I promise we won't drag you into another Dungeon dive," Tom said, raising his hands in mock surrender. "But only if you promise to go out with some of the teams more often to level up. You need these skills to survive. You can't hide in the ivory tower all the time. Eventually, the fight will come to us."

Brian sighed deeply, weighing his options. "Fine," he agreed reluctantly, the tension easing from his shoulders.

With a resigned breath, he took his coin, slid it into the slot, and pulled the lever. The reels spun wildly before coming to a stop, and a can clattered into the tray. Brian grabbed it and opened it, watching the puff of smoke dissipate to reveal… a single gold earring.

"You've got to be fucking kidding me," Brian muttered, glaring at the tiny piece of jewelry in his hand.

Tom laughed. "Things aren't always what they appear to be. *Inspect* it," he advised, a knowing grin spreading across his face.

Communication Network

Item Type: Accessory - Earring
Rarity: Epic
Description: The Communication Network earring is a powerful tool used by commanders and generals across the universe to maintain contact and control over their forces. When worn, this earring can be paired with life signatures, allowing the wearer to monitor whether the life essence of each connected individual is still active. In addition, the earring grants the ability to initiate one-way telepathic communication with any of the paired life signatures, making it ideal for giving commands, coordinating strategies, or checking in on the status of allies from any distance.

Effect:

- Life Essence Detection: Displays the status (active or inactive) of paired life signatures within the user's mental interface.
- One-Way Telepathic Communication Initiation: Allows the wearer to send telepathic messages to any of the paired life signatures. Communication can only be initiated by the wearer, and only one line of communication is possible at a time.
- Pairing Process: To connect with a life signature, both the wearer and the target must be within 10 yards and willingly initiate the pairing process.

Note: Extremely effective for military operations, rescue missions, and covert coordination.

"That actually seems really handy," Brian admitted after reading the description several times. "Especially for my job. No more tracking people down."

With Brian's turn complete, Derek stepped up and grabbed the last coin from the table. He held it up for a moment, feeling its weight in his hand, before glancing back at his friends with a confident smirk. Then, with a swift motion, he slid the coin into the slot and yanked down on the lever.

The reels spun, but unlike the others, they kept going and going, longer than any of the previous spins. An air of anticipation settled over the group, their eyes locked on the machine as though willing it to stop. Suddenly, all three reels halted simultaneously, as if someone had pressed a quick-stop button.

This time, a loud siren blared to life, and the lights on top of the machine erupted in a flurry of colors, far more intense than any of the previous spins.

The can that dropped out looked different from the others. Unlike the previous ones that bore a label with an image of the item inside, this one was completely blank—its metal surface unmarked and enigmatic. Derek picked it up, his brow furrowing in confusion as he turned it over in his hands.

"What's with the blank can?" he asked, glancing at the others, who shrugged in response. Realizing there was only one way to find out, Derek braced himself and cracked the can open.

A plume of smoke erupted from the can with a hiss, and then the distinct sound of clanging metal echoed through the void. As the smoke dissipated, the group's eyes widened at what they saw lying before them: a full set of blackened armor, polished to a brilliant shine, glinting ominously in the strange light of the void.

Derek's mouth fell open slightly, his eyes running over the intricate, almost otherworldly designs etched into the armor's surface. The plates were sleek yet heavy-looking, with dark, metallic hues that seemed to shift and ripple like oil on water.

"Whoa," Tom whispered, breaking the silence. "That's... definitely not from our planet."

Dreadnought Armor

The Dreadnought Armor is a masterfully crafted suit of full plate armor, originally forged for Donovan Bartol, the renowned Dreadnought Cleric who led his people through countless victories. Enchanted and blessed by the divine, this armor was believed to be lost for millennia after Donovan vanished in a brutal battle. The set retains its legendary durability and power, making it highly sought after by warriors who seek to withstand overwhelming odds. Rumored to contain secrets and abilities yet to be unlocked, the armor is a testament to the glory of its original wearer.

After carefully *Inspecting* each piece, Derek realized that the armor set offered three times the defense of his current gear, yet felt significantly lighter. As he more closely examined the helmet, he noticed what appeared to be some sort of digital screen embedded inside, hinting at advanced technology.

Curiosity piqued; Derek decided to immediately equip the armor. One by one, he strapped on each piece, marveling at how comfortably they fit. The plates seemed to perfectly mold to his body, offering both mobility and protection. When he finally slid the helmet over his head, he heard a soft hiss as it sealed into place, and then the display inside the visor flickered to life.

Lines of data scrolled across the screen, and a heads-up display appeared, showing vital signs, a mini-map, and targeting reticles. It was like something out of a sci-fi movie.

"Holy shit..." Derek exclaimed, his voice echoing slightly inside the helmet.

"What?" Tom asked, excited.

Derek's voice echoed with a hollow menace that was unable to fully restrain the man's obvious joy. He flexed one arm.
"I'm the Juggernaut, bitch!"

Chapter 42

Dungeon #2

Dreadnought Armor

Set Components:

1. **Dreadnought Helm**
   - *Special Ability:* **Divine Awareness** - Grants the wearer a warning of impending danger, giving them a moment of heightened reflexes and increased movement speed for 5 seconds. *(Cooldown: 1 hour)*
2. **Dreadnought Chestplate**
   - *Special Ability:* **Bulwark of Faith** - Reduces incoming physical and magical damage by 20%.
3. **Dreadnought Gauntlets**
   - *Special Ability:* **Hammer of Justice** - Increases the wearer's melee damage by 15%.
4. **Dreadnought Leg Guards**
   - *Special Ability:* **Charge of the Ancients** - Allows the wearer to rush forward with divine speed, knocking back enemies in a 10-yard path.
5. **Dreadnought Boots**
   - *Special Ability:* **Divine Grounding** - Immunity to knockback effects and increased stability on uneven terrain.

Set Bonus:

5-Piece Bonus: Legacy of Donovan - The full potential of the Dreadnought Armor can only be unlocked by those who have proven their worth in battle and resonate with the spirit of Donovan Bartol.

Item Type:	Armor
Durability:	10,000/10,000

Defense:	+500
Item Quality:	Master Craft
Item Rarity:	Legendary

"Get that off and give it to me right now!" James yelled, his voice echoing through the empty chamber as he glared at Derek.

"Fuck you. This armor is mine!" Derek shot back, his eyes darting around the empty space. The display before him was surreal, almost like viewing the world normally through an open-face helmet. There was no sense of enclosure or inhibited peripheral vision like he would have expected from wearing such a suit.

"This is awesome! We never had anything like this except in VR," Derek commented, moving himself around, testing the suit. He could feel it reading his movements, responding perfectly, and moving with him in a way that felt completely natural and fluid. Excited, he decided to give the suit a more serious test. He crouched slightly, readying himself, and then pushed off with his back foot, rocketing forward.

The world around them began shifting and changing; the Dungeon dissolving away as they were transported back to reality. Unfortunately, Derek found himself rushing straight toward a wall. His eyes widened as he flailed in panic, desperately trying to stop the suit's forward momentum. Unable to arrest the movement in time, Derek screamed as he smashed through the wall, plowing straight into the next one. The impact left a comical, human-shaped outline in the thick stone.

"It's like Wile E. Coyote got his hands on Master Chief's armor," Tom commented offhandedly, chuckling.

Peeling himself away from the wall, Derek shook himself off, still a bit dazed. "I'm sure it's just going to take some getting used to," he replied, his voice tinged with a mix of excitement and embarrassment.

"Hopefully the learning curve isn't too steep. Alright, everyone, good job on this Dungeon. We just have one more to run," Tom said, turning toward the Dungeon door. He walked over, placed his hand on the wall next to the frame, and closed his eyes, concentrating on claiming it for Azroc. A symbol of Azroc giving a thumbs up appeared on the wall, just like in the other Dungeons they had conquered.

"Oh no, you are going to drop me back at the Guild first. I'm not doing that shit again," Brian protested, raising his hand as if to ward off the very idea.

"I know. We need to swap you out for someone else. Plus, we need to check in with everyone. We were in there quite a while," Tom said, looking outside and noticing that the sun was already up.

The team left the aquarium Dungeon and headed back to the Guild base. When they arrived, the guard on duty, Brandon, looked at them, his expression puzzled.

"Hey, Brandon. What's the matter? You look like you weren't expecting to see us," Tom said, noticing the confused look on the guard's face.

"I wasn't. Weren't you guys heading out to run a Dungeon?" Brandon asked, still looking bewildered.

"We did. We already finished it. Why?" Tom asked, now more curious than ever about why Brandon seemed so confused.

"I expected you to be gone a lot longer. Was the Dungeon that easy?" Brandon asked, his face lighting up at the possibility of easy loot.

"What are you talking about? We were in there for almost two days," Tom said in shock, his voice rising slightly.

"Two days? You just left a few hours ago. What the hell are you talking about?" Brandon asked, now just as shocked as Tom.

"There must be some kind of time dilation in the new Dungeon," Derek offered, trying to make sense of the situation.

"But… how is that even possible?" Tom asked, clearly struggling to wrap his head around the concept.

"Seriously? You can shoot fireballs and heal wounds in seconds, and you're hung up on time-dilation magic?" Kiera interjected, her voice dripping with sarcasm.

"It just seemed like something that shouldn't be possible. But I guess, with magic…" Tom trailed off, contemplating the implications of what this could mean for their future Dungeon runs.

"Actually, it's theoretically possible," Brian began, slipping into lecture mode. "As you get closer to the speed of light, time slows considerably. So, if we were moving that fast, we could potentially reach a point where time barely passes for us."

"And you know this how?" Jay asked, raising an eyebrow at Brian.

"I'm a reader. It's literally called the time dilation effect in physics. The concept comes from Einstein's Theory of Relativity. Special relativity infers that if two people were to watch a clock and one was moving at tremendous speeds, the person moving would see the clock move more slowly than the person standing still due to their relative perspective, or if you will, velocity," Brian explained briefly. "I don't think we were somehow traveling at light speeds, but if physics can explain it, then magic should be able to do it."

"Well, then, I guess we don't need to worry that something happened while we were inside, do we?" Tom asked, looking at the group. "Thanks, Brandon, for the update, and keep up the good work here."

Walking into the Guild building, the team went to the security room.

"You guys look like shit warmed over. And you're back sooner than I thought. Rough time?" TJ asked, leaning back in an office chair in front of the security camera monitors, not missing a beat.

"Yeah, yeah, yeah, time dilation, physics, magic, blah, blah, blah. We need to replace Brian because he's being a little chicken shit about going into Dungeons," Jay said quickly, hoping to skip the physics lecture again.

"Hey—" Brian complained.

"Oh, shut your beautifully butterscotch-accented mouth. You know it's true," Jay cut him off before he could continue. "Who you got for us?"

"Well, since you came back so fast, I'm not sure who's here right off hand. A lot of people went out with their teams for training. Let me see who we have," TJ said, reaching across the table in front of the monitors for a clipboard. Reading over the list carefully, he came to rest on one name in particular.

"Looks like Michael is in training with Graham. He's your best bet for people here who can handle the first run of a new Dungeon," TJ said, looking from the papers to the team.

"Great! Can you get him to meet us here?" Tom asked, his tone eager.

"Sure thing. Just give me a few minutes," TJ said, rolling his chair over to the PA system and calling for Michael to join them.

"I'm going to shower and try to scrub away the terror from myself. Probably need new clothes at this point too," Brian said sullenly as he bid the team farewell and left the room.

Not long after, Michael entered the room, his intimidating appearance and size making Tom glad he was on their team once again. "What's up? You all needed me? I was training with Graham. Is everything okay?" Michael asked, seeming genuinely concerned.

"We need another member for a Dungeon dive. We want you to join us," Tom explained straightforwardly.

"Oh, hell yeah! I'm totally in! Where's it at?" Michael asked, his excitement evident.

The other members of the team looked at each other suddenly as Derek facepalmed. "Guess we need Brian back after all," Derek said with a huge sigh.

"No need. I have it marked here. You can take this and add it to your map," TJ said, holding up a piece of paper.

"What do you mean add it to our map?" Tom asked, looking confused.

"Your System map. Don't you have it turned on?" TJ asked.

"We have a System map?" Tom asked again, still confused.

"Oh, man. You mean you all have been running around without your map on?" TJ asked, trying not to laugh.

"Just tell us what we need to know, please. All this bullshit with stuff we couldn't possibly know…" Jay began to grumble as he tried to urge TJ forward.

"Just think about your display and think about a mini-map like in video games. It should appear in your vision, then you can move it in the display to wherever you want. You can scan other maps by looking at them and thinking about adding the info to your map. It will show kind of a grey covering over an area you haven't visited before and lighter where you have been. You can also mentally put pins in it to show a destination you want to reach," TJ explained, and each of the team began to put the map into their displays.

"This could've been really handy so many times," Kiera complained, frowning at how much easier things might have been.

"Like running from zombies through an urban environment?" Jay said in agreement.

"You can also view a larger map by focusing on the mini-map, and it'll bring up a layout you can zoom in and out on. But it covers most of your vision, so be careful where you use it," TJ continued.

Tom took the map from TJ and looked it over. He thought about adding the details to his map, and a circle appeared in the middle of his vision, laid over the map, showing the progress of the map scan. When it reached one hundred percent, the circle disappeared, and he pulled up his own map. It had all the items on the map TJ had given him and even looked the same.

He again thought about making it more like the digital maps from apps he had used on his phone, and the System again gave him a loading icon. When it was completed, he was looking at a clean, easy-to-read map with all the locations on TJ's map. Tom passed the map on to the others to scan as well.

Focusing on the marker TJ had indicated for the second Dungeon, the icon had words added to it, saying, "Dungeon #2."

Minimizing the map back to its miniature form, Tom addressed the others. "Excellent! Are we ready to set out? Michael, do you need anything?" Tom asked.

"I'm ready. Let's do this shit!" Michael said excitedly, pumped up for the new challenge.

Gathering everyone together, they left the security room. Tom offered to take the GS2 this time, as the distance was a little further away, and walking seemed like a pain since the day was getting away from them. Heading to the garage, they piled in, and Tom started the engine, the rumble of the GS2 echoing in the garage.

Upgrades Available
You currently have upgrade points available for the Goblin Slayer 2.0. Would you like to allocate your points now to enhance your vehicle's performance and capabilities?

Yes	*No*

"Guess I haven't been spending these points like I should. One minute, guys, while I handle this," Tom said, selecting "Yes" and browsing through the upgrade options.

Tom scrolled through the available upgrades, eyeing the high-end items. Almost all of them required prerequisite purchases. He had his sights set on the Gatling gun, so he opted to invest in the reinforced upgrades for the entire vehicle. That left him with enough points for two more upgrades, so he added armor plating for the driver's and passenger side doors. With the upgrades confirmed, he put the vehicle in reverse, backed out of the parking space, and drove out of the parking garage.

The second Dungeon was located on the west side of town, closer to Shandra's neighborhood. They had to be cautious about their route, not wanting to provoke Stormcrusher's gang by straying into their territory. Fortunately, the old bank building seemed distant enough from Stormcrusher's area to avoid any immediate conflict.

About half an hour later, they arrived and parked the GS2 in a parking garage across the street, trying to keep it out of sight. They walked over to the bank. Its doors had been pried open—whether by looters, rival Guild members, or monsters, Tom couldn't tell. Either way, it made for easy entry.

Walking toward the back of the bank, Tom spotted a door near the drive-through window area. A sign on it read "Dungeon," with a smaller one beneath saying, "Beware of Animals."

"That's new. Never seen the second sign before," Tom remarked, squinting at the signs.

The others just shrugged. Tom opened the door, revealing a staircase leading down into a dimly lit hallway. The steps were stone, and an ornate sconce at the top held an electric light.

"Electricity? Here?" Tom said, surprised to see a light that wasn't a torch.

"Magic Dungeon, Tom. Let's go," Jay urged, growing impatient.

"You can't just say everything is magic when you don't get it," Tom scoffed at Jay's casual explanation.

"I can, and I will. Now get your ass in gear!" Jay replied, giving Tom a light push.

Tom steadied himself against the stone walls and continued down, deciding it wasn't worth debating right now. Reaching the bottom, the door behind them shut automatically.

The team moved down the hall until they entered a vast room, its ceiling soaring three stories high. In the center lay a massive, fur-covered creature curled up on the floor. A heavy chain with links as large as a man's hand stretched from the wall, disappearing behind the beast's body.

As they cautiously equipped their weapons and entered the room, the creature began to stir. It uncurled, stood up, and turned to face them.

"What the actual fuck is that?" Tom asked as the creature rose to its full height and stared at them.

Chapter 43

Dungeon of the Mad Scientist

Goatamus
Born from the twisted experiments of a Mad Scientist, the Goatamus is a formidable hybrid abomination combining the stubborn determination of a goat with the raw power and ferocity of a hippopotamus. With the head and horns of a goat and the massive, muscular body of a hippo, this creature is driven by a relentless territorial instinct and a fury that few can withstand. The Goatamus is a highly aggressive predator, capable of inflicting devastating damage on anyone foolish enough to enter its domain. Its powerful legs can stomp with earth-shattering force, and its curved horns are deadly in close combat. Most dangerous of all is its charge—once it locks onto a target, it barrels forward with unstoppable momentum. Approach with extreme caution and be prepared to evade its attacks!

HP:	1860/1860
MP:	0/0
SP:	1590/1590
Attacks:	Stomp, Gore, Charge

The creature reared up to its full height on two hind legs, towering like a small mountain. It let out a deep, resonant bellow that shook the very air around them, then dropped back down to all fours with a ground-shaking thud. Its shorter-than-expected forelegs lashed out in a sudden, aggressive kick, each movement packed with raw power. When it landed, the earth trembled slightly under the immense weight, causing loose stones to bounce and dust to rise. Tom's eyes quickly scanned the creature, trying to assess the threat it posed and form a plan.

The beast was a grotesque amalgamation of forms: it had the head and curling horns of a goat, with the massive, barrel-like body of a hippopotamus. Coarse, bristly fur covered its bulk, matted and caked with dirt. The horns were enormous, jutting out from its skull and curving outward to the sides, giving it a menacing reach that extended well beyond its already formidable frame. It stood nearly ten feet tall at the shoulder, and its sheer mass suggested it weighed close to ten thousand pounds. Muscles bulged beneath its shaggy hide, promising terrifying strength. The creature lowered its head, snorting and pawing at the ground like a bull preparing to charge.

Suddenly, it lunged forward, barreling toward them with surprising speed for something so large. The ground quaked beneath its thunderous steps. But just as it was about to close the distance, the creature jerked to a halt, a heavy iron chain snapping taut and pulling it back. The chain, as thick as a man's wrist, stretched from a metal collar around its neck to a massive anchor embedded in the stone wall. It let out a frustrated roar, thrashing its head, the horns slicing through the air.

"Holy shit, this thing is huge! It's going to be a problem. Anyone got any ideas?" Tom asked, his eyes still fixed on the creature.

"If we can get on its back, we can probably do a lot of damage in a place it can't reach," Jay suggested, eyeing the beast's broad, fur-covered spine.

"The old prison-piggyback trick, eh?" James noted, nodding his approval. "I think you're right. If it works for those corn-fed bastards in the slammer, it'll work here."

Jay narrowed his eyes at James for a moment before shrugging agreeably.

"Okay, good plan for now," Tom agreed. "Let's get someone up there and start hacking away. Everyone else, keep it distracted. Confuse it, draw its attention away." He equipped his sword from his Inventory, its blade gleaming in the dim Dungeon light.

"Who's going up there?" Derek asked, scanning the group to determine the best candidate for the task.

"Probably Jay. He's the most agile," Tom replied, locking eyes with Jay. "Better switch to a sword, too. You'll need something to cut through that thick hide."

"Or a chainsaw," James offered.

"Really? Why don't you guys hop up on that death trap?" Jay protested, looking around for some support from the others.

"Sorry, man. You signed up for this. Plus, you're the sneakiest. You can get around it and climb up without being noticed," Tom said, a smirk spreading across his face.

Tom looked over and saw that James was idly painting the target with his laser pointer.

"What are you doing?" he asked.

"Actually, I was just thinking…" James said.

"Shit, I just remembered I have a colonoscopy scheduled today," Jay said before James could say anything else. "I should probably head over that way—"

"I was just *thinking*," James repeated emphatically, "that this bastard is chained up like it's their kink. Why can't we just kill it from here?"

Jay reached into his pocket. Pulling out his cellphone, he held the blank screen up to his ear? "Doctor Kavorkian? I was just heading—what's that? You need to cancel? Damn, okay. Yeah, we can reschedule." Jay was nodding seriously. "Yeah, that works. Thanks. Bye."

Everyone was now looking at the Rogue.

"Well, would you look at that?" Jay chirped. "Looks like I'm free today. Let's go with James' plan."

The group paused, staring first at James, then at Jay, and finally at the chained beast still struggling against its bonds.

"Well... shit... I don't see why not," Tom said, realization dawning on him. "Alright, everyone, stop feeling stupid and take it down."

With a unified nod, they all switched to their guns and took aim. The roar of gunfire filled the room as they unloaded their magazines at the Goatamus. But as the bullets sped toward the creature, a shimmering, magical barrier suddenly flared to life, separating them from the beast and sealing the entrance to the room. The bullets ricocheted off the barrier, clattering harmlessly to the floor with soft tinkling sounds.

A glowing message appeared in their displays as they ceased fire, realizing their efforts were in vain:

Ah, Ah, Ah! You didn't enter the room!

To engage this monster in combat, you must step inside its designated area. This creature's movement is restricted to its chamber, and ranged attacks from outside will not trigger battle mode. Nice try, but you'll have to face it head-on! Enter the room to proceed with combat.

"Damn. Worth a shot, though. Alright, back to the original plan," Tom said, switching back to his greatsword.

Suddenly, Jay started patting down his pants as though searching for a ringing phone.

"Don't even think about it," Tom growled. "You're going in there and mounting that bastard like it's that thing's wedding night."

James stared at Tom, slack jawed. Tom stared back.

"What?" Tom gently shoved James away from himself.

"I'm just..." James wiped a fake tear from his eye. "So proud. My baby boy found his sense of humor." His voice was cracking with emotion. "I just... never thought I'd see the day..."

James wrapped his arms around Jay, sobbing hysterically. Jay patted the man consolingly as if to say "there there. It's going to be okay."

Tom rolled his eyes and held up his greatsword. "You ladies getting to work, or what?"

James straightened out and smoothed the imaginary tear stains from Jay's clothes and thanked him. He turned and gave a thumbs up to Tom.

"I'd rather get my hands dirty anyway," Michael added, pulling out two heavy axes, his eyes gleaming with anticipation of the battle ahead.

As soon as the barrier disappeared, Michael took off first, charging into the room with a roar that echoed through the chamber, challenging the beast awaiting them. The Goatamus answered with its own defiant bellow, a deep, rumbling sound that reverberated through their bones, and the fight began. The creature lunged at Michael, its massive frame barreling forward like a freight train. Michael swiftly sidestepped to the right, narrowly avoiding the charge. The Goatamus stumbled, crashing to the ground as it tried to adjust to Michael's quick movement.

Seizing the opportunity, Michael planted his feet and pivoted, launching himself toward the beast's exposed right side. Both axes swung down in a deadly arc, their blades flashing in the dim light before sinking deep into the creature's flesh. Large gashes opened, and blood began to pour out, matting the thick fur in streams of dark red. The Goatamus howled in a mix of rage and pain, its head whipping around to strike at Michael.

But the team was relentless. As the beast turned to focus on him, Tom darted to its left, his greatsword slashing across its side. The blade carved a deep wound from its shoulder down to its midsection, and the Goatamus screamed again, this time with a mix of pain and fury.

James stood back, firing his gun to provide covering fire while moving to flank the beast. His bullets barely penetrated the thick hide, but small drops of blood sprayed from where they struck. Seeing an opening, James moved behind the creature and aimed carefully. He unleashed a volley of shots directly at the creature's groin, hitting it squarely in the enormous nutsack dangling between its legs. The Goatamus let out an ear-splitting roar of rage, its eyes glowing an intense red as it thrashed in blind fury.

"Great! You can't just leave well enough alone, can you?!" Derek yelled at James, right before trying to dodge out of the way of a retaliatory swipe. He wasn't quick enough—a horn clipped him, sending him flying across the room and crashing into the wall with a sickening thud.

"DEREK!" Tom shouted as he saw Derek's body flung aside like a ragdoll.

"I'm okay… that hurt like hell, though," Derek groaned, pushing himself up to his feet, trying to reassure the team despite the pain.

Meanwhile, Kirsten and Kevin sheathed their weapons and dashed forward, each grabbing one of the beast's horns. With a coordinated effort, they pulled downward, forcing the Goatamus' massive head to the floor. The creature's momentum was halted, and it let out a desperate bleat of distress. Jay took this chance, sprinting straight at the beast's face and leaping onto its back, driving his sword between its shoulder blades and holding on tight.

The Goatamus screamed in agony, the sound filled with both fury and pain. It reared up on its hind legs, lifting the two Barbarians still clinging to its horns. Kevin was thrown off first, sent flying across the room in a wild cartwheel, his loincloth flapping as he crashed into the far wall. Kirsten, however, managed to keep her grip, pulling herself up onto the horn and crouching low, clinging for dear life.

"Thank god there was an undercarriage for that loincloth," James commented as he continued to fire at the creature.

With its head weighted down to one side, the beast struggled to balance. Desperate, Kirsten waited for a brief pause in its violent thrashing and then drove her fist directly into the creature's eye with all her might. The fragile membrane burst under the impact, and thick fluid poured down its face. The Goatamus let out an ear-piercing shriek and thrashed even more violently, shaking its head in wild circles. Kirsten quickly jumped from the horn, barely escaping as it swung its head like a wrecking ball.

The rest of the team, except for Jay, who was still clinging to his embedded sword, backed away to avoid the chaotic flailing. Jay had no choice but to hang on, unable to free his weapon or himself. Suddenly, from the side of the room, a blur of motion shot past Tom—a figure clad in heavy battle armor. With a force like a battering ram, the armored form crashed into the Goatamus' side, knocking it off balance and sending it toppling over with a tremendous crash. The sickening sound of ribs cracking echoed in the chamber.

"What the hell?!" Tom shouted, spinning around to see Derek in his battle armor, withdrawing from the impact zone. "I need some of that damn armor!"

Standing back, Tom called out to the others, "Keep it busy!"

The team sprang into action, most leaping on top of the fallen creature to try to pin it down. Tom stepped back, charging up his *Final Flash* spell, his hands glowing with accumulating energy. He kept his distance, wary of needing to dodge an attack. Jay was still nowhere in sight, likely lost somewhere on the beast's back when it was knocked over. The Goatamus thrashed wildly, trying to roll back onto its feet. Its short legs scrambled uselessly, and one of its horns had embedded itself deep into the stone floor like a nail driven into wood, preventing it from moving freely.

After what felt like an eternity in the chaos of battle, Tom's spell reached full power. He shouted for everyone to clear out, then released a concentrated beam of energy straight at the creature's exposed underside, pouring more mana into the spell for maximum impact. The beam pierced through the air and struck the beast squarely in the chest, punching through its thick hide and erupting out the other side.

A surprised scream erupted from Jay as he narrowly dodged the beam. "Watch where you're pointing that thing, you fucker!" he shouted at Tom as the beam faded away. "You'll put someone's eye out!"

The creature let out a weak, pitiful sound, almost like a mewl, as it took its last breath and fell silent. The team cautiously gathered around the fallen beast, staring at it for a long moment.

"That was fun," Michael said with a broad grin.

"You're in for a lot of 'fun' on this team, then," Jay replied, looking at Michael like he was insane and making air quotes around the word fun.

Surveying the body, the team realized they could harvest several useful parts for crafting. They took its thick hide, complete with fur, its massive horns, and even some of the meat for food. Once they finished, they noticed the only exit from the room was at the far end, opposite where they had entered.

"Maybe this was like the guard dog?" Tom mused, glancing between the beast and the exit.

"Probably. And if that's the guard dog, I bet we're in for some real treats inside," Derek said, his voice slightly distorted through his armor.

"Sounds like fun to me," Michael said, already heading for the exit.

Seeing no reason to linger, the rest of the team followed him. As they stepped through the doorway, they found a hallway with several branching paths on either side, leading up to what seemed to be a room lit up at the end of the hall. It was hard to see from this distance what exactly was inside.

"Should we explore each of the halls since they appear to be staggered?" Tom asked the team.

"That's for the best. We don't want anything sneaking up behind us if we just go straight to the end," Derek suggested.

As they continued down the hall, the first side path came up on the left. The team paused briefly before turning to explore the new route. The hall grew darker as they proceeded, prompting Jay to pull out a flashlight from his Inventory and shine it down the path.

"Where'd you get that?" Tom asked.

"One of the buildings we went through. Back in Flagstaff, actually. Lots of stuff there, and since they were being raided, I figured they wouldn't miss it. Now that they came with us, I know they won't," Jay explained, sweeping the beam back and forth along the walls, looking for any threats.

The light passed over a statue on the right, revealing a bat-like figure perched on top. Suddenly, a creature fluttered out from behind it, its cries piercing the silence like a baby's wail. In the low light, it was hard to make out what it was.

Michael tracked the fluttering movement with his eyes and swung his axe. The crying abruptly stopped as the creature fell to the floor, dead. Jay's flashlight beam settled on it, revealing a grotesque sight: a creature with the furry body, feet, and wings of a large bat, but with the head of a small child. Michael's blow had nearly severed it in two across the neck and chest, and it lay in a spreading puddle of blood.

"What the hell?!" James exclaimed, his voice trembling.

"It looks like some kind of human-bat hybrid," Tom said, stepping closer but not too close. "That's sick."

"What kind of monster would create something like this?! It's just wrong!" James shouted, his face pale with horror.

"Don't worry, we'll find out," Tom said, placing a reassuring hand on James' shoulder.

James jerked away from the touch, his eyes wide with fear. "I don't know if I can do this. This is too much," he said, taking a step back.

Suddenly, more cries echoed down the hallway. The sounds grew louder, drawing nearer. More of the creatures were coming.

Chapter 44

Bat, Bat, Man

The crying sounds grew louder and more dissonant as the creatures drew nearer, filling the air with a cacophony of wails. It was as if all the toys had been snatched from a daycare, and children of every age were screaming in protest, their voices layered in a maddening chorus. Soon, the rapid flapping of wings surrounded the party as the bat-like monsters swarmed, their grotesque forms darting in and out of the dim light.

The adventurers swung their weapons furiously, trying to fend off the onslaught of creatures. Swords, axes, and maces sliced and smashed through the air, striking down any monster that ventured too close. All except James. He crouched on the floor, hands clamped over his ears, screaming in terror at the chaos enveloping him.

"Son of a bitch!" Kiera yelled as one of the creatures latched onto her shoulder, its tiny human-like teeth sinking into her neck. She grabbed the bat-human hybrid by its head, tore it off her shoulder, and slammed it to the ground with all her strength. She then stomped on its writhing body, crushing it instantly. Glancing at her display, she noticed a small blood drop icon appear beneath her HP bar. She focused on the icon, trying to fend off more attackers while deciphering the status effect. What she saw made her curse again.

"Shit! These fuckers cause bleeding when they bite you!" Kiera shouted to the others.

The team continued their defensive tactics, swinging weapons, shields, and even their arms to keep the bats at bay. Derek's mace collided with one of the creatures, sending it crashing to the ground right in front of James. His screams fell silent as he stared at the grotesque creature, its small child-like head now bleeding from its mouth, nose, and eyes.

Without a word, James stood, his eyes wide with horror, and turned to sprint away from the hall, a yell of pure terror escaping his lips as he ran.

"What's his deal?" Jay called out, swatting at bats with one hand and slicing with his Ninjato in the other.

"If we finish off these bats, we can go ask him," Derek grunted, holding his shield up as another creature slammed into it and fell to the ground, stunned.

After several more intense minutes, the swarm began to thin out, with fewer bats left attacking. The remaining creatures were quickly dispatched, and the team paused to catch their breath.

"Guess we should go see what got into shithead back there," Kiera said, leaning over, her hands on her knees.

"I think I know, but you all need to be nice. It's not a fun subject," Tom said, straightening up and heading down the hall in the direction James had fled.

They found James around a corner at the end of the hall, sitting on the floor with his knees pulled to his chest, his arms wrapped tightly around his legs, his head buried in his knees. He was sobbing uncontrollably. Tom crouched down beside him and placed a hand gently on his shoulder.

"Hey, bud. Is this about Anthony?" Tom asked softly.

James nodded, his head never lifting from his knees.

"Who is Anthony?" Jay asked quietly, trying to be sensitive to the situation but feeling awkward seeing this vulnerable side of James.

"Anthony was James' kid brother. An oops-baby when James was about twelve," Tom began, watching James to see if he wanted to continue. When James didn't, Tom went on, "James loved that kid. They did everything together. Anthony looked up to him like a hero."

"You keep using past tense," Jay said, his face slowly registering understanding.

"When James was seventeen and Anthony was four, they were playing outside when a van pulled up," Tom continued, glancing at James, who seemed to be pulling himself together enough to speak.

James wiped his face, his voice breaking as he recounted, "Two men jumped out and grabbed Anthony. I tried to stop them, but they were too strong. They took him. The police searched for days. Everyone in the city was on alert. Texas Rangers came in to help."

"It's okay, James. We're your family now. You don't have to carry this alone," Tom consoled him, squeezing his shoulder reassuringly.

"On the sixth day, after barely sleeping or eating, I was out hanging up flyers. The police came to the house. They'd found his body in a ditch, nearly a hundred miles away. He'd been tortured… and worse, before they killed him. It was…" James's voice broke as fresh sobs wracked his body.

A heavy silence fell over the group, each person's head bowed in sorrow. After a long moment, James took a deep breath, steadying himself.

"I haven't been the same since. I see his face in every kid I see. I was there. I should have been able to do something," James said, his voice filled with guilt.

"You did everything you could. You were just a kid. Evil people do evil things, and it's not on you," Kiera said, kneeling beside him and placing a comforting hand on his other shoulder.

"I saw the faces on those bats, and it brought back everything—every memory, every feeling, every sleepless night and every numb day where I had to go through life with a smile plastered on my face," James said, his voice quivering as he let the words spill out. "It reminded me of standing in the morgue. Of them pulling back the sheet over his small body so we could identify him. His cold, lifeless, and broken little body just lying there." James' voice trembled as the full weight of his trauma came flooding back, the pain raw and unfiltered.

Kiera pulled James into a tight hug, holding him close as she rocked gently back and forth. James' sobs grew louder, the weight of his past grief crashing over him like a tidal wave, impossible to resist. She continued to hold him as he cried, feeling the decades-old sorrow pour out like a phantom wound reopening.

"We're here with you, James. You're not alone anymore," Kiera whispered, her voice soothing. "I'm glad you opened up to us. We're bound together now. You can always count on us. Trauma is a part of life; we all carry something that haunts us. Some traumas are deeper, but sharing the burden rather than hiding behind humor is the first step to healing." She gave him a final squeeze, then pulled back, holding him at arm's length and locking eyes with him.

James nodded, wiping his eyes. "I don't know if I can ever get over the loss. Some days, it feels like the wound is closed, just scar tissue. Then, out of nowhere, something reminds me of his laugh or the games we used to play, and it feels as fresh as the day we got the call," he said, his voice barely above a whisper.

"We all handle loss and trauma differently, but bottling it up, burying it deep, only makes it fester," Derek offered, his voice calm but firm. "This chink in your armor has shown us who you really are underneath, and we still accept you, no matter what happened. Talking about it is the only way to start the healing process."

"I don't know if I can do that," James admitted, sniffling as he wiped his nose on his sleeve.

"You can't—not on your own," Jay said softly, leaning in to meet James' gaze. "That's why you've got us. We're here to help carry the load. No matter how big a dickhead you are, we're not going anywhere."

A small smile broke across James' face despite the tears. "I don't think I can face those creatures," he said, his voice still shaky.

"That's fine. I'll kill every last one of them so you don't have to," Jay replied with a fierce determination. "Nobody messes with my family." He stood up straight, his hands planted firmly on his hips.

"Thanks, Jay. I really appreciate that," James said, his voice steadier, but still fragile.

"Kiera, can you stay here with James? The rest of us can take care of this," Tom suggested to Kiera, who was still beside James.

"Sure. We'll stay here and catch our breath," Kiera replied, rubbing James' back in comfort.

"Alright then, let's go fuck up some monsters," Jay said, turning and striding back down the hall toward where the bats had been.

Michael, Tom, Derek, Kevin, and Kirsten followed close behind, their faces set with determination. They picked up their pace to a light jog, eager to get to the end of the hall and finish what they'd started. As they passed the scattered bodies of the bat creatures, they pushed on into the darkness. Jay's flashlight was the only source of light in the pitch-black corridor, casting eerie shadows on the walls as they moved.

Up ahead, the beam of light revealed an archway that opened into a larger chamber. They slowed their approach, wary of rushing headlong into danger. At the archway, Jay peeked carefully around the corner into the room beyond. He pulled back quickly, his face serious.

"Not good. There are a lot of them," Jay whispered.

"How many?" Derek asked, his voice low.

"More than I care to count. Hundreds, maybe," Jay replied, his face grim.

"Shit. Any ideas?" Tom asked, looking around at the group.

"Yeah, dumbass, the tattoo! Use the damn tattoo!" Jay snapped. "We don't have any other big area-of-effect options here."

"Right, right! Good call," Tom said, nodding. "Alright, let's light this birthday candle." He stepped into the room, moving cautiously toward the center.

The floor was covered in a thick layer of guano from the bats clinging to the ceiling above. The soft cries of a few baby bats echoed in the cavernous space, crawling around blindly. Stopping in the middle of the room, Tom readied his greatsword, inhaling deeply before realizing it was a mistake to do so in the middle of a dung pile. He nearly gagged, but steeled himself and activated his *Tattoo of Life Absorption*.

Instantly, several bat creatures fell from the ceiling, their bodies hitting the ground with soft thuds as the first pulses of damage took effect. The rest erupted into a cacophony of screeches, their cries mixing with the sound of flapping wings as they descended upon him. Power surged through Tom as he began unleashing *Eldritch Blasts* toward the ceiling, green flames igniting the clustered masses of bats. Bodies plummeted to the floor, still ablaze with ghostly green fire.

The room took on a ghastly green hue from the burning bodies, casting grotesque shadows that danced along the walls in a grim spectacle. The surviving bats swooped down, launching frenzied attacks at Tom from all directions. One bat shot toward the back of Tom's head, but Michael intercepted it, cleaving it in two with a well-timed swing of his axe.

The rest of the team surged into the room, weapons swinging as they joined the fray. Suddenly, a low growl resonated from the back of the chamber. Two piercing red eyes blinked open on the far wall. Large, leathery wings unfurled as a roughly human-sized but monstrous creature, crawled down the wall and began to stalk across the floor toward Tom.

"SHIT!" Jay shouted, his eyes widening. "Looks like Grandpa woke up, and he's as mad as he is ugly!"

"Well, fuck up his day then!" Tom shouted back, too busy fending off the swarming bats as most of them zeroed in on him, seeing him as the primary threat.

The giant bat, now crawling on the ground, lumbered closer to Tom, its blood-red eyes locked on him. It seemed to recognize him as the greatest danger to its brood. Jay quickly stepped in between the monster and Tom, slicing through a bat mid-flight just in front of the boss creature. The severed halves of the smaller bat hit the ground with a wet splat. The boss glanced down at its fallen offspring, then turned its furious gaze to Jay, baring its jagged teeth in a low, menacing growl.

"I might have fucked up. Can we reset the encounter?" Jay asked with a forced grin, but the monster responded by lunging at him, fangs aimed at his throat. "I guess not!"

Jay dodged to the side just in time, countering with a quick slash across the beast's face, opening a deep gash along its cheek.

"Tough old bastard," Jay muttered, sidestepping a swipe from the claw on its right wing. "Guess that leathery skin has more uses than just making you look like an elephant's ass."

"Take out its wings so it can't get any height advantage!" Derek shouted from the other side of the room. He had given up on dodging the smaller bats, relying on his armor to shield him. He grabbed two bats out of the air, crushed them in his hands, and hurled their bodies at two more bats, knocking them to the ground. Tom's tattoo drained the remaining life from the downed creatures.

Realizing his greatsword wasn't effective in the chaos, Tom stored it away and began conjuring an *Eldritch Blast* in each hand. He aimed the crackling energy at the bats around him, the green flames spreading between clustered targets. Holding the spells required a constant stream of mana, but with his tattoo siphoning life force from the fallen, his mana reserves were full and ready.

"Flaming fists could have been fun," Tom mused, briefly considering his other tattoo options.

Meanwhile, Jay continued to dart around the boss bat, narrowly avoiding its snapping jaws and sweeping claws. After dodging another bite, he lunged to the side and drove his sword into the thin flap of skin connecting its wings. As he sprinted along its side, he dragged his blade, tearing a massive gash in the membrane. The creature shrieked in pain, its cry eerily human, like that of an old man.

It whipped around with unexpected speed, catching Jay off guard, and lunged. They went down in a tangled heap.

"JAY!" Tom shouted, his heart pounding in his chest.

Chapter 45

Amalgamations

Tom tried to push through the chaos to reach Jay, but the swarm of smaller bats between them was too dense, blocking his path. Frustrated, he realized he couldn't make it to Jay in time. Desperate to understand their enemy better, Tom activated *Inspect* on the creature, hoping to get a clearer sense of what they were truly up against.

Elder Bat Abomination	
Born from the twisted ambitions of a Mad Scientist obsessed with genetic manipulation, the Elder Bat Abomination is a nightmarish fusion of human and bat DNA. This grotesque creature, standing at human height but possessing the monstrous features of a giant bat, represents the horrific culmination of decades of unethical experimentation. Its humanoid body is covered in leathery skin, with oversized, membranous wings that unfurl like the cloaks of the damned. Sharp, yellowed fangs protrude from a distorted mouth, and its eyes burn with a feral intelligence that hints at the human DNA buried within its monstrous form. This abomination should never have seen the light of day, and its very existence is a blasphemy against nature.	
HP:	895/1250
MP:	400/500
SP:	450/500
Attacks:	Claw, Vampiric Bite, Ultrasonic Blast

Tom could only catch glimpses of the battle through the jagged tear Jay had slashed in the monster's wings. The brief flashes of movement showed Jay pinned beneath the creature, struggling to defend himself. "Someone get to Jay *now!*" Tom shouted, swinging his flaming fists to punch bats out of the air.

The floor was becoming increasingly treacherous, littered with the shriveled bodies of fallen bats from Tom's tattoo effects. Kevin suddenly charged across the room, ignoring the bites and scratches tearing at his skin. With a powerful lunge, he slammed into the massive bat, locking it in a bear hug. The impact sent both of them rolling off Jay, who was on the ground with his hands shielding his face from the creature's attacks. Tom caught sight of deep gashes across Jay's torso, his clothes stained with blood.

Swatting two more bats out of the air, Tom unleashed an *Eldritch Blast* at a nearby target, then quickly cast *Dark Healing* on Jay. As he channeled the spell, he unintentionally directed some of the excess energy into it, feeling the pull of the chaotic mana surging through him. Trying to fend off the attacking bats with one hand, Tom could feel sharp bites piercing his skin. Suddenly, a System prompt appeared in his view, interrupting his focus.

Spell Evolution!

Dark Healing has evolved into Dark Restoration!

Your mastery and continuous use of Dark Healing, combined with the application of advanced magical principles, have caused the spell to evolve into Dark Restoration! You can now channel additional mana into the spell to amplify its healing effects. Be aware: the longer you maintain the spell, the more mana it will consume to stay active. Use this newfound power wisely!

Tom quickly minimized the System prompt to review later and yanked a bat off his shoulder with his flame-covered hand. The creature sizzled and screeched in agony as it burned, and Tom flung it away with a flick of his wrist. Suddenly, Jay shot up from the floor, his eyes wild and darting around.

"SHUT IT OFF!" he shouted at Tom, his voice almost a roar. "I feel like someone injected adrenaline straight into my heart! HEEEERRRRAAAAAAAAAAGGGHHHH!"

With a primal scream, Jay launched himself at the Elder Bat, his fists flying as he pummeled the creature's stomach like a boxer attacking a speed bag. Realizing the spell's effect, Tom immediately cut off *Dark Restoration* and instead activated his *Fear* Skill. Instantly, the bats swooping toward him shrieked in terror and veered away, their human-like eyes wide with fear as they desperately tried to escape his presence.

In their panic, many of the bats became disoriented, colliding with walls and each other. Meanwhile, Jay's relentless punches were starting to enrage the Elder Bat. Seeing the change in its demeanor, Jay shifted tactics, switching to punch daggers. With the blades gripped between his middle and third fingers, he began driving them into the creature's flesh, then tearing his hands sideways to maximize the damage. Kevin, noticing the opportunity, switched his grip from a bear hug to a full nelson, exposing the Elder Bat's torso even more.

Gash after gash appeared across the monster's body, blood pouring from its wounds. It sagged in Kevin's grip, its strength fading rapidly from blood loss. Its head slumped forward, and it began to lose consciousness. Sensing it was near death, Kevin released his hold slightly, grabbed the creature by the chin with one hand and a shoulder with the other, and pulled with all his might. The Elder Bat's head tore free with a sickening rip, a section of its spine coming out with it. No blood gushed from the neck—the earlier draining by Jay had left it nearly dry.

The remaining bats in the room went into a frenzy at the sight of their leader's death. They flew around erratically, their desperation evident, but Tom's tattoo, which he reactivated, continued to drain their life force by the dozens. Within moments, only a few bats remained fluttering weakly, and the team swiftly picked them off.

"Fucking hell! We need more AOE shit for these damn swarms," Jay muttered, sliding down against a wall, exhausted now that the excess energy coursing through him had finally burned off.

"Agreed," Tom replied, slumping down to catch his breath as well. "Next time we're back at the Guild, we should check the vending machines for anything useful."

After a few minutes of rest, the team stood up and began searching the room for loot. The smaller bats didn't have anything worth taking, but Tom's eyes were drawn to a hidden nest behind the statue where the Elder Bat had perched. He moved over and rummaged through it, finding several large gemstones nestled among the debris.

"What are these for?" Tom asked, holding up a sapphire the size of an orange, inspecting it closely in the dim light.

<table>
<tr><td colspan="2" align="center">Infused Sapphire</td></tr>
<tr><td colspan="2">

A gemstone of extraordinary beauty and power, the Infused Sapphire has been meticulously crafted and infused with potent mana, enhancing its natural properties. This sapphire's deep blue hue is amplified by the magical energy coursing through it, making it a valuable component in both crafting and smithing. When used in the creation of weapons, armor, or magical items, it provides a significant boost in power and can even imbue the item with special skills or abilities. Its flawless clarity and excellent cut further amplify its effectiveness, making it highly sought after by artisans and enchanters alike.

Note: The Infused Sapphire's potential varies based on the crafting skill of the user and the quality of the materials it is combined with. Use it wisely to maximize its effects!

</td></tr>
<tr><td align="center">Rarity:</td><td align="center">Epic</td></tr>
<tr><td align="center">Clarity:</td><td align="center">Flawless</td></tr>
<tr><td align="center">Cut:</td><td align="center">Excellent</td></tr>
</table>

"Great. Just one more thing I don't understand about this System," Tom thought as he turned the gem over in his hand. It was an absolute monster of a gemstone, its size and flawless cut making it a rare treasure.

For a moment, Tom thought he'd struck it rich with such a find. Then he remembered that traditional money was worthless now—Monster Cores were the currency of the new world—so that dream died almost immediately. Maybe Roland could make something worthwhile with these. He grabbed each gem and carefully placed them in his Inventory.

With nothing else of value in the room, the team made their way back down the hallway to where Kiera and James were waiting. James was still sitting on the floor, rocking back and forth. As he saw the others approaching, he stopped and slowly got to his feet.

"You got them?" James asked, his voice tentative.

"We got them all. You don't have to worry about those things anymore," Tom said, placing a reassuring hand on James' shoulder. "And maybe it's best you skip this Dungeon in the future."

"Yeah, I don't want to see that again," James muttered, looking down at his shoes. "Hopefully there aren't any more of them."

"If there are, we'll take care of it," Tom assured him, pulling him in for a hug.

James hadn't expected the hug and froze for a moment, but then he wrapped his arms around Tom. "Thank you," he whispered quietly in Tom's ear.

After a moment, they pulled away and the team regrouped, ready to move on to the next area. Further down the main corridor, they turned right into another hallway. Jay took point with his flashlight again, illuminating the path ahead. When they reached the end, they found the room already lit with torchlight, so Jay put his flashlight away.

Inside, a cluster of enormous conch shells lined the floor, each large enough to house a creature that could pose a severe threat to humans. The shells, towering at about five feet tall and eight feet long, gleamed in the flickering light. They were still, showing no signs of movement.

"What the hell are these things?" Kiera asked, running a hand over one of the shells' intricate patterns. "They're actually quite beautiful."

Tom decided to use *Inspect* on the shells, hoping to gain some insight into what they were dealing with.

Giraffe Conch

The Giraffe Conch is yet another twisted creation of the Mad Scientist, designed to wreak havoc on the realms with its unnatural form and deadly capabilities. Appearing at first as a large, beautifully patterned conch shell, this creature conceals a long, retractable neck that allows it to strike with incredible reach. The elongated neck, resembling that of a giraffe, can rapidly extend from the shell, catching prey off guard. Its unique and striking appearance is deceiving, as this abomination is capable of launching toxic

---

projectiles from a distance, making it a serious threat to any adventurer who gets too close.	
HP:	400/400
MP:	10/10
SP:	50/50
Attacks:	Skull Bash, Poison Missile

"That's strange," Tom muttered, studying the information the System provided about the creature.

Derek walked over, curiosity piqued, and used *Inspect* to see the stats for himself. "Why would they have such odd stats? This seems like... AH!" He yelped suddenly as something struck his armor with a sharp, metallic ping, nearly knocking him off balance.

Tom's eyes darted to the creatures and saw a yellow and brown tube-like appendage retracting back into the shell of the nearest one. His gaze dropped to the floor, where he noticed a six-inch-long spike, its tip coated in a dripping purple liquid. He crouched down, picked up the spike carefully, and *Inspected* it more closely, his brow furrowing with concern.

Giraffe Conch Spine
The Giraffe Conch Spine is a deadly projectile fired from the Giraffe Conch, a creature engineered for maximum lethality. The spine is barbed and rigid, designed to pierce armor and flesh with ease. What makes this item truly dangerous, however, is the coating of one of the world's most potent poisons. Even a single drop of this toxic substance is lethal enough to kill over one hundred adult males of any species not resistant to poison. Handle with extreme caution; this spine is not just a weapon—it's a death sentence.

"Oh, shit," Tom muttered under his breath as he saw the danger unfolding.

Suddenly, long giraffe-like necks began protruding from the conch shells, their heads emerging as the team instinctively took a few steps back.

"Watch out for the spines they shoot! They're deadly poisonous!" Tom shouted to the others.

As if on cue, the giraffe heads began to inhale deeply, their necks arching back one by one.

"DODGE!" Tom yelled, recognizing the movement. It was almost like the way he and his friends used to lean back to spit watermelon seeds in the fields as kids.

A volley of spines launched from the mouths of the creatures, hurtling through the air with a deadly hiss. The team leapt aside, narrowly dodging the projectiles. After the attack, the necks remained still, their eyes fixed on the adventurers.

"Was that it?" Jay asked, his voice filled with a mix of skepticism and relief.

"Maybe we should—" Tom started, but his words trailed off as he noticed a bulge moving up one of the giraffe necks. "What the hell is that?"

He pointed at the creature, and the others followed his gaze. As the lump reached the creature's mouth, the tip of another spine began to emerge.

"So, there's a tell," Derek observed, a keen gleam in his eye. "Looks like they need time to reload. When they fire the spines, that's our chance to attack."

The team braced themselves, watching closely for the next signs of attack. When the necks jerked back to fire, everyone dove out of the way as another barrage of spines shot toward them. The moment they recovered, they charged at the creatures, hacking and slashing at the vulnerable necks. Within a minute, all the heads lay severed on the floor, and the Giraffe Conches were dead, leaving behind pools of purple blood that seeped into the stone, staining it.

Jay pulled a mason jar from his Inventory and began collecting the spines scattered around the room.

"What are you doing with those?" Tom asked, watching him carefully.

"Saving them for poison making. Could come in handy one day—you never know," Jay replied. He then moved over to one of the conch shells and stuck his hand deep inside, his arm disappearing up to the shoulder.

"Oh, that's just gross. Now what are you after?" Tom asked, grimacing as he watched Jay rummaging around.

"The poison gland. They've got to have one. I can use that too," Jay said, his tongue sticking out slightly in concentration. "Aha! There it is!"

He pulled out a small, purple sack filled with a liquid that looked disturbingly like a water balloon. Carefully, he placed it inside another mason jar from his Inventory. Once he had filled the jar, he motioned for the team to head back to the hallway.

They took the next path, which diverted to the left. Inside, they found a room filled with raccoons, each one with a rattlesnake for a tail.

Diamond-Back Raccoons

The Diamond-Back Raccoon is a twisted creation resulting from the Mad Scientist's relentless experiments to fuse the traits of different species into one unpredictable creature. This abomination features the body of a raccoon, complete with its dexterous paws and masked face, but with the tail replaced by a living rattlesnake. The snake tail retains all the dangerous features of a rattlesnake, including venomous fangs and a swift strike that can deliver a toxic bite. These creatures are highly unpredictable, combining the cunning and curiosity of a raccoon with the deadly venomous strike of a rattlesnake.

HP:	150/150
MP:	0/0
SP:	100/100
Attacks:	Venomous Bite, Claws, Poison Spray

These creatures weren't very effective fighters, except for their snake-tail bites. Derek told the others to stay back and went on a stomping spree, his armor protecting him completely from the bites. No one wanted anything from this room; the only items of interest were shiny rocks the creatures had hoarded in a hole dug into the Dungeon wall.

The last room in the hall before reaching the end was on the right. When they entered, they found twelve men standing there, motionless. Confused, Tom used *Inspect* to get more information on them.

Minotaur-Centaur Hybrids	
The Minotaur-Centaur Hybrid is a bizarre and ultimately failed experiment by the Mad Scientist, who sought to combine the strength and endurance of a Minotaur with the speed and agility of a Centaur. The goal was to create a powerful creature with horns and sturdier legs that would not easily break under stress. However, the experiment was a disappointment—every offspring produced by these hybrids was born as a regular human, lacking any of the desired traits of either species. Though not particularly formidable, they are aggressive and will use basic attacks to defend themselves if provoked.	
HP:	250/250
MP:	100/100
SP:	300/300
Attacks:	Punch, Kick, Bite, Scratch

With no real threat from the rabid men in the room, the team quickly dispatched them. The hybrids attacked with the ferocity of wild animals but lacked any of the skill or instinct that true beasts possessed. Their movements were erratic and uncoordinated, suggesting they had never learned how to interact with others, retaining only a primal, feral behavior.

Once the hybrids lay dead, the team moved cautiously toward the last room at the end of the hall. Nothing could have prepared them for what awaited them beyond the door.

Chapter 46

Laboratory

What met their eyes was a maze of tables, each one covered in a chaotic array of beakers, test tubes, Erlenmeyer flasks, and every conceivable piece of equipment needed for a fully functioning laboratory. Along the far wall stood a series of imposing metal chambers, their surfaces gleaming under the dim lights.

"This must be the lab of the Mad Scientist I keep reading about in the System messages," Tom said, his voice tinged with awe as he took in the sheer volume of equipment.

"Sounds about right," James muttered, pushing past Tom and striding into the room. Pulling a mace from his Inventory, he raised it high and smashed one of the Erlenmeyer flasks on a nearby table.

"NO! Don't do that! We should take the equipment back to the Guild!" Tom shouted, rushing over to stop James from causing more damage.

"But this bastard is messing with nature! We can't let him keep doing this!" James snapped back, his eyes blazing.

"And I agree. But I think those are the incubation chambers on the wall over there. Smash those instead, so whatever's growing in there doesn't come after us. This lab equipment, though—it could be useful for making medicines or maybe even alchemical potions, but we definitely need it at the Guild," Tom reasoned, directing James' attention to the metal chambers lining the wall.

Sure enough, inside each chamber, visible through glass panels, were creatures in various stages of growth.

Seeing them, James' anger flared. Visions of the human-headed bats filled his mind, triggering more memories of Anthony. With a roar, he swung his mace and shattered the first chamber, spilling its contents across the floor.

Fueled by rage, James went from chamber to chamber, smashing each one to pieces. Meanwhile, the others scrambled to load as much of the lab equipment as they could into their Inventories. After James destroyed a few more containers, an alarm blared through the room, and a hidden compartment in the ceiling opened to reveal a blinking red light, flashing in sync with the alarm's piercing sound.

"Well, that was unexpected," Tom muttered, unsure of what to do next.

"This is usually when I yell, 'Book it before the fuzz shows up.' But now?" Kiera asked, her voice filled with uncertainty.

Suddenly, a door slid open on the right side of the room, and the sound of deep, menacing barking echoed out. Emerging from the new opening were three massive, three-headed dogs, each the size of a horse. Thick drool dripped from their bared teeth as they growled and locked eyes on the intruders.

"Shit," Tom breathed out in resignation.

Squirrel, who had been sticking close to James like a loyal guardian, now jumped in front of him, baring his own teeth in response. In a flash, Squirrel grew to the size of a small SUV and leaped at the monstrous dogs. Jerky, suddenly appearing on Tom's shoulder, grabbed Tom's head and yanked it toward him.

"Jerky and Squirrel kill doggies. You get stuff," Jerky said, squeezing Tom's cheeks together with his scaly hands, making his mouth pucker like a fish.

With a shriek, Jerky leaped from Tom's shoulder, wings unfurling as he glided down to join Squirrel, who was battling all nine heads at once. Beams of energy shot from Jerky's eyes, targeting the rear flank of one of the beasts. Tom, realizing the seriousness of the situation, quickly used *Inspect* on one of the three-headed dogs.

Puddles - Cerberus

Puddles is the beloved yet troublesome pet of the Mad Scientist who resides in this Dungeon. Named for his unfortunate habit of relieving himself indoors without any regard for designated spaces, Puddles is nonetheless a formidable guardian. As a Cerberus, he possesses three heads, each with its own distinct personality and level of aggression. When all three heads work in unison, Puddles can be an overwhelming force on the battlefield. However, this strength can also be a weakness, as the heads often act independently, leading to confusion and infighting.

Special Traits:
- **Head Disunity:** Each head can act independently, sometimes resulting in a lack of coordination that can be exploited in battle. However, when synchronized, Puddles becomes a highly dangerous adversary.

HP:	800/800
MP:	250/250
SP:	950/950
Attacks:	Bite, Claw, Fire Breath

As Tom read the information on Puddles, a burst of fire erupted from one of the Cerberus' heads, aimed directly at Squirrel. The dire wolf swiftly shrank in size and dodged the blast, which ended up squarely hitting one of the other Cerberus' heads. The attack seemed to have little effect, indicating to Tom that these creatures had some level of fire resistance. As Squirrel landed from his dodge, he expanded to the size of a city bus, slamming the Cerberus against the wall. Then, shrinking back to SUV size, he bit down on one of the creature's necks, violently shaking his head back and forth.

Another Cerberus quickly recovered and lunged to bite Squirrel's hindquarters. Jerky reacted instantly, summoning a magical barrier that the creature bit into, cracking some of its teeth. Squirrel's eyes began to glow a fierce red when he turned to face the Cerberus that had dared to attack him. A powerful wind whipped up around him, sending loose research papers flying around the room.

Tom could feel the immense power building in Squirrel, his fur rippling as if charged with energy. Suddenly, Squirrel opened his mouth wide and let out a ferocious howl. A glowing orb formed at the back of his throat and then shot out, followed by two more, zigzagging wildly through the air before exploding on impact with the Cerberus' three heads. The monster whimpered in pain as it was blasted back into a wall, collapsing into a lifeless heap.

Another Cerberus took advantage of the chaos, leaping onto Squirrel's back and sinking its teeth into his flesh. Squirrel howled in pain and shook furiously, flinging the Cerberus off. It hit the ground hard, then started to get up, pieces of Squirrel's fur still clutched in its mouths. The final Cerberus saw its chance and bit down on Squirrel's leg. This, however, proved to be its undoing. Squirrel let out a yelp, and Jerky conjured an ice spike in midair, hurling it with magic.

The spike pierced through the Cerberus' back and out its chest. The beast released Squirrel and stumbled, blood pouring from its middle mouth before collapsing on its side.

"That was new," Derek remarked, noticing Jerky's spell.

"He's been hunting more often and picked up some new tricks," Tom explained with a grin, still hurriedly stuffing his Inventory with lab equipment.

Realizing that its companions had been dispatched quickly, the remaining Cerberus began to circle Squirrel cautiously, searching for an opening. Jerky fired a beam at it, but the creature leapt over the blast. Squirrel seized the opportunity, diving at the Cerberus. He grew to an enormous size, catching the three-headed dog in his mouth midair and thrashing it around like a chew toy.

Tossing the now-limp creature aside, Squirrel shrank back to his normal size and limped over to Derek.

"Good job, Squirrel. You too, Jerky," Derek praised as he cast a healing spell on the dire wolf. Squirrel tested his once-injured leg, then padded over to James, who was still busy smashing the last of the glass containers. Jerky landed back on Tom's shoulder, looking quite pleased with himself.

"I see you've been practicing your new spells," Tom commented as he placed the last of the equipment into his Inventory.

"Jerky gets strong, like master. Jerky helps," Jerky said proudly, puffing out his chest.

"You're definitely getting stronger. You've earned a treat when we get back to the Guild," Tom praised, scratching Jerky behind his horns.

Jerky rubbed his hands together excitedly, then turned invisible again, hiding from sight.

"HUUURRAAAAGGHH!" James bellowed as he smashed the last of the glass. "I don't know how you guys keep swinging these weapons around."

"You could have just shot out all the glass," Derek suggested.

James paused, looking at the shattered glass on the floor and then at the mace in his hand.

"Well... fuck. That would've been easier," James said, shaking his head at his oversight.

"Probably faster, too," Kiera said.

"And less messy," Jay chimed in.

"But less cathartic," Kiera admitted.

"Could have done it from a distance," Tom pointed out.

"Alright, I get it. Stupid James and his stupid ideas. Can we just move on?" James grumbled after the remarks.

"Sorry, James. Old habit of ribbing you. What matters is that it's done," Tom said, feeling a bit guilty after James' recent trauma.

"No, it's fine. I don't want you all treating me like I'm made of porcelain," James replied. "Let's just find this guy and blow his head off."

"There's the old James," Jay said with a grin.

James stopped, glared at Jay for a moment, then turned away to search for an exit.

"The only way out seems to be where the dogs came from. Guess we head that way," Derek observed, pointing to the door that had opened when the alarm sounded.

James made a beeline for the doorway and went through. Moments later, as the others rushed to follow, they heard a scuffle from the passage just before James was tossed back into the room, crashing onto a table and breaking it.

"James! Are you okay?" Tom shouted, rushing over to check on him.

"Fucker hits like a semi-truck," James groaned, rubbing his jaw.

"Who does?" Tom pressed for answers.

A roar, ending in a high-pitched squeak, echoed from the hallway as a creature crouched to enter the room. Standing up to nearly eight feet tall, the creature had horns like a bull, the body of a man, and the feet of a large rodent. Its face looked eerily familiar, like something Tom had seen before. He quickly used *Inspect*.

Chipmotaur

The Chipmotaur is the chaotic culmination of years of twisted experimentation and selective breeding, merging the brute strength and rage of a Minotaur with the manic energy and speed of a hyperactive chipmunk. This unnervingly powerful hybrid creature is notorious for its erratic behavior and boundless stamina, making it a formidable opponent in any encounter.

With a muscular, bull-like body and the oversized, twitchy eyes of a chipmunk, the Chipmotaur is constantly on edge, ready to unleash its fury at a moment's notice. It is particularly protective of its food stores—especially its nuts. Approach with extreme caution and, above all, **DO NOT TOUCH THE CREATURE'S NUTS!**

HP:	2480/2480
MP:	500/500
SP:	8000/8000
Attacks:	Gore, Bite, Claw, Charge, Nutshot, Rage

"Mongo! Don't forget your weapon!" came a high-pitched voice from the hallway behind the creature.

A man in a lab coat, thick horn-rimmed glasses, and hair and a mustache reminiscent of Albert Einstein emerged from the hall, dragging a monstrous greataxe with two massive blades behind him.

"Here, Mongo. Kill the intruders for me, please. I have much work to do," the little man said as he handed the greataxe to the Chipmotaur.

As the man turned to leave, a gunshot echoed through the room. The bullet ricocheted off the wall, just inches from his head, causing him to freeze in his tracks.

"Are you the Mad Scientist?" James shouted from behind him.

"That is a terribly undignified name. I don't know who came up with that. I'm Percival McNulty—genetics genius and scientist extraordinaire!" the man, Percival, announced loudly, his pride evident.

James fired another shot, this time hitting Percival in the shoulder.

"AAAAHHHHHHH!" Percival screamed, clutching his wounded shoulder as blood seeped onto his pristine white lab coat. "What the hell did you do that for?!"

"You're a monster, that's why," James retorted. "Someone with no morals, no respect for nature or the way of the world. You're playing god, creating beings that were never meant to exist. I bet you have a pile of failed experiments somewhere, crying out in pain or horror at their mere existence. You're the definition of evil, and someone needs to put you down." James steadied his aim at Percival. "I don't know if I believe in hell, but if it exists, it's made for people like you."

James fired again, but this time a massive hand moved between Percival and the bullet. The shot bounced off the Chipmotaur's skin, landing on the floor with a light metallic clink. Momentarily stunned, James' shock quickly turned to fury. He drew his second gun and fired shot after shot at the beast, but every bullet bounced off its thick hide.

The Chipmotaur threw its arms back—one still gripping the giant axe as if it were a feather—and let out a bellowing roar that echoed like a bull in mating season. The roar ended with a sharp squeak, and then its eyes locked on James. It charged at him, its rodent feet pounding the ground.

Percival chuckled darkly as he slipped back through the doorway and disappeared down the hall. James tried to dodge, but the Chipmotaur extended its free arm and clotheslined him, sending him flipping end over end before crashing onto his chest with a painful grunt.

Struggling to catch his breath and rise to his feet, James looked up just in time to see the creature raise its axe high above its head, preparing to bring it down with deadly force.

The axe whistled through the air as it plummeted toward him. Realizing the danger, James stared up in horror, his eyes wide as the gleam of the blade closed in on him.

Chapter 47

The Mad Scientist

As the axe continued its deadly descent toward him, James, still struggling to get off the ground, closed his eyes and braced for the inevitable.

I've lived a good life, he thought.

In the end, he had even managed to help people. His life had meant something. Now, he could finally find peace and let his worries drift away like a leaf on a river.

A sudden metallic clang jolted him back to reality. His eyes flew open, and he saw Derek standing over him, blocking the massive axe. Derek's arms were crossed in front of him, and the blade was caught on the bracers of his battle armor, sparks flying from the impact.

"Move your ass!" Derek growled through gritted teeth.

James scrambled out from under the Chipmotaur, just as Derek was shoved backward by a surge of strength from the creature. With a roar of frustration at losing its kill, the Chipmotaur turned its attention to the others. A clicking sound echoed in the room, and Percival's voice crackled through a speaker.

"Ohhhh, that was close! You'll have to be faster than that to beat Mongo!" Percival's taunting voice filled the room.

Tom's eyes scanned the laboratory, realizing it was two stories tall. Near the ceiling on the right side, he spotted a blacked-out window. A light flickered on, revealing Percival's face grinning down at them with twisted delight, a microphone in his hand.

"Hehehehehe. Mongo was designed for maximum devastation, and he's practically invincible!" Percival cackled, his voice dripping with arrogance.

James aimed his gun at the window and fired. The bullet ricocheted off, leaving not even a scratch.

"Ah, ah, ah. Unbreakable glass! Your puny projectiles won't work," Percival jeered, prancing back and forth in his room, gloating over his assumed victory.

"I really don't like that guy," Tom muttered, staring up at Percival, who continued to make a mockery of himself.

The Chipmotaur let out another deafening roar, and the team quickly regrouped for the fight. Tom summoned Bron and barked out rapid orders.

"Bron, Kevin, and Kirsten! Keep that thing busy! Derek, we need you tanking—your new armor can take a beating." Tom's voice cut through the chaos as he directed his team. "James, Kiera, see if anything will pierce its skin. Jay, find and exploit its weak spots! I'll back you up with whatever strategies I can."

The team responded immediately, forming into small groups and diving into the fray. As they moved, Tom took a deep breath and shouted a challenge at the monstrous beast.

"COME AND GET SOME, YOU FUGLY SON OF A BITCH!" Tom roared with all his might.

The Chipmotaur's head snapped toward him at the sound of his voice. The moment their eyes met, Tom activated his *Fear* Skill on the creature. A System prompt immediately appeared in his view.

Mongo cannot be affected by Fear

Due to having activated its rage ability, Mongo can no longer be affected by most status effects. Fear has failed.

"Dammit!" Tom cursed under his breath, realizing it had no effect. "It's got a rage ability! Be careful!"

Kevin and Kirsten rushed in with their greataxes gleaming. Kirsten struck first, but Mongo blocked her blow with his axe. She rotated her body, using the force of Mongo's block to throw it off balance. Seeing Kevin rushing in from behind, the creature had no time to react.

Kevin activated his *Sunder* ability, his new mythril greataxe gleaming as he slashed across Mongo's body, drawing a thin line of blood.

Mongo roared in surprise and pain, clearly not accustomed to being hurt.

"It can be hurt! Kill it!" Tom shouted, activating his *Tattoo of Strength* and charging in.

His sword flared to life as he activated its *Dark Inferno* ability.

Then a thought struck him.

I wonder...

Tom cast *Dark Flame Weapon*, layering it over the existing enchantment.

The flames on his sword exploded outward, a roaring inferno surging around the blade.

Almost immediately, he felt his skin tighten, the heat sucking the moisture from the air.

His MP bar plummeted.

"NOPE!" Tom yelped, cutting the spell off instantly. "Don't do that again."

Still, his blade burned with dark fire as he slashed at Mongo's exposed back, the flames licking at the beast's fur.

The blade bit deep, searing the flesh as it burned.

Mongo reared back with a bellow, instinctively throwing Tom off and sending him sprawling across the battlefield.

Seeing Tom on the ground, Mongo turned and charged, lowering its head to gore him. Tom tried to roll out of the way but was caught on the side by one of Mongo's horns, lifting him into the air. Tom flailed, struggling to keep his grip on his weapon. As he began to fall, he saw Mongo beneath him, ready to catch him on its horns.

A gray blur slammed into the monster from the side, knocking it off balance and allowing Tom to crash to the ground with a thud, momentarily knocking the wind out of him. Derek had tackled the beast but was quickly overpowered as they wrestled on the floor. Mongo pinned Derek beneath him, raining blows down on Derek's head, his axe lost in the struggle.

From the shadows, Jay appeared, driving two daggers into Mongo's groin, aiming low for the dangly bits and scoring a critical hit. The Chipmotaur let out a piercing bellow of pain. Jay leaped back as Mongo swung at him, giving Derek a chance to roll free and get to his feet.

"This is for James!" Derek shouted, delivering a swift kick to Mongo's groin, driving the daggers deeper. Mongo's body spasmed, curling into a fetal position, but it quickly recovered due to its rage. It charged at Derek again, but Tom intercepted, jamming his sword into Mongo's side, throwing the creature off balance.

Derek pounced, smashing Mongo in the nose with his mace. Tears formed in the beast's eyes as it thrashed under the two fighters. Kevin and Kirsten joined the fray, and chaos erupted as they struggled to subdue the creature. James tried to move in, but Mongo's strength was overwhelming, leaving Kiera no choice but to buff the party. She sang a fast-paced song of heroism, boosting everyone's strength.

Moments later, power radiated from Mongo, and a wave of energy blasted everyone off. Tom, Derek, Kevin, and Kirsten hit the ground hard, rolling to their feet. Mongo stood, radiating a visible red aura.

"Oh, you've gone and done it now! This is my creation's ultimate form—Raging Bull and Hungry Chipmunk style!" Percival gloated.

The Chipmotaur's eyes began to glow red as it scanned the room. Its gaze landed on James off to the side of the room, and it locked on him.

"Uh, oh," James said as he stared back, eyes growing wide with worry.

"James… why are your pants glowing?" Kiera asked suddenly.

Looking down, James noticed that his crotch had a faint red glow. Looking back up quickly at the monster, he threw himself to the side just as an acorn the size of an orange shot at him with incredible speed.

"What the fuck?! That's *my* move!" James cried out.

Derek stepped forward to intercept the monster, trying to redirect its attention. Mongo blurred with speed, punching Derek in the stomach and sending him flying.

"Holy shit! I didn't even see it move!" Tom exclaimed.

"Time to slow him down!" Jay shouted, pulling out his kama and chain and swinging it overhead.

Mongo blurred again, grabbing Kevin and lifting him overhead. Jay released his chain, wrapping it around the creature's legs. Tom grabbed the chain, and together they pulled, tightening it around Mongo's legs. Mongo lost its balance, dropping Kevin and crashing to the ground.

The team pounced again, weapons raised, and struck with ferocity. Stabs, cuts, and blunt force trauma battered the creature as it flailed wildly. Managing to toss the fighters off, Mongo staggered to its feet, bruised and bleeding. It roared defiantly, moving to attack Kevin, who was still reeling.

Kirsten leaped onto Mongo's back. "You leave him alone!" she screamed, biting, scratching, and pulling on its ear.

Mongo tilted away from Kevin, arms flailing, eyes shut. Tom forced himself up, ignoring his wounded side, and charged. With a knuckle duster in hand, he darted under Mongo's swinging arm and drove it up under its chin. It pierced through skin and bone, sending a shock through its body.

Mongo went rigid, swayed, and then collapsed, dead.

Kirsten kept pounding its head, screaming vengeance for Kevin. The others sighed in relief.

"NOOOOOOOO! MONGOOOOO!" Percival shrieked, pressing his hand against the glass.

James walked toward the door Percival had gone through. The others remained behind, healing each other. A moment later, James appeared in the window, and they heard Percival begging for his life. The light went out, followed by the sound of a microphone hitting the floor and screams echoing through the room.

"Should we do something?" Derek asked.

"Like what? Tell him not to kill the guy we were probably here to kill?" Tom replied from his seated position.

"Maybe stop him from torturing him?" Derek suggested as another scream erupted.

"Nah. Let him have it. Good to get it out of his system, and that bastard deserves it," Tom said. "Besides, he's just a Dungeon mob in the end."

"Yeah, I guess you're right," Derek agreed, moving to help others heal.

Kirsten had stopped hitting Mongo and was tending to Kevin. Kiera stood watch with her rifle, while Jay leaned against a wall, cleaning his daggers.

After a while, the screams stopped, and a vending machine appeared on the far side of the room.

"Looks like he's done. Time to get some loot," Tom said, heading over.

James returned from upstairs, choosing his item last, storing it without a word.

"You okay?" Tom asked him.

"Better. That was cathartic," James replied, not meeting his eyes.

"We're here for you. Lean on us," Tom said, placing a hand on his shoulder.

"Thanks. I know I need to. Just don't like reliving those memories," James said, his face heavy with emotion.

"No one does, but burying it won't help. Gotta let it out," Tom advised.

"I'll try. But there'll still be jokes," James said, a small smile breaking through.

"Wouldn't have it any other way," Tom smiled back.

"I think it's time to get back to the Guild," Derek said. "We need to prep for the war."

"You had to bring that up," Tom grumbled. "Fine, but we stop at the entrance again. Azroc's orders."

With that, the team began their trek back to the Dungeon entrance.

Chapter 48

Guild Preparations

After Tom and his companions stopped near the entrance, he placed a hand on the wall next to the door. An image of Azroc giving a thumbs up appeared under his touch, the enchanted mark lighting up briefly with a soft glow.

"That never gets old. Azroc is one classy dude," James commented, admiring the mark with a grin. He ran his fingers through his hair, still slightly sweaty from the Dungeon crawl.

"Feels a bit narcissistic to have your face on the mark, though, doesn't it?" Derek replied, raising an eyebrow as he wiped grime from his hands.

"I don't know. Plenty of people have their faces on brands. Famous people would do endorsements and the like. Why not Azroc? Why don't you bring it up next time you see him?" Tom suggested with a sly smile, his eyes gleaming with a playful challenge.

"No thanks. I think I'll stick to not poking a bear with that much power," Derek said, shaking his head as he gave up on his line of thought. He stretched his arms, trying to work out the tension from the recent fight.

Leaving the building, the team hopped into the GS2, the engine roaring to life as Tom revved it up. They sped back toward the Guild building, the headlights cutting through the twilight as the day transitioned into night. It was getting dark, and the fatigue of the day's battles weighed on everyone. The energy in the car was low, but the sense of accomplishment was palpable. They were tired but satisfied; it had been a good run in the Dungeon. For Tom, the XP gain had been substantial, and he could almost feel the invisible bar nudging closer to the next level. Just a bit more, and he'd hit level twenty-seven, a milestone that would bring more Attribute Points and new possibilities.

Leveling up had always been one of the best ways to get a significant stat boost. While the training regimens they followed helped improve their individual stats slowly over time, there was nothing quite like the surge of power that came with gaining ten Attribute Points from leveling up. That immediate boost in Strength, Agility, or whatever they needed most was always a game changer.

As the Guild building came into view, its stone walls illuminated by the dim lights around the perimeter, Tom slowed down to chat with the guard on duty. They exchanged some light banter, mostly about the recent Dungeon exploits, the guard expressing a mix of awe and envy. After a few moments, the guard lifted the barrier arm, and Tom drove into the parking garage, the tires squeaking slightly on the concrete floor.

Everyone climbed out, their muscles aching from the day's exertion. Most of the party members decided to split off to tend to their own affairs, each of them heading toward different parts of the Guild hall. Tom, Derek, and James decided to head to the security office to see what had been going on in their absence. However, upon arrival, they noticed something unusual: the room was empty of the usual high-ranking team members.

"Where's TJ?" Tom asked, a puzzled look crossing his face. TJ was almost always here, overseeing the security of the Guild with a watchful eye.

"He went to grab some dinner. You should be able to find him in the cafeteria," replied one of the security officers, glancing up from his desk where he was monitoring the security feeds.

"And Brian?" Tom asked, curious about their other team member.

"Not sure. He might have gone to bed. Said you all wore him down to nothing with all the 'torture,'" the guard replied with a chuckle, recalling Brian's earlier complaints.

"What a baby. Oh well, it was good for him. We'll try to catch TJ in the cafeteria," Tom said, waving to the guards and thanking them for their hard work before heading out.

They made their way down the hallway to the cafeteria, their stomachs rumbling with anticipation. Ready for a meal, they joined the queue, the delicious scents of various dishes wafting through the air. Quite the contrary to how they clearly smelled, given the people's reactions around them. When they reached the servers, they were handed plates of rice accompanied by a hearty bowl of vegetable stew.

"No meat tonight?" Tom asked, eyeing the plate and noticing the absence of any protein. He knew meat had been scarce, but he hoped for a surprise.

"Not much coming in right now, so we're rationing it," explained a woman behind the counter, a hairnet keeping her graying hair neatly tucked away. "They're working on the livestock issue, but until we get it sorted and the animals are breeding, we're limited to what we bring in."

"Ah, makes sense. Too bad, but I'm glad someone's on it. When Charlene gets a moment, could you have her come by my table? Just let her know it's Tom," he requested, picking up his tray and moving to an open table.

As the others joined him, they dug into their food, talking about the Dungeon run, rehashing their tactics, and analyzing what they could do better next time. Midway through the meal, Charlene appeared from the kitchen, wiping her hands on a towel stained with various splatters from the evening's work. She took a seat near Tom, a tired but warm smile on her face.

"What can I do for you, Tom?" Charlene asked, adjusting the towel over her shoulder.

"I've got a bunch of meat we can add to the food stores. Where would you like me to put it?" Tom asked, setting his fork down and turning his full attention to her.

"We could store it in the freezer, depending on how much you've got," Charlene said, her curiosity piqued. "How much are we talking?"

"Thousands of pounds," Tom replied, his eyes sparkling with a bit of amusement at her wide-eyed reaction. "We took down a pretty big creature in a Dungeon. Decided to harvest it."

"Wow. What kind of creature? And are you sure it's safe to eat?" Charlene questioned, her voice tinged with a mix of skepticism and intrigue.

"It's called a Goatamus—a weird cross between a goat and a hippo, but much bigger," Tom explained. "And yeah, it's safe. We checked for toxins—nothing harmful."

"Okay, I can work with that. As long as it's not poisonous or venomous," Charlene said, still a bit wary.

"Nope, nothing like that," Tom assured her.

"Great! Let's get it in the freezer," Charlene agreed, standing up to guide him. She noticed Jerky perched on Tom's shoulder, his eyes wide with interest.

Charlene opened the door to the walk-in freezer, a gust of cold air spilling out. She pointed to a set of metal shelves near the back. "You can stack it here. If it overflows, use the next set of shelves."

Jerky, ever curious, leaped off Tom's shoulder, eager to explore. Charlene chuckled and added, "Oh, and Jerky, I've got your meal waiting in the kitchen. Why don't you come with me while Tom unloads the meat?"

Jerky nodded vigorously, his wings fluttering with excitement as he followed her back into the kitchen. Tom began the laborious task of unloading the vast amount of Goatamus meat from his Inventory, stacking it neatly on the shelves, trying to keep the different cuts organized by where they came from on the creature's body.

It took almost half an hour to finish. By the time Tom was done, not only were all five sets of shelves filled, but the floor space was piled high with cuts of meat that didn't fit on the shelving. Wiping a bit of sweat from his brow, he exited the freezer and asked Charlene if everything was arranged to her liking.

"Holy cannoli! That's a lot of meat, Tom!" Charlene exclaimed, eyes wide with astonishment.

"Didn't I mention it was a huge goatamus?" Tom chuckled, watching her reaction as they closed the freezer door.

"This will last us at least a week! We should send out some teams to find more of these creatures," Charlene suggested, already calculating how to best use the haul.

"That's easier said than done," Tom cautioned. "It's not a monster we've encountered anywhere but this Dungeon. But with some planning, we could farm it, provided the team is careful. It was pretty tough to bring down."

"If there's any way to do it, it would be a huge help until we get the livestock sorted," Charlene pleaded, her eyes hopeful. "Though, people will likely get tired of only eating goatamus meat all the time."

"If they want something different, they can get out there and find something themselves. We're doing the best we can. I'll talk with Brian, see if we can assign some backup teams to farm the Dungeon for food," Tom offered. "If they're careful, they might be able to farm the first monster and then get out."

"Thank you, Tom. That would really take a load off my mind," Charlene sighed with relief. "Some of the Guild members are already grumbling about there not being meat in tonight's stew."

"You're doing great work, Charlene. But remember, you need to level up too. Otherwise, you'll stagnate," Tom reminded her, his tone serious.

"I know. It's hard to leave when I've got to prepare meals, but Phyllis is proving to be a fast learner. I could probably leave her in charge when I need to train," Charlene said, sounding a bit reluctant but aware of the necessity.

"Good. We want everyone to be prepared, just in case," Tom said firmly, crossing his arms to emphasize his point.

"Alright, alright, I promise. I'll make time for training," Charlene agreed, albeit reluctantly.

"Good to hear. And keep up the amazing work. You're a pillar here, and we need you safe," Tom said warmly, giving her a nod of appreciation.

Returning to his table, Tom found his stew had gone cold, but he ate it anyway.

Jerky reappeared, munching on a chunk of meat, and hopped up onto the table beside him.

"So, Squirrel evolved. Think Jerky will too?" James asked, his eyes on the little creature tearing at his food.

"Hard to say. It would be cool if he did, but I like him just the way he is. He's already gotten better at fighting, and that's enough for me," Tom replied, grinning as he watched Jerky.

"Would be cool if he turned into a giant demon you could fly on," James joked with a laugh.

Jerky glanced up, frowning at James with an almost comically serious expression.

"Yeah, I don't think he's on board with that idea," Tom chuckled.

"I'm sure if Jerky evolves, he'll be amazing no matter what," Kiera chimed in, reaching out to give Jerky a scratch behind his horns.

Jerky purred contentedly, rubbing his head against her arm.

"Hey, guys! Glad you made it back safe," TJ greeted, approaching their table.

"Just the guy we needed. How's everything going?" Tom asked.

"Everything's moving according to plan. But I think you might want to head down to the basement and talk to Roland and Herbert," TJ said, a knowing smile on his face.

"Herbert?" Tom questioned, raising an eyebrow.

"Yeah, you haven't met him? He's another engineer, brought in by Harold. Used to work on government projects—mainly weapons. He's got some ideas cooking for the Space Pirates," TJ explained with a grin.

"Sounds like both fun and trouble," Tom admitted, intrigued.

"Yeah, we need every edge we can get. Can't just sit around and wait for them to land," TJ said, his tone serious.

"Alright, I'll go see what he's got. Can you tell Brian I want to meet with him tomorrow?" Tom asked, finishing his meal.

"Sure thing," TJ agreed and moved on to talk to another Guild member.

Tom stood up, motioning for Derek to join him. "Let's go see what Roland and Herbert are up to," he suggested.

Derek nodded, deciding to accompany Tom to keep up with the progress on the Guild's defenses. The others excused themselves to freshen up and rest after the long day.

Descending the stairs to the basement, Tom and Derek entered the expansive open space that had been created with Guild points. The clang of hammer on metal echoed through the chamber as they spotted Roland hard at work on an anvil.

"Hey, Roland! How's it going?" Tom called out, his voice carrying across the room.

"Tom! Good to see you!" Roland boomed, his face lighting up. "I have somesing for you—or raser, for your tiny demon friend," he said, setting down his hammer. Reaching into a crate, he pulled out several small pieces of finely crafted armor.

"Is that... tiny demon armor?" Tom asked, his eyes widening as he inspected the pieces.

"Ja! Tiny demon armor!" Roland confirmed proudly. "I vanted to give your little friend somesing to help him stay safe."

Tom examined the chest piece, noticing the intricate filigree work. "This craftsmanship is incredible, Roland," he complimented.

"Du schmeichelst mir," Roland replied, smiling. "Please, try it on your little friend."

Jerky, standing beside Tom, approached Roland, who helped him into the armor. Jerky now sported a sleek half breastplate, greaves, and bracers. The fit was perfect.

"Give it a test run, Jerky," Tom suggested.

Jerky immediately took off, darting around on two legs, then switching to all fours. He jumped, rolled, and flipped through the air, even testing his gliding ability. Landing smoothly, he looked up at Tom with a nod and a grin.

"He approves! Thank you, Roland," Tom said, shaking the big man's hand.

"It vas mein pleasure," Roland said, beaming with pride.

"By the way, do you know where Herbert is? TJ said I should talk to him," Tom asked.

"He's in ze back, opposite corner from vhere Harold is set up," Roland informed them.

"Thanks, Roland," Tom said, waving as they headed off.

They made their way across the vast room, finally spotting a man hunched over a desk, his face illuminated by a single desk lamp. As they approached, the sound of their footsteps made him turn.

"You must be Tom. I've heard a lot about you," the man said, standing up.

"And you must be Herbert. I've heard exactly nothing about you," Tom replied with a chuckle. "But that's not your fault."

"Well, I don't envy your workload," Herbert replied, shaking hands with both Tom and Derek.

"I heard you've got something to show me?" Tom inquired, eager to see what new developments were underway.

"That depends," Herbert replied, a devilish grin spreading across his face. "How do you feel about explosions?"

Chapter 49

Countermeasures

"I think my feelings on explosions can be summed up with: Love to watch them, not a fan up close," Tom said cautiously, watching Herbert closely. Herbert seemed to be studying him, looking for any signs of discomfort or hesitation.

"Excellent! Then you'll love these," Herbert replied with a gleam in his eye. He moved to a long workbench that stood adjacent to his cluttered desk.

The table had something large covered with a cloth, its shape obscured by the draping fabric. The contours hinted at something interesting, but Tom couldn't make out what the item might be. With one swift motion, Herbert pulled the sheet back, revealing a set of four surface-to-air missiles, sleek and intimidating.

"Are those real?!" Tom gasped, instinctively stepping back. His heart skipped a beat at the sight of the deadly weaponry.

"Of course they're real. How else are we supposed to fend off Space Pirates coming from outer space without something capable of taking down a flying craft?" Herbert replied, his tone tinged with annoyance as if the answer were obvious.

"Are they safe?" Tom asked, still uneasy about having such dangerous explosives in the Guild's basement.

"They're perfectly safe," Herbert insisted, waving a dismissive hand. "Something would have to do some serious damage to them to make them go off."

Derek, less alarmed than Tom, moved closer to inspect the missiles. "How do you plan to get the missiles to the ships?" he asked, leaning in for a better look at the sleek metal surfaces.

Tom paled. "That's the least of our worries, Derek."

"What the hell are you talking about, Tom?" Derek scowled. "Why do you look like you just saw a ghost? This is some real fire power at a time we can desperately use it."

"That's my point," Tom said, his shaking hand pointing at the weapons. "James can never find out about these things."

There it is. Tom swallowed, finally noting the alarm he felt transfer itself to Derek's face.

Derek whirled on the creator of their doom.

"What the hell were you thinking?!" Derek shouted. "Why don't you just go work for our enemies while you're at it?"

"I… think I missed a memo." Herbert's smile slowly faded. "Is this James some kind of terrifying villain bent on our total destruction?"

"Worse," Derek spoke, finally getting a handle on his panic. "Much worse."

Tom nodded, opening his mouth to speak.

"He's our best friend."

As he began to explain, horror began to grow on the Engineer's face.

"Okay." Herbert exhaled. The bags under his eyes spoke of the effort he'd put forth. "I've added a biometric failsafe which its primary function, above all else, is to prevent James from using any of these weapons."

Tom and Derek's shoulders slumped in relief. They'd been up all night, working long into the next day, frantically trying to prevent disaster.

"Of course, it also allows us to ensure that our enemies can't use them against us and allows us to police who has the authorization to utilize these weapons," Herbert added with obvious pride in his voice. "Now that we've averted our probable demise… where were we?"

Tom rubbed his face, trying to remember where they'd left off. "You were asking a question, Derek. What was it?"

"Hmm?" Derek jerked awake, having started to nod off. He furrowed his brow, clearly trying to remember. After a moment, he brightened. "Oh, right! I was asking how we plan to get the missiles to the ships."

"Right!" Herbert smiled. "That's what I'm still working on," Herbert admitted, rubbing his chin thoughtfully. "I'm thinking of using some of Harold's research on mana as an energy source to make these babies fly with magic. If it works, we could open up all sorts of possibilities for guidance systems and enhanced capabilities."

Tom's brows furrowed. "And where exactly did you get these?" he asked, concern still evident in his voice.

"Oh, just some old warehouse. That part's not important. What matters is that we now have a starting point for developing countermeasures," Herbert replied, waving off the question as if it were trivial.

Tom still wasn't convinced but decided to focus on the more pressing issues. "And how are you planning to make sure these missiles can penetrate magical defenses? These were designed to hit aircraft with metal hulls, not magic shields," he pointed out.

"That's exactly what I was working on," Herbert explained, his eyes lighting up. "We want to give them some form of magical piercing or nullification capability. If we could create a kind of magic EMP to knock out the shields, then the missile would strike directly."

"And if the missile is powered by magic too, wouldn't it shut itself off?" Derek interjected, pointing out the flaw in the plan.

"That's the issue we're facing." Herbert sighed. "In current tech, we use a Faraday cage to protect against EMPs, so there must be a magical equivalent we can put around our equipment. We just have to figure out what that is. Bohdan's been helping us with potential solutions."

"Do you have anything else up your sleeve?" Derek asked, eyes gleaming with interest.

"Isn't a bunch of deadly missiles enough?" Tom asked nervously, eyeing the imposing weapons on the table.

"We need to be ready for anything. No telling if it's one ship or thousands coming. We need more backup," Derek replied, following Herbert as he moved away from the table.

Herbert continued, "I've got a few other concepts in the works, but nothing concrete yet. I'm working on a laser cannon that can target airborne ships. The main problem is finding a power source big enough to keep the laser going long enough to do real damage without overheating."

"So, you got the laser part to work?" Derek asked, genuinely impressed.

"Yeah, that was the easy part," Herbert nodded, but his face darkened. "But it melts the housing and connections if we run it too long. If we dial down the power, it's not effective enough to cause damage. It's a problem we haven't solved yet. I'm hoping we find a stronger material than what we've been using."

"We've gotten weapons that claim to be made of mithril from vending machines. I bet the machines sell the raw metal too, for crafting. You could work with Roland to make something out of it," Derek suggested.

Herbert's eyes widened. "Really? That would be incredible! A new metal to experiment with," he murmured, his mind already spinning with possibilities, momentarily drifting away from the conversation.

"What about defensive measures?" Derek pressed, bringing him back.

"Hmm? Oh, right," Herbert said, snapping back to reality. "We're also working on a mana-powered shield that could cover the entire building in case of an attack. That's coming along pretty well, actually. We're close to finishing the proof of concept. After that, we just need to scale it up."

"You guys have been busy!" Tom exclaimed, genuinely surprised by all the progress.

"The Profession path gives us a lot of information, and the rewards usually lead to even more knowledge," Herbert explained. "Every time we create something new, we get insights into other potential projects. It's all moving much faster than I ever thought it would. But that's probably due to our engineering backgrounds before all this started."

"So, your previous knowledge carried over to the System?" Derek asked, intrigued.

"When I chose my Profession, I got a manual that I could absorb. It was overwhelming at first, but about half of it I already knew from my studies and work before the apocalypse. Then, when I complete a quest for the Profession, I get more books with specialized knowledge," Herbert said, pacing as he spoke, clearly energized by the topic.

"You get quests for Professions?" Tom asked, his interest piqued.

"Yes. It's another way to level up and advance your Profession. The quests usually tie into the projects we're working on. You can have up to ten active quests at once, which lets us simultaneously tackle multiple projects. It's probably different for Professions because we don't go out and kill monsters for XP," Herbert continued. "I've learned so much about topics I was already passionate about. It's a mix of our old technology and what the System calls Magi-Tech."

"Magi-Tech—like a combination of magic and technology?" Derek guessed.

"Exactly. Think about it—if you showed a medieval person a cell phone, they'd think it was magic. Here, magic is just another form of science, one we don't yet fully understand. But if we can harness and study it, the applications are nearly limitless," Herbert explained, his enthusiasm growing.

"And you've already learned a lot about these energies?" Tom asked.

"Absolutely. Mana has clearly demonstrated itself as the fifth Fundamental Force." Herbert began ticking off from his fingers. "Gravitational, electromagnetic, strong nuclear force, weak nuclear force, and now, lastly—mana. Over the course of human history, we have learned a tremendous amount of information about the reality we exist in. And now, we get to expand that understanding into this new and exciting frontier of mana." His eyes burned with enthusiasm. "We already know some things about it—many things, even. It's not visible to the naked eye unless processed, but it contains all forms of magic—much like how white light contains all colors. By using what the System calls a Mana Diffuser Mesh, or MDM, we can separate mana into its core components: Life, Death, Fire, Water, Earth, Air, Light, and Dark," Herbert said, his voice filled with a teacher's excitement.

He led them to another nearby table and pulled a sheet off of a small setup. Beneath it was a clear box, similar to a vacuum chamber, with a metallic mesh on one end.

"When we channel mana into the MDM, it separates like this," Herbert said, flipping a switch on a nearby device. A beam of white energy shot into the mesh filter, and from there, it split into eight different colors, each one bouncing around the chamber like a contained light show.

Tom watched, fascinated. "But if mana contains all types of magic, how do I cast a spell from a specific school?" he asked, his curiosity getting the better of him.

"That's a great question, and also—I believe—where the System comes into play. Your body works as a natural MDM filter," Herbert explained. "When mana enters your body, it's processed into its distinct types. Ancient Chinese teachings on chi possessed a similar concept. Different points in your body process different types of mana. Your lower core processes fire, the hands handle water, the feet manage earth, the lungs deal with air, the heart is life, the intestines death, the brain light, and the stomach dark."

"That doesn't quite line up with what I remember about chi," Derek said, skeptical.

"Not exactly, no. They didn't have all the information we now have. But it's a familiar point of comparison. Each area has a core that stores that type of energy. When you cast a spell, it draws from that core. The more you use those cores, the stronger and more efficient they become," Herbert continued, his passion evident.

"So, do we need to meditate or something?" Derek asked.

"Not quite. The System's level-up process handles most of that growth. However, you can improve your *control* over mana by focusing on its flow within these cores. This allows for greater precision and can even lead to creating new spells," Herbert explained, his excitement palpable as he shared his knowledge.

"And you learned all this from the System's books?" Tom asked.

"Yes, and by working closely with Bohdan, Harold, and Bob. That old man is a well of knowledge," Herbert replied. "It's been a collaborative effort, pooling what we know from our different Classes and Professions."

"We're building our own little scientific community here," Derek mused, his mind racing with ideas. "This information has given me some ideas for my own magic."

"And we're just scratching the surface," Herbert said, his eyes alight with excitement. "There's so much more to learn, and it makes me eager to jump out of bed every day to work on new projects!"

"Since you've been down here working, I think we have some things you might appreciate," Tom said, beginning to pull the lab equipment they had taken from the Mad Scientist's Dungeon out of his Inventory.

Harold's eyes widened as he saw the various beakers, tubes, and machines appear on the floor. Derek joined in, adding more equipment to the growing pile.

"Where did you get all this? Did you raid a laboratory or something?" Herbert asked, picking up a beaker and examining it closely.

"A Dungeon, actually," Tom replied with a grin.

"A Dungeon laboratory," Derek clarified.

Tom nodded. "There was a scientist experimenting with genetically modified monsters, and we took everything we could carry."

"This is fantastic! We've been making do with what we could scrounge or build. This equipment will be a huge help," Herbert said, his voice brimming with excitement as he inspected a complex-looking apparatus.

"I'll send the others down to bring the rest of what we grabbed. We had to move fast to avoid the monsters, so we split up the loot." Tom chuckled, recalling their frantic scramble to grab everything they could.

"Thank you, this is like Christmas morning!" Herbert beamed, still marveling at the equipment.

"If you need anything else, just let us know. We'll do what we can to keep you supplied. It's the least we can do for all the work you're doing to protect us," Tom said.

"Hmm? Oh, yes, that would be great," Herbert muttered, already absorbed in examining a strange-looking machine.

"Let's leave him to his toys," Derek suggested, smiling at Herbert's enthusiasm.

As they headed out, Tom and Derek made their way back upstairs. At the top, they said their goodnights, both feeling the weight of the long day. With the time dilation in the Dungeon, it felt like two days crammed into one. Tom's bed was calling to him.

Reaching his quarters, Tom took a quick shower to wash away the grime and sweat of the day. Exhausted, he collapsed into bed. His eyes were already half-closed as he murmured a goodnight to Jerky, who had curled up at the foot of his bed.

Within seconds, he was out cold, drifting into a deep and peaceful sleep.

Chapter 50

Plans to Actions

As the teams continued their rigorous training, the days passed by with a mostly routine schedule. Occasionally, there were skirmishes with Stormcrusher's faction and The Master's forces, but these encounters were minor, resulting in minimal injuries or casualties on either side. Still, tensions simmered beneath the surface, like a pot ready to boil over.

Several weeks went by before a viable plan to take down The Master began to take shape—one that wouldn't lead to massive losses for both sides. During this time, Tom's impatience grew steadily. The slow progress gnawed at him; he felt as if he were failing those he had promised to save. Each day that passed without decisive action seemed like another day lost, another step further from the promise of freedom that the slaves had to endure.

Despite his growing frustration, Tom found some solace in his personal growth. The continuous Dungeon runs for loot and XP proved invaluable for the teams. Each delve into the depths honed their skills, toughened their bodies, and sharpened their minds. The intense encounters had molded them into a more cohesive and deadly unit. The accumulation of powerful items from the Dungeons and leveling up brought significant boosts in Attributes and abilities, which was a much-needed morale boost.

One notable change during this period was James' refusal to re-enter The Mad Scientist's Dungeon. No one blamed him; the trauma of what he had faced there was still too fresh, too raw. Instead, Graham had taken his place on several of their expeditions into the twisted lair. His presence was a welcome addition; Graham's expertise in various fighting styles and weapon techniques turned out to be a massive boon for the team. He patiently taught the others how to wield their weapons with more finesse and adaptability, focusing on tactics that could counter unpredictable opponents.

Graham had also worked alongside Tom, Derek, Chris, and Zach to compile a comprehensive compendium of battle tactics. Together, they developed a guide, detailing the most effective team compositions for handling different types of monsters.

Once finalized, this information was distributed among the various fighter groups, ensuring they had a solid foundation for dealing with the threats they might face. The compendium covered optimal party formations, coordinated attack patterns, and strategies to maximize each team member's abilities. By studying these tactics, the teams could adapt quickly, increasing their chances of survival in any scenario they had anticipated.

In addition to Dungeon runs, Tom continued to summon Bron daily. The warrior Summon had become a steadfast mentor, introducing the team to new training techniques that pushed their limits further. These sessions often left them exhausted but filled with a sense of accomplishment. Tom could see the results—stronger strikes, faster reflexes, more endurance, and better teamwork. The progress they were making was tangible, and it filled him with a quiet satisfaction.

Despite his lingering impatience and concern for their ultimate goal, Tom began to feel they were getting closer to being ready. His stats had grown significantly, and his abilities had evolved to the point where he could face challenges that once seemed insurmountable. The same could be said for his companions; they were becoming a well-oiled machine, each one playing off the others' strengths and covering their weaknesses.

With every passing day, Tom felt his resolve hardening. He knew they were getting closer to the moment when they could finally strike at The Master and bring an end to his reign. But until then, he would continue to push himself and his team to become stronger, faster, and smarter. The time was coming, and when it did, they would be ready.

Tom Harris	
Race: Human	**Class:** Warlock
Level: 29	**Total XP:** 1,116,250
XP To Next Level: 156,750	**HP:** 570/570
MP: 500/500	**SP:** 410/410
Attributes:	**Unused Attributes Points:** 0
Strength: 51	**Constitution:** 57
Dexterity: 38	**Endurance:** 41
Intelligence: 50	**Wisdom:** 50
Charisma: 105	**Luck:** 30
Non-Combat Skills:	
Inspect	**Level:** 12 **Rank:** Novice
Combat Skills:	
Vehicular Homicide	**Level:** 24 **Rank:** Initiate
Swords	**Level:** 23 **Rank:** Initiate
Summon Demonic Creature	**Level:** 32 **Rank:** Initiate
Fear	**Level:** 10 **Rank:** Novice
Corruption	**Level:** 10 **Rank:** Novice
Spells:	

Eldritch Blast	**Level:** 18 **Rank:** Novice
Dark Ball	**Level:** 12 **Rank:** Novice
Dark Mending	**Level:** 17 **Rank:** Novice
Lightning Strike	**Level:** 12 **Rank:** Novice
Doppelganger	**Level:** 10 **Rank:** Novice
Dark Flame Weapon	**Level:** 15 **Rank:** Novice
Final Flash	**Level:** 12 **Rank:** Novice
Tattoos:	
Tattoo of Brute Strength	Tattoo of Life Absorption
Tattoo of Magic Nullification	Tattoo of the Summoner

Reaching one hundred in Charisma had provided Tom with a noticeable boost to his spells that relied on this Attribute. It also increased the likelihood that his interactions with others would go more smoothly. But this raised unsettling questions for him—how exactly did Charisma affect others? Did this mean the System was manipulating the way people perceived and responded to him? If so, could it actually alter how they thought? That idea was unnerving. The implications of such power were frightening to consider.

Tom had also noticed subtle changes in his appearance. Those extra points from working out with Bron had not only made him feel better, but also seemed to improve his looks. His facial features had become more defined, with sharper cheekbones and a stronger jawline. His body, honed from relentless training, now looked like it had been sculpted from stone, each muscle more pronounced than before. He couldn't ignore the fact that more people in the Guild seemed to stare at him when he entered a room. At first, he brushed this off as the natural response to him being the Guild leader. However, one day, standing before his bathroom mirror, he couldn't help but acknowledge that he looked more attractive—like one of those influencers on social media who seemed to have an almost magnetic pull on people simply because of their looks.

As he made his way downstairs toward the lobby for his routine training, he heard hurried footsteps behind him. He turned to see Brian rushing up, slightly out of breath and looking like he had something urgent to say.

"Wait! Tom!" Brian called out, his voice strained as he tried to catch up.

"What's up, Brian?" Tom asked, turning to face him with a raised eyebrow.

"You need to get to the basement. Herbert and Bohdan have something for you," Brian said, leaning over with his hands on his knees, still panting heavily.

Tom chuckled. "And you need to get out and train some more. It's not good that you're winded just from running down here."

"Fuck you. I'm administration," Brian shot back with a scowl.

Tom laughed. "Doesn't matter. If you need to run from a monster, you can't be caught out of breath." He gave Brian a firm pat on the back and headed off toward the basement stairs, leaving his friend to catch his breath.

When Tom reached the bottom of the stairs, he waved to Roland, greeting him with a cheerful "Guten Morgen." He had been trying to pick up on a little German to better communicate with the Smith.

"Ah! Guten Morgen, Tom. Wie geht es dir?" Roland beamed back at him.

"Mir geht es gut, wie geht dir?" Tom replied, asking how Roland's morning was in return.

"Dein Deutsch wird besser," Roland said, smiling widely at Tom.

Tom stood there awkwardly, having used most of his conversational German in those previous sentences.

Roland laughed heartily at Tom's discomfort. "Your German is getting better. Sorry for zat. I get carried avay in mein native tongue sometimes."

Tom bid him farewell, hurrying to the back of the basement. There, he found Herbert, Bohdan, and Harold huddled together, their backs turned, intently focused on something laid out on a table.

"Hey, guys. Whatcha got for me?" Tom asked as he approached, curious about their latest creation.

"This," Harold said, turning to reveal a small device that looked like a metal ball with interlocking pieces. A button on top blinked intermittently with a green light.

"You're gonna have to give me more to go on," Tom replied, scrutinizing the device in Herbert's hand.

"We're calling it an anti-magic grenade," Harold explained. "You press this button on top, it blinks red for three seconds, and then it casts the anti-magic field spell that Bohdan showed us. Here, give it a try." He placed the sphere into Tom's hand.

Tom examined the device closely, feeling its weight and the cold, smooth metal under his fingers. He turned, pressed the button, and watched as the light began blinking red. With a swift motion, he hurled it like a baseball. The grenade flew across the room with a high-pitched whistle, propelled by Tom's enhanced strength. Suddenly, it froze midair, emitting a series of beeps. The interlocking parts of the sphere expanded, releasing a burst of golden light that formed a cube of energy, hovering in the air. The cube marked the boundaries of an anti-magic field.

"Mein schmiede!" Roland cried out, his voice a mix of surprise and dismay.

Tom realized he had thrown the grenade too far, catching Roland and his equipment within the anti-magic zone. Apparently, Roland's forge was powered by some kind of magic, as the flames in the forge flickered out the moment the field took effect.

"Sorry, Roland! How long will it stay like that?" Tom asked, wincing at his mistake.

"It lasts for the same duration as the spell," Harold answered, "but you can press the button again to deactivate it."

"That's amazing! But how does it just float there like that?" Tom inquired, his interest piqued.

"That part was a pain to figure out," Herbert admitted. "Before we added the floating effect, it would just sit on the floor, and the spell radius would only reach about halfway up a human's height. We used some of the stored mana to cast a stasis spell, specifically targeting the shell of the grenade. Fortunately, the stasis spell is a targeted type rather than an area of effect."

"Wait, the stasis spell still works in the anti-magic field?" Tom asked.

"That's one of the mysteries we've uncovered," Herbert explained. "If we activate the components in a specific sequence and trigger a chain reaction, the spell can still function—even in the field. It's designed to suppress any magic that isn't part of itself; otherwise, the anti-magic effect would cancel itself out. By chaining the spells together, much like how lightning spells can arc between targets, the stasis spell is interpreted as an extension of the original. The field doesn't recognize it as foreign, so it doesn't shut it down."

"That's genius! And is it a one-time-use item?" Tom continued, fascinated by the intricacy of the device.

"No, it's rechargeable," Bohdan explained. "You just hold it and channel your mana into it. Since the base Intelligence for a person is ten, it requires less than one hundred mana to recharge. But just barely." He ran to get the sphere back, pressed the button to deactivate it, and demonstrated how to recharge it by holding it in his hand and letting mana flow into it. The light on top blinked yellow before returning to its steady green flash as it charged.

"Awesome! So, it's really casting two spells instead of one?" Tom asked, marveling at the complexity.

"Exactly," Harold said. "We enchanted a module with a rune to cast the spell when enough mana is available. It stores this mana in a small battery. When you press the button, the mana discharges into the runes, activating the spells. The three-second delay is actually the casting time for the anti-magic field spell, but it also gives you time to throw it."

"Excellent work! I know this must have taken a lot of time to get right, but it was totally worth it. Could we do this with other spells too?" Tom's mind raced with possibilities, thinking about the utility of a fireball or other offensive spells in grenade form.

"We can enchant it with any spell as long as we have the corresponding rune," Harold replied. "Bohdan's knowledge of magic was crucial for that part, and Herbert's experiments with how magic works were invaluable."

Tom nodded, impressed by the teamwork. "And how long does it take to produce these? We're going to need quite a few," he said, thinking about the upcoming raid on The Master's base.

"Now that we've perfected the process, the only bottleneck is production time. With Roland crafting the necessary parts, we should be able to ramp up production to about fifty grenades a day. We're already working on more parts to keep up the pace," Harold said, considering the logistics.

"Would adding more people help speed up production?" Tom asked, probing whether they needed additional manpower.

"Possibly," Harold answered carefully. "But bringing new people up to speed would actually slow us down initially. If we had other engineers, we could probably get them up to speed faster. But for now, it's better for the three of us to handle the assembly."

"Understood. If that changes, let Brian or me know, and we'll get you any help you need. This is priority number one right now," Tom said, making sure they understood the importance of their task.

"We'll definitely let you know if we need more hands," Harold added.

Tom thanked each of them for their hard work, then turned to help Roland relight his forge. Once his mistake was corrected and Roland was back to hammering away on his anvil, Tom headed upstairs. His next stop was the security room. He asked TJ to call all the members of his party and Brian for a meeting.

About half an hour later, everyone was assembled, waiting for Tom's directions.

"Herbert, Bohdan, and Harold have developed a working anti-magic field device that we can use. This means that in just a few days, we need to be ready to assault The Master's base of operations," Tom began, pacing in front of the group. "This will be risky, but it's necessary. The people there have suffered long enough while we've prepared. All the training we've been doing is about to come into play.

"We're going to use a plan similar to our last one, but this time, the focus is solely on The Master. Kiera, I want you on top of a closer building. Do you have silencers for those rifles? I don't want them knowing where their minions are getting sniped from," Tom said, locking eyes with her.

"Yeah, we can get those. I also have three more people I want to bring with me. We'll need as much firepower as possible," Kiera replied.

"Jay, your job is to disarm any barriers and traps The Master might have in place. Bron is going with you to handle the gates," Tom continued.

"Roger that. We got it," Jay said, giving a quick salute.

"TJ, I need Chris to get all our defense teams ready to go—the ones that clear out monsters. We need every fighter we can spare who isn't critical to the base's defense. And make sure everyone else is on standby in case Shandra decides to strike while we're engaged," Tom added, laying out the plans he'd been formulating for weeks.

"Understood," TJ said, jotting down notes on the paper in front of him.

"We have to prepare for this to go one of a few ways," Tom continued. "The Master could send his horde at us, merge them into that Hulk monster Jay saw, or do a combination of both. I want heavy firepower for the latter and AOE options for the former. Also, if things aren't going well for him, we have to assume he'll use his slaves as shields or fighters. That's where the devices come in."

"I'll take Michael and Bron with me. We'll be the strike team going directly after The Master," Tom concluded, turning to face his group.

"Are you sure you shouldn't have a few more people with you? Just in case?" Jay asked, his concern evident.

"We need every person to help fight off the hordes. A smaller team will be able to break away more easily," Tom replied, knowing the battle ahead would be tough enough with just the three of them.

"What about Bohdan? Could you take a spell slinger with you?" Kiera suggested.

Tom considered it for a moment. "I can ask. It's not a bad idea to have a backup mage," he agreed. "Alright, now is the time to poke holes in the plan. I want as few surprises as possible."

"How many fighters do we have now?" Derek asked.

"Let's see… one hundred and forty-eight, according to Chris' numbers," TJ said, consulting a clipboard.

"That's better than I thought! More than enough," Tom said, feeling a rush of optimism.

"Chris has been working overtime to make sure everyone who joins contributes, and Graham has been training them before sending them out. Not everyone is as seasoned as you guys, but they can fight zombies," TJ confirmed.

That meant more than ten percent of the Guild was made up of able-bodied fighters. Tom would have preferred closer to fifty percent, but given the circumstances, he'd take what he could get. The military hadn't been fifty percent of the population before the apocalypse, so this was acceptable.

Suddenly, Chris burst into the security office, looking urgent.

"Oh, good, you're all here. Tom, you're going to want to see this," Chris said before turning and rushing back out of the room.

Chapter 51

So it Begins

Tom and the others rushed outside, drawn by the rising clamor echoing through the compound. The air was thick with tension, the kind that prickled at the skin like static before a storm.

The newly built wall, a hard-won upgrade from the Guild's relentless efforts, loomed over the perimeter—a solid barrier against the horrors outside. Reinforced gates now sealed them in, sturdy and unyielding, but in the face of what lay beyond, they suddenly felt fragile.

Tom took the stairs two at a time, his boots thudding against salvaged wood, each step carrying the weight of unspoken dread. When he reached the top, Chris and Brandon were already there, standing like statues, their expressions grim as they gazed out over the cityscape.

Then Tom saw it.

A roiling mass of undead, packed so tightly that they seemed to merge into a single writhing entity, stretched as far as the eye could see. Their dead, hollow eyes gleamed in the dim light, fixed unblinkingly on the wall, on them. The air carried the wet, fetid stench of decay, and somewhere within the throng, low, guttural moans weaved together into a sound both mindless and ominous.

And then, the sea of corpses began to part.

Slowly, unnervingly, the dead shuffled aside, peeling away like a rotting tide. From the depths of the horde, a figure emerged.

The Master.

He strode forward, untouched and unfazed, his movements deliberate. There was no urgency, no aggression—only the cold arrogance of a man who knew he was in control. A faint smirk tugged at his lips as he approached the gate, as though the very sight of them amused him.

Tom's fingers curled into fists. His pulse hammered. He already knew what was coming, and he had no intention of letting it play out the way The Master intended.

Tom barely registered the tension in his fingers as they moved on instinct, summoning a pistol from his Inventory. His breath came slow and steady, his focus narrowing to a single point—The Master's forehead.

He fired.

The gunshot shattered the silence, a deafening crack that echoed across the streets.

Chris flinched at the sudden blast. "Jesus, Tom! What the hell?!"

The bullet never found its mark.

A shimmering blue shield materialized around The Master in an instant, a translucent barrier humming with arcane energy. The shot ricocheted off harmlessly, embedding itself in the skull of a nearby zombie. The creature barely had time to react before it crumpled lifelessly to the ground.

Tom exhaled sharply, lowering the gun but not holstering it just yet.

"Damn," he muttered. "Of course, it couldn't be that easy."

Beside him, Chris let out a slow breath, his posture stiff with unease. "I think he came to talk to us." His voice carried an edge of uncertainty, as if he wasn't sure whether to be relieved or even more afraid.

Tom scoffed, his jaw tightening. "You know what he's done. I wasn't going to waste the chance." His grip on the pistol flexed before he finally slid it back into his Inventory. "Didn't think it'd work, but I had to try."

His eyes never left The Master, and in that moment, Tom knew—with absolute certainty—that the necromancer had been expecting this. The smirk, the slow, arrogant advance… This was all a performance. He wanted them to know they couldn't touch him.

Jay had been watching The Master the entire time, his expression shifting from wary to exasperated as the necromancer sauntered toward the gate like a preacher approaching his congregation.

"Uh-oh." Jay let out a long, suffering sigh. "I know that look. Everyone, buckle up. Monologue incoming."

The Master's lips curled into an amused smile as his gaze flickered to Jay, but he chose not to acknowledge him—whether out of restraint or arrogance was unclear. Instead, his focus settled back on Tom, his voice as smooth as silk and just as dangerous.

"Now, now, Tom. Is that any way to greet a guest?" he called, his words dripping with mock civility. His tone was a slow-acting poison—polite on the surface, but laced with something dark underneath.

Tom leaned casually against the wall, but his hand remained ready for another shot if he saw an opening.

"My finger slipped." His voice was all sarcasm, but his eyes were sharp. "Normally, *guests* get an invitation. You didn't. That makes you an intruder, and—funny thing—I'm a big supporter of Make My Day laws."

The Master chuckled, the smirk never leaving his face. "Oh my! Do you get many intruders here? Must be a sign the neighborhood's going downhill."

Tom tilted his head in mock thought. "You're right. It *has* been getting worse. I'd say it started… oh, just a few hours ago." His voice was calm, but the anger underneath it simmered like a slow-burning fuse. "Don't worry, though—I plan on cleaning up the streets. See, there's this real bastard going around forcing people to do things against their will." He let his gaze linger on The Master before adding, deadpan, "You should be careful. I hear he's a giant cockholster."

Jay cocked his head, rubbing his chin as if deep in thought. "You know… I've never really understood the term cockholster." He gestured vaguely. "Like, is it about holding cocks, or is there some deeper meaning I'm missing?"

James stepped forward with a knowing smirk. Adjusting an imaginary tie, he took on the air of an esteemed professor about to educate his class.

"Ah, my dear boy, you've come to the right place." He cleared his throat dramatically. "In this particular context, the subject in question is, indeed, a *holder* of cocks—so to speak. And not just metaphorically, mind you."

The smirk deepened as James leaned forward, tapping his chin in exaggerated contemplation. "Now, the ideal positioning—one might argue—requires being on one's knees." He sighed, placing a hand on his lower back. "Alas, I am not as limber as I once was, so you shall have to imagine the man in question assuming the correct stance."

Jay nodded, attentively solemn. "I'm with you so far."

"Splendid," James continued. "Once in position, a line will inevitably form—an eager congregation of participants, as it were." He made a sweeping gesture toward The Master's undead horde, his tone dripping with faux admiration. "And then, dear boy, the holstering begins."

With that, James tilted his head back, opened his mouth slightly, and proceeded to make the most obscene, exaggerated gargling noise imaginable.

Jay, for his part, had pulled a thick notebook from his Inventory and was taking notes—his eyebrows raising occasionally in enlightenment as he furiously scribbled in the margins. Occasionally he would mimic James' movements and chew the eraser of his pencil as though trying to figure out the words to describe what he was seeing.

The display went on for an uncomfortably long time. James shook his head theatrically, flailed his hands as if overwhelmed, and finally staggered back, wiping his mouth like a man who had just barely survived a near-drowning.

"If one intends to monetize such efforts, I highly recommend a thick application of waterproof mascara," he concluded, voice hoarse but authoritative. "Presentation is everything, after all."

Jay, who had been nodding along enthusiastically, clasped his hands together in sudden realization. "Wow. That actually clears up so much." He turned back to The Master, his eyes full of mock understanding. "Everything makes so much sense now. Thank you."

James gave an exaggerated bow. "My pleasure, good sir."

The Master, who had been watching in stone-faced silence, finally let out a slow chuckle—but there was a flicker of irritation behind his amusement.

"How... quaint." His smirk returned, but it was thinner now, his patience tested. "This individual in question can't be all bad, I should think. It sounds as though he merely wishes to provide his followers with a sense of purpose. A home, even."

"He is!" James agreed, brightly. "You saw the demonstration. He tries really hard. In fact, I admire his dedication and enthusiasm."

The Master fought to hide his scowl.

"It's clear that he's not out to provide purpose for his followers," Tom shot back, his expression hardening. "More like taking away their free will and ability to choose for themselves. Did you come here just so we could dance around the fact that what you're doing is wrong?"

"No, of course not," The Master replied, his smile fading. "I came here to extend you an offer. Help me defeat Shandra, and I'll leave the city."

"Alone?" Tom asked, his voice flat and unreadable.

"Me and all my minions," The Master clarified, his smirk returning.

"Just the undead ones?" Tom pressed, narrowing his eyes.

"Anyone I control," The Master answered, but there was a slight twitch at the corner of his mouth.

"No deal," Tom said without hesitation, his tone cold as steel.

"And if I give you the living humans?" The Master inquired, his tone growing more suspicious.

"Still no deal. Sorry, but the only way you're leaving is in a body bag," Tom stated firmly, feeling the anger simmering within him starting to boil over.

"Come now," The Master said, his voice trying to sound reasonable. "You can't be so unreasonable. We have a common enemy and should focus on the greater threat."

"You're right. Shandra's Guild is a threat," Tom agreed, "but I wouldn't call it greater than someone who enslaves people." His voice was rising, his patience thinning.

"You really think that bitch is any different? With her threats of violence on anyone not willing to bend to her will? I give them purpose!" The Master's voice lost its calm, becoming more impassioned. "I give them a life with meaning when this world has treated them with nothing but disdain and apathy. I am the only one who is willing to do what needs to be done to rebuild this world into a form more fitting of its discarded refuse. I alone am the one who strives to see a world where the little man no longer gets stepped on and forgotten!"

"You alone have been the one I see making people do things they don't want to," Tom countered, pointing down at him. "The ultimate form of bullying, the puppet master looking for validation in a world that probably shit on him from a great height. But that doesn't excuse your actions. You'll pay for what you've done." He paused, then added with venom, "At least Shandra merely asked us to join her."

"You dare compare me to that troglodyte who prances around as though her pathetic 'might' gives her the right to rule this city? I am far above that barbaric whore and her constant need for violence!" The Master shouted, his voice trembling with fury. "This is not over! I will free this city from its burdens and shape it into the glorious place it should have been from the beginning!"

"Such ironic talk of freeing a city you plan to enslave," Tom said, his lip curling in disgust. "If you want to settle this here and now, we'll be happy to oblige. Open the gates."

The moment the gates creaked open, The Master's smirk widened. But it faltered—just slightly—as he took in the army waiting for him.

Nearly a thousand Guild members stood ready, their weapons gleaming in the light, their faces set with grim determination. Some held rifles, others had swords and spears, but they all had one thing in common—they were here to fight.

Tom didn't wait for The Master's reaction.

He leaped from the wall, his boots slamming into the ground with a heavy thud. Dust and loose debris kicked up around him as he stalked forward, greatsword already in hand. The tension in the air snapped like a coiled spring as the battle erupted.

The horde surged forward, crashing into the Guild's front line like a tide of rotting flesh. The clash of steel and bone rang out as gunfire roared through the streets. Screams and battle cries blended into a deafening cacophony.

Tom didn't break stride. His blade sang through the air, cutting down the first wave of zombies with brutal efficiency. Limbs severed, torsos cleaved in two—he carved a path of destruction straight toward The Master, his focus a singular, burning point.

The necromancer saw him coming.

Instead of retreating, The Master raised a hand. A swirling mass of dark energy crackled to life in his palm before launching forward.

Tom barely managed to sidestep, feeling the searing energy hiss past him. The moment he recovered, The Master was already moving—his hands weaving complex sigils in the air, summoning spectral chains that lashed out like living whips.

Tom brought up his sword just in time, slashing through the first chain, but the second coiled around his arm, yanking him off balance.

The Master lunged.

With surprising speed, he summoned a curved dagger from his robes and drove it toward Tom's ribs. Tom twisted, narrowly avoiding a fatal strike, but the blade bit deep into his side, tearing through his armor.

A grunt escaped him, but he didn't hesitate—he countered instantly, bringing his greatsword down in a vicious arc.

The Master dodged, but not fast enough—Tom's blade raked across his shoulder, slicing through his elegant robes and drawing dark, almost oily blood.

The Master hissed in irritation, his mask of smug control cracking ever so slightly.

"You're stronger than I expected," he admitted, voice smooth but carrying an undercurrent of frustration.

Tom didn't respond—he just pressed the attack.

He switched gears, his sword movements flowing seamlessly into brutal strikes and sudden, deceptive feints. The Master, for all his arrogance, was fast—his shield flickered to life at just the right moments, absorbing some of the blows, but not all.

Tom's blade tore through fabric and flesh again, a shallow but painful wound blooming across The Master's forearm.

The necromancer's eyes narrowed.

Then, he struck back—hard.

A shockwave of necrotic energy erupted from his body, forcing Tom to brace himself.

In that instant, The Master vanished—reappearing behind him, his dagger flashing downward in a vicious, calculated strike.

Tom twisted at the last second, the blade grazing his shoulder instead of piercing his back. He spun, lashing out with a sweeping horizontal strike, but The Master was already moving, his cloak billowing as he phased backward in a flicker of shadow.

For a moment, they stood at a stalemate—both warriors breathing hard, watching each other.

Then The Master smirked again, though this time it lacked some of its former confidence.

"You know," he mused, absently wiping blood from his sleeve, "this isn't quite the effortless victory I had envisioned."

Tom's grip tightened on his sword. "I could say the same."

The Master chuckled, rolling his shoulders. "I could keep this up all day… but frankly, I have more important matters to attend to."

He raised his hand, and suddenly the zombies surged forward, throwing themselves between him and Tom. A strategic wall of bodies—not to shield himself, but to stall Tom just long enough.

Tom hacked through the undead, carving a path toward The Master, but the necromancer was already retreating.

The Warlock growled in frustration at being stymied by the undead. He studied the necromancer as he withdrew, noting the calm and calculating air the man was putting on. However, he still caught it—a flicker of unease in The Master's eyes. It was just for a split second, before it was buried beneath his usual smirk.

The sight made Tom smile as he continued to swing his greatsword with enthusiasm.

The Master had learned enough, he decided.

Slipping between his thronging minions like a fish through the sea, he calmly removed himself from the confrontation. The bodies of the dead were more than eager to plug the gap and therefore slow and stall the foolish Guild leader of the aptly named Vanguard.

Vanguards were the first to die in battle, after all.

To be clear, he was not fleeing—no, flight would imply fear.

He was withdrawing, his movements deliberate, his expression thoughtful rather than desperate.

A tactical retreat. A necessary retreat.

But not one he had planned on making, he admitted—if only to himself. Yet he could see it in the foolish Warlock's eyes.

Tom knew it.

And so did The Master.

He activated his ability that allowed him to switch places with a waiting undead that had been positioned overlooking the engagement. The necromancer watched the battle unfold for a time, gauging the strengths and weaknesses of his horde of undead. He had to admit that they simply didn't measure up to the forces arrayed against them—*yet.*

"Barely worthy to be considered my opponent," he muttered as he watched the simple-minded Warlock slashing away like a simple Barbarian. Who had ever heard of such a thing?

It's a disgrace, he sniffed.

He had been sure he'd found a kindred spirit in the naive leader whose powers were so obviously similar to his own.

Enslavement? The *gall.* The hypocrisy. A Warlock who feared and doubted his own strength? Who would rather undermine his own power and System-given Class to pathetically imitate another?

The Master shook his head. "The fool."

With a final, lingering glance, the necromancer faded into the shadows.

If mere numbers are not the answer, then perhaps... His thoughts had already moved on to the future.

The necromancer smiled.

He had plans to make.

Tom exhaled sharply, gripping his wounded side, eyes still locked on where The Master had vanished. His fingers clenched into a fist, frustration coiling tight in his chest. The bastard had slipped away—but the battle wasn't over.

He turned his gaze back to the battlefield. The chaos still raged, but the tide was shifting. The Master's retreat had left his forces vulnerable. Without their commander orchestrating their movements, the undead moved with mindless aggression but no strategy. And against Tom's fighters, that was a fatal weakness.

Snapping himself out of his momentary pause, Tom tightened his grip on his sword and pushed forward.

Tom's forces fought with unmatched ferocity, pushing through the mass of undead with the sheer power of their rage and determination. Derek, Jay, Kiera, and the others were a force of nature, cleaving, slashing, and shooting anything that moved against them. Soon, they began to circle around, flanking the horde and tightening the noose around The Master's forces.

The zombies were no match for the sheer will and strength of Tom's Guild. One by one, the undead fell, bodies piling up in the streets, and the remaining zombies were surrounded. The members of the Guild, fueled by their anger and their desire for justice, showed no mercy. Even the non-combatants— tailors, cooks, janitors—joined the fray, wielding makeshift weapons with the ferocity of seasoned warriors. Iron skillets cracked skulls, wooden clubs smashed bones, and a rain of bullets and arrows filled the sky. One woman was even seen beating a cowering zombie with a flip-flop, screaming at the creature in Spanish, showing that even in the apocalypse, the power of La Chancla lived on.

Tom's heart swelled with pride as he saw his people fighting with such courage, but the pride was tempered with his own frustration. The Master had slipped through his fingers. He gritted his teeth and forced himself to focus, driving back the last of the zombies. As the last of them fell, Tom took a moment to catch his breath, his chest heaving. His arms burned from the effort of wielding two greatswords, but his anger refused to let him rest.

Derek, his armor covered in gore and grime, jogged over to him. "Tom!" he called out, concern in his eyes. "Are you alright?"

Tom nodded, but his jaw was clenched tight. "I'm fine. I can't believe he got away," he growled, his voice rough with frustration.

"It's okay," Derek said, his tone soothing. "We played everything perfectly. Everyone was on standby and came to help. He's slippery. We couldn't have expected that to have worked fully."

"I know," Tom replied, his fists tightening around the hilt of his sword. "But I was so close…"

"You almost had him. And that means you'll be ready for the fight when we take it to him," Derek said, giving Tom's shoulder a reassuring squeeze. "This is just the beginning."

Tom took a deep breath, letting Derek's words sink in. He nodded slowly. "You're right," he said, his voice steadying. "We have things to do. We strike in a week. As soon as the grenades are ready." His eyes burned with a fierce resolve.

Derek nodded, his own face set with determination behind his helmet. The others began to gather around them, tired but victorious. Jay, blood-splattered but grinning like a madman, clapped Tom on the back.

"Hell of a fight, boss," he said. "Did you see that abuelita? I do NOT wanna get on her bad side."

Tom chuckled, but his mind was already racing with the plans to come. "We need to regroup. Assess our injuries and gear up for the final push," he said. "This was just the warm-up. The next time we meet The Master, he won't get away."

The team returned to the compound, battered and bruised, but with their spirits high. They had faced down The Master and his undead horde, and they were still standing. They knew the fight was far from over, but now they had a taste of victory, and it was intoxicating.

Back in the safety of the compound, Tom immediately called for a debriefing. He wanted every detail of the skirmish—what went well, what didn't, where they could improve. As the leaders gathered, Tom stood at the head of the table, his face stern but focused. "We did good today, but we could have done better," he started, his voice steady. "The Master got away, but we made it clear that we're not to be trifled with."

Kiera, leaning back in her chair with her sniper rifle leaning against the table, nodded. "Those silenced rifles worked like a charm. We took out a lot of zombies before they even knew what hit them. I'm just upset I didn't have a clear shot on that Master son of a bitch."

"Good," Tom said, acknowledging her report. "Jay, you and Bron did a great job with the gates. We need that kind of precision if we're going to break into The Master's stronghold."

Jay smirked, still riding the adrenaline high. "You know me, always happy to break and enter. What about the traps? You think he'll have more waiting for us?"

"Definitely," Tom replied. "That's why I want to bring Bohdan along this time. He'll be able to counter any magical traps or barriers."

"Speaking of magical defenses," Brian chimed in, "I think we need to talk more about those anti-magic grenades. We saw today how effective magic is in combat. If The Master or his minions have anything up their sleeve, those could turn the tide."

"Agreed," Tom said. "I'll talk to Bohdan and the others about ramping up production. We need as many of those as we can get."

For the next hour, they discussed tactics, formations, and the logistics of their next move. The room buzzed with energy. Tom could see it in their eyes— they were ready. His people were fighters, survivors, and now they were a force to be reckoned with.

After the meeting, Tom went to the basement to check on the progress of the anti-magic grenades. As he entered, the familiar sounds of hammering and machinery greeted him. Roland was hard at work, hammering away at a new piece of metal, his face streaked with soot and sweat.

"Roland," Tom called out over the noise.

The big man looked up, a broad smile breaking across his face. "Tom! Just ze man I vanted to see!"

"How's production going?" Tom asked, walking over to the forge.

"Ve are vorking as fast as ve can. Already made about sirty of zem. Should have more by ze end of ze day," Roland replied, his voice a deep rumble.

"That's good to hear. I need you to keep pushing. We're going to need every single one," Tom said, his tone serious.

"Ve von't let you down," Roland said, turning back to his work with renewed vigor.

Tom continued deeper into the basement, heading toward Harold's workspace. He found Harold and Bohdan huddled over a table filled with blueprints and notes. The two men looked up as Tom approached.

"Tom," Harold said, his voice tinged with excitement. "We've been working on something new."

Tom raised an eyebrow. "Oh? What have you got?"

Harold grinned and motioned for Tom to come closer. "It's a bit of a surprise. Just a little something that might give us the edge we need."

Tom listened as Harold began to explain their latest innovation, his mind already whirring with the possibilities. The battle today had been a taste of what

WAR

was to come, and Tom was determined to be ready. The next time they faced The Master, it would be the last.

The clock was ticking. The war for the city was far from over, but Tom knew one thing for certain—they were ready to fight. And they would win.

Chapter 52

Restful Preparations

A week passed in the blink of an eye. Tom did nothing but train during the time they had spent waiting for Herbert, Bohdan, and Harold to complete the creation of the anti-magic field grenades. Bron had spent hours each day with Tom, teaching him advanced techniques and putting him through even more intensive training regimens. The sessions were grueling, pushing Tom's endurance, reflexes, and strength to their absolute limits. Sweat poured from his body, and his muscles burned with every movement. Yet, he persisted, refusing to relent, driven by the need to be stronger, faster, and smarter than ever before.

On the morning of the final day, Bron appeared, as usual, when Tom summoned him. The massive Mastadonian warrior looked at Tom with a discerning eye, noticing the exhaustion etched into his features. Bron placed a heavy hand on Tom's shoulder, his touch both comforting and commanding.

"You must take today to rest and recover," Bron said, his deep voice resonating with a calm yet forceful tone. "You have been pushing so hard that you will crack if you continue. Rest is just as much a part of the training process as the actual training itself."

Tom shook his head, his expression tense. "I can't. I have to be the best that I can be. I can't fail again," he replied, looking away from Bron in shame. His eyes stared at the floor, frustration evident in his posture.

Bron watched him quietly for a moment, his gaze steady. "Did you do everything you could last time?" he asked suddenly, catching Tom off guard.

"Yes," Tom answered hesitantly, his brow furrowing in confusion.

"Then you didn't fail," Bron said with a gentle smile under his trunk. "You may not have achieved the goal you were looking for, but you still managed to do something no one else has so far."

Tom's eyes narrowed slightly, skeptical. "And what's that?" he asked, feeling a bit patronized.

"You made The Master feel fear," Bron replied, his chest puffing out slightly as he stood tall, pride evident in his stance.

Tom paused, the words sinking in slowly. He mulled over what Bron was saying. The Master must have felt fear before, right? Yet, as he thought back, he couldn't recall a time when he had seen The Master as anything but haughtily confident. That arrogance probably stemmed from the fact that he could summon hordes of zombies and control people's minds with his collars. But the last battle… Yes, there had been a moment—a flicker of panic in The Master's eyes when Tom had broken through the zombie lines and reached him.

"I hadn't thought of it like that," Tom admitted begrudgingly, his voice softer now, his mind turning over the idea.

"It's okay not to hit the clouds when you shoot for the heavens," Bron continued, ensuring Tom's attention stayed on him. "But it's not okay to hold it over yourself and push to the breaking point. Then you are of no use to anyone."

Tom let out a deep sigh, the weight of the past week's relentless drive pressing down on him. "I just don't want to let people down," he confessed, his voice tinged with frustration. "We could have ended it all, and he slipped through my fingers."

Bron nodded understandingly. "Your people do not see you as a failure. If they did, they would not follow you. You give them hope—the inspiration to be more than they would be by themselves. Never forget the feeling of wanting to be a leader they can follow. But always remember to be accountable not only to them but to yourself."

Tom took a deep breath, feeling some of the tension in his shoulders begin to ease. "You're right," he sighed, his head hanging slightly. "You're not the first one to say something similar to me. I put so much pressure on myself that I forget to think about what we've done together so far."

A broad smile spread across Bron's face. "Good. Now, it's time for recovery. Hot shower, followed by a cold shower, then I want you to eat as many grains as you can. Tomorrow, you fight for your people, and you will be victorious," Bron said with a prideful force, his words infectious.

"Yeah! We can do this. That son of a bitch won't know what hit him!" Tom replied, a surge of confidence and adrenaline rushing through him.

Following Bron's orders, Tom took a hot shower, letting the heat soothe his aching muscles. After several minutes, he switched to a cold shower, the icy water shocking his system, but also rejuvenating him. His skin tingled, and his mind cleared as the chill drove away the fatigue. Once finished, he laid on his bed, stretching his limbs and letting his muscles relax completely. He could feel how the weeks of intense training had changed his body, chiseling it to a form that was stronger and more capable than ever before. He knew he had almost overdone it this week, pushing himself to the brink.

After a period of rest, he left his room and made his way to the cafeteria. As he entered, he was greeted by the warm, inviting aroma of freshly prepared food. Charlene was waiting for him and waved enthusiastically when she spotted him. Her smile was wide, her energy infectious.

"Hey, Tom! So glad to see you giving the training a bit of a break," Charlene said, her voice light and cheerful. "Bron came by and talked with me and many of the others. Such a helpful… What is he again?"

"Mastadonian," Tom replied with a chuckle. "Just think Mastodon—an elephantine creature from the Ice Age. That's how I remember it."

"That's right," Charlene said, snapping her fingers as she remembered. "Well, today we're carb-loading. Bron just kept calling it grains, but I think that's because they don't know what carbs are wherever he's from."

Under most circumstances, Tom would have been annoyed at her continued talking, but he had come to realize that many people were nervous around him. They saw him as a role model or some sort of superhero. Tom knew he wasn't either, but if it gave them hope, he was willing to live up to their expectations.

"So, what do you have for us today?" Tom asked, eagerly holding his tray out for the food.

"Pancakes, waffles, pasta, and fresh baked sourdough bread!" Charlene announced proudly. "We can't have it often, but Joe had a container with leaven in it, so we now have bread!"

"That's awesome," Tom said, his eyes lighting up. "But, what exactly is leaven?"

"Oh!" Charlene exclaimed, clearly excited to share. "That's the yeast mixture that grows to give sourdough bread its distinct flavor. It's also sometimes called a starter."

Tom nodded in understanding. "I see now. Well, I'll take some of everything, please!" he said, his mouth watering at the thought of freshly baked bread.

Charlene loaded up his tray with a generous helping of each dish. The pancakes were golden brown and fluffy, the waffles crispy on the outside and soft on the inside, the pasta perfectly cooked and covered in a light sauce, and the bread—oh, the bread—was a golden-crusted masterpiece that sent his senses into overdrive. As he poured syrup over his pancakes, he could feel his mouth watering in anticipation.

Tom took his first bite, and the flavors burst in his mouth like a symphony. The pancakes were soft and buttery, the syrup sweet but not overwhelming. He savored each bite, allowing himself to enjoy the moment of peace and satisfaction that came with a good meal. He hadn't realized just how much he'd missed simple pleasures like this.

First-world problems, eh? Tom thought to himself, chuckling at the idea. It seemed so absurd now, yet it was a reminder of what they were fighting for— the ability to enjoy the little things.

Charlene hovered nearby, watching him enjoy the meal. "Charlene, I could kiss you. Has anyone told you how wonderful you are?" Tom asked her between bites. "Or how much of an impact you have on this Guild and everyone in it?"

Charlene blushed slightly, her smile growing even wider. "Well, I hear it from time to time. But I'm never gonna say no to a few more compliments!" She giggled.

"We are so lucky to have you," Tom said sincerely, making sure to look her in the eyes so she could see he meant every word.

After finishing his breakfast, Tom went around to check on several other Guild members. He wanted to ensure everyone had what they needed for the coming battle. As he walked through the compound, he noticed people diligently working—some cleaning their weapons, others practicing combat maneuvers, and a few simply offering words of encouragement to their peers. It warmed his heart to see the camaraderie and determination in everyone's eyes.

But as he continued his rounds, Tom realized he didn't actually have much to do. His preparations were complete, his body needed rest, and his mind was set on the task ahead. Not wanting to be a nuisance or overbearing, and knowing that people wouldn't tell him to leave except for his closest friends, Tom decided to take Bron's advice to heart. He returned to his room and lay down, allowing himself to relax fully.

Tom slept for sixteen straight hours. He couldn't believe he'd let himself rest for so long, but his body clearly needed it. He awoke with a start, his mind immediately on high alert. The sun was still down, but the faint light of dawn crept into the sky. He knew there was no going back to sleep now.

After a quick wash, Tom dressed and headed downstairs to the security office. There, he found Brian and TJ already at work, both sipping coffee and poring over various notes and plans.

"What are you two doing here so early?" Tom asked, surprised to see them.

"We're just getting everything ready for the strike and making sure everyone is good to go," Brian replied, not looking up from his clipboard. "Oh, by the way, I need you to just stand still for a second, if you could. Yeah, just like that. Don't move."

"What are you doing?" Tom asked, arching an eyebrow.

"I need to get your life signature for my Communication Network item. I have everyone else already; you're the last one," Brian explained.

"And this is for…?" Tom questioned, still not fully understanding.

"So I can communicate with you as well as track your movements. It'll let me help with the plans and know who needs help where," Brian said impatiently. "Now don't move, don't talk."

Tom stood still, feeling an odd energy ripple up and down his body. It settled on his chest, lingering for a moment before it suddenly vanished.

"All done," Brian said, looking satisfied. "Now we're ready for the attack. Everything else is in place. The others should be up and moving within the hour to prepare."

"That felt weird," Tom commented as he walked over to a chair and sat down.

"What? You felt something?" Brian asked, suddenly very interested. "When I did the scan?"

"Yeah, like some kind of energy moving over my body, then it stopped on my chest," Tom explained.

"Interesting," Brian murmured, rubbing his chin thoughtfully. "No one else said they felt anything at all. I wonder if they did and just didn't want to tell me, or if this is unique. I'll have to do some research. But for now, let's focus on today."

Brian and Tom walked out to the courtyard, where they were surprised to see several Guild members already up and preparing. Jay was among them, leading his team through a series of stretches to stay agile.

"You're up awfully early, Jay," Tom commented, smiling as he watched the team go through their routines.

"We have a lot to do to get ready," Jay replied with a grin. "And I don't want to miss the chance for pre-battle stretching. You think you have to worry about pulling a hammy in a football game? Try doing it when someone's about to stab you."

"Very true," Tom chuckled. "I think I should join you as well."

As more people gathered, the courtyard buzzed with energy and anticipation. Finally, Herbert, Bohdan, and Harold arrived, bringing with them the crates filled with the newly crafted anti-magic grenades. They carefully set them up on tables that Brian had arranged.

Almost one hundred and sixty people were assembled, each one buzzing with a mix of anxiety and excitement. The Engineers had managed to create three hundred and twelve of the anti-magic grenades—enough for nearly two per person.

Tom stood at the front, his eyes scanning the crowd. "I want you all to remember that these grenades are meant to be used when you see humans with the collars on them," he instructed, his voice carrying over the murmuring crowd. "Make sure you do not use them on the zombies. They might have an effect, and they might not, so we don't want to waste them."

"Did we test it on one of them?" someone from the crowd asked.

"No. We didn't know the implications of that kind of testing. If The Master has some kind of connection to the zombies, he might've known what we were planning. Also, everyone went a little hog wild and killed all the zombies before we could capture one. That's beside the point. We really need to focus on only trying to use these on the enslaved people. They are our main priority," Tom explained.

He paused, letting his words sink in. "You're all here because we have a job to do. We have to free those who can't help themselves. This is our chance to show them there's a better life now—that they don't have to live their lives ruled by some tyrant who tricked them. We will set them free!"

The crowd erupted in a cheer, a unified roar of determination and defiance.

Tom felt a swell of pride and responsibility in his chest. "I'm proud to call you my brothers and sisters!" he shouted, his voice filled with emotion. "And I'll stand beside you in the battle, and we'll destroy this monster's reign of terror!"

Another cheer erupted, louder and more passionate than before. Tom looked around at the faces of his friends, comrades, and newfound family. They were ready. They were determined. And most importantly, they were united.

With that, Tom and his teams moved out, weapons in hand, hearts full of courage, to face their most hated enemy. The final battle against The Master was about to begin.

Chapter 53

War... Again, Again... For Real This Time

Jay moved ahead of the group with his team of Rogues, stealthily scouting the path to The Master's base. Their mission was to infiltrate the enemy's stronghold, disarm as many traps as possible, and remain unseen while causing maximum chaos when the battle erupted. Jay relished his role as the master of stealth and subterfuge for the Guild. There was a thrill in the challenge of sneaking, spying, and outmaneuvering the enemy. He had gathered around him a team of like-minded individuals who shared his love for the shadows, and together, they ensured the battle would start with every advantage in their favor.

The team moved silently through the deserted streets, each step purposeful and light, keeping to the shadows and using the cover of darkness to their advantage. The recent implementation of mana collectors had significantly reduced the number of random monster spawns in the area, making their path less treacherous. With additional Guild teams patrolling daily to hunt monsters for XP, the streets were finally beginning to remain mostly clear. This was a welcome change, allowing Jay and his Rogues to move more swiftly and silently.

As they neared the imposing walls of The Master's base, Jay raised a hand, signaling his team to halt. The breaking dawn cast long, eerie shadows against the towering structure. He scanned the surroundings for any signs of movement. Seeing nothing amiss, he gestured to the team to proceed. Moving as one, they pulled out their grappling hooks, launching them with precise aim to latch onto the wall's edge. One by one, they scaled the wall with the agility of seasoned climbers, slipping over the top and descending quietly on the other side.

Landing softly on the ground inside the perimeter, Jay led his team toward the gate. They crouched low and stayed close to the walls, their eyes darting around for any signs of sentries or patrols. The atmosphere inside the base was tense and foreboding, but strangely quiet. Reaching the gate, they wasted no time. With practiced efficiency, Jay and his Rogues quietly removed the heavy wooden barricade and dislodged the iron bar that locked the doors in place. The gates were now unsecured, ready to be opened at a moment's notice when the rest of the Guild arrived. The battle would soon begin.

"Alright, phase two," Jay whispered to his team, his voice barely audible but firm. "We need to take out the barbed wire and watch for traps. Everyone ready for what comes next?"

His team nodded in unison, their expressions serious but confident. They knew the risks—one wrong step, one careless move, and everything could fall apart. But that was the life of a Rogue, always walking the razor's edge between success and disaster.

They fanned out, keeping their movements slow and deliberate, eyes sharp for any tripwires or hidden snares. Jay felt a rush of adrenaline. This was his domain—the silent shadows, the hidden dangers, the pulse-pounding anticipation of what lay ahead.

After Jay and his spies set off, Kiera moved out with her team of snipers. She had recently added two more sharpshooters to the squad, and they had been training tirelessly for weeks to prepare for this attack. Pride swelled in her chest as she thought of the progress her team had made. She was confident they were ready to play their part from the rooftops, providing overwatch and critical fire support.

Kiera had meticulously scouted three buildings surrounding The Master's base, each offering strategic vantage points to cover the battlefield from multiple angles. Tom had insisted that every sniper be equipped with silencers for their rifles to minimize muzzle flash and noise, making it difficult for the enemy to pinpoint their positions. She took his suggestion a step further by splitting the team into three groups, each assigned to a different location. This way, even if one position was compromised, such as with the goblins last time, the others could continue to rain down fire on the enemy without being detected.

To ensure everything went smoothly on the day of the assault, Kiera had drilled her team relentlessly. Every day for the past week, she had them run the fastest routes to their designated sniper points, over and over, until they could do it without a moment's hesitation. As they approached the first building on this day, just as they had practiced, the three teams silently split off, heading for their respective rooftops.

Kiera chose to set herself up in the second building to be in the thick of things and to confirm that at least two of the sniper nests were operational and ready before the battle commenced. She sprinted up the stairs of the semi-crumbling structure, her breath steady and controlled, her rifle clutched tightly in her hands. The dusty air filled her lungs, but she had no time to worry about that. Reaching the rooftop, she immediately knelt down at the wall, setting up her sniper rifle and adjusting the sights for the perfect angle to fire down on the enemy below.

Tina, one of her most reliable snipers, took up a position next to her. Once both were settled and their rifles were ready, Kiera gave Tina a nod. Without a word, Tina pulled out a small mirror. As the first rays of the sun began to rise, she used the mirror to flash a signal toward the first and third buildings. Moments later, two small flashes returned from both directions, confirming that the other teams were in place and prepared.

WAR

Kiera exhaled slowly, peering through her scope. She swept her gaze over the base, taking in every detail. For a moment, it seemed like all was quiet, but then she spotted them—Jay and his team, moving silently through it, diligently working to disarm traps and clear paths for the main assault. She could feel her pulse quicken with a mix of anticipation and anxiety. The snipers would play a crucial role, providing covering fire and taking out high-priority targets. The success of this operation rested heavily on their shoulders.

As she scanned the area, Kiera could see that the base was still mostly calm. The tension in the air was palpable, like the feeling before a violent storm. She steadied her breathing and steadied her aim, muscles taut with readiness. Her mind drifted for a moment, silently hoping that everything would go according to plan. She had grown close to her team and cared deeply for each of them. She wanted them all to come back safely, and she was determined to do her part to ensure that happened.

"We're ready, Kiera," Tina whispered, breaking the silence.

Kiera nodded, still looking through her sights. "We've trained for this. Trust in your skills and your instincts. We've got each other's backs."

She continued to monitor the base, waiting for Tom's signal to begin their part of the operation. In the back of her mind, she made a silent wish: that her new friends would survive the day, and that she would have the strength and focus to protect them from up high.

Tom led his forces on foot, moving at a steady pace through the streets. Derek moved alongside him, helping to organize the fighters into teams to ensure they stuck together for party XP and bonuses. There was no need to rush to The Master's base—better to give Jay, Kiera, and the others time to prepare. The measured pace added to the tension, building a sense of anticipation for what was to come.

An electric energy buzzed in the air as everyone gripped their weapons tightly, ready for whatever might be waiting for them. Each step forward was a step toward freeing those The Master held captive and preventing anyone else from falling under his control. Tom's heart was filled with a steely determination, his eyes ablaze with purpose. He moved with confidence, knowing deep down that they were fighting for what was right.

The group advanced through the city like a silent, seething force of righteous anger, prepared to fight for justice and freedom. Their numbers and intent sent small groups of goblins scrambling away in the distance, too frightened to challenge such a large, organized crowd of well-armed warriors.

As the sun began to rise, it bathed the world in a soft, golden light. The sunlight glinted off the polished metal of the armor worn by some of the fighters, making them appear like a shimmering wave of defiance as they marched onward. This was more than just a fight; it was a statement of unity and purpose, a chance for them to show their commitment to their cause and the values that had drawn them to Vanguard.

When they finally neared the gates of The Master's base, Tom stopped and turned to face his people. He scanned the sea of faces, feeling a deep sense of pride. So many had chosen to stand with him, knowing the risks. He never forced anyone to fight if they weren't ready—despite what Brian might have thought after their Dungeon expedition. Each of these fighters had made a choice, and that choice was their own.

"You've all chosen a path that might lead to death," Tom began, his voice strong and clear. "But it's an honorable death, one of our choosing. We've all seen the oppression at the hands of The Master, and it has ignited a fury in us that can only be quelled by righting this wrong against our fellow humans. It's one thing to use necromancy to control the dead, but to enslave the living, to strip them of their free will and force them to act against their nature—that's an offense we cannot forgive."

The crowd erupted into a cheer, their voices united in agreement and defiance.

"Today, we end that nightmare," Tom continued, his voice rising with each word. "Today, we bring justice to those who have suffered. We'll ensure this atrocity can never happen again. Today, we fight for what we know is right! FOR FREEDOM! TO PROTECT THOSE WHO CANNOT PROTECT THEMSELVES!"

His final words rang out over the assembled fighters, who responded with an even louder roar of agreement that seemed to shake the very ground beneath them. The echoes of their shouts carried through the area, ensuring there was no way The Master could ignore the presence of an angry force right outside his gates. This was what Tom wanted—to put The Master on the defensive, to make him feel the same dread his victims must have felt when they realized their fate was no longer their own. Tom was certain that after their last encounter and The Master's near defeat at his hands, the man would be feeling both fear and anger. With luck, those emotions would lead him to make mistakes.

Tom turned his gaze back to the base and took a step forward. As he did, a sudden explosion shattered the tense silence. He looked up to see a cloud of smoke rising from within the base walls, a sign that the chaos had already begun.

"Fucking shitstains!" Jay cursed as an explosion detonated at the end of the barbed wire he was holding, forcing him to jump back with a startled shout. His ears rang from the blast, and he felt a sharp sting of heat on his face. They had been rolling up the barbed wire on wooden rods they'd brought along, carefully working to clear the barriers. But as he pulled on one of the wires to straighten it out, something had triggered—an explosive trap hidden at the end of the line.

"Well, there's no point in being sneaky now. Get those wires out of the way, whatever the cost!" Jay shouted to the others, knowing the element of surprise was now blown—literally.

The team didn't hesitate. With a renewed sense of urgency, they continued pulling at the remaining barbed wire, ripping it away from its anchors even as more explosions erupted around them. The sharp, deafening blasts sent chunks of dirt and debris flying, and the acrid smell of smoke and burnt metal filled the air. Almost immediately, zombies began pouring out of the main building and from other structures scattered around the compound, drawn to the noise like flies to a carcass.

"Shit. Change of plans! Time to meet up with Tom! Make a dash for the gate, and then do what we do best!" Jay shouted, pivoting to a new strategy. Dropping their bundles of wire, they began a tactical retreat toward the gate.

No one questioned Jay's command. His team immediately abandoned their task and sprinted toward the entrance. As they ran, several zombies lunged out from nearby alleys and doorways, trying to block their path. Jay raised his right arm, aiming the small launcher attached to his gauntlet, and fired off two smoke pellets. They hissed through the air and struck the ground in front of the approaching zombies, erupting into thick, swirling clouds of smoke.

The zombies, blinded by the sudden haze, staggered and flailed as they tried to find their way through the dense fog. Jay and his team deftly maneuvered around them, slipping through the smoke like shadows, their footsteps light and precise. Ahead of them, the massive gates of the compound came into view, and Jay spotted Tom heaving the heavy doors open, his group of fighters already forming up, ready to charge in.

"This is about to be a whole lot of fun," Jay muttered to himself, a fierce grin spreading across his face as he sprinted toward the reinforcements.

"Idiots!" Kiera muttered as she watched the first explosion rip through the base via her rifle's scope. "That asshat is gonna get himself killed." Her voice was barely more than a hiss, frustration simmering just beneath the surface. She watched Jay's team scramble, their previously stealthy approach now blown to bits—literally.

Through her scope, Kiera saw zombies emerging from every possible hiding place within the compound. They poured out of alleys, doorways, and even from behind crumbling walls, charging toward Jay and his team. Fortunately, Jay had enough sense to abandon the plan and make a break for the gates. She could see Tom's team arriving, preparing to storm the base even as Jay's team sprinted toward them.

The situation was rapidly spiraling into chaos, but the overall plan was still intact. Kiera adjusted her scope, tracking the movement of a group of zombies hot on Jay's heels. She exhaled slowly, her finger squeezing the trigger. A soft crack rang out, and the head of the zombie closest to Jay exploded in a mist of blood and brain matter, the lifeless body crumpling to the ground.

Kiera's team of snipers joined in, methodically picking off the zombies chasing after Jay's retreating group. The rifle shots were crisp and precise, and more undead dropped in quick succession. Suddenly, another wave of zombies spilled into Jay's path. She lined up her shot on the first one when a thick cloud of smoke bloomed into her view, obscuring her line of sight.

"That sneaky bastard," Kiera murmured, a hint of a smile touching her lips. "Way to go, Jay."

She watched as Jay and his team maneuvered around the smoke screen, cleverly evading the zombies and making it to the safety of Tom's forces. She could see them blending into the larger group, preparing to move on to the next phase of their plan.

"Be safe," Kiera whispered, more to herself than anyone else, as she refocused her scope, searching for fresh targets. The real battle was just beginning, and she was ready to make every shot count.

Tom heaved against the massive gates, muscles straining as he pushed them open. If everything had gone according to plan so far, they should be unlocked and ready for their assault. The hinges groaned under the sudden movement, but the doors slowly began to give way. Relief washed over Tom as he realized this part of the plan was actually going smoothly. As he continued to push, putting his full weight into the effort, others joined him, their combined strength forcing the gates open wider until they created a large enough opening for the entire group to enter.

Just as the fighters began to pour into the base, Tom spotted Jay sprinting toward them, a horde of zombies in hot pursuit. Jay's face was set with determination, his eyes scanning for any possible escape route as the undead closed in behind him.

"FOR VANGUARD!" Tom roared, thrusting his greatsword high into the air.

The battle cry echoed across the battlefield, and a chorus of fierce replies erupted from the rest of the Vanguard fighters. The energy was palpable, electrifying the air around them. With a unified shout, they charged forward, surging into the base like an unstoppable wave. Tom led the charge, his eyes fixed on Jay and his team, who were closing the distance fast. As they passed, Tom turned on his heel and swung his greatsword in a wide arc, catching a zombie just behind Jay and slicing its head clean off in one swift motion.

Tom's eyes narrowed as he focused on the larger contingent of zombies rushing in from the shadows, their numbers swelling with every second. His adrenaline surged, and he didn't break stride. Charging headlong into the mass of undead, he unleashed a sweeping horizontal slash with his greatsword, cutting through four zombies in a single, brutal swing. As the blade cleaved through decaying flesh and bone, Tom activated his *Tattoo of Brute Strength*, feeling a sudden surge of raw power flood through his veins. His muscles bulged with newfound might, making the heavy sword feel light as a feather in his grip.

With the additional strength coursing through him, Tom seamlessly transitioned to wielding his greatsword with one hand. His team crashed into the zombie ranks around him, their own weapons flashing and cutting through the horde. With his free hand, Tom summoned Bron, the towering Mastadonian warrior appearing from the summoning circle beside him. The two exchanged a nod—a silent agreement to unleash havoc.

What followed was a whirlwind of violence. Tom and Bron moved together in a deadly dance, their weapons weaving through the growing mass of zombies. Tom's greatsword became a blur of lethal steel, cleaving through anything in his path. Bron, with his own massive warhammer, swung in wide, devastating arcs, shattering bone and sending bodies flying.

The battlefield around them erupted into chaos, but in the midst of it, Tom and Bron carved a path of pure destruction. They were an unstoppable force, a pair of warriors whose movements were perfectly synchronized, tearing through the ranks of the undead like a storm that could not be tamed.

Chapter 54

The Hunt for The Master

Chaos was the only way to describe the scene unfolding inside the walls of The Master's base. The air was thick with the acrid stench of burning flesh, ozone from spell discharges, and the metallic tang of blood. The sounds of battle merged into a cacophony of screams, roars, and the relentless clang of steel against bone. Spells flew across the battlefield like deadly fireworks, their explosions casting eerie shadows across the ruined walls. Gunshots rang out sporadically, echoing off the stone, while swords, axes, and maces swung relentlessly, cleaving through undead flesh. Zombies hissed, bit, and clawed at the living with an insatiable hunger that defied death.

Tom stood back-to-back with Bron, both wielding their massive weapons like extensions of their own bodies. Each swing was a blend of precision and brute force, hacking and slashing at anything that got too close. The ground beneath them was slick with blood and littered with the severed limbs of their enemies. The zombies swarmed from all sides, their rotting, reeking bodies pressing in, driven by some unseen force to crush the life out of the living. The noise was deafening—a chorus of growls, screams, and the sickening crunch of bone.

Tom felt his heart pounding in his chest, but he kept his movements steady and controlled. With a surge of will, he activated his second tattoo, the one that allowed him to drain the very essence of life from his enemies. A greenish, inky aura began to pulse around him, and he felt the familiar pull as the zombies' vitality began to siphon into him. Instinctively, the zombies seemed to sense this new threat. Their lifeless eyes locked onto Tom as they felt their energy being ripped away, and a low, guttural growl emanated from their throats. They grew more frantic, clawing and pushing toward him, driven by a primal need to snuff out the source of their pain.

Seeing an opportunity, the Vanguard fighters exploited this distraction. Blades flashed like lightning, arrows and bullets whistled through the air, and spells detonated with explosive force, cutting down the distracted zombies in droves. Tom and Bron sensed the shift, their bond forged in countless hours of training guiding them as they carved a path through the throng of undead. They fought like men possessed, their movements a terrifying symphony of destruction. Tom swung his greatsword in a broad arc, the blade slicing through multiple bodies with a single, powerful sweep, while Bron's massive hammer came down with bone-crushing force, sending zombies flying like ragdolls.

Amid the chaos, the tide of battle suddenly shifted.

It was as if an invisible hand had seized control, commanding the zombies to halt their frenzied attacks. In eerie unison, the undead turned, their gazes locking onto a single point near the back of their ranks. There was a palpable tension in the air, a brief, terrible calm before the storm.

"They're forming the Hulk! Prepare raid battle formations!" Derek's voice boomed above the chaos, cutting through the noise like a blade.

Tom watched, his eyes wide with a mix of awe and horror, as the zombies began melding together. Their bodies fused into one grotesque, writhing mass of rotting flesh and bone. The mass swelled like a bloated, pulsating tumor, its size growing with each added body. It twisted and contorted, limbs snapping and fusing in unnatural ways. The shape began to solidify into the hulking figure Jay had described. Long, apelike arms extended outward, ending in massive, clawed hands. Its legs were short but grotesquely powerful, supporting the immense weight of its muscled, misshapen torso. Jagged bone protrusions jutted from its elbows and ran down its spine like a grotesque armor.

Then, its head emerged—a giant, skull-like visage atop broad shoulders, its hollow eyes burning with a malevolent, unnatural light. The creature let out a deafening roar that shook the very ground. The roar was so loud that fighters had to cover their ears, some dropping their weapons to shield themselves from the noise. The force of the roar sent a gust of fetid air rushing over the battlefield, and for a moment, everything seemed to freeze. A few Vanguard fighters stumbled back, their faces pale with shock.

Suddenly, a loud crack cut through the roar as something struck the beast on the side of its head, causing it to reel slightly. Smoke billowed from the impact site.

"That's the first signal! Mages, let loose your volley!" Derek commanded from somewhere amid the chaos.

Fireballs, ice spikes, lightning bolts, and energy orbs of every imaginable color soared through the air. The barrage struck the hulking abomination in rapid succession, the impacts throwing up plumes of smoke and dust. The combined force of the spells seemed to halt its advance. But then, with another enraged roar that sent tremors through the ground, it charged forward again, its massive arm swinging down like a battering ram.

The front line of fighters scattered, but not fast enough. Screams filled the air as men and women were flung like ragdolls, their bodies tumbling through the air to land with bone-crunching thuds. Tom winced as he saw two fighters he knew well—Janice and Rob—crash to the ground, their bodies crumpling awkwardly.

"Clerics! Healing now!" Derek shouted, his voice thick with urgency. A group of healers broke off from the main force, rushing to tend to the injured and pull them back to safety. The Clerics' hands glowed with soft white light as they murmured spells of restoration, their faces grim and focused.

"Now's our chance. Time to split off. Bohdan! Michael! To me!" Tom bellowed over the din, his voice carrying authority and urgency. Bron nodded in agreement, and they began to push their way through the chaos toward the main building.

"You pulled me away just when it was getting good," Michael grumbled with a half-smile, his tone mocking despite the danger around them.

"Trust me, there's plenty more where that came from," Tom replied, his eyes fixed on their destination.

Reaching the stone steps leading to the main doors, Tom took them two at a time, his heavy boots clanging against the stone. He threw his weight against the massive wooden doors, first pushing, then pulling, but they didn't budge. Locked tight. Growling with frustration, Tom grabbed both handles and heaved with all the strength his tattooed muscles could muster. The wood around the locks splintered and cracked under the strain, and with a final, mighty pull, the doors burst open in a shower of broken wood and iron.

Inside, they found a group of men and women wielding makeshift weapons—hammers, saws, and chisels. Their eyes were wide with fear, but they stood their ground, the collars around their necks glowing ominously.

Sweat dripped down their faces, and their hands trembled, but they were ready to defend their master even to death. Tom stowed one of his greatswords in his Inventory and summoned an anti-magic grenade. He pressed the button and tossed it into the room. It bounced once before the stasis spell triggered, causing it to rise into the air. The grenade expanded, releasing a yellow field that covered the room in a shimmering anti-magic barrier.

"You can drop your weapons now," Tom said firmly, his voice echoing in the now-silent room. "This field will stop the effects of the collars."

A moment of hesitation passed, then relief washed over the faces of the enslaved men and women. They dropped their tools, the clattering echoing off the walls as they fell to their knees.

"Thank you!" one of the men sobbed, tears streaming down his face as he stared at his hands. He looked up at Tom as if seeing him for the first time, his eyes filled with a mixture of fear and gratitude.

"Don't thank us yet. We still have to find The Master," Tom cautioned, his tone sharp and direct. "If you stay here, the field will protect you for the next hour."

The freed captives nodded, moving to one side of the room, some huddling together for comfort, others still in shock.

"Where is The Master now?" Tom asked, scanning the group.

"His chambers are down the hall, last door on the right. If he's not there, check the basement," one of the women said, her voice trembling. She kept glancing around as if expecting an ambush at any moment.

"Great, there's a basement. Alright, thank you. We'll come back for you." Tom turned to his team, his expression hardening. "Let's move."

As they stepped out of the anti-magic field, Bohdan muttered a quick incantation, and a soft, shimmering light enveloped them.

"What was that?" Michael asked, feeling a rush of energy coursing through his limbs.

"A haste spell. It'll help us move faster," Bohdan replied, a satisfied grin on his face.

Tom noticed a small, pink stopwatch icon at the top of his display, with motion lines indicating speed. As they moved, he felt the magic taking effect—his feet seemed to fly across the ground, his movements more fluid and agile.

"This is the kind of thing we need more often!" Tom grinned, feeling the adrenaline rush.

They reached the end of the hall, and Tom didn't hesitate. With a powerful kick, he sent the door flying inward.

They rushed inside, their eyes quickly scanning the room. It was an opulent chamber, with lavish furnishings that seemed almost absurd in the middle of a war zone. A four-poster bed draped in rich fabrics stood against the back wall, its sheets rumpled. Fur rugs covered the floor, and a fire crackled in a stone hearth, casting flickering shadows across the space.

A high-backed leather chair was positioned near the fire, with a small round table beside it. On the table rested a half-eaten steak, a glass of wine, and an open book. Tom could almost picture The Master sitting there, gloating over his evil plans. His grip tightened on his greatsword.

"He must have been here and heard the commotion," Tom muttered, his eyes narrowing. "Looks like he's not so keen on meeting us face-to-face. The coward."

A voice suddenly filled the room, seemingly coming from all directions at once. "Oh, a coward, am I? You have meddled in my plans for the last time, Tom. I will not forgive this intrusion."

Tom's eyes darted around, searching for the source of the voice. "What's the matter? Don't like unexpected guests? And what are you gonna do about it, huh? Run away again?" he taunted.

"Oh, I have plenty of surprises planned for you and your friends," the voice continued, dripping with contempt. "You aren't the only one who's been looking forward to this moment."

Tom sneered. "Yeah? Well, your plans haven't worked out so far, have they? You're just a sad little man trying to play god."

"You still don't see the bigger picture," The Master's voice replied, condescending. "You think you're the hero in this story, but you're just another obstacle. Another failure. Just like all the others before you, there are many paths to power, but only one that ensures you keep it."

Tom was done listening to this drivel. He focused on his surroundings, searching for hidden doors or passages. His eyes caught something—a latch behind one of the bookshelves. He reached out and pulled. With a click, the shelf swung open, revealing a narrow, dark stairwell descending into the depths.

"Found you," Tom growled. He turned back to his team, his eyes blazing with determination. "It's time to end this."

No more taunts came. The group descended into the blackness, Bohdan's magical light hovering above them, casting eerie, shifting shadows. The air grew colder, more oppressive, as they descended deeper. At the bottom, they found themselves in a narrow stone hallway that twisted sharply to the right.

"Clear," Bohdan whispered after peering around the corner. They advanced cautiously, their footsteps echoing off the damp, cold stone. Another door loomed ahead, larger and more imposing than the last.

Tom held up a fist, signaling them to stop. He pressed his ear to the door but heard nothing. His instincts screamed that something was behind it.

"Smash it down," Bron said with a nod. "Let them know we're not here to play."

Tom drew back and kicked the door with all his might. The door exploded inward, wood splintering, and the group rushed in, weapons ready. Four hulking figures turned to face them—zombies, but these were different. Larger, more grotesque, their decaying bodies reinforced with bony protrusions and covered in patches of thick, leathery skin.

"Time to dance," Tom said with a predatory grin, his eyes gleaming with anticipation. Bron grunted in agreement, and together, they surged forward, weapons raised, ready to unleash hell.

Chapter 55

Plans Unfold

"Druids, try to slow that thing down! Barbarians, aim for the legs! Mages, keep hitting the head to distract it!" Derek bellowed across the battlefield, his voice cutting through the chaos as he crouched down to heal another wounded fighter. A soft, golden glow emanated from his hands, spreading over the body of a man with a broken leg, who had been flung away like a ragdoll by the creature's sweeping arm.

This fight was not going the way Derek had hoped. The undead monstrosity was massive, its defense impossibly high, and their efforts felt like trying to chip away at a mountain with a toothpick. They were doing their best just to keep people alive while holding the creature at bay, but they were running out of steam. Wounded fighters were being brought back to a central location, hastily healed, and then sent back into the fray—but this wasn't a sustainable strategy. They needed a game-changing move, and they needed it fast.

"I wish Tom was here with his *Final Flash* spell," Derek muttered under his breath, frustration etched on his face as he finished healing the fighter. "That would really come in handy right about now."

"If big and flashy is what you need, we could always use the undead strategy," Chris suggested, stepping up from the back where he had been coordinating efforts. His face was grim but determined, his eyes scanning the chaotic battlefield.

"What's the undead strategy?" Derek asked, desperate for any idea that might turn the tide.

"You and the other Clerics have holy magic. So do the Paladins. It's the bane of undead existence," Chris began, speaking quickly but clearly. "If we can create an opening for both Classes to strike at once, it should do a tremendous amount of damage. The mages can hit the head with spells to disorient it, and then you all run in, strike, and retreat. That should give the other fighters a chance to move in after for some cleanup."

Derek nodded, the plan already forming in his mind. "Not saying it will kill it, but it should give us an advantage," Chris continued.

"Good plan. Let's get the word spread to the others and give it a go. You relay the orders and let me know when we're ready," Derek agreed, lacking any better alternative.

Chris darted off, moving quickly between groups of Clerics and Paladins, issuing instructions. He gestured to another team member to spread the word to the mages, ensuring everyone was prepared for a coordinated assault. Derek finished his healing, helping the man to his feet with a strong grip.

As Derek surveyed the battle, he saw their fighters holding a ragged line with shields, making quick strikes whenever they saw an opening. But they weren't making any real progress against a creature this size. The monster's sheer bulk and thick skin turned most attacks into mere annoyances. As word of the new strategy spread, Derek watched as Clerics and Paladins began to pull back from the front lines, replaced by other fighters who stepped up to hold the line.

He knelt beside another wounded Warrior, extending his hands and letting a white light flow from them. The glow enveloped the woman on the ground, mending her cuts and bruises, setting broken bones. The warmth of his healing power flowed through her body, knitting torn muscles and tissue back together. As he finished, Chris returned, panting slightly but with a fire in his eyes.

"We're ready. Give the word and we'll execute the plan," Chris reported, saluting with a quick, determined nod.

"Right. Let's do this," Derek replied, pulling a mana potion from his Inventory. He removed his battle armor helmet, downed the potion in one go, and felt the invigorating warmth spread through him as his mana reserves refilled. It was a brief respite, but it would have to be enough.

Jogging toward the front lines, Derek equipped his shield and mace. The heavy weight of the shield felt strange in his hand, given he was more accustomed to his battle suit's sleek movements. But he needed it for the most powerful holy strike in his arsenal. The Skill, called *Defense of the Faithful*, required both a shield and a weapon to channel his deity's fury against the undead. Paladins had a similar Skill, *Smite the Wicked*, but they didn't require a shield for it. Combining these two holy Skills against the undead seemed like their best bet. He wished he had access to a *Turn Undead* spell like in the tabletop games he used to play before the apocalypse, but this would have to suffice.

A loud horn blasted from the rear lines, signaling the mages to unleash their most powerful spells. Fiery explosions, ice shards, and crackling arcs of lightning converged on the undead monstrosity's upper torso and head. The creature reeled back, its massive form stumbling a few steps as the onslaught of magic disoriented it.

As the spells impacted, Derek activated his Skill, summoning the holy power within. A brilliant white light flared around him, blazing with righteous fury. The air crackled with divine energy, charged with the power of his deity's wrath against the evil that animated the undead behemoth.

"DEFENSE OF THE FAITHFUL!" Derek shouted, his voice booming over the battlefield as he leaped into the air, his shield glowing like a miniature sun.

Across the field, other Clerics and Paladins echoed his cry, their voices rising in a symphony of divine power. A wave of brilliant white light bathed the front lines as beams of pure energy descended from the heavens onto the Paladins, their auras radiating holy might. The intensity of the combined light was blinding. The hulking monstrosity raised a massive arm to shield its face, its growls turning to pained howls as the light seared its undead flesh.

One by one, every Cleric and Paladin leapt toward the Hulk, raining down blows imbued with holy energy. Their attacks struck like bolts of lightning, each one burning the creature's corrupted flesh, driving it back inch by inch. The ground trembled with the force of their strikes, and the air was filled with a cacophony of holy incantations and the monstrous roars of the beast. Smoke and steam rose from its decaying form as if the very air were rejecting its existence.

The creature screamed in pain, its body shuddering under the relentless barrage, and finally, it toppled backward. The earth shook as it crashed to the ground, its body writhing as dark smoke billowed from the wounds.

Druids immediately seized the opportunity, chanting in unison as thick, thorn-covered vines erupted from the ground, coiling around the creature's limbs like constricting serpents, binding it in place. The Hulk struggled to rise, bellowing in rage, but its awkward position on its back made it difficult to regain its footing.

"Barbarians, Warriors—move in! Attack the limbs!" Derek called out, sweat pouring down his face from the exertion and heat of the battle.

Barbarians and Warriors rushed forward with a collective roar, slashing and hacking at the creature's limbs, trying to sever or cripple them. Jay and his Rogues flanked from the sides, tossing smoke bombs to disorient the creature further, making it harder for the monster to see through the haze. Bards in the back ranks played a war song, their music infusing the fighters with renewed vigor and strength.

A sudden rumble shook the battlefield as Squirrel, now the size of a school bus, leapt onto one of the creature's massive arms. He clamped down with his powerful jaws and began tugging and shaking his head like a wolf tearing at its prey, keeping the Hulk from freeing its arm from the vines. The beast thrashed, trying to dislodge him, but the dire wolf held firm, his teeth tearing into its rotting flesh.

Derek used *Inspect* on the creature, and a grim line settled on his lips. The health bar hovered around fifty percent.

"This is going to be a long battle," he muttered under his breath, charging forward to deliver another series of holy strikes. He could only hope Tom was having better luck.

Meanwhile, on the rooftop positions, the snipers faced their own frustrations. Since the zombies had melded together into the Hulk form, their ability to provide effective support had been diminished. The creature's massive form shrugged off their bullets as if they were no more than mosquito bites.

"This sucks!" Tina complained after firing another shot, her frustration evident. "We're barely making a dent in that thing."

"We have a job to do," Kiera replied firmly, her eye never leaving her rifle scope. "We don't know what'll happen next, and we need to be ready. Hold your position."

"Kiera, do you have an update?" Brian's voice resonated in her mind, a product of his mental communication network.

"We can't do much from here; it's too big," Kiera replied mentally, her voice tight with frustration. "But we shouldn't abandon our position if we might be needed later."

"Hold on, let me see if there's something we can do," Brian responded before falling silent.

Kiera kept her focus, taking potshots at the massive creature whenever she saw an opening. Beside her, Tina glanced over, a glimmer of hope in her eyes. Both of them understood the importance of holding their position, but frustration gnawed at them. The comms item Brian had found in the Dungeon allowed for swift communication across the battlefield—a godsend in the chaos—but she didn't envy Brian's job of keeping everyone coordinated.

"Okay, Derek agrees there's not much you can do from there. His orders are to get inside the base and have your grenade launchers ready," Brian finally reported.

"Excellent. Relay the orders to the rest of my team. Tina and I are heading out now," Kiera responded.

"On it," Brian confirmed, his voice fading away.

"Alright, Tina. We're moving to the gates," Kiera said, standing up and slinging her rifle back into her Inventory. "Get your grenade launcher ready. It's time to join the fight up close."

With her team now mobilizing to join the melee inside the walls, Kiera couldn't help but feel a surge of adrenaline. She knew the fight was far from over—and that the real challenge had only just begun

.

Derek had never been so relieved to hear Brian's voice crackling through his communication network. Kiera and her team had been all but useless in their current position, their sniper rifles ineffective against the hulking monstrosity dominating the battlefield. Getting them up close, where they could leverage their grenade launchers and provide much-needed firepower, was exactly the shift in strategy they needed.

Now back to healing the wounded, Derek glanced over at the Hulk, which had managed to get back on its feet. It was locked in a fierce grapple with Squirrel, the giant dire wolf, who, though not nearly as strong as the undead giant, was far more agile. It was like watching a massive ape trying to swat a darting, slippery weasel. The battle between them had turned into a frustrating game of cat and mouse, with neither side gaining a decisive advantage.

WAR

With the cooldown times on their most powerful Skills, they wouldn't be able to execute another coordinated holy strike for quite some time. They needed a new strategy, something to keep the beast occupied and weakened until they could strike again. Derek hoped that Kiera's arrival would tip the scales with her team's firepower, but he wasn't confident it would be enough to turn the tide.

His mind raced through possible tactics, searching for a stopgap measure that could buy them more time. For now, they were playing a defensive game—and it wasn't one they were likely to win. The creature was too strong, its attacks too devastating. They were managing to hold it at bay, but just barely.

"Tom, wherever you are, you need to hurry the fuck up. We can't do this all day," Derek muttered under his breath as he laid his hands on another injured fighter, his healing magic flowing through his palms and into the man's wounds.

The strain was beginning to take its toll. Derek could feel the fatigue seeping into his bones from the constant use of healing spells, coupled with the energy-intensive attacks he'd had to throw out earlier while wearing his battle armor. He was one of the few who could withstand the creature's assaults and provide healing, which meant he'd been juggling two exhausting roles for the duration of the fight. The ground around him was littered with empty mana potion cans, each one drained to the last drop. With only three potions left, he had to use them sparingly and rely more on his natural mana regeneration.

A few moments later, Kiera appeared, jogging over to him with a determined look on her face. She didn't waste a second, pulling him into a quick, tight hug.

"I'm so glad you're still okay," she said, her breath a bit ragged from the sprint. "What can we do?"

Derek pulled back and gave her a weary but resolute nod. "Use those grenade launchers to keep it off balance. Buff the team when you can, but don't take unnecessary risks. We're in a bit of a stalemate here that we likely won't win if it keeps dragging on. Just hoping Tom can come through for us," he explained, trying to sound more optimistic than he felt.

"Thanks for not sugar-coating it," Kiera said with a wry smile. She clapped a hand on his shoulder, squeezing it briefly before jogging off to join her team in the thick of the battle.

Seconds later, Derek heard a series of explosions rip through the air, followed by the familiar boom of grenades detonating. He glanced up, watching as Kiera and her team launched an assault, providing some much-needed firepower that sent waves of shrapnel and debris cascading through the battlefield. He couldn't help but feel a small spark of hope as he moved on to the next wounded fighter, letting out a sigh of exhaustion.

"Everything alright, Derek?" Chris asked, approaching him with a concerned expression.

"I'm just running low on energy," Derek admitted, his voice tinged with fatigue. "This is taking a lot out of me, and I'm almost out of mana potions." He tried to keep his tone light, but the strain was evident. The weight of his responsibilities pressed down on him, making him feel heavier than his armor.

"We've got more potions. I brought extras for the mages, but you're welcome to as many as you need," Chris replied, pulling a mana potion from his

Inventory and handing it over. "Without you and the other Clerics, we'd be in a much worse spot right now."

Derek took the can with a grateful nod. "You really thought of everything, didn't you, Chris?" He chuckled, his spirits lifting slightly as he cracked open the can and downed it. The familiar warmth of restored mana coursed through him, giving him a second wind.

"I try to be prepared," Chris said with a faint smile. "We knew this was going to be a tough fight, so I stocked up on healing potions too, just in case we get overwhelmed."

Derek nodded, his mind already shifting back to the battle. "Any other ideas? Your last one worked better than I could've hoped," he said, setting his helmet back on his head and moving to heal a man writhing on the ground with broken ribs.

"Not just yet," Chris replied, his eyes scanning the battlefield, never lingering on one point for too long. "But I'm keeping a close watch. If I see any openings, I'll let you know. Sometimes, we just have to wait for the right moment."

"Good. As soon as you spot something, let me know," Derek said, finishing the healing spell and leaning back on his haunches to rest. He removed his helmet, wiped a bead of sweat from his forehead, and tried to conserve his strength.

Chris nodded, his gaze lingering on the massive undead creature thrashing against the fighters holding it back. "I just hope Tom's doing alright," he murmured, his tone grave.

"Me too, Chris. Me too," Derek replied quietly, his eyes flicking back to the monster. He couldn't help but feel the same. Wherever Tom was, they needed him to succeed—and fast.

Chapter 56

Fighting Through

"Michael, Bron, would you like to go first?" Tom offered, gesturing toward the undead creatures blocking their path.

"With pleasure," Michael said, stepping forward with a grin, his twin axes gleaming menacingly in the light of Bohdan's floating spell. The tension in the air was palpable, like the moment before a lightning strike.

The undead creatures sensed his approach, turning toward him with hollow eyes, suddenly burning with an unnatural hatred and hunger. These were smaller versions of the monstrous Hulk outside, but no less terrifying with their jagged claws and twisted features. Without hesitation, they charged; their growls echoing off the walls.

Michael's grin widened, his blood thrumming with excitement. He crouched into a ready stance, muscles coiling like springs. As the first creature lunged at him, he sidestepped with a quick spin to the right, narrowly avoiding the sweeping claws. He retaliated with a swift downward slash, embedding his axe deep into the spine of the first monster. It let out a low gurgle as its body convulsed.

The second creature lunged, its talons aimed at his chest. Michael deftly parried with his other axe, deflecting the blow and stepping aside to maintain his momentum. But as he turned to face his new attacker, the third creature charged at his exposed back, jaws wide and ready to tear into him.

Before it could strike, Bron barreled into it like a living battering ram. The force of his charge sent the undead creature hurtling into a stone wall with a sickening crunch. The room trembled with the impact, and the creature slumped to the ground, dazed. Bron wasted no time, his massive frame moving with surprising speed and grace. His greataxe arced through the air and cleaved the creature's head clean from its shoulders. Gore splattered across the stone as the body collapsed.

Bron turned back to check on Michael, who was now engaged in a furious dance of death with the remaining two monsters. Michael's movements were a blur—his axes a whirlwind of steel that struck with deadly precision. The fourth creature, witnessing Bron's display of raw power, hesitated. It cautiously approached him, eyes narrowed, saliva dripping from its rotten jaws.

Bron stood his ground, his eyes locked onto the creature, his lips curled in disdain. This undead was sluggish and predictable, a puppet on strings. It was nothing more than a mindless husk, and Bron intended to send it back to the grave. Suddenly, it sprang forward, leaping through the air with a screech.

Bron's hand shot out like a viper, catching the creature around the throat in mid-air. With a thunderous roar, he slammed it into the ground, the stone floor cracking under the impact. Without a moment's pause, he lifted the creature and smashed it headfirst into the ground again. This time, its skull burst apart like an overripe melon, painting the floor with blackened gore. Bron rose to his full height, wiping his hand clean, and turned back to the ongoing fight.

Meanwhile, Micahel blocked a vicious overhead swipe from one of the undead with his crossed axes. He then swept his leg out in a low kick, knocking one of its legs out from under it and sending it crashing to the ground. Spinning on his heel, Michael ducked under a second attack from the other monster and unleashed a slash with each weapon, his axes cutting deep into both its thighs. The creature's strike, aimed at his chest, whistled through the empty air where he had just been.

The second creature tried to step forward for another attack, but its legs, now torn and bleeding, gave way beneath it. Michael sidestepped as it clawed desperately at the ground to pull itself closer. He turned back to the first creature still struggling to get up, its body flailing awkwardly. With a savage overhand chop, Michael buried both axes into its skull. The creature convulsed, a low hiss escaping its lips. Michael planted a boot on its chest, yanked his axes free, and swiftly decapitated it with a clean stroke.

He turned back to the crawling creature, disgust etched across his face. He kicked it hard in the face, snapping its head back with a sickening crack. As it continued its pathetic crawl, its legs dragging uselessly behind, Michael stepped around it with ease and lopped its head off with a single fluid motion.

"Where's the next ones?" Michael asked, turning to Tom and Bron with a wild grin, his face smeared with blackened blood and gore.

"Dude, bring it down three creepy notches," Tom said, chuckling despite himself.

The group continued down the next hallway, their boots echoing off the cold stone. The path led them down a long, narrow corridor that suddenly veered to the left, opening into another large, dimly lit room. Here, they found twenty more undead—goblins and wolves—aimlessly shuffling about like nightmarish marionettes awaiting orders.

"My turn," Bohdan said, stepping forward with a calm determination. His eyes narrowed in concentration as he pushed past Tom and Bron, raising his hands toward the ceiling. A soft red glow enveloped his palms as he muttered an incantation under his breath. With a sudden roar, torrents of flame erupted from his hands, shooting out like hellish fire-hoses. Only many times more literal.

The gouts of fire bathed the undead in a scorching inferno, their flesh blistering and burning in an instant. They screeched in agony, their bodies twisting and contorting as they tried to flee the onslaught. One by one, they crumbled to the floor, reduced to smoldering husks. The acrid stench of burnt flesh filled the room.

"Remind me not to get on your bad side, Bohdan," Tom muttered, placing a hand on Bohdan's shoulder and staring wide-eyed at the charred remains.

They pressed on, navigating a maze of rooms filled with more zombies, each one clearly designed to delay them. After what felt like the seventh room of mindless undead, they finally entered a vast chamber. At its center stood a creature that dwarfed even the ones they had seen in the previous rooms—a massive undead Hulk.

"So, you've made it this far, but will you be in time to save your friends outside?" The Master's voice echoed mockingly around them, seemingly coming from every corner of the room. "They don't seem to be doing so well. They might even be dead by the time you get back to them."

The enormous creature took a single, thunderous step toward them, its eyes glowing with a malevolent light.

"My friend here is going to keep you busy while they die at the hands of my ultimate creation. Don't worry, you will soon join them in the afterlife." The Master's voice descended into a manic cackle as the Hulk lumbered closer, its heavy footsteps shaking the ground.

Bron dashed forward, his face set in grim determination. He pulled a second greataxe from his Inventory, his massive legs pounding the stone floor as he charged. The monster met him head-on, its gigantic, clawed hands catching his axes in mid-swing. They were locked in a brutal struggle, each one straining to overpower the other. Bron's muscles bulged with effort, veins standing out like cords as he fought to press the creature back.

Tom activated his *Tattoo of the Summoner*, giving Bron an additional boost of power. With a sudden twist, Bron pivoted to the right, letting the creature's weight carry it forward. Seizing the opening, he drove one of his axes deep into the monster's back. The beast roared, shrugging off the pain like a mere annoyance, and swung a massive hand that collided with Bron's head, sending him stumbling backward.

Michael leapt into the fray, his body a blur of motion. He hurled one of his axes with all his strength, embedding it deep in the creature's shoulder. Then, gripping his remaining axe with both hands, he brought it down in a savage arc across the monster's side. Both weapons sank deep, but the beast retaliated with a bone-rattling backhand that sent Michael crashing to the ground.

Bron, regaining his balance, took advantage of the distraction. He stowed one of his axes and delivered a bone-crunching punch to the side of the Hulk's head. The impact spun the creature sideways, and it staggered a few steps, dazed but not defeated. Before it could recover, Bron charged again, tackling the monstrosity to the ground. They rolled, a chaotic tangle of limbs, each trying to gain the upper hand. Bron pinned the creature beneath him, raining down blows on its head with his powerful fists.

Suddenly, the creature's clawed foot kicked up from beneath, smashing into Bron's skull and sending him sprawling. As Bron rolled away, Michael sprang from a crouched position, launching himself into the air. He drove his heel down onto the creature's stomach with all his might, forcing a whoosh of air from its lungs as it curled itself around the blow. Seizing his axes from the beast's flesh, he prepared for another strike. But the creature rolled to the side, forcing Michael to jump back to avoid being crushed.

Bron was ready again, landing a left hook that snapped the monster's head to the right. It staggered, only to be met with a vicious right hook from Michael. Back and forth they went, the two warriors delivering a relentless barrage of punches, their fists smashing into the creature's skull like hammers against stone.

Despite their ferocity, the beast's resilience seemed endless. Its body swayed, but it would not fall. Not waiting for it to recover, Tom had been charging up his most powerful spell. Feeling the energy peak in his hands, he held it back just enough to prevent the spell from releasing prematurely.

"Hold its arms!" Tom shouted to Michael and Bron, his voice carrying over the din of the battle.

Without hesitation, Michael and Bron moved in unison, each grabbing one of the creature's massive arms. With all their strength, they pulled, forcing the beast's limbs outward and leaving its chest wide open and exposed.

Tom steadied himself, his eyes narrowing with focus. His hands, glowing with the power of the charged spell, crackled with blue and white arcs of energy. He positioned his hands at his hip, the orb of energy between them now pulsating like a living thing, its brightness growing to almost blinding levels. He could feel the heat emanating from it, the air around him sizzling with raw, untamed power.

"FINAL FLASH!" Tom roared, thrusting his hands forward and unleashing the pent-up energy. The blast tore from his palms, a blinding beam of white-hot light that widened from the size of a grapefruit to that of a beach ball within seconds. The sheer force of the spell sent shockwaves rippling through the air, a deep, rumbling boom echoing off the walls.

The creature's eyes, which had been filled with rage and malevolent fire, widened in a sudden flash of fear as the beam struck it dead center in the upper torso. The impact was immediate and catastrophic. The blast disintegrated the Hulk's head and part of its chest in a single, violent moment, vaporizing everything in its path. The heat of the beam left nothing but a deep, smoldering indention in its body where the head and shoulders once were.

As the light of the spell faded, a stunned silence fell over the room. The massive body of the creature remained kneeling for a moment, its arms still stretched out by Michael and Bron. Then, almost in slow motion, the creature's lifeless body slumped forward, crashing what would have been face-first onto the ground with a heavy, resounding thud. Smoke rose from the cauterized edges of its wounds, the remnants of Tom's spell still hissing and sizzling.

"Remind me not to make you mad as well," Bohdan muttered, his voice filled with awe as he stared at the smoldering corpse.

Tom panted, sweat pouring down his face, his body trembling from the energy expenditure. "That… took a lot more out of me than I thought," he admitted, shaking his hands to dispel the tingling numbness that remained from channeling so much power.

"Well, what do you think of that, Master?" Michael taunted, his chest heaving from the fight. "Still think you can win this?"

For a moment, there was only silence, the tension in the room palpable. Then, The Master's voice returned, filled with incredulous anger.

"What the hell kind of monsters are you?" the voice boomed, resonating with frustration. "You come here to ruin my plans for making this city a peaceful place to exist, and show off by killing anything in your path. You call me the villain, but all I see are people looking for chaos!"

Tom's breathing steadied, and his eyes narrowed. "The peace that you're seeking is the peace of the grave," he shot back. "You're looking to enslave people, not help them."

"Enslave?" The Master sneered. "I'm giving them the power they crave! I am setting them *free* from the day-to-day dangers by protecting them. I provide them with purpose. You promise nothing but death from the danger you continually bring to your doorstep."

Tom paused, a flicker of doubt crossing his mind. Was there a sliver of truth to The Master's words? Had he, in his relentless pursuit of freedom and justice, inadvertently brought danger to his people? He thought of Seth and the others who had died or been injured because of the battles he chose to fight. Had his desire to be a hero made things worse for those he sought to protect?

"Fuck that," Michael said sharply, his voice cutting through Tom's thoughts. "Freedom isn't free. It never has been. Each and every letter of the words of the Constitution of this great nation was written in the scarlet blood of men and women who all held the same belief." Michael's voice had taken on an aspect that felt greater than himself. His mouth firmed behind the bristles of his thick beard— his voice booming out into the world around him, saturated with a confident, quintessential faith. "We hold these truths to be self-evident, that all men are created equal, that they are endowed by their Creator with certain unalienable Rights, among these are Life, Liberty and the pursuit of Happiness." Michael's voice was filled with passion. "Those words get bandied about as casually as you please. We've lost the awe and respect of the deep truth behind them. This world is filled with danger. We had to fight to survive far before Tom showed up, and we'd still be fighting if he died or ran off. Tom doesn't bring danger to us; he stands in the gap to be a shield for those who can't defend themselves. Tom has never once promised anyone peace, prosperity, or power—only the possibility of a better tomorrow."

"You are a naive fool who loves the thrill of battle," The Master scoffed. "You cannot possibly understand."

Michael's eyes blazed with defiance. "So I like jumping into the fray. But you're wrong about one thing. I don't do it just for the thrill. I do it because people are counting on us. People who can't fight for themselves."

"He's right," Tom said, his voice stronger now, as if Michael's words had reignited a fire within him. "I'm not the one causing this. I allow every one of my Guildmates to choose their path. You, however, force them into servitude. You may call it protection, but you're forcing them to do what you want instead of giving them the choice. I bet most of them would rather be out in the wilds, fighting for their lives, than here with you."

There was a heavy pause, and then a mechanical sound filled the room. A door slid up at the back, revealing twelve men and women who marched in. Each of them wore the familiar collars, like the one Lily had been wearing when she escaped and came to their Guild. They looked haggard and worn, their clothes ragged and dirty, their bodies gaunt from malnutrition. Tom's rage, which had momentarily cooled, surged back with a vengeance at the sight of these broken souls.

After they formed a line in front of the doorway, The Master himself stepped out from the shadows. He wore a pinstriped suit, meticulously pressed, with a pair of white gloves that gleamed in the dim light. His hair, slicked back with an unnatural sheen, was perfectly in place, his smile twisted with self-satisfaction. Adjusting his glasses up onto his nose with a gloved hand, he looked down his nose at Tom and his companions.

"Well then," he said, his voice dripping with condescension. "Shall we see whose resolve is stronger?"

Chapter 57

Freedom

The Master had put Tom in an impossible situation.

He stood behind a human shield of twelve captives, using them as a living barrier, their bodies a twisted fortress of flesh and fear. At first glance, it looked like they were simply terrified hostages, their heads bowed, their shoulders hunched. But then Tom noticed something off.

The way eleven of them stood rigid but not panicked. Their eyes were blank, unwavering, not pleading for rescue but waiting—watching The Master in quiet anticipation, as if expecting instruction.

Only one person in the group broke the pattern.

A woman—thin, malnourished, and frantically shifting her gaze between Tom and The Master. Her fingers twitched, curling into fists before releasing again, as if she were trying to gather the courage to act. Her eyes weren't blank. They were alive—desperate.

She saw this for what it was. An opportunity. A chance to escape.

Tom was about to speak when she suddenly turned to the others, voice trembling but urgent.

"This is it," she whispered, just loud enough for them to hear. "We can go. He's losing. He's—"

A sharp, panicked gasp cut her off.

"Don't," one of the others hissed, their voice tight with fear—not of The Master, but of her words. "Just listen to him. Do what he says."

"Are you serious?" she demanded, her whisper turning harsh. "He's using you as meat shields! He doesn't care about you!"

One of the men standing beside her shook his head, his expression unreadable. "That's not true. He's always protected us. As long as we listen, we're safe."

Safe.

The word made something twist in Tom's gut.

These people weren't just scared—they had been conditioned. They believed obedience meant survival.

The woman saw it too. Her expression turned desperate. "We're not safe! Look at what's happening! We have a chance, but we have to take it now—"

A low, amused chuckle cut through the air.

The Master had been watching.

He took a single step forward, slow and deliberate, placing a hand gently on the shoulder of the man who had defended him. "Now, now. This is unfortunate." His voice was mocking—almost disappointed, like a parent scolding a foolish child.

His hand tightened.

"Kill her."

The command was calm, effortless—like he had just told them to fetch him a drink.

The shift was instant.

The eleven snapped into motion, moving as one unit, their hesitation vanishing.

The woman's eyes went wide. "No—"

The first blow came fast, a brutal strike to her stomach, knocking the breath from her lungs. She staggered, doubling over. A second later, another hit—a knee to the ribs.

One of them grabbed her arm. Another drove a fist into her face.

Tom's stomach plummeted.

They weren't just obeying. They weren't reluctant. They were following orders like machines.

And The Master? He simply watched, smiling.

Tom's team reacted at once.

Michael gasped, stepping forward as if to intervene, but Bron caught his arm, his expression dark and tense. Bohdan let out a curse, fists clenched so hard his knuckles went white.

Tom felt something hot rise in his chest.

Not just rage.

Something worse.

This wasn't mind control. This wasn't a spell forcing them to comply. These people believed in The Master. They had been twisted into thinking this was right.

They had been broken long before this moment.

And Tom felt helpless to help. If he stepped in, what was to stop them from being ordered to attack him? Or worse, they simply chose to attack him out of fear of retribution.

Tom gritted his teeth so hard he thought they might crack. He had to try.

He took a single step forward.

"Ah, ah, ah. No interfering," The Master said, snapping his fingers.

A set of grotesque undead hands reached up from the ground and grabbed his ankles, holding him in place.

The woman coughed, blood dripping from her lips as she tried to push away—tried to fight—but there were too many of them. The blows kept coming.

Until she stopped moving.

Until her body hit the floor with a dull thud.

Only then did The Master raise a hand, halting them.

Silence crushed the room.

For a few terrible seconds, no one spoke.

Then The Master sighed, shaking his head as if disappointed. "A shame. Some people simply don't learn."

He snapped his fingers again and the hands released Tom's ankles, disappearing back into the ground.

His foot nudged the woman's motionless body, then he looked up at Tom, his smile returning.

"But that can be fixed," The Master lowered his head as the light glinted off his glasses, giving him a menacing look.

His hand wove in a complex series of movements. Tom and his team braced for the spell. Greenish light shot from his hand into the fresh corpse of the slave.

Suddenly, it began to stir. Twitching at first, then moving as if trying to stand up without using its arms.

Once the spell fully took hold, it raised itself to a standing position, blood and spittle mixing into a drooling mess, dripping from its broken jaw.

"That's better. Truly obedient now," The Master chuckled.

Tom stared in horror at the poor creature. It had been a human moments ago. Now its will was as empty as the look in its eyes.

"Now… Where were we? Ah yes, I remember. How will you save them if you can't even save yourself?" The Master taunted, his laughter grating and filled with malice. The door behind him slowly closed, sealing off the only other exit from the room. As it clicked shut, The Master's sneer grew wider, his eyes never leaving Tom and his companions.

"People like you make me sick," The Master continued, his voice dripping with contempt. "You, with your self-righteous ideals and charismatic bravado, are worse than even that detestable Shandra. At least I can respect her ruthless pursuit of power in this unforgiving world." He paced back and forth behind his human shield, hands clasped behind his back, looking like a lion behind glass at the zoo, predatory. "You pretend that you care for other people and pretend they are on the same level as you when we all know they are just weak examples of human flesh who don't deserve to be the ones calling the shots for their lives."

His gaze bore into Tom as he continued, his eyes flashing with fury and disgust. "You treat them with kindness, which does nothing but make them weaker, giving them the delusion that they too can make a difference. It's ridiculous! You think of yourself as some kind of messiah when, in reality, you are nothing more than an idealist who is going to get them killed."

The Master's tirade paused for a moment as he noticed Tom moving out of the corner of his eye.

"What… what are you doing?" he asked, his tone faltering slightly.

Tom feigned innocence, shrugging his shoulders casually. "What? Us? Oh, nothing. Continue. You were saying something about us making you sick and me thinking I'm Jesus or something? Kinda blasphemous if you ask me."

"Not *Jesus*, you buffoon!" The Master snapped, his frustration bubbling to the surface. "I said… never mind. That's not the point!"

"Oh, I'm so glad. I'd hate for lightning to strike me for standing too close to you. That would be such a bummer," Tom said, his tone light and mocking.

"You think you can kill me? HA! You can't even save your friends. What do you think you will do here?" The Master sneered, dismissing Tom's words with a wave of his hand.

"It's gonna happen. Just give it time. And it's going to be slow. I want to enjoy the moment." Tom's expression shifted from playful to deadly serious, his eyes hardening into a look that spoke of a man who had walked through fire and come out stronger on the other side.

The Master stopped pacing, his confidence wavering for just a second. He stared at Tom, trying to read the calm menace in his gaze, but finding it too unsettling to maintain eye contact. He quickly tried to recover his composure.

"It will not be you who ends up killing me. I promise you that," The Master said, forcing his voice to stay steady, though a hint of uncertainty crept in. "You have no hope here, and not only will I kill you, but your friends above will die as well. After that, I will march on your Guild and destroy them all. Everything you know and love will perish because of you."

"I guess we'll see, won't we?" Tom replied, his tone shifting back to casual nonchalance.

"You are so infuriating! I have you by the literal balls in this situation, bearing down on you with your own destruction, and you still seem to feel like you are going to come out on top!" The Master shouted, his agitation reaching a fever pitch.

"That's because I know something you don't," Tom said, lifting a small, metallic orb for The Master to see, a cold grin creeping across his face.

The Master's eyes narrowed in suspicion. "What is that?"

Tom clicked the activation switch with his thumb. The device whined, arcs of golden energy rippling across its surface.

"You'll find out soon enough," Tom replied. And then, he threw it.

The grenade ripped through the air, heading straight for The Master.

The necromancer moved instantly, yanking one of his loyal followers in front of him. The enslaved man flinched but made no attempt to resist, standing willingly as a human shield.

Then the grenade detonated mid-air.

A pulse of golden energy burst outward, flooding the room with blinding light. The air hummed, vibrating like a tuning fork struck with raw, disruptive force.

Tom didn't wait for the effect to take hold.

"NOW!" he barked.

Bron charged forward like a battering ram, his massive frame cutting through the battlefield like a wrecking ball. Michael was right behind him, a wickedly curved blade flashing in his grip. Bohdan, his eyes alight with arcane focus, lifted his staff—prepared to strike while The Master was exposed.

They were going to end this now.

But something was wrong.

No one moved.

WAR

The enslaved people—they should have reacted. Should have gasped, panicked, screamed, broken free—but they just stood there. They had been freed from their shackles—from the oppressive tyranny of slavery.

The golden light bathed them, the energy crawling over their skin, yet they did not run.

They did not fight.

They simply stared ahead, silent, waiting for The Master to tell them what to do.

Tom's stomach dropped.

No.

This wasn't like before. It wasn't mind control holding them in place.

It was belief.

They were choosing to stay. Choosing not to move, because obedience had always kept them safe before.

The Master let out a slow, mocking laugh.

"You really thought that would work, didn't you?" he sneered, stepping forward, the golden glow reflecting in his cold, dark eyes.

But Tom saw it—the slight tremor in his fingers, the way his stance shifted ever so slightly.

The grenade had worked—partially.

The Master had felt it, his magic flickering just for a moment, his grip over the room weakening.

But he clearly wasn't beaten yet.

His hand shot up, fingers curving into a claw, and suddenly the air in the room shifted.

A black, writhing aura coiled around his arm, swirling in defiance against the anti-magic field. The golden energy flickered, collapsing inward, and then— it cracked apart like shattering glass.

Tom's breath hitched as the anti-magic field dissipated, fading like mist in the wind.

The Master grinned, rolling his shoulders. "Clever. But I am not so easily undone."

He lifted his hands again, and this time, his magic answered the call.

Shadows swelled around his body, dark tendrils snapping outward like living whips. A pulse of pure, violent energy shot toward Tom's team, forcing them to scatter.

Tom quickly regained his feet. The moment The Master's magic stopped, he rushed forward, his greatsword cleaving through the air in a brutal arc. If he could end this quickly, he could stop The Master before he recovered his full power.

But The Master wasn't done yet.

Just before Tom's blade found its mark, The Master twisted, sidestepping at an unnatural speed. Dark energy coiled around his body, and with a flick of his hand, a shockwave erupted outward.

Tom barely had time to throw his arms up before he was blasted backward, his boots skidding across the stone floor.

The Master straightened, rolling his shoulders as his aura grew denser— the very air around him hummed with power.

"You thought I was finished?" he hissed, his voice carrying a sharp edge of contempt. "Pathetic."

He lashed out, sending bladed tendrils of darkness shooting toward Tom.

Tom dodged the first, but the second caught his side, searing pain ripping through his ribs. He gritted his teeth, swinging his sword in a desperate counter, but The Master was already moving, weaving around the attack with unnatural grace.

Then, from the corner of his vision—

Bron roared, swinging his axe like a falling star.

The Master vanished in a blur, reappearing behind Bron, palm outstretched. A burst of black energy surged forward, slamming into Bron's back. The Mastadonian let out a pained grunt, his body crashing into the ground like a felled tree.

Michael lunged next, his blade glinting as he aimed for The Master's throat.

A cruel smile flickered across The Master's face.

A sharp, twisting motion, and suddenly Michael froze mid-air, his body locked in place, suspended by tendrils of shadow magic wrapping around his limbs.

The Master tightened his grip—the shadows constricted, and Michael let out a choked gasp as he was slammed into the ground with bone-crushing force.

Bohdan made his move.
 The mage's hands flashed through a series of sigils, summoning a spiraling arcane circle above him. With a cry, he unleashed a piercing lance of raw energy—white-hot and blinding.

The Master turned abruptly, eyes gleaming. His hand snapped upward, and a swirling black vortex burst into existence. It tore through the air like a living thing, devouring Bohdan's spell in an instant. The raw magic vanished into the dark spiral, consumed entirely.

Tom narrowed his eyes. That spell wasn't just a shield—it was hungry.

Before the vortex could continue its destructive path, Tom clenched his fist, calling forth one of his Skills. "Corruption!" he shouted, and a pulse of dark energy surged from his outstretched hand, targeting The Master and the minions surrounding him. Veins of writhing shadow crawled across their forms, sapping their strength and disrupting their mana flow.

The vortex flickered—then faltered.

Tom sprinted forward, sword gripped tight. As he neared, a glimmering mana field around The Master snapped into view—his final defense.

Tom's sword struck the barrier.

The impact resonated like a bell toll, cracking through the field as Tom poured everything he had into the strike. Mana backlash erupted, a blast of arcing energy rebounding into The Master. He staggered, momentarily stunned, the vortex behind him unraveling into nothing.

That was the opening Tom needed.

His *Tattoo of Brute Strength* flared to life, muscles surging with raw power. He triggered *Dark Inferno*, the spell-enhanced enchantment in his sword igniting in a storm of inky red flames.

The greatsword blazed like a falling star, and Tom charged in to end it.

Tom swung.

The Master's eyes widened in shock as the blade took him in the neck. His head snapped to one side as the sword stuck viciously into the necromancer's spinal column. With hate-fueled strength, The Master ripped the weapon from his body.

Black blood fountained from the bastard's mouth, and yet he still smiled.

Tom didn't like that smile.

With casual arrogance, The Master raised his hand, his fingers limned in a black half-light as he gestured toward one of his followers standing nearby. As he did so, his wound began to heal. His neck sutured together with a sickening slurp and The Master tilted his head toward one side then the other, casually working out the kinks.

Horrifyingly, however, the nearby follower's neck split in the exact same place. Blood fountained from the wound as the woman fell to her knees, her eyes never leaving the necromancer as they filmed over in death.

"It is wonderful to have good help in these troubled times, is it not?" The Master said mockingly. "If only you had such faithful minion—"

The tip of a blade erupted from his robed chest. Michael stood behind the necromancer, his grin fierce and bloody.

"We're not minions, you piece of shit," he growled.

The Master took the deathblow surprisingly well. He glanced down at the sword that had impaled him and then back at the Warrior behind him.

"Are you not?" he asked, his eyes questioning. "You are bound by shackles no weaker than my own, and yet you fail to see them." His chuckling voice felt like blackened bile and blood. "Even I find it difficult to counter the Warlock's admittedly overwhelming Charisma. A decidedly devious Attribute, is it not?" He turned his attention toward Tom. "In fact, I commend you. Had I known its power and capabilities, perhaps I would have never needed these collars to begin with." His smile was acidic. "After all, *yours* seems to work even better than my own."

Tom's mind froze as he considered the implications of the words the necromancer spoke.

Is that true? he wondered. *Are all of these people following me caught up in the wake of some disgusting, mind-bending Attribute of the System?*

He thought back to his interactions with the people he led. Were all of those moments false? Tainted by some magically imbued social equivalent of a ruffie?

In some dark part of Tom's mind, it made sense. Why else would anyone follow him? Of course it would be because of some kind of System-induced super-pheromone, or however the result was managed.

He was not allowed to wallow in his despair for long, however.

This time, the necromancer snapped his fingers and disappeared. He reappeared a short distance away, where a man had been standing.

The Master straightened his clothes casually, frowning at the large hole in his robes, but clearly unbothered by any damage.

Instead, the man that had been standing there was now impaled on Michael's blade. Both hands gripped the sword that would end his life. Fear and confusion reigned in the man's gaze for a moment, until he looked over to where The Master was now standing. As he saw the necromancer, the look in the follower's eyes changed to that of acceptance.

The Master nodded grimly, raised one hand and snapped his fingers once more.

The living corpse exploded.

Michael was thrown backwards, his limp body rolling and twisting against the hardened ground. As his body slid to a stop, Tom couldn't tell whether the man was dead or alive—only that he lay there, unmoving.

Tom felt his heart sink.

They were losing.

One by one, his team was falling.

And now, The Master turned to him, his dark eyes glowing with triumph.

"You fought well," he said mockingly. "I'll even admit you were… impressive."

His hand rose, fingers curling into a claw, and a void of writhing darkness formed above him—power coiling like a storm, ready to be unleashed.

"But now, you have my permission to die."

Tom's mind raced.

Nothing was working. Their attacks weren't enough. Their magic was being consumed.

He needed something else.

Something new.

Something that The Master couldn't predict.

His eyes narrowed.

Desperation fueled him, his mind snapping to two spells he knew well—*Dark Ball* and *Lightning Strike*. Mentally, he grabbed both spells and shoved them together with a maniacal resolve.

For a moment, it seemed impossible—like forcing oil and water to mix. Light and dark. Static and shadow. The spells fought each other like cats in a sack.

Good. That was exactly what he wanted.

He'd already been warned of the ramifications of playing with magic—particularly the dangers involving opposing magics. Bob had warned him of the repercussions of this kind of playing with magic, but he didn't have time to think about the consequences. That warning gave him the kick start for this idea. He needed that destructive capability, and he needed it now.

He had to act.

Tom gritted his teeth, pushing his willpower to the limit, channeling both conflicting forces at once.

Darkness pooled in one hand. Lightning crackled in the other.

The energies fought, clashing like two wild animals. The spell resisted him, struggling against its own unnatural existence.

But Tom held it together.

And then—

It snapped into place.

A surging, crackling sphere—a ball of black lightning, arcs of violet electricity dancing wildly inside its core.

A new spell.

A spell made from desperation and fury.

A spell that could end this.

As the spell coalesced, time seemed to hold its breath. Tom turned his gaze toward the deadly necromancer, but his eyes passed by the gloating face easily.

No, the more difficult part was taking in each of the remaining nine followers who still stood by their vaunted Master. Tom's gut churned and his heart ached for each one of them.

He could see himself in their place. Powerless. Tortured. Haunted. Bent toward a will greater than their own. With this spell, he knew that it wouldn't be only The Master who suffered his wrath. These innocents, too, would pay the price.

Yet, were they innocent? Tom thought. *If the saying that all it takes for evil to win is for good men to do nothing is true, then what does it mean to actively support evil?*

It means that they share the same blood on their hands regardless of how they might try to justify themselves. They've made their choice, and now I've made mine.

With grim finality, Tom's voice ripped through the air—

"VOID STORM!"

He threw it forward, and the room erupted.

The attack howled like a hurricane, a swirling storm of lightning and darkness that shredded through the air like a banshee's wail. The Master's eyes widened in shock, his instincts screaming at him to move—but it was too late.

The *Void Storm* slammed into him, sending tendrils of black lightning surging through his body.

The Master let out a guttural cry, his form convulsing violently as the energy tore into him, burning and unraveling his magic simultaneously.

He hit the ground, writhing, his body smoking from the attack.

The spell didn't end there, however, it swept through the necromancer and beyond, smashing into the nearby followers and sending them flying like bowling pins. None rose from where they had fallen.

Tom schooled his expression at the sight. It had been necessary. What was obvious to Tom was that the necromancer could keep swapping injuries with that crowd all day. Understanding that, Tom knew that he would have to remove them from the equation. He tried hard to put just the right amount of magic into the spell to put each of them down without killing them, but he also knew that the line between knocking someone unconscious and killing them was a line measured in hairs. What's more, he knew that he could neither be squeamish nor overly merciful if he were to win.

What bothered him the most, however, was that he was still unsure of The Master's full capabilities. For all he knew, The Master could feel each heartbeat in the room. It meant that Tom would need to—at the very least, injure each of these people to a degree where swapping injuries would never make sense.

It was, perhaps, a coldly logical choice, but Tom knew it was the right one to make, no matter how hard it was to do so.

"You… killed them," The Master said, horrified.

"They joined the war as my enemies when they willingly served your orders and as your get out of jail free card," Tom said frostily.

He didn't hesitate.

Tom closed the distance, gripping his sword with both hands.

The Master tried to push himself up, his body weak, twitching. He looked up, and for the first time—

There was true fear in his eyes.

Tom's blade came down.

"AHHHHHHHHHHH!!" The Master's agonized scream tore through the room as he stared in disbelief at his severed wrist, blood pouring from the stump. With another clean motion, Tom chopped off The Master's other hand, a look of utter hatred on his face.

Tom loomed over him, his expression unyielding, a cold fury burning in his eyes. "You know what I hate more than anything else in the world? Well, when they put lettuce on my tacos, I guess, but right after that? People who think they can play god with other people's lives."

The Master's sobs grew louder, his body writhing in agony. Tom placed the point of his sword on The Master's left shoulder and pressed down, leaning his weight into the blade. Blood seeped through the fabric of The Master's suit, and he let out another wretched scream.

"You really thought you could keep doing this, didn't you?" Tom said, his voice eerily calm—almost disappointed.

The Master lay before him, writhing, his body weak and broken, struggling to even lift his shaking, severed arms. The once-mighty necromancer, reduced to nothing but a man bleeding out on the floor.

Tom exhaled slowly, shaking his head.

"Let me tell you why you lost," he said, crouching just enough to look The Master in the dying glow of his eyes.

"You built yourself for right now. Every Skill you chose, every ability you unlocked—it was all about immediate power. You saw something strong, and you grabbed it, thinking that was all that mattered. But you never thought ahead. You never asked yourself what those choices would mean later."

The Master gritted his teeth, eyes burning with rage and denial, but Tom kept going.

"You didn't build a foundation. You built a house of cards—and it's collapsing around you.

"You focused everything on magic, but did you ever consider what would happen if someone took that magic away? Did you ever think, 'What if I face someone who's ready for me?' Or were you so convinced of your own superiority that you believed you'd never have to adapt?"

The Master let out a pained breath, but he had no answer.

Tom smiled, but it wasn't mocking—it was cold, sharp, the smile of a man who had already won before the fight even started.

"That's the difference between you and me," he said. "You were chasing power. I was building something greater.

"Every stat I've put points into, every Skill I've unlocked, every ability I've honed—it wasn't just for me. It was for my Guild. It was for our future. I didn't just think about what makes me strong now—I planned for what makes us unstoppable later."

The Master's breathing was ragged, his mind racing, trying to find something—anything—to throw back at Tom.

But there was nothing left.

"You kept taking the fastest road to power," Tom continued, his voice dropping lower, colder. "But the fastest road always ends at a cliff.

"And guess what, asshole?"

Tom leaned in.

"You just ran out of road."

The Master let out a strangled, bitter laugh, his lips curling in defiance. "Even... now... you're still just... talking..."

Tom's expression didn't change.

"No," he said simply.

Tom ripped his sword free from The Master's shoulder, the blade slick with blood. A broken, pitiful whimper escaped the necromancer's lips, his shaking body barely able to move. He lay sprawled on the cold stone floor, defeated, his severed wrists twitching uselessly at his sides.

Tom exhaled slowly, rolling his shoulders, his grip tightening on his sword. When he spoke, his voice was low, unyielding—not with rage, but with a cold, final certainty.

"You make me sick."

The Master groaned, his breathing ragged, but he couldn't lift himself up.

"You had so many choices," Tom continued. "You could have been better. But instead, you let your own weakness define you."

Tom crouched slightly, just enough to look The Master in the eye, watching the way his pale, blood-drained face twitched at his words.

"Let me guess," Tom continued, his tone shifting into a mocking drawl. "You were bullied, right? Someone shoved you into a locker? Called you names? Tossed you in a dumpster? So you spent your whole life waiting for the moment you could do it to someone else."

The Master's jaw clenched, his fingers twitching, but he had no words.

Tom's lips curled in disgust.

"Pathetic."

The word landed like a hammer, heavier than anything Tom had said before.

"You could have proven them wrong. You could have built something real—for yourself, for others. Instead, you just became what you hated. The second you got a taste of power, you clawed for more, forcing people to kneel to you so you'd never feel small again."

The Master's breath shuddered, but it wasn't from pain—it was from the weight of truth settling over him.

Tom lifted his sword again.

"All that power," he muttered, almost to himself, "and this is how you end up."

Then, with a brutal swing, he severed The Master's right leg just above the knee.

The necromancer's scream was deafening, his body convulsing violently as blood pooled around him. His remaining leg jerked instinctively, but there was nothing left to push against.

Tom towered over him, his silhouette stretching across the blood-streaked floor like a shadow of judgment.

"It's over," he said simply. "But you're right about one thing. I've done enough talking."

He raised his sword high over his head.

The Master's mouth opened, maybe to beg, maybe to curse him one last time—

But the blade fell.

A sharp, brutal slice cleaved through flesh, muscle, and bone in a single, merciless stroke. The grotesque sound of the severed neck echoed through the chamber, followed by the heavy clang of metal on stone.

The Master's head rolled, leaving a dark, wet trail in its wake, his lifeless eyes still frozen in an expression of shock and denial.

And just like that—

The nightmare was over.

A heavy silence settled over the room.

The only sound came from the slow drip of blood pooling across the stone floor and the ragged breathing of those still alive.

Groaning, and knowing that his magic wouldn't work on Michael, but he had a feeling it would work on these others… He had been relieved when he noticed that the man's health bar was still present and had stopped falling, which had been making Tom panic for the past few minutes.

Tom raised his hand, pushing the last of his magic into healing the bodies of the fallen. The spell didn't work on all of them. Some were too far gone even for the miracles of the System.

Tom accepted it, and continued on until the ones he could save had risen unsteadily to their feet.

The freed captives—if they could even be called that yet—stared at the mutilated corpse of their former master, their expressions frozen somewhere between horror and disbelief.

None of them spoke.

None of them moved.

Even though the collars had lost their power, even though they were no longer bound by The Master's will, they remained rooted in place, stiff, uneasy, afraid.

But not of The Master.

Of Tom.

One of them—a thin man with sunken eyes—shook his head slowly, as if trying to clear away the reality of what he had just seen. "You..." His voice quivered, barely more than a whisper. "...killed him. Killed *us*..."

Tom glanced down at The Master's mangled remains and those of whom he couldn't extend mercy to in the moment, before looking back up. "Yeah," he said simply. "I did."

The group flinched, as if expecting something worse to follow.

No celebration. No relief.

Just disgust.

A woman near the front wrapped her arms around herself, eyes darting between the bloodied sword in Tom's hands and The Master's severed head lying only a few feet away. Her skin paled, and she looked like she was going to be sick.

Tom could see it in their faces—the way their bodies stayed tense, the way they subconsciously edged away from him, trying to put space between themselves and the man who had butchered their captor.

"You think I'm a monster," Tom said, his voice steady but tired.

No one answered.

He sighed, wiping the blood from his blade before returning it to his Inventory. He didn't want them to see it anymore—to see him holding the weapon that had just ended their master's life.

"You're free," he said firmly, keeping his tone measured, calm. "You're not his property anymore. You don't have to stay here. You don't have to listen to anyone."

A few of them exchanged uncertain glances, but still, no one spoke.

Tom took a slow step forward, keeping his movements deliberate, making sure he didn't do anything sudden that might make them think he was about to hurt them next.

"I know you don't trust me," he continued, meeting their wary gazes one by one. "I get it. You spent who knows how long thinking that listening, obeying, and keeping quiet was the only way to survive. And now, you just watched me..." His voice trailed off, and he exhaled sharply. "...do what I had to do."

Still, no one moved.

His fingers tightened slightly at his sides. He had fought for them. Killed for them. Nearly died for them. And yet, in their eyes, he was just another monster.

It stung more than he expected.

But that didn't matter.

What mattered was getting them out.

"Look," he said, rubbing a hand across his face before leveling them with a steady gaze. "I don't care if you hate me. I don't care if you never want to see me again after this. But I'm going to get those collars off you, and I'm going to get you out of this hellhole."

He reached into his Inventory and pulled out a pair of bolt cutters, holding them up.

"You want to leave? Let me help."

The group hesitated.

Then, finally—one woman stepped forward.

She looked just as wary as the others, but her hands shook as she touched the metal collar around her throat, her fingers brushing against the cold steel.

"It's really over?" she asked, her voice barely above a whisper.

Tom gave a small nod. "Yeah."

A long pause. Then, slowly, she turned her back to him, exposing the lock on her collar.

Tom didn't waste a second.

The metal snapped with a clean crack, the collar falling away from her neck and clattering against the floor.

The woman let out a sharp gasp, her hands flying up to her throat, as if expecting some invisible force to punish her for removing it.

When nothing happened, her breath hitched, her fingers trembling as she felt her own skin without cold metal pressing into it for the first time in years.

The other captives stared.

A few more hesitantly stepped forward.

And then, the rest followed.

Tom and Bohdan worked quickly, breaking off the remaining collars. One by one, the oppressive steel bindings hit the floor, each one a small victory, though no one seemed quite ready to celebrate yet.

Once the last one was gone, Tom let out a slow breath. "Alright," he said. "You're free. You can leave whenever you want, or stay with us if you need a place to go."

Silence.

Then—

"There are more."

Tom's head snapped up, locking eyes with the woman he had freed first.

She swallowed, her voice thick with something between uncertainty and obligation. "There are more of us," she said, glancing toward a heavy wooden door near the back of the room. "He kept them locked up in there. Down the hall."

Tom's expression hardened.

"How many?"

"I don't know. Dozens, maybe more."

Tom didn't hesitate. He rose to his feet, turning to Bron and Bohdan. "Get ready. We're not done yet."

He turned back to the captives, his voice firm but softer than before.

"You don't have to trust me," he said. "But you can help us save them."

WAR

"Bron, can you take out that door?" Tom asked, nodding toward the heavy stone barrier that blocked their way.

Bron, his massive form casting a shadow over the group, gave a curt nod. He strode over to the door, swapping his greataxe for a warhammer that would have looked almost comically oversized in anyone else's hands. Hefting the weapon, he drew it back, muscles rippling, and swung it with all his might. The hammer connected with a deafening crash, sending cracks spider-webbing across the stone surface. With another mighty swing, the door shattered inward, a cloud of dust and debris billowing out.

Tom immediately moved forward, leading the way into the now-exposed hallway beyond. It was dark and narrow, the walls slick with grime. The smell of mildew and unwashed bodies clung to the air like a thick fog. At the end of the corridor was a wooden door, heavily worn and patched in places. Wasting no time, Tom lifted his boot and kicked the door in, sending it flying off its hinges.

Inside was a sight that twisted his stomach.

The room was barely lit by a single dim candle hanging from the ceiling. The floor was littered with filth, the stench of human waste and rotten food thick in the air. Huddled together in the furthest corner were about thirty more people, their eyes wide with fear and exhaustion. They flinched at the sudden intrusion, pressing themselves further back against the cold stone wall, some raising their arms in a futile attempt to shield themselves.

"It's okay," Tom said softly, raising his hands to show he meant no harm. "You're all free now. The Master is dead, and we're here to help you. Come with me, and we'll get those collars off."

For a moment, there was no response, just the sound of ragged breathing and a few muffled whimpers. Then, the woman who had spoken to Tom earlier burst into the room, her face bright with relief. She rushed to one of the huddled figures and enveloped them in a tight embrace.

"It's true! He saved us!" she cried out, turning to the others. "We're free!"

The expressions on the captives' faces shifted from confusion to disbelief and finally to joy as they slowly began to realize what had happened. One by one, they tentatively stood up, testing their newfound freedom, their movements stiff and cautious from days, perhaps weeks, of confinement. They shuffled out of the dark room, some leaning on others for support, all desperate to escape the prison that had held them for so long.

Back in the larger room, Tom and Bohdan went to work, removing the oppressive collars from each of the newly freed captives. As the metal restraints fell to the ground, clattering against the stone floor, many of them wept openly, overcome by the sudden release from their bondage.

"Come with me," Tom said once they were all freed. "We'll bring you somewhere safe where you can clean up, get new clothes, and then you can choose how you want to live your lives."

Tom took the lead, guiding the group back through the winding corridors, retracing their steps past the mangled corpses of the zombies they had fought through earlier. The air was still thick with the stench of decay, the walls smeared with old blood and filth, but for the first time, the path led toward something other than misery.

The former captives followed closely, their movements hesitant, cautious, as if they expected at any moment to be dragged back into the darkness.

Some of them stole glances at the bodies, their expressions a mix of relief and unease. They had spent so long under The Master's rule, under his cruelty, that seeing his forces destroyed so utterly felt unreal.

Step by step, they moved closer to the exit, the air growing less stale, the distant sounds of battle above no longer muffled by thick stone.

The captives they had encountered at the beginning were still at the entrance, dutifully waiting, though they shrunk back from Tom as they took in his appearance. Tom nodded to them before reaching for the door.

And then—

They emerged into the open air.

The moment they stepped outside, sunlight crashed against their skin like a tidal wave.

Several of them flinched, instinctively raising their arms to shield their eyes. Some let out small, startled gasps, as if they had forgotten what the sun felt like.

For some, it was likely the first time in years they had been outside those dank, oppressive walls.

Tom let them take it in, his own gaze sweeping across the battlefield, taking in the wreckage, the bodies, the Guild fighters scattered in the aftermath of war.

But his focus wasn't on the carnage.

It was on what came next.

And with that thought, Tom kept walking, leading the freed captives toward whatever awaited them beyond this fight.

Chapter 58

Hulking Defeat

Derek's arms felt like lead weights.

Every swing of his mace was slower than the last, every breath came harder, his body screaming at him to stop, rest, collapse—but he couldn't. Not yet. Not with that thing still standing.

The Hulking Zombie Abomination loomed over them, a grotesque fusion of flesh, rot, and unholy power. The holy light from the Clerics and Paladins had scorched it, but it refused to fall. Every time they thought they had an advantage, it adapted, shifting its grotesque mass to compensate for the damage.

Another roar shook the battlefield, a sound so deep it rattled Derek's ribs, and he barely had time to throw himself aside as a massive, rotting limb smashed into the ground where he had just been standing. The impact sent a shockwave of dust and broken stone outward, throwing several fighters off their feet.

"How is this thing still moving?!" Chris shouted, slashing at one of the zombie creatures still crawling from the monster's body.

"It shouldn't be!" Derek panted, wiping sweat from his brow. "That last hit should've ended it!"

But it hadn't.

The abomination lurched forward, its movements erratic but no less deadly. The ground beneath them was littered with corpses, both undead and human alike.

Derek stole a glance toward Kiera's sniper team. They had switched from precision shots to rocket launchers, raining explosive fire at the monster. But even that wasn't enough.

Derek gritted his teeth. He could see it on everyone's faces—the creeping edge of hopelessness.

Tom, where the hell are you?

The monster reared back, its twisted maw opening wide, ready to unleash another devastating attack—

And then—

It froze.

For just a second, its entire body spasmed, a violent shudder running through its massive form. Its glowing, corrupted veins pulsed wildly, flickering between unnatural hues, and then—

It lurched forward, collapsing to one knee.

Derek didn't dare breathe.

The battlefield fell into eerie silence, the remaining undead staggering, as if suddenly disoriented.

"What the…?" Chris whispered.

Another violent convulsion rippled through the abomination's form. Its flesh began to rot away at an accelerated rate, its massive limbs shriveling, the arcane energy that held it together beginning to flicker and die out.

Derek took a cautious step forward, still gripping his weapon. "Did we…?"

The abomination let out a gurgling wail—not a roar of defiance, but of dissolution.

Chunks of its own body started falling away, hitting the ground with sickening squelches, its bones cracking under their own weight. The necrotic magic that had given it life was unraveling, dissolving into nothingness.

And then—it collapsed.

A cloud of putrid dust rose as the monstrosity crashed into the ground, its massive form breaking apart as if something had just severed its connection to the world entirely.

For a moment, nobody moved.

Then—

"What the hell just happened?!" Chris asked, his voice sharp with disbelief.

Derek stared at the crumbling remains, his heartbeat pounding in his ears. "I don't know," he admitted. "But I don't think it was us."

Chris wiped sweat and grime from his face, looking around at the other fighters, who were just as stunned as they were. "You think… Tom?"

Derek's gut twisted.

Tom.

Whatever had just happened, it had started from inside the building. That couldn't be a coincidence.

"We need eyes on the entrance," Derek ordered, turning toward the main structure.

The remaining fighters shifted uneasily, the tension not fully lifting despite the abomination's fall. Some of them were too exhausted to think, while others seemed almost afraid to see what would come out of that building next.

Then—

The doors opened.

And out stepped Tom.

At first, it was just Tom—his armor scuffed, his face grim.

Then Bron, Michael, and Bohdan followed, looking just as battered.

But what made the fighters stiffen—what sent a wave of unease rippling through the already shaken group—was the dozens of figures trailing behind them.

The former captives.

Their clothes were tattered, their faces gaunt, their expressions vacant. They didn't look relieved. They didn't look grateful.

They looked haunted.

Derek felt his stomach sink.

Something had happened down there—something worse than anything they'd seen up here.

Tom stopped a few feet away from them, his gaze sweeping across the battlefield, taking in the exhausted fighters, the scattered remains of the abomination, the wary expressions of his allies.

Nobody spoke.

And then—

Chris exhaled, running a hand down his face. "Jesus, man. Took you long enough."

The tension fractured, if only slightly, but Derek could see it—Tom wasn't laughing.

He was processing.

Derek stepped forward, lowering his weapon. "You did this, didn't you?" He gestured to the rotting remains of the abomination.

Tom let out a slow breath. "Yeah."

Chris let out a low whistle, shaking his head. "Well, damn. Whatever you did, remind me never to piss you off."

A few tired chuckles rippled through the remaining fighters, but it was half-hearted, filled more with relief than humor.

Tom's eyes flickered toward the freed captives, and Derek could see it— he wasn't just thinking about the battle.

He was thinking about what came next.

Derek nodded toward the people behind him. "Are they—"

"Alive," Tom confirmed. "That's all I can say for now."

Derek studied him for a long moment before exhaling sharply. "Then let's get the hell out of here."

No one argued.

Without another word, the survivors and fighters began moving, leaving the battlefield behind—but not the weight of what had happened here.

Chapter 59

Aftermath

War Victory Against The Master!

Congratulations, Vanguard! Your Guild's decisive victory against The Master and his forces has earned you the following rewards for all members:

- **XP:** 75,000 (Base 50,000 + 50% bonus for achieving all primary objectives and surviving with 90% of your forces)
- **Item:** 1 random weapon suitable for your Class
- **Monster Cores:** 1 Rare Monster Core

Bonus Reward:
For defeating The Master and liberating his captives, each member also receives:
- **Guild Reputation:** +500
- **Unique Title:** "Liberator of the Enslaved" (Grants a small bonus to Charisma when dealing with freed or enslaved persons)

Continue to bring justice to this world and strengthen the guild!

You Have Defeated an Enemy Guild Leader!

For your pivotal role in defeating the enemy Guild leader, you have earned extra rewards! Continue to lead your troops from the front lines to achieve even greater victories!

- **XP:** 500,000 (Base 250,000 + 100% bonus for dealing the first and final blows personally)
- **Item:** 1 Horn of Retribution (A powerful artifact that can rally your forces and unleash a devastating counterattack)
- **Monster Cores:** 1 Legendary Monster Core

WAR

- Guild Points: 250,000 (Base 150,000 + 66.67% bonus for maintaining over 90% unit survival rate)

Keep leading with valor and reap the rewards of your courageous actions!

Level Up!

You have earned enough XP to advance to the next level. You are now level 30! Continue to work hard and push yourself to gain more XP to continue to level up. You receive 10 Attribute Points to distribute as you see fit.

Level Up!

You have earned enough XP to advance to the next level. You are now level 31! Continue to work hard and push yourself to gain more XP to continue to level up. You receive 10 Attribute Points to distribute as you see fit.

Bonus!

For reaching level 30, you have received the Warlock Skill Dark Shroud. Dark Shroud will allow the user to shroud themselves in darkness, making them 10% harder to hit. As this Skill levels, the percentage will grow as well.

Tom flipped through his notifications in amazement at the rewards he had received. He hadn't even been able to declare war on The Master because they hadn't known what Guild he belonged to—or even if he had managed to form one. But the System seemed to understand the nature of the conflict and dispensed rewards as if it had been a proper Guild war. This was valuable information for the future. He made a mental note to ask Bob about this when they returned to the Guild.

Across the battlefield, spirits were lifting as nearly everyone seemed to have gained at least one new level. It helped soften the blow that they had lost twelve members of their Guild in the battle against the giant undead creature. Derek had given Tom a quick rundown of the events and promised a full report once they were back at the Guild.

Tom felt the immense weight of the losses pressing down on him. Even though each person had chosen to fight alongside him, he couldn't help but feel responsible for their deaths. Derek had tried to console him, reminding him it could have been much worse and that they had saved forty-two people from the collars' control, but it only lifted Tom's spirits a little. He couldn't ignore the guilt gnawing at him.

As Tom walked Derek through the details of what had transpired in The Master's base, others gathered around, eager to hear the story. Tom promised to share the full account after they returned to the Guild. For now, the focus had to be on making sure nothing of value was left on the bodies or in the building. Derek quickly organized teams, and they set off to search the entire compound.

Another group was tasked with escorting the newly freed slaves back to the Guild once all the collars were removed. The ex-slaves were overjoyed to be free and each one wanted to express their gratitude to Tom. Some of his men tried to block them from approaching, but Tom insisted they be allowed through. They came up to him in turns; some shook his hand with vigor, while others embraced him, tears streaming down their faces. Tom made sure to assure each of them that they were now free and safe.

After they had all spoken with him, they were led to the team assigned to escort them back. Tom wanted them to feel comfortable, to know they were no longer under anyone's control. With that settled, he turned his attention to helping with the search.

The zombies, being mindless undead, didn't have much of value on them; most of the spoils were limited to Monster Cores. Inside the base, however, they found a cache of treasures that The Master had hoarded for himself. Unfortunately, the hoard was mostly comprised of things that the System had rendered useless in this new world—diamond rings, large gems, gold bars, coins, and other items that would have been worth a fortune before. These were hidden in a concealed compartment in The Master's quarters.

Bohdan explained that while these items no longer held any monetary value, they could be invaluable for enchanting practice. Enchanters could use them to hone their Skills, adding bonuses that could prove beneficial in future battles. Tom decided to give all the items to Bohdan to take to an Enchanter who could make good use of them.

With the search complete, the remaining forces gathered their fallen comrades and began the journey back to their base. The mood was a complex mix of joy and sorrow. Conversations were mostly light, filled with relief and stories of camaraderie, but there were also quiet moments where they shared memories of those who had given their lives. A more formal celebration of their lives would be held once they were all settled back at the Guild.

Upon their return, Tom, and the rest of the leadership team met in the security room to share the full details of what had happened. Brian had a team ready to receive the dead and wounded, taking them to be either healed or prepared for the evening's memorial service.

"How soon do we hold the service for the fallen?" Tom asked, his voice heavy.

"We'll do it tonight. I had Charlene and her staff prepare a feast. It'll be both a celebration and a memorial," Brian replied as he scanned his notes on a clipboard.

"A feast? What if we had lost?" Tom inquired, surprised by the foresight.

"I figured it would go one of two ways," Brian began, "either you'd win and come back a hero, or you'd all die, they'd come for revenge, and again two scenarios: we win and celebrate, or we all die, and then it wouldn't have mattered what we did before that. After the scuffle at the gates with The Master, my money was on you winning. You really gave him an ass beating that day." Brian smirked at the memory.

"I'm glad you had so much faith in us. I wasn't feeling so sure," Tom admitted, though he couldn't help but smile at Brian's confidence in their victory.

"Thank you for believing in us. I'm sure it helped the others fight harder, knowing someone had that kind of faith in them," Tom said.

"Spirits were high going into the battle. I couldn't have asked for more, truth be told," Derek added. "Everyone fought with determination and a thirst for vengeance."

"Be prepared, Tom. You'll have to give a speech," Brian mentioned, still going through his checklist.

"What? Why me?" Tom asked, caught off guard.

"Because you're the Guild leader. People will expect you to speak to honor the fallen. It's only right," Brian replied.

"He's right," Kedron chimed in. "You led them into battle; and knowing the risks they still followed you. You should speak to their sacrifice."

"I'm giving more eulogies post-apocalypse than I ever did before," Tom grumbled. "Fine, I'll do it. What else?"

"We need to compensate any families for their loss," Brian added, not looking up from his list.

"And how do we do that? Money doesn't mean anything anymore," Tom retorted.

"Maybe with Monster Cores, or a new room. At the very least, some kind of memorial object where we carve their names," Brian suggested.

"Monetary compensation feels meaningless now. But a memorial sounds perfect. We could create a monument where we place the names of all the fallen," Kedron added.

"Alright, let's make it a monument. Do we have someone who can make that?" Tom asked, looking at Brian again.

"The Crafters have been making great strides in their Professions. I'm sure they can handle it," Brian replied. "I heard you gave the spoils to them, too. That'll make them happy, and the rewards from the System should keep the fighters satisfied. I even leveled up from that XP bonus."

"Those rewards were something else. I couldn't believe how much XP we got. And that was on top of the kill XP," Tom commented.

"Alright, it's settled. We'll have the feast and the memorial tonight to honor our victory and the sacrifices made. Now, let's hear exactly what happened from Derek and Tom," Brian said, wrapping up the discussion points.

Derek recounted the day's events, with others chiming in to add their perspectives on their parts of the battle. Jay and Kiera shared details about their respective roles. Derek finished by describing how the giant undead creature had collapsed when Tom killed The Master.

Tom took his turn, detailing the events inside the base, including the maze of rooms, the hidden zombies, and the showdown with The Master. He retold the tale of everything they had to do. How the Master had killed one of the slaves and resurrected them right in front of them.

"Honestly, that bastard got what was coming to him. Maybe he didn't suffer enough," Jay said after Tom finished.

"I didn't want to sink further than I did. I just wanted it to be over. But I wanted him to feel the fear he inflicted on others," Tom said, his anger simmering as he remembered The Master's arrogance.

Their ideals had clashed, and a confrontation had been inevitable. Tom reflected on how simple differences in beliefs could lead to such violent outcomes. It was hard to accept that someone could take things so far, but history had shown that conflicts often erupted over the smallest disagreements.

He snapped out of his thoughts when he noticed everyone was preparing to leave. "I'm going to take a shower and clean up. I'll see you all before the gathering," Tom said, excusing himself.

Back in his room, Tom shed his armor and clothes, stepping into the shower. Jerky, sensing his turmoil, climbed onto his shoulder and nuzzled against his face as warm water cascaded over them both.

"Thanks, buddy. I know you understand. I'm lucky to have found you," Tom said, scratching Jerky behind the horns.

"Master, good," Jerky said in his broken English.

At that moment, Tom's emotions overflowed. His heart, full of love and sorrow, cracked open as he began to cry. The warm water washed away more than just the grime and blood—it also broke down the wall he had built around his feelings, letting them pour out freely.

Chapter 60

Celebrating Goodbye

Returning to the lobby several hours later, Tom felt a sense of relief from the cleansing shower, as if part of the weight on his shoulders had been lifted through the release of his emotions. Earlier, he had been worried about getting through the upcoming ceremony with all the emotions swirling around inside him—the pain of losing members of the Guild and the near loss of control when confronting The Master. Now, with his mind clearer, he felt more in control and ready to face the celebration and memorial ahead.

Guild members were bustling about, moving quickly from one task to another as they worked to make the event special while adding the final touches to the preparations. It had been decided that the gathering would take place in the courtyard to allow for more space; the only other option was the gym, which would have felt like cramming sardines into a ring box to fit everyone in.

Stepping outside, Tom spotted Brian standing just outside the doors, overseeing the arrangements and barking orders with his usual no-nonsense demeanor.

"Yes, the food tables will be over there. No, further! We're going to have a thousand people here trying to get food. We can't have them crowding the doors!" Brian directed, his voice carrying authority as he pointed to where he wanted things placed. "Julias! Why are you arranging flowers? Yes, I know it's a memorial, but really, man? This is the apocalypse! Let it go! No, I don't care what you did before this all happened—don't be daft!" Brian continued to call out as people rushed around, setting up tables and arranging chairs for the elderly or handicapped to sit in.

The courtyard was gradually transforming into a proper venue for a gathering. Tables were being arranged in neat rows, chairs were set up along the perimeter for those who might need to sit, and a large space was cleared in the center for people to mingle and share stories. Colorful banners, scavenged from nearby buildings, added a surprisingly festive touch, fluttering lightly in the breeze.

Seeing Tom exit the building, Brian waved and hurried over, his clipboard clutched to his chest like it was a lifeline.

"Tom! Are you ready for your speech?" Brian asked, his voice filled with hope as he reached him.

"Sure," Tom replied, exhaling slowly. "Still not sure how good I'll be at it, but I'm ready."

"Good! It's important you speak to them as the leader. You got this. They already look up to you, and you've become immensely popular since the dispatching of The Master," Brian said, his tone trying to put Tom at ease.

"Really? Well, I'm glad they supported that decision. I was worried they might think it was a personal vendetta," Tom admitted, glancing down at his shoes, a bit of self-doubt still lingering.

"Not at all. They respect your sense of right and wrong and fully support your call to free those enslaved. No one who's decent wants to see others suffer like that," Brian reassured him.

"Thanks for the encouragement. I needed that," Tom said, offering a grateful smile.

"Don't mention it. Now, just be ready—I'll call you up when it's time for the speech. For now, why don't you rest and get some food before everyone else comes so you can mingle," Brian suggested, gently guiding him toward the tables where the kitchen staff were laying out food.

Moving over to the food area, Tom was greeted with a delicious spread. Several dishes featured Goatamus meat prepared in different ways, accompanied by a variety of fruits, vegetable medleys, and a selection of desserts. The sight and smell reminded him of the award banquets he used to attend in high school. But this time, he wasn't just a guest going up to receive a perfect attendance or honor roll award—this time, he was the leader, the one everyone looked up to. That realization made his nerves tingle, but he focused on letting the excitement drive him forward.

He filled a plate and moved to a table set up for those who couldn't stand for the entire event, savoring every bite of his food. The meat was perfectly tender, with a light glaze that gave it a hint of sweetness, reminiscent of a good barbecue sauce. The Goatamus meat had enough fat to burst with flavor in every bite. Paired with fried potatoes and a sautéed vegetable medley, the meal was a comforting balance of taste and nutrition.

Tom had always been impressed by Charlene's relentless drive to ensure every meal was not only delicious but also nutritious. She put her heart and soul into feeding the Guild, making sure everyone was well taken care of. He knew he had to find a way to express his gratitude to her for all her hard work.

As he finished his meal, a young boy rushed by and took his plate before he could even stand up. "Thanks!" Tom called out to him, smiling at the boy's eagerness to help. Feeling more energized, he moved back to the entrance of the Guild building to begin greeting people. Soon, Guild members began arriving in waves. Each one shook his hand or offered their thanks, their faces lit with smiles. The atmosphere was overwhelmingly positive, though he could see the pain etched on the faces of those who had lost loved ones in the battle—a natural response, he thought.

A line began to form at the tables as the members of Vanguard queued up for food. The kitchen staff stood behind the tables, serving portions and making sure there was enough for everyone. There was chatter everywhere, a lively buzz that filled the courtyard. Tom continued to greet each member as they exited the building. His personal touch seemed to lift spirits even more; he noticed several people looking back at him after they walked away, smiling or whispering to a friend.

Many of the Guild members hadn't personally met him before, and he could see some of them pointing at him, explaining to their companions that they had just met the Guild leader for the first time. He realized he needed to make more of an effort to know everyone, but given the sheer number of members and the constant demands for his attention, he knew it might be a pipe dream.

As the crowd continued to grow, Tom noticed the former captives of The Master arriving together. They had been cleaned up and given new clothing, though many still looked gaunt and appeared jittery, their eyes darting around as if expecting some new threat to emerge. Tom couldn't blame them; the horrors they had endured would leave anyone paranoid and scarred. When they saw him, their faces brightened with recognition and gratitude. They eagerly approached, many trying to speak to him all at once. Rebecca, who was escorting them, gently guided them past Tom when they began to hold up the line with their excitement.

"I know it weighs on you, but we did a good thing in rescuing them, despite the cost," Derek said, walking up behind Tom and placing a comforting hand on his shoulder.

"I know. And that's probably the only reason I'm able to stand here and do this," Tom replied, continuing to greet people as they filed out of the building.

"Good. Because I can't get you out of this one. I'm glad you seem to be handling this better. If you need to talk, we're all here for you," Derek said, pulling Tom around to face him.

Tom paused, locking eyes with Derek, and saw the sincerity and shared pain in his friend's gaze.

"Thanks, Derek," Tom said, pulling him into a tight hug.

As the line dwindled and everyone had been served, Tom looked out over the sea of faces filling the courtyard. It struck him just how many people had chosen to join them in this effort to rebuild something meaningful. His heart swelled with pride. These were people who had decided to work together to make life a bit better, despite all they had been through. In a world that had been torn apart by chaos, they were proving that community, compassion, and cooperation were still possible.

Brian moved to a microphone set up near the building's entrance and began to speak, his voice amplified to reach everyone.

"Thank you all for coming today. We wanted to make sure we showed our appreciation for everything you've done to make Vanguard what it is today. We achieved a great victory, but it came at a cost. One we'll have to ask ourselves if we're willing to make far more often than we would have had to endure before the System. I asked Tom, our Guild leader, if he would be willing to say a few words to you all," Brian said, stepping back and motioning Tom forward. "Tom, if you would."

Tom approached the microphone, taking a deep breath to steady himself. The sight of all those faces, filled with expectation, made his heart race.

"Hello. As Brian said, I'm Tom, for anyone I haven't had the pleasure to get to know better yet. And I'm sorry for that. But I want to do better. I can't tell you how proud I am of everyone here. We've all come together from different places, different lifestyles, and different backgrounds to build something special—a place where we can start to feel safe again, where we can set up a new sense of normal in this world. You all show me that we can be better if we work together," Tom began, his voice gaining strength.

"When someone threatened the peace we strive for, we banded together and rose to meet the challenge. It filled me with pride to see zero hesitation to fight for what we're working to build here. But my heart is heavy with the price that was paid to achieve our victory. Those who gave their lives so that others might be free will never be forgotten. Their legacy will live on in our memories as well as in the lives of those who were spared and set free." Tom paused, scanning the crowd, seeing a mix of grief, admiration, and resolve in their eyes.

"We have a choice in every action we take. Some believe that every decision we make creates new timelines, alternate realities where different choices lead to different outcomes. While I don't know if that's true, I do know that those who fought to give the enslaved a chance at freedom did so knowing the risks. They knew the price might be their lives, but they fought anyway, for something greater than themselves." Taking a deep breath, Tom saw Derek giving him an approving nod from the front row.

"A friend of mine said something recently that really resonated with me, and I'm going to shamelessly steal it for my speech." He waved at Michael. "Thanks, Michael."

The audience laughed.

"That saying is this: freedom is never free. It's paid for with the blood of those willing to stand against tyranny, those who refuse to let others dictate their choices. I know it sounds cliché, but I never truly felt its meaning until recently. I didn't serve in the military, so I didn't see my friends die in combat before the world changed. Now, I've felt that pain. I bear the burden that we all share now— the loss of good people, friends, allies, family. But I urge each of you to remember them and their sacrifices. They were not in vain; they were for our betterment, for our dream of a life where we stand up for each other and become strong together." Tom finished, stepping back from the microphone.

There was a moment of silence before applause started, slowly at first but quickly swelling until people were cheering. Tom could see tears in some eyes, while others looked inspired, fired up as if ready to head back out into battle. He understood that feeling; sometimes, his own anger almost drove him back to violence, a burning desire to avenge those they had lost. But he knew there was no solace in that path, so he tried to find healthier ways to cope with his grief.

"Thanks for speaking, Tom. Now, a few housekeeping items..." Brian began as he went through a list of things that needed to be addressed for the evening.

Tom moved away from the spotlight and grabbed a piece of meat from the serving table. He took a few steps, then turned back and grabbed an extra piece for Jerky. His familiar appeared on his shoulder and eagerly devoured the meat, its little jaws working furiously. Chuckling at the now-armored Quasit, Tom made his way over to the memorial pillar that had been created for the occasion and began reading each of the names engraved on it, taking a moment to honor each fallen Guild member silently.

As the sun dipped lower in the sky and a cool breeze swept through the courtyard, a funeral pyre was constructed close to its center. The bodies of the fallen were respectfully carried out of the building and placed on the logs. Tom, standing at the front with his Guildmates, used his *Eldritch Blast* spell to ignite the pyre. The flames roared to life, casting a warm, flickering light over the gathering, and the entire Guild shared a long moment of silence, heads bowed in memory of those they had lost.

Chapter 61

Party Interruptions

"Okay, everyone. I have a special surprise in store for the evening," Brian announced, his voice amplified through the microphone after the solemn memorial ceremony. "While much looting went on in the city during the initial System integration, I managed to put together a team that hit a liquor store and found a large supply of spirits. I held them back for an occasion just like this. So tonight, we're opening the bar up for drinks in celebration of our first big victory!"

A wave of cheers erupted from the Guild members gathered in the courtyard. The sudden shift from the earlier somber tone to one of celebration was palpable. It was clear that everyone welcomed this momentary escape from the grim realities they faced daily—a chance to let loose and celebrate their hard-won success.

"Please head to the stations around the courtyard to get drinks, and let's begin the real celebration!" Brian concluded. He turned to a makeshift music machine hooked up to a set of speakers and pressed play, filling the air with the upbeat and familiar tune of Journey's "Don't Stop Believin'".

The iconic opening notes resonated throughout the courtyard, and a collective cheer went up as everyone began to sing along. The infectious energy of the song seemed to wash away the remaining shadows of the memorial, transforming the mood into one of camaraderie and joy. Voices harmonized, rising in excitement at the well-loved lyrics, their spirits visibly lifting with each verse.

As the crowd continued to belt out the chorus, the atmosphere morphed into one of unity and pure exhilaration. People began dancing, moving together in a rhythm that spoke to the shared relief of this brief respite from the harsh world outside. Tom stood back, watching the transformation unfold with a smile tugging at his lips.

Nothing brings people together quite like a sing-along, Tom thought to himself, his grin widening as he watched the crowd sway and sing with abandon.

Following Journey's anthem, the unmistakable tune of Neil Diamond's "Sweet Caroline" began to play, prompting another uproar of excitement. As if by instinct, everyone shouted the famous "bah, bah, bah" in unison. People threw their arms over each other's shoulders, swaying side to side as if they were long-time friends at a karaoke bar, rather than survivors of an apocalypse. The sense of unity and shared experience was palpable, radiating from every corner of the courtyard.

With the drinks flowing freely, the night continued to evolve. Tom and a select team of security remained sober, keeping vigilant in case of an unforeseen attack. But for most, the evening was about releasing pent-up tension. The playlist rolled on, featuring songs like "I'm Sexy and I Know It," "Uptown Funk," and "Party Rock Anthem," which brought the crowd together in laughter and dance. People gathered in the middle of the courtyard, dancing with wild enthusiasm as their inhibitions faded into the night.

The energy shifted again as the playlist moved to group dances. The beats of "The Electric Slide" and "Cha Cha Slide" had nearly everyone joining in, forming lines and moving in sync, step-by-step. Even those who were shy or unsure couldn't help but be pulled in by the infectious spirit of the dance. And when Garth Brooks' "I've Got Friends in Low Places" came on, it was as if the entire courtyard turned into a single, unified choir. Long lines of people linked arms, swaying and shouting the lyrics with all their might.

Tom continued to stand back and watch, leaning against a wall as he took it all in. He saw people of all walks of life—farmers, teachers, former office workers, and students—coming together, united by this brief, precious moment of joy in a world now riddled with danger. His heart filled with pride. These were the moments worth fighting for, the flashes of humanity that made all the struggles worthwhile. He caught sight of James near the dance floor, singing his heart out with a drink in hand, moving with the others to the beat. Tom smiled, his chest tightening with an emotion he couldn't quite place—a mixture of pride, nostalgia, and perhaps a little envy.

"He does a pretty good job with parties, doesn't he?" Derek's voice cut through Tom's thoughts as he joined him, leaning against the wall with a casual ease.

"You' re not partaking?" Tom asked, giving Derek a curious look.

"Nah. I gave up alcohol a long time ago," Derek replied, his eyes still scanning the crowd. "Besides, I figured you could use some company."

Tom nodded, appreciating the gesture. "I'm trying to enjoy this, but it's hard, you know? I feel like we've accomplished something great, but then my mind keeps drifting to the next challenge. I have no idea how we're going to deal with Shandra."

Derek nodded, understanding. "I get it. The fight never really ends. When you're in a place where the normal rules of society have been thrown out the window, you try to hold onto the good moments. But there's always another threat lurking around the corner. I went through it when I was deployed in Iraq," he said, his voice tinged with memories of a different kind of battlefield.

Tom turned to him, curious. "What did you do to keep going?"

Derek paused, his gaze distant for a moment. "Mostly what you see here," he said, gesturing to the crowd. "We had drinks on base, or we went to bars in safe cities when we could. Celebrations like this keep morale high. A man can endure almost anything if he knows there's hope on the other side. Right now, they have hope," Derek said, nodding toward the people singing and dancing.

Tom watched the crowd for a moment, taking in Derek's words. "I wish I could feel the same level of excitement they do," he admitted, his shoulders sagging slightly under the weight of his responsibilities.

"So did the commanding officers," Derek continued. "They had to be the realists, always looking ahead, always planning for the next fight. It's a heavy burden, but if we keep morale high, we can overcome just about anything. Just remember not to lose sight of what we've accomplished. These people all have a safe place to live and grow. That's no small feat, considering what we've been through."

"That's true," Tom agreed, nodding slowly. "It's good to be reminded of how far we've come, especially when there are dark clouds looming ahead."

He thought back to their first days in this strange, new world. He and James had panicked, jumping into his car and running over anything green and moving, terrified out of their minds. He chuckled softly, remembering how scared he had been back then—how weak those monsters seemed now compared to what they faced regularly. He couldn't help but shudder to think what might have happened if they had encountered some of the larger beasts they'd fought more recently.

"We'll get through this," Derek said during a lull in the conversation. "We're so much stronger now."

"Yeah," Tom replied, his mind drifting. "And then we have the space pirates to look forward to."

Derek laughed, shaking his head. "See, that's what I'm talking about. You're focused on what's next when you should be focused on now. Worry about that tomorrow. Be present in this moment."

Tom smirked, realizing Derek was right. "Yeah, yeah, I know. I just can't stop thinking about it."

"Life's a balancing act," Derek said, his voice calm and wise. "You can't lose sight of the bigger picture, but if that's all you focus on, you'll lose sight of the present and you'll spiral."

The sun had set a while ago, and Brian's team had set up strings of lights over the courtyard. The warm glow bathed the party in a cozy ambiance, creating a scene that felt like a late-night backyard gathering on a perfect summer evening. Shadows danced along the ground as people moved about, their laughter and chatter filling the air.

"Thanks for checking in with me," Tom said, breaking the comfortable silence that had settled between them. "I feel like we're so busy all the time, I forget to stop and smell the roses."

"Anytime," Derek replied, his smile sincere. "And don't keep your feelings bottled up. Let us help share the burden. We're all here for you." He gave Tom a reassuring pat on the back. "Now, if you'll excuse me, I'm going to check the walls."

As Derek walked off toward the perimeter, Tom continued to lean against the wall, watching the party unfold. The joy on his Guildmates' faces was infectious. Suddenly, he saw Derek pause and put a finger to his ear, listening intently. His expression shifted to one of concern, and he turned back to Tom.

"Teams on the wall have spotted movement outside. Let's go investigate, but stay cool. We don't want to panic anyone here just yet," Derek said, gesturing for Tom to follow.

Tom nodded and pushed off the wall, walking as casually as he could to avoid drawing attention. They reached the wall and climbed the stairs to meet one of the security guards on watch.

"Report," Derek said firmly, his eyes already scanning the darkness outside the walls.

"We spotted someone moving in the shadows. Probably just Stormcrusher spies keeping an eye on things, but with everyone distracted, we didn't want to take any chances," the guard explained.

"Good call. Where did you last see them?" Derek asked, his eyes still sweeping the dimly lit landscape.

"Just to the right of that building there. In the alley," the guard said, pointing across the street.

"I'll check it out," Tom offered, moving swiftly and hopping down off the wall.

"No, Tom… never mind," Derek sighed, knowing it was futile to try and stop him. In fact, the infuriating man was already disappearing from sight.

"Is he always like that?" the guard asked, watching Tom land and move quickly toward the building.

"Yup. A man of action," Derek replied with a smirk, staring off at their hapless Warlock chieftain. "Good leadership quality, bad strategy."

Landing softly in a crouch to absorb the impact, Tom crept across the street, his eyes locked on the darkened alley. He didn't expect to find anything, but his senses were on high alert. His breath caught when a figure stepped out of the shadows, a man cloaked in black from head to toe, with a mask covering all but his eyes.

"Hello, Tom," the man said calmly.

Tom's muscles tensed, ready for a fight. "And who might you be?"

"Now, now, calm down. I'm not here for a fight," the man responded, raising his hands in a gesture of peace. "My name is Sean, and I have a message from Shandra."

Tom blinked, surprised by the civility in Sean's tone, so unlike Shandra's usual brute force approach. "Go on," he said cautiously.

"She wishes to send her congratulations on eliminating The Master and his forces. She also extends one more invitation to join Stormcrushers before it's too late," Sean explained, his voice surprisingly refined, almost cultured.

Tom scoffed, crossing his arms over his chest. "And why would I do a thing like that? We just took out a Guild with minimal casualties, and now she wants us to submit to her tyrannical rule?"

"Shandra simply wishes to avoid further bloodshed. She's offering you a position at her side, leading your people to a more peaceful time," Sean continued. "Wouldn't you like to end all this fighting? To work together to rid this city of the plague that has fallen over it?"

Tom raised an eyebrow, unimpressed. "And how exactly does she plan to rid the city of whatever plague she thinks she can fix? The System created this chaos. We can't undo that."

"With your people working alongside ours, we can push the monsters out of the city," Sean replied, though his confidence seemed to waver slightly.

Tom let out a humorless laugh. "Did any of you actually read the tutorial? Monsters are random spawns due to the mana concentration in the area. Even if you kill every monster here, more will spawn by morning."

Sean hesitated, his brow furrowing as he considered Tom's words. Sensing an opportunity, Tom pressed further.

"Look, it sounds like she's not giving you the full picture. Maybe she's looking for a patsy to find real answers," Tom suggested. "How about I make you an offer? Join us. Leave Shandra. We have creature comforts here you can only dream of with her lot."

Sean seemed genuinely conflicted now, his eyes darting around as if searching for an answer in the shadows.

"It can't be easy living without power, probably surviving off rations. We have a Rogue team that would welcome someone like you," Tom added, trying to entice him further.

Sean paused, clearly torn. "I'll need time to think about it," he finally said. "Shandra would put out an immediate hit on me if I left."

"It just means you'd fit right in with the rest of us." Tom chuckled, nodding. He sensed that he was close. "We've defended against every attack so far. Stay here, and we'll keep you safe. Did I mention everyone gets a mattress?"

Sean's eyes widened slightly. "A real mattress?"

"Yep. And hot meals," Tom continued, adding just a bit more bait. "You'll even get personal training."

Sean looked down, considering his options for a long moment. Finally, he looked back up, a determined look in his eyes.

"Deal."

Chapter 62

Insight

Tom escorted Sean to the gates of the Vanguard base and called for them to be opened. The heavy metal gates groaned and slid back from the inside, creating a metallic grinding sound that cut through the night air. Tom walked in first, his eyes scanning the courtyard for any signs of concern. The sudden movement of the gate caught everyone's attention; the lively activities of the party came to a halt as all eyes turned toward the entrance, the music still playing softly in the background.

Sean leaned in close to Tom, his voice barely above a whisper.

"This is what you do with your time?" His tone was laced with curiosity, his eyes darting around the scene of celebration.

"It's not what it looks like..." Tom began, trying to find the right words to explain, but Sean cut him off before he could finish.

"This is fantastic!" Sean's voice, once low and skeptical, suddenly rose with genuine excitement. "That uptight Shandra would never have allowed us to cut loose like this!" His tone was filled with an almost childlike glee.

Tom paused mid-stride and turned his head to stare at Sean, a mixture of surprise and confusion on his face. Though Sean's features were mostly hidden beneath his dark hood and mask, the twinkling in his eyes was unmistakable. It was like watching someone see sunlight for the first time after years underground. Tom continued to observe as Sean pulled his hood back, revealing hair that had gone prematurely gray, and removed the mask covering his face. His face was thin but not unhealthy; his nose slightly pointed, giving him a sharp, fox-like appearance, and his jawline was strong and defined. As he turned to Tom, he smiled—a genuine, broad smile that lit up his face. A single tear rolled down his cheek, catching Tom off guard.

"You don't know what it's like out there," Sean said, his voice trembling slightly. "To see people happy here, enjoying themselves in a semblance of what life used to be like... I'm just lost for words." His voice broke on the last word, and he quickly wiped the tear away with the back of his hand.

Tom felt a pang of sympathy, recognizing the emotional weight behind Sean's words. "Well, you're home now," he said softly, his voice filled with understanding. "None of that matters anymore."

Tom turned his attention to the rest of the Guild members, who were still staring, confused about what was happening. Their faces ranged from curious to cautious, each one trying to make sense of the unexpected guest in their midst.

"Everyone," Tom called out loudly, his voice echoing across the courtyard, "this is Sean. He'll be joining the Guild. Please treat him like the family we all have become."

A wave of applause and cheers erupted from the crowd, glasses raised high in a gesture of welcome. The atmosphere shifted again, from uncertainty to acceptance. People were quick to approach Sean, offering introductions, pats on the back, and even a few hugs.

But amidst the celebration, Derek's voice broke through the commotion, cutting sharply with an unmistakable urgency.

"Tom, a word," he said in a tone that brooked no argument.

He led Tom away from the crowd, his face a mask of concern. A few of the more curious Guild members continued to gather around Sean, offering him a drink and peppering him with questions.

Once they were about a dozen paces away, Derek turned to Tom, his eyes blazing with intensity.

"What do you think you're doing?!" he whispered harshly, his tone a mixture of frustration and incredulity.

Tom raised an eyebrow, genuinely perplexed by Derek's reaction. "I'm introducing the newest member of the Guild to the others," he replied, his voice calm but firm.

Derek's expression hardened. "Did you invite him, and he accepted?" he questioned, his eyes narrowing.

Realization dawned on Tom. "Oh! No, I haven't done that yet." Quickly, he pulled up the Guild tab of his interface, his fingers moving swiftly across the screen. Within seconds, he sent Sean an official invite to join the Guild.

Across the courtyard, Sean's eyes unfocused briefly as the notification appeared in his vision. A moment later, his face lit up with a wide smile, and he looked back at Tom with a nod of approval. Almost simultaneously, Tom received a confirmation message that Sean had accepted the invite.

"There, now he's a part of Vanguard. Thanks for catching that," Tom said, giving Derek a grateful nod and turning to leave.

But Derek wasn't finished. He grabbed Tom by the elbow, his grip firm.

"Oh, we are *far* from done. Do you even know who that is?!" Derek demanded, his voice a harsh whisper.

"Sure do. He's Sean, the leader of Shandra's spies," Tom replied nonchalantly.

"*Just* the leader of the enemies' spies, he says! That doesn't give you any reason to suspect anything?" Derek pressed, leaning in closer, his frustration evident as he tried to lead Tom to the logical conclusion.

Tom sighed, his shoulders slumping slightly. "You want me to toss him out because he might have ulterior motives, don't you?"

Derek's eyes bore into Tom's.

"That's one of the many thoughts that crossed my mind the instant I knew he worked for Shandra," he said, his hands now on his hips, his posture tense with defiance.

Tom leaned in closer, his tone softer but still resolute. "*Worked* for Shandra. Now he works for us."

Derek didn't budge. "And how do we know this isn't a ploy to get information from us and send it back to her? What if he's just getting close to assassinate someone?" His eyes flicked over to the crowd, gesturing subtly to the partygoers.

Tom nodded, acknowledging the concern. "The thought crossed my mind too, but I can't explain it—something tells me this is real. They don't have electricity over there. Shandra is a complete tyrant, as we already know, and Sean seemed genuinely unhappy. I couldn't turn him away if there was a chance he could help us. Besides, if he is sincere, we could use his knowledge."

Derek's face remained stony, but Tom could see the gears turning behind his eyes. He continued to stand there for a long moment, his facial expressions shifting as he weighed the risks.

"You know I trust you, right?" Derek asked, his voice softer now, almost pleading.

Tom nodded. "I do."

"Then I need to verify this. We can't just assume the best and not prepare for the worst," Derek said, his voice steady but tinged with concern as he turned slightly away, crossing his arms over his chest in contemplation.

Tom smiled, knowing they balanced each other out. "And this is why we're in this together. You, the ever-pessimistic watchdog always looking out for us; me, the overly optimistic guy always trying to help; and James—the one who keeps looking at the glass asking who drank his booze." Tom chuckled, trying to lighten the mood.

"Sean! Can you come over here?" Tom called out.

Sean looked up from where someone had just offered him a drink. Seeing Tom's wave, he excused himself from the group and walked over to where Tom and Derek were standing.

"Hey, what's up? Everything alright?" Sean asked, his tone friendly but cautious.

Tom gestured to Derek. "This is Derek. He's my general in the Guild. He manages all the forces and ensures we don't do stupid things. He's raising the obvious concern. Can you give us some additional assurances of your change of heart? I hate to ask, but I hope you understand why there might be some worry."

Sean nodded, not at all surprised by the question. "No worries. I figured this would come up." He paused, gathering his thoughts. "Shandra is losing control over there. People are leaving left and right, and those who are staying are only doing so out of fear—especially after she killed that guy she caught trying to sneak out the other day."

Derek's eyes narrowed. "If people are leaving, why haven't we seen anyone else looking to join us?"

Sean shrugged slightly. "Most are trying to get as far away from her as possible. They're not going to hang out near the lion's den; they're leaving the city altogether, going into hiding. She's been forcing us to hunt down the others.

I was planning to bail soon myself and skip town, but Tom's offer was too good to pass up."

Derek, still skeptical, asked, "And now that you've left, she's obviously going to know you're gone. What's she likely to do next?"

Sean's eyes flickered with realization. "Oh, she's gonna lose her shit. She'll probably lash out at something… like you guys… oh shit."

"Oh shit is right," Derek agreed. "Sean, you come with me. We're going to the security office to talk about her forces. Tom, you need to shut this party down, get everyone inside, try to sober them up, and get them ready."

Tom started to protest. "Aw, but they're having such a good time—"

"Tom," Derek interrupted in that stern, parental tone that left no room for negotiation.

Tom sighed but quickly switched to leadership mode. "Yeah, yeah, I know. At least make sure you see about having Sean go be a double agent for us."

"That won't actually be possible. See, Guild leaders get notifications when people leave the Guild. It made Shandra pissed when she saw them. So, I don't want to go back in there knowing she'll want me dead for betraying her," Sean explained.

"Fuck. Alright, fine. Everyone! We gotta shut the party down. I know, I know, but this is for safety. There might be an attack coming in the not-too-distant future, and we can't be caught out here partying. Brian, get the music shut off and meet with Derek in the security office! Kiera, Jay, Kevin, Kirsten, and Michael, help me get everyone to the cafeteria. Kedron, get your team and help with tear down from the party. Charlene, we need coffee!"

The music cut off abruptly, and the atmosphere shifted from festive to urgent. People began to move inside, sensing the seriousness of Tom' s tone. Not a single cry of disappointment was heard; they knew the dangers they faced and moved with purpose. Some, more drunk than others, staggered but still found their way toward the building.

Tom stayed behind to make sure everyone got in safely. He continued to oversee the efforts, helping take down tables and load them onto carts to be brought inside. Once the courtyard was cleared, he made his way to the security office. Inside, Brian and Derek were deep in conversation with Sean, who was gesturing animatedly as he explained the current situation. Brian was taking notes furiously.

"So, what did I miss?" Tom asked, pulling up a chair and sitting down with a grunt.

"A lot, actually," Derek replied, sounding more surprised than frustrated. "I don't have any way of substantiating what he says, but it sounds right. We've got intel on pretty much everyone there."

"Of course you can't verify anything," Sean chimed in with a slight smirk. "If you did, I'd have been terrible at my job."

"TJ," Derek called out to one of the guards nearby, "double up the guards on rotation for now. We need eyes out there. Sean's defection will have been a big blow to Shandra's ego. She's likely to do something rash."

"You got it," TJ said as he moved to the radio to relay the orders.

"Well, I'll be the first to say it—I think this was actually a good idea," Derek admitted, though begrudgingly. "I don't like it, and I would've preferred to be consulted, but I think we have a pretty good chance of taking Shandra down."

"Great, though I'd like to minimize the casualties," Tom added.

"I… I can't promise that, Tom. We have to strike them while they're in disarray," Derek countered.

"Then we aren't hitting them now. Sean said a lot of people want to leave. I don't want them dead because they got stuck in a bad situation. That's not okay," Tom said firmly.

Derek sighed, rubbing his temples. "See what I have to deal with?" he muttered to Sean.

Sean chuckled, nodding. "I'm beginning to. And honestly, I feel more and more like I made the right decision listening to him. Shandra wouldn't have hesitated to crush you. But that's part of why the Guild is so unhappy and beginning to crumble."

"So, what do we know, then?" Tom asked, steering the conversation back on track.

"There are only a few people we really need to be wary of," Derek began. "Shandra herself, obviously. Keith, the Barbarian—"

Tom snorted. "What's with everyone with a K name being a Barbarian?"

"No idea. I don't think that means anything, though it's odd. Anyway, there's also Claude, who's a wizard, and Bill, who's a Cleric. These make up Shandra's core team. Sean was a part as well, but we know what happened there. Keith is loyal to a fault. He won't ever leave Shandra's side. Claude and Bill though…" Derek trailed off, looking to Sean for more information.

"They could go either way," Sean continued. "Though Bill is a complete ass."

"Okay. I'm good with not relying on winning them over. How many people are left in the Guild?" Tom asked.

"About a hundred and fifty. Give or take. A lot are lower levels, comparatively speaking of course, but many are not. Honestly, most left are those who are looking to gain favor with Shandra and are no loss to society, if you catch my meaning," Sean said, trying to be helpful.

Tom nodded thoughtfully, his mind racing through possible strategies. "What was it you did before this all happened, Sean?" he asked, a sudden curiosity piqued.

"Umm, well, I worked for the FBI. I was stationed in Fort Worth, but I had business with the Dallas Police the day of the integration," Sean replied.

Tom's eyes widened. "Seriously? Damn, that's cool," he said, genuinely impressed. "So, you did all this stuff before and just continued here?"

Sean chuckled. "I was more focused on solving crimes, but I had a lot of connections and learned how to use them. So, kind of?" He smirked. "And before you ask, no, there is no Mulder or Scully."

Tom burst out laughing. "Well, that's too bad. And exactly what they would want you to think."

Sean laughed uneasily, not sure how to take Tom's joke.

"You'll get used to that. It's how a lot of people cope around here," Derek interjected. "If we could get back to the issue at hand?"

"Sure, sure. Go on," Tom conceded, still chuckling.

"Now, with roughly one hundred and fifty people, we could likely crush them easily. The team with Shandra is the wild card. We could lose a lot of people taking them down. So, we have to get them alone," Derek explained.

"But we don't want to kill everyone," Tom said, thinking aloud. "We need to force a meeting. With her whole Guild."

Derek looked at him skeptically. "And just how do you propose we do that?"

Tom's face broke into an evil grin. "We fire a cannonball across her port bow."

Derek frowned. "Tom." He drew the word out in warning. "You know I don't like it when you start in on the pirate lingo."

Tom's grin could have put Davy Jones to shame.

Chapter 63

Artillery

"Avast, ye land-lubbers!" the Warlock-pirate shouted, his voice echoing down into the depths of the Guild house.

Tom descended the stairs in the lobby to the basement early the next morning, his footsteps echoing off the walls in the stillness. Even though nothing had happened overnight from the Stormcrushers, the tension was still palpable in Vanguard. Security measures remained tight, and the air was thick with a mix of anxiety and readiness. As Tom reached the expansive underground space, he saw Roland, the large Smith, hammering away on a new project. Sweat glistened on Roland's muscled arms as he focused intently on his work, his hammer strikes ringing like a steady drumbeat in the dimly lit basement.

Tom raised a hand in greeting and called out a friendly, "Yo-ho!"

Roland barely paused, looking up just long enough to offer a quick wave before returning his attention to the red-hot metal on his anvil. His silence spoke volumes; whatever he was working on was important enough to keep him from his usual jovial banter.

Tom frowned.

Must be an important project, he thought, smiling to himself as he continued through the basement. He didn't want to interrupt the giant Smith at his craft, knowing full well how Roland could get when he was in the zone.

As Tom made his way toward the back half of the basement, Herbert came bounding over, almost colliding with him in his excitement. Herbert's face was alight with a manic energy that made his wild, curly hair seem to vibrate.

Tom approached the man with a rolling gait.

"Is that…?" Herbert squinted. "What *is* that?"

"Dead men tell tails!" squawked Jerky, who was perched on Tom's shoulder. Its head was snapping around as though searching for enemies. "Jerky no see any tails here…" the Quasit muttered, not quite under its breath. It pecked mulishly at Tom as it pouted. "You said there be tails." The Quasit fluffed its own tail to serve as an example.

Jerky was shapeshifted into the form of a parrot, only…

"Are those… *teeth* inside that bird's beak?" Herbert said, confusedly scratching his head. "And how many eyes is a parrot supposed to have?"

Tom couldn't help smiling at his familiar.

Jerky—bless the Quasit's soul. Tom mentally chuckled, remembering the last few hours. *He really did try to take on a picture-perfect form of a macaw. Only, this version has a startling purple hue, and yes—the teeth and extra eyes are rather disconcerting to boot.* Tom smiled. *I tried to tell him, but I'll be damned if he wasn't convinced that he had 'inside intel' on 'parrots.'*

Tom later found that the 'intel' was a rather well-made if... *eccentric* child's drawing of a bird. The Warlock took another look at his preening familiar.

He actually nailed it, honestly, Tom admitted, if only to himself.

"It's 'dead men tell *no* tales,'" Tom corrected, scratching Jerky on his neck.

"That make no sense," Jerky replied, clacking its beak. "How dead man tell if creature has tails?" The bird paused, clearly thinking. "Why dead man care at all?"

Tom smiled, his shoulders shaking as he held in his laughter.

"Nevermind your strange bird," Herbert waved off the distracting antics. His eyes were bright with fanaticism. "Are you here for the testing?" he nearly shouted, practically bouncing up and down like a child on too much sugar.

"I am, but I don't see how we're going to test them down here," Tom replied, his brow furrowing with concern as he looked around the cluttered space filled with crates, machinery, and the scent of metal and oil.

Herbert grinned, a mischievous twinkle in his eyes. "Oh, we aren't. We'll be taking the elevators up to the site for testing," he explained, nodding toward the far side of the basement where a set of industrial elevators stood.

"Walk the plank!" Jerky chimed in.

Tom raised an eyebrow, a bit annoyed. "Well then, why couldn't I have just met you up there?"

Herbert's grin widened, and his tone took on a mockingly innocent quality. "Because then you wouldn't have been able to help carry the ammunition," he replied, his voice tinged with a 'duh' implication that made Tom roll his eyes.

"You don't need me to carry anything. You have a blasted Inventory, Herbert," Tom quipped back, crossing his arms.

Herbert suddenly stopped rummaging through a nearby crate and turned toward Tom, a sly smile spreading across his face.

"Oh, really? Well then, Mr. Bigshot Inventory, go ahead—put it in your Inventory." He gestured dramatically at a massive crate lying on the floor.

Curious, Tom stepped closer and peered inside. His eyes widened, and his jaw dropped. Inside was a bullet, scaled up to a monstrous six feet in length, looking like something out of a sci-fi movie.

It was easily the size of a small tree trunk.

"Holy fuckin' shit," Tom breathed out in disbelief, staring at the oversized projectile.

Herbert's grin turned into a full-blown smirk. "Yeah, so if you'd like to get to using those muscles, I'd really appreciate it," Herbert said, his voice almost sing-song. "We don't have the right equipment down here for the transport we'd normally use in a warehouse. So, you're my workhorse."

Tom shot him a glare, feeling a mixture of irritation and embarrassment. He did not want to be lugging this giant artillery round up several flights of stairs, but he couldn't see a better option. The thing was too big for any of their elevators to handle in one piece without someone guiding it.

"Fine," Tom grumbled. "We just need the one?" He positioned himself to lift the massive ammunition, mentally preparing for the weight.

"No, we have two, but I have Kevin here to help us take the other one," Herbert replied casually, his focus already shifting back to his crate.

"Kevin's here?" Tom asked, glancing around the busy basement, half-expecting Kevin to suddenly pop out from behind a pile of scrap metal.

"Not yet, but he will be shortly. Now come on, lift with your back, not your legs," Herbert called out, already moving away toward the stairs.

"Isn't it supposed to be the other way around?" Tom shouted after him, his voice dripping with sarcasm.

"I don't know; I'm more of an equipment doctor, not a people doctor," Herbert called back over his shoulder without missing a beat.

Just as Tom positioned himself to lift, Herbert turned back, almost as if remembering something crucial. "Oh, and don't drop it. It needs to stay intact so it doesn't damage the barrels." He said one last thing with an overly casual air, "Also, they're explosive, naturally."

Tom's eyes widened, his stomach dropping as the implication sank in.

"Fantastic," he muttered to himself, carefully getting his arms under the massive round.

It was heavier than he anticipated but still manageable with his enhanced strength, thanks to the points he'd invested in Strength since the System integration. *Thank God I put points in Strength,* he thought as he hoisted it up onto his shoulder like a hefty log.

Tom paused mid-struggle, sweat already forming at his brow.

"Wait… why the hell am I doing this myself?"

He shook his head at his own stupidity, then quickly wove his hands through the familiar summoning pattern. Moments later, Bron materialized, his massive form towering over Tom.

Bron blinked lazily, looking down at him. "What now?"

Tom gestured at the ridiculously heavy shell he had just set down. "Hey, Bron, could you carry this for me?"

Bron looked at the object. Then at Tom.

Then back at the object.

Then snorted loudly through his trunk. "Oh. I see. So now I'm just a beast of burden?"

Tom rolled his eyes. "No, it's just really—"

"No."

Tom blinked. "Wait, what?"

Bron crossed his arms, looking entirely too amused. "It will be good training for you. If you can't lift that, then what good is that oversized toothpick you call a sword?"

Tom gawked at him. "Dude. Really?"

Bron didn't even bother responding—he just leaned against the wall, arms still crossed, and began examining his nails like they contained the secrets of the universe.

Tom let out a long, suffering sigh. "Unbelievable."

Still muttering under his breath, he bent down and hefted the shell onto his shoulder again, groaning as he adjusted its weight.

Bron didn't move. Didn't react. Didn't even acknowledge him.

Until—

"Good form," he said dryly.

Tom shot him a glare.

Bron just grinned.

As he made his way up the stairs, he noticed Kevin descending toward him, his face breaking into a grin when he saw Tom. "Hey, Tom!" Kevin shouted, waving energetically. "That is one giant bullet!" Kevin's eyes gleamed with fascination as he got closer, practically drooling over the sight of the artillery round.

"You like ammunition?" Tom asked, somewhat surprised by Kevin's enthusiasm.

Kevin shook his head, still marveling at the oversized round. "No, but I like explosions, and this one looks like it'll make a doozy!"

Tom chuckled, shaking his head. "Well, there's one more in a crate somewhere near the smithy. Can you grab it and bring it up to wherever this demo is taking place?"

Kevin nodded enthusiastically. "Oh, I know where it's going. I helped bring up the other parts. Third from the top floor. I'll meet you there."

With that, he jogged off, his excitement palpable as he went to retrieve the second round.

Tom continued up the stairs, grumbling under his breath, "Feels like everyone knows what's going on except me."

When he finally reached the lobby, Herbert was already waiting impatiently by the elevators, his foot tapping rapidly against the floor.

With a grunt, Tom maneuvered the massive round into a vertical position to fit it into the elevator. The doors slid shut, and Tom felt the familiar sensation of his stomach dropping as the elevator began its ascent.

When they reached the designated floor, a soft chime sounded, and the elevator doors slid open. Tom stepped out and immediately froze, his eyes widening in disbelief. The scene before him looked like something straight out of a military action film. At each of the four corners of the floor stood small freight elevators, each one just the right size to accommodate the massive artillery round he carried. The entire space buzzed with activity; men and women in uniforms and utility belts rushed around, checking various pieces of machinery and monitoring control panels. The air was filled with the hum of generators and the low rumble of mechanical systems coming to life.

Near one of the elevators, two shirtless Barbarians, their muscles bulging and glistening with sweat, stood waiting for orders. They were imposing figures, well over six feet tall.

"When the hell did you have time to build all this?!" Tom exclaimed, his voice filled with a mix of awe and disbelief. His gaze darted around the room, taking in the complex web of machinery and the scale of the operation.

Herbert turned to him, beaming with pride. "Oh, *I* didn't build these," he said with a grin. "I just provided the blueprints, and our team got to work. These are part of our new defense system," he continued, patting one of the elevators affectionately as if it were a prized racehorse. "I got the idea when the Space Pirates announcement came through and figured we'd need something hefty to defend our territory. We've only now finalized the design and manufacturing. Today's the first trial run."

Tom's eyes sparkled with a mix of excitement and curiosity. His mind raced with the possibilities these massive weapons presented.

"Can… I fire one?" he asked, his voice almost childlike in its enthusiasm.

"No," came the immediate, flat response from Herbert, his tone brooking no argument.

Tom's shoulders sagged with disappointment. "What? Why not?" he asked, his earlier excitement now replaced with a tinge of frustration.

"Because these are *military-grade* weapons," Herbert explained, his expression turning serious. "And I need someone familiar with them at the controls. Nick will be handling the firing." He glanced over his shoulder and nodded toward the stairs leading up. "I'll introduce you to him in a moment when we get upstairs. For now, just give these gentlemen your round."

Tom nodded, still feeling a bit deflated but understanding the logic. He walked over to the Barbarians, who towered over him, their eyes sizing him up with a mixture of curiosity and respect. He carefully handed the enormous bullet to the larger of the two, who accepted it without a word. The Barbarian placed the heavy round into the waiting elevator. The door closed with a heavy thud, and a deep, mechanical whirring filled the air as the lift ascended. Moments later, the chime sounded again, and the lift returned to their level. The second Barbarian, just as large and imposing as the first, hefted a massive cardboard cylinder—another piece of the artillery system—and loaded it into the elevator before sending it up to the floor above.

"Follow me," Herbert said, gesturing for Tom to accompany him. His steps were quick, his demeanor suggesting that he was eager to show off his latest creation.

As they climbed a set of metal stairs in the center of the room, Tom noticed the scent of machine oil and fresh paint hanging in the air. The stairwell was narrow, and the sound of their boots echoed off the steel walls. When they reached the top, Tom stepped out onto a floor where all of the windows had been removed, replaced by heavy steel beams to hold up the next level, but still providing a view of the outside. At each of the four corners of the building stood massive twin-barreled turrets, their dark barrels gleaming ominously in the sunlight.

Tom' s mouth fell open in slack-jawed wonder at the sheer size of the weapons. Each turret was mounted to a reinforced platform, bolted securely into the structure of the building. The barrels were at least twenty feet long, the steel reinforced to withstand the immense pressure and heat of a high-caliber discharge. The sight of them, jutting out over the city, was both awe-inspiring and terrifying. They looked like something ripped straight from the deck of a battleship and planted atop a skyscraper.

"Impressive, aren't they?" Herbert said with a hint of smug satisfaction. "Let me introduce you to Nick. He's our gunnery specialist and the one in charge of overseeing the firing of these beasts," he added, waving a hand toward a man sitting at a control panel behind one of the turrets.

The man, Nick, was tall and lean, with a weathered face that spoke of experience. He offered a polite smile as he approached.

"Pleasure to meet you, Tom. Sorry we haven't been properly introduced before. Been a bit busy, haven't we?" Nick's English accent and cheery demeanor were disarming, and Tom found himself immediately liking the guy.

"Yeah, nice to meet you too, Nick," Tom said, shaking his hand. "So, I'm guessing you were in the military?"

"Indeed, mate. Served in Her Majesty's service before I made my way to the States. Can't tell you how honored I am to be here, helping keep folks safe again," Nick replied warmly.

"Glad to have you on board," Tom said sincerely. "Now, does everyone know what they're doing?"

"Absolutely," Herbert chimed in, unable to contain his excitement. "We're sending a warning today. We've got the perfect building picked out— close enough that she's going to feel the tremors. Shandra is absolutely going to snap!"

The elevator dinged again, and Kevin emerged, having already dropped his round off with the other Barbarians. He walked over to Herbert, who was already fiddling with some controls at the panel Nick had been standing at.

"Ah, perfect timing! If you both would follow me over here, we need to be at a safe distance from the operators so as not to be in their way, and then we'll give this baby a proper test run!" Herbert's voice was practically vibrating with excitement.

Herbert moved to a space with a yellow square painted on the ground and footprints painted inside. He stood on one set of footprints, pulling out a pair of safety glasses and ear covers and putting them on.

"Put these on, and stand here," Herbert said, indicating the other sets of footprints. When they had complied, Herbert gave Nick a thumbs up. "Okay! Let's light this candle!"

Tom looked around, realizing he hadn't been given any protective gear. "Where's my protection?" he asked, irritation creeping into his voice.

Herbert looked at him, incredulous. "You didn't bring any?" he shouted, his voice muffled by his ear covers.

"No! I wasn't told I needed them!" Tom shouted back, his frustration evident.

Herbert rolled his eyes. "I kind of figured that firing a giant cannon would mean you obviously need hearing protection," he said, giving Tom a look that reminded him of his mother's exasperation whenever he did something particularly dim-witted.

"Whatever, just fire the damn thing. I want to get this party started because I have to be ready for Shandra's retaliation," Tom said, brushing off the criticism.

Herbert nodded, giving him a thumbs-up, and then signaled Nick, who donned his own protective gear and took his place at the controls. The cannon powered up with a low hum, the barrels rotating and adjusting as Nick moved the joysticks with practiced precision.

"Preparing fire one! Target acquired and locked!" Nick shouted over the whirring noise.

"FIRE ONE AND TWO!" Herbert yelled, his voice tinged with almost childlike glee.

Nick pulled the triggers, one at a time, and the cannons roared to life. Both barrels fired consecutively, recoiling back with immense force. The blast was deafening, a thunderous boom that shook the very foundation of the building. Tom felt a sharp pain in his ears as blood trickled down the side of his face. The concussive force of the blast nearly knocked him off his feet.

Grabbing his ears, Tom looked back to see Herbert, still grinning like a madman, picking himself up off the floor. Ignoring the pain, Tom hurried over to the now-open window space to watch the rounds' trajectory. In the distance, there was an explosion, and smoke began to billow up from a building. Birds scattered, and distant animals shrieked in fear.

Guild Admin Notice:

Your Guild has destroyed a goblin orphanage. Congratulations! You receive 1,000 XP!

"What the actual fuck?!" Tom shouted, his eyes darting back to the notification that flashed in his vision. He read it again, unable to believe what he was seeing. "There was a goblin orphanage in that building?!"

Herbert, still grinning with the adrenaline of the test, pulled off his ear protection, his face slowly shifting from excitement to a more neutral expression. "*Was*," he said nonchalantly, clearly unfazed by the situation. "But not anymore."

Tom, however, was still struggling to hear over the intense ringing in his ears.

"What?" he yelled, his voice louder than necessary, his hearing temporarily dulled from the cannon's thunderous blast.

Herbert gestured to Tom's ears, realizing the issue. Tom, catching on, quickly cast *Dark Healing* on himself. A cooling sensation washed over him as the spell took effect, and within moments, his hearing returned to normal. He could hear the distant crackle of burning wood and stone where the artillery round had hit, and the subtle rustle of the wind around them.

"What did you say?" Tom asked again, now calmer but still tense.

"I said there were some sort of goblins there before. That's just one more reason we picked that building," Herbert repeated, his tone pragmatic and devoid of emotion.

"But it was an *orphanage*?!" Tom's voice rose again, his initial shock giving way to anger. His mind conjured images of goblin children, scared and helpless, caught in the blast.

Herbert looked at him, surprised by his reaction.

"Tom. We're *Americans*—maybe," he hedged, tilting a hand side-to-side uncertainly—clearly unsure as to how the System had affected the state of the union. "Hell, the Taliban used to make them their bases. I wouldn't be surprised if they *built* the damned things just to hide inside of them. But that's beside the point: You're getting upset over goblins?" he asked, genuinely taken aback. "The same creatures that have been raiding settlements, stealing children, and killing thousands of people all around the city since the integration?"

Tom paused, his anger warring with his logic. He took a deep breath, realizing Herbert had a point. The word "orphanage" in the System notification had triggered something in him—a knee-jerk reaction to the idea of harming innocents. But these were goblins, creatures that had been a constant threat, wreaking havoc wherever they went.

"Sorry," Tom said after a moment, exhaling deeply. "I think it was the word 'orphanage' in the System notice that threw me off. You're right; these aren't human kids we're talking about." He took another breath, calming himself. "Thanks for the reality check."

Herbert nodded, satisfied. "No worries. I get it. Words like that carry weight. But we have to remember—this is war now. And those things? They're not going to lose sleep over wiping out one of our own if they get the chance."

Tom still wasn't sure how he felt about it. The word "orphanage" suggested helplessness, innocence—even if the reality was different. He decided to push those thoughts aside for now. He could think about it later, when there wasn't so much to manage. Right now, they needed to assess the damage and consider their next steps.

"*America!*" a voice called out in sing-song as James stepped into view.

"Fuck, yeah!" Jay chorused, following after him.

Kiera swaggered in shortly after. Tom made a face at the sniper.

"What?" She scowled.

"I just figured you'd be able to keep these two in line." Tom said.

Kiera raised an eyebrow so high that Tom was worried it would get lost in her hairline. "You try keeping a leash on these two."

Tom froze.

"Yeah." He sighed. "That's fair."

Kiera sniffed, unfolding her arms—magnanimous in her victory.

"Still. What the hell are you guys doing here?"

James responded by wrapping an arm around Tom's neck. "*Explosions*, Tom." He splayed out the fingers on each hand in pantomime. "You thought you'd just hog all the fun? Is that it?"

Tom simply rolled his eyes.

The cityscape was unnervingly quiet in the aftermath. Before the System integration, an explosion of this magnitude would have brought sirens, news choppers, and swarms of first responders. Now, all he could hear was the faint crackling of burning debris and the low hum of smoke rising into the sky. There were no cries of panic, no organized emergency response—just the eerie, quiet aftermath.

Herbert surveyed the smoking ruins with a satisfied smile. "I'd say that was a great success. These cannons are going to be invaluable when the space pirates make their move," he said, clearly proud of his handiwork. "Nick, fantastic job with the firing."

Nick, still standing at the controls, gave a thumbs up, a broad grin on his face. "Glad to be of service! Always happy to help keep us all safe."

Tom nodded, still staring out at the distant plume of smoke. His mind wasn't on the pirates, though; it was on Shandra. He knew her too well by now— her arrogance, her temper. She wouldn't let this slide. "Now, we just wait and see what her next move will be," he said, his voice low but firm. "She has to respond. She's too rash not to. And when she does, we'll be ready."

He gazed out over the city, his eyes narrowing as if he could see Shandra's reaction miles away. He knew that rattling her like this would provoke a response, and he wanted her to know they were ready for it.

"Come and get some, bitch," Tom muttered under his breath, a grim determination settling over his features. He could almost feel the weight of the city pressing down, the quiet tension before the storm.

Tom took a deep breath.

His heart was ready. *He* was ready to face whatever came next.

His reverie was suddenly interrupted by the cheerful sound of James' voice.

"Yeah! Tell 'em, Tom!" James praised the Warlock. "We'll teach that bitch a lesson, am I right?" He stepped closer to the mortar, tilting his head to one side as he examined the deadly weapon. "Now, where's the button for this damned thing?"

Five voices shouted in unison as each person reflexively tackled James to the ground.

"NOOO!"

Chapter 64

Applying Pressure

No immediate response came from Stormcrusher after Vanguard's cannon fire leveled the distant building.

Derek remained vigilant, monitoring every possible movement from their rival Guild. Sean's knowledge and experience had proven invaluable, especially in interpreting Shandra's behavior and potential tactics. His familiarity with her mindset and the inner workings of Stormcrusher helped them plan traps and counters more effectively. Sean's integration into Vanguard had also gone better than anyone expected. He had quickly found a role alongside Jay, co-captaining the Rogue team and providing new insights into their training.

At first, Jay had been resistant to sharing leadership. He had built his team from the ground up, earning their respect through hard-fought battles and countless hours of training. Handing over some of that control didn't sit right with him. However, it didn't take long for Sean to prove his worth. His time as an FBI agent had given him skills and tactics that Jay hadn't considered, and Sean was more than willing to learn from Jay's combat experience in return. Their collaboration added a new layer of depth to their Rogue team's capabilities, combining Jay's guerrilla tactics with Sean's strategic planning and stealthy maneuvers.

Over several reconnaissance missions, Sean and Jay scouted Shandra's base, searching for any signs of movement or potential weaknesses. To their frustration, they found none.

Shandra was either biding her time, keeping all her forces locked down, or she had grown wise to their surveillance and adapted to stay hidden. Not wanting to reveal their hand, Vanguard's leadership decided not to post a permanent watch outside her base. They wanted to give the illusion of lax defenses, a window of opportunity Shandra might think she could exploit.

This strategy seemed to be paying off. Shandra adjusted her tactics, adopting a more guerrilla style of warfare, launching surprise attacks on isolated Vanguard teams caught training or hunting in the outskirts. Her strikes were precise and deadly, targeting weaker teams to instill fear in the others and destabilize their morale.

When one of Vanguard's teams was ambushed and a junior member killed, the loss hit them all hard. The air in the Guild was heavy with grief and anger. Tom called an emergency meeting and issued new orders: all groups leaving the Guild building would be paired with a senior team for protection.

"That bitch hit us again!" Kiera shouted, slamming her fist on the table in the security office. The heavy oak surface groaned under the force, her eyes wild with rage. "How many more of our people need to die before we just storm in and take her out?"

Tom sat at the head of the table, his elbows on the surface, fingers pressing into his temples. Derek stood beside him, arms folded, trying to keep a level head. "I get it, Kiera," he said in a calm but firm tone. "But if we go in like that, it'll be a massacre. And not just for us. Remember, there are people over there who are looking for a way out. We can't just bulldoze through them."

Kiera scoffed, her face flushed with frustration. "Yeah, and how many more of our people have to die while we're playing this game? A game that *she's* winning, by the way."

"Kiera's not wrong, man," Jay said, leaning against the wall with his arms crossed, his voice steady but laced with an undercurrent of anger. "If we hit them hard and fast, yeah, there'll be casualties, but think of how many lives we'd save by ending it now. People are tired of this. They want it over."

Tom looked up, his eyes tired but resolute. "We can't know that for sure, Jay. If we can provoke her enough, maybe we can draw her out and get her to amass her forces. That's when we strike. Create chaos on her side, give the people who want out a chance to slip away."

"What about something different?" Kedron suggested, leaning forward in his chair with a thoughtful expression. "Can you challenge her to single combat? I mean, she's proud and reckless. She might actually go for it."

The room fell silent, everyone mulling over the suggestion. Tom looked over at Bob, their System expert, who had been quietly flipping through his notebook.

"Bob?" he asked, hoping for some clarity.

Bob adjusted his glasses and nodded, his expression thoughtful. "There *is* a dueling function in the System. You can issue a formal challenge to her, and terms can be set for the duel. But if you initiate the challenge, she gets to set the initial terms. You then have the right to amend them, and it goes back and forth until both sides agree."

"There we go!" Kiera exclaimed, a grin spreading across her face. "Challenge her, kick her ass, and we're done with this whole mess."

"It's not a bad option," Tom agreed, rubbing his chin thoughtfully. "But let's not jump the gun. We need to be sure this is the best move. What else do we have on the table?"

"Not much, to be honest," Brian replied, glancing at his clipboard. "We're still training up our fighters, fortifying the building's defenses, and working on weapons development for when those damn Space Pirates arrive. That's going to be a nightmare if we're not ready."

"Any progress on air or space combat vehicles?" Derek asked, tapping his finger against the table. "If we're stuck on the ground when they show up, we're screwed."

Brian flipped through his notes again, his brow furrowed. "We've been working on some designs, but we're pretty far behind. Other species integrated into the System have had centuries to develop this stuff. Harold found some schematics in the vending machine for a massive battleship, but building one would take years."

"And what about smaller fighters? X-wings or something more agile?" Tom asked, half-joking but still hopeful.

"Nothing yet, but we're scouring every option," Brian said. "The vending machine has a ton of weird stuff, but nothing like what we're hoping for yet."

"So, in the meantime, we're focused on ground-to-air defenses?" Derek inquired, his tone all business.

"Exactly," Brian confirmed. "Herbert has some expertise in that area from before the integration, so he's been cranking out ground-to-air missiles and other defenses. We should have some serious firepower ready for when the pirates show up."

Tom nodded, absorbing the information. "Alright, the challenge duel might be our best shot at forcing Shandra's hand. If we can set the right terms, maybe we can avoid an all-out bloodbath. But I know she's not going to take it lying down. Sean's been clear about that. Still, we have to try. If there's even a small chance to prevent more deaths, we have to take it."

Kiera practically bounced in her seat, her enthusiasm overflowing. "Finally! Send it now! I swear, if I stand outside, I might hear her scream from here!"

Tom chuckled, the tension in the room easing slightly. He pulled up his interface and navigated to the relations section, finding the dueling option. The dropdown list of names appeared, and he mentally searched for Shandra's name. After selecting it, he hit the "Challenge" button.

A notification appeared: *Challenge Sent Successfully.*

"Okay, now we just wait to see…" Tom began, but he was cut off as another notification popped up almost instantly. *Shandra has accepted your challenge.*

"Uh, Bob?" Tom asked, his voice edged with surprise. "What happens if she just accepts the duel without setting any terms?"

Bob looked up, his face a mix of surprise and concern. "Oh, that's unusual. If she does that, it means you get to set all the terms. She… really should have read the details before hitting accept."

"Ooooh, she's *pissed*," Kiera said.

Tom's eyes widened.

He quickly opened the duel menu, seeing a new field labeled "Set Terms."

He typed in carefully: *If I win, Shandra gives up being a Guild leader forever, disbands her Guild immediately upon System confirmation of her loss, leaves Dallas, and all her people are free to choose their path. If she wins, Vanguard merges with Stormcrusher, and we come under her leadership.* He hesitated, weighing the terms, then hit send.

Within seconds, a new message popped up: *Terms Accepted.*

"Damn. Maybe I should have asked for more," Tom muttered under his breath.

"What's going on?" Derek asked, sensing Tom's apprehension.

"She accepted my terms, like, immediately. There's no way she read through them," Tom explained, a slight frown creasing his brow.

Derek's face tightened with worry. "What were your terms, exactly?"

"If I win, she disbands Stormcrusher and leaves town. If she wins, Vanguard merges with her Guild, and we follow her lead," Tom summarized.

Derek's eyes widened in disbelief. "You did *what?* Why would you risk all of us like that?"

Tom raised a hand to calm him. "We need this to be enticing for her, or she'd never agree. If I lose...well, we'll deal with that bridge when we come to it."

"Just make sure you follow through," Bob interjected, his tone serious. "The System doesn't take kindly to broken agreements. The consequences could be… severe."

"Noted," Tom said, trying to sound more confident than he felt. "Shandra might have a backup plan if she loses. She's always been crafty."

"Right," Jay added, his usual laid-back demeanor giving way to a more serious expression. "Expect the unexpected."

"Next step is setting the time and place," Bob noted, his eyes still on his book.

Tom opened the interface again, selecting a neutral location halfway between their bases and setting the duel for tomorrow at noon. He confirmed the details, and the fields merged into a single reminder of the duel's time and location.

"This has been a long time coming," Tom said with a sigh, feeling the weight of the situation settle over him like a heavy cloak. "I'm ready for it to be over, one way or another."

"You've got this, Tom," Jay said, shooting him a double thumbs up. "We believe in you."

"Thanks, Jay. I think I'm ready too," Tom replied, a small, resolute smile forming on his lips. "At least, I hope I am."

"If anyone can beat her, it's you," Derek said, his voice firm but supportive. "It had to be you. In fact, this is the only way this could have worked. She's always hated you the most."

Brian, who had been quiet for a while, spoke up. "Alright, we need to plan for tomorrow. I suggest every available strike team be in the vicinity. Not all in plain sight—just close enough to intervene if things go south. Shandra is unstable, and she might react violently if she loses."

Tom nodded, appreciating the foresight. "Good idea. Let's be ready for anything. This could get ugly fast."

Kiera punched the air with her fist. "Hell yeah! I've been waiting too long to see her go down."

"Let's not get ahead of ourselves," Derek cautioned. "Some of her people are just as reckless. We need to be ready to counter any move they make."

"Let them try," Kiera said with a wicked grin, clearly eager for the confrontation.

Tom glanced around the room. "Alright, anything else we need to cover?"

Brian flipped through his notes one last time. "If we can find some farm animals, that would help our long-term food supply. The area out back is almost ready. We could start breeding them for food once everything's set up."

Tom nodded, adding it to his mental checklist. "Okay, after this duel, we'll focus on that. One thing at a time."

Jay, who had been listening quietly, spoke up. "I can drive a truck if we find a livestock hauler. Used to do it for a living. We could head out of town, find some animals, and bring them back."

Tom looked at him, impressed. "You were a trucker?"

"Yep. Hauled up and down I-35 to Missouri for years," Jay said, leaning back with a satisfied grin.

"And now you're a Rogue…" Tom's voice was flat.

Jay shrugged. "Everyone needs a hobby."

"Well, that's one problem solved," Tom said, standing up and stretching. "This has been a productive meeting. Let's all prepare for tomorrow."

"You know, when you guys put your heads together, you actually get a lot done," Brian commented, a smirk on his face. "Instead of sitting around complaining."

"Alright then, let's get to work," Tom said with renewed determination. "I've got time for one more training session with Bron before the big showdown. Let's make sure everything's set."

As the group began to disband, Derek called out to Tom. "Just remember, Tom—don't let your guard down."

Tom turned back, offering a confident grin. "Never do."

Chapter 65

Duel

Bron had decided that Tom needed light training rather than a grueling session. "I don't want you pulling a muscle or injuring yourself right before the fight," Bron had explained, his deep voice echoing in the training hall. "A strained ligament or a misstep could be the difference between victory and death." After a brief sparring session—where Tom had come tantalizingly close to landing a single blow on Bron—Bron shifted the focus to stretching exercises. He wanted Tom as limber as possible for the duel ahead.

"You're going up against a woman who rules her Guild with sheer force and a ruthless desire for power," Bron said, his tone grave as he watched Tom stretch. "That force will not be relegated merely to personality. She will be a formidable opponent, and you cannot afford to take anything for granted. Strike hard, strike true, and show no mercy, for you will be shown none in return."

Tom paused mid-stretch, his eyes meeting Bron's intense gaze. "Is there anything I should know about the duel? Rules, loopholes, pitfalls?"

"The rules of a duel, set by the System's Administrators, are ironclad and binding," Bron explained, folding his massive arms across his chest. "If you do not show up for the duel, you lose. If you refuse to fight, you lose. If anyone interferes, the System deals out… extreme consequences. Terms can't be changed once agreed upon. It's a matter of honor. While tactics in a duel are broad, it's seen as dishonorable to win through deceit."

Tom smirked, his lips curving into a mischievous grin. "So, shoving a grenade down her pants, kicking her to the ground, and hopping back is off the table?"

Bron's serious expression softened for a moment, and he snorted in reluctant amusement. "Not illegal, but definitely frowned upon by the System and other combatants. Just fight with honor, and you'll be fine. You've come a long way since we started."

Tom grinned, a genuine warmth in his eyes. "That's all thanks to your teaching."

Bron looked away, pretending to notice something on the far side of the training hall. For a brief moment, Tom could almost imagine the big guy blushing if he were capable of it. "Just don't get yourself killed, kid. There's still a lot more I've got to teach you." The serious air that the Mastadonian had adopted began to thaw as he smiled. "With that said, however, this should be—as you humans say- a cake walk for you."

"Mmm?" Tom asked, suddenly getting a bad feeling.

"Well," Bron grinned. "I heard that this… *Shandra* simply accepted the terms of the duel without reviewing them."

Tom scratched his head. "Well… yeah…"

"And you obviously set the duel up to be something like magic only, or summoned creatures only." Bron's loud, boisterous laughter echoed throughout the training hall. He paused to wipe tears of mirth from his eyes.

"… Uhhhh"

Bron blinked, studying the Warlock. "I am by no means an expert in human body language, but I can't help but think that you seem… uncomfortable." The Mastadonian began to adopt a vaguely disapproving body language of his own. "You *did* set the terms in your favor, *didn't* you? You *were* the only one to moderate those terms, right?"

The Warlock kicked at the floor of the training hall, embarrassed.

"Tom…" Bron's voice was raised in warning.

Tom threw up his hands and shouted. "Well, how was I supposed to know!? There's not a 'System Duel's for Dummies' book I can just check out of the local library for crying out loud!"

The Mastadonian face-palmed, his large hand easily covering his entire face.

Tom winced, but couldn't help but be proud of how quickly his Summon was picking up on aspects of human culture.

As the sun rose over the city, Tom stood outside the Vanguard Guild building, soaking in the fresh morning air. The horizon was painted in a breathtaking palette of orange, yellow, and red, mingling with the fading purples, blues, and blacks of the night. The first rays of sunlight broke through the city's skyline, reflecting off the shattered windows of abandoned buildings like glittering jewels scattered across the concrete jungle.

Tom took a deep breath, closing his eyes as he felt the warmth of the sun's rays wash over him. He held his breath for a moment, letting the calmness seep into his bones before exhaling slowly. His heartbeat steadied, and he focused on the task ahead. Today, he would face Shandra in a duel that could determine the future of Dallas. He didn't have to put anyone else's life in danger; it was just him and her. The weight was on his shoulders, but for once, that felt like a relief.

He imagined Shandra's face when she received his duel invitation, the fury twisting her features at the thought of being challenged. She probably saw this as her chance to finally put him "in his place." This would be a clash for the ages, a turning point for the city and its factions.

"You ready?" Derek's voice broke through Tom's thoughts. Tom turned to see his friend standing beside him, hands in his pockets, his face set in determination.

"Yeah," Tom replied, a serene smile touching his lips. "I thought I'd be more nervous or scared, but I'm oddly at peace." He turned back to the sunrise, watching as the sky's fiery hues began to give way to the bright light of day.

Derek nodded, his eyes following Tom's gaze.

"Good. You've put in the work. You've trained hard for this. Besides, someone's gotta put that bitch in her place," he added with a smirk, trying to inject some levity into the moment.

Tom chuckled, appreciating the attempt at humor. Derek was trying to channel his inner James, who was always the one to lighten the mood with a joke. "Alright, I'm gonna grab some breakfast. Need to be fueled up. Don't want to go in there with an empty stomach."

"I'll join you. Low blood sugar's no joke," Derek said, falling in step with Tom as they headed inside.

In the cafeteria, Tom grabbed a tray and was about to tell the server what he wanted when she held up a hand to stop him. "Charlene says you get the special breakfast this morning. Need you at your best," she said, piling his plate high with bacon, sausage, eggs, and two biscuits.

"What about pancakes?" Tom complained, eyeing a stack of fluffy pancakes on a nearby table.

"You had your carb load yesterday," Charlene called from the kitchen, her voice stern but caring. "If you do that this morning, you'll just feel bloated."

"But… pancakes." The Warlock made grabby-hands towards a nearby plate.

The woman to whom the plate belonged to gave him a look and slid the plate further away from Tom. She also turned her back on him, despite him not even being *that* close to her to begin with…

Tom sighed, relenting. "Fine, fine. You're right."

He made his way to a table where Bobby and Kedron were deep in conversation, and he and Derek joined them.

"Hey, settle an argument for us," Kedron said as Tom sat down. "If Terry Crews were here right now, he'd be a Paladin, right? All that Charisma, those muscles."

Before Tom could respond, Bobby jumped in. "Oh, no way. He'd be a Barbarian. Always taking his shirt off, flexing, high Strength."

Tom chuckled, thinking for a moment. "I think you're both wrong. He'd be a Bard. Charisma, yeah. Muscles, yeah. But also, he plays the flute. So, a Bard—high Charisma, looks good, takes his clothes off, and plays an instrument."

Laughter erupted around the table, easing some of the tension of the day. As more Guild members joined them, the banter continued, and for a brief moment, everything felt normal—like they weren't about to face a life-and-death duel. But the reality was always there, lurking beneath the surface. Eventually, Derek gave Tom a nudge, reminding him it was time to go.

Back in the lobby, the strike force teams were assembling. They would follow Tom to the duel, staying mostly out of sight but close enough to intervene if things went sideways. Jay and Sean's team would scout the area for any traps or ambushes, while Kiera's snipers would keep a sharp eye out for anyone trying to interfere.

After reviewing the plan one more time, the teams dispersed, each heading in different directions. Tom's core group—Derek, James, Kevin, Kirsten, Michael, Kedron, Bobby, Austin, Clay, Graham, DeeDee, and Briana—walked with him as they approached the abandoned parking lot where the duel would take place. Shandra arrived shortly after, flanked by what looked like her entire Guild, all armed and ready.

"That's a lot of people for a duel," Tom noted, his eyes scanning the crowd.

"They're just here to make sure you don't try anything," Shandra snapped back, her voice dripping with contempt.

Tom chuckled at her response, shaking his head. "Really? You're the one who's been skulking around, attacking the weakest of us, and you're worried about us playing dirty?"

"I don't trust you, Tom," Shandra shot back, venom in her voice. "You could have been great if you'd joined us. Instead, you chose to play leader to this pathetic band of misfits."

"The same misfit's you are now trying to recruit from," Tom scoffed. His patience was wearing thin. "Alright, enough with the speeches. Let's get this over with. I'm tired of your attitude."

Shandra smirked, her eyes gleaming with malice. "So eager to die. I almost pity you for it."

"Oh, please. I fought worse than you during our skirmish with The Master, and those were just zombies." He sniffed the air, wrinkling his nose in distaste. "In fact, you kind of remind me of them," Tom shot back at her, watching her response.

She did not disappoint. Shandra turned so red Tom thought steam was going to shoot out of her ears.

They moved to the center of the parking lot, about ten yards apart. A gong sounded in the distance, marking the start of the duel. A shimmering blue dome appeared above them, slowly descending to encase the area. When it settled on the ground, the barrier became invisible, but the outline remained visible as a faint shimmer, showing the boundaries of their combat area.

Both combatants stood still, sizing up each other. Tom drew his greatsword, feeling its weight in his hands as he swung it in a slow arc. He had just begun to step forward when he caught a glint of metal from the corner of his eye. Shandra had drawn a gun and fired.

Tom's instincts kicked in, and he tried to dodge, but the bullet struck his shoulder, the impact sending him sprawling to the ground. He landed hard, pain flaring through his arm, and he rolled onto his back, clutching his wound.

Shandra walked toward him, her gun still aimed at his head. "You're so naive, Tom," she taunted, her voice cold and mocking. "You thought this would be a fair fight? For all your talk about being noble and just, you're nothing but a fool."

"You really think murdering anyone who doesn't agree with you is the path to power?" Tom growled, gritting his teeth against the pain. His sword lay just out of reach, and he could feel his blood trickling down his arm. "That kind of leadership only leaves you isolated, surrounded by enemies. One day, someone will put a knife in your back while you sleep."

As he spoke, he activated a Skill he'd been preparing. A glyph appeared on the ground behind Shandra, and one of her men shouted a warning. She turned her head just as an Abyssal Chicken burst from the glyph, lunging at her. She dodged, but the chicken latched onto her hand, the one holding the gun, and began biting down.

She screamed in rage, dropping the gun, and slamming the chicken against the ground repeatedly to dislodge it. Tom seized the moment, casting *Dark Healing* on himself. He felt the healing energy surge through him, and the bullet was pushed out of his shoulder, clattering onto the pavement.

Shandra finally crushed the chicken under her boot, turning just in time to see Tom charging her. She pulled a sword from her Inventory and blocked his strike with her good hand, their blades clashing with a metallic ring. She was strong—maybe even stronger than Tom—and she began to push him back, her face twisted with fury.

Tom knew he had to get creative. Shifting his weight, he feigned a stumble, then suddenly kicked up with his left foot, catching her injured hand. She screamed, stumbling back, breaking the deadlock. For a moment, they stared at each other, both breathing heavily.

"Surprised? I clawed my way to the top," Shandra snarled, her eyes blazing with hatred. "I've fought for *everything* I have. And now you think you can take it all away?"

"I'm not here to take what's yours, Shandra," Tom replied, his voice steady and firm. "I'm here to stop you from turning this city into a wasteland, ruled by fear and bloodshed. You see everyone as an enemy, and that'll leave you standing on top of a pile of ashes, all alone."

"SHUT UP!" Shandra screamed, her face contorting in rage. "I will *kill* you for standing in my way!"

And with a roar, she launched herself at him once more, her eyes wild and desperate.

Chapter 66

Titans Clash

Tom watched her come, the air shimmering with magic, the ground beneath her cracking with each step.

Shandra moved like a force of nature, a living storm of strength and fury, her sword raised high, energy coiling around the blade like lightning. She was too fast for someone that size.

Tattoo of Brute Strength activated. Tom barely had time to bring his sword up before she was on him, her first strike slamming into his blade with bone-jarring force. The shock of impact rattled through his arms, his boots grinding into the dirt from the sheer weight of it—but this time, he matched her power.

The tattoo pulsed, a surge of raw strength flooding his muscles, letting him absorb the impact without losing ground. His boots dug into the earth, his grip steady.

She didn't let up.

Blow after blow came down, her blade flashing in a relentless storm of steel and raw aggression. Each strike carried the kind of weight meant to break through anything standing in her way—a relentless, overpowering assault meant to end this fast.

But Tom didn't break.

He dug in, gritting his teeth as he absorbed each impact, adjusting his footing just enough to keep from being overwhelmed.

She's trying to end this quickly. Typical.

"You think you're so great. Better than everyone else," she growled, her voice thick with bitterness.

Tom shook his head, his expression one of frustration and pity. "You're projecting. I've never thought I was better than anyone," he replied, his voice steady, but carrying an edge of weariness. "I merely refused to join your tyrannical Guild. We could have been allies, but your obsession with control and your disregard for reason made that impossible."

Shandra rushed him again, continuing her barrage of attacks.

"You always fight like this?" he grunted, deflecting a brutal downward slash before pivoting to dodge her next strike.

Shandra's eyes flashed. "Only when I want someone dead."

WAR

Tom let out a sharp exhale, shaking the ache from his arms. "Wow. And here I thought you didn't like me."

Her snarl was almost animalistic, her next strike coming even harder. No hesitation. No mercy.

Because Shandra never hesitated.

Her father had beaten that out of her a long time ago.

The memory came rushing back, unbidden, unrelenting.

The taste of blood on her tongue. The sting of failure in her bones.

Shandra was fifteen, standing in the middle of a private training hall, her body bruised, aching, her vision swimming from the last hit she had failed to block.

Across from her, Val stood with his hands clasped behind his back, watching her with the kind of cold, emotionless calculation that made her feel like a test subject rather than a daughter.

"Again," she gritted out, tightening her grip on her sword, trying to push past the tremble in her arms. "I'll get it this time."

Her father didn't move, didn't blink, didn't acknowledge her effort.

"You still don't understand," he said, his voice measured, calm, cutting. "That is why you will never be great."

Shandra's stomach twisted, but she refused to let it show.

"I'm getting stronger," she shot back, setting her stance again. "I'll beat anyone in my way."

That earned her a reaction.

A slow, deep sigh, the kind that carried the weight of disappointment.

"Still thinking like a dog."

He took a single step forward, and it felt like the entire room shifted with his presence.

"You think power is about winning fights? Overcoming one enemy at a time?" His hand moved suddenly, a blur of motion—Shandra's blade was wrenched from her grip, her wrist twisted, her body spun off-balance before she even registered what had happened.

The sword clattered to the ground.

She froze.

Val didn't even look at it.

"You think too small," he said, his voice void of warmth.

His open palm struck her cheek, a sharp, precise snap that sent pain lancing through her jaw. Not enough to break anything. Just enough to humiliate her.

Shandra staggered, but didn't fall.

He stepped closer, his fingers gripping her chin, forcing her to look up at him.

"Power means building a world where you don't have to fight at all." His grip tightened. "Do you know why people fear me?"

Shandra didn't answer.

"They fear me because I do not waste my energy swinging at obstacles," he said. "I shape the battlefield before the fight even begins, both in any fight and in the office. I create obstacles for others—while ensuring I have none of my own."

He released her roughly, his presence looming as she swallowed the sting of the lesson.

"If you only train to fight," he said, turning away, "then you will always be a soldier in someone else's war. Until you learn to think beyond yourself, to plan beyond this fight, beyond this decade, you will always be small."

The memory burned through her mind like a firestorm.

Tom sidestepped, but this time—Shandra was already adjusting, her blade pivoting into a perfect follow-through arc that forced him to parry harder than before.

Her magic surged, a violent aura of crimson and silver coiling around her sword like serpents of energy. The air between them crackled, the battlefield itself shuddering as her power spread.

And then—she disappeared. No—not disappeared. The battlefield warped. The space around him rippled, distorted, as if reality itself had become unstable.

A blurred afterimage flickered to his left—then his right—then above—too fast to track. Shandra wasn't just moving fast. She was controlling space itself.

Tom's instincts screamed, but before he could react, her blade struck from his blind spot. He barely brought his sword up in time, the impact sending a violent shockwave up his arm.

She came at him again—another impossible angle, another twisting step through warped space.

He was being funneled, every dodge forcing him into a worse position, the battlefield shaping itself around her attacks.

Tom gritted his teeth.

Fine. If she wanted to bend the battlefield, he'd burn through it.

Dark Inferno—Activate.

His blade ignited, black fire roaring to life, dark energy crackling along the edge like a living thing.

And as she struck again—

He slashed straight through the distortion. The space warped around his flames—then shattered like glass. Shandra's eyes widened in shock for just a fraction of a second—enough time for Tom to step forward, blade already swinging.

Steel clashed.

He pushed into her guard, the force of his strike sending her skidding backward, her boots grinding against the ground.

She barely caught herself, eyes narrowing as she reevaluated him.

"Not bad," Tom admitted, rolling his shoulders. "But you're still not thinking far enough ahead."

Shandra grinned, her magic flaring even higher. "Then let me show you just how far ahead I'm thinking."

Her magic spiked again, the energy around her warping the air itself—and then she activated the second phase of her attack.

Shandra was everywhere at once. Her afterimages flickered, her *Distortion Step* warping her presence, making it feel like he was fighting ghosts.

Tom was forced onto the defensive, barely keeping up as her blade slashed from angles that shouldn't have been possible.

A sharp pain shot across his forearm as he barely managed to turn aside a near-fatal strike, the edge of her blade biting through fabric and skin.

Shit.

He was losing ground. Each attack funneled him, each strike was meant to control space, and now he was running out of it.

Tom gritted his teeth. He had to change the tempo.

Instead of waiting for her to finish a full attack sequence, he stepped in early, twisting through her next strike before it fully formed.

A risky move—but it paid off.

Shandra's blade skimmed past his ribs, missing a clean cut by a fraction of a second, while Tom closed the distance, his own blade already swinging.

A brutal counter.

Shandra's eyes flashed with surprise—but she wasn't slow.

She wrenched her body back, her sword coming up just in time to meet his attack.

Steel clashed.

The impact sent her skidding backward, boots grinding against the ground as she absorbed the force. She slid to a halt, her free hand brushing the dirt, and when she looked back up—

She was grinning.

"Clever," she admitted, shaking out her arm. "But not clever enough."

Tom exhaled, rolling his shoulders. "Well, I try."

Shandra's magic flared again—but this time, it was different. The very air around them shuddered, like reality itself was being dragged against its will.

Tom's stomach dropped.

What the hell is she—

The ground exploded beneath him. A wave of force surged upward, violent and raw, throwing him off balance as the battlefield twisted around them. Shandra wasn't just warping her own movement anymore. She was warping the battlefield itself.

Tom barely had time to register it before she vanished again—and then she was above him, descending like a razor-edged executioner, blade poised to cleave him in two.

He twisted in midair, barely bringing his sword up in time to block the strike—the collision sending shockwaves through his bones.

Tom hit the ground hard, rolling to absorb the impact as the battlefield continued to warp around him.

His mind raced. She wasn't just faster—she was controlling the space itself, bending the very ground beneath him. It wasn't just unpredictable. It was oppressive.

Shandra descended again, her blade whistling through the air, and Tom had just enough time to roll aside, feeling the shockwave of her strike explode against the ground where his head had been seconds earlier.

He pushed himself up, breathing hard, scanning the warping space around them.

There. A pattern.

She wasn't just warping randomly—she was controlling her position relative to him, using the distortions to funnel him into disadvantageous spots.

Tom adjusted his stance, letting his breathing steady.

Alright. Time to break the pattern.

Shandra surged forward again, closing the distance in a blink. This time, Tom didn't react to her movements. He moved first.

Instead of waiting for her attack, he stepped in before she fully repositioned, disrupting her intended path before she could force him into another bad spot.

Her blade still came—but this time, his sword was already there to meet it.

Steel clashed.

A spark of shock flashed through Shandra's eyes.

Tom pushed in, twisting his blade inside her guard, forcing her to break away.

She skidded backward, boots grinding into the dirt, and this time, she wasn't grinning.

"You really don't like being predictable, do you?" Tom exhaled, shifting his grip.

Shandra's jaw clenched.

"You think you've figured it out?" she spat, her magic spiking violently.

The temperature around them dropped. Tom's body tensed as he felt a new shift in energy. Something was coming.

Shandra lifted her free hand, and for the first time in the fight, her magic manifested into a physical form. Black chains erupted from the ground, coiling like serpents, writhing with raw energy.

Shit.

Tom jumped back, but one snapped toward him, latching around his ankle and yanking him off his feet.

Another shot out, this time for his wrist—he barely twisted away in time.

Shandra strode forward, the chains rattling like a thousand whispered voices, her eyes glowing with something dark and triumphant.

"You forced me to use this," she said, voice steady, unshaken.

She flexed her fingers.

The chains tightened.

Tom gritted his teeth.

Alright. New problem.

Tom braced himself, testing the chains. They weren't just physical—they were sapping his strength, draining the energy from his limbs.

Shit.

She had planned for this.

He dug his boots into the dirt, trying to yank free, but the more he struggled, the tighter they wound, constricting like serpents made of raw magic.

Shandra took another step forward, raising her sword high.

"It's over," she said.

Tom exhaled sharply.

"You really don't get how stubborn I am, do you?"

He stopped struggling.

Instead—he reached deep into his core, summoning his highest-level spell.

Eldritch Blast.

Dark energy crackled at his fingertips, raw and unstable.

The chains reacted, their magic trying to consume the power before it could be released—

But Tom detonated it anyway.

A blast of raw, eldritch force exploded outward, shattering the chains in a violent eruption of energy.

The backlash sent both of them flying.

Tom barely caught himself with a midair twist, landing in a low stance, his sword already raised.

Shandra landed several feet back, boots skidding against the ground, her teeth clenched in frustration.

Her eyes flashed with something unreadable—anger, disbelief, something else.

"That was a mistake," she muttered, more to herself than to him.

She took a slow breath.

And then—

The ground cracked beneath her feet.

Tom tensed. Something was wrong. Shandra's magic didn't just spike—it changed. The very air around her distorted, warping like heat waves over stone, but far more unnatural.

Her aura darkened, flickering between her usual crimson energy and something deeper, heavier—like ink swallowing light.

Tom's stomach tightened.

No. This isn't normal. This is something else.

Shandra's breathing turned sharp, her muscles locking up for a fraction of a second—then she let out a low, guttural sound, like she was forcing something back down.

"You're strong," she admitted, voice lower than before. "Stronger than I expected."

Tom narrowed his eyes. "Not to be rude, but you look like you're about to pass out."

She let out a sharp breath—half a laugh, half something else.

Then she lifted her free hand, palm open, and the battlefield shuddered beneath them.

"SOVEREIGN DOMAIN!"

A pulse of pure, crushing force exploded outward.

It wasn't just magic. It was pressure—a gravity-like weight pressing down on everything, pulling the air taut, making Tom's limbs feel like lead.

He gritted his teeth, pushing against it, feeling the sheer density of the attack.

"Not bad," he managed. "But this feels a lot like desperation."

Shandra's eyes flashed.

"This is what it means to be above others," she said, and her aura surged to its peak.

The entire battlefield became hers.

Tom gritted his teeth as the world around him crushed down like an invisible mountain.

His lungs felt tight, his limbs dragged against his will, every motion ten times heavier than it should have been.

This ability wasn't just magic—it was absolute control.

Shandra walked forward slowly, her presence unshaken as the very battlefield bent to her will.

Tom could see it now. This was her world.

"This is where you fall," she said, voice sharp and unwavering. "You can't freely move anymore. You don't get to fight on your own terms."

Tom forced himself to step forward, every motion like wading through stone. He wasn't done. But damn, it was getting harder to move.

Shandra's sword flashed forward, impossibly fast despite the crushing gravity.

Tom blocked, but the impact rattled his bones, driving him down to one knee. The ground cracked beneath him from the sheer force of it.

Shandra grinned.

"This is over."

She drove forward, sword poised to finish it—

Tom gritted his teeth.

Alright. If he couldn't fight this gravity, he'd just have to steal enough energy to withstand it.

Tattoo of Life Absorption—Activate.

A pulse of sickly dark energy rippled outward, subtle, almost invisible—but Tom felt it instantly. Strength flowed into his limbs. His muscles stopped trembling, his breathing steadied, and suddenly—the unbearable weight of *Sovereign Domain* didn't seem as crushing.

Shandra didn't notice. She was too focused on ending this.

Her sword came down.

But Tom moved.

Not a dodge. Not a block.

He stepped into her attack.

Shandra's blade cut deep into his shoulder, pain exploding through him—

But his own sword was already swinging.

Her eyes widened in shock.

A perfect counter.

She had overcommitted.

Tom's blade slammed into her side, sending her skidding backward, blood spraying in an arc.

The pressure around him wavered.

She had felt that one.

She caught herself, barely staying on her feet, her breathing ragged now.

Tom forced himself up, rolling his shoulders, the pain already dissipating from the health he was stealing.

"You're strong," he admitted. "But this"—he exhaled sharply, gripping his sword tighter—"is taking a lot out of you, isn't it?"

Shandra's expression flickered—a fraction of uncertainty. She knew it too. *Sovereign Domain* was draining her. It wasn't just weighing him down—it was straining her own body to sustain it. She just hadn't expected the fight to last this long.

"You think this is enough to stop me?" she snapped, trying to push through it.

Her aura flared dangerously—but for the first time, it stuttered.

Tom noticed.

And that meant—

She was about to break.

But she wasn't done yet. With a sharp breath, Shandra clenched her fist, and the battlefield shuddered again. Tom barely had time to react before a final wave of force slammed into him.

He hit the ground hard, rolling with the impact, but he could feel it—

Sovereign Domain was collapsing. Her control was slipping. She clearly knew it too. That's why she wasn't holding back anymore. She let out a raw, defiant cry, her sword burning with crimson light, and she charged.

Tom exhaled sharply, gripping his blade.

Alright. Time to finish this.

He raised his free hand, dark energy crackling at his fingertips.

Not just *Dark Ball*. Not just *Lightning Strike*.

Void Storm.

Shandra closed the gap in an instant, blade arcing toward his throat—

Tom unleashed the spell.

A vortex of crackling black lightning roared to life, tendrils of dark energy spiraling outward, consuming the very air.

Shandra's eyes widened. She tried to block. It wasn't enough. The impact slammed into her full force, lifting her off her feet. She hit the ground hard, skidding across the battlefield, her sword clattering from her grasp.

For a moment, silence.

Then—

A cough. A slow, weak movement. Shandra pushed herself up onto one elbow, breathing raggedly. Her aura was gone. *Sovereign Domain* had shattered completely.

She looked up at Tom, and for the first time, there was no defiance in her eyes. Only realization. She had lost.

Tom approached slowly, sword still raised, his expression unreadable.

Shandra let out a weak, bitter chuckle.

"So that's it, huh?"

Tom didn't answer immediately. He exhaled, rolling his shoulders.

"You weren't planning for the future," he said finally. "That's why you lost."

Shandra's gaze flickered. She clenched her jaw, but she didn't argue. She had spent everything she had, trying to dominate here and now. Tom had been building for what came next. She looked down, her hands trembling.

"My father was wrong," she muttered. "All this power… and it still wasn't enough." She closed her eyes. "Just get it over with."

Tom lifted his sword—

Shandra didn't move.

She simply watched him, her breathing slow, steady. A part of her already knew this was the end. But she refused to look away. Even in death, she wouldn't cower.

Tom exhaled sharply.

"You could have been better than him," he said.

A flicker of emotion passed through her eyes. Regret? Maybe. But it was too late now.

"Maybe," she admitted. "But I wasn't."

The sword fell.

A clean, decisive strike.

Shandra's body went still.

Then came the notification.

Duel Victory: Tom of Vanguard

You have defeated your opponent in single combat. As per the agreement, your conditions have been granted.

WAR

Tom dismissed the System prompt hovering in his vision as he stood over Shandra's lifeless body. The barrier that had surrounded them glowed a bright blue for a moment, then shattered outward in a cascade of motes of light, like a thousand fireflies released into the evening air. The lights drifted lazily on an invisible breeze, casting an ethereal glow across the battlefield. For a brief moment, it felt as if time itself had paused, and all eyes were on the tiny flickering embers dancing in the aftermath of the duel.

"Rest in peace, Shandra," Tom murmured, his voice almost lost in the silence. "I will keep leading them to be better."

He took a deep breath, turning his gaze to survey the battlefield. The brawl between the Guilds had slowed to a near halt, both sides caught in the awe of the shimmering lights that marked the end of the fight. Faces that had been contorted with rage and fear now reflected a strange, almost serene curiosity. But the calm didn't last.

A deafening roar shattered the stillness. "SHANDRAAAAAAA!"

The guttural scream cut through the air like a blade. Tom's attention snapped to the source: a massive man, his face twisted in a mask of agony and rage, eyes blazing an unnatural red. The veins across his neck and arms bulged grotesquely, and his muscles seemed to swell and ripple as tendrils of dark energy radiated off him, twisting like smoke in the wind.

Tom's stomach tightened in fear. He'd seen this transformation before—this was *Berserker's Rage*, a deadly state where reason was lost, replaced by pure, uncontrollable fury.

"Watch out! He's going berserk!" Kevin's shout carried over the tense silence.

The massive Barbarian, now fully consumed by his rage, charged directly at Tom. His footsteps pounded the ground like the beat of a war drum, each step faster than the last. Before he could close the distance, Kirsten dove in from the side, tackling him with all her might. The two rolled across the dirt, locked in a violent struggle. Despite her strength, she was no match for the Barbarian's monstrous power. With a growl, he threw her off like she was weightless, sending her skidding across the ground. He regained his footing and continued his charge, his eyes locked on Tom.

A sharp crack echoed through the battlefield as Kiera fired a shot from her sniper rifle. The bullet struck the side of the Barbarian's head with a metallic ping, knocking him sideways. Tom's eyes widened in horror as the man staggered but showed no signs of serious injury. No blood flowed from the wound. Three more shots rang out in quick succession, each one bouncing harmlessly off the Barbarian's skin as if he were made of iron.

"HOW DARE YOU KILL HER?! YOU MONSTER!" the man bellowed, his voice unnaturally deep, echoing with layers of distortion as if multiple voices were speaking at once.

Tom knew he needed help. He quickly summoned Bron, who appeared beside him, taking in the chaotic scene in an instant.

"No," Bron whispered, his voice barely audible but laced with dread. His eyes were fixed on the Barbarian, a man now lost to his own consuming rage, his hatred for Tom blazing like a firestorm. "He's beyond saving. We have to destroy him now!"

Before Tom could react, the Barbarian launched himself with a powerful leap, covering the distance between them in the blink of an eye.

Tom barely managed to roll to the side, narrowly avoiding the brutal impact as the Barbarian crashed to the ground where he had just been standing. The earth beneath them cracked under the force, sending up a cloud of dust and debris.

Bron wasted no time. With a roar, he swung his massive greataxe, the blade flashing in the light as he brought it down on the Barbarian's back. The ground trembled with the impact, and a sickening crunch followed. The brute let out a painful grunt, almost like a cough, his eyes bulging wide with shock. Despite the force, the blade barely cut into his thick skin, leaving only a shallow wound.

The Barbarian's recovery was immediate. He lashed out with a vicious kick, catching Bron in the leg and sending him crashing to one knee.

Tom saw his chance.

He surged forward, activating his sword's *Dark Inferno* ability. The blade ignited with a dark, fiery aura as he brought it down in a powerful overhand strike. The Barbarian raised his shoulder to take the blow, grinning madly, but his smile twisted into a howl of pain when the sword bit into his flesh and black flames began to eat away at his skin.

Tom's victory was short-lived. With a wild swing of his massive arm, the Barbarian swatted Tom aside like a rag doll. The blow hit Tom square in the chest, and he felt the wind rush out of him as he was hurled through the air, landing hard on his back. Stars danced in his vision as he gasped for breath, the pain radiating through his ribs.

Bron tried to capitalize on the Barbarian's distraction, driving a fist into his face. But instead of dazing him, the blow only seemed to fuel his rage. The Barbarian snarled and retaliated with a bone-shaking punch, sending Bron spinning away, skidding across the ground.

Kevin, Kirsten, and Michael saw their chance and rushed in from behind, leaping onto the Barbarian and trying to subdue him with sheer force. Their efforts were in vain. With another ear-splitting roar, the Barbarian grabbed each of them one by one, ripping them off his back and throwing them aside like toys. They crashed to the ground, groaning in pain, but managed to scramble away before he could crush them underfoot.

The Barbarian's body began to pulse rhythmically, each beat of his heart visible as his muscles swelled even further. Veins bulged grotesquely across his skin, and his eyes blazed like burning coals. His gaze locked onto Tom, who was still struggling to rise. With slow, deliberate steps, he advanced, each step sending tremors through the earth.

Tom barely managed to push himself to his knees when a massive hand clamped around his throat, lifting him effortlessly off the ground. His feet dangled helplessly as the Barbarian held him aloft, squeezing with crushing force.

WAR

"You will pay for what you have done. The hour of reckoning is now."

Chapter 67

Final Confrontation

Tom's lungs screamed for air as he writhed in the crushing grasp of the Barbarian. The giant's hands were like iron, squeezing the life out of him with a force that could bend steel. His vision blurred, black tendrils creeping in from the edges, threatening to pull him into unconsciousness. Desperate, he gathered the last of his strength, drawing his leg back as far as it would go. With every ounce of force he could muster, he drove his boot into the man's most sensitive parts.

The Barbarian's eyes went wide, a primal groan tearing from his throat. The grip around Tom's neck slackened, just enough for him to gulp in a breath of sweet, life-giving air. The relief was fleeting.

Still reeling from the pain, the brute's face contorted back into a mask of fury, and his hands began to tighten once more, cutting off Tom's windpipe.

Suddenly, a dark blur shot across the battlefield, and a thunderous impact slammed into the Barbarian's side. It was Derek, using the full power of his suit to launch himself at the giant like a human cannonball. The force of the collision knocked the Barbarian off his feet, sending both men crashing to the ground. Tom collapsed, gasping and coughing, his lungs burning with every breath.

Derek, atop the Barbarian, wasted no time. He rained down a flurry of punches, each one landing with bone-crushing force. The giant's head snapped back and forth under the onslaught, but his rage seemed to fuel him more than anything else. He bared his teeth, and with a sudden movement, caught Derek's right hand, then his left. His massive fists closed around Derek's hands like a vise.

Derek's eyes went wide as he felt the strength of the hand grabbing him. He let out a cry, more from frustration than fear. At that moment, Bron appeared, his shadow looming large. With a powerful leap, he delivered a kick that would have put any pro athlete to shame. The Barbarian's head snapped to the side with a sickening crack that seemed to echo across the battlefield.

The giant's grip loosened, and Derek took his chance, rolling off him and scrambling away. The Barbarian, shaking his head to clear it, rolled to his knees and slammed a fist into the pavement, sending cracks radiating out like a spiderweb.

Bron stepped forward, his greataxe stowed away, ready to engage the Barbarian with his bare fists. Kevin and Kirsten flanked him on either side, their muscles bulging as they activated their own rage abilities, veins standing out like cords on their skin.

The Barbarian, eyes wild with fury, got to his feet and let out a roar that shook the air around them. Without warning, he charged.

Bron sidestepped deftly, landing a solid punch to the man's face, narrowly dodging the counter-swing. Kevin, seizing the moment, leaped forward, bringing both of his hands down in a hammer blow onto the back of the Barbarian's neck. The giant staggered forward, right into a well-timed roundhouse kick from Kirsten that connected with his jaw.

The impact lifted the Barbarian off his feet and sent him crashing to the ground, the concrete cracking beneath his weight. Bron, Kevin, and Kirsten didn't press the advantage, choosing instead to hold back, their chests heaving as adrenaline surged through their veins. They circled him, ready to react to his next move.

Across the parking lot, a different battle played out between the two Guilds. While the intensity wasn't as fierce as the clash between the Barbarians, the tension was still palpable. Scuffles and fistfights had erupted after the death of a Stormcrusher member, but most of Shandra's followers had lost their will to fight after witnessing her defeat. Now, they watched with wide eyes, uncertain of their next move.

Briana saw the opportunity and quickly cast a shimmering barrier between the Barbarian and Bron's team. The Barbarian got to his feet and hammered his fists against the barrier, causing cracks to spread across its surface like a shattered mirror. His eyes, glowing with fury, locked onto Briana. Her breath caught in her throat as she realized what was about to happen.

With a deafening roar, he shattered the barrier into a thousand glittering shards. Briana cried out, collapsing to her knees as the magical backlash hit her like a physical blow. Kedron caught her just in time, his face contorted with concern.

"Damn it! We can't just stand here!" Kedron shouted, his eyes blazing with determination. He released Briana and stepped forward, but Bobby grabbed his shoulder, holding him back.

"You'll just get in the way. They need space to move around that beast," Bobby said, his voice calm but firm.

"Fine, then we use spells!" Kedron snapped, pulling free of Bobby's grip. "Mages! Hit that bastard with every debuff you've got!"

Kedron's hands wove an intricate pattern through the air, his voice a low, urgent chant. Other mages joined in, and the Barbarian's skin began to pulsate with a kaleidoscope of colors as layers of debuffs settled on him. His movements slowed, his muscles straining under the weight of a dozen curses.

Snarling, he turned toward the mages, coiling to leap.

Before he could, Bron's massive fist collided with his jaw once again, this time, sending him sprawling to the ground. Bron had used the distraction to shift the fight's focus back to himself and his team. With a grunt, the Barbarian struggled back to his feet, only to be met with a punch from Kevin, then Kirsten. They took turns, darting in with quick strikes before retreating out of range.

The giant suddenly stood upright, spinning around with both fists extended like a living cyclone. His arms caught all three of his attackers, knocking them back a few steps. He panted heavily, each breath a ragged gasp. The debuffs were taking their toll, slowing him further.

"Grab him and hold him down!" Tom shouted, his voice commanding as he began to draw upon his own power.

Bron, Kevin, and Kirsten lunged in unison, grabbing both arms and one of his legs. The Barbarian roared and fought against them, his muscles bulging as he tried to bring his arms together. Inch by inch, he began to force them closer, his strength still immense despite the magical weakening.

"Now! Get back!" Tom commanded, his voice urgent.

Bron gave a nod, and Kevin and Kirsten responded instantly. The three released the Barbarian simultaneously, falling back to the ground. Tom thrust his hands forward, a surge of energy building within him.

"FINAAAAAAAAAL FLAAAAAAAAAAASH!" he roared, and a brilliant beam of energy erupted from his palms, hurtling toward the Barbarian.

The beam struck the Barbarian square in the chest, and for a moment, it seemed to halt, as if hitting an immovable wall.

Almost delicately, with a burst of power, it surged through him, blasting out of his back in a brilliant explosion of light. The force of the blast illuminated the battlefield, sending debris flying and causing everyone nearby to shield their eyes.

"HAAAAAAAAAAAAAAA!" Tom's voice rose to a crescendo as he poured everything into the attack—his anger, his frustration, his fear, and his determination. The beam widened, engulfing the Barbarian, whose scream rose to a high-pitched wail before the energy cut through him entirely, severing his body in two across the middle.

The blinding light slowly dimmed, and Tom dropped to one knee, completely drained. The two halves of the Barbarian lay on the ground, his legs twitching and convulsing while his upper body spasmed in shock. Tom, catching his breath, forced himself back to his feet and approached what remained of the massive warrior. His muscles had shrunk back to normal, the *Berserker's Rage* fading as the life ebbed from his opponent.

"Keith, I presume?" Tom asked, his voice barely more than a whisper, tinged with exhaustion.

Keith's eyes rolled wildly, his mouth opening and closing as he struggled to take in a breath, but his lungs and diaphragm were too damaged to function. With great effort, he managed a slight nod.

"You don't have long," Tom said softly, his expression heavy with regret. "I'm sorry. It wasn't supposed to be like this."

Keith's eyes flicked around, a wild, desperate movement as he realized the end was near. Tom could see the fear in them, the realization of mortality hitting hard. He pulled out his gun, the weight of it suddenly immense in his hand.

"I wish things could've been different," Tom murmured, and with a single shot, he ended it. Keith's body went still, the life leaving him with a final, soft exhale. He knelt down, closing the man's eyelids over his glassy gaze. "She was right," he sighed. "Some enemies you just can't let live—no matter how hard you try."

Tom turned away, his shoulders sagging under the weight of his actions. The battlefield seemed to go silent, his heartbeat pounding in his ears. He fell to his knees, deactivating his tattoos, his breath coming in ragged, uneven gasps. His emotions were a chaotic storm within him, a mix of sorrow, relief, and a gnawing emptiness.

"Why did it have to be like this?" Tom whispered to himself, staring down at the cracked pavement beneath him, seeking some meaning in all the violence.

A heavy hand rested on his shoulder. Bron knelt beside him, his presence grounding.

"Do you think you did the right thing?" Bron asked, his voice low and steady.

Tom took a long breath, feeling the weight of the question settle over him. "I… don't know. I did what needed to be done… But… that's not the same thing, is it?"

"No. It is not." Bron's gaze was heavy. "Yet, still I tell you: rise, warrior. You did what was necessary. This could have escalated into a war, with far more bloodshed as a result. But you stopped that. Do not second-guess yourself when you've done what you believe is right." Bron's words were firm, resolute, and as he stood, Tom felt a small measure of strength return to him.

Bron moved to address the remaining members of Stormcrusher. "You have all seen what pride and blind loyalty do to those in power. Stop this pointless fighting and come together. The world is dangerous enough without us fighting amongst ourselves."

The crowd hesitated, torn between their loyalty to their fallen leader and the reality before them. Bron's words carried weight, and slowly, many of them lowered their weapons. The tension hung thick in the air, a fragile moment of decision that could shatter at any second.

"If any of you want to leave now, I suggest you go. The rest of you will be welcome to apply to Vanguard if you so choose," Tom said, his voice gaining strength as he stood beside Bron.

There was a murmur among the remaining members of Stormcrusher. Two of them turned and fled, unwilling to face the new reality. The rest stayed, storing their weapons and stepping forward.

"We don't want to fight anymore," one man said, looking around at the others and then at Tom. "It's been hell under Shandra. No one could speak out against her. We all saw what happened to those who did."

"I'd rather not fight any more, either. Yet fight we must," Tom replied. "Though I agree with the hope that it won't be against each other in the future. We can build something better together. No more infighting. We have bigger threats to face."

With that, he turned to head back to Vanguard, his Guild members following close behind. A few stragglers from Stormcrusher joined them, but the somber atmosphere was thick, the weight of what had transpired still heavy on everyone's minds.

"You okay?" Derek asked as he caught up, concern etched on his face.

Tom nodded, his eyes forward. "I'll be fine. Just need to get back home and figure out what comes next."

He knew the path ahead would be fraught with more challenges, but for now, they had survived—and that, in itself, was a victory.

Chapter 68

Next Steps

When they finally returned to the Guild base, the air was filled with a mixture of relief and cautious optimism. Members who had stayed behind greeted those who had gone to battle with hugs and handshakes, sharing stories in excited murmurs that rippled through the crowd like a current. There was a sense of victory, albeit a bittersweet one, as people spoke of what had happened and what it meant for their future. But in the midst of the reunion, Tom broke away from the crowd, heading directly for the security office with a heavy expression. He pushed the door shut behind him with a soft click.

Seeing Tom retreat, Derek and James exchanged a glance and followed. They knew him well enough to understand that while everyone else was busy decompressing, Tom needed space to process what had happened. Inside the security office, they found him standing with his back to the door, his shoulders tense, his hands on the edge of a table. A dim overhead light cast shadows across his face, accentuating the weariness in his eyes.

"Hey, dude. You okay?" James asked gently as he stepped inside, his voice filled with concern.

Tom didn't respond immediately. He raised a hand, signaling them to hold on for a moment. His notifications had been flashing incessantly since the duel, a bright, blinking glow in his peripheral vision that he had tried to ignore. Now, with the room quiet and his friends waiting, he decided to check them.

Taking a deep breath, he pulled up his interface, bringing the notifications to the forefront of his vision. Lines of text scrolled before his eyes, detailing the aftermath of the battle, the System's responses, and various rewards and penalties. His brow furrowed as he read, his eyes narrowing in concentration.

Derek and James waited in silence, their expressions reflecting a mixture of concern and patience. They knew Tom well enough to understand that he needed to go through this in his own time. The silence in the room felt heavy, almost tangible, a stark contrast to the celebratory atmosphere outside.

War Victory Against Stormcrusher!

Congratulations, Vanguard! Your Guild's decisive victory against Stormcrusher has earned you the following rewards for all members:

- **XP:** 50,000
- **Item:** 1 random weapon suitable for your Class

    - **Monster Cores:** 1 Rare Monster Core

Continue to bring justice to this world and strengthen the Guild!

You Have Defeated an Enemy Guild Leader!

For your role in defeating the enemy Guild leader, you have earned extra rewards! Continue to lead your troops from the front lines to earn even more rewards!

    - **XP:** 250,000
    - **Guild Points:** 150,000
    - **Monster Cores:** 1 Epic Monster Cores

Level Up!

You have earned enough XP to advance to the next level. You are now level 32! Continue to work hard and push yourself to gain more XP to continue to level up. You receive 10 Attribute Points to distribute as you see fit.

"Sorry, I just wanted to clear those damn notifications. They were driving me crazy with all the blinking," Tom muttered as he dismissed the last of them. "Yeah, I'm alright. Still a bit shaken up, but more tired than anything else right now."

He leaned back in his chair, his eyes narrowing slightly. His mind buzzed with the remaining points he needed to allocate from the System rewards.

I'll deal with those later, maybe when I get back to my room tonight, he thought.

"Man, that was really something," James said, leaning against the doorframe.

Tom chuckled, but it was a dry sound, lacking its usual warmth. "It wasn't easy, for sure. We've been training hard, and having an actual trainer like Bron instead of just running around and getting ourselves beaten to get better—that made a huge difference."

"Bron has helped us more than we could ever repay him for," Derek agreed, his tone full of respect.

"Yeah," Tom nodded, his expression softening a bit. "But right now, I need some time to myself. There's so much to think about, and it feels like we're still not ready for everything that's coming."

Derek and James exchanged a quick glance. They understood where he was coming from.

"Just don't forget to celebrate the victory, Tom," Derek reminded him. "The others will be looking to you to say something to them. They need to see you're still in this."

"Sure," Tom replied, rubbing his eyes. "Just set something up and I'll be there. Have it where we had the other party. They should be able to drag the stuff back out, right?" He looked between Derek and James, seeking confirmation.

"Probably," Derek said with a nod. "Shouldn't be too much trouble. I'll talk with Brian, and we'll get something going."

As Derek left the room, Tom turned his attention to James, studying his friend's face. "And how are you holding up?" he asked pointedly.

James hesitated, his eyes dropping to the floor. "Better… but not great. I'll get over it eventually."

Tom's gaze softened. "Don't just 'get over it.' You have to get through it. You need to feel it, not avoid it. That's something I'm learning, too. Remember, you're not alone in this. You can always talk about it."

James took a deep breath, his shoulders sagging slightly as he pulled up a chair next to Tom and leaned forward. "I keep seeing his face, everywhere I look. Anytime I see a kid, it's him. When does that stop?"

Tom sighed, his expression thoughtful as he considered his words carefully. "Probably as soon as you forget him," he said, shrugging as he leaned back, putting his hands behind his head. "But I don't think you're supposed to forget. That's the point. You get through it, you don't get over it. Eventually, the rawness of it will fade, and you'll learn how to handle those feelings. But you can't do that if you don't let yourself feel them."

James nodded, his eyes distant. "I hate feeling like this."

"Everyone does," Tom said quietly. "Because it sucks. It's supposed to suck. But the reason it hurts so much is because you've been trying not to deal with it. It will get easier, but it won't happen overnight."

James looked up, his eyes meeting Tom's. "Are you dealing with this too?"

Tom gave a small, weary smile. "Yeah, I am. Not doing a great job of it right now, but it's always worse in the beginning. I'll learn to handle it better in time. We both will. We just have to keep at it because people are counting on us. Working through it will make us stronger."

James tilted his head, curiosity in his eyes. "How do you figure?"

Tom leaned forward, his voice taking on a more encouraging tone. "It's like working out, right? You build up your body by pushing through the tough parts. Same thing here. You work on how you react to situations, build up emotional resilience. Eventually, it won't be something that can be used against you. And don't worry—I'm here with you every step of the way."

A small smile tugged at James' lips. "Thanks, Tom. For always being there."

"Anytime," Tom said with a grin. "Now go on, get some rest. You've earned it."

James stood up, smiling a bit more genuinely now. As he reached the door, he turned back. "You better be drinking tonight. No need for you to be on guard, right?"

Tom chuckled, waving him off. "Alright, I will. Get me something tall and strong."

James nodded and left, leaving Tom alone with his thoughts. Tom leaned back in his chair, his eyes wandering to the security monitors showing various parts of the base. He watched for a moment, seeing his people—his family—moving around, some laughing, others deep in conversation. When the lobby had mostly cleared, he decided it was time to go to his room.

Stripping off his clothes, Tom stepped into the shower. The hot water was a welcome relief, cascading down his tired muscles. For a moment, he half-expected Jerky to join him as the little creature usually did, but it seemed his companion was off somewhere else, probably enjoying a snack. Tom scrubbed himself clean, letting the water wash away the grime and tension of the day.

After drying off, he flopped onto his mattress, staring up at the ceiling. The events of the day replayed in his mind, every decision, every action, every word spoken. After what felt like hours, his eyes grew heavy, and he drifted off into a restless sleep, still in his thoughts.

A light knock on his door woke him.

Tom stirred, wiping a trail of drool from the corner of his mouth, groggy from his nap.

"Tom? You in there? The party's ready for you to come and join in," Derek's voice came muffled through the closed door.

"Uh… right. I'll be down soon. Meet you there," Tom called back, his voice thick with sleep.

"Alright. Be quick, we don't want to keep people waiting," Derek replied before his footsteps faded away.

Tom rolled out of bed, feeling a bit disoriented. He pulled out a pair of socks and shoes from his Inventory, slipping them on. As he did, he realized he could probably just equip them directly using the System, but he decided against it, preferring the routine of doing it manually.

He headed into the bathroom, relieved himself, and stared at his reflection in the mirror. He barely recognized the man staring back. His face was leaner, more hardened, but his eyes still carried that weight of doubt. "No sense in dwelling on what's done. Just have to move forward," he muttered to himself.

Taking one last deep breath, he exited his room and took the elevator down to the ground floor. As the doors opened, he was met with a deafening roar of voices.

"TOM!" the crowd cheered in unison.

Tom blinked, taken aback by the outpouring of energy. "What is all this?" he asked, a bit overwhelmed.

Derek grinned at him from across the room. "We wanted to do something for you tonight. We're not just celebrating our victory; we're celebrating you. You don't get enough credit around here, you know."

"Somebody get this man a drink!" Jay's voice boomed, laughing as he saw Tom's slightly embarrassed reaction.

As everyone began moving outside, Brian hit the music, and the unmistakable anthem of Queen's "We Are the Champions" blared from the speakers. The crowd erupted in laughter and cheers. James approached, holding two drinks. He handed one to Tom, who took it with a nod of thanks, taking a cautious sip. He winced as the alcohol burned down his throat.

"Holy shit, that's strong," Tom said, coughing slightly.

"Long Island iced tea. You'll learn to love it after about three of them," James chuckled, taking a swig of his own drink.

The celebration continued long into the night. Music filled the air, people danced and laughed, and for the first time in a long while, Tom allowed himself to be part of it. He even joined in on the Cha Cha Slide, moving with the beat, his usually serious demeanor softened by the camaraderie and the buzz of the alcohol. He met the newest members of the Guild, many of whom approached him with heartfelt gratitude, thanking him for what he had done to help them.

By the end of the evening, Tom felt tipsy but lighter than he had in a while. Standing back, he watched everyone enjoying themselves, feeling a rare moment of contentment wash over him. For once, the weight of leadership felt a little less crushing.

But just as he was beginning to truly enjoy this rare peace, a message popped up in his field of vision. He tried to swipe it away, eager to get back to the party, but the System wouldn't allow it. Frustrated, he opened the message, his eyes scanning over the text. His expression turned serious, his heart dropping as he read its contents.

The night, which had been so full of celebration and release, took a sudden turn. Tom's mind raced as he processed the new information, knowing that this peace might be shorter lived than any of them hoped.

Administrator Call Incoming:	
Administrator #53 would like to speak with you about the approaching Space Pirate invasion. Accept the call?	
Yes	*No*

"Oh, shit."

End of Book 2

<u>Special Thanks:</u>

To Geneva, Chrissy, and Jez at Legion Publishing—thank you once again for everything you do to bring these books to life. Your tireless efforts, support, and belief in this series continue to amaze me. Without you, I wouldn't be standing at this point in the journey. You've made it possible for these stories to reach readers, and I'm forever grateful.

To my D&D group—you wonderful, patient, chaotic band of adventurers. Thank you for putting up with me, for letting me sneak in mechanics and ideas from the book during our sessions, and for being my creative safe space. You are my closest friends, and I love you all dearly. This series is better because of you.

To James (yes, *that* James)—thank you for being the constant spark of inspiration and a lifeline of encouragement. You get my spicy brain, laugh at my dumb jokes, and remind me that it's okay to be exactly who I am. I don't know if I'd still be writing without the ability to talk through every wild idea and twist with you. I love you, buddy.

Invasion

Book 3

Grand System Vending

By

Ryan Maxwell

The good news: Tom and his guild won the war for Dallas.
The bad news: Space pirates are still on their way—and they aren't bringing a gift basket.
After blasting vending machine monsters, fighting in a Mexican standoff, and surviving the least user-friendly apocalypse imaginable, Tom thought he'd finally get a break. Instead, he's knee-deep in problems that can't be solved with sword swings or witty sarcasm.
There's a city to rebuild, guild members to train, and a never-ending list of disasters to manage. With problems like a ghost in the Guild hall, a murder mystery unfolding in the middle of town, and someone, somehow, trying to organize a committee meeting about snack distribution, Tom must rely on his friends to help organize the Guild so they aren't destroyed from within.
Worse, the pirates haven't given up. Their ships are getting closer, their tech is terrifying, and Tom's pretty sure a vending machine just called him expendable.
With time running out and doomsday on the calendar—again—Tom and his friends must race to prepare for Earth's next unwanted DLC. Because when galactic war comes knocking, you don't get a patch. You get patch notes. On fire.
The war for Earth isn't over. It's just changing terms and conditions.

Pre Order Now!

Rise of Mankind : Age of stone

By Jez Cajiao

In all the games Matt has played, Dungeons are places to raid, places you dream of conquering, but when the world is stripped of electricity, and the first mana-twisted beasts start to prowl, the games all come to an end...

Matt's just an ordinary guy, but when he's beaten, robbed, and left for dead, bleeding out at the bottom of a gully, it all has to change as he grasps frantically at his only chance for survival, coming as it does in the form of a glowing, dangerously pulsing light.

With his reality forever altered, Matt must quickly find a suitable place to deploy the Dungeon Core, fighting his way through the hundreds of people between him and safety, because if he doesn't do it soon, a Core Detonation will solve all of his problems for him… permanently.

Welcome to the New World.

Experience a dark apocalyptic LitRPG Dungeon Core tale, Matt is a normal guy, pushed into terrible situations, and without anyone to hold his hand and explain the system. This is a weak-to-strong tale about doing what's right, not what's easy, in a nightmarish world. Fans of Dungeon Core stories, progression fantasy and strategy real time expansion games are sure to love it.

Order Now!

Theft of Decks

By Lars Machmüller

When the deck is stacked against you? Change the game!

In the frontier town of Isarn, Chase will never be more than the lowly Darkborn thief he is. Banned from training, banned from acquiring better cards, if the Lightborn had their way, he'd be banned from life itself.

He's not alone though, and the one thing he and his friends have is determination. Losing a hand to a brutal punishment only fueled his obsession to get access to his own amazing, reality-bending cards.

That is the path to power and a future for them all. Nobody cares where you came from when you're rich enough. For now, though, they're facing both established powers, churches and age-old prejudices. It's time to get to work, and if the Lightborn won't share and play nice?

Sometimes the only way to get dealt a better hand is to steal the whole damn deck!

Buy on Amazon

Quest Academy

By Brian J. Nordon

A world infested by demons.
An Academy designed to train Heroes to save humanity from annihilation.
A new student's power could make all the difference.

Humans have been pushed to the brink of extinction by an ever-evolving demonic threat. Portals are opening faster than ever, Towers bursting into the skies and Dungeons being mined below the last safe havens of society. The demons are winning.

Quest Academy stands defiantly against them, as a place to train the next generation of Heroes. The Guild Association is holding the line, but are in dire need of new blood and the powerful abilities they could bring to the battlefront. To be the saviors that humanity needs, they need to surpass the limits of those that came before them.

In a war with everything on the line, every power matters. With an adaptive enemy, comes the need for a constant shift in tactics. A new age of strategy is emerging, with even the unlikeliest of Heroes making an impact.

Salvatore Argento has never seen a demon.
He has never aspired to become a Hero.
Yet his power might be the one to tip the odds in humanity's favor.

Buy on Amazon

Wandering Warrior

By Michael Head

A divine quest to deliver justice.
One year to accomplish his mission.
After nineteen planets, there's something different about this one.

James Holden has reached the maximum level there is for a human. That's perfect, since he's the only one of his kind. A wandering warrior, without control of his destination, tossed between universes by gods who've failed to tell him why. James is the lone Judge on a new world in need of someone to balance the scales. He isn't afraid to do so with extreme prejudice. As the Chief Justice, he has to right the wrongs the innocent can't fix themselves.

As James quickly discovers, the roots of corruption run deep. Guilds choose to protect themselves rather than the people. Monsters roam the wilderness unchecked. Judgment is usually a decision between right and wrong, but nothing is ever that simple. This time, being the strongest human won't be enough to punish the guilty. James might have to recruit some new blood, even if he prefers to work alone.

On his twentieth world, he is going to win, no matter the cost. James will have to find a way to break past the limits of the system if he's going to have a chance at making a difference.

Buy on Amazon

Knights of Eternity

By Rachel Ní Chuirc

When Zara awoke in chains she thought she'd gone mad.

She was Zara the Fury - mistress of flame and fear. Her name was whispered across the land, from ramshackle taverns to the royal court. Even the heroic Gilded Knights thought twice before crossing her path.

She was feared—*respected.*

Now she was curled up on a dirt floor on her fiancé's orders. Valerius, leader of the Gilded, mocks her cries for help. And the kingdom is on the brink of war over the missing Lady Eternity…

But that wasn't why Zara thought she had gone mad.

The reason why is that the last thing she remembered was blood, an arcade screen, and the gun that changed everything.

But no chains can hold the Fury, and when she gets out? The world is going to *burn*.

Buy on Amazon

Scarlet Citadel

By Jack Fields

Gormon Hughes is 19, thin as a broom, and has—not for the first time in his life—been swept into the path of trouble. Poor, recently heartbroken, and indebted to the sort of people who file their teeth into needle points and devour wriggling bloated spiders for fun, Hughes sets his sights on salvation.

That salvation is the Scarlet Citadel, a wealthy organization of pageant fighters, monster hunters, and secret keepers. With the aid of strange oracles, rare good fortune, and a unique power that bubbles like champagne in the core of Hughes' being, he must join the Citadel and advance himself.

But the ladder of progression is harsh and dark. The rungs are slippery.

And falling means disaster…

Buy on Amazon

<u>LITRPG!</u>

To learn more about LitRPG, talk to other authors including myself, and to just have an awesome time, please join the LitRPG Group

<u>www.facebook.com/groups/LitRPGGroup</u>

Facebook

There's also a few really active Facebook groups I'd recommend you join, as you'll get to hear about great new books, new releases and interact with all your (new) favorite authors! (I may also be there, skulking at the back and enjoying the memes…)

https://www.facebook.com/groups/LitRPGlegion/

https://www.facebook.com/groups/GamelitSociety

https://www.facebook.com/groups/LitRPG.books

https://www.facebook.com/groups/LitRPGforum/

RYAN MAXWELL
RHINO WRITING